THE FU MANCHU OMNIBUS

VOLUME II

THE AUTHOR

Sax Rohmer was the pen name of Arthur Sarsfield Ward, who was born in Birmingham in 1866 of Irish parents. For many years he lived in New York. He worked as a journalist on Fleet Streeet before he made his name as the creator of the Dr Fu Manchu thrillers.
He died in 1959.

THE FU MANCHU OMNIBUS

Sax Rohmer

VOLUME II

THE DAUGHTER OF FU MANCHU

THE MASK OF FU MANCHU

FU MANCHU'S BRIDE

a&b

This omnibus edition first published in Great Britain in 1997 by
Allison & Busby Ltd
114 New Cavendish Street
London W1M 7FD

Reprinted 2001

Daughter of Fu Manchu first published in Great Britain in 1931
by Cassell & Co. Ltd.
The Mask of Fu Manchu first published in USA in 1932
by PF Collier & Son Corporation
by special arrangement with
Doubleday, Doran & Company, Inc.
Fu Manchu's Bride first published in 1933
by PF Collier & Son Corporation
by special arrangement with
Doubleday, Doran & Company, Inc.

The moral right of the author is asserted

This book is sold subject to the condition that it shall not, by way of trade
or otherwise, be lent, resold, hired out or otherwise circulated without the
publisher's prior written consent in any form of binding or cover other than
that in which it is published and without a similar condition including this
condition being imposed upon the subsequent purchaser.

A catalogue record for this book is available from the
British Library

ISBN 0 74900 222 0

Designed and typeset by N-J Design Associates
Romsey, Hampshire
Printed and bound in Great Britain by
Mackays of Chatham plc

DAUGHTER OF
FU MANCHU

CONTENTS

PART ONE

CHAPTER
1   THE LIVING DEATH
2   RIMA
3   TOMB OF THE BLACK APE

PART TWO

4   FAH LO SUEE
5   NAYLAND SMITH EXPLAINS
6   THE COUNCIL OF SEVEN

PART THREE

7   KÂLI
8   SWÂZI PASHA ARRIVES
9   THE MAN FROM EL-KHÂRGA

PART FOUR

10 ABBOTS HOLD
11 DR. AMBER
12 LORD OF THE *SI FAN*

PART ONE

CHAPTER FIRST—*The Living Death*

CHAPTER SECOND—*Rima*

CHAPTER THIRD—*Tomb of the Black Ape*

Chapter First

THE LIVING DEATH

Just in sight of Shepheard's I pulled up.

I believe a sense of being followed is a recognised nervous disorder; but it was one I had never experienced without finding it to be based on fact.

Certainly what had occurred was calculated to upset the stoutest nerves. To lose an old and deeply respected friend, and in the very hour of the loss to be confronted by a mystery seemingly defying natural laws, is a test of staying power which any man might shirk.

I had set out for Cairo in a frame of mind which I shall not attempt to describe; but this damnable idea that I was spied upon—followed—asserted itself in the first place on the train.

In spirit still back in camp beside the body of my poor chief, I suddenly became conscious of queer wanderers in the corridor. One yellow face in particular I had detected peering in at me, which possessed such unusual and dreadful malignity that at some point just below Beni Suef I toured the cars from end to end determined to convince myself that those oblique, squinting eyes were not a product of my imagination. Several times I had fallen into a semi-doze, for I had had no proper sleep for forty-eight hours.

I failed to find the yellow horror. This had disturbed me, because it made me distrust myself; but it served to banish my sleepiness. Reinforced with a stiff whisky-and-soda, I stayed very widely awake as the train passed station after station in the Nile Valley and drew ever nearer to Cairo.

The squinting eyes did not reappear.

Then, having hailed a taxi outside the station, I suddenly became aware, in some quite definite way that the watcher was following again. In sight of Shepheard's I pulled up, dismissed the taxi, and mounted the steps to the terrace.

Tables were prepared for tea, but few as yet were occupied. I could see no one I knew, but of this I was rather glad.

Standing beside one of those large ornamental vases at the

head of the steps, I craned over, looking left along Sharia Kamel. I was just in time. My trick had its reward.

A limousine driven by an Arab chauffeur passed in a flash.

But the oblique, squinting eyes of its occupant stared up at the balcony. It was the man of the train. I had not been dreaming.

I think he saw me, but of this I couldn't be sure. The car did not slacken speed and I lost sight of it at the bend by Esbekiyeh Gardens.

A white-robed, red-capped waiter approached. Mentally reviewing my condition and my needs, I ordered a pot of Arab coffee. I smoked a pipe, drank my coffee, and set out on foot for the club. Here I obtained the address I wanted. . . .

In a quiet thoroughfare a brass plate beside a courtyard entrance confirmed its correctness. In response to my ring a Nubian servant admitted me. I was led upstairs and without any ceremony shown into a large and delightfully furnished study.

The windows opened on a balcony draped with purple blossom and overhanging the courtyard where orange trees grew. There were many books and the place was full of flowers. In its arrangement, the rugs upon the floor, the ornaments, the very setting of the big writing-table, I detected the hand of a woman. And I realised more keenly than ever what a bachelor misses and the price he pays for his rather overrated freedom.

My thoughts strayed for a moment to Rima, and I wondered, as I had wondered many times, what I could have done to offend her. I was brought back sharply when I met the glance of a pair of steady eyes regarding me from beyond the big writing-table.

The man I had come to see stood up with a welcoming smile. He was definitely a handsome man, grey at the temples and well set up. His atmosphere created an odd sense of security. In fact my first impression went far to explain much that I had heard of him.

"Dr. Petrie?" I asked.

He extended his hand across the table and I grasped it.

"I'm glad you have come, Mr. Greville," he replied. "They sent me your message from the club." His smile vanished and his face became very stern. "Please try the arm-chair. Cigars in the wooden box, cigarettes in the other. Or here's a very decent pipe mixture"—sliding his pouch across the table.

"Thanks," I said; "a pipe, I think."

"You are shaken up," he went on—"naturally. May I prescribe?"

I smiled, perhaps a little ruefully.

"Not at the moment. I have been rather overdoing it on the train, trying to keep myself awake."

I filled my pipe whilst trying to muster my ideas. Then, glancing up, I met the doctor's steady gaze; and:

"Your news was a great shock to me," he said. "Barton, I know, was one of your oldest friends. He was also one of mine. Tell me—I'm all anxiety to hear."

At that I began:

"As you may have heard, Dr. Petrie, we are excavating what is known as Lafleur's Tomb at the head of the Valley of Kings. It's a queer business, and the dear old chief was always frightfully reticent about his aims. He was generous enough when a job was done and shared the credit more than fairly; but his sense of the dramatic made him a bit difficult. Therefore, I can't tell you very much about it. But two days ago he shifted the quarters, barred all approaches to the excavation, and generally behaved in a way which I knew from experience to mean that we were on the verge of some big discovery,

"We have two huts, but nobody sleeps in them. We are a small party and under canvas. But all this you will see for yourself—at least, I hope I can count on you? We shall have to rush for it."

"I am coming," Dr. Petrie replied quietly. "It's all arranged. God knows what use I can be. But since he wished it. . . ."

"Some time last night," I presently went on, "I heard, or thought I heard, the chief call me: 'Greville! Greville!' His voice seemed strange in some way. I fell out of bed (it was pitch dark), jumped into slippers, and groped along to his tent."

I stopped. The reality and the horror of it stopped me; but at last:

"He was dead," I said. "Dead in his bed. A pencil had dropped from his fingers and the scribbling block which he used for notes lay on the floor beside him."

"One moment," Dr. Petrie interrupted me; "you say he was

dead. Was this impression confirmed afterwards?"

"Forester, our chemist," I replied sadly, "is an M.R.C.P., though he doesn't practise. The chief was dead. Sir Lionel Barton—the greatest Orientalist our old country has ever produced, Dr. Petrie. And he was so alive, so vital, so keen and enthusiastic."

"Good God!" Dr. Petrie murmured. "To what did Forester ascribe death?"

"Heart failure—a quite unsuspected weakness."

"Unaccountable! I could have sworn the man had a heart like an ox. But I am becoming somewhat puzzled, Mr. Greville. If Forester certified death from syncope, who sent me *this*?"

He passed a telegram across the table. I read it in growing bewilderment:

"Sir Lionel Barton suffering catalepsy. Please come first train and bring antidote if any remains."

I stared at Petrie; then:
"No one in our camp sent it!" I said.
"What!"
"I assure you. No member of our party sent this message."

I saw it had been delivered that morning and had been handed in at Luxor at six a.m. I began to read it aloud in a dazed way. And, whilst I was reading, a subdued but particularly eerie cry came from the courtyard. I stopped. It startled me; but its effect upon Dr. Petrie was amazing. He sprang up as though a shot had been fired in the room and leaped towards the open window.

§ 2

"What was it?" I exclaimed.

Whilst the cry had not resembled any of the many with which I was acquainted in that land where the vendor of dates, of lemonade, of water, of a score of commodities has each his separate song, yet, though weird, it was not in itself definitely horrible.

Petrie turned, and:

"Something I haven't heard for ten years," he replied——and I saw with concern that he had grown pale—"which I had hoped never to hear again."

"What?"

"The signal used by a certain group of fanatics of Burma loosely known as dacoits."

"Dacoits? But Dacoity in Burma has been dead for a generation!"

Petrie laughed.

I made that very statement twelve years ago," he said. "It was untrue then, it is untrue now. Yet there isn't a soul in the courtyard."

And suddenly I realised that he was badly shaken. He was not the type of man who was readily unnerved, and I confess that the incident—trivial though otherwise it might have seemed—impressed me unpleasantly.

"Please God I am mistaken," he went on, walking back to his chair. "I must have been mistaken."

But that he was not, suddenly became manifest. The door opened and a woman came in, or rather—ran in.

I had heard men at the club rave about Dr. Petrie's wife, but the self-chosen seclusion of her life was such that up to this present moment I had never set eyes on her. I realised now that all I had heard was short of the truth. It is fortunate that modern man is unaffected by the Troy complex; for she was, I think, quite the most beautiful woman I had ever seen in my life. I shall not attempt to describe her, for I could only fail; but, seeing that she had not even noticed my existence, I wondered, as men will sometimes wonder, by what mystic chains Dr. Petrie held this unreally lovely creature.

She ran to him and he threw his arms about her.

"You heard it!" she whispered. "You heard it!"

"I know what you are thinking, dear," he said. "Yes, I heard it; but after all it isn't possible."

He looked across at me, and suddenly his wife seemed to realise my presence.

"This is Mr. Shan Greville," Petrie went on, "who brings me very sad news about our old friend, Sir Lionel Barton. I didn't mean you to know, yet. But——"

Mrs. Petrie conquered her fears and came forward to greet me.

"You are very welcome," she said.

She spoke English with a faint fascinating accent.

"But your news—do you mean——?"

I nodded.

Into the beautiful eyes watching me I saw the strangest expression creeping. It was questioning, doubting; fearful, analytical. And suddenly Mrs. Petrie turned from me to her husband, and:

"How did it happen?" she asked.

As she spoke the words, I thought she seemed to be listening.

Briefly, Dr. Petrie repeated what I had told him, concluding by handing his wife the mysterious telegram.

"If I may interrupt for a moment," I said, taking out of my pocket-case, "Sir Lionel must have written this at the moment of his fatal seizure. You see—it tails off. It was scribbled on the block which lay beside him. It was what brought me to Cairo."

I handed the pencilled message to Petrie. His wife bent over him as he read aloud, slowly:

"Not dead . . . Get Petrie . . . Cairo . . . amber . . . inject . . ."

She was facing me as he read—her husband could not see her face; but he saw the telegram slip from her fingers to the carpet.

"Kara!" he cried. "My dear! What is it?"

Her wonderful eyes, widely opened, were staring past me through the window out into the courtyard; and:

"He is alive!" she whispered. "Oh God! He is alive!"

I wondered if she referred to Sir Lionel; when suddenly she turned to Petrie, clutching the lapels of his coat and speaking eagerly, fearfully.

"Surely you understand? You *must* understand. That cry in the garden, and now—this! It is the Living Death! It is the Living Death! He knew before it claimed him. '*Amber— inject.*'" She shook Petrie with a sudden passionate violence. "Think! . . . The flask is in your safe."

And, watching Petrie's face, I realised that what had been unintelligible to me, to him had brought light.

"Merciful heavens!" he cried, and now I saw positive horror

leap to his eyes. "I can't believe it—I won't believe it."

He stared at me, a man distracted; and:

"Sir Lionel believed it," his wife said. "He wrote it. This is what he means."

And now I remembered those hideous oblique eyes which had looked in at me during my journey. I remembered the man in the car who had passed me at Shepheard's. Dacoits! Bands of Burmese robbers! I had thought of them as scattered. Apparently they were associated—a sort of guild. Sir Lionel knew the Far East almost better than he knew the Near East. So, suddenly I spoke—or rather I cried the words aloud:

"Do you mean, Mrs. Petrie, that you think he's been murdered?"

Dr. Petrie interrupted, and his reply silenced me.

"It's worse than that," he said.

If I had come to Cairo bearing a burden of sorrow, I thought, looking from the face of my host to the beautiful face of his wife, that my story had brought their happy world tumbling about them in dust.

§ 3

The train to Luxor was full, but I had taken the precaution of booking accommodation before leaving the station. And, as I was later to learn, I had been watched.

I was frankly out of my depth. That Petrie was deeply concerned for his wife, who seemed now to be the victim of a mysterious terror, he was quite unable to conceal. The object locked in the safe referred to by Mrs. Petrie proved to be a glass flask sealed with wax and containing a very small quantity of what might, from its appearance, have been brandy. However, the doctor packed it up with the greatest care and placed it in his professional bag before leaving.

This, together with the feverish state of excitement into which I seemed to have thrown his household, was sufficiently mystifying. Coming on top of a tragedy and a sleepless night, it was almost the last straw.

Petrie explored the train as though he expected to find Satan in person on board.

"Are you looking for my cross-eyed man?" I asked.

"I am," he returned grimly.

And somehow, as his steady glance met mine, it occurred to me that he was hoping, and not fearing, to see the oblique-eyed spy. It dawned upon me that his fears were for his wife, left behind in Cairo, rather than for us. What in heaven's name was it all about?

However, I was too far gone to pursue these reflections, and long before the attendant had come to make the bed I fell fast asleep.

I was awakened by Dr. Petrie.

"I prescribe dinner," he said.

Feeling peculiarly cheap, I managed to make myself sufficiently presentable for the dining car, and presently sat down facing my friend, of whom I had heard so much and whom the chief had evidently regarded as a safe harbour in a storm.

A cocktail got me properly awake again and enabled me to define where troubled dreams left off and reality began. Petrie was regarding me with an expression compounded of professional sympathy and personal curiosity; and:

"You have had a desperately trying time, Greville," he said; "but you can't have failed to see that you have exploded a bombshell in my household. Now, before I say any more on the latter point, please bring me up to date. If there's been foul play, is there anyone you could even remotely suspect?"

"There is certainly a lot of mystery about our job," I confessed. "I know for a fact that Sir Lionel's rivals—I might safely call them enemies—have been watching him closely—notably Professor Zeitland."

"Professor Zeitland died in London a fortnight ago."

"What!"

"You hadn't heard? We had the news in Cairo. Therefore, he can be ruled out."

There was a short interval whilst the waiter got busy, and then:

"As I remember poor Barton," Petrie mused; "he was always surrounded by hosts of strange servants. Are there any in your camp?"

"Not a soul," I assured him. "We're a very small party. Sir Lionel, myself, Ali Mahmoud, the head man, Forester, the chemist—I have mentioned him before; and the chief's niece, Rima, who's our official photographer."

I suppose my voice changed when I mentioned Rima; for Petrie stared at me very hard, and:

"Niece?" he said. "Odd jobs women undertake nowadays."

"Yes," I answered shortly.

Petrie began to toy with his fish. Clearly his appetite was not good. It was evident that repressed excitement held him— grew greater with every mile of our journey.

"Do you know Superintendent Weymouth?" he asked suddenly.

"I've met him at the club," I replied. "Now that you mention it, I believe Forester knows him well."

"So do I," said Petrie smiling rather oddly. "I've been trying to get in touch with him all day."

He paused, then:

"There must be associations," he went on. "Some of you surely have friends who visit the camp?"

That question magically conjured up a picture before my mind's eye—the picture of a figure so slender as to merit the description serpentine, tall, languorous; I saw again the brilliant jade-green eyes, voluptuous lips, and those slim ivory hands nurtured in indolence. . . . Madame Ingomar.

"There is one," I began—I was interrupted.

The train had begun to slow into Wasta, and high above those curious discords of an Arab station, I had clearly detected a cry.

"Dr. Petrie! A message for Dr. Petrie."

He, too, had heard it. He dropped his knife and fork and his expression registered a sudden consternation.

§ 4

As Petrie sprang to his feet, a tall figure in flying kit came rushing into the dining car, and:

"Hunter!" Petrie exclaimed. "Hunter!"

I, too, stood up in a state of utter bewilderment.

"What's the meaning of this?" Petrie went on.

He turned to me, and:

"Captain Jameson Hunter, of Imperial Airways." he explained—"Mr. Shan Greville."

He turned again to the pilot.

"What's the idea, Hunter?" he demanded.

"The idea is," the airman replied, grinning with evident enjoyment, "that I've made a dash from Heliopolis to cut you off at Wasta! Jump to it! You've got to be clear of the train in two minutes!"

"But we're in the middle of dinner!"

"Don't blame me. It's Superintendent Weymouth's doing. He's standing by where I landed the bus."

"But," I interrupted, "where are we going?"

"Same place," said the airman, grinning delightedly. "But I can get you there in no time; save you the Nile crossing and land you, I believe, within five hundred yards of the camp. Where's your compartment? You have to run for your things or leave them on the train. It doesn't matter much."

"It does," I said. I turned to Petrie. "I'll get your bag. Fix things with the attendant and meet me on the platform."

I rushed out of the dining car, observed in blank astonishment by every other occupant. Our compartment gained, I nearly knocked over the night attendant who was making the bed. Dr. Petrie's bag I grabbed at once. Coats, hats, and two light suitcases were quickly bundled out. I thrust some loose money into the hand of the badly-startled attendant and made for the exit.

Petrie's bag I managed to place carefully on the platform. The rest of the kit I was compelled to throw out unceremoniously—for the train was already in motion. I jumped off the step and looked along the platform.

Far ahead, where the dining-car had halted, I saw Petrie and Jameson Hunter engaged apparently in a heated altercation with the station-master. Heads craned through many windows as the Luxor express moved off.

And suddenly, standing there with the baggage distributed about me, I became rigid, staring—staring—at a yellow, leering face which craned from a coach only one removed from that we had occupied.

The spy had been on the train.

I was brought to my senses by a tap on the arm. I turned.

An Airways mechanic stood at my elbow.

"Mr. Greville," he said, "is this your baggage?"

I nodded.

"Close shave," he commented. He began to pick up the bags. "I think I can manage the lot, sir. Captain Hunter will show you the way."

"Careful with the black bag!" I cried. "Keep it upright, and for heaven's sake, don't jolt it!"

"Very good, sir."

Hatless, dinnerless, and half-asleep I stood, until Jameson Hunter, Dr. Petrie, and the station-master joined me.

"It's all settled," said Hunter, still grinning cheerfully. "The station-master here was rather labouring under the impression that it was a hold-up. I think he's been corrupted by American movies. Well, here we go!"

But the station-master was by no means willing to let us go. He was now surrounded by a group of subordinates, and above the chatter of their comments I presently gathered that we must produce our tickets. We did so, and pushed our way through the group. Further obstruction was offered . . . when all voices became suddenly silent.

A big man, wearing a blue serge suit, extraordinarily reminiscent of a London policeman in mufti, and who carried his soft hat so that the moonlight silvered his crisp white hair, strolled into the station.

"Weymouth!" cried Petrie. "This is amazing! What does it mean?"

The big, genial man, whom I had met once or twice at the club, appeared to be under a cloud. His geniality was less manifest than usual; but the effect of his arrival made a splendid advertisement for the British tradition in Egypt. The station-master and his subordinates positively wilted in the presence of this one-time chief inspector of the Criminal Investigation Department now in supreme command of the Cairo Detective Service.

Weymouth nodded to me, a gleam of his old cheeriness lighting the blue eyes; then:

"I don't begin to think what it means, Doctor," he replied, "but it was what your wife told me."

"The cry in the courtyard?"

"Yes; and the telegram I found waiting when I got back."

"Telegram?" Petrie echoed. He turned to me. "Did you send it, Greville?"

"No. Do you mean, Superintendent, you received a telegram from Luxor?"

"I do; I received one to-day."

"So did I," said Petrie, slowly. "Who, in sanity's name, sent those telegrams, Greville?"

But to that question I could find no answer.

"It's mysterious, I grant," said Weymouth; "but whoever he is, he's a friend. Mrs. Petrie thinks——"

"Yes," said Petrie, eagerly.

Weymouth smiled in a very sad way, and:

"She always knew in the old days," he added. "It was uncanny."

"It was," Petrie agreed.

"Well, over the phone to-night she told me——"

"Yes?"

"She told me she had the old feeling."

"Not——"

"So I understood, Doctor. I didn't waste another minute. I 'phoned Heliopolis and by a great stroke of luck found Jameson Hunter there with a bus, commissioned to pick up an American party now in Assouan. He was leaving in the morning, but I arranged with him to leave to-night."

"Moonlight is bad for landing unless one knows the territory very well," Jameson Hunter interrupted. "Fortunately I knew of a good spot outside here, and I know another just behind Der-el-Bahari. If we crash, it will be a bad show for Airways."

We hurried out to where a car waited, Dr. Petrie personally carrying the bag with its precious contents; and soon, to that ceaseless tooting which characterises Egyptian drivers, we were dashing through the narrow streets with pedestrians leaping like hares from right and left of our course.

Outside the town we ran into a cultivated area, but only quite a narrow belt. Here there was a road of sorts. We soon left this and were bumping and swaying over virgin, untamed desert. On we went, and on, in the bright moonlight. I seemed to have stepped over the borderline of reality. The glorious blaze of stars above me had become unreal, unfamiliar.

My companions were unreal—a dream company.

All were silent except Jameson Hunter, whose constant ejaculations of "Jumping Jupiter!" when we took an unusually bad bump indicated that he at least had not succumbed to that sense of mystery which had claimed the rest of us.

On a long, gentle slope dangerously terminated by a ravine, the 'plane rested. Our baggage was quickly transferred and we climbed on board. A second before the roar of the propeller washed out conversation:

"Hunter," said Weymouth, "stretch her to the full. It's a race to save a man from living death...."

CHAPTER SECOND

RIMA

IT WAS bumpy travelling, and I had never been a good sailor. Jameson Hunter stuck pretty closely to the river, but saved miles, of course, on the many long bends, notably on that big sweep immediately below Luxor, where, leaving the Nile Valley north of Farshût, we crossed fifty miles of practically arid desert, heading east-south-east for Kûrna.

I was in poor condition, what with lack of sleep and lack of meals; and I will not enlarge upon my state of discomfort beyond saying that I felt utterly wretched. Sometimes I dozed; and then Rima's grave eyes would seem to be watching me in that maddeningly doubtful way. Once I dreamed that the slender ivory hands of Madame Ingomar beckoned to me. . . .

I awoke in a cold perspiration. Above the roar of the propeller I seemed to hear her bell-like, hypnotic voice. . . .

Who was this shadowy figure, feared by Petrie, by his wife—by Weymouth? What had he to do with the chief's sudden death? Were these people deliberately mystifying me, or were they afraid to tell me what they suspected?

Forester was convinced that Barton was dead. I could not doubt it. But in the incomprehensible message scribbled at the last, Petrie seemed to have discovered a hope which was not apparent to me. Weymouth's words had reinforced it.

"A race to save a man from living death."

Evidently he, too, believed . . . believed what?

It was no sort of problem for one in my condition, but at least I had done my job quicker than I could have hoped. Luck had been with me.

Above all, my own personal experience proved that there was something in it. Who had sent the telegrams? Who had uttered that cry in the courtyard? And why had I been followed to Cairo and followed back? Thank heaven, at last I had shaken off that leering, oblique-eyed spy.

Jameson Hunter searched for and eventually found the landing-place which he had in mind—a flat, red-grey stretch east of the old caravan road.

I was past reliable observation, but personally I could see nothing of the camp. This perhaps was not surprising as it nestled at the head of a wâdi, represented from our present elevation by an irregular black streak.

However, I was capable of appreciating that the selected spot could not be more than half a mile west of it. Hunter brought off a perfect landing, and with a swimming head I found myself tottering to the door.

When I had scrambled down:

"Wait a minute," said Petrie. "Ah, here's my bag. You've been through a stiff time, Greville. I am going to prescribe."

His prescription was a shot of brandy. It did me a power of good.

"If we had known," said Hunter, "some sandwiches would have been a worthy effort. But the whole thing was so rushed—I hadn't time to think."

He grinned cheerfully.

"Sorry my Phantom-Rolls isn't here to meet us," he said. "Someone must have mislaid it. It's a case of hoofing, but the going's good."

Carrying our baggage, we set out in the moonlight. We had all fallen silent now, even Jameson Hunter. Only our crunching footsteps broke the stillness. I think there is no place in the world so calculated to impress the spirit of man as this small piece of territory surrounding those two valleys where the quiet dead of Egypt lie. At night, when the moon sails full, he would be a pitiful soul who, passing that way, failed to feel the touch of eternity.

For my own part, as familiar landmarks appeared, a dreadful unrest compounded of sorrow and hope began to take possession of me. Above all, selfishly no doubt, I asked myself again and again—had Rima returned?

We were not expected until morning when the Cairo train arrived. Consequently I was astounded when on mounting the last ridge west of the wâdi I saw Forester hurrying to meet us. Of course, I might have known, had I been capable of associating two ideas, that the sound of our approach must have aroused the camp.

Forester began to run.

Bad news casts a long shadow before it. I forgot my nausea, my weariness. It came to me like a revelation that something fresh had occurred—something even worse than that of which I had carried news to Cairo.

I was not alone in my premonition. I saw Weymouth grasp Petrie's arm.

Forester began shouting:

"Is that you, Greville? Thank God you've come!"

Now, breathless, he joined us.

"What is it?" I asked. "What else had happened?"

"Only this, old man," he panted. "We locked the chief's body in the big hut, as you remember. I had serious doubts about notifying the authorities. And to-night, about dusk, I went to . . . look at him."

He grasped me by both shoulders.

"Greville!" Even in the moonlight I could see the wildness in his eyes. "His body had vanished."

"What!" Weymouth yelled.

"There isn't a trace—there isn't a clue. He's just been spirited away!"

§ 2

"If only Nayland Smith could join us," said Weymouth.

Dr. Petrie, looking very haggard in the lamplight, stared at him.

"The same thought had just crossed my own mind," he replied. "I am due to sail for England on Thursday. I had been counting the days. He's meeting me in . . ."

I knew that I could never again be present at so singular a scene. The hut was in part a laboratory, one end being devoted to Forester's special province, and containing a table laden with jars, test tubes, and other chemical paraphernalia. In part it was a museum. There were plans, diagrams, and photographs—Rima's photographs—pinned on the walls: lumps of stone bearing labels stacked upon the floor; and in open cases were all sorts of fragments found during the earlier stages of our excavation and duly tabulated in the same way.

There was a very dilapidated mummy case at the farther

end of the hut, which we had taken over from the Egypt Exploration people and had not troubled to remove. The lid rested against the wall. Then there was a long, bare table, very stoutly built, upon which finds were stacked at the end of the day, examined, and sorted according to their value. This, particularly, was my job. But at the moment, as I have said, the table was empty. When I had seen it last before leaving for Cairo, the body of Sir Lionel Barton lay upon it, covered by a grey blanket.

Now, in almost complete silence, for twenty minutes or more, I had watched a one-time chief inspector of Scotland Yard carrying out a detailed investigation in that strangest of settings.

Weymouth had not confined his inquiries to the hut alone; but, assisted by a flash-lamp, had examined the lock of the door, the windows, the path outside; but had finally returned and stared at the table.

Now he fixed his eyes upon me, and:

"Mr. Greville," he said, "you are not prejudiced by certain suspicions of mine which are shared by Dr. Petrie. I asked Mr. Forester to see to the comfort of Jameson Hunter because I wanted just the three of us alone here. Now, you look pretty well whacked, but I know how you feel about this thing; so I am going to ask you a few questions."

"As many as you like," I replied.

Superintendent Weymouth sat down on the bench just beside the door and knitted his brows; then:

"Where is the headman Ali Mahmoud?" he asked.

"Forester tells me he sent him across to Luxor to-night with a letter for our friend the manager of the Winter Palace. Forester asked him, in the letter, to call you, Superintendent, in Cairo, and to explain what had happened. Ali should be back now."

Weymouth nodded thoughtfully.

"Leaving out for the moment the circumstances of Sir Lionel's death," said he, "how long a time elapsed between your finding him in his tent and the removal of his body to this hut?"

"Roughly, two hours," I replied after a few moments' thought.

"During those two hours someone was always in sight of the tent?"

"Certainly."

"When was it decided he should be moved?"

"When I made up my mind to go to Cairo. I gave instructions for his body to be placed in this hut . . . I am second in command, you know. Forester agreed, although he swore that life was extinct. I personally superintended the job. I locked the hut, handed the keys to Forester, and turned in, hoping for some sleep before starting for Luxor."

"Did you sleep?"

"No; I lay awake right up to the time I had to set out."

"Did anything unusual occur during the night?"

I thought hard, and then: "Yes," I replied; "there was a queer howling of dogs. Ali Mahmoud turned out. He said the sound had not been made by dogs; but of course he was rather strung up. We all were. We searched but found nothing."

"H'm! What time was this?"

"I am afraid I can't tell you; but some time before dawn."

"Did you open this hut?"

"No."

"Ah!" said Weymouth meditatively. "That was a pity. And now, Mr. Greville, there's another point I'm not clear about. You spoke of Sir Lionel's niece. Where is she, and where was she at the time of the tragedy?"

I had expected the question, of course. Nevertheless I didn't quite know how to meet it. I saw Dr. Petrie regarding me curiously, and at last:

"I don't know where she is!" I replied—and recognised how strange the words must sound.

"What!" Weymouth exclaimed. "But I thought she was official photographer?"

"She is; but . . . Well! we had a quarrel. She went across to Luxor on Tuesday at midday. I haven't seen her since!"

"Oh, I see," said Weymouth. "Forgive me. I hadn't grasped the position. Sir Lionel knew of her absence?"

"He treated it as a joke. That was his way. She often stayed in Luxor and worked here during the day."

"Did he approve of the—understanding?"

"Yes; at least I think so."

"I suppose, as she hasn't come back, that she doesn't know what's happened?"

"I suppose so; but I am very anxious. . . ."

"Naturally." Weymouth looked suddenly grave; and then:

"Perhaps, Mr. Greville," he said, "you would ask Forester to come in?"

I opened the door and walked out in the dense shadow of the wâdi. A new atmosphere invested it, an atmosphere to which, even mentally, I didn't like to give a name, but which nevertheless was an atmosphere of terror.

What was the meaning of the disappearance of Sir Lionel's body? Whom could it benefit? Most damnable mystery of all—what was the information clearly shared by Weymouth and Petrie which they were suppressing?

So my thoughts ran as I walked through the shadows. The moon was out of sight from the wâdi, but the stars were wonderful; and suddenly the natural law of things had its way. I began to think of Rima, to the exclusion of everything else.

Her empty tent—the tent which she occupied when she spent the night in camp—was on the slope directly ahead. Moonlight touched it at one point, but the front was in shadow.

"If I am in the way," I seemed to hear her voice saying again, "I can go——"

If she was in the way! What had she meant? I had had no chance to find out. She had gone. Undoubtedly she was labouring under some strange delusion. But where was she—and did she know what had happened?

I was abreast of her tent, now, and something—an empty longing, no doubt—prompted me to peep inside. As I did so, an incredible thing happened—or, rather, two incredible things.

The mournful howling of a dog arose, apparently quite close to the camp. And in the darkness of the tent something stirred!

I suppressed a cry, bent forward with outstretched arms . . . and found a slim soft body in my embrace!

Even then, I couldn't believe what was true, couldn't appreciate the nature of my capture, until:

"Shan! Shan!" came a stifled cry. "You're hurting me dreadfully!"

"Rima!" I exclaimed—and wondered if my heart or hers throbbed the more wildly.

I said not another word. Stooping, I kissed her with a desperation which probably sprang from a submerged fear that she would never give me an opportunity of kissing her again.

But, thank heaven, that doubt was groundless. She threw her arms around my neck, as the mournful howling died away, and:

"Shan," she said, "I'm terrified, Shan dear!"

But her kisses had given me the right to console her, and when we presently reverted to sanity;

"When did you arrive, darling?" I asked.

"I came back with Ali. He told me—everything about it. So, of course, I had to come."

"But what made you go?"

She nestled her adorable little tousled head against me.

"I won't be scolded," she said—"although I am to blame! No, please, Shan. I truly meant what I said. I did really think I was in the way."

"In whose way?"

"If you talk to me like that I won't answer. Besides, there isn't time now. I should have come back to-night even if I had had to come alone. I have something most extraordinary to tell you. . . ."

But now came the sound of voices.

"I tell you it wasn't a dog," I heard Forester say.

"It wasn't either!" Rima whispered. "But you must go, Shan. I'm all right, now. Who is in the big hut?"

"Dr. Petrie and Superintendent Weymouth——"

"They were old friends . . . weren't they——"

"Yes, darling. Don't despair. It sounds absurd to say so, but they have a theory that the chief——"

"Please tell me."

"It's hardly fair, Rima. I don't believe it, myself. But they think he may be alive!"

She clung to me very tightly, and then:

"But I think so, too!" she whispered.

§ 3

"Do you know, Greville," said Forester. "I never liked this job. Lafleur's Tomb has a bad name."

We were walking back to the hut.

"What do you mean?"

"Well, you know as much as I do. Nobody has tackled it since Lafleur's time. But old Zeitland was planning to come out."

"He died recently in London."

"I know! And what about the Frenchman——"

"Do you mean Lafleur?"

"Yes, somewhere in 1908—or 1909, wasn't it? Well, I may be wrong"—Forester halted just as we reached the hut—"but didn't Lafleur disappear?"

I racked my memory for some moments. Lafleur was before my time and the facts were hazy. But at last:

"Yes," I replied slowly. "I believe there was some mystery, Forester. Though oddly enough it had never occurred to me before."

"It never occurred to *me* until we made that astounding discovery to-night. Why should it? But in view of what's happened, it's more than odd, don't you think?"

"We must tell Weymouth."

We went into the hut. Weymouth was sitting where I had left him, his brows still wrinkled in thought. . . . Dr. Petrie was pacing slowly up and down. As we entered, Weymouth raised his kindly blue eyes to Forester, and:

"Did you catch that dog?" he asked.

"No," said Forester, staring hard. "Did it sound like a dog to you?"

"It wasn't a dog," Weymouth replied simply. "This camp is being watched! Has anything occurred which might account for this signalling?"

"Yes," I broke in; "Ali Mahmoud has returned—and Rima Barton is with him."

"Ah!" Weymouth murmured. "I am glad to hear it. . . ."

"Greville and I have been thinking——" Forester began, when:

"One moment!" Weymouth raised his hand. "We shall get muddled. You can help me most, Forester, by letting me plod through the inquiry in my own way. I have the facts up to the time Mr. Greville left last night; now I want to know what happened afterwards."

"It's painfully simple," Forester replied. "Everything we might be likely to want was moved from here, naturally; so there was no occasion for anyone to enter the place. But death, of course, in the climate up here ought to be notified and dealt with promptly."

Weymouth nodded.

"Greville got me to agree to be quiet for the present, and nobody else knew, except Ali."

"You're sure no one else knew? What about the men?"

"They live in Kûrna. None were in camp. We removed the chief in the darkness—didn't we, Greville? and next morning I gave out that he had gone across to Luxor with Greville, here, and was proceeding down to Cairo. I stopped all work, of course."

"Yes, I see."

"At about dusk to-night—I should say last night—I thought it advisable to—er—inspect the body."

"Quite!"

"I opened the door, looked in, and . . . the hut was as you see it now."

"What about the blanket?"

"The blanket had disappeared, as well as the body."

"You're sure the door was locked?"

"Perfectly sure. I unlocked it."

"The window?"

"Fastened on the inside as you found it."

"Thank you," said Weymouth quietly.

He stared across at Dr. Petrie and there was a silence of some seconds' duration; a very odd silence, in which I sensed a mental communion going on between these two men, based upon some common knowledge which Forester and I didn't share. But at last it was broken by Dr. Petrie.

"Strangely like his handiwork!"

I began to be a bit ruffled. I thought the time had come for pooling of the known facts. Indeed I was about to say so, when

Weymouth spoke again.

"Was there anyone in the habit of visiting this camp?"

"No," said Forester; "the chief wouldn't allow a soul past the barriers." He stared across at me. "I except Madame Ingomar," he added. "But Greville can tell you more about the lady than I can."

"Why do you say that?" I cried angrily.

"Evidently because he thinks so," said Weymouth in a stern voice. "This is no time, gentlemen, for personal matters. You are assisting at an official inquiry."

"I am sorry." Forester replied; "my remark was quite out of place. The truth is, Superintendent, that neither Greville nor I know very much about Madame Ingomar. But she seemed to favour Greville's society, and we used to pull his leg about it...."

My thoughts began to stray again. Had I been blind? And where I had been blind, had Rima seen?

"Who is this woman?"

Weymouth's terse query brought me back to the job in hand.

Forester laughed dryly, and:

"A question I have often put to Greville," he replied; "but which I know he was no more able to answer than anyone else, except the chief."

"Oh, I see. A friend of Sir Lionel's?"

I nodded. Weymouth was staring in my direction.

"What nationality?"

I shook my head blankly.

"I always said Hungarian," Forester declared; "simply because of her name. Greville thought she was Japanese."

"Japanese!" Dr. Petrie rapped the word out with startled suddenness. "Why Japanese?"

"Well," said Forester, "it isn't an unreasonable guess, because her eyes did slant slightly."

Weymouth exchanged a rapid glance with Dr. Petrie and stood up.

"An attractive woman—young?" he challenged—for the words were spoken almost like a challenge.

"Undoubtedly," I replied. "Smart, cultured and evidently well-to-do."

"Dark?"

"Very."

"What coloured eyes?"

"Jade-green," said Forester.

Again I detected a rapid exchange of glances between Petrie and Weymouth.

"Tall?" asked the former.

"Yes, unusually tall."

"An old friend of Sir Lionel's?"

"We were given to understand," said Forester "that she was the widow of a certain Dr. Ingomar, whom the chief knew well at one time."

"Was she staying at one of the Luxor hotels?" Weymouth asked.

"I'm afraid I can't tell you," I replied. "She wasn't staying at the Winter Palace."

"You mean neither of you know. Does Miss Barton know?"

"I have never asked her."

"When was she last here?"

"On Monday," Forester answered promptly; "the day the chief switched the quarters around and put up barricades."

"But did Sir Lionel never speak of her?" asked Dr. Petrie.

"No," I said. "He was a man who gave few confidences, as you are aware."

"Was there any suggestion of intimacy between them?" Weymouth was the speaker. "Did Sir Lionel show any jealousy, for instance?"

"Not that I ever noticed," Forester replied. "He treated her as he treated everybody—with good-humoured tolerance! After all, the chief must have said good-bye to sixty, Weymouth!"

"Stranger things have happened," Petrie commented dryly. "I think, Weymouth, our next step is to establish the identity of this Madame Ingomar. Do you agree with me?"

"I do," said Weymouth; "absolutely"—and his expression had grown very grim.

He stared from me to Forester, and:

"You're both getting annoyed," he said. "I can see it. You know that the doctor here and I have a theory which we haven't shared with you. Very well, you shall know the facts. Ask Miss Rima Barton to join us, and arm Ali Mahmoud. Tell him to mount guard and shoot anything he sees moving!"

"What on earth does this mean?" Forester demanded.

"It means," said Petrie, "that we are dealing with agents of Dr. Fu Manchu. . . ."

§ 4

Dr. Fu Manchu! When that story was told, the story which Weymouth unfolded in the hut in the wâdi, whilst I can't answer for Forester, personally I was amazed beyond belief.

Rima's sweet face, where she sat half in shadow, was a fascinating study. She had ridden up from Kûrna with Ali Mahmoud. In the tent, when I had found her in my arms, she had worn riding kit; but now she had changed into a simple frock and had even made some attempt to straighten the tangle of her windblown hair. The night ride had whipped a wild colour into her tanned cheeks; her grave Irish eyes seemed even brighter than usual as she listened spellbound.

Some of the things Weymouth spoke of aroused echoes in my memory. I had been too young at the time to associate these events one with another. But I remembered having heard of them. I was considering the advantages of a legal calling when the war disturbed my promising career. The doings of this great and evil man, some of whose history I learned that morning, had reached me merely as rumours in the midst of altogether more personal business.

But now I grasped the fact that if these two clever and experienced men were correct in their theories, a veritable plague was about to be loosed upon the world.

Dr. Fu Manchu!

"Sir Lionel and I," said Dr. Petrie, "and Nayland Smith were last of those on the side of the angels to see him alive. It's possible he survived; but I am not prepared to believe it. What I am prepared to believe is that someone else may be carrying on his work. What was a dacoit—probably a Burman—a professional robber and murderer, doing in the courtyard of my house in Cairo last night? We know now, Greville, he was following you. But the cry points to an accomplice. He was not alone! The old net, Weymouth"—he turned to the latter—"closing round us again! Then—this camp is watched."

"I have said it before," Weymouth declared, "but I'll say it again; if only Nayland Smith could join us!"

"You refer, of course, to Sir Denis Nayland Smith," said Forester, "one of the assistant commissioners at Scotland Yard? I know people who know him. Used to be a police official in Burma?"

"He did," Petrie replied. "He also saved the British Empire, by the way. But if we have many unknown enemies, we have at least one unknown friend."

"Who is that?" I asked.

"The well-informed stranger," Petrie replied, "who wired me in Cairo—and who wired Weymouth. Whoever he may be, he takes no chances. Dr. Fu Manchu was master of a method for inducing artificial catalepsy. It was one of the most dangerous weapons in his armoury. I alone, as I believe, possess a drop of the antidote. The man who sent that telegram knew this!"

"So much for unknown friends," said Weymouth. "As to unknown enemies, either you have a Dacoit amongst your workmen or there was a stranger in camp last night."

"You've found a clue!" Rima cried.

"I have, Miss Barton. There's only one fact of which I have to make sure. If I am wrong in that, maybe all my theory falls down."

"What's the fact?" Forester asked, with an eagerness which told how deeply he was impressed.

"It's this," said Weymouth. He fixed a penetrating gaze upon me. "Was Sir Lionel completely undressed when you found him?"

"No," I replied promptly. "It was arranged that we all turned out at four to work on the job."

"Then he was fully dressed?"

"Not fully."

"Did he carry the key of this hut?"

"He carried all the keys on a chain."

"Was this chain on him when you found him?"

"Yes."

"Did you detach it?"

"No; we laid him here as we found him."

"Partially dressed?"

"Yes."

Weymouth slowly crossed to the mummy case at one end of the hut. The lid was detached and leaned against the wall beside the case.

"Both you, Greville," he went on, turning, "and Forester were present when Sir Lionel's body was brought in here?"

"Ali and I carried him," Forester returned shortly.

"Greville supervised."

"Did Ali leave when you left?"

"He did."

"Good," Weymouth went on quietly; "but I am prepared to swear that not one of you looked into the recess behind this sarcophagus lid."

I stared blankly at Forester. He shook his head.

"We never even thought of it," he confessed.

"Naturally enough," said Weymouth. "Look what I found there."

A lamp stood on the long table; and now, taking a piece of paper from his pocket, and opening the paper under the lamp, the superintendent exposed a reddish, fibrous mass. Rima sprang forward and with Forester and myself bent eagerly over it. Petrie watched.

"It looks to me like a wad of tobacco," said Forester, "chewed by someone whose gums were bleeding!"

Petrie bent between us and placed a lens upon the table.

"I have examined it," he said. "Give me your opinion, Mr. Forester. As a physician you may recognise it."

Forester looked, and we all watched him in silence. I remember that I heard Ali Mahmoud coughing out in the wâdi and realised that he was keeping as close to human companionship that night as his sentry duties permitted.

Shrugging, Forester passed the glass to me. I peered in turn, but almost immediately laid the glass down.

Petrie looked at Forester; but:

"Out of my depth!" the latter declared. "It's vegetable; but if it's something tropical, I plead ignorance."

"It *is* something tropical," said Petrie. "It's betel nut."

Weymouth intruded quietly, and:

"Someone who chewed betel nut," he explained, "was hiding

behind that sarcophagus lid when you brought Sir Lionel's body into this hut. Now, I'm prepared to hear that before that the door was unlocked?"

"You're right," I admitted; "it was. We locked it after his body had been placed here."

"As I thought."

Weymouth paused; then:

"Someone who chewed betel nut," he went on, "must have been listening outside Sir Lionel's tent when you decided to move his body to this hut. He anticipated you, concealed himself, and, at some suitable time later, with the key which Sir Lionel carried on his chain, he unlocked the door and removed the body!"

I entirely agree," said Forester, staring very hard, "and I compliment you heartily. But—betel nut?"

"Perfectly simple," Petrie replied. "Many dacoits chew betel nut."

At which moment, unexpectedly:

"Perhaps," came Rima's quiet voice, "I can show you the man!"

"What!" I exclaimed.

"I think I may have his photograph . . . and the photograph of someone else!"

Chapter Third

TOMB OF THE BLACK APE

I MIGHT have thought, during that strange conference in the hut, that life had nothing more unexpected to offer me. Little I knew what Fate held in store. This was only the beginning. Dawn was close upon us. Yet, before the sun came blushing over the Nile Valley, I was destined to face stranger experiences.

I went with Rima from the hut to the tent. All our old sense of security was gone. No one knew what to expect now that the shadow of Fu Manchu had fallen upon us.

"Imagine a person tall, lean, and feline, high shouldered, with a brow like Shakespeare and a face like Satan . . . long, magnetic eyes of the true cat-green . . ."

Petrie's description stuck in my memory; especially "tall, lean, and feline . . . eyes of the true cat-green . . ."

A lamp was lighted in Rima's tent, and she hastily collected some of her photographic gear and rejoined me as Ali came up shouldering his rifle.

"Anything to report, Ali Mahmoud?"

"Nothing, Effendim."

When we got back to the hut I could see how eagerly we were awaited. A delicious shyness which I loved—for few girls are shy—descended upon Rima when she realised how we were all awaiting what she had to say. She was so charmingly petite, so vividly alive, that the deep note which came into her voice in moments of earnestness had seemed, when I heard it first, alien to her real personality. Her steady grey eyes, though, belonged to the real Rima—the shy Rima.

"Please don't expect too much of me," she said glancing around quickly. "But I think perhaps I may be able to help. I wasn't really qualified for my job here, but . . . Uncle Lionel was awfully kind; and I wanted to come. Really, all I've done is wild-life photography—before, I mean."

She bent and opened a paper folder which she had put on the table; then:

"I used to lay traps," she went on, "for all sorts of birds and animals."

"What do you mean by 'traps' Miss Barton?" Weymouth asked.

"Oh, perhaps you don't know. Well, there's a bait—and the bait is attached to the trigger of the camera."

"Perfectly clear. You need not explain further."

"For night things, it's more complicated; because the act of taking the bait has to touch off a charge of flash powder as well as expose the film. It doesn't work very often. But I had set a trap—with the camera most cunningly concealed—on the plateau just by the entrance to the old shaft."

"Lafleur's Shaft!" I exclaimed.

"Yes; there was a track there which I thought might mean jackal—and I have never got a close-up of a jackal. The night before I went to Luxor something fell into my trap! I was rather puzzled, because the bait didn't seem to have been touched. It looked as though someone might have stumbled over it. But I never imagined that anyone would pass that way at night—or at any other time, really."

She stopped, looking at Weymouth; then:

"I took the film to Luxor," she said; "but I didn't develop it until to-day. When I saw what it was, I couldn't believe my eyes! I have made a print of it. Look!"

Rima laid a photographic print on the table and we all bent over it.

"To have touched off the trigger and yet got in focus," she said, "they must have been actually coming out of the shaft. I simply can't imagine why they left the camera undisturbed. Unless they failed to find it or the flash scared them!"

I stared dazedly at the print.

It represented three faces—one indistinguishably foggy, in semi-profile. That nearest to the camera was quite unmistakable. It was a photograph of the cross-eyed man who had followed me to Cairo!

This was startling enough. But the second face—that of someone directly behind him—literally defeated me. It was the face of a woman—wearing a black native veil but held aside so that her clear-cut features were reproduced sharply. . . .

Brilliant, indeterminably oblique eyes . . . a strictly

chiselled nose, somewhat too large for classic beauty . . . full lips, slightly parted . . . a long oval contour. . . .

"That's a dacoit!" came Petrie's voice. "Miss Barton, this is amazing! See the mark on his forehead!"

"I have seen it," Rima replied, "although I didn't know what it meant."

"But," I interrupted excitedly, as:

"Greville," Forester cried, "do you see!"

"I see very plainly," said I. "Weymouth—the woman in this photograph is Madame Ingomar!"

§ 2

"What is Lafleur's Shaft?" Weymouth asked. "And in what way is it connected with Lafleur's Tomb?"

"It isn't connected with it," I replied. "Lafleur's Tomb—also known as the Tomb of the Black Ape—was discovered, or rather suspected to exist, by the French Egyptologist Lafleur, about 1908. He accidentally unearthed a little votive chapel. All the fragments of offerings found were inscribed with the figure of what appeared to be a huge black ape—or perhaps an apeman. There's been a lot of speculation about it. Certain authorities, notably Maspero, held the theory that some queer pet of an unknown Pharoah had been given a freak burial.

"Lafleur cut a shaft into a long zigzag passage belonging to another burial chamber, which he thought would lead him to the Tomb of the Black Ape. It led nowhere. It was abandoned in 1909. Sir Lionel started from a different point altogether and seems to have hit on the right entrance."

"Ah!" said Weymouth. "Then my next step is clear."

"What is that?"

"I want you to take me down to your excavation."

"Good enough," said I; "shall we start now?"

"I think it would be as well." He turned to Forester. "I want Greville to act as guide, and I want you and Petrie to look after Miss Barton in our absence."

"We shall need Ali," I said, "to go ahead with lights."

"Very well. Will you please make the necessary arrangements?"

Accordingly I relieved Ali Mahmoud of his sentry duties and had the lanterns lighted. They were kept in the smaller hut. And presently Weymouth and I were on the ladders....

The first part of our journey led us down a sheer pit of considerable depth. At the bottom it gave access to a sloping passage, the original entrance to which had defied all our efforts to discover it.

This was very commonplace to me, but I don't know how that first glimpse of the pit affected Weymouth. The night was black as pitch. Dawn was very near. Outlined by the light of the lanterns Ali carried, that ragged gap far below, to reach which we had been at work for many months, looked a likely enough portal to ghostly corridors.

An indescribable smell which characterises the tombs of Upper Egypt crept up like a hot miasma. Our ladders were fairly permanent fixtures, sloping down at easy gradients from platform to platform. The work had been fenced around; and, as we entered the doorway, watching the Arab descending from point to point and leaving a lantern at each stopping place, a sort of foreboding seemed to grab me by the throat.

It was unaccountable, or so I thought at the time, but it was well founded, as events were soon to show. I glanced at Weymouth. The big man was looking doubtfully at the ladders, but:

"It's safe enough," I said, "even for your weight. The chief is as heavy. I'll lead the way."

And so we set out, descending slowly. When at last the rubble-covered floor of the tunnel was beneath our feet, Weymouth paused, breathing deeply.

"That's the way to the original entrance," I said, pointing, "up the slope; but it's completely blocked fifteen yards along. There must be a bend, or a series of bends, because where it originally came out heaven only knows. However, this is our way."

I turned to where the shadowy figure of Ali waited, a lantern swinging in either hand so that the light shining up on to his bearded face lent it an unfamiliar and mask-like appearance. I nodded; and we began to descend the tunnelled winding slope. At a point just before we came to the last bend, Ali paused and held up one of the lanterns warningly.

"There's a pit just in front of us, Weymouth," I explained.

"It doesn't lead anywhere, but it's deep enough to break one's neck. Pass to the left."

We circled cautiously around the edge of this mysterious well, possibly designed as a trap for unwary tomb robbers. Then came the sharp bend, and here Ali left one of his two lanterns to light us on our return journey. The gradient became much steeper.

"We were starting on a stone portcullis which the chief believed to be that of the actual burial chamber," I explained, as we stumbled on downward in the wake of the dancing lantern. "He had a system of dealing with these formidable barriers which was all his own. Probably a few hours' work would have seen us through. Here we are!"

Ali paused, holding the lantern above his head..... And, as he did so he uttered a loud cry.

I pushed past Weymouth in the narrow passage and joined the headman. He turned to me in the lamplight. His face was ghastly.

"Good God!" I clutched the Arab's arm.

A triangular opening, large enough to admit a man, yawned in the bottom left-hand corner of the portcullis!

Ali raised his lantern higher. I looked up at a jagged hole in the right top corner....

"What does this mean?" Weymouth demanded hoarsely.

"It means," I replied, in a voice as husky as his own, "that someone has finished the job ... and finished it as Sir Lionel had planned!"

§ 3

The tomb of the Black Ape was extraordinary.

Whilst structurally it resembled in its main features others with which I was familiar, it was notable in its possession of an endless fresco of huge black apes. There were no inscriptions. The sagging portcullis, viewed from the interior of the chamber, created an odd hiatus in the otherwise unbroken march of the apes.

Low down in the corner of one wall was a square opening which I surmised must lead to an antechamber, such as is sometimes found. The place contained absolutely nothing so far as I could see except a stone sarcophagus, the heavy lid of which had been removed and laid upon the floor. Within was a perfectly plain wooden mummy case, apparently of sycamore, its lid in position.

I was defeated. Either the mummy case was the least valuable object in the burial chamber, and everything else had been looted, or the thieves had been interrupted in the very hour of their triumph!

I hope I have made the scene clear, Ali standing almost as still as a statue, holding his lantern aloft; Weymouth a dim figure at one end of the sarcophagus, and I facing him from the other; the black apes marching eternally around us. Because this was the scene, deep there in the Egyptian rock, upon which eerily a sound intruded. . . .

"What's that?" Weymouth whispered.

We stood listening, reduced to that frame of mind which makes sane men believe in ghosts.

And, as we listened, the sound grew nearer.

It was made by soft footsteps. . . .

Weymouth recovered himself first; and:

"Quick," he whispered to Ali, "through the opening!"

He pointed to that square gap which I have mentioned and which I supposed to communicate with an antechamber.

"Quiet!" he added. "Not a sound!"

Led by Ali, we crossed the chamber, and as the headman stooped and disappeared only a dim and ghostly light shone out to guide us.

"Go on!" Weymouth urged.

I ducked and entered. Weymouth followed.

"Cover the lantern!"

Ali began to speak rapidly in Arabic, but:

"Cover the lantern!" Weymouth repeated angrily. "Be quiet!"

Ali threw something over the lantern and we found ourselves in utter darkness.

In a low tone, the headman began to speak again, but:

"Silence!" Weymouth ordered.

Ali Mahmoud became silent. He was one of the bravest men I have ever known, but now his broken tones spoke of fear. Partially, I had gathered what he wanted to say. My recognition only added to the horror of the situation.

That quiet shuffling had ceased. The air was indescribably stuffy, as one finds in such places. I knelt, resting my shoulder against the side of the opening, hoping that I might have some view of the outer chamber if anyone carrying a light should enter it.

Hard breathing in my ear told of Weymouth's nearness.

Of the size or shape of the place in which we were hiding I had formed no impression whatever.

Then, they began to advance again . . . soft footsteps.

"Whoever comes," Weymouth whispered, "don't stir!"

There was absolute silence. If found myself listening to the ticking of my wrist-watch. A minute passed.

Then dawned a dim light. It outlined the triangle beside the portcullis.

The light increased. I recognised it as the ray of an electric lamp. And in some strange way this discovery was a relief. I suppose, without recognising the fact, I had been in the grip of superstitious fear. God knows what I had expected! But the approaching threat became less horrible at the moment I realised the presence of modern science in its equipment.

Weymouth's breathing had ceased to be audible.

A figure appeared in the opening . . . a fan of white light spread itself across the floor.

The figure stooped and entered. . . . I saw an Arab woman robed in shapeless black, her pose furtive. She held a flashlamp, casting its ray all about the burial chamber. This was anomaly enough. But I was less concerned with it than with the hand that held the torch. . . .

A delicate slender hand it was, nurtured in indolence—an unforgettable hand, delicious yet repellent, with pointed, varnished nails: a cultured hand possessing the long, square-jointed thumb of domination; a hand cruel for all its softness as the velvet paw of a tigress.

My breath came sharply. Weymouth's fingers gripped my shoulder.

Had he seen what I had seen? Did he understand?

The woman crossed in the direction of the sarcophagus. I saw that she wore loose slippers—that her ankles were of that same dull ivory as the chaste, voluptuous hand.

She disappeared. Only by those shadows which the torchlight cast could I judge of her movements. She went all but silently in those soft slippers, but I thought that she had stooped to examine the sarcophagus. Apparently she made no attempt to raise its wooden lid. The light grew brighter—ever brighter.

She was approaching the low entrance to that antechamber in which we crouched!

At the very threshold she paused.

The light of her lamp painted a white fan which extended to within a few inches of my knees, touching nothing but rugged floor. By cheer chance—as I thought, then—no one of us came within its radius.

It moved, shining now directly upon the triangular opening beside the portcullis. I could see the woman's body as a dim outline. She stooped and went out. I listened to the rubble moving beneath her slippered feet as she mounted the sloping passage. Weymouth's breathing became audible again close to my ear. The sound receded . . . receded . . . and ceased; then:

"Quiet!" Weymouth whispered. "Don't move until I give the word."

My legs were aching because of the discomfort of my position, but I stuck to it, still listening intently.

Absolute silence. . . .

"Ali," Weymouth directed. "Uncover the light."

Ali Mahmoud dragging his robe from the lantern, dim yellow light showed us the low-roofed, rough-hewn chamber in which we crouched.

"Effendim!" Ali exclaimed, in quivering tones. "I saw him when first we came in. Look!"

Face downwards upon a mound of rubbish in an angle farthest from the entrance was a brown man, naked except for his loincloth and dark turban knotted tightly about his head!

"He is cold," Ali continued; "and as I knelt in the darkness I had to support my weight upon his dead body. . . ."

§ 4

On hands and knees I crawled out into the passage. I contrived to make no sound.

I looked to my left.

Ali's lantern was just visible at the bend. Standing upright, I headed for it, stepping warily. At the corner I dropped to my knees again and stared up the slope. She was not in sight: I could trace the path beyond the wall to the next bend.

I proceeded. . . .

In view of the ladders I pulled up. A vague light, moon rays on black velvet, broke the darkness. I thought perhaps it came down the shaft . . . but it began to fade.

I hurried forward. I reached our excavation and looked up. No one was on the ladders.

Hopelessly puzzled I stood, listening.

And in that complete stillness I heard it again . . . the sound of footsteps softly receding. . . .

She had gone up the steep slope which led to the former entrance—but which now ended in an impassable mass of rock!

I had her!

Weymouth's instructions were forgotten. I meant to make a capture! This woman was the clue to the mystery. . . . It was she who had stolen the chief's body—and even without the clue provided by Rima's camera, I should have known her in spite of disguise.

Madame Ingomar!

Scrambling over irregular masses of stone, I had not gone five paces, I suppose, before a definite fact intruded itself. Whereas the air in the lower passage was fetid, almost unbreathable, here it was comparatively fresh.

I came to the angle, rounded it, and stopped. . . . I shot the ray of a torch ahead, expecting a wall of rock.

An irregular opening, some five feet high, yawned, cavernesque, right of the passage!

Running forward, I climbed through, throwing the ray of my torch before me. This opening had been completed at some earlier time, closed up and camouflaged.

I stood in a shallow pit. A ladder rested beside me, rearing its length into the darkness above. All this I saw as I stared upward, intently.

Light in hand, I mounted the ladder. . . . I found myself in a low tunnel. I stood still, listening, but could detect no sound. I pushed on, cautiously, the air growing ever fresher, until suddenly recognition came.

Switching off the light, I stared up to an opening where one pale star hung like a diamond pendant.

The passage ahead of me was empty. But I knew, now, where I stood, and I knew how the woman had escaped. . . .

This was Lafleur's Shaft!

§ 5

Weymouth nodded, looking very grim.

"We are dealing with a she-devil," he said, "and I suppose she came to look for her servant."

He shone a light upon the upturned face of the man we had found in that chamber. It was a lined, leering face, hideous now by reason of the fact that the man had died from strangulation. Between the brows was a peculiar, coloured mark—how produced I could not imagine. But it appeared to have been seared in the yellow flesh, and then enamelled in some way.

"A Burman," Weymouth went on, "and a religious dacoit."

He touched the mark with his finger, then stood still, listening. We all three listened, breathlessly—yet I dare swear no one of us knew what he expected to hear.

I thought as I looked down at those distorted features that if the slanting eyes were opened, this might well be a twin brother of the malignant creature who had followed me to Cairo.

"What does it all mean?" I asked.

"It means that our worst suspicions were correct," Weymouth replied. "If ever I saw one, this is a servant of Dr. Fu Manchu! This carries me back, Greville, to a scene in Sir Lionel's house late in 1913—the death of the Chinaman, Kwee. It may be a coincidence but it's an odd one. Because Kwee met his death when he was engaged on the same duty which I presume brought this yellow demon here."

"The murder of Barton?"

Weymouth nodded.

"Precisely. It's more than strange, and it's very horrible."

"Yet surely there's hope in it," I exclaimed excitedly. "This man belonged to the enemy. He has been strangled. It is just possible. . . ."

"By heavens! it is!" he took me up. "After all he didn't die at the hands of his own friends."

"One thing is fairly certain," I said; "he came by the same route as the woman—by Lafleur's Shaft. What isn't certain is when a way was forced through."

"Nor why a way was forced through," Weymouth added. "What in heaven's name were they after? Is it possible"—he lowered his voice, staring at the procession of hideous, giant apes which marched eternally round the walls of the chamber—"that there was something in this tomb beyond. . . ." He nodded in the direction of the sarcophagus.

"Quite possible," I replied; "but lacking special information to the contrary the first thing any excavator would do would be to open the mummy case."

"This seems to have been done."

"What!" I cried. "What!"

"Look for yourself," Weymouth invited, a curious expression in his voice.

He directed a ray on one end of the sarcophagus; whereupon:

"Good God!" I cried.

The wooden rivets had been removed, the lid raised and then replaced! Two wedges prevented its falling into its original position, leaving a gap of an inch or more all around. . . .

I stared in utter stupefaction, until:

"Have you any idea why that should be done?" Weymouth asked.

I shook my head. "Unless to make it easier to lift again," I suggested.

"If that was the idea," Weymouth went on quickly, "we will take advantage of it." He turned to Ali. "Hold the light—so. Now, Greville, get a grip with me, here. Don't move to any other part of the lid if you can avoid it—there may be fingerprints. And now . . . see if we can raise it."

In a state of such excitement as I cannot describe, I obeyed. Simultaneously we lifted, steadily. It responded to our efforts, being lighter than I had supposed. . . .

I fixed a half-fearful gaze upon its shadowy interior.

It appeared to contain a dull, grey mass, irregular in contour, provokingly familiar yet impossible to identify in that first dramatic moment. The very unexpectedness of its appearance destroyed my reasoning powers, temporarily defeating recognition.

When we had the lid at an angle of about forty-five:

"Hold it!" I called. "I'll take the other end."

"Right!" Weymouth agreed.

"Now!"

We lifted the lid bodily and laid it on the floor.

I could not have believed that that night of mystery and horror had one more thrill for my jaded nerves. Yet it was so, and it came to me then—an emotion topping all the others; such a thing as no sane man could have conjured up in his wildest imaginings. . . .

Amazed beyond reasonable articulation, I uttered a sort of strangled cry, staring—staring—down into the sarcophagus.

Overstrain and the insufferable atmosphere of the place may have played their parts. But I must confess that the procession of apes began to move about me, the walls of the tomb to sway.

I became aware of a deadly sickness, as I stared and stared at the grey-white face of Sir Lionel Barton, lying in that ancient coffin wrapped in his army blanket!

PART TWO

CHAPTER FOURTH—*Fah Lo Suee*

CHAPTER FIFTH—*Nayland Smith Explains*

CHAPTER SIXTH—*The Council of Seven*

Chapter Fourth

FAH LO SUEE

"Better turn in, Greville," said Dr. Petrie rapidly.

"Lie down at any rate. Can't expect you to sleep. But you've had enough for one night. Your job is finished for the moment. Mine begins."

How the others had reacted to our astounding discovery I am quite unable to relate. I was in no fit condition to judge.

Petrie half supported me along the sloping passage, and administered a fairly stiff peg from his flask which enabled me with Ali's aid to mount the ladders. I was furious with myself. To have to retire when the most amazing operation ever attempted by a surgeon was about to be performed—the restoring of a dead man to life! . . . But when at last I dropped down on my bed in the tent, I experienced a moment of horrible doubt—a moment during which I questioned my own sanity.

Ali Mahmoud's expression, as he stood watching me anxiously, held a certain reassurance, however. That imperturbable man was shaken to the depths of his being.

"Effendim," he whispered, "it is Black Magic! It is Forbidden this tomb!" He grasped an iron ring which he wore upon his right hand, and pronounced the *takbîr*, being a devout Moslem. "Everyone has told me so. And it is true!"

"It would seem to be," I whispered. "Go back. You will be wanted."

I had always loved the chief, and that last glimpse of his grey-white face, under the astounding circumstances of our discovery, had utterly bowled me out. The things I had heard of Dr. Fu Manchu formed a sort of dizzy background—a moving panorama behind this incredible phantasy. There was no sanity in it all—no stable point upon which one could grasp.

Was Sir Lionel dead, or did he live? Dead or alive, who had stolen his body, and why? Most unanswerable query of all—with what possible object had he been concealed in the sarcophagus?

A thousand other questions, equally insane, presented

themselves in a gibbering horde. I clutched my head and groaned. I heard a light footstep, looked up, and there was Rima standing in the opening of the tent.

"Shan, dear!" she cried, "you look awful! I don't wonder. I have heard what happened. And truly I can't believe it even now! Oh, Shan, do you really, really think——"

She fell on her knees beside me and grasped my hand.

"I don't know," I said, and scarcely knew my own voice. "I have had rather a thick time, dear, and I, well . . . I nearly passed out. But I saw him."

"Do you think I could help?"

"I don't know," I replied wearily. "If so, Petrie will send for you. After all, we're quite in his hands. I don't want you to hope for too much, darling. This mysterious 'antidote' seems like sheer lunacy to me. Such things are clean outside the scope of ordinary human knowledge."

"Poor old boy," said Rima, and smoothed my hair caressingly.

Her touch was thrilling, yet soothing; and I resigned myself very gladly to those gentle fingers. There is nothing so healing as the magnetism of human sympathy. And after a while:

"I think a cigarette might be a good idea, Rima," I said. "I'm beginning to recover consciousness!"

She offered me one from a little enamelled case which I had bought in Cairo on the occasion of her last birthday—the only present I had ever given her. And we smoked for a while in that silence which is better than speech; then:

"I saw something queer," said Rima suddenly, "while you were away with Mr. Weymouth. Are you too weary—or do you want me to tell you?"

Her tone was peculiar, and:

"Yes—tell me what you saw," I replied, looking into her eyes.

"Well," she went on, "Captain Hunter came along after you had gone. Naturally, he was as restless as any of us. And after a while—leaving the hut door open, of course—I went and stood outside to see if there was any sign of your return. . . ."

She spoke with unwonted rapidity and I could see that in some way she had grown more agitated. Of course I had to allow for the dreadful suspense she was suffering.

"You know the path, at the back of the small hut," she

continued, "which leads up to the plateau."

"The path to Lafleur's Shaft?"

Rima nodded.

"Well, I saw a woman—at least, it looked like a woman—walking very quickly across the top! She was just an outline against the sky, and I'm not positive about it at all. Besides, I only saw her for a moment. But I can't possibly have been dreaming, can I? What I wondered, and what I've been wondering ever since is: What native woman—she looked like a native woman—would be up there at this time of night?"

She was sitting at my feet now, her arm resting on my knees. She looked up at me appealingly.

"What are you really thinking?" I asked

"I'm thinking about that photograph!" she confessed. "I believe it was—Madame Ingomar! And, Shan, that woman terrifies me! I begged uncle not to allow her to come here—and he just laughed at me! I don't know why he couldn't see it . . . but she is dreadfully evil! I have caught her watching you, when you didn't know, in a way. . . ."

I bent down and rested my head against her tangled curls.

"Well?" I said, my arm about her shoulders.

"I thought you . . . found her attractive. Don't get mad. But I knew, I knew, Shan, that she was dangerous. She affects me in the same way as a snake. She has some uncanny power. . . ."

"Irish colleens are superstitious," I whispered.

"They may be. But they are often wise as well. Some women, Shan—bad women—are witches."

"You're right, darling. And it was almost certainly Madame Ingomar that you saw!"

"Why do you say so?"

Then I told her what had happened in the tomb, and, when I had finished:

"Just as she disappeared," Rima said, "I heard footsteps—quick, padding footsteps—on the other side of the wâdi. I called out to Dr. Petrie, but the sound had died away . . . . I'd had one glimpse of him, though—a man running."

"Did you recognise him?"

"Yes."

"What!"

Rima looked up at me reflectively, and:

"Do you remember the Arab who came into camp some days ago and insisted that he must see uncle?"

I nodded.

"I think I know the man you mean—the chief asked me to find out what he wanted?"

"Yes."

"A gaunt-faced fellow—steely piercing eyes? Spoke very queer Arabic and denied all knowledge of English. Told me quite bluntly he had nothing whatever to say to me, but must see Sir Lionel. I finally told him to go to the devil. Why, good heavens, Rima . . . . that was the evening before the tragedy!"

"Well," said Rima in a very low voice, "this was the man I saw running along the ridge to-night!"

"I don't like the sound of it," I admitted. "We have trouble enough already. Did he see you?"

"He couldn't have done. Besides, he was running at tremendous speed."

Even as she spoke the words, my heart seemed to miss a beat. I sprang up. Rima clutched me, her beautiful eyes widely opened.

Racing footsteps were approaching the tent!

I didn't know what to expect. My imagination was numb. But when the flap was dragged aside and Ali Mahmoud unceremoniously burst in, I was past reprimand, past any comment whatever.

"Effendim! Effendim! Quick, please. They tell me not to disturb Forester Effendim and Captain Hunter. . . His camp bed!"

"What!—the chief's?"

"I am ordered to carry it up to the mouth of the old shaft!"

"Ali Mahmoud!"

Rima sprang forward and grasped the headman's shoulders.

"Yes! Yes!" His eyes were gleaming madly. "It is true, lady! It is Black Magic, but it is true."

Of all the queer episodes of that nightmare business there was none more grotesque, I think, than this of Ali and I carrying Sir Lionel's camp bed up the steep path to that gaunt and desolate expanse upon which Lafleur's Shaft opened. As we had come out of the chief's tent, I had heard the voices of Jameson Hunter and Forester in the big hut.

I was literally bathed in perspiration when we reached our goal. Dropping down upon the light bed, I stared out over that prospect beneath me. Right at my feet lay the Sacred Valley of Der-el-Bahari; to the right the rugged hills and ravines of this domain of the dead. Beyond, indicated by a green tracing under the stars, the Nile wound on like a river of eternity. For a few moments I regarded it all, and then Rima's fingers closed over my own.

A lantern stood at the mouth of Lafleur's Shaft.

We began to descend—to where a group awaited us.

Never, to the end of everything, shall I forget that moment when Weymouth and Dr. Petrie lifted Sir Lionel, still swathed in his worn army blanket, and laid him on the camp bed. Ali Mahmoud, who possessed the lean strength of a leopard, had carried him up the short ladder on his shoulders. But the effort had proved dangerously exhausting to the sufferer. Anxiety was written deeply upon Petrie's face as he bent over him.

Rima was almost as ghostly pale as he who had been plucked out of the gates of death. She was staring at Petrie fearfully, as one who glimpses a superman. But my own feelings were oddly compounded of joy and horror—joy because the dear old chief had been given a chance to live; horror, because I recognised a scientific miracle—and suddenly, awfully, appreciated the terrifying genius of Dr. Fu Manchu.

At which moment, Sir Lionel opened his eyes—gazed vacantly, and then saw us.

"Cheer up, Rima—child," he whispered. "God bless you fellows." And to me: "Thanks for the dash to Cairo. Good scout!"

He closed his eyes again.

§ 2

"Well, Nurse," said Petrie, as Rima came out and joined us on the hotel terrace, "what do you think of our patient?"

Rima, a delicious picture in a dainty frock which had taken the place of the rough kit she wore in camp, fixed that grave look of hers on the speaker.

Then she turned swiftly aside, and I saw a threat of tears in her eyes.

"Yes," Petrie murmured. "I don't quite know what to make of him. I'm only an ordinary practitioner, Rima, and although I've searched every hotel in Luxor, this is an off season. There isn't a man in Upper Egypt whose opinion I could take. And the only likely Cairo man, as bad luck would have it, is away on leave."

Silence fell between us. Sir Lionel Barton—first perhaps of modern Orientalists—lay in his room in a state of incomparable coma, a mysterious secret locked in his memory. Petrie had rescued him from death—dragged him back, indeed from the other side of that grim Valley—by virtue of an unnamed drug prepared by the greatest physician the world had ever known.

Strange, tragic, that so mighty a brain as that of Dr. Fu Manchu should be crooked—that an intellect so brilliant should be directed not to healing but to destruction. He was dead. Yet the evil of his genius lived after him. . . .

In a few weeks now this quiet spot in which we sat would be bustling with busy, international life. The tourist season would have set in. Dragomans, sellers of beads, of postcards and of scarabs would be thick as flies around the doors of the hotels. Dahabîyehs would moor at the landing-places; fashionable women would hurry here and there, apparently busy, actually idle: white-suited men, black-robed guides—bustle—excitement. . . .

Even now, as I stared across the nearly deserted roadway and beyond old peaceful Nile to where crags and furrows marked the last resting place of the Pharoahs, even now I could scarcely grasp the reality of it all.

What was the secret of the Tomb of the Black Ape? Careful examination had enabled us to prove that Lafleur at the time his excavation was abandoned—that is, at the time of his disappearance in 1909—had got within a few yards of the passage leading to the burial chamber. Some unknown hand had completed the work and then had so carefully concealed the opening that later Egyptologists had overlooked it. Or had the hand been that of Lafleur himself?

More astounding still: the inner stone door, or portcullis, had been opened before! And it had been reclosed—so cunningly that even the chief had thought it to be intact! We were not the first party to reach it.

Therefore . . . when had the tomb been emptied? In Lafleur's time or a week ago whilst I was in Cairo? Who had reclosed it, and why had he done so? Above all—what had it contained?

Maddening to think that poor Sir Lionel might know . . . but was unable to tell us. . . .

My musings were interrupted.

"Next to Brian Hawkins of Wimpole Street," came Petrie's voice, "there's one man with whom I'd give half I possess to have ten minutes' conversation."

"Who is that?" Rima asked.

"Nayland Smith."

I looked across.

"Not as a professional consultant," Petrie added. "But somehow, in the old days, he seemed to find a way."

"Uncle was always talking about him," said Rima. "And I've hoped we should meet. He's chief of some department of Scotland Yard, isn't he?"

"Yes. He finally left Burma five years ago. And I'm looking forward to meeting him in England."

"Weymouth cabled him," said I, "but had no reply."

"I know." Petrie stared vacantly before him. "It's rather queer and quite unlike Smith."

"Is there really nothing we can do?" said Rima.

She rested her hand suddenly on Petrie's arm and I knew she feared that she might have offended him.

"I didn't mean you're not doing everything that's possible— I just mean do you think we're justified in waiting?"

"I don't !" he replied honestly; for honesty was the keynote of his character. "But I doubt if either of the men I mentioned could indicate any treatment other than that which we're following. Physically, Sir Lionel is gaining strength day by day, but his mental condition puzzles me."

"Is it contrary to your experience, Doctor?" I asked; "I mean your experience of this strange drug which must have been used in his case?"

Petrie nodded.

"Quite contrary," he assured me. "The crowning triumph of Fu Manchu's methods was their clean-cut effects. His poisons served their purpose to a nicety. His antidotes restored to normal."

A thick-set figure rounded the corner of the building and bore down upon us.

"Ah, Weymouth!" said Petrie. "You look as though a long drink with a lump of ice in it would fit the bill."

"It would!" Weymouth confessed, dropping into a cane chair. He removed his hat and mopped his forehead.

"Any luck?" said I.

Whilst Petrie gave an order to a waiter, Weymouth shook his head sadly.

"Madame Ingomar is known to a number of people in Luxor and neighbourhood," he replied, "but not one of them can tell me where she lives!"

"It's therefore fairly obvious that she must have been either living in the native quarter or renting a villa!"

Weymouth looked at me with a tolerant smile, and:

"I agree," he replied. "My best local agent reported this morning, and you can take it for granted that madame has not been living in the native quarter. I have personally just returned from a very tiring inspection of a list of the available villas in and about Luxor. I can state with a fair amount of certainty that she did not occupy any of these."

A gentle rebuke which I accepted in silence. Dr. Petrie put the whole thing right, for:

"Scotland Yard methods have been pretty harshly criticised," said he, "generally by those who know nothing about them. But you must agree, Greville, that they don't fail in thoroughness."

He paused suddenly, arrested I suppose by my expression. I was staring at a tall Arab who, approaching the hotel, pulled up on sighting our group. His hesitation was momentary. He carried on, swung past us, and went in through the swing doors.

Rima sprang up and grasped my arm.

"The Arab," she cried; "the Arab who has just passed! It's the man I saw in camp. The man who ran along the top of the wâdi!"

I nodded grimly.

"Leave him to me!" I said, and, turning to Weymouth: "A clue at last!"

"Is this the mysterious Arab you spoke about?" excitedly.

"It is."

I dashed into the hotel. There was no sign of my man in the big lobby, in which only vedettes of the tourist army, mostly American, were to be seen. I hurried across to the reception clerk. He knew me well, and:

"A tall Arab. Just come in," I said quickly. "Bedoui, Fargâni, or Maazâi, for a guess. Where's he gone?"

An assistant manager—Edel by name—suddenly appeared behind the clerk and I thought I saw him grip the latter's shoulder significantly; as:

"You were asking about an Arab who came in, Mr. Greville?" said he.

"I was."

"He is employed by one of our guests—a gentleman of the Diplomatic Service."

"That doesn't alter the fact that he's been prowling about Sir Lionel's camp," I replied angrily. "There are one or two things I have to say to this Arab."

Edel became strangely embarrassed. His expression mystified me. He was Swiss and an excellent fellow; but reviewing what I had heard of the methods of Dr. Fu Manchu I began to wonder if my hitherto esteemed acquaintance might be a servant of that great evil man!

"What's the name of the diplomat?" I asked rather shortly. "Do I know him?"

Edel hesitated for a moment; but at last:

"He is a Mr. Fletcher," he replied. "Please forgive me, my dear Mr. Greville, but I have orders in this matter."

Now definitely angry, but realising that Edel wasn't to blame, I turned. Weymouth stood at my elbow.

"I respect your orders, Edel," I said, "but there can be no possible objection to my interviewing Mr. Fletcher's Arab servant?"

"May I add," said Weymouth harshly, "that I entirely agree with what Mr. Greville has said."

Edel recognised Weymouth; which seemed merely to add to his confusion of mind.

"If you will excuse me for a moment, gentlemen," he murmured, "I shall phone from the private office."

He withdrew—followed by the reception clerk who obviously dreaded cross-examination.

I exchanged glances with Weymouth.

"What the devil is this all about?" he said.

There was an interval during which Dr. Petrie came in with Rima. At which moment Edel reappeared, and:

If Mr. Greville and Dr. Petrie would be good enough to go up to Number 36," he requested, "Mr. Fletcher will be pleased to see them."

§ 3

"God knows we have trouble and enough," said Petrie, as the lift carried us to the third floor, "without the appearance of this unknown diplomat. I've never met a Mr. Fletcher. Can you imagine any reason why he should ask *me* to accompany you?"

"I can't," I admitted, and laughed, but not too mirthfully.

As we reached the third floor the Nubian lift-boy conducted us to the door of Number 36, pressed the bell, and returned to the lift.

The door opened suddenly. I saw a clean-shaven thick-set man, wearing a very well cut suit of the kind sometimes called "Palm Beach." With his black brows and heavy jaw, he more closely resembled a retired pugilist than any conception I might have formed of a diplomat.

Petrie stared at him in a very strange fashion; as:

"My name is Fletcher," he announced. "Dr. Petrie, I believe?" And then to me: "Mr. Greville? Please come in."

He held the door open and stepped aside. I exchanged glances with Petrie. We walked into the little lobby.

It was a small suite with a sitting-room on the left.

Why did Mr. Fletcher open his own door when he employed an Arab servant?

I was gravely suspicious, for the thing was mysterious to a degree, but:

"Come right through!" cried a voice from the sitting-room.

Whereupon, to add to my discomfort, Petrie suddenly grasped my arm with a grip which hurt. He stepped through the open doorway, I following close at his heels.

A window opened on to a balcony and to the right of this window stood a writing-table. Seated at the table, his back towards us, was the tall Arab whom we were come to interview!

I noted with surprise that he had removed his turban, and that the head revealed was not shaven, as I might have anticipated, but covered with virile, wavy, iron-grey hair.

Fletcher had disappeared.

As we entered, the man stood up and turned. The deep brown colour of his skin seemed in some way incongruous, now that he wore no turban. I noted again the steely eyes which I remembered; the lean, eager face—a face hard to forget once one had seen it.

But if I was perplexed, my companion had become temporarily paralysed. I heard the quick intake of his breath—turned . . . and saw him standing, a man rigid with amazement, positively glaring at the figure of the tall Arab beside the writing-table!

At last, in a whisper, he spoke.

"You!" he said, "you, old man! Is this quite fair?"

The Arab sprang forward and grasped Petrie's hand. Suddenly, seeing the expression in those grey eyes, I felt an intruder. I wanted to look away; but:

"It isn't!" I heard; "and it hurts to hear you say it. But there was no other way, Petrie. By heaven, it's good to see you again, though!"

He turned his searching glance upon me.

"Mr. Greville," he exclaimed, "forgive this comedy, but there are vast issues at stake."

"Greville," said Petrie, continuing to stare at the speaker with an expression almost of incredulity, "this is Sir Denis Nayland Smith."

§ 4

"I felt sure you would recognise Detective Inspector Fletcher," Nayland Smith declared. "You once spent a night with him, Petrie—in the Joy Shop, down Limehouse way: Detective-Sergeant Fletcher he was then. Have you placed him?"

Petrie's puzzled expression suddenly changed, and:

"Of course!" he cried. "I knew I'd seen him somewhere—Fletcher! But what on earth is he doing here?"

"Ask what I'm doing here," snapped Nayland Smith. "One answer covers both questions. Fletcher's in my department of the Yard, now: you may remember he always specialised in Oriental cases. He's been posing as the principal, very successfully, whilst I, in the capacity of an Arab with whom he had confidential business, have been at liberty to get on with my job."

"But I don't understand," said I, "just what your job has been. I can't make out what a senior official of Scotland Yard is doing here in Luxor. It surely isn't usual? I mean, you've been hanging about our camp for some time past, sir."

Nayland Smith smiled; and—a magic of all rare smiles—my impression of his character was radically altered. I found myself for the first time at my ease with this grim Anglo-Indian. I saw behind the mask and I loved the man I saw.

"Damned *un*usual," he admitted, "but so are the circumstances." He turned to Petrie. "I didn't recognise Weymouth. I passed you very quickly. We must send for him. Fletcher can go."

He began to pace up and down the room, when:

"Smith!" Petrie exclaimed. "I don't understand. We're all in together. What had you to gain by this secrecy?"

Nayland Smith pulled up in front of him, staring down hard, and:

"Do you quite realise, Petrie," he asked, "with whom we're dealing?"

"No," Petrie replied, bluntly, "I don't"

Nayland Smith stared at him for a while longer and then turned to me.

"How much do you know of the facts, Mr. Greville?" he snapped.

"I have heard something of the history of Dr. Fu Manchu," I replied, "if that's what you mean! But Fu Manchu is dead."

"Possibly," he agreed, and began to walk up and down again—"quite possibly. But"—he turned to the doctor—"you recognise his methods, Petrie?"

"Undoubtedly. so did poor Barton! By sheer luck, as you know, I had a spot of the antidote. But whilst it has worked the old miracle, there are complications in this case."

"There are," said Smith. And stepping to the writing-table he began to load a large and very charred briar with coarse-cut mixture from a tin. "It may be that the stuff has lost some if its potency in years—who knows? But one thing is certain, Petrie. I address you also, Mr. Greville."

He broke two matches in succession, so viciously did he attempt to strike them, but he succeeded with a third.

"All that fiendish armament is about to be loosed on the world again—perhaps reinforced, brought up to date. . . . And that's why I'm here."

Neither Petrie nor I made any comment. Nayland Smith, his pipe fuming between his teeth, resumed that restless promenade; and:

"You must know all the facts, Greville," he said rapidly. "Then we must form a plan of campaign. If only we can strike swiftly enough, the peril may be averted. It seems to be Fate, Petrie, but again I'm too late. Reports reached me from China, then from nearer home; from Cairo; from Moscow; from Paris and finally from London. Doubting everybody, I took personal action. And I definitely crossed swords with her for the first time at a popular supper restaurant in Coventry Street."

"Crossed swords with whom?" Petrie demanded, voicing a question which I myself had been about to ask.

But Nayland Smith, ignoring Petrie's question, continued to stride up and down, seemingly thinking aloud.

"New evidence respecting the sudden death of Professor Zeitland, the German Egyptologist, came to hand. I was satisfied that she was concerned. I sent Fletcher to interview her. . . .

"She had disappeared. We lost track of her for more than a week. All inquiries drew blank; until, by a great stroke of luck, the French police identified her at Marseilles. She had sailed for Egypt.

"Good enough for me! I set out at once with Fletcher! Perhaps I shall be better understood if I say that the chief commissioner sent me. Since our one and only meeting, further advices from China had opened my eyes to the truth.

"I arrived in Port Said two weeks ago to-day. I had nothing to go upon—no evidence to justify summary action; only one fact and a theory. . . ."

His pipe went out. He paused to relight it.

"Do I understand, Sir Denis," I said, "that you're speaking of Madame Ingomar?"

He glanced at me over his shoulder.

"Madame Ingomar? Yes. That's a nom-de-guerre. Her dossier is filed at Scotland Yard under the name of Fah Lo Suee. You'll recognise her when you see her, Petrie!"

"What!"

"You met her once, some years ago. She was about seventeen in those days; she's under thirty, now—and the most dangerous woman living."

"But who is she?" cried Petrie.

Nayland Smith turned, a lighted match held between finger and thumb.

"Dr. Fu Manchu's daughter," he replied.

CHAPTER FIFTH

NAYLAND SMITH EXPLAINS

"THE TRAIL led me from Cairo to Luxor," said Nayland Smith. "Information with which I was supplied from day to day clearly pointed to some attempt on Sir Lionel Barton.

"Professor Zeitland, I had learned, from facts brought to light after his sudden and mysterious death, had been studying the problem presented to Egyptologists by Lafleur's Tomb, or the Tomb of the Black Ape. He had contemplated excavations. He deeply resented what he looked upon as Sir Lionel's intrusion. Did you know this?"

He turned to me suddenly. His skin, as I new realised, had been artificially darkened. Looking out from that brown mask, his eyes were unnaturally piercing.

"Perfectly well."

Superintendent Weymouth, whose unexpected meeting with Sir Denis had reduced him to an astounded silence, now spoke for the first time since he had entered the room.

"Probably some of the professor's notes were stolen," he said.

"They were!" rapped Nayland Smith: "which brings us to Barton. Are his notes intact?"

He shot the question at me with startling rapidity.

"He made few notes," I replied. "He had a most astounding memory."

"In short, his memory was his note-book! This explains much. . . ."

He paused for a moment, and then:

"I immediately adopted the device which you know," he went on. "Fletcher installed himself here, and I used these rooms as my base of operations. I had first to track Fah Lo Suee to her lair. I use the term advisedly, for she is the most dangerous beast of prey which this century has known."

"I simply cannot understand," cried Petrie, "why Sir Lionel never suspected this woman!"

Nayland Smith shook his head irritably.

"I think he did—but too late. However—naturally I distrusted everybody, but I decided to take Barton into my confidence. It was on that occasion, Greville, that we met for the first time. I bear you no ill will, but I could have strangled you cheerfully. Short of revealing my identity, I was helpless . . . and I decided to stick to my disguise. . . ."

He shrugged his shoulders.

"I was wrong. The enemy struck. Forthright action might have saved him. I must have failed to do even what little I did do, for all the odds were against me, were it not that that very night I made up my mind to try to get to Sir Lionel secretly whilst the camp was sleeping.

"In one of your workmen, Greville—Said by name—I recognised an old friend! Said was once my groom in Rangoon! I dug him out of his quarters at Kûrna and appointed him my liaison officer.

"Then, with Said in touch, I started. I had found one man I could trust. . . .

"I reached Barton's tent three minutes too late. He had just scrawled that last message——"

"What!" Weymouth interrupted excitedly. "You actually saw the message?"

"I read it," Nayland Smith replied quietly. "Barton, awakened by the needle, miraculously realised what had happened. I am prepared to learn that he expected it . . . that, at last, he had begun to distrust 'Madame Ingomar.' It had just dropped from his hand as I entered.

"It was *my* voice, Greville, not his—that awakened you. . . ."

Nayland Smith ceased speaking, and stepping up to the table, began to knock ash from the steaming bowl of his briar, whilst I watched him in a sort of stupefaction. Petrie and Weymouth were watching him too. Truly, here was a remarkable man.

"I slipped away as quietly as I had come. I watched for developments . . . then I set out for the head of the wâdi, where Said was watching. And Said had news for me. Someone had passed his hiding place ten minutes before— someone who slipped by rapidly. Said had not dared to follow. His orders were to wait . . . but I guessed that he had seen the agent of Fah Lo Suee who had entered Barton's tent ahead of me, and who had done his appointed work. . . .

"'He was Burmese,' Said assured me. 'and I saw the mark of Kâli on his brow!'

"In a deep hollow, by the light of my torch, I wrote a message to Fletcher. Said set out for Luxor. I was taking no chances. The result of that message, Petrie, you know—you also, Weymouth. Fletcher despatched two telegrams.

"Then I returned, and from the slope above Sir Lionel's tent, overheard the conference. I still distrusted everybody. As early as Lafleur's time, a certain person was interested in the Tomb of the Black Ape. Of this I am confident. The nature of his interest it remains for us to find out. In the meantime, a member of the family of that great but evil man has penetrated to the Tomb——"

"Smith!" Petrie interrupted. "Some age-old secret—probably a ghastly weapon of destruction—has lain there, for thousands of years!"

Nayland Smith stared hard at the speaker; then:

"Right," he snapped—"as regards the first part. Wrong as regards the second."

Giving us no chance to ask him what he meant:

"My point of vantage regained," he went on rapidly, "I saw all that took place. I saw the hut opened and two lanterns placed inside. I realised that it was proposed to carry Sir Lionel there. I saw the body placed in the hut, and the door locked. I could do no more—for Barton."

§ 2

"Since it seemed fairly certain that the objective of these mysterious crimes was the Tomb of the Black Ape, I now made my way round to the enclosure. The door was locked, but I managed to find a spot where I could climb up the fencing and look over. I stared down into the pit and listened intently. In that silence, any movement below must have been clearly audible. But I could not hear a sound.

"I was mystified—utterly mystified. I began to wonder if poor Barton had been mistaken in his own symptoms. I began to think he might really be dead! Perhaps the man whom Said had seen had had no connection with the matter. For I confess I could imagine no object in inducing that form of artificial catalepsy of which we know Dr. Fu Manchu to have been a master.

"Crawling above the camp like a jackal, I taxed my brain to discover some line of action.

"None of you sleep much that night, and I had to watch my steps. It was a nerve-racking business, especially as I suspected that a trained assassin was prowling about somewhere—and possibly covering my movements.

"Failure seemed to threaten me again. I had failed in London. I had failed here. But I was expecting the return of Said at any moment, now, and presently I heard our prearranged signal: the howling of a dog.

"He, at least, had done his job. I replied.

"Perhaps my imitation was a poor one. All I know is that you, Greville, and others, came out into the wâdi with lanterns, and began to search all about the camp."

"We did," I interrupted. "That howling was unnatural. Dogs never came as near to the camp at such an hour."

"You found nothing," Nayland Smith went on; "and when all was quiet again, I crept round and rejoined Said. He had more news. As he had pulled across from Luxor to Kûrna, and in sight of the landing place, a motor-boat had passed, heading upstream. Note that, Weymouth. Standing in the bows was the Burman whom Said had seen near Sir Lionel's camp!

"This set me thinking. I came back here and turned up some recent reports. I discovered, Weymouth, that a certain Sheikh Ismail—who once slipped through our fingers in London—was living in the Oasis of Khârga. This venerable gentleman, for he must be well past eighty, I believe to be the present holder of the title of Sheikh al-Jébal, or head of the murderous sect of the *Hashishîn!*"

"A member of the old group!" said Weymouth excitedly.

"Exactly! And an associate of Dr. Fu Manchu! As a result, after a few hours' rest, I started for Esna. And I spent a very profitable day there."

"Esna!" I exclaimed. "Why Esna?"

"Because the old caravan road to the oasis starts from there, and because Esna is upstream. But whilst I was so employed, there's little doubt, I think, that Fah Lo Suee and her party, operating from Lafleur's Shaft, were completing the work begun by Barton...."

"Amazing," I interrupted, "but fate, I suppose, that not a soul went down all day. The men, of course, were given a holiday."

"I know," Smith said. "Said was with me. However, I got back just before dusk and went straight to the camp to see how the land lay. Everything seemed to be quiet, and I was following the edge of the wâdi and had reached a point just above the hut in which Sir Lionel's body lay, when I pulled up....

"It must have been inaudible from the tents. It came from directly below me—a soft, wailing cry. But I knew it! Good God, how well I knew it!...

"The call of a dacoit!

"Over these dangerous madmen, Greville, as well as the thugs and the hashishîn, the late Dr. Fu Manchu had acquired a mysterious control. I dropped flat on the ground, wriggled to the edge and looked down. Nothing moved—the place was dark and silent. But I continued to watch and presently I saw a seeming miracle.

"The door of the hut was open! I clenched my fists and stared. It was as though the gate of a tomb had opened. I did not know *what* to expect. But what I saw was this:

"A thick-set brown man, naked except for his loin-cloth, came out, bending double in the manner of a laden Eastern porter, and carrying on his shoulders the body of Sir Lionel Barton wrapped in a grey blanket!

"On the threshold, he laid him down. He locked the door with a key he carried, shouldered the body again, and set off up the wâdi.... How had he got into the hut and where had he obtained the key?"

"Weymouth has solved that mystery," Petrie interrupted. "The key was on Sir Lionel's chain. He had only partially undressed on the previous night, and the dacoit must have slipped in between the time that the hut was opened and the time that Sir Lionel was carried there."

Nayland Smith tugged at his ear, a nervous mannerism which I had already observed, and turning to Weymouth:

"Congratulations!" he said. "What was your clue?"

"The man had been chewing betel but. I found some...."

"*Chunam*! Brilliant, Weymouth! No school to equal that of

experience. But do you grasp the astounding fact that he had stuck to his post for some twenty hours, with nothing but betel nut to sustain him! Yet he still had the strength of a tiger—as I was to learn! . . .

"I started to follow. By the smaller hut, as you know, Greville"—turning to me—"there's a steep path leading to the plateau: it begins as a sort of gully. And in the dense shadow there my dacoit stopped.

"Need I say that I was searching madly for a proper plan of action? What was the right course? Barton, if not dead, was palpably unconscious. What was the purpose of this mysterious body-snatching? Even if they knew that you, Petrie, had been sent for——"

"They did!" I interrupted. "I was followed to Cairo!"

"Even so, I argued, it must be as Barton himself had believed. Someone needed him—alive! My decision was made. I would not arouse the camp—my first, natural impulse—nor interfere in any way. I would follow and see where he was being taken.

"At which moment I nearly made a fatal mistake. I was on the point of moving from the deep belt of shadow in which I lay concealed, when a second soft call drew my gaze upward to where the path ceased to be a ravine and topped the slope above.

"Another dacoit was descending, almost silently, but very swiftly.

"I shrank back.

"A low-toned conversation took place in the darkness beneath me; and then the pair raised the body of Sir Lionel and carried it rapidly up the slope and over the top.

"I gave them twenty seconds. I could risk no more. Then, fairly silent in my soft slippers, I raced up and threw myself prone on the crest. . . . They were heading westward across the plateau.

"Naturally, I had made myself acquainted with the outstanding peculiarities of the district immediately surrounding Sir Lionel's excavation; and in a flash, as I lay there, plainly visible in the moonlight should either of the dacoits have looked back, the truth dawned upon me. I knew where they were making for.

"They were carrying him to Lafleur's Shaft!"

§ 3

"When at last, using what little cover I could find, I ventured to approach the entrance to the shaft—which, I discovered, is a long, sloping tunnel—the dacoits were already far ahead of me. I could just see the moving light of a lantern.

"I stopped, lying flat by the entrance and looking down. What should I do next?

"For one moment the dreadful idea came to me that they were going to bury him—alive! I had it in mind to rush back to the camp for assistance, since I was single-handed and had no notion how many the enemy numbered.

"Wiser second thoughts prevailed. Sir Lionel lived. And they needed his knowledge. . . .

"Of Lafleur's Shaft I knew next to nothing. From what little I had gathered of its history, I understood that it was an abandoned cutting, terminating in a dead-end some forty feet below the level of the plateau.

"I waited—until I thought I might venture to descend the shaft to the first bend. It was hot and still—very still. No light showed ahead of me nor could I hear a sound. My sense of mystification increased. Where had they gone? What was their purpose?

"Risking everything, I flashed a light along the sloping path below me. I saw a rough tunnel terminating in another bend. I began to descend it. Sometimes my foot slipped and I stopped, listening. . . . Not a sound. I descended still further. Lafleur's Shaft, I learned, forms roughly a slanting figure Z. At last I came to a yawning pit. One fact my lamp revealed—the fact that a ladder rested in it. I stood in darkness, listening again.

"I could hear nothing.

"Using my lamp sparingly, I found my way to the head of the ladder and climbed down. On an irregular mass of stone at the base I paused. So far as my scanty information carried me, this was the end of Lafleur's Shaft. It was empty!

"Where had the dacoits gone?

"I knew, from experience of these wiry little Burmans, that they possessed a gorilla-like strength and that for one to have carried even so heavy a man as Sir Lionel Barton down the ladder slung across his shoulders was not an impossible task.

"But where had he gone?

"Cautious examination discovered a ragged gap in one wall of the pit, or well, in which I stood. I groped my way through and found myself in a slanting passage running, roughly, parallel with the tail of the Z of Lafleur's Shaft, but hewn in the solid rock and obviously of very early origin.

"Far below to my right, a vague light showed. . . .

"I stood still again, listening.

"Voices . . . then a crashing, booming sound.

"I crept down the slope. I came to a second ladder, and looking up saw the stars. This was Barton's excavation! A dim perception of the truth began to dawn on me. I stole down a little further. I lay flat in the passage—watching.

"In the light of several lanterns I saw a party of half-naked men working feverishly to break a way through the wall! They worked under a woman's direction! I heard her voice—an unforgettable, bell-like voice. . . ."

"Madame Ingomar!" I shouted, excitedly, jumping up and staring at Sir Denis.

"Undoubtedly, Fah Lo Suee. She was questioning Barton, who lay in the passage . . . *and Barton was answering her!*"

§ 4

"Beyond doubt they had been at their task for hours. Barton, unwillingly—perhaps unwittingly—helped them to complete it. They forced the opening. They all went through—four men led by Fah Lo Suee. Sir Lionel was left where he lay.

"I began to move back to the ladders. I had them in a trap! Not daring to use a light, I groped my way to the foot of the pit. I climbed to the first platform. Now using my torch, I went up to the second.

"Switching off the torch, I pressed myself against the side of the excavation.

"Three lanterns passed the gap below. I counted them. Their bearers were heading for Lafleur's Shaft. There was an interval. Then, a fourth light shone out into the pit; it grew brighter.

"A woman, in native dress, looked up to where I crouched on the platform. . . .

"She withdrew, and went on. I heard a vague shuffling—a distant voice. Silence came. . . . Three men and one woman. Where was the fourth man—and Barton?

"The answer was all too obvious. . . . Barton had served the purpose of Fah Lo Suee: his usefulness was ended. Whatever she had sought, she had found. And now I realised that my immediate duty was to Sir Lionel. I crept down again, rung by rung. And, just as I reached the jagged opening, an explanation of the mystery of the fourth man burst upon me with icy certainty. . . .

"Already it might be too late! Barton had served the purpose for which he had been kept alive. Now, a dead man—not a synthetically dead man—he was to be replaced in the hut. This was the task of the dacoit who had carried him to Lafleur's Shaft, and who had remained behind to carry him back!

"A dim light shone through the newly made opening. I crawled nearer; so near that at last I could touch Sir Lionel's body.

"The dacoit came out, stooping and holding the lantern. He would have been an easy shot but I had decided against the use of firearms. The professional strangler never had a chance; because I'd got my thumb on his jugular and my knee between his lean thighs almost before he suspected I was there. I had little compunction; but these people are queerly situated. This fellow had sinews like iron wire and the strength of a tiger. Yet, when I removed my grip and wondered how I should tie him up . . . he was dead!

"Perspiration blinded me and I was shaking with my exertions. I stood there, the fallen lantern at my feet, looking down at those two ghastly companions—the one indisputably dead; the other, for all his rigour and grey-white face, alive for all I knew to the contrary. Certainly, I had heard his voice not long since. . . .

"Taking up the lantern, which had remained alight, I stooped and went in through the triangular opening which had been made in the wall. . . . I found myself in the Tomb of the Black Ape!

"I need not describe it. The great sarcophagus was open—the

wooden lid roughly in place, the stone one lying on the floor. I raised the sycamore covering. The mummy case was empty.

"Observing in a corner a cavern-like opening, I crossed and explored it. It proved to be a low antechamber. Into this I dragged the dacoit so that he should be out of my sight. Then, I stood in the tomb, endeavouring to make up my mind what I should do about Barton.

"My brain was not at its best. But nevertheless I had to imagine what would happen when the dacoit failed to report. Also, I had to take it for granted that my theory respecting his orders was correct; namely that his job was to carry Barton back to the hut, relock the door, and rejoin Fah Lo Suee wherever she might be.

"Suppose one of the enemy returned in my absence and found Barton where he lay? It was a dreadful possibility.

"First I thought of dragging him into the antechamber with the dead dacoit. Then I realised that this would be useless. My second idea, wild though it sounds, was a good one. They would never think of looking in the sarcophagus! . . .

"The task was a heavy one. But I managed it. I replaced the lid, using some wedges which I found inside to prevent it closing entirely and to allow of air reaching the interior.

"I came out of Lafleur's Shaft. I heard the sound of a descending plane! At first, I couldn't believe my ears. Then came the explanation.

"And just as I grasped the fact that help for poor Barton—if he had not passed beyond its reach—had arrived, I heard a second sound . . . Said's signal!

"Appreciating his state of anxiety—I had been missing for hours—I circled round the camp and joined him. He had heard the decent of the plane, of course, but he was even more urgently concerned about a party of three men and a woman, the men bearing heavy burdens, who at that very moment, I gathered, were setting out on camels for Kûrna!

"I weighed the chances—and the stakes. I came to a speedy decision. Leaving Said on duty, I set out for a point on the Kûrna road—where Fletcher was posted. . . .

"Needless to add, I failed to overtake Fah Lo Suee. Fletcher had noted the mysterious caravan, but naturally had not challenged it. I returned, and made my return known to Said. . . ."

"You alarmed the whole camp!" I broke in. "We had learned to recognise that false dog's howling!"

"Quite!" Nayland Smith smiled his rare, revealing smile. "But Said informed me that Rima Barton, who had been here, in Luxor, was back in camp with Ali Mahmoud and that you three fellows were with Forester in the big hut....

"Dead beat though I was, another job remained: to enable you to find Barton! I sent Said out scouting. The last thing I desired was to make a dramatic entrance that night. Said presently returned to report that you, Weymouth, and Greville had gone to the excavation with Ali Mahmoud.

"I ordered Said to creep down Lafleur's Shaft and watch....

"He was back in less that seven minutes by my watch! He had met a woman coming out! He thought that she had not seen him. She had gone towards the Valley....

"My fatigue forgotten, I set out racing along the top of the wâdi——"

"Rima saw you!" I interrupted.

"Very likely. I observed that the door of the hut was open....

"A wild-goose chase! Madame had vanished! With characteristic cool courage she must have returned to find out what had become of her missing servant.

"When the news reached me that Barton lived, I was worse than dog-tired; I was exhausted. And that night I shared a humble shakedown with Said."

§ 5

"I dislike dividing our forces at this stage of the campaign," said Nayland Smith, "but there's nothing else for it. I had intended to send a message down, Petrie, if you hadn't anticipated me. As a matter of fact"—he glanced at the table—"I was writing it when the manager rang me up. I can play my lone hand no longer.

"Fletcher must stay on guard. We can't leave Sir Lionel unprotected. Rima, of course, must remain also. Indeed it would be useless to ask her to do otherwise. And I want you, Greville, to act as guide. It's a pretty desperate expedition. But there's a chance we may be able to strike quickly and strangle this dreadful business at the hour of its birth."

"Just a moment, Sir Denis," Weymouth interrupted. "Where do I come in?"

Smith turned to him, and:

"Glad to have you with me," he replied, "although your actual duty doesn't call for it."

"Thanks," said Weymouth dryly.

Smith met Dr. Petrie's fixed stare.

"Your leave starts next Thursday," he said. "And I can imagine how Kâramanèh is looking forward to seeing London again. . . ."

There was a short silence, then:

"Is that all you have to say?" asked the doctor.

Nayland Smith grasped his shoulders impulsively.

"We stuck together pretty closely in the old days," he said. "But, now, I daren't ask you——"

"You don't have to!" Petrie declared truculently. "I'm coming!"

"But where are we for?" I asked.

"For the house at present occupied by Fah Lo Suee."

"What!" Petrie exclaimed. "Then where is this house?"

"Near the Oasis of Khârga—which accounts for Weymouth's inability to trace it!"

"But Khârga's surely a hundred and fifty miles!"

"There's a sort of railway," I said, "and a train about twice a year, from somewhere down Farshût way."

"Not our route," snapped Nayland Smith. "We're going from Esna."

"But that's just a caravan road—and a bad one too. The chief and I went once—he had an idea of working on the Temple of Hibis there—and I'm not likely to forget it! Sir Lionel loves camels—and so we went on camels. It took us three days to get to Khârga and three days to get back!"

"What I wanted to know! We're going by car."

"Gad! There are some nasty bits!"

"There may be. But if Fah Lo Suee can do it, we can do it! The only car I could beg, borrow, or steal was a hard-bitten Buick about six years old. But I've got it parked in a quiet spot. I completed arrangements this morning. You might glance over this map."

From the table drawer he produced a large-scale map, when: "What on earth are we going for?" Weymouth demanded.

"We're going to spy! To-night, I have reason to believe, the powers of hell will be assembled in el-Khârga."

§ 6

I went along to the room occupied by the chief, quietly opened the door, and looked in. He lay as I had last seen him, haggard, and pale under his tan. But his expression remained untroubled, and his strong, bronzed hands, crossed, rested quietly on the sheet.

Rima was sitting by the open window, reading. She looked up as I entered, shook her head and smiled rather sadly.

I went across to her.

"No change, dear?"

"Not the slightest. But you look excited, Shan. What is it? Something that extraordinary man Nayland Smith has told you?"

"Yes, darling. He has discovered what we wanted to know. We start in an hour."

Rima grasped my arm. Her eyes opened widely and her expression grew troubled; then:

"Do you mean—her?"

I nodded.

"Where she is?"

"Yes."

"Oh, that woman terrifies me! . . . . I hate the thought of your going."

I put my arm around her shoulders.

"You have none of your old doubts, darling, have you?" I asked.

She shook her head, then nestled against me.

"But I'm afraid of her," she explained—"desperately afraid of her. She is evil—utterly evil. Where is this place?"

"In the Oasis of Khârga."

"What! But that's miles and miles away in the desert! However are you going to get there?"

I briefly explained Nayland Smith's plan; and when Rima

understood that he as well as Weymouth and Petrie were coming with the party, she seemed to grow easier in mind. Nevertheless, I could see that she was very troubled. And I have often wondered since if some moment of prevision came to her—if she foresaw, dimly, that a dreadful danger lay awaiting me in the Oasis of Khârga....

"To-night . . . the powers of hell will be assembled . . ."

Nayland Smith's strange words recurred to me.

A sound of footsteps on the gravel in the garden below brought my mind sharply to present dangers. I crossed to the balcony and looked down. One glance was sufficient to reassure me. Of course, I might have known!

Fletcher, pipe in mouth, was slowly pacing up and down—a sure guard, if ever a man had one.

"He stays there all the time. until the windows are closed," Rima explained. "Then he comes up and remains in the corridor."

I stooped for a moment over the chief, wondering what secrets were locked up in that big brain of his; wondering what had really happened down there in the Tomb of the Black Ape, and how much he knew regarding the missing contents of the sarcophagus. Rima stood beside me, and:

"You must be dreadfully tired, dear," I said.

"Oh, I get plenty of sleep," she replied, "in little bits. Nurse and I watch, turn and turn about, you know. I shouldn't be happy if I weren't doing it."

She looked up at me in that grave way which always made me ashamed of myself, made me feel that in some spiritual sense I was infinitely less than she. She lifted her lips to mine and I took her in my arms....

Having little enough to do in the way of preparation, I might not have torn myself away so quickly had it not been for the arrival of the nurse, a stout and capable Scottish woman, well-known to the management.

Perhaps it was as well. Rima clung to me almost pitifully.... Yes! I think some Celtic premonition must have warned her.
. . .

Downstairs I found Petrie waiting. Nayland Smith had disappeared; but:

"We are to join him at Esna," Petrie explained, "and for

some reason which I should regard as lunatic in any other than Smith, we are to pose as natives!"

"What!"

"Complete outfits—of which he has quite a wardrobe—are ready in his rooms. Weymouth is up there, now . . . and Said is standing by to guide us to the meeting place."

We stared hard at one another. But neither of us was in jesting mood; and:

"Please God we all get back safe," said Petrie simply.

CHAPTER SIXTH

THE COUNCIL OF SEVEN

THAT JOURNEY across the desert was strange in many ways—stranger and more horrible in its outcome than a merciful Providence allowed me to foresee. Nevertheless it aroused within me that sort of warning sixth sense which once before, on the train to Cairo, had advised me of the fact that I was spied upon. Possibly those religious fanatics guarding the extraordinary woman who called herself Madame Ingomar, and whom I knew claimed a sort of divine ordinance for their ghastly crimes, reacted upon me in some odd way. All I know is that I seemed to have developed a capacity for smelling them out; as will presently appear.

Weymouth, Petrie, and Nayland Smith rode in the back of the car, and I sat in front with Said. The starting place outside Esna has been cunningly chosen and we had every reason to believe that the outset of our journey had been managed without attracting attention.

Our disguises were passably good. Both Weymouth and Petrie were well sun-browned, and I had the complexion which comes with months of exposure to the weather. Petrie's distinguished appearance was enhanced by a tarbûsh and we had agreed to address him as "Bey." Weymouth, his robes crowned by a small white turban, resembled a substantial village sheikh; and I knew I could pass anywhere for a working Arab. Nayland Smith had retained the dress he was wearing at our first meeting.

Clear of the cultivated land that borders the Nile, and well out upon that ancient route which once had known no passage more violent than that of the soft padding camels and the tinkling of the camel bells, we met never a soul for thirty miles.

An hour, and another hour, we carried on, over desolate, gravelly, boundless waste. The sun blazed down mercilessly, although it was dipping to the western horizon. On we went, and on; until, having mounted a long slope, I saw a wâdi ahead.

Nothing moved within my view, although I searched the prospect carefully through Nayland Smith's field-glasses. The ground was hard as nails. But at the bottom of this little valley, I spied a clump of palms and knew that there must be water.

A sentinel vulture floated high overhead.

We bumped on merrily across the wildest irregularities. In no sense was this a motor road. And, having carefully studied the map, I had serious doubts of its practicability beyond the site of some Roman ruins merely marked "el-Dêr."

Down we swept into the wâdi, Said driving in that carefree manner which characterises the native chauffeur for whom tyres are things made to be burst, and engines, *djinns* or powerful spirits invulnerable to damage. However, we carried three spares and could only hope for the best.

I don't know what it was, unless perhaps the smoother running of the car, which drew my attention to the path ahead. We were now in the cup of the valley and rapidly approaching that clump of palms which I had noted. Suddenly:

"Pull up," rapped Nayland Smith.

His hand gripped my shoulder. Said pulled up.

"Look!"

We all stood and stared ahead. Nayland Smith pointed. The surface was comparatively soft here; and clearly discernible upon the road, crossing and recrossing, were many tyre marks!

"Fah Lo Suee!" said Smith, as if answering my unspoken query. "You can set your mind at rest, Greville. The road to Khârga is practicable for driving.

It was a curious discovery, and it set me thinking, hard. When Madame Ingomar had visited the camp, had she come all the way from the oasis, and had she returned there? Presumably, this was so. And, as always happened when my thoughts turned to this phenomenal woman, a very vivid mental picture presented itself before my mind. Her long, narrow, jade-green eyes seemed to be staring into mine. And I saw one of those small cigarettes which she loved, smouldering in a long engraved holder between delicate ivory fingers.

We passed the tree-shaded well, and mounted a stiff slope

beyond. I cannot answer for the others, but, as I have indicated, my own thoughts were far away. It was just as we reached the crest, and saw a farther prospect of boundless desert before us, that I became aware, or perhaps I should say conscious, of that old sense of espionage.

Nothing moved upon that desolate expanse, over which the air danced like running water. But a positive conviction seized me—a conviction that news of our journey had reached the enemy, or would shortly reach the enemy. I began to think about that solitary Pharoah's Chicken—that sentinel vulture—floating high above the palms. . . .

"Stop!" I said.

"What is it?" snapped Nayland Smith.

"May be nothing," I replied, "but I want to walk back to the brow of the hill and take a good look at the wâdi through which we have just come."

"Good!" He nodded. "I should have thought of it myself."

I got out the glasses, slung them across my shoulder, and walked rapidly back. At a point which I remembered, because a great blackened boulder lying straight across the road had nearly brought us to grief, I stooped and went forward more slowly. This boulder, I reflected, might provide just the cover I required. Lying flat down beside the stone, to the great alarm of a number of lizards who fled rapidly to right and left, I focused my glasses upon the clump of trees below me.

At first I could see nothing unusual. But the vulture still floated in the sky and the significance of his presence had become unmistakable. . . . Some living thing was hidden in the grove!

Adjusting the sights to a nicety, I watched, I waited. And presently my patience was rewarded.

A figure came out of the clump of trees!

I could see him clearly and only hoped that he could not see me. He might have passed muster, except for his tightly knotted blue turban. Emphatically, he was not an Egyptian. Standing beside the irregularly marked path, he placed a box upon the ground. I studied his movements with growing wonderment.

What could he be about? He seemed to be fumbling in the box.

Then suddenly he withdrew his hand, raised it high above his head—and a grey pigeon swept low over the desert, rose up and up, higher and higher! It circled once, twice, three times. Then, straight as an arrow it set out . . . undoubtedly bound for the Oasis of Khârga!

§ 2

"Very clever," said Nayland Smith grimly. "We shall therefore be expected. I might have guessed she wouldn't be taken unawares. But it confirms my theory."

"What theory?" Petrie asked.

"That to-night is a very special occasion at the house of the Sheikh Ismail!"

"We're running into a trap," said Weymouth. "Now that we know beyond any doubt that we're expected, what are our chances? It's true there's a railway to this place—but it's rarely used. The people of the oases have never been trustworthy—so that our nearest help will be a hundred and fifty miles off!"

Smith nodded. He got out and joined me where I stood beside the car, loading and lighting his pipe. He began to walk up and down, glancing alternately at me, at Weymouth, and at Dr. Petrie. I knew what he was thinking and I didn't interrupt him. He was wondering if he was justified in risking our lives on so desperate a venture; weighing the chances of what success might mean to the world against our chances of coming out of the job alive. Suddenly:

"What's the alternative?" he snapped, peering at Weymouth.

"There isn't one that I can think of."

"What do you say, Petrie?"

Petrie shrugged his shoulders.

"I hadn't foreseen this," he confessed. "But now that it's happened . . ."

He left the sentence unfinished.

"Get the map out, Greville," Nayland Smith rapped. . . . "Here, on the ground."

I dived into the front of the car and pulled out the big map.

This we spread on the gravelly path, keeping it flat by placing stones on its corners. Weymouth and Petrie alighted; and the four of us bent over the map.

"Ah!" Nayland Smith exclaimed and rested his finger on a certain spot. "That's the danger area, isn't it, Greville? That's where we might crash?"

"We might!" I replied grimly. "It's a series of hairpin bends and sheer precipices, at some points fourteen hundred feet up. . . ."

"That's where they'll be waiting for us!" said Nayland Smith.

"Good God!" Petrie exclaimed.

I exchanged glances with Weymouth. The expression in his blue eyes was enigmatical.

"Do you agree with me?" rapped Smith.

"Entirely."

"In short, gentlemen," he went on, "if we pursue our present route it's certain we shall never reach el-Khârga."

There was an interval of silence; then:

"We might easily break down before we get to the hills," I said slowly. "No one at the other end would be the wiser, except that we should never enter the danger zone. Now"—I bent and moved my finger over the map—"at this point, as you see, the old caravan road from Dongola to Egypt is only about thirty miles off. It's the Path of the Forty, formerly used by slave caravans from Central Africa. If we could find our way across to it, we might approach Khârga from the south, below the village marked Bûlag—it means a détour of forty or fifty miles, even if we can do it. But . . ."

Nayland Smith clapped me on the shoulder.

"You've solved the problem, Greville!" he said. "Nothing like knowledge of the geography of a district when one's in difficulties. We're in luck if we make it before dusk. But how shall we recognise the Path of the Forty?"

"By the bleached bones," I replied.

§ 3

Sunset dropped its thousand veils over the desert. The hills and wâdis of its desolate expanses passed from a glow of gold through innumerable phases of red. We saw crags that looked yellow under a sky of green: we saw a violet desert across which the ancient route of the slave traders stretched like a long-healed scar. There were moments when all the visible world resembled the heart of a tulip. But at last came true dusk with those scattered battalions of the stars set like pearls in a deep, velvet-lined casket.

Wonderful to relate, we had forced the groaning Buick over trackless miles south-west of the road, had found a path through the hills and had struck the Darfûr caravan route some twenty miles below el-Khârga. A difference in the quality of the landscape, a freshening and a cleanness in the air, spoke of the near oasis. Then, on a gentle slope:

"A light ahead!" Weymouth cried.

I checked Said. We all stood up and looked.

"That must be Bûlag," said Nayland Smith. "The house of the sheikh lies somewhere between there and el-Khârga."

"It's a straight road now," Petrie broke in. "Thank heaven, there's plenty of light. I'm all for blazing through the village as hard as we can go and then finding some parking place outside the town."

"Pray heaven the old bus can stand it!" Weymouth murmured devoutly.

And so, headed north, we set out. The road was abominable, but fairly wide where it traversed the village. Nayland Smith had relieved Said at the wheel and the scene as he coaxed a way through that miniature bazaar was one I can never forget. Every man, woman, child and dog had turned out. . . .

"They may send the news to el-Khârga," said Smith, as we finally shook off the last pair of staring-eyed Arab boys who ran after us, "but we've got to chance it."

We parked the doughty Buick in a grove of date-palms just south of the town. Weymouth seemed to anticipate trouble with Said, but I knew the man and had never doubted that he would consent to stand by. We left him a charged repeater and spare shells, and there were ample rations aboard to sustain him during the time he might have to mount guard. We marked an hour on the clock when, failing our reappearance, he was to push on with all possible speed to the post office at el-Khârga and communicate with Fletcher. How he carried out these orders will appear later.

As the four of us walked from the palm grove:

"It's a good many years," said Weymouth, "since I disguised myself!"

I looked at him in the moonlight, and I thought that he made a satisfactory and most impressive sheikh. True, his Arabic was bad, but so far as his appearance went, he was above criticism. Dr. Petrie was a safe bet; and Sir Denis, as I knew, could have walked about Mecca unchallenged. For my own part I felt fairly confident, for I knew the ways of the desert Arabs well enough to be capable of passing for one.

"We may be too late," said Nayland Smith; "but I feel disposed, Greville, to make straight for the town; otherwise we might lose ourselves. Then, you acting as spokesman, since you speak the best Arabic, we can inquire our direction boldly."

"I agree," said I.

And so it was settled.

§ 4

El-Khârga, as I vaguely remembered, though a considerable town of some seven or eight thousand inhabitants, consisted largely of a sort of maze of narrow streets roofed over with palm trunks so as to resemble tunnels at night. We penetrated, and presently found our way to the centre of the place. A mosque and two public buildings attracted my attention; and:

"Down here," I said, "there's a café, where we shall learn all we want to know."

Two minutes later we were grouped around a table in a small smoke-laden room.

"Look about," said Nayland Smith. "Kismet is with us. Whatever is going on in el-Khârga is being discussed here, to-night."

"I told you this was the place," said I.

But I looked about as he had directed. Certainly we had discovered the one and only house of entertainment in el-Khârga. . . . Little did I realise, as I considered our neighbours, where my next awakening would be!

Here were obvious townspeople, prosperous date-merchants, rice growers, petty officials and others, smoking their pipes in evening contentment. A definite odour of *hashish* pervaded the café. But the scene looked typical enough, until:

"Those fellows in the corner don't seem quite in the picture," said Weymouth.

I followed the direction of his glance. Two men were bending over a little round table. They smoked cigarettes, and a pot of coffee stood between them. In type, they were unfamiliar; unfamiliar in the sense that one didn't expect to come across them in an outpost of Egypt. In Cairo, they might have passed unnoticed, but their presence in el-Khârga was extraordinary. I turned to Nayland Smith, who was glancing in the same direction; and:

"What are they?" I asked.

"Afghans," he replied. "The great brotherhood of Kâli is well represented here."

"Remarkable," I said, "There can be few relations between Afghanistan and this obscure spot."

"None whatever!" Weymouth broke in. "And now, Greville, follow the direction in which my cigarette is pointing."

Endeavouring not to betray myself, I did as he suggested.

"A group of three," he added for my guidance.

I saw the group. I might have failed to identify them, but my memory was painfully fresh in regard to that dead man in the Tomb of the Black Ape. They wore their turbans in such a manner that the mark on the brow could not be distinguished. But I knew them for Burmans; and I did not doubt that they belonged to the mysterious fraternity of the dacoits! At which moment:

"Don't turn around until I give the signal," Nayland Smith rapped—"but just behind us."

I watched him as he glanced about, apparently in search of a waiter, then caught his signal. I looked swiftly into an alcove under the stairs . . . and then turned aside, as the gaze of a pair of fierce, wild-animal eyes became focused upon mine. The waiter arrived and Nayland Smith ordered more coffee. As the man departed to execute the order:

"Thugs!" he whispered. He bent over the table. "There are representatives of at least three religious fanatical sects in this place to-night. Dacoity is represented, also Thugee. The two gentlemen from Kandahar are *phansigars*, or religious stranglers!" He stared at Weymouth. "Does this suggest anything to you?"

Weymouth's blue eyes were fixed on me and:

"I confess, Greville," he said, "that I feel as you do.... And I can see that you're puzzled."

"I am," I agreed.

Nayland Smith raised his hand irritably and tugged at the lobe of his left ear; then:

"You understand, Petrie?" he jerked.

I looked at Dr. Petrie and it was unnecessary for him to reply. I saw that he did understand.

"Any doubt I may have had, Smith," he said, "regarding the purpose of this expedition, is washed out. In some miraculous way you have brought us to what seems to be the focus of all the dangerous fanatics of the Eastern world!"

"I don't claim all the credit," Smith replied; "but I admit that the facts confirm my theory."

"And what was your theory?" I asked.

"My theory," Smith replied, "based on the latest information to hand, and, as Weymouth here knows, almost hourly reports from police headquarters as widely divided as Pekin and Berlin, was this: That some attempt was being made to co-ordinate the dangerous religious sects of the East together with their sympathisers in the West. In short that the organisation once known as the *Si Fan*—you, alone, Greville," he turned to me, "fail to appreciate the significance of this—is in process of reconstruction! Something vital to the scheme was hidden in the Tomb of the Black Ape. This—and I can only blame myself—was removed under my very nose. The centre of the conspiracy is Fah Lo Suee—Dr. Fu Manchu's daughter, whose temporary headquarters I know to be here. To-night, at least, I am justified. Look around."

He bent over the table and we all did likewise, so that our four heads came very closely together; then:

"We are not too late," he said earnestly. "A meeting has been called . . . and we must be present!"

§ 5

The two Indians in the alcove stood up and went towards the door. As the pair disappeared:

"They lead, and we follow!" said Nayland Smith. "Go ahead, Weymouth, and act as connecting link."

He stood up, clasping his hands for the waiter. Weymouth had his meaning in a moment, nodded, and went out.

"Follow him, Greville!"

I grasped the scheme and went out behind the superintendent. The spirit of the thing was beginning to get me. Truly this was a desperate adventure ... for the stakes were life or death!

We were dealing with savagely dangerous characters who were, moreover, expert assassins to a man. Possibly those we had actually identified in the café represented only a small proportion of the murderous fanatics assembled that night in el-Khârga. ...

Weymouth led and I followed. I had grasped Nayland Smith's routine—and I knew that Petrie would be behind me. The score discharged, Smith would track Petrie.

I saw the bulky form of the superintendent at the far side of the square. By a narrow street he paused, peered ahead, and then glanced back.

I raised my hand. Weymouth disappeared.

Reaching the street in turn, I looked along it. I saw a sheer tunnel, but recognised it for that by which we had reached the square. There was an open space at the further end; and I saw Weymouth standing there in the moonlight and knew that I must be visible to him—as a silhouette.

He raised his arm. I replied. Then I looked back.

Dr. Petrie was crossing the square!

We exchanged signals and I followed Weymouth. The chain was complete.

For a time I thought that the house of the Sheikh Ismail might be somewhere on the road we had pursued from the palm grove to the town. But it was not so. Weymouth, ahead of me, paused, and gave the signal: left.

A narrow path through rice fields, with scanty cover other than that of an occasional tree, proved to be the route. If the men walking a few hundred yards ahead of Weymouth looked around, they could scarcely fail to see him! I only prayed, should they do so, that they would take it for granted he was bound upon business similar to their own.

Where an acacia drooped over a dome, very white in the moonlight, which marked the resting place of some holy man, the path seemed to end. So also did the cultivated land. Beyond stretched the desert away to distant hills.

By the shrine Weymouth paused, turned, and signalled. I looked back. Petrie was not in sight, I waited, anxiously ... and then I saw him, just entering the rice field.

We exchanged signs and I passed on.

Left of the cultivated land, and invisible from the rice, was a close grove of dôm palms. As I cautiously circled around the shrine and saw nothing but desert before me, instinctively I looked to the right and left. And there was Weymouth, not fifty yards away!

I joined him, and:

"The house is just beyond the trees," he said. "There's a high wall all around it. The two Indians have gone in."

We waited for Petrie. Then Nayland Smith joined us. He turned and stared back along the path. Evidently no other party was on the way yet. The track through the rice field was empty as far as the eye could see.

"What next?" said Smith. "I'm afraid I've left too much to chance. We should have visited the mudîr. The thing begins to crystallise. I know, now, what to expect."

He turned, and:

"Weymouth," he said, "do you remember the raid on the house in London in 1917?"

"By God!" cried Weymouth. "You mean the meeting of the Council of Seven?"

"Exactly!" Smith rapped.

"Probably the last."

"In England, certainly."

"The Council of Seven?" I said. "What is the Council of Seven?"

"It's the *Si Fan!*" Petrie replied, without adding to my information.

But the tone of his voice turned me cold in spite of the

warmth of the night.

"The Council of Seven," Weymouth explained, in his kindly way, "was an organisation with headquarters in China...."

"In Honan," Smith jerked.

"The president, or so we always believed," Weymouth continued, "was Dr. Fu Manchu. Its objects we never learned except in a general way."

"World domination," Petrie suggested.

"Well, that's about it, I suppose. Their methods, Greville, included wholesale robbery and murder. Everybody in their path they removed. Poison was their favourite method, animal or vegetable, and they apparently controlled in their campaign the underworld of Europe, Asia, Africa, and America. They made the mistake of meeting in London, and"—his tone grew very grim—"we got a few of them."

"But not all," Nayland Smith added. He suddenly grasped my shoulder, and: "Are you beginning to understand," he asked, "what was hidden in the Tomb of the Black Ape?"

I looked at him in blank surprise.

"I can see no connection," I confessed.

"Something," he went on tensely, "which has enabled the woman you know as Madame Ingomar, after an interval of thirteen years, to summon the Council of Seven!"

§ 6

In the shadow cast by a lebbekh tree we all crouched, Nayland Smith having his glasses focused upon the door in a long high wall.

The two Afghans had approached and now stood before this door. So silent was the night that we distinctly heard one of them beat on the panels. He knocked seven times....

I saw the door open. Faintly to my ears came the sound of a strange word. It was repeated—by another voice. The murderous Asiatics were admitted. The door was closed again.

"Representatives of at least two murder societies have arrived," said Smith, dropping the glasses and turning. "We are learning something, but not enough. In short, how the devil are we going to get into that house?"

There was a pause and then:

"Personally," said Dr. Petrie, "I think it would be deliberate suicide to attempt to do so. We have not notified the officials of el-Khârga of our presence or our business; and as it would appear that the most dangerous criminal group in the world is assembling here to-night, what could we hope to do, and what would our chances be?"

"Sanity, Petrie, sanity!" Nayland Smith admitted. But the man's impatience, his over-brimming vitality, sounded in his quivering voice. "I've bungled this business—but how could I know? . . . I was guessing, largely."

He stood up and began to pace about in the shadow, carefully avoiding exposing himself to the light of the moon; then:

"Yes," he murmured. "We must establish contact with el-Khârga. Damnable!—because it means splitting the party. . . . Hello!"

A group of three appeared, moving like silhouettes against the high, mud-brick wall—for the moon was behind us. Nayland Smith dropped prone again and focused the glasses. . . .

"The Burmans," he reported. "Dacoity has arrived."

In tense silence we watched this second party receive admittance as the first had done. And now I recognised the word. It was *Si Fan!* . . . Again the great iron-studded door was closed.

"We don't know how many may be there already," said Petrie. "Possibly those people we saw in the café—"

"Silence!" Smith snapped.

As he spoke, a tall man dressed in European clothes but wearing no hat appeared around the corner of the wall and approached the door. He had a lithe, swinging carriage.

"This one comes alone," Nayland Smith murmured. He studied him through the glasses. "Unplaceable. But strangely like a Turk. . . ."

The tall man was admitted—and the iron-studded door closed once more.

Nayland Smith stood up again and began beating his fist into the palm of his left hand, walking up and down in a state of tremendous excitement.

"We must do something!" he said in a low voice—"we must do something! Hell is going to be let loose on the world.

To-night, we could nip this poisonous thing in the bud, if only . . ." he paused. Then: "Weymouth," he rapped, "you have official prestige. Go back to el-Khârga—make yourself known to the mudîr and force him to raise a sufficient body of men to surround this house! You can't go alone, therefore Dr. Petrie will go with you. . . ."

"But, Smith! . . ."

"My dear fellow"—Nayland Smith's voice altered entirely—"there's no room for sentiment! We're not individuals to-night, but representatives of sanity opposed to a dreadful madness. Greville here has a peculiarly intimate knowledge of Arab life. He speaks the language better than any of us. This you will both admit. I must keep him by me, because my job may prove to be the harder. Off you go, Weymouth! I'm in charge. Get down the dip behind us and circle round the way we came. Don't lose a moment!"

There was some further argument between these old friends, but finally the dominating personality of Nayland Smith prevailed; and Weymouth and Dr. Petrie set out. As they disappeared into the hollow behind us:

"Heaven grant I haven't bungled this thing!" said Nayland Smith and gripped my arm fiercely. "But I've stage-managed it like an amateur. Only sheer luck can save us now!"

He turned aside and focused his glasses on the distant angle of the wall. A minute passed—two—three—four. Then came a sudden outcry, muffled, but unmistakable.

"My God!" Smith's voice was tragic. "They've run into another party! Come on, Greville!"

Breaking cover we hared across in the moonlight. Regardless of any watcher who might be concealed behind that iron-studded door in the long wall, we raced headlong to the corner. I was hard and fit; but, amazing to relate, I had all I could do to keep pace with Nayland Smith. He seemed to be a man who held not sluggish human blood but electricity in his veins.

Around the corner we plunged . . . and almost fell headlong over a vague tangle of struggling figures!

"Petrie!" Nayland Smith cried. "Are you there?"

"Yes, by the grace of God!" came pantingly. . . .

"Weymouth?"

"All clear!"

Dense shadow masked the combatants; and, risking everything, I dragged out my torch and switched on the light.

Dr. Petrie, rather dishevelled and lacking his tarbûsh, was just standing up. A forbidding figure, muffled in a shapeless camel-hair garment, lay near. Weymouth was resting his bulk upon a second.

"Light out!" snapped Nayland Smith.

I obeyed. Weymouth's voice came through the darkness.

"Do you remember, Sir Denis, that other meeting in London? There was only one Lama monk there. There are two here!"

His words explained a mystery which had baffled me. These were Tibetan monks!

"They must have heard us approaching," Petrie went on. "They were hiding in the shadows. And as we climbed up onto the path, they attacked us. I may add that they were men of their hands. Personally I'm no means undamaged, but by sheer luck I managed to knock my man out."

"I think I've strangled mine!" said Weymouth grimly. "He was gouging my eye," he added.

"Petrie!" said Nayland Smith. "We're going to win! This is the hand of Providence!"

For one tense moment none of us grasped his meaning; then:

"By heavens, no. It's too damned dangerous," Weymouth exclaimed. "For God's sake don't risk it!"

"I'm going to risk it!" Smith snapped. "There's too much at stake to hesitate. If they were in our place, there'd be two swift executions. We can't stoop to that. Gags we can improvise. But how the devil are we going to tie them up?"

At which moment the man on whose body Weymouth was kneeling uttered a loud cry. The cry ceased with significant suddenness; and:

"Two of us wear turbans," said Weymouth: "that's twelve feet of stout linen. What more do we want?"

We gagged and bound the sturdy Tibetans, using torchlight sparingly. One of them struggled a lot; but the other was still. Petrie seemed to have achieved a classic knockout. Then we dragged our captives down into the shadow of the hollow; and Nayland Smith and I clothed ourselves in those hot, stuffy, camel-hair garments.

"Remember the sign," he rapped—"*Si Fan!* . . . then the formal Moslem salute,"

"Good enough! But these fellows probably talked Chinese. . . ."

"So do I!" he rapped. "Leave that to me."

He turned to Weymouth. "Your job is to raise a party inside half an hour. Off you go! Good luck, Petrie. I count on you, Weymouth."

But when a thousand and one other things are effaced—including that difficult parting—I shall always retain my memories of the moment, when Nayland Smith and I, wearing the cowled robes of the monks, approached that iron-studded door.

My companion was a host in himself; his splendid audacity stimulated. I thought, as he raised his fist and beat seven times upon the dun-bleached wood, that even if this adventure should conclude the short tale of my life, yet it would not have been ill-spent since I had met and been judged worthy to work with Sir Denis Nayland Smith.

PART THREE

CHAPTER SEVENTH—*Kâli*

CHAPTER EIGHTH—*Swazi Pasha Arrives*

CHAPTER NINTH—*The Man from el-Khârga*

Chapter Seventh

KÂLI

ALMOST immediately the door opened.

Conscious of the fact that our hoods were practically our only disguise, that neither of us possessed a single Mongol characteristic, I lowered my head apprehensively, glancing up into a pair of piercing eyes which alternately regarded my companion and myself.

The keeper of the door was a tall, emaciated Chinaman!

"*Si Fan*," said Nayland Smith, and performed the salutation.

"*Si Fan*," the doorkeeper replied and indicated that he should enter.

"*Si Fan*," I repeated; and in turn found myself admitted.

The Chinaman closed and bolted the door. I discovered myself to be standing in a little arbour within a gateway. The shadow of the wall lay like a pall of velvet about us, but beyond I saw a garden and moon-lighted pavilions, and beyond again a courtyard set with orange trees. The house embraced this courtyard, and from mûshrabîyeh windows dim lights shone out. But there was no movement anywhere. No servants were visible, other than the tall, emaciated Chinaman who had admitted us. I clutched my monkish robe, recovering some assurance from the presence of the repeater which I carried in my belt.

Extending a skeleton hand, the keeper of the gate indicated that we were to cross the garden and enter the house.

I had taken my share of ordinary chances, having lived anything but a sheltered life. Yet it occurred to me, as I stood there beside Nayland Smith, looking in the direction of the tree-shaded courtyard, that this was the wildest venture upon which I had ever been launched.

Our wits alone could save us!

In the first place it seemed to me that survival hung upon one slender point: Were the Mongolian monks known personally to anyone in the house? If so, we were lost! The several groups assembled in the café at el-Khârga obviously had been strangers one to another . . . but there might be—must be— some central figure to whom they were all known.

We had searched the Tibetans for credentials but had found none. And now, suddenly, shockingly, I remembered something!

"Sir Denis!" We had begun to pace slowly across the garden. "We're trapped!"

"Why?" he jerked.

"The elder of those monks wore a queer silver ring on his index finger, set with a big emerald. I noticed it as I helped to tie him up."

Nayland Smith shot his hand out from a loose sleeve of the camel-hair garment. I saw the emerald glittering on his index finger!

"His evidence of identity?" he suggested. "It was!"

We crossed the courtyard in the direction of an open doorway. I saw a lobby lighted by one perforated brass lamp swung on chains. There were doors right and left—both of them closed.

On a divan a very old Chinaman was seated. He wore a little cap surmounted by a coral ball. His wizened face was rendered owlish in appearance by the presence of tortoiseshell-rimmed glasses. A fur-trimmed robe enveloped his frail body, his ethereal hands relaxed upon his crossed knees. I saw that on an index finger he wore just such a ring as that which Nayland Smith had taken from the Tibetan monk! A silver snuff-bowl rested upon the divan beside him; and as we entered:

"*Si Fan*," he said in a high, thin voice.

Nayland Smith and I went through the prescribed formula. Whereupon, the Chinaman spoke rapidly to my companion in what I presumed to be Chinese, and extended his right hand.

Nayland Smith stooped, raised the emaciated hand, and with the ring upon its index finger touched his brow, his lips his breast.

Again, the high, sibilant voice spoke; and Sir Denis extended his own hand. The ritual was repeated—this time, by our singular host. To my intense relief, I realised that I had been taken for granted. Evidently I was a mere travelling companion of my more distinguished compatriot.

Raising a little hammer, the aged Chinaman stuck a gong which stood beside him. He struck it twice. The door right of the divan opened.

He inclined his head, we both acknowledged the salute and, Smith leading, walked in at the open doorway. As we crossed the threshold he fell back a step, and:

"The Mandarin Ki Ming!" came a whisper close to my ear. "Pray heaven he hasn't recognised me!"

I found myself in a large salon, scantily furnished as was the lobby. At the further end, approached by three carpeted steps were very handsome double doors, beautifully carved and embellished with semi-precious stones in the patient Arab manner. The place was lighted by a sort of chandelier hung from the centre of the ceiling: it consisted of seven lamps. There were divans around the walls and two deep recesses backed by fine, carved windows.

Seven black cushions placed upon silk-covered mattresses were set in a crescent upon the polished floor, the points of the crescent toward the double doors. Beside each mattress stood a little coffee table.

Four of the mattresses were occupied and in the following order:

That on the left point of the crescent by the tall, distinguished-looking man whom Nayland Smith had surmised to be a Turk; the second by two of the Burmans I had seen in the café. Then, centre of the crescent, were three vacant places. The next mattress was occupied by the Afghans, and that on the right horn of the crescent by the appalling thugs.

Four of the Seven were present. We, fifth to arrive had been announced by only two strokes of the gong.

Which of those three vacant places were we intended to occupy?

This difficulty was solved by the hitherto invisible custodian of the door—who now proved to be a gigantic Negro. Bowing reverently, he led us to the mattress adjoining that of the Afghans. As we crossed, the four groups assembled stood up unanimously, the leaders each raising a right hand upon which I saw the flash of emeralds.

"*Si Fan!*" they cried together.

"*Si Fan.*" Nayland Smith replied.

We took our seats.

§ 2

One of the most dreadful-looking old men I had ever seen in my life entered to the sound of three gongs. As cries of "*Si Fan*" died away, he took his place on the mattress one removed from ours. He was a Syrian, I thought, and of incalculable age. His fiercely hooked nose had a blade-like edge and from under tufted white brows hawk eyes surveyed the assembly with an imperious but murderous regard.

Beyond doubt this was the Sheikh Ismail, lineal successor of the devilish Sheikh al-Jébal, and lord of the *Hashishîn*!

Upon ourselves, particularly, that ferocious gaze seemed to linger. The atmosphere was positively electrical. It contained, I believe, enough evil force to have destroyed a battalion. I simply dared not contemplate what our fate would be in the event of our discovery. Our lives were in the hands of Weymouth and Petrie!

One place remained—that in the centre of the crescent.

A gong sounded—once.

The Mandarin Ki Ming came in and seated himself upon the vacant mattress....

I realised that having admitted the mandarin, the Negro doorkeeper had retired and closed the door. A hush of expectancy came. Then, from somewhere beyond the end of the saloon a silver bell sounded—seven times; and the beautiful doors swung open.

A woman appeared at the top of the steps, facing us but backed by shadow....

Her hair was entirely concealed beneath a jewelled headdress. She wore jewels on her slim, bare arms. A heavy girdle which glittered with precious stones supported a grotesquely elaborate robe, sewn thickly with emeralds. From proudly raised chin to slight, curving hips she resembled an ivory statue of some Indian goddess. Indeed, as I watched, I knew she was Kâli, wife of Siva and patronne of thugs and dacoits, from whom they derived their divine right to slay!

All heads were lowered and a word sounding like a shuddering sigh, but to me unintelligible, passed around the assembly.

I was fascinated—hypnotised—carried out of myself—as from under the sheltering cowl I looked and looked . . . into those brilliant jade-green eyes of Kâli . . . *Madame Ingomar!*

We had posed ourselves in imitation of the other groups: Nayland Smith reclining beside the black cushion so that his elbow could rest upon it, and I crouching behind him. Any exchange of words at that moment was impossible.

In such a silence that I believe one could have heard the flight of a moth, Fah Lo Suee began to speak. She spoke first in Chinese, then in Turkish, of which I knew a few words. Her audience was spellbound. Her silver bell voice had a hypnotic quality utterly outside the range of my experience. She employed scarcely any gesture. Her breathing could not visually be detected. That slender body retained its ivory illusion. The spell lay in her voice . . . and in her eyes.

She uttered a phrase in Arabic.

Two strokes of a gong sounded from behind me.

The Mandarin Ki Ming stood up. Fah Lo Suee ceased speaking—and I heard the high, sibilant tones of the Chinaman.

I saw Sheikh Ismail leap to his feet like the old panther he was. I saw his blood-lustful gaze fixed upon mine.

We were discovered! Two gong strokes!

The real Tibetans had escaped—were here!

A sickly sweet exotic perfume came to my nostrils. I experienced a sudden sense of pressure. . . .

§ 3

The illusion persisted. It seemed to have recurred at intervals for many nights and days, many weeks—for an immeasurable period. . . .

Always, that vague exotic perfume heralded the phase. This, invariably, seemed to arouse me from some state of unconsciousness in which I thought I must have been suspended for long ages. Once, I became victim of a dreadful idea that I had solved the mystery of perpetual life but was condemned to live it in a tomb. . . .

Then, next I saw her—the green goddess with eyes of jade. I knew that her smooth body was but a miraculous gesture of some Eastern craftsman immortalised in ivory; that her cobra hair gleamed so because of inlay and inlay of subtly chosen rare woods: her emerald robe I knew for an effect of cunning light, her movements for a mirage.

But when she knelt beside me, the jade-green eyes held life—cold ivory was warm satin. And slender insidious hands, scented lotus blossoms, touched me caressingly. . . .

At last came true awakening—and memories.

Where was I? Obviously, I must be in the house of the Sheikh Ismail where the Council of Seven had met. I lay on a divan propped up with many cushions, in a room small enough to have been called a cabinet.

If it were day or night I had no means of judging. Heavy plush curtains of green and gold completely obscured what I assumed to be the window. And I felt as weak as a kitten. In fact, when I tried to sit up in order to study my strange surroundings, I failed to do so.

What had happened to me?

I saw that the floor was covered with a thick green carpet, and directly facing the divan on which I lay was a magnificent ormolu piece occupying the whole of one wall. A square lamp or lantern hung from the centre of the ceiling and flooded the room with amber light.

An ebony carved chair, evidently of Chinese workmanship, stood near me beside a glass-topped table upon which were phials, instruments, and other surgical items!

Weakly, I looked down at my body. I wore unfamiliar silk pyjamas and on my feet were soft Chinese slippers!

What in heaven's name had happened to me?

Now, memory began to function. . . .

Nayland Smith!

I remembered! I remembered! We had been betrayed—or had betrayed ourselves at that incredible meeting of the Council outside el-Khârga! I recalled the high, soft voice of the dreadful mandarin who had denounced us; the staring eyes of the terrible Sheikh. . . . I could recall no more.

Where was Nayland Smith? And where were Petrie and Weymouth?

Clearly had some time elapsed, a fact to which my inexplicable change of attire bore witness. But why had no rescue been attempted? Good God!—a truly horrible doubt came—Weymouth and Petrie had fallen into a trap!

They had never reached el-Khârga!

A dreadful certainty followed. They were dead! I alone had been spared for some unknown reason; and apparently I had been, and still remained, very ill.

Inch by inch—in some way I seemed to have lost the power of co-ordinating my muscles—I turned, seeking a view of that side of the room which lay behind me. All I saw was a flat green door set in the dull gold of the wall. There was a second such door, which I had already noted immediately before me.

As I reverted, laboriously to my previous position the latter door opened. It was a sliding door.

A Chinaman came in! He wore a long white coat of the kind used by hospital attendants, He closed the door behind him.

One swift look I ventured—noting that he was a comparatively young man with a high intellectual forehead, that he wore black-rimmed spectacles and carried a notebook. Then I closed my eyes and lay still.

He took the chair beside me, raised my wrist, and felt the pulse. As he dropped my hand I ventured on a quick glance. He was recording the pulse in his note-book.

Next, unbuttoning the jacket of my silk pyjamas, he inserted a clinical thermometer under my left armpit and, leaving it there, dipped the point of a syringe into a glass of water and carefully wiped it on a piece of lint. This, also, I witnessed, without being detected.

Engrossed in his tasks, he was not watching me. I saw him load a shot of some nameless drug into the syringe on the table.

I reclosed my eyes.

The Chinese surgeon removed the thermometer and recorded my temperature.

There was a long, silent interval. I kept my eyes closed. Something told me that he was intrigued, that he was studying me.

Presently, I felt his head close to my bare chest. He pressed his ear against my heart. I lay still, until:

"Ah, Mr. Greville," he said, with scarcely a trace of accent, "you are feeling better, eh?"

I opened my eyes.

The Chinaman was still watching me. His face was quite expressionless as his tones had been.

"Yes," I said . . . and my voice refused to function higher than a whisper!

"Good." He nodded. "I was becoming anxious about you. It is all right now. The artificial nourishment, I think we may dispense with. Yes, I think so. Do you feel that some very savoury soup and perhaps a small glass of red wine would be acceptable?"

"Definitely!"

My whispering voice positively appalled me!

"I will see to it, Mr. Greville."

"Tell me," I breathed, "where is Nayland Smith?"

The Chinese surgeon looked puzzled.

"Nayland Smith?" he echoed. "I know no one of that name."

"He's here . . . in el-Khârga!"

"El-Khârga?" He stopped and patted me on the shoulder. "I understand. Do not think about this. I will see that you are looked after."

§ 4

A little, wrinkled Asiatic, who either was deaf and dumb or who had had orders to remain silent, brought me a bowl of steaming soup and a glass of some kind of light Burgundy. It was a vegetable soup, but excellent, as was the wine.

And presently I found myself alone again.

I listened intently, trying to detect some sound which should enable me to place the location of this extraordinary green and gold room in which I found myself. Any attempt to escape was out of the question. I was too weak to stir from the divan.

Apart from a vague humming in my aching head, no sound whatever could I hear.

Was I in the house of the Sheikh Ismail? Or had I been smuggled away to some other place in the oasis? An irresistible drowsiness began to creep over me. Once, I aroused with a start which set my heart beating madly.

I thought I had heard a steamer's siren!

Of course (I mused) I had been dreaming again. A sudden, acute anger and resentment stirred me. I was thinking of my companions. I groaned because of my great weakness. . . . I dozed.

Good heavens! What was that?

My heart beating wildly, I tried to sit up. Surely a motor horn! I lay there sweating from the shock of the effort.

I closed my weary eyes. . . .

Divining, rather than knowing, that the door behind me had opened, I kept my lids lowered—but watched.

A faint perfume—which I later determined was rather an aura than a physical fact—reached me. I knew it. This was the herald of another of those troubled visions—visions of the goddess Kâli incarnated.

She stood beside me.

The mythical robes—perhaps never more than figments of delirium—were not there. She wore a golden Chinese dress not unlike a pyjama suit and little gold slippers. The suit was silk of so fine a texture that as she stood between me and the light I could detect the lines of her ivory body as though she floated in a mist of sunrise.

A soft hand touched my forehead.

I raised weary lids and looked up into jade-green eyes.

She smiled and dropped into the chair.

So it was Madame Ingomar that I had to thank for my escape!

"Yes," she answered softly in her strange bell-like voice. "I saved your life at great peril to my own."

But I had not spoken!

Her hand caressed my brow.

"I can tell what you are thinking," she said. "I have been listening to your thoughts for so long. When you are strong again, it will not be so—but now it is."

Her voice and her touch were soothing—magnetic. I found my brain utterly incapable of resentment. This woman, kin of the super-devil, Fu Manchu, my enemy, enemy of all I counted worth while—petted me as a mother pets her child!

And a coldness grew in my heart—yet I remained powerless to resist the spell—because I realised that if she willed me not to hate, but to love her, I should obey . . . I could not refuse!

I dragged my gaze away from hers. Irresistible urges were reaching me from those wonderful eyes, which had the brightness of polished gems.

She stooped and slipped her arms under my head.

"You have been very ill", she whispered. Her lips were almost touching me. "But I have nursed you because I am sorry. You are so young and life is good. I want you to live and love and be happy. . . ."

I struggled like a bird hypnotised by a snake. I told myself that her silver voice rang false as the note of a cracked bell; that her eyes were hideous in their unfathomable evil; that her red lips would give poisoned kisses; that her slenderness was not that of a willow but of a poised serpent. And then, as a worshipper calls on his gods, I called on Rima, conjuring up a vision of the sweet, grave eyes.

"The little Irish girl is charming," said that bell voice. "No one shall harm her. If it will make you happy, you shall have her. . . . And you must not be angry, or get excited. You may talk to me for a few minutes and then you must sleep. . . ."

§ 5

My next awakening was a troubled one. The strange room looked the same. But she had gone. How long? . . .

I had lost all track of time.

What had I imagined and what was real?

Had I asked her, or only dreamed that I had asked her, of the fate of my friends? I thought I had done so and that she had told me they were alive, but had refused to tell me more.

Alive—and, I could only suppose, prisoners!

She had assured me, unemotionally, one arm pillowing my head and those magnetic fingers soothing my hot brow, that it was blind folly to oppose her. She wielded a power greater than that of any potentate living. Her strange soul was wrapped up in world politics. Russia, that great land "stolen by fools," was ripe for her purpose. . . .

The present rulers? Pooh! Her specialists (calmly she spoke of them and I supposed her to mean professional assassins) would clear away such petty obstacles. Russia awaited a ruler. The ruler had arisen. And, backed by a New Russia, which then would be part and parcel of Asia—"*my* Asia"....

China, after many generations, was to be united again. Japan, in the Far East, Turkey, in the Near East, must be forced into submission. Already the train was laid. Kemal stood in her way. Swâzi Pasha, his secret adviser, must be removed....

"But I am so lonely, Shan. Your name is sweet to me, because it is like my own Chinese. Sometimes I know I am only a woman, and that all I see before me ends in nothing if it brings me only power and no love."

Now I was alone.

This was a superwoman into whose hands I had fallen! And what blindness had been upon me during our earlier if brief association to close my eyes to the fact that she had conceived a sudden, characteristically Oriental infatuation?

Perhaps a natural modesty. I had never been a woman's man and counted myself negligible when female favours were being distributed. Or, possibly, my preoccupation with Rima. Certainly, from the first moment I had met her, I had not so much as noticed any other woman's existence or bothered myself to wonder if any other woman had noticed mine.

Yet, as I recalled again and again, Madame Ingomar had chosen me to show her over the excavation and had sought me out many times. Yes, I had been blind....

Now, too late, I saw.

Beyond any dispute, she sprang from generations of autocrats; power was in her blood. She had selected me, for no reason that I could imagine; and I had read in those strange green eyes, as clearly as though she had spoken, that if I rejected her I must die!

I knew, also, intuitively, that she had experienced love. Judged by Western standards, she was young. But judged by any standard she was old in knowledge. However I chose, my triumph would be a short one.

So musing, and weak as a half-drowned cat. I lay staring around my gold and green prison.

The door behind me opened and the Chinese doctor came in.

"Good morning, Mr. Greville."

I glanced at the heavy curtains. No trace of light showed through them.

"Good morning," I said.

My voice was stronger. The Chinaman went through the ritual of taking pulse and temperature; then:

"A great improvement," he announced. "You have an admirable constitution."

"But what has been the matter with me?"

He moved his hands in a slight, deprecatory gesture.

"Nothing, in itself, serious: a small injection. But it was necessary to renew it. . . . However, I am going to get you on your feet, Mr. Greville."

He clapped his hands sharply, and the silent man entered. Together, and skilfully, they raised me from the divan and carried me into a beautifully equipped bathroom which adjoined the green and gold apartment.

"You must not object to our assistance in your toilet," said the doctor. "Because, although unknown to you, we have so assisted before!"

I submitted to the ordeal of being groomed. I had never been seriously ill before, and the business was new to me and utterly detestable. Then I was carried back to bed.

"A lightly boiled egg, and toast," the Chinaman declared, "will not be too severe. Tea—one cup—very weak. . . ."

Presently this was brought and set upon the table beside me. Propped by cushions, I now found it possible to sit up.

With some trace of returning appetite I disposed of this light breakfast. The tray was removed by the dumb man and I lay waiting. Watching the doors alternately, I waited . . . for her. And I waited in a steadily mounting horror. In some way which I had never hitherto experienced, this woman, for all her exotic beauty, terrified me.

The door opened . . . the dumb man came in with a number of books, a box of cigarettes, and other small comforts.

There was no clock in the room and my wrist-watch had been removed. . . .

I saw no one but this silent Asiatic all day, of the progress of which I could judge only by the appearance of regular meals.

Several times, but more faintly than on the first occasion, I could have sworn I heard river noises, and once what strangely resembled a motor horn.

The Chinese surgeon attended me after I had dealt with a

dinner excellently prepared, and "groomed" me for the night. When he had gone, I lay smoking a final cigarette and wondering if....

"Turn out the light when you are tired," had been his final injunction.

§ 6

Lying there in silence and darkness, I almost touched rock bottom. Despair drew desperately near. I was utterly at the mercy of this woman. Whatever had happened to me had left me weaker than a child. And that damnable mystery, the true nature of my illness, was not the least of my troubles.

I suffered no physical pain, except for a throbbing head; I could recall no blow . . . *what* had been done to me?

Sleep was out of the question; but I had tried to find relief from the inexorable amber light. Why, I wondered wearily, had I imagined riverside and street sounds and now imagined them no longer?

And, whilst I turned this problem over in my mind, came a sound which was not imaginary.

It was muffled. But I had learned that all sounds reached the green and gold room in that way. Nevertheless, dim though it was, I knew it . . . an eerie minor cry—the cry I had heard in Petrie's courtyard in Cairo. . . .

The call of a dacoit!

Good God! Had this she-fiend been mocking me? Was I to be strangled as I lay there helpless?

My hand reached out for the switch. I was trembling wildly. Weakness had destroyed my nerve. I grasped it—a pendant—pressed the button. . . .

No light came!

At which I nearly lost myself. I suppose for the first time in my life, I was delirious, or hysterical.

"Smith!" I cried. "Weymouth! Help! . . ."

My voice was a husky whisper. Weakness and terror had imposed on me that crowning torture of nightmare—inability to summon aid in an emergency.

But this was the peak of my sudden, childish frenzy. The fit passed. Nothing further happened. And I grew cool enough to realise that perhaps my enforced silence had been a blessing in disguise. Smith! Weymouth! . . . Heaven only knew where my poor friends were at that hour.

The door behind my couch opened.

I lay still—resigned, now, to the inevitable. I did not even attempt to look around, but stayed with half-closed eyes prepared for death.

A dim light appeared.

Watching, I lost faith in myself. I was altogether too exhausted, in my low state, to experience further fear; but I determined that my brain was not so completely to be relied upon as I had supposed. Actually, I was not awake; I hovered between two states in a borderland of hideous fancy.

An outré figure carrying a lantern came into the room. The light of the lantern cast a huge, misshapen image of its bearer on the golden wall.

This was a hunchbacked dwarf—epicene, revolting. His head was of more than normal size; his grey-black bloated features were a parody of humanity; his eyes bulged, demoniac, from a vast skull. He wore indoor Arab dress, a huge tarbûsh crowning his repulsive ugliness.

Never so much as glancing in my direction, he crossed to the door on the other side of the room and went out.

Both doors remained open. Sounds reached me.

First among these I detected voices—subdued but keyed to excitement.

They were voices of delirium, I decided. They spoke a language which conveyed nothing to me.

A man wearing an ill-fitting serge suit and a dark blue turban raced through the room in the wake of the dwarf. He carried an electric torch. Its reflection, diffused from the golden walls, exhibited a yellow, tigerish face, lips curled back and fanglike teeth bared in a sadistic grin. . . .

The dacoit who had followed me to Cairo!

It was a procession of images created by a disordered brain. Yet I was unconscious of any other symptoms of fever.

Two kinds of sounds came to me now: the excited voices, growing louder, and a more distant, continuous disturbance difficult to identify. Then came a third.

A pulsing shriek quivered through the house . . . and died into wordless gurgling.

The dacoit reappeared. He carried a short, curved knife, its blade red to the hilt. . . . His squinting bloodshot eyes fixed themselves upon me. He drew nearer and nearer to the divan upon which I lay helpless.

Out of the babel of voices, one voice detached itself; a harsh, metallic voice. It cried three words.

The dacoit passed me—and returned by the way he had originally entered.

A sustained, harsh note . . . a flat, surely unmistakable note—that of a police whistle!

I smiled in the darkness.

Clearly, high fever had claimed me. But this ghastly delirium must soon end in unconsciousness. I touched my forehead. It was wet, but cold.

The indistinguishable voices grew faint—and died away.

But that queer, remote booming continued.

And now I determined that it came not from the door behind me—that by which the dacoit had gone out—but from that which faced the foot of the divan . . . the door through which the hunchback had fled.

A dim crash sent ghostly echo messengers through the building.

Shouts followed. But now I could pick out certain words. . . .

"Easy at the landing sir! Wait for me . . ."

A sound of clattering footsteps, apparently on a staircase. . . .

"You take that door! I'll take this!"

Surely I knew that great, deep voice.

More ghostly crashing.

"Nothing here!"

"Next floor!"

A background of excited conversation; then:

"Nayland Smith!" came the great voice—"are you there, sir? Shan Greville! Are you there?"

I *did* know that voice!

"Silence!" it commanded. "Listen!"

In the interval of stillness which followed, I tried to reply. My heart was beating like a racing engine. My brain had become a circus. And the answering cry died in my throat.

"Carry on!"

Clattering of footsteps was renewed. They were somewhere outside the green-gold room, when:

"God's mercy!"

They had found the hunchback. Sudden silence fell.

Subdued voices broke it, until, above them:

"There's another room!" came a cry.

Holding an electric lamp, the speaker burst through the doorway. . . .

Delirium was ended: this was reality!

"Greville!"

"Weymouth!" I said faintly and stretched out a shaking hand.

CHAPTER EIGHTH

SWÂZI PASHA ARRIVES

PERHAPS the presence of blue-uniformed and helmeted constables in a measure prepared me. But, looking back, I realised that this anomalous intrusion upon the oasis did not register a hundred per cent of its true force at the time.

I was weak in a degree which I simply couldn't believe or accept. The idea of mirage remained. When they carried me through a queer room adjoining that in which I had suffered—a room where something lay covered by a piece of ornate tapestry torn from the wall—I was still no more than half alive to facts.

That the house of the Sheikh Ismail had been raided in the nick of time was clear enough. What had become of Petrie I failed to imagine, nor could I account for the presence of London policemen. Also, I was dreadfully concerned about Nayland Smith.

Weymouth's appearance—he wore dinner kit—also intrigued me. But I remembered that at least two days had elapsed; and in some way, I supposed wearily, this hiatus must explain these seeming discrepancies.

Then we reached the outside of the house. A big grey car stood before the door. There was a crowd. I saw several constables.

I saw the street. . . .

I saw a long, neglected wall. From a doorway in this wall I had been carried out to the car. Adjoining was a row of drab two-storied houses. Similar houses faced them from across the narrow way. Some of the doors were open and in the dim light shining out groups were gathered.

They were Chinese—some of them. Others were nondescript. The crowd about the car, kept in check by two constables, was made up of typical East End London elements!

I was placed comfortably on the cushions. A man whom I suddenly recognised as Fletcher seated himself in front with the chauffeur. Weymouth got in beside me. The car moved off.

"You're all at sea!" he said, and rested his hand reassuringly on my arm. "Don't think too much about it yet. I'm going to take you to Dr. Petrie's hotel. He'll get you on your feet again."

"But . . . where am I?"

"You're in Limehouse at the moment."

"What!"

"Keep cool! You didn't know? Well, it is so."

"But two days back, I was in Egypt!"

As the car swung into a wide, populous thoroughfare—West India Dock Road, I learned later—Weymouth turned to me. His expression, blank at first, gradually changed, and then:

"Good heavens, Greville," he said, "I'm just beginning to understand!"

"I wish I could!"

"Brace yourself up—because it's going to be a shock; although the facts must have prepared you for it. You said, which you can see now is impossible, that you were in Egypt two days back. . . . Can you stand the truth? You left Egypt a month ago!"

§ 2

A week elapsed. Petrie's treatment worked wonders. And a day came when, looking down from a hotel sitting-room on the busy life of Piccadilly, I realised that the raw edges of the thing had worn off.

I had lost a month out of my life. I had been translated in the manner of the old Arabian tales from the Oasis of Khârga to some place in Limehouse. The smooth channel of my ways had been diverted; and the shock of recognising this had staggered me. But now, as I say, I was reconciled. Also, better equipped to cope with it: indeed, nearly fit again.

"My extraordinary experience with Sir Lionel," said Petrie, who stood just behind me, "was of enormous assistance in your own case, Greville."

"You mean the success of the new treatment suggested by Sir Brian Hawkins?"

"Yes . . . at least, so I believed."

I turned away from the window and stared at Petrie curiously. His expression puzzled me.

"I don't understand, doctor. You sent a telegram from Luxor to Sir Brian in London, giving him full details about the chief. He cabled back saying that he had communicated these particulars to a Dr. Amber—a former assistant—who was fortunately then in Cairo and who would ring you up."

"Quite so, Greville. And this Dr. Amber did ring up, discussed the case with me, said he agreed with Sir Brian's suggestions and despatched, express, a small box. It contained a third of a fluid drachm of some preparation, labelled 'One minim per day subcutaneously until normal.' After four injections, Sir Lionel fully recovered—except that he had no recollection of what had taken place from the time of the attack to that when he opened his eyes in his room at the Luxor hotel."

"That's plain sailing enough, Petrie, and a big success for Sir Brian Hawkins. You came to the conclusion that I was suffering from the effects of overdoses of the same drug——"

"And so I tried the same cure—with equally marvellous results."

He paused, staring me hard in the face; then:

"When we got down to Cairo," he went on—"as you know, I postponed sailing—Dr. Amber had left his hotel. And when we reached London, Sir Brian Hawkins was abroad. He came home this morning."

"Well?" I said, for he had paused again, staring at me in that peculiar manner.

"Sir Brian Hawkins never received my telegram."

"What!"

"He was unacquainted with anyone called Dr. Amber—and the preparation, a specimen of which I had taken with me, was totally unknown to him!"

"Good God!"

"Don't let it worry you, Greville. We've been the victims of a cunning plot. But the unknown plotter has saved two valuable lives—and defeated Fah Lo Suee! Excuse me if I run away now. Please stay here and make yourself at home. My wife wants to do some shopping, and I never allow her out alone, even in London. You know why," he added significantly.

I nodded, as:

"Rima and Sir Lionel are due to-morrow," he said, "and I know how you're counting the hours."

§ 3

So whilst it was true that to Petrie and to Weymouth I owed the fact that I now stood staring down again on the busy life of Piccadilly, I owed even more to . . . someone else! I was all but fit. I had taken a stroll in the Park, and with decent precautions for a week or two was competent to take up once more the battle of life. But—who was Dr. Amber?

Almost a deeper mystery than that of the hiatus, to me represented by a blank in my existence; and this, heaven knows was strange enough!

The house of the Sheikh Ismail had been raided by a party under the mudîr of Khârga. This official, it seems, was already suspicious of the strange visitors to the town.

They found not a soul on the premises!

El-Khârga was combed carefully. No trace. The mudîr got in touch with Esna, and all roads were watched. Nothing resulted. The dreadful Seven had dispersed—into thin air! Nayland Smith was missing, I was missing; and Said had disappeared with the car. . . .

Weymouth set the official wires humming. Too late, it had occurred to him that Fah Lo Suee might have retired not upon Esna but upon Asyût. Later, this theory was proved to be the correct one.

A dead man, a piece of baggage, I had been carried across the desert to Asyût, entrained for Port Said, and shipped to England, as cargo is shipped! Three days too late to hold her in the Egyptian port, Weymouth, inspecting the books of the Suez Canal Company, discovered that a Clyde-built steamer chartered by a Chinese firm for some private enterprise had passed through the Canal and cleared Port Said at a date which corresponded with his suspicions. Radio was set humming all over the Mediterranean; and the suspected craft was finally boarded off Cherbourg by the French police.

Her papers were in order; but consignments of goods and a number of her people had already been dispatched overland.

This was the state of affairs when the party reached England. Weymouth, of course, had secured leave of absence in the circumstances; and acting upon the policy adopted by poor Nayland Smith in earlier days, had succeeded with the backing of Scotland Yard in keeping all publicity out of the press.

It was the efficiency of Detective-Inspector Yale and of K Division which led to my rescue. For some time they had been watching certain premises in the Limehouse area. Apart from consignments of suspicious goods and of the presence, particularly at night, of Asiatics of a character not usual in that district, a smartly dressed woman had visited the place.

Now, furnished by Weymouth with particulars of those goods sent overland from Cherbourg, Yale secretly inspected some of the crates and packing cases stored in the yard of the suspected premises. As a result of what he found, I was rescued from the green and gold room, and restored to health by Dr. Petrie. But a shadow lay upon all of us—one indeed, which had retarded my convalesence.

§ 4

"Our last battle against Fu Manchu," said Weymouth sadly, "has opened with a big score for the enemy. We've lost our field-marshal."

Detective-Inspector Yale nodded gloomily. I had met him several times before, and I knew that with Fletcher he had been put in charge of this case, which, in his eyes, had neither beginning nor end."

"It's a blank mystery to me," he confessed. "Excepting one badly murdered dwarf, there wasn't a thing of any use to us in the Limehouse raid."

"You're rather overlooking me!"

Detective-Inspector Yale smiled; Weymouth laughed aloud.

"Sorry, sir," said Yale. "But the fact remains—we drew blank. The house was undoubtedly used by these *Si Fan* people. But where are they? I knew when Sir Denis took personal control there was something serious in the wind. He was overdue leave, it's true, but he was a demon for work; and I saw when he started for Egypt with Fletcher he'd gone for business, not pleasure. Besides, there was a big dossier accumulating."

He smiled again, turning slightly in my direction.

"The death of Professor Zeitland was a bad show for the Yard," he admitted. "It was long after the event that we realised his death wasn't due to natural causes. This in strict confidence, Mr. Greville. There's been no publicity about the absence of Sir Denis, because we've kept on hoping from day to day, and his instructions on that point were explicit. But personally. . . ."

He turned aside and stared out of the window.

"I'm afraid so," Weymouth whispered.

"It's a job," Yale went on, "which I admit is above my weight. Most extraordinary reports are accumulating and the Foreign Office has nearly driven me crazy. I never knew very much about this Dr. Fu Manchu, outside department records. I was just a plain detective officer in those days. But it looks to me—and this is where I am badly out of my depth, Superintendent—as though this delayed visit of Swâzi Pasha comes into the case!"

"I'm sure it does!" I replied. "The woman you knew as Madame Ingomar regards the present rulers of Turkey as her enemies. Swâzi Pasha is probably the biggest man in Stamboul to-day. She told me with her own lips that he was marked!"

"Amazing!" said Yale. "He is to occupy Suite Number 5 in this hotel, and apart from routine measures, I'm going to satisfy myself about the staff."

I accompanied Weymouth and Yale on their tour of inspection. The suite was on the floor below, and we went down the stairs. Yale had the key and we entered. Everything had been prepared for the comfort of the distinguished visitor and his confidential private secretary.

Suite Number 5 consisted of a reception room entered from a lobby, a dining room, and two bedrooms with bathrooms adjoining. Swâzi Pasha had been detained by illness in Paris, so the Press informed us, but would arrive at Victoria that evening.

Detective-Inspector Yale seemed to suspect everything in the place. The principal bedroom he explored as though he anticipated discovering there trap-doors, sliding panels, or other mediæval devices. He even turned on the electric heater, an excellent imitation of a coal fire, and considered it carefully; until:

"Once he gets here," said Weymouth, "he's safe enough. It's outside that he's in danger."

Yale turned to him, one eyebrow raised interrogatively, and:

"Queer *you* should say that," he replied. "I've been going carefully through the records—and you ought to know better than I do that if we're really up against this Asiatic group the best hotel in London isn't safe!"

I glanced at Weymouth, and saw his expression change.

"True enough," he admitted. "Dr. Fu Manchu got a man in the New Louvre once, under our very eyes. Yes, you're right."

With enthusiasm he also began to sound walls and to examine fittings, until:

"I have had painful personal evidence of what these people can do," I said, "but I rather feel that any attempt on the life of Swâzi Pasha will be made outside."

Yale turned and:

"Outside," he assured me stolidly, "short of a fanatic who is prepared to pay the price with his life, Swâzi Pasha is as safe as any man in Europe. But in the absence of Sir Denis, I'm responsible for him and, knowing what I know now, I'm prepared for anything."

§ 5

When presently I left Weymouth and Yale, I became selfishly absorbed in my own affairs again. The chief had engaged rooms by radio for himself and Rima here at the Park Avenue, and as I wandered back to my own apartment I found myself wondering which rooms they were. Indeed, a perfectly childish impulse prompted me to go down and inquire of the office.

As I entered the corridor in which my own quarters were located as well as those of Dr. Petrie and his wife, I saw a figure hurrying ahead of me. Reaching the door next to my own, he inserted and turned the key in the lock. As he did so, I had a view of his face in profile. . . .

Then he went in, and I heard the door shut.

Entering my own room, I sat down on the bed, lighted a cigarette, and wondered why this chance encounter seemed so important. It was striking discords of memory which I couldn't solve. I smoked one cigarette and lighted a second, thinking hard all the time, before the solution came, then:

"I've got it!" I cried.

This man in the next room was the Turk who had attended the Council of Seven!

I glanced at the telephone. Here was a mystery completely beyond my powers—something which Weymouth and Yale should know about at once. I hesitated, realising that in all probability they were on their way to Victoria. A tremendous unrest seized me. What did it mean? That it meant mischief—and bloody mischief—I felt certain. But what should I do?

I lighted a pipe and stared down into Piccadilly. Inaction was intolerable. What could I do? I couldn't give this man in charge of the police. Apart from the possibility of a mistake, what evidence had I against him? Finally I grabbed my hat and went out into the corridor. I had detected no sound of movement in the neighbouring room.

Walking over to the lift, I rang the bell. The cage had just arrived and I was on the point of stepping in, when I thought someone passed swiftly behind me.

I turned. My nerves were badly overtuned. The figure had gone, but:

"Who was that?" I said to the lift-boy.

"Who do you mean, sir," he asked. "I didn't see anyone."

I thought that he was looking at me rather oddly, and:

"Ground floor," I said.

Had this thing got me more deeply than I realised? Small wonder if it were so, considering my own experience. But was I beginning to imagine creatures of Dr. Fu Manchu, shadows, menaces, where really there was no physical presence? It was a dreadful thought, one to be repelled at all costs by a man who had passed through the nightmare of that month which I had survived.

For I had been dead and I lived again.

Sometimes the horror of it wakened me in the middle of the night. A drug, unknown to Western science, had been pumped into my veins. The skill of an Asiatic physician had brought me back to life. Petrie's experience—aided by the mysterious "Dr. Amber"—had done the rest. But there might be an aftermath, beyond the control even of this dreadful Chinaman whose shadow again was creeping over Europe.

My present intention was to walk across to Cook's and learn at what time the s. s. *Andaman*, in which Sir Lionel and Rima were travelling, docked, and when the boat-train arrived. I was in that state of anxiety in which one ceases to trust that high authority, the hotel hall porter.

This purpose was frustrated by the sudden appearance, as I came down the steps, of Dr. Petrie and his wife. I was instantly struck by the fact that something had terrified Mrs. Petrie. The doctor was almost supporting her....

"Hello, Greville," he said. "My wife has had rather a shock. Come back with us for a minute."

The fact was obvious enough. Filled with a sudden new concern, I realised, as I took Mrs. Petrie's arm and walked back up the hotel steps, that she was in a condition bordering on collapse. Well enough I knew that this could mean only one thing. As I had suspected, as Weymouth had suspected—the enemy was near us!

In the lobby she sat down and her husband regarded her anxiously. Normally, she had the most wonderful flower-like complexion—I mean naturally, without artificial aid—of any woman I had ever met. Now she was pale, and her wonderful eyes mirrored a sort of mysterious horror.

"Are you sure, Kara? Are you sure?" Petrie asked with deep concern.

"Could I ever be wrong about him?"

"When you are safely upstairs, dear," he replied, "I am going back to confirm your suspicion—or disprove it."

"But," I exclaimed, "whatever is wrong?"

"*He* is here."

"What do you mean, Mrs. Petrie? Who is here?"

She looked up at me, and for all her pallor I knew how beautiful she was. I thought that if those strange, wonderful eyes had beckoned to me before I had known Rima, I should have followed wherever they led. She was, indeed, very lovely, and very terrified; and:

"It seems like madness," she whispered; "but about this I can never be mistaken. If I had not seen, I should have felt. But I saw."

"Do you understand, Greville," Petrie interrupted tersely, "my wife saw—I can't doubt her; she has never been wrong on this point—someone looking out from a window above a shop in Burlington Arcade."

"I know it is madness, but I know it is true," she said.

"When?" I demanded.

"A moment ago."

"But do you mean——"

Mrs. Petrie nodded.

Her eyes were tragic. She stood up.

"I am going upstairs," she said. "No, truly, I'm quite all right again. Go back, or it may be too late. But take Mr. Greville with you."

She walked towards the lift, whilst Petrie and I watched her. As she entered and the lift went up:

"It seems simply incredible to me," I declared. "But do you mean that in a room over a shop in Burlington Arcade——"

"A dealer in Oriental jewellery, yes!" Petrie took me up quickly. "I could see nothing—the room above was in darkness—but Kâramanèh saw *Dr. Fu Manchu* looking down!"

§ 6

I wondered if Nayland Smith would have approved of Petrie's method of inquiry. Personally, I thought it admirable, for as we entered the establishment, oddly reminiscent, as many are in the Arcade, of a shop in an Eastern bazaar:

"My wife came along this afternoon," said Petrie, "and noticed a large Chinese figure in the room above. She asked me to call and learn the price."

The salesman, who would not have been out of place in any jewel market of the Orient, except for the fact that he wore a well-cut morning coat, raised his eyebrows in surprise. He was leaning upon a case containing typical Levantine exhibits, and all sorts of beaded necklaces framed him about. I thought that, saving the presence of civilised London around us, he might, considered alone, have been termed a sinister figure.

"The room above, sir," he replied "is not my property. It is used as a store-room by another firm. See"—he turned—"the stair is there, but the door is locked. I have a case upon it as you may observe for yourself. That door is very rarely opened. And I assure you it contains no Chinese figure."

He made no attempt to sell us anything.

But outside, in the Arcade, we both stared up at the window above the shop. The room to which it belonged appeared to be empty. Petrie shrugged.

"She has never been wrong before," he said significantly. "And the gentleman with whom we have been chatting gives one the shudders."

"I agree, but what can we do?"

"Nothing," he replied.

Turning, we walked back to the Park Avenue Hotel. The journey was a short one, but long enough for me to tell Petrie of my encounter in the corridor. He stopped as we reached the corner of Berkeley Street, and:

"There's some very black business underlying all this, Greville," he said. "We've lost the best man of the lot already. Now it looks as though the arch-devil had taken personal charge. Where's Weymouth?"

"Gone to Victoria, I expect. Yale was with him."

Petrie nodded.

"If *you* weren't mistaken, Greville, it looks as though the danger to Swâzi Pasha is here, in London. If my wife isn't mistaken—it's a certainty! We can at least learn the name of the man you saw; because in dealing with Dr. Fu Manchu and his Burmans I don't believe in coincidences!"

We consulted the reception clerk and learned without difficulty that the room, of which I naturally remembered the number, was occupied by a Mr. Solkel, of Smyrna.

"Has he stayed here before?" Petrie asked.

No. It was Mr. Solkel's first visit.

"Thank you," said Petrie, and as we walked towards the lift:

"Mr. Solkel, of Smyrna," he mused. "I don't like the sound of him."

"*I* don't like the look of him!"

"Yet it is just possible you were wrong; and so—what can we do?"

We went up to Petrie's sitting-room where his wife, apparently recovered, was waiting to receive us.

She smiled, her gaze set on Petrie's face; and I wondered if Rima would greet me with a smile like that. He simply shook his head and ran his fingers through her beautiful hair.

"I knew," she whispered; and although she continued bravely to smile, there was horror in her eyes.

"He is so clever! But I was right!"

A nameless but chill foreboding possessed my mind. I believe the others shared it. I was thinking of the man who had gone out to meet this menace, and had come to his end, alone against many, in that damnable house in Khârga. But, Petrie now ringing for cocktails, we all tried to show a bold front to our troubles. Yet even as I raised my glass I seemed to detect, like a sort of patrol, the approach of something; not as a memory, but as words spoken eerily, to hear a bell-like voice:

"I am so lonely, Shan. . . ."

For days and nights, for weeks, I had lain in her power . . . the witch-woman; daughter of this fiend incarnate, Dr. Fu Manchu. "She is evil, evil . . ." Rima had said. And I knew it for truth. Much as we had all suffered, I felt that worse was to come. I could hear the cheery, familiar roar of London's traffic beneath me; sometimes, dimly, I could catch snatches of conversation in the adjoining apartment, occupied by an enthusiastic American traveller and his wife.

Everything was so safe, so normal. Yet I knew, I could not venture to doubt, that some climax in the incredible business which had blotted out a month of my life and had brought Sir Lionel Barton to the edge of eternity, was creeping upon us.

§ 7

"Thank goodness that part of the business is over," said Weymouth. "There were no official formalities, as the Pasha is still indisposed. He was all silk mufflers and fur collar. He has only one secretary with him. The other members of his suite are staying at the Platz over the way. He's safe indoors, anyhow."

"Safe?" Mrs Petrie echoed and laughed unhappily. "After what I have told you, Superintendent?"

Weymouth's kindly face looked very grim, and he exchanged a troubled glance with Petrie; then:

"She never used to be wrong, doctor," he confessed. "Honestly, I don't know what to make of it. I sent a man around directly I got the news. But of course the shop was closed and locked. I don't know what to make of it," he repeated. "The woman was rapidly becoming a nightmare to me, but if the Doctor in person has appeared on the scene . . ."

He spread his hands in a helpless gesture; and we were all silent for some time. Then Weymouth stood up:

"It's very nice of you, Mrs. Petrie," he said, "to ask me to dine with you. I have one or two little jobs to do downstairs, first—and I'm going to have another shot to get a look at Mr. Solkel. It isn't really my case." He smiled in the awkwardly boyish manner which made the man so lovable. "But I've been retained as a sort of specialist, and Yale is good enough to be glad."

"I suppose," said Petrie, as Weymouth made for the door, "there are detectives on duty in the hotel?"

"Five, with Fletcher in charge. That should be enough. But I'm worried about Mr. Solkel. His official description doesn't correspond with yours, Greville. For one thing, they tell me he wears glasses, is in delicate health, and keeps to his room constantly. However. . . ."

He went out.

Petrie stared hard in my direction.

"There's absolutely no doubt," he said slowly, "that Madame Ingomar's campaign has opened well, for her. Her astonishing indiscretion, I can only ascribe to"—he paused, smiling, and glanced at his wife—"a sudden and characteristically Oriental infatuation."

She flushed, glancing at him, and:

"Nayland Smith once said that about me!" she replied.

"I'm glad he did!" Petrie returned. "But if the daughter is anything like the father, I confess even now I don't envy Swâzi Pasha's chances. Just check up on madame's record, and you will see what I mean. Apart from certain mysterious movements last year, in such widely divided places as Pekin, Turkestan, Siberia, and the northern provinces of India, we may take if for a fact that Professor Zeitland fell a victim to this Chinese she-devil. He stood in her way. He knew something about Lafleur's Tomb which she wanted to know. Having learned it, it became necessary that he should be blotted out. This duly occurred, according to schedule. Barton was next in her path. He served her purpose and escaped by a miracle. She got what she wanted—the contents of the tomb. If we could even guess the importance of these, we might begin to understand why she stuck at nothing to achieve her end."

He paused to light a fresh cigarette, and then:

"I believe poor old Smith knew," he went on. "He was the one man in the world she had really to fear. And he . . ." the sentence remained unfinished.

"That she regarded Swâzi Pasha as an obstruction," I said, "she was good enough to tell me herself."

Petrie glanced at his wife, whose expressive eyes registered a deep horror; then:

"I said a while ago," he added, "that I don't give very much for his chances. Selfishly, I can find it in my heart to wish that he had chosen another hotel. Kâramanèh has lived in the storm centre too long to want any further experiences."

This, then, was the atmosphere which surrounded us all that evening in a London hotel; this the shadow under which we lay.

During dinner—which was served in Petrie's sitting-room, for Weymouth had had no opportunity of dressing:

"I suppose," said I, "that Mr. Solkel is receiving suitable attention?"

Weymouth nodded.

"He hasn't gone out," he replied. "But I hear that a new wardrobe trunk was delivered and taken up to his room this afternoon. This suggests that he is leaving shortly. If he goes out he will be followed. If he rings for anything, the waiter will be a Scotland Yard man."

Weymouth had secured a small room right up under the roof, for London was packed. But I drew a great sense of security from his presence in the building. At his wife's request,

Petrie had abandoned a programme for the evening, arranged earlier, and had decided to remain at home.

When we said good night to our host and hostess, Weymouth came along to my room. Pausing in the corridor, he stared at the door of Number 41; but not until we had entered my adjoining apartment and lighted our pipes, did he speak; then:

"Swâzi Pasha has cancelled an engagement to dine with the Prime Minister to-night, owing to the delay in Paris," he said. "He's not going out and is receiving no one. Even the Press have been refused. But Yale's job starts tomorrow. The Pasha has four public appointments."

"You feel fairly confident, then, of his safety to-night?"

"Perfectly," Weymouth replied grimly. "I feel so confident about it that I'm going to patrol the hotel in person! You turn in, Greville. You're not really fit yet. Good night."

§ 8

Sleep was a difficult problem. Apart from a morbid and uncontrollable apprehension, I was intensely strung up by reason of the fact that Rima was due in the morning. I tried reading, but simply couldn't concentrate upon the printed page.

The jade-green eyes of Fah Lo Suee began to haunt me, and in the dialogue of the story I was trying to read I seemed to hear her voice, speaking the lines in that bell-like, hypnotic voice.

I relived those ages of horror and torment in the green-gold room: I saw again the malignant dwarf— "A *hashishîn*," Weymouth had told me. "They belong to the Old Man of the Mountain—Sheikh Ismail." I heard the creature's dying shrieks; I saw the dacoit return, carrying his bloody knife....

Throwing down the magazine disgustedly, I began to pace my room. I contemplated another whisky-and-soda, but realised in time that it would be a poor cure for insomnia. The after-theatre rush was subsiding. Piccadilly was settling down into its nightly somnolence. That inner circle of small, expensive streets containing the exclusive dance clubs would be full of motor traffic now, for London's night life is highly centralised, the Bohemia of Soho impinging on the white-shirted gaiety of Mayfair; two tiny spots on the map; sleepless eyes in a sleeping world.

I wondered if Petrie and his wife were awake—and I wondered what Weymouth was doing. This curiosity about Weymouth grew so intense that I determined to ring and find out . It was at this moment that I first heard the sound.

It was difficult to identify. I stood still, listening—all those doubts and surmises centred now upon my mysterious neighbour, Mr. Solkel. What I heard was this:

A dim, metallic sound, which might have been made by someone slightly shaking a sheet of thin metal. Next, a faint sibilance which oddly suggested paying out a line. Then came silence. . . .

My brain was functioning at high pressure. Whereas, in the foggy stage that followed my dreadful experience, I should have been incapable of thinking consistently about anything, now a dozen theories sprang to my mind. I decided to stand still—and to listen.

The sound was renewed. It came from beyond the fireplace!

An electric radiator, which I had had no occasion to use, stood there. Stooping, I quietly placed it on the rug; and kneeling down I pressed my ear to the tiles of the recess in which it had rested.

Whispering!

And at this very moment a fact occurred to me . . . a startling fact!

My room was directly above Suite Number 5!

The connection defied me, but of one thing I was sure: these strange noises, which had temporarily ceased, portended some attempt on Swâzi Pasha's apartments below.

I came to a swift decision. Walking silently in my slippers, I crossed to the door, opened it cautiously, and peeped out into the corridor. It was empty and dark save for one dim light at the end. Leaving my door ajar, I started for the staircase. . . .

A sense of urgency possessed me—I must find Weymouth or Fletcher! The fate not only of a Turkish statesman but perhaps of Europe depended upon promptitude.

Silence everywhere as I hurried along the corridor to the

staircase. I raced down in semi-darkness. I reached the corridor below, lighted only by one dim lamp just above the elevator shaft. I looked right. The corridor was empty. I looked left. There was no one.

Hesitant, I stood debating my course. I might ring for the lift-man. I might race on down into the lobby and summon the night porter. The result would have been better accomplished had I used my own room telephone. No doubt I had counted too confidently on meeting Fletcher or Weymouth.

I determined to take the matter into my own hands. I turned left, and walked swiftly in the direction of the door of Suite Number 5.

Even at the moment that I reached it I hesitated again. Of the fact that some deadly peril, urgent, insistent, threatened Swâzi Pasha, I seemed to have occult information. But, as I realised, my facts were scanty. If I roused him, I might save his life. On the other hand, I might make myself ridiculous.

There was a bell-push outside the door, and my hand was raised to press it. Suddenly, silently, the door opened . . . and I found myself staring into the gaunt, angular face of Nayland Smith!

Chapter Ninth

THE MAN FROM EL-KHÂRGA

With one significant gesture, Nayland Smith silenced the words on my lips. He took a quick step forward into the corridor and I saw that he was barefooted. Then, his lips very close to my ear:

"Lucky I heard you," he whispered. "One ring would have ruined everything! Come in. Be silent. . . . Whatever happens, do nothing."

He stepped back, pointing urgently to my slippers. I removed them and tiptoed into the lobby. Nayland Smith reclosed the front door without making a sound and led me into the principal bedroom. Except for a faint streak of light coming through the curtains, the room was in darkness. He pushed me down into a corner near the foot of the bed and disappeared.

To say that I was astounded would be to labour the obvious. I actually questioned my sanity. That Nayland Smith was alive made me want to shout with joy. But what in heaven's name was he doing in Swâzi Pasha's apartments? Where had be been and why had he failed to notify us of his escape? Finally, what was it that I had nearly ruined by my unexpected appearance and for what was he waiting in the dark?

Where Smith had gone and why we were concealing ourselves, I simply couldn't imagine; but, my eyes growing used to the gloom, I peered carefully about the bedroom without moving from the position in which he had placed me. I could see no one, hear nothing.

Then all my senses became keyed up—alert. I had detected a sound of soft footsteps in the corridor outside! I waited—listening to it drawing nearer and nearer. The walker had reached the door, I thought. . . . But he did not pause, but passed on. The sound of footsteps grew faint—and finally died away.

Silence fell again. The window behind those drawn curtains was open at the top, and sometimes faint street noises reached my ears: the hooting of a passing taxi, the deeper note of a private car; and once, rumbling of what I judged to be a string of heavy lorries. But in the building about me, complete silence prevailed. I found myself looking across an eiderdown bedspread in the direction of the fireplace. Except that it was more ornate, it closely resembled that in my own room. The shock of meeting Smith, the present horrible mystery, keyed up my already wide-awake brain. I began to form a theory. . . .

At which moment, as if to confirm it, came a faint sound. Something was shuffling lightly behind the electric radiator!

This was backed by green tiles, or imitation tiles which I judged to be stamped on metal. The deep recess which they lined resembled a black cavity from where I crouched. I could just detect one spot of light on the metal hood of the radiator.

Following some moments of tense silence, came a second sound. And this . . . I recognised.

It was the same subdued, metallic clang which had arrested my attention in the room above!

I thought that the darkness behind the radiator had grown even denser. I scarcely breathed. Fists clenched, I watched, preparing to duck if any light should come in, since my discovery was clearly the last thing Nayland Smith desired.

The spot of high light on the hood moved outwards, towards me. I was afraid to trust my sight—until a very soft padding on the carpet provided an explanation of this phenomenon.

Someone had opened the back of the fireplace and now was lifting the radiator out bodily. . . .

Who, or what, had crept out into the room?

Nothing moved again, but I thought a figure stood between me and the recess. Whatever it might be, it remained motionless, so that, after I had concentrated my gaze, it presently took shape in the dusk—but such horrible shape, that, divided only by the width of the bed from it, I shrank involuntarily.

It was a spiritual as well as a physical shrinking, such as I had experienced in that room in Limehouse, when, on the night of horror which had led to my release, a ghastly yellow dwarf had crossed my room, carrying a lantern. Of the fate of that misshapen thing I had seen bloody evidence. This figure now standing silent in the darkness—standing so near to me—was another of the malignant killers; one of those

Arabian abominations attached to the Old Man of the Mountain ... he whose blazing eyes, as he sprang up from his mattress when the Mandarin Ki Ming denounced us, formed my last memory of the Council of Seven. ...

A sickly sweet exotic perfume stole to my nostrils. ... I knew it!

To crouch there inactive, with definite terror beginning to claim me, was next to impossible, and I wondered why Nayland Smith had imposed so appalling a task. I wondered if he had seen what *I* could see—knew what I knew.

The answer came swiftly, almost silently. I heard a dull, nauseating thud, followed by a second, heavier thud on the carpet. Nayland Smith's voice came in a tense whisper:

"Don't stir, Greville."

My heart was beating like a sledge-hammer.

§ 2

I began to count the seconds. ... Fully a minute passed in absolutely unbroken silence.

Nayland Smith, I realised now, had been concealed in one of two recesses flanking the projecting fireplace. This same formation occurred in my own room, and might betoken a girder or platform, or possible a flue. Formerly, the Park Avenue had been fitted with open coal-fires.

Another minute passed. Nothing happened. The suspense began to grow intolerable. A third minute commenced—then a sound broke that electric stillness; a soft shuffling sound, like that which had heralded the approach of the Arabian dwarf. It was all the more obvious now since the back of the fireplace had been displaced, and it resembled that of a heavy body moving in a narrow space.

Sounds of movement grew suddenly louder and then ceased altogether.

Silence fell again. This, I believe, was the least endurable moment of all. Every sense told me that someone was peering out into the room. But I hadn't the slightest idea what to expect—nor, if attack were coming, what form it would take!

Soft padding. Silence. A whispered phrase came like a hiss

out of the darkness:

"*Enta raih fēn?*" (Where has he gone?) The words were Arab—but not spoken by an Arab!

Yet I gathered that the speaker, in what I judged to be a state of excitement, had abandoned his own tongue in favour of that of the murderous dwarf, whose absence clearly puzzled him. But I had little time for thought.

There came a rush, and a crash which shook the room . . . a shot!— a flash of dim light and the tinkle of broken glass! The bullet had shattered the window above my head. . . . Then:

"The switch, Greville!" came Nayland Smith's voice. "Over the bed!"

I sprang up as well as my cramped limbs would permit, jumped onto the bed, and groped for the pendant switch.

A sound of panting and gurgling came from somewhere down on the carpet between the bed and the fireplace; loud banging on the floor. Presently I found the switch, and was dazzled when the room became flooded with light. I jumped across to the other side of the bed. I could hear racing footsteps in the corridor outside, excited voices, movement all about. . . .

At my feet sprawled a man in pyjamas, his head thrown back and his eyes staring upward, almost starting from their sockets. Nayland Smith knelt upon him, his right hand clutching the throat of the prostrate man, his left pressing to the floor sinewy brown fingers in which a pistol was gripped.

"Get his gun!" he snapped, without releasing that stranglehold.

I slipped around the combatants and snatched the pistol from that virile grasp. As I stooped, I had my first proper view of the captive. . . . He was the man I had seen in the corridor— Mr. Solkel!

A bell was ringing furiously. Someone was banging on the outer door. "Open!" Smith panted. Half under the bed lay the hideous dwarf, motionless.

Weymouth's voice was raised outside in the corridor now:

"Hello, there!" he bellowed. "Open this door! Be quick, or we shall have to force it!"

"Open!" Smith rapped irritably.

I turned and ran to the door.

One glance of incredulity Weymouth gave; then, followed by Fletcher and two others who wore the Park Avenue livery, he rushed past me.

"Good God!" I heard. "Sir Denis!" Then:

"Are you mad, sir? You're strangling *Swâzi Pasha!*"

§ 3

"Our first captures!" said Nayland Smith.

An overcoated figure in charge of two detectives dressed as footmen disappeared from the suite.

"Your mistake, Weymouth, was natural enough. In appearance he *is* Swâzi Pasha."

"He is," said Dr. Petrie, who had joined us in the apartment—all the hotel had been aroused by the shot. "I met Swâzi in Cairo only a year ago; and if the man under arrest is not Swâzi Pasha, then I shall never trust my eyes again."

"Really, Petrie?" said Nayland Smith, and smiled in that way which lent him such a boyish appearance. "Yet"—he pointed to the open fireplace—"the metal back of this recess has been removed very ingeniously. It has been reattached to the opening which it was designed to mask, but to-night as you see it hangs down in the ventilation shaft by reason of the fact that a stout piece of canvas has been glued to the back so as to act as a hinge.

"Can you suggest any reason why Swâzi Pasha should remove the back of his fireplace and why he should climb down a rope ladder from the apartment of a certain Mr. Solkel in the middle of the night?"

It was Weymouth who answered the question, and:

"I admit I can't, Sir Denis," he said.

"No wonder! The details of this amazing plot are only beginning to dawn upon me by degrees. In addition to the ladder which undoubtedly communicates with Room 41 above us, there's this stout length of rope with a noose at the end. Can you imagine what purpose it was intended to serve?"

We all stared into the recess. As Smith had said and as we all had noticed, such a ladder as he described hung in the shaft, possibly as a means of communication between the two floors. A length of rope had been carried into the room. The noose with which it ended lay upon the carpet at our feet.

"I shall make a suggestion," Smith went on. Mr. Solkel has been occupying Number 41, I understand, for a week past. He has employed his time well! We shall find that the imitation tiling at the back of his fireplace has been removed in a similar fashion to this . . . because Suite Number 5 was reserved for Swâzi Pasha as long as a month ago. The purpose of the ladder is obvious enough. A moment's consideration will convince us, I believe, of the use to which this noose was intended to be put. The business of the dwarf, a highly trained specialist—now in Vine Street Police Station—was quietly to enter Swâzi Pasha's room and to silence him with a wad of cotton-wool which you recall he clutched in his hand, and which was saturated with some narcotic. The smell is still perceptible. Possibly you, Petrie, can tell us what it is?"

Petrie shook his head doubtfully; but:

"I have preserved it," he said. "It's upstairs. Some preparation of Indian hemp, I think."

"*Cannabis indica* was always a favourite, I seem to recall, with this group," Smith said grimly. "Probably you are right. The pasha being rendered quietly unconscious, it was the duty of the dwarf to slip the noose under his arms and to assist the man waiting in the room above to haul the body up. These dwarfs, of whom the first living specimen now lies in a cell in Vine Street—the only *hashishîn*, I believe ever captured by European police—have the strength of gorillas, although they are of small stature. The body of the insensible man being carried up to Number 41 by this dwarf on the rope ladder, assisted by the efforts of 'Mr. Solkel' above, the pasha was to be placed in bed. Once there, no doubt it was their amiable intention to dispose of him in some manner calculated to suggest that he had died of heart failure.

"Solkel would have taken his place.

"The distressing death of an obscure guest from Smyrna would have been hushed up as much as possible by the hotel authorities—and Mr. Solkel would have lunched with the prime minister in the morning. I am even prepared to believe that the back of the fireplace in Number 41 would have been carefully replaced; although I fail to see how the same could have been done for this one. The dwarf, no doubt, could have been dispatched by the new pasha in a crate as a piece of baggage to some suitable address."

"But how did the dwarf get in?" I exclaimed.

"Almost certainly in the wardrobe trunk which Mr. Solkel received to-day," Weymouth answered.

"You're right," Smith confirmed.

"But," I cried, "how could the impostor, granting his extraordinary resemblance to Swâzi Pasha, have carried on?"

"Quite easily," Smith assured me. "He knew all that Swâzi knew. He was perfectly familiar with the latter's movements and with his peculiarly secluded life. He was intimately acquainted with his domestic affairs."

"But," said Petrie, "who is he?"

"Swâzi Pasha's twin brother," was the astonishing reply; "his deadly enemy, and a member of the Council of Seven."

"But the real Swâzi Pasha?"

"Is at the Platz Hotel," Smith replied, "masquerading as a member of his own suite."

He was silent for a moment, and then:

"The first time I ever used a sandbag," he said reflectively, weighing one of those weapons in his hand. "But having actually reached Victoria without incident, I determined that this was the point of attack. A transfer of overcoats was made on the train, and the muffled gentleman who entered the Park Avenue was not Swâzi Pasha, but I! Multân Bey, the secretary, escaped at a suitable moment and left me in sole possession of Suite Number 5.

"I didn't know what to expect, but I was prepared for anything. And you must remember, Petrie"—turning to the latter— "that I had had some little experience of the methods of this group! I heard the sound, faint though it was, high up in the ventilation shaft—the same which disturbed you, Greville. Then a hazy idea of what to expect dawned on my mind. A sandbag, the history of which I must tell you later, was in my trunk in the lobby. As I came out to secure it, since I considered it to be the most suitable instrument for my purpose, I heard your soft but rapid footsteps, Greville. I realised that someone was approaching the door; that he must be stopped knocking or ringing at all costs, since my purpose was to catch the enemy red-handed."

There was a pause, and then:

"It's very late," said Dr. Petrie slowly, his gaze set upon Nayland Smith; "but I think, Smith, you owe us some further explanation."

"I agree," Nayland Smith replied quietly.

§ 4

It was a strange party which gathered in the small hours in Dr. Petrie's sitting-room. Petrie's wife, curled up in a shadowy corner of the divan, seemed in her fragile beauty utterly apart from this murderous business which had brought us together. Yet I knew that in the past she had been intimately linked with the monstrous organisation which again was stretching out gaunt hands to move pieces on the chessboard of the world. Weymouth, in an armchair, smoked in stolid silence. Petrie stood on the hearthrug watching Nayland Smith. And I, seated by the writing-table, listened to a terse, unemotional account of an experience such as few men have passed through. Nayland Smith, speaking rapidly and smoking all the time—striking many matches, for his pipe constantly went out—paced up and down the room.

"You have asked me, Petrie," he said, "to explain why I allowed you to believe that I was dead. The answer is this: I had learned during my investigations in Egypt that an inquirer who has no official existence possesses definite advantages. My dear fellow"—he turned impulsively to the doctor—"I knew it would hurt, but I knew there was a cure. Forgive me. The fate of millions was at stake. I will tell you the steps by which I arrived at this decision.

"I don't know how much you recall, Greville, of that meeting at the house of the Sheikh Ismail. But you remember that I recognised the venerable mandarin who received us in the lobby? It was none other than Ki Ming, president of the Council of Seven! You remember the raid in London, Weymouth, and the diplomatic evasion by which he slipped through our fingers?"

"Very clearly," Weymouth replied.

"One of the finest brains and most formidable personalities in the world to-day. I rank him second only to Dr. Fu Manchu. I have yet to test the full strength of the lady known as 'Madame Ingomar,' but possibly she is deserving of a place. We shall see. I doubted if he knew me, Greville. Even had I been sure, I don't know what I could have done. But at least I knew my man and saw our danger."

"I had seen it all along," I interrupted.

Nayland Smith smiled, and:

"A V.C. would not be too high a reward for your courage on that occasion!" he said. "Had the mandarin been sure, he would never have admitted us to the council. He only suspected; but he took instant steps to check these suspicions. I didn't like the way Sheikh Ismail looked at us when he came in.

"A messenger had been dispatched to el-Khârga to make sure that the Tibetan deputies had actually set out. He found them on the way. They must have succeeded in attracting his attention. That messenger was the third member of the Burmese party—the dacoit who was absent from the council.

"The two gong notes told me what had happened. As Ki Ming began to speak—denouncing us—I glanced back.

"That gigantic Negro door-keeper—he had entered and approached us silently as a cat—was in the act of throwing a silk scarf over your head! . . . the third dacoit stood at my elbow.

"One's brain acts swiftly at such times. I realised that the mandarin's orders were that we be taken alive. But simultaneously, I realised that the Sheikh al-Jébal had his atrociously wicked eyes fixed upon me in an unmistakable way.

"These thoughts, these actions, occupied seconds. I could not possibly save you. Resistance to such men and such numbers was out of the question. I could only hope to save myself and to rescue you by cunning."

Such a statement, spoken incisively, coolly, from another than Sir Denis Nayland Smith must have sounded equivocal. Coming from him, it sounded what it was—the considered decision of a master strategist.

"You remember our position, Greville? We weren't ten paces from the steps on the top of which Fah Lo Suee stood. Anticipating the intention of the Old Man of the Mountain and of the Burman who now sprang like a leopard, I ducked. He missed me . . . and I raced across the floor, up the steps, and before madame could realise my purpose, had one arm around her waist and the muzzle of a pistol tight against her ear!"

Nayland Smith paused for a moment, and we remained silent, spellbound, until:

"She is not human, that woman," came a hushed voice. "She is a vampire—she had *his* blood in her."

All eyes turned in the direction of the divan. Mrs. Petrie was the speaker.

"I agree with you," Nayland Smith replied coolly. "A human woman would have screamed, fought, or fainted. Fah Lo Suee merely smiled, and scornfully. Nevertheless, I had won, for the moment. Her lips smiled, but her cold green eyes read the truth in mine.

"'Tell them,' I directed her, 'that if anyone stirs a finger I shall shoot you!'

"She continued to smile, and 'Please move your pistol,' she asked, 'so that I may speak.' I moved the pistol swiftly from her head to her heart. She looked aside at me and paid me a compliment which I shall always value: 'You are clever,' she said. Then she spoke to the petrified murderers in the room below.

"I risked one swift glance. . . . You had disappeared, Greville. The Negro had carried you out! . . . Fah Lo Suee began to speak. The cloak of her father has fallen upon her. She spoke as coolly as if I had not been present. First in Chinese, then in Hindustani, and thirdly in Arabic.

"Then: 'Order all to remain where they are,' I said—'except one, who is to give instructions for my friend to be brought to meet me outside the house.' She gave these orders—and the frustrated dacoit, who still crouched on the mattress where he had fallen, went to carry out my directions.

"'Lead the way!' I said.

"She turned; I knew I was safe for the moment. We entered a little room upon which the big doors opened. This room was not empty. . . . She was well guarded. And never can I forget her guards! Half a dozen words, however, reduced them to impotence. I could not afford to take my eyes off Fah Lo Suee for long; but nevertheless, as we passed through that anteroom, I solved a mystery. I grasped the explanation of something which has been puzzling us since it became evident that the first step in this new campaign of devilry was directed towards the Tomb of the Black Ape."

He paused, beginning to knock out his pipe, and:

"Yes, Sir Denis," I said eagerly, "go on!"

He turned to me, smiling grimly.

"This is your particular province, Greville," he continued, "which fate brought into mine. It isn't any secret of the ancient Egyptians; it's something more dangerous—more useful. For in that room, Petrie"—he turned now to the doctor—"were phials, instruments, and queer-looking yellow-bound books. Also several caskets, definitely of Chinese workmanship."

"I'm afraid I don't understand," Petrie confessed.

"Possibly I can enlighten you," said Nayland Smith, "for I think I have solved the mystery. At some time between his supposed death in 1917 and this year, Dr. Fu Manchu concealed there the essential secrets of his mastery of the Eastern world; the unique drugs, the unknown works dealing with their employment—and the powers, whether tangible—amulets and signets—or instructional and contained in his papers, which gave him control of practically all the fanatical sects of the East."

"Good God!" Weymouth murmured.

"This was what Dr. Fu Manchu's daughter went to Egypt to recover. This was why Professor Zeitland was murdered. Barton escaped by a miracle. Their possession, you understand. . . ."

He paused in his restless promenade and looked about from face to face.

"Their possession made her mistress of the most formidable criminal organisation in the world!"

§ 5

"I walked with Fah Lo Suee through that strange house, across a path to a garden at the back—not that through which we had entered—and out on to a narrow road bordering the wall on the side which faced the palm grove. This path was deserted.

"'Where is he?' I demanded.

"Fah Lo Suee smiled a mocking smile, and:

"'You must be patient,' she replied. 'They have to bring him a long way.'

"I pocketed my pistol and contented myself with keeping an arm around her. It was a natural gesture, but one for which I was to pay a high price, as I shall tell you.

"Two men appeared around the angle of the wall carrying a limp body. They hesitated, looking towards us. Madame raised her hand. They came on. . . . I saw you, Greville, lying on the sandy path at my feet, insensible.

"I continued to clutch Fah Lo Suee tightly, and now I reached for my pistol. I had detected one of the Negro bearers looking across my shoulder in a curiously significant way. . . ."

He paused and struck a match; then:

"It was short warning," he added, "but it might have been enough. If I had had the pistol against Fah Lo Suee's ribs, to-day the world would be rid of a very dangerous devil.

"Someone dropped from the wall behind me . . . and a swift blow with a sandbag concluded this episode!"

Nayland Smith raised his hand reflectively to his skull.

"I woke up amid complete silence, my head singing like a kettle. I was slow to realise the facts; but when I did I was appalled. That lonely house is shunned by all, I have learned; for the Sheikh Ismail has an evil reputation as a dealer in Black Magic. I was a prisoner there. What were my chances?

"I was in a cell, Greville"—he suddenly turned to me in the course of his ceaseless rambling walk—"some three yards square. I was lying on the hard mud floor. Not a thing had been taken from me; even my pistol remained in my belt . . . and the sandbag which had downed me lay close by! A subtle touch, that—but to-night I capped the jest! A window, just beyond reach, admitted light. There wasn't a scrap of furniture in the place. It had a heavy door reinforced with iron. I was desperately thirsty . . . and on the ledge of the window above me, I saw a water-jar standing on a tray.

"Knowing myself to be in Egypt and failing my experience of Chinese humour, I might have questioned the meaning of all this. But, looking at the lock of the door, and taking out my pistol—to learn that the shells had been withdrawn—I knew. And I resigned myself.

"It was physically impossible to reach the water-jar on the window-ledge.

"I had been judged worthy of that Chinese penalty known as The Protracted Death...."

§ 6

"Perhaps I groaned when these facts forced themselves upon me. You see, Greville, as we entered the saloon I had recognised another undesirable acquaintance . . . Ibrahîm Bey—Swâzi's twin brother!

"I have known Swâzi Pasha for many years and in my newer capacity at Scotland Yard have had intimate dealings with him. Beyond doubt he stands between Turkey and that indeterminable menace which some believe to emanate from Moscow and others from elsewhere—but which includes Turkey in its programme.

"Recognising now the fact that Ibrahîm—a cold-blooded sedition monger—was a member of the Council of Seven, I knew! Here was the clue to those mysterious movements—of which you, Weymouth, had news, and which were painfully familiar to myself in the Near and Far East.

"Swâzi Pasha was doomed! . . . So, likewise was I—the one man who might have saved him!

"You tell me, Weymouth, and you also, Petrie, that you searched the sheikh's house from roof to cellar. One spot of cellar you overlooked—the spot in which *I* awakened!

"I had no means of knowing how long I had been unconscious. My wrist-watch remained but had been smashed, doubtless as I fell. I had no means of learning if the raid had taken place. Two ideas were paramount. First, your fate, Greville. Second, Swâzi Pasha.

"I considered the window carefully. It was some two feet square, protected by rusty-looking iron bars, and from the nature of the light which it admitted, I determined that I was in a cellar and that the time was early morning. I determined, also, that the window was inaccessible. A careful examination of the door convinced me that I had no means of opening it. And since not a sound reached me, it was then I resigned myself to that most horrible of deaths—starvation and thirst. . . . Thirst, with a moist jar of water standing on the ledge above me!

"From my condition I judged that only a few hours had elapsed, and I detected a sporting gesture on the part of Fah Lo Suee—a gamble characteristically Chinese. If anyone chanced to pass that way I might be rescued! All this was surmise, of course, but I decided to test it. My eyes were burning feverishly. My head throbbed madly. But otherwise I was vigorous enough. Loudly I cried for help in English and in Arabic. Then, I listened intently.

"There was no sound.

"A Buddhist-like resignation was threatening me more and more. But I was by no means disposed to abandon myself to it. To sit down was impossible, otherwise than on the floor— and I felt peculiarly limp. I leaned up against the door and weighed my chances.

"And it was at this moment that a good man announced his presence. Failing him I shouldn't be here to-night!

"I heard the howl of a dog!

"Said!"

"In that moment, Petrie"—instinctively Nayland Smith turned to his old friend—"the face of the world changed for me! The mood of resignation passed. Standing immediately under the window I howled a reply.

"The signal was repeated. I answered it. And two minutes later I heard Said's voice above.

"Details are unnecessary, now. He had to go back to the car for gear and a rope. Scrambling down the shallow well with which the window communicated, he succeeded in wrenching the bars loose.

"And so I climbed out, to find myself on the fringe of the palm grove. I can't blame you, Weymouth, for failing to discover this far-flung chamber of the Sheikh's house. Undoubtedly it had been designed for a dungeon. I can only suppose the iron-barred door communicated with a tunnel leading to the cellars.

"My mind was made up. Beneath my monkish cowl I was

an Arab, and an Arab I would remain! I was heart-sick about you, Greville, but knew that I could do nothing—yet. Stamboul was my objective. The reason you failed to find the car in the gully was that I commandeered it for the overland journey to the railroad!

"I had realised the efficiency of the organisation to which I was opposed. My funds were fortunately sufficient for my purpose, and I reached Stamboul a week after the raid on the house of the Sheikh Ismail. Officially, I was not present in Constantinople. But I acquainted myself with the latest news in the possession of Scotland Yard—through the medium of Kemal's police. Acting upon this, I checked his journey in Paris. The rest you know."

Nayland Smith ceased speaking, and:

"Something you do not know," said Mrs. Petrie from her shadowy corner on the divan. "I have seen him—Fu Manchu—in London to-night!"

Nayland Smith turned to her.

"You were never at fault, Kâramanèh," he said. "Dr. Fu Manchu occupied rooms next to those of Swâzi Pasha in Paris!"

A taxi hooted outside in Piccadilly. . . .

PART FOUR

CHAPTER TENTH—*Abbots Hold*

CHAPTER ELEVENTH—*Dr. Amber*

CHAPTER TWELFTH—*Lord of the Si Fan*

Chapter Tenth

ABBOTS HOLD

"It all seems so peaceful," said Rima, clinging very tightly to my arm; "yet somehow, Shan, I never feel safe here. Last night, as I told you, I thought I saw the Abbots Hold ghost from my window. . . ."

"A natural thing to imagine, darling," I replied reassuringly. "Every one of these old monastic houses has its phantom monk! But, even if authentic, no doubt he'd be a jovial fellow."

As is the fashion of such autumn disturbances, a storm which had been threatening all the evening hovered to the west, blackly. Remote peals of thunder there had been during the dinner, and two short but heavy showers. Now, although angry cloud banks were visible in the distance, immediately overhead the sky was cloudless.

We sauntered on through the kitchen garden. A constant whispering in the trees told of moisture dripping from leaf to leaf. But the air was sweet and the path already dry. Rima's unrest was no matter for wonder, considering the experiences she had passed through. And when Sir Lionel had suggested our leaving London for the peace of his place in Norfolk, no one had welcomed the idea more heartily than I. In spite of intense activity on the part of Inspector Yale and his associates, all traces of Madame Ingomar—and of her yet more formidable father—had vanished,

But Nayland Smith considered that Sir Lionel, having served Fah Lo Suee's purpose—might now be considered safe from molestation and we had settled down in Abbots Hold for a spell of rest.

"The queer thing is," Rima went on, a deep, earnest note coming into her voice, "that since Sir Denis joined us I have felt not more but less secure!"

"That's very curious," I murmured, "because I've had an extraordinary feeling of the sort, myself."

"I suppose I'm very jumpy," Rima confessed. "But did you notice that family of gypsies who've camped beyond the big plantation?"

"Yes, dear. I passed them to-day. I saw a boy—rather a good-looking boy he seemed to be, but I was some distance off—and an awful old hag of a woman. Do they worry you?"

Rima laughed, unnaturally.

"Not really. I haven't seen the boy. But the woman and man I met in the lane simply gave me the creeps——"

She broke off; then:

"Oh, Shan! what's that!" she whispered.

A deep purring sound came to my ears—continuous and strange. For a moment I stood still, whilst Rima's fingers clung close to mine. Then an explanation occurred to me.

Not noticing our direction, we had reached the corner of a sort of out-house connected by a covered passage with part of the servants' quarters.

"You understand now, darling," I said, and drew Rima forward to an iron-barred window.

Bright moonlight made the interior visible; and coiled on the floor, his wicked little head raised to watch us, lay a graceful catlike creature whose black-spotted coat of gold gleamed through the dusk.

It was Sir Lionel's Indian cheetah—although fairly tame, at times a dangerous pet. Practical zoology had always been one of the chief's hobbies.

"Oh, thank heaven!" Rima exclaimed, looking down into the beautiful savage eyes which were raised to hers—"I might have guessed! But I never heard him purring before."

"He is evidently in a good humour," I said, as the great cat, with what I suppose was a friendly snarl, stood up with slow, feline grace, yawned, snarled again, and seemed to collapse wearily on the floor. The idea flashed through my mind that it was not a bad imitation of a drunken man!

This idea was even better than I realised at the time.

We walked on, round the west wing of the rambling old building, and finally entered the library by way of the french windows. Sir Lionel had certainly changed the atmosphere of this room. The spacious apartment with its oak-panelled walls and the great ceiling beams displayed the influences of the Orientalist in the form of numberless Eastern relics and curiosities, which seemed strangely out of place. Memories of the cloister clung more tenaciously here—the old refectory—

than to any other room in Abbots Hold.

A magnificent Chinese lacquer cabinet, fully six feet high, which stood like a grotesque sentry-box just below the newel post of the staircase, struck perhaps the most blatant discord of all.

The library was empty, but I could hear the chief's loud voice in the study upstairs, and I knew that Nayland Smith was there with him. Petrie and his wife had been expected to dinner, but they had telephoned from Norwich to notify us that they would be detained overnight, owing to engine trouble.

Mrs. Oram, Sir Lionel's white-haired old housekeeper, presently came in; and leaving her chatting with Rima, I went up the open oak staircase and joined the chief in his study.

"Hullo, old scout!" he greeted me as I entered. "If you're going to work with me in future, you'll either have to chuck Rima or marry her!"

He was standing on the hearthrug, dominating that small room, which was so laden with relics of his extensive and unusual travels that it resembled the shop of a very untidy antique dealer.

Nayland Smith, seated on a corner of the littered writing-table, was tugging at the lobe of his left ear and staring critically at the big brown-skinned man with his untidy, grey-white hair and keen blue eyes who was England's most intrepid explorer and foremost Orientalist. It was a toss-up which of these two contained more volcanic energy.

"Smith's worried," Sir Lionel went on in his loud rapid manner. "He thinks our Chinese friends are up to their monkey tricks again and he doesn't like Petrie's delay."

"I don't," snapped Nayland Smith. "It may be an accident. But, coming to-night, I wonder—"

"Why to-night?" I asked.

Nayland Smith stared at me intently; then:

"Because to-night I caught a glimpse of the Abbots Hold ghost."

"Rot!" shouted Sir Lionel.

"The monk?" I asked excitedly.

Nayland Smith shook his head.

"No! Didn't look like a monk to me," he said. "And I don't believe in ghosts!" he added.

§ 2

When I rejoined Rima, her restless mood had grown more marked.

"I'm so glad you're here, Shan," she said. "Dear old Mrs. Oram has gone to bed; and although I could hear your voices in the study I felt quite ridiculously nervous. I'm terribly disappointed about the Petries."

During their short acquaintance Rima and Mrs. Petrie had established one of those rare feminine friendships which a man can welcome. In Mrs. Petrie's complex character there was a marked streak of Oriental mysticism—although from her appearance I should never have suspected Eastern blood; and Rima had that Celtic leaning towards a fairyland beyond the common ken which was part and parcel of her birthright.

"So am I, darling," I said. "But they'll be here in the morning. Have you been imagining things again?" I glanced at the french windows. "Peters has locked up, I see. So you can't have been nervous about gypsies!"

It was strange that Rima, who had shared our queer life out in the Valley of the Kings, should be so timorous in a Norfolk country house; should fear wandering gypsies who had never feared Bedouins!

"No." She looked at me in her serious way, apparently reading my thoughts. "I'm not afraid of gypsies—really. I have spent too many nights out there in the wâdi in Egypt to be afraid of anything like that. It is a sort of silly, unreal fear, Shan! Will you please do something?"

"Anything! What?"

Rima pointed to the Chinese cabinet at the foot of the stairs. "Please open it!"

I crossed to the ornate piece of furniture and flung its gold-lined doors open. The cabinet was empty—as I had expected.

Rima thanked me with a smile, and:

"I've been fighting a horrible temptation to do just that," she confessed, "for a long time! Thank you, Shan dear. Don't think I'm mad but, truly"—she held out the book she had on her knees—"for ever so long past I have been sitting here reading and re-reading this one line—and glancing sideways at the cabinet. You seemed to wake me out of a trance!"

I took the book—a modern novel—and glanced at the line upon which Rima's finger rested. It was:

"I am near you. . . ."

"Could anything be more absurd?" she asked pathetically. "What's wrong with me?"

I could find no answer, then—except a lover's answer. But I was to learn later.

When at last we said good night, I noticed as Rima stood up that she had a scent spray on the cushions beside her, and laughingly:

"What's the idea?" I asked.

She considered my question in an oddly serious way. In fact, her mood was distrait in an unusual degree; but finally:

"I had almost forgotten," she replied, with a far-away look; "but I remember, now, that there was a fusty smell, like decaying leaves. I thought a whiff of eau-de-Cologne would freshen the air."

My room was on the south-west front of Abbots Hold. It was one of those in the Georgian wing, and an ugly stone balcony stretched along before it. Beneath this balcony ran a sort of arcade behind which iron-barred windows belonging to the domestic quarters faced on sloping lawns. Above were these fine, spacious rooms reserved for guests, and the prospect was magnificent. Next to me was Nayland Smith; then there was a vacant room, and then Rima's.

On entering I did not turn up the light. There was a private plant in Abbots Hold installed by Sir Lionel. But, groping my way across, I raised the blind and looked out.

Opening the french window, I inhaled the fragrance of moist loam and newly wetted leaves. Away on the right I had a view of a corner of the terrace; directly before me the ground dropped steeply to a belt of trees bordering the former moat; beyond, it rose again, and two miles away, upstanding weirdly beyond distant park land, showed a ruined tower, one of the local landmarks, and a relic of Norman days.

At first my survey of the prospect was general and vague; indeed, I had opened the window more to enjoy the coolness of the night air and to think about Rima than for any other reason. But now, suddenly, my entire interest became focused upon the ruined tower rising ghostly above surrounding trees.

Clearly visible against a stormy backing, one little point of light high up in the tower appeared and disappeared like a winking eye!

I clenched my teeth, craning out and watching intently. A code message was being transmitted from the tower! For a while I watched it, but I had forgotten Morse, and the dots and dashes defeated me. Then came inspiration: someone in Abbots Hold must be receiving this message!

Instant upon the birth of the theory, I acted.

The geography of the neighbourhood, which I knew fairly well, told me that this message could only be intended for Abbots Hold. Neglectful of the fact that the leaves were drenched with rain, I quickly got astride of the ledge and began to climb down the ivy to the shrubbery beneath.

I dropped into wet bushes without other mishap than the saturating of my dinner kit, and keeping well within the shadow of the house I began to work my way round in the direction of the terrace. I passed the dining-room, glancing up at the rooms above it, and proceeded. The whole house was in darkness.

Below the terrace I paused, looking again toward the distant tower.

The top remained just visible above the trees... and there, still coming and going, was the signal light!

I stepped out farther from the building, cautiously looking upward to the left.

"Ah!" I muttered.

Dropping down upon the sloping lawn, its turf still wet from the recent downpour, I crept farther northward, until I could obtain a clear view of the study window.

The room was in darkness, but the curtains were not drawn. A light, probably that of an electric torch, was coming and going, dot and dash, *in the chief's study!*

I came to the end of the terrace, and taking advantage of a bank of rhododendrons, crept farther away from the house, until I could see, not merely the reflection, but the actual light being operated.

Faintly as it glowed in the darkness, I could detect the figure of one who held it.... And at first I was loth to credit what I saw.

The legend of Abbots Hold; Rima's fears; memories—dreadful memories—of my own, must certainly, I determined, be influencing my imagination.

The man signalling to that other on the distant tower—for man I assumed the signaller to be—was wrapped in a sort of cowl . . . his head so enveloped in the huge hood that in the dim reflection of the torch it was quite impossible to detect his features.

"Good God!" I muttered. "What does this mean!"

Stooping below the level of the bushes, I turned. Regaining the shelter of the terrace, I ran for twenty paces. Then, leaping into the shrubbery, I located the thick branch of ivy which was a ladder to my window, and began to climb up again, my heart beating very fast, and my thoughts racing far ahead of physical effort.

Scrambling over the stone balustrade, I stepped towards the open french window of my room. . . .

Out of the shadows into the moonlight a figure moved.

It was Nayland Smith!

§ 3

"Ssh! Speak quietly, Greville!"

I stared in amazement, standing there breathing heavily by the open window, then:

"Why!" I asked in a low voice. "What's happened?"

"Close the window," said Smith.

I obeyed, and then, turning:

"Did you see me climbing up?" I asked.

"No. I heard you. I was afraid to show myself. I was expecting someone else! But you are bursting with news. Tell me."

Quickly I told him of the light beyond the valley—of the cowled figure in the study.

"Too late to trap him now, Sir Denis!" I finished, starting for the door.

He grabbed my arm.

"Not too late!" he rapped. "Here he is!"

I threw a quick and startled glance around the room, as:

"Where?" I demanded.

"There!"

Nayland Smith pointed to my bed.

Amazed to the verge of losing control, I stared at the bed. A rough, camel-hair garment lay there.... I moved, touched it. Then I knew.

"It's the robe of a Lama monk!"

Nayland Smith nodded grimly.

"Together with a certain sandbag," he said, "it has formed part of my baggage since that eventful meeting of the Council of Seven at el-Khârga!"

"But——"

"Why did I play ghost? Very simple. I suspected that some member of the household was in league with the enemy. I believe, now, I was wrong. But I knew that wherever my private inquiries led me, no one would challenge the hooded monk of Abbots Hold!"

"Good enough," I admitted. "But you were signalling from the study!"

"I was!" Nayland Smith rapped. "I was signalling to Weymouth who was watching the tower."

"To Weymouth!"

"Exactly! Weymouth reported in that way to me—as had been arranged; and I gave him certain instructions in return."

I looked him squarely in the face, and:

"Does the chief know that Superintendent Weymouth is standing by?" I asked.

"He does not!" Nayland Smith smiled, and my anger began to melt. "That rather takes the wind out of your angry sails, Greville!" He grasped my shoulder. "I don't trust Barton!" he added.

"What!"

"I don't trust you.... Both have been under the influence of Fah Lo Suee. And to-night I don't trust Rima!"

I had dropped down on to the bed, but now I started up. Into the sudden silence, like a growling of angry beasts, came an echo of thunder away eastward.

"What the devil do you mean?"

"Ssh!" Nayland Smith restrained me; his gaze was compelling. "You heard me say to-night that I had had my first glimpse of the ghost?"

"Well?"

"It was true. The ghost slipped through my fingers. But the ghost was *Fah Lo Suee!* . . . Don't raise your voice. I have a reason for this. Just outline to me, without any reservation, what took place from the time that you left Barton's study to the time that you said good night to Rima."

I stared blankly for a moment, then:

"You are her accepted lover," he added, "and she is very charming. I congratulate you . . . and give you my permission to leave out the kisses. . . ."

§ 4

"Rima was obsessed with the idea," I said, "that someone was hiding in the big lacquer cabinet. But her frame of mind seems to have been such that she wouldn't stoop to test this suspicion."

"Very characteristic," Nayland Smith commented. "You may remember that I left Barton's study some time ahead of you?"

"Yes."

"The cabinet in question stands beside the newel post of the staircase, and as the library was lighted to-night, in deep shadow. It had certain properties, Greville, with which I am acquainted but which may be unfamiliar to you. It's a very old piece and I had examined it in the past. It has lacquered doors in front and a plain door at the back!"

"Do you mean——"

"Precisely! As I came out of the study, I noticed a curious passivity in Rima's attitude which aroused my interest. Also, she was not reading, as your account would lead one to suppose—but, twisted around her chair, was staring rigidly at the french windows! The staircase, you remember, is not visible from outside!"

"Then——"

"Her suspicion—which came later—was based on fact. *I was in the cabinet!*"

"But when——"

"Did I withdraw? Husband your blushes. I escaped at the

moment you entered the room, and slipped unnoticed through the door leading to the servants' quarters below the staircase. I went back to the study by way of the east wing, and waited for Weymouth's signal. I had another small problem to investigate en route and so grabbed my useful ghostly disguise!"

"What was the small problem?"

"The cheetah!"

"The cheetah?"

"A tame cheetah, Greville, is more sensitive than any ordinary domestic animal to the presence of strangers. He is used to Barton's guests, but an intruder would provoke howls calculated to rouse the house. I suspected that the cat had been doped."

"By heaven, you're right!"

"I know I'm right! When I went round there in my monkish disguise he was snoring like an elephant! But please go on."

To the best of my ability I outlined what Rima had told me of her mood of passive terror. I tried to explain that I had reassured her and had finally parted from her confident that she was restored to normal; but:

"There's something wrong," Nayland Smith rapped irritably; "and time is important. She went out of the library—I'll swear, to fetch something—just before you came in, and she opened and then reclosed the windows."

"I'm sorry!" I exclaimed.

"Ssh!"

"I had overlooked it, Sir Denis—although it isn't of the slightest importance. She had gone to her room to get a scent-spray containing eau-de-Cologne."

Nayland Smith, who had been walking across and across the rug beside the bed, pulled up with a jerk.

"Not of the slightest importance? It's what I've been waiting to hear! At least I understand the strong smell of eau-de-Cologne which I detected on the terrace outside the library. . . . Quick! You are privileged. . . . Steal along to Rima's room. Take your shoes off. Go by the balcony. Her window is open, no doubt. If she's awake—which I think unlikely—ask her for the eau-de-Cologne bottle. Explain things how you like. If she's asleep, find it—and bring it to me! Take this torch. . . ."

150

§ 5

The strange theft was accomplished without a hitch. Rima slept soundly. Although her dressing-table was littered with bottles, I found the spray easily enough—for it was the only one of its kind there. I hurried back to my room.

Nayland Smith took it from my hands as though it had been a live bomb. He opened the door and went out. I heard him turn a tap on in the bathroom. Then he returned—carrying the spray. I saw that it was still half full.

"Take it back," he directed.

And I replaced it on Rima's dressing-table without arousing her.

"Good," Smith acknowledged. "Now we enter a province of surmise."

He began to pace the mat again, deep in thought; then:

"I am the likeliest!" he snapped suddenly; and although I couldn't imagine what he meant, went on immediately: "Conceal yourself in the south corner of the balcony. The ivy is thick there. Keep your shoes off. We must be silent."

As the paving was still wet, my prospect was poor; but:

"If anyone moves in Rima's room," he continued rapidly, "don't stir. If anyone comes out on to the balcony—watch. But whoever it is, do nothing. Just watch. If necessary, follow, but don't speak and don't be discovered. Off you go, Greville!"

I had already started, when:

"It may be a bit of an ordeal," he added, "but I count on you."

Past the open window of Smith's room I went and past that, closed, which belonged to the vacant room. Then, creeping silently, I went by Rima's window and crouched down among a tangle of wet ivy in the corner formed by a stone balustrade.

The sky directly above was cloudless again, and part of the balcony gleamed phantomesque in silvery moonlight. But, another part, including the corner in which I lay concealed, was in deep shadow. From somewhere a long way off—perhaps over the sea—came dim drumming of thunder. About me whispered leaves of rain-drenched foliage.

I saw Nayland Smith go into his room.

What were we waiting for?

Abbots Hold was silent. Nothing stirred, until a soft fluttering immediately above me set my heart thumping.

An owl swept out from the eaves and disappeared in the direction of the big plantation. From some reed bed of the near-by river a disturbed lapwing gave her eerie, peewit cry. The cry was repeated; then answered far away. Silence fell once more.

My post was a cold and uncomfortable one. It was characteristic of Nayland Smith that he took no count of such details where either himself or another was concerned. The job in hand overrode in importance any such trivial considerations.

Presently I heard the big library clock strike—and I counted the strokes mechanically.

Midnight.

I reflected that in London, now, folk would just be finishing supper.

Then . . . I saw her!

I suppose—I hope—I shall never again experience just the sort of shock which gripped my heart at this moment. Vaguely, I had imagined that our purpose was protective; that I was on guard because Rima's safety was at stake in some way. To the mystery of Nayland Smith's words, "I am the likeliest," I had failed all along to discover any solution.

Now, the solution came . . . hazily at first.

Rima, a fairy gossamer figure in the moonlight, came out barefooted on to the terrace!

Unhesitatingly, she turned right, passed the vacant room and entered the open window of that occupied by Nayland Smith! I could not believe the evidence of my senses. Just in the nick of time I checked her name as it leaped to my lips.

". . . You must be silent. It may be a bit of an ordeal—but I count on you. . . ."

Rising slowly to my feet, I stole along the terrace. The moon shone into Smith's room as it shone into mine. Just before reaching the window, I dropped down on my knees and cautiously craned forward to peer in.

Nayland Smith was in bed, the sheets drawn up to his chin. His eyes were closed . . . and Rima stood beside him.

Something that had puzzled me in that first stunning

moment now resolved itself—grotesquely. I had realised that Rima carried a glittering object. I saw it clearly as I peered into the room.

It was the scent-spray!

And, as I watched, I saw her stoop and spray the face of the motionless man in the bed!

She turned.... She was coming out again.

I drew back and hurried to my shadowy corner. Rima appeared in the moonlight. She looked unnaturally pale. But with never a glance to right or left she walked to her room and went in. Her eyes were wide-open—staring.

Absolute silence....

Then Nayland Smith appeared. He was fully dressed but he had removed his shoes.

He signalled to me to approach Rima's window. A man stupefied—horror, amazement, incredulity, each fighting for a place—I obeyed. Dropping to my knees again, I peered in....

Rima, at the green marble wash-basin, was emptying the scent-spray! She allowed hot water to run for some time, and then carefully rinsed the container and the fitting. Replacing the latter in position, she put the bottle on the dressing-table where I had found it... and went to bed!

Nayland Smith beckoned to me. I rose and walked very unsteadily along the terrace to his room.

§ 6

"Rima!" I said. "Rima! My God, Sir Denis, what does it mean?"

He grasped by shoulder hard.

"Nothing," he replied.

His keen eyes studied my amazement.

"Nothing?"

"Just that—nothing. I warned you it might prove to be an ordeal. Sit down. A peg of whisky will do us both good...."

I sat down without another word. And Nayland Smith brewed two stiff pegs. Handing one to me:

"Here's part of the explanation," he jerked—and held a book under my nose. "Smell. Only one sniff!"

A sickly-sweet odour came from the open pages. The book was that which Rima had been reading in the library.

"Familiar?"

I nodded; and took a long drink. My hand was none too steady. It was a perfume I could never forget. It formed my last memory of the meeting of the Seven at el-Khârga; my first memory of that dreadful awakening in the green-gold room in Limehouse!

"*Hashish!*" snapped Nayland Smith—"or something prepared from it. Rima, by means of this doped book, was put into a receptive condition. It's a routine, Greville, with which Petrie is unhappily familiar . . . hence Petrie's detention on the way!

"Fah Lo Suee is an accomplished hypnotist! For this piece of knowledge I am also indebted to the doctor: he once all but succumbed to her . . . and she was only in her teens in those days. She was posted outside the closed french windows of the library to-night. In some way, and at the psychological moment, she attracted Rima's attention—and obtained mental control over her."

"But . . . is this possible?"

"You have seen it in full operation." he answered. "Rima was given hypnotic orders to go to her room for a scent-spray. She obeyed. That was when, from my post in the Chinese cabinet, I heard her hurry upstairs. She brought the spray, opened the window—I heard her—and gave it to Fah Lo Suee—whose name, by the way, means 'Sweet Perfume'. It was emptied, recharged and returned to her. She reclosed the window . . . having received those detailed post-hypnotic instructions which we have seen her carry out to-night."

"But—my bewilderment was increasing—"I spoke to her after this! I even asked why she had fetched the scent-spray, and she said she had detected a sickly smell—like decaying leaves—and thought it would freshen the air."

"Part of her orders!" he rapped. "Next, she was instructed to go to bed and sleep until midnight; then to spray me with the contents—which I preserved for analysis and replaced with water!—and then to remove all traces—as we know she did do! My dear fellow, Rima is utterly unaware that she has played this part . . . and doubtless it would have been an easy death!"

"You mean, when she wakes, she will know nothing about it?"

"Nothing whatever! Unless, perhaps, as in Petrie's case, the memory of a troubled dream. However, I have hopes . . . if my Morse orders were promptly obeyed."

"You mean your signal to Weymouth?"

He nodded, and:

"The 'gypsies,'" he rapped.

"What!"

"Three are dacoits—one posing as an old hag! The 'boy' of the party is Fah Lo Suee!"

CHAPTER ELEVENTH

Dr. AMBER

"I CAN'T blame myself," said Weymouth, staring disconsolately out of the window. "She's slipped through our fingers again. A real chip of the old block," he added. "It took a load off my mind, after the Limehouse raid, to hear that Nayland Smith had seen Fu Manchu himself, in person, in Paris—and lost him! . . ."

The "gypsy" caravan behind the big plantation which formed a western boundary to Sir Lionel's Norfolk place had been seized by a party of constabulary under Weymouth's command—and had proved to be empty. This had happened three days before, but it still rankled in the superintendent's mind.

"I can't hang on here indefinitely," he explained, "I'm badly needed in Cairo at the moment. The disappearance of Sir Denis and yourself was the real excuse for my leave, but now. . . ."

His point was clear enough. Weymouth was a staunch friend, but he loved his job. He had come to England in pursuit of a clue which suggested that Nayland Smith and I had been smuggled into Europe. We were found. Duty called him back.

"It isn't your present job, I admit," said I; "but it's the tail end of an old one, after all!"

He turned and stared at me across the room. I was back at the Park Avenue looking after a hundred and one interests of the chief's which centred in London. He, with Rima, remained in Norfolk—where, now that Nayland Smith had left, he might count on peace. Of Nayland Smith's present movements I knew nothing.

"You've hit it!" Weymouth admitted. "I'd like to be in at the death."

Certainly it was a queer situation for him—for all of us. Dr. Fu Manchu, most formidable of all those greater criminals who from time to time disturb the world, was alive . . . and his daughter, no poor second to this stupendous genius, had already proved that she was competent to form subject of debate in the councils of the highest.

Weymouth's expression struck me as ominous; and:

"The death is likely to be that of Nayland Smith," I said, "judging from our experience at Abbots Hold."

Weymouth nodded.

"He stands between her and all she aims for," he replied. "He's countered two of her first three moves and he's promised me word within the next hour. But"—he stared at me very grimly—"you and I, Greville, know more about the group called the *Si Fan* than most people outside it."

I laughed—somewhat hollowly, perhaps.

"Get back to Cairo," I advised. "It's probably safer than London at the moment—for you."

Weymouth's sense of humour on such points always failed him. His blue eyes hardened; he literally glared at me; and:

"I never ran away from Dr. Fu Manchu," he replied. "If you think I'm going to run away from his daughter you're wrong."

At that I laughed again, and this time my laughter rang true. I punched the speaker playfully.

"Don't you know when I'm pulling your leg?" I asked. "I'd put my last shilling on your being here, job or no job, until the end of this thing is clearly in sight!"

"Oh!" said Weymouth, his naïve smile softening the hard mask which had fallen when I had suggested his retiring to Cairo. "Well, I don't think you'd lose your money."

But when he had gone, I took his place at the window and stared down on the panorama of Piccadilly. I was thinking of Nayland Smith. . . . "He stands between her and all she aims for.". . . How true that was! Yes, he held most of the strings. Fah Lo Suee had started with a heavy handicap. Ibrahîm Bey occupied a prison cell in Brixton Prison. He would be tried and duly sentenced for attempted robbery with violence. The public would never learn the whole truth. But Ibrahîm Bey might be counted out of the running. The Egyptian authorities, working in concert with the French in Syria, were looking for Sheikh Ismail; and the Mandarin Ki Ming would have to hide very cleverly to escape the vigilance of those who had been advised of his aims. . . .

My phone bell rang. I turned and took up the receiver.
"Yes?"
"Is Mr. Shan Greville there?"

"Speaking."

The voice—that of a man who spoke perfect English but who was not an Englishman—sounded tauntingly familiar.

"My name will be known to you, I believe, Mr. Greville. I am called Dr. Amber."

Dr. Amber! The mysterious physician whose treatment had restored Sir Lionel—whom I had to thank for my own recovery!

"Owing to peculiar circumstances, which I hope to explain to you, I have hitherto been able to help only in a rather irregular way," he went on. "Because of this—and of the imminent danger to which I am exposed—I must make a somewhat odd request."

"What is it?"

"It is this: All I have to tell you is at your disposal. But you must promise to treat myself as non-existent. I have approached you in this way because the life of Sir Denis Nayland Smith is threatened—to-night! My record backs my assurance that this is a friendly overture. Have I your promise?"

"Yes—certainly!"

"Good. It will be a short journey, Mr. Greville—not three minutes' walk. I am staying at Babylon House, Piccadilly; Flat Number 7. May I ask you to step across? You have ample time before dinner."

"I'll come right away."

Dr. Amber! Who was Dr. Amber? Where did he fit into this intricate puzzle which had sidetracked so many lives? Whoever he might be, he had shown himself a friend, and without hesitation, but fired by an intense curiosity, I set out for Babylon House—a block of service flats nearly opposite Burlington Arcade.

A lift-man took me to the top floor and indicated a door on the right.. I stepped up to it and rang the bell.

The elevator was already descending before the door opened . . . and I saw before me the Chinese physician who had attended me in that green and gold room in Limehouse!

Fear—incredulity—anger all must have been readable in my expression, when:

"You gave me your promise, Mr. Greville," said the Chinaman, smiling. "I give you mine, if it is necessary, that you are safe and with a friend. Please come in."

§ 2

The typical and scanty appointments of the apartment into which I was shown possessed a reassuring quality. From a high window with a narrow balcony I could see the entrance to Burlington Arcade and part of one wall of the Albany.

"Won't you sit down?" said my host, who wore morning dress and looked less characteristically Chinese than he had looked in white overalls.

I sat down.

A small writing-desk set before the window was littered with torn documents, and a longer table in the centre of the room bore stacks of newspapers. I saw the London *Evening News*, the *Times of India*, and the Chicago *Tribune* amongst this odd assortment. Certain paragraphs appeared to have been cut out with scissors. The floor was littered with oddments. I noticed other definite evidences of a speedy outgoing. A very large steamer trunk bearing the initials L. K. S. in white letters stood strapped in a corner of the room.

"It is my purpose, Mr. Greville," said Dr. Amber, taking a seat near the desk and catching me steadily, "to explain certain matters which have been puzzling yourself and your friends. And perhaps in the first place, since I wish to be perfectly frank"—he glanced toward the big trunk—"I should tell you that 'Dr Amber' is a pseudonym. I am called Li King Su; I hold a medical degree of Canton; and I once had the pleasure of assisting Dr. Petrie in a very critical major operation. He will probably remember me.

"You are quite naturally labouring under the impression that I belong to the organisation controlled by the Lady Fah Lo Suee. This is not so. I belong to another, older, organisation. . . ."

He stared at me intently. But I didn't interrupt him. I was considering that curious expression—"the Lady Fah Lo Suee."

"I was—shall we say?—a spy in the house in which you first met me. The lady called Fah Lo Suee has now discovered the imposture, and——"

Again he paused, indicating the steamer trunk.

"My usefulness is ended. I am a marked man, Mr. Greville. If I escape alive I shall be lucky. But let us talk of something else. . . . The Tomb of the Black Ape has proved something of a puzzle to Sir Denis Nayland Smith. The solution is simple: A representative of that older organisation to which I have referred was present when Lafleur opened the place many years ago. By arrangement with that distinguished Egyptologist, it was reclosed. Later—in fact, early in 1918—a prominent official of our ancient society, passing through Egypt, had reason to suspect that certain treasures in his possession might be discovered and detained by the British Authorities—for these were troubled times. He proceeded up the Nile and successfully concealed them in this tomb—the secret of which had been preserved with just such an end in view. . . ."

I suppose I must have known all along; but for some reason at this moment the identity of "a representative of that older organisation" and "a prominent official of our ancient society" suddenly burst upon me with all the shock of novelty; and, meeting the glance of those inscrutable eyes which watched me so intently:

"You are speaking of Dr. Fu Manchu!" I said.

Li King Su permitted himself a slight deprecatory gesture.

"It is desirable," he replied, "that those of whom I speak should remain anonymous!"

But I continued to stare at him with a sort of horror. "By arrangement with that distinguished Egyptologist," he had said smoothly. Good God! What kind of "arrangement"!

"It was the intention of the hider," he went on, "that those potent secrets should remain concealed for ever. The activities of Professor Zeitland and Sir Lionel Barton created an unforeseen situation. It was complicated by the action of the Lady Fah Lo Suee. She had recently learned what was hidden there, but she was ignorant of how to recover it. . . . Professor Zeitland imparted his knowledge to her—then came Sir Lionel Barton. . . ."

He paused again, significantly.

"We moved too late, Mr. Greville. An old schism in our ranks had made an enemy of one of the most brilliant and dangerous men in China—the exalted Mandarin Ki Ming. He gave the Lady Fah Lo Suee his aid. But we wasted no more time. I succeeded in gaining admittance to their councils. It was by means of their organisation that I intercepted Dr. Petrie's telegram to Sir Brian Hawkins. You know the use which I made of my knowledge.

"Your present English Government is blind. You will lose Egypt as you have lost India. A great federation of Eastern States affiliated with Russia—a new Russia—is destined to take the place once held by the British Empire. You have one chance to recover. . . ."

The man's personality was beginning to get me. I had forgotten that I sat, inert, listening to a self-confessed servant of Dr. Fu Manchu: I only knew that he was raising veils beyond which I longed to peer.

"What is it?" I asked.

And, as I spoke a chill—not figurative but literal—turned me cold. I had detected Li King Su in the act of glancing toward a partially opened door which led to the bedroom. . . .

Definitely someone was listening!

As if conscious of the fact that he had betrayed himself, "Dr. Amber" went on immediately:

"A counter alliance! But we are getting out of our depth, Mr. Greville. To return to more personal matters: The schemes of the Lady Fah Lo Suee were not approved by us. The authority she has stolen must be restored to those who know how to wield it. In other words, Sir Denis Nayland Smith's aim and our own are identical—at the moment. But he is marked down!"

"He knows it!"

"He may know it—but to-night he is walking into a trap! Since he left Norfolk—where he failed to arrest the prime mover—you have lost touch with him. He is following up a clue discovered by Inspector Yale. It is a false clue . . . a snare. He stands in the way: she is afraid to move until he is silenced.

"Here"—he handed me a slip of paper—"is the address to which he is going to-night. Death waits for him."

I glanced at the writing.

"The garden of this house adjoins the Regent Canal," Li King Su went on. "And it is intended that Sir Denis's body shall be found in the Canal in the morning! Here"—he passed a second slip—"is the address at which Sir Denis is hiding."

The second address was that of a Dr. Murray in a southwest suburb.

"Dr. Murray bought Dr. Petrie's practice," the even voice continued, "when the latter went to Egypt. I must warn you against any attempt to communicate by telephone. The Lady Fah Lo Suee has a spy in the house! Take what steps you please, Mr. Greville, but move quickly! For my own part, I leave London in an hour. I can do no more. It is unnecessary to remind you of our bargain."

§ 3

At the very moment that I entered the lift, that occult knowledge of being watched left me. It was the same—but intensified—as that which had warned me in Cairo, and later on the road to el-Khârga. Li King Su, on acquaintance, was a remarkable man. But some vastly greater personality had been concealed in that inner room. I could not forget that Dr. Fu Manchu had been seen a stone's throw from Babylon House!

Could I trust Li King Su?

Simple enough to test his statements. I had only to take a taxi to Dr. Murray's address.

But, as I thought, as I walked out into Piccadilly, a mistake now might carry unimaginable consequences; better to consult Weymouth or Yale before I committed an irreparable blunder.

Dusk was falling. I saw that the lamps in Burlington Arcade had been lighted as well as those in the Piccadilly Arcade which forms a sort of abbreviated continuation of the older bazaar and breaks through to Jermyn Street. Deep in thought I passed the entrance to the latter. A French sedan was drawn up beside the pavement.

I was level with it when an exclamation of annoyance checked me sharply—and just prevented my collision with a woman who, crossing before me, had evidently been making for the car.

She was a fashionable figure, wearing a fur-trimmed coat, and a short veil attached to her close-fitting hat quite obscured her features. She carried several parcels, one of which she had dropped almost at my feet.

Stooping, I picked it up—a paper-wrapped package fastened with green tape and apparently containing very light purchases. The chauffeur sprang down and opened the door of the car, as:

"Thank you very much," said the laden lady. "Will you be so kind as to hand it in to me?"

She entered the car. I followed with the dropped package and bent forward into the dark interior. Through the opposite windows I saw the sign above a popular restaurant suddenly become illuminated. I detected a damnably familiar perfume. . . .

I was enveloped. I felt a sudden paralysing pressure in my spine—a muscular arm levered me into the car . . . and I realised that I had been garroted in Piccadilly, amid hundreds of passers-by and in sight of my hotel!

§ 4

I shot up from green depths in which I had been submerged for an immeasurable time. I had dived into a deep lake, I thought, and had become entangled in clinging weeds which sprang from its bed. I could not free my limbs; I knew that I was drowning—that never again should I see the sun and the blue sky above. . . .

Then, the clasp of those octopus tentacles was relaxed. And I shot to the surface like a cork. . . .

Green! . . . Everything about me was green!

What had happened? Where was I?

Great heavens! I was back in Limehouse! . . . But no—this place was green and gold, but smaller—much smaller than the room of my long captivity.

It was a miniature room—something was radically wrong with it. There were tow windows, draped in those heavy gold curtains which I remembered; a tracing of green figures was brushed across the gold. There was a tall lacquer cabinet and upon it stood a jade image of Kâli . . . tiny, minute. There were flat green doors and a green carpet; golden rugs. An amber lamp gave green light. Upon a black divan was a second, larger figure of Kâli . . . as large as a carnival doll.

But, no! This figure resembled Kâli only in her features: she wore a green robe and high-heeled black shoes. In one slender hand, a soft hand nurtured in luxury, was a long cigarette holder. I could see the smoke from the burning cigarette. . . . A doll—but a living doll!

The picture grew smaller yet. The doll became so tiny that I could no longer discern her features. I was a giant in a microscopic room!

And then—the colours became audible!

"I am green" said the carpet. "We are gold," the miniature curtains replied. . . .

Raising both hands I clutched my head!

I was mad! I knew it—because I wanted to laugh!

The room began to increase in size! From the dimensions of a doll's house fashioned by gnomes it swelled to those of a gigantic palace! . . . I was a mere fly in an apartment which could scarcely have found ground space in Trafalgar Square!

But, now—I recognised that green-draped figure on the black divan. It was Fah Lo Suee!

The mighty roof, higher than that of any mosque, of any cathedral in the world, began to descend: the walls closed in . . . huge pieces of furniture were pushed towards me. Fah Lo Suee towered above my shrinking body, her monstrous cigarette sending up a column of smoke like that of a sacrifice. . . .

I cried out . . . and saw the cry!

"God help me!"

It issued from my lips in squat green letters! I closed my eyes, and:

"So you are awake, Shan?" said a bell-like voice.

But I was afraid to raise my eyelids.

"Look at me. You are all right now. . . ."

I looked.

My head was swimming and every muscle in my body ached—but the room had taken on normal proportions. It was a large room, filled with modern furniture, except that its scheme was severely green and gold and that there were Oriental pieces placed about.

Fah Lo Suee watched me ... but the jade-green eyes were hard.

"You are better," she continued. "*Cannabis indica* produces strange delusions—but as *we* use it, there is no drug so swift to serve our purpose."

I considered the situation. I was seated in a big armchair facing the divan upon which Fah Lo Suee reclined indolently watching me. The damnable fumes of the drug began to leave my brain. Fah Lo Suee, slender, sinuous, insolent, was a woman—but a deadly enemy. I knew what Nayland Smith would have done!

Preparatory to a spring, I drew my feet together ... a certain distance. Then—

My ankles were fastened to the chair!

Fah Lo Suee dropped ash from her yellow cigarette into a copper bowl upon the low table beside her. I watched the elegant, voluptuous movements of that feline hand with a queer sense of novelty. What a tigress she was!

"The chief purpose of my visit to England," she said, speaking as though nothing unusual existed between hostess and visitor, "was defeated by Sir Denis Nayland Smith. My further plans are in abeyance—pending his suppression."

My head ached as though my brain were on fire, but:

"He is by way of being rather a nuisance?" I suggested viciously.

Fah Lo Suee smiled, a smile of contempt.

"I could have dealt with him—alone. But one of my own people proved treacherous. In your pocket, Shan, you had two addresses. One was that of Dr. Murray—in whose home your brilliant friend is hiding; the other was that of this house."

She continued to smile—and she continued to watch me. I tried to conquer my wandering ideas. I tried to hate her. But her eyes caressed me, and I was afraid—horribly afraid of this witch-woman who had the uncanny power which Homer gave to Circe, of stealing men's souls.

If I could trust Li King Su, Nayland Smith was coming here—to this house—where death awaited!

And now I was powerless to stop him!

"Li King Su was a traitor." Through the beats of a sort of drumming which had started in my brain I heard the bell-like voice. "No doubt he counted on a great reward."

She ceased speaking and clapped her hands sharply.

That gigantic Negro who had been the door-keeper in el-Khârga, and who had overpowered me at the meeting of the Seven, came in!

Fah Lo Suee addressed him rapidly. She spoke in a sort of bastard Arabic—the Nubian dialect; and I found time for wonder. I knew North Africa from the inside; but I had never learned that queer lingo of the Nubians. Yet this woman—who was Chinese—used it familiarly!

The Nubian went out. Fah Lo Suee removed the stump of a yellow cigarette from her long holder, selected a fresh one from a cloisonné box, and fitted it into place. She ignited it with an enamelled lighter.

A dragging sound came.

I saw the Nubian pulling a heavy trunk through the door and across the carpet. This trunk was vaguely familiar. Then, on top, I saw white painted initials: L.K.S.

The Negro removed the straps and threw the lid back.

"Look," said Fah Lo Suee. "He was a traitor."

Li King Su lay in his own trunk—dead!

§ 5

Not until I found myself aloud could I think my own thoughts, uninfluenced by the promptings of those jade-green eyes. But when the door closed behind Fah Lo Suee, I began desperately to weigh my chances.

Nayland Smith was doomed!

This was the thought which came uppermost in my mind. The clue upon which he was working, and which would lead him that night to this house, was a false clue—a bait!

And that our enemies did not spare those who crossed their path I had learned.

The trunk had been dragged from the room.... But I could still see, in imagination, that strangled grin on the dead man's face.

I tried to reconstruct the details of our interview in Babylon House. Had I detected, or only deluded myself that I had detected, a swift exchange of signs between Li King Su and someone concealed in an inner room? Had I merely imagined the presence of this other?... Or had I been right in supposing someone to be there but wrong in my natural deduction that he was a friend of the Chinese doctor?

Had the hidden man murdered Li King Su and caused his body to be removed in the big trunk?...

"The garden of this house adjoins the Regent Canal," he had said.

The Regent Canal! A gloomy whispering waterway, now little used, and entering a long tunnel somewhere near this very spot where I found myself a prisoner!

I bent forward to inspect the fastenings which confined my ankles... I was checked.

In the mad fantasies attendant upon my recovering from the effects of *hashish*, and afterwards under the evil thrall of Fah Lo Suee, I had failed to note a significant fact.

A rope was around my waist, binding me to the heavy chair!

True, my hands were free, but I could neither reach my ankles nor the knots fastening the line about my body, which were somewhere under the back of the chair.

A coffee-table on which were whisky and soda and cigarettes stood conveniently near. I was about to take a cigarette ... when I hesitated. Reaching to my pocket I took out my own case and with a lighter which lay on the table started a cigarette.

At all costs I must keep my head. Upon me, alone, rested the fate of Nayland Smith—perhaps the fate of a million more!

I smoked awhile, sitting deliberately relaxed, and thinking ... thinking. My bonds occasioned me no inconvenience provided I remained inactive. Short of a painful, tortoise-like progress across the room, dragging the heavy chair with me, it became increasingly clear that to move was a physical impossibility.

The house was silent—very silent. Those heavy gold draperies seemed to exclude all sound.

For a long time I sat there smoking cigarette after cigarette. Then I heard something.

One of the two doors opened.

The huge Nubian came in, carrying a tray upon which were sandwiches and fruit. He set the tray on the table beside me. His girth of shoulder was amazing; and as he stooped he gave me a wicked glance of his small, sunken, bloodshot eyes.

Without a word, he went out again, quietly closing the door.

Was I being watched? Having avoided the cigarettes and the whisky, was this a further attempt to dope me? I considered the facts. . . .

What had they to gain? I was utterly at their mercy. Secret poisoning was unnecessary.

I ate a sandwich and drank a glass of whisky and soda.

Silence. . . .

The figure of Kâli on the lacquer cabinet engaged my attention. I found myself studying it closely—so closely that I began to imagine it was moving. . . .

Kâli—symbol of this hellish organisation, the *Si Fan* into whose power I had fallen. . . .

The door opened, and Fah Lo Suee came in.

"I am glad to see that you have called on your philosophy," she said. "You will need it. Unless you are prepared to face another injection of *F. Katalepsis* you must give me your parole for half an hour. . . ."

She stood in the open doorway, one slender hand, its polished nails gleaming like gems, resting on her hip. Her eyes were mercilessly hard.

I can't say what it was in her bearing that told me; but I knew, beyond any shadow of doubt, that all was not going smoothly with Madame Ingomar.

"Naturally, I must decline."

"You mean it?"

"Definitely."

She smiled. Her passionate lips betrayed a weakness which was not to be read in those jade-green eyes. She clapped her hands. The big emerald which she wore on an index finger glittered evilly.

The huge Nubian entered. Fah Lo Suee spoke rapidly, and he crossed to me.

"Don't resist," she said softly. "It would be merely melodrama. He could strangle you with one hand. Do as I ask. I am being merciful."

My wrists were firmly knotted behind me. Those lashings which held me to the heavy chair were cast off. Then the black picked me up as one might raise a child and carried me out of the room!

"In half an hour," said Fah Lo Suee, "I will free you again—and we will talk."

Clenching my teeth grimly—for curses, execrations, torrents of poisonous, futile words, bubbled up in me—I was borne across an elegantly furnished lobby. Everywhere I detected an ultra-modern note, in spite of the presence of old Oriental pieces.

Upstairs I was carried, and into a dark little room opening off the first floor landing. I was laid down, prone, on a narrow settee. The Nubian went out and locked the door. . . .

Trussed as I found myself, it was no easy matter to regain my feet. But I managed it, and stood staring around me in semi-darkness. The only light, I saw, came through a window which, on the outside, was reinforced with iron bars. And this light was the light of the moon.

The place seemed to be a small writing-room. There was a bureau at the end near the window, closed, a square Cubist-looking chair before it. The black-and-gold walls were bare. There was a closed bookcase, a low stool of Arab workmanship, and the narrow settee upon which I had been placed.

I contrived to get to the window.

It overlooked a neglected garden . . . and at the end of the garden I saw the Canal!

Dropping into the chair, I began to taste that most bitter of all draughts which poor humanity knows—despair. I remembered Nayland Smith's story of the house at el-Khârga: . . . "A Buddhist-like resignation was threatening me more and more. . . ."

Nayland Smith!

Whilst I sat here, a fiery furnace raging within, but nevertheless useless as any snared rabbit, he was walking into a death trap!

She would have no mercy. I had seen how she dealt with those who crossed her: I had read his sentence in her glittering eyes. This time, there would be no "sporting gesture." And I . . . I should awake somewhere in China, as a male concubine of this Eastern Circe!

I bent down, resting my throbbing head on the bureau. . . . Then came sounds.

Somewhere a bell rang. There were voices. I heard movements—I divined that some heavy burden had been carried in.

The sounds died away. Silence fell again.

How long I sat there, in a dreadful apathy, I had no means of judging. But suddenly the door was unlocked, and I started up.

Fah Lo Suee came in, carrying a long-bladed knife.

§ 6

She stood watching me.

"Well?" I said. "What are you waiting for?"

She smiled, that one-sided voluptuous smile which was never reflected in her eyes; then:

"I am waiting," she replied—her bell-like voice very soft—"to try to guess what you will do when I release you."

She came forward, bent so that her small, shapely head almost rested on my shoulder, and cut the lashings which confined my wrists. Her left hand grasped my arm as she stooped. Dropping to her knees, with two strokes of the keen blade she cut away the ropes binding my ankles.

Then she stood upright, very near to me, and met my stare challengingly.

"Well?" she said in mockery.

My first impulse—for I had been thinking about Nayland Smith almost continuously—was to be read in my glance.

"It can never happen twice to me, Shan," said Fah Lo Suee.

She called a name.

The door opened—and I saw the giant Nubian looking in.

Fah Lo Suee gave a brief order. The Negro retired, closing the door.

"Does no more subtle method occur to you?" she asked, her voice softer than ever. "I am as ready to be lied to as any other woman, Shan—by the right man—if he only tells his lies sweetly."

And, face to face with this evilly beautiful woman, knowing, as I knew too well, that my own life was at stake, that possibly I could even bargain for that of Nayland Smith, I asked myself—why not? With her own lips she had reminded me of that old adage, "all's fair in love and war." With her it was love—or the only sort of love she knew; with me it was war. Perhaps, on a scruple, hung the fate of nations!

She drew a step nearer. The perfumed aura of her personality began to envelop me. Choice was being filched from the bargain. Those mad urgings which I had known in the green-gold room in Limehouse began to beat upon my brain.

I clenched my fists. I could possibly but the safety of the Western world with a kiss! Tensed fingers relaxed. In another instant my arms would have been around that slender, yielding body; when:

"Greville!" came a distant cry. *"Greville!"*

And I knew the voice!

I sprang back from Fah Lo Suee as from a poised cobra. Her face changed. It was as though a mask had been dropped. I saw Kâli—the patronne of assassins. . . .

She snapped her fingers.

Before I could move further, collect my scattered thoughts, the Nubian was on me!

I got in one straight right, perfectly timed. It didn't even check him. . . .

As his Herculean grip deprived me of all power of movement, Fah Lo Suee turned and went out. She hissed an order.

The Nubian threw me face downward on the settee. Never, in the whole of my experience of rough-houses, had I been so handled. I was helpless as a rat in the grip of a bull terrier. My knowledge of boxing as well as a smattering of jiu-jitsu were about as useful as botany!

I honestly believe he could have broken any normally strong man across his knee.

One of the ghastly Burmans, with the mark of Kâli on his forehead, came to assist. I was trussed up like a chicken, tossed on to the Negro's mighty shoulder, and carried from the room.

This was the end.

I had played my hand badly. On me the ultimate issue had rested . . . and I had failed. That swift revulsion, at the sound of my name—that sudden, irrational reversion to type—had sealed the doom of . . . how many?

Helpless, a mere inanimate bundle, I was carried down to the room where the image of Kâli sat on a lacquer cabinet.

The Nubian threw me roughly on the divan, so that I had no view beyond that of the lacquer cabinet and the wall against which it stood. He withdrew. I heard the closing of a door.

I turned. . . .

In the big, carved chair which formerly I had occupied, Nayland Smith was firmly lashed! There were bloodstains on his collar.

"Sir Denis! How did you know I was here?"

He glanced down at the coffee-table.

"You left you cigarette case!" he replied. "I shouted for you—but a dacoit"—he indicated the bloodstains—"silenced me."

I stared at him. No words came.

"Weymouth and Yale," he went on, and the tone of his voice struck the death-knell of lingering hope, "are watching the wrong house. I have made my last mistake, Greville."

Chapter Twelfth

LORD OF THE *SI FAN*

"I THOUGHT I had found a secret base of operations," said Nayland Smith. "It's one I have used before—the house of Dr. Murray who bought Petrie's practice years ago. Evidently it's been known for some time past that I employed it in this way. I discovered—too late—that a parlour maid in Murray's service is a spy. She doesn't know the real identity of her employers, but she has been none the less useful to them. . . ."

As he spoke, he was studying every detail of the room in which we lay trapped. Apparently he had accepted his fastenings as immovable; and evidently divining my thoughts:

"These lashings are the work of a Sea-Dyak," he explained— "palpably a specialist. Though seemingly simple, no one except the late Houdini could hope to escape from them."

"A fellow with the mark on his forehead? He tied me up! I mistook him for Burmese!"

Nayland Smith shook his head irritably.

"A member of the murder group—yes. But no Burman. He belongs to Borneo. . . . The story of my stupidity, Greville, for which so many may be called upon to pay a ghastly price, is a short one. Yale brought me a clue to-day. Its history doesn't matter—now. It was a fake. But it consisted of fragments of torn-up correspondence written in Chinese and a few cipher notes in another hand. I grappled with it: no easy task. But by about four o'clock I saw daylight. I phoned Weymouth to stand by between six and seven."

"He told me so."

"Yale also was in touch. At six o'clock I had got all the facts—including an address in Finchley Road; and at six-thirty I called Weymouth at the Park Avenue giving him full instructions. I arranged to meet him outside Lord's at half-past nine to-night.

"By sheer accident, ten minutes later, I caught Palmer, the parlourmaid, at the telephone. Murray was in his consulting-room, and there was nothing in itself remarkable about the girl's presence at the phone. She makes appointments and receives patients.

"But I heard my own name mentioned!"

"I taxed her—and she got muddled. She was clever enough to wriggle out of the difficulty, verbally; but I had become gravely suspicious. Bearing this in mind, Greville, it's all the less excusable that I should have fallen into the trap planted for me.

"Murray's house overlooks a common, and it's usually safe to trust to picking up a taxi on the main road, although sometimes one has to wait. During dinner I said nothing about Palmer, being still in two minds as to her complicity. But when I left, I made a blunder for which I should certainly condemn the rawest recruit.

"The door of Murray's house opens on a side turning—and as I came out a taxi, proceeding slowly in the direction of the common, passed me. The man looked out as I came down the steps and slowed up. I counted it a stroke of luck, said 'Lord's cricket ground—main entrance'—and jumped in."

Nayland Smith smiled. It was not the genial, revealing smile that I knew.

"End of story!" he added. The windows were unopenable. As I closed the door, which locked automatically, a charge of gas was puffed into the interior. That taxi, Greville, had been waiting for me!"

"Then Weymouth and Yale—"

"Weymouth and Yale, with a Flying Squad party, are covering the house of some perfectly harmless citizen in Finchley Road! What they'll do when I fail to turn up, I can't say. But they haven't a ghost of a clue to this place—wherever it is!"

"It's beside the Regent Canal," I replied slowly. "That's all I know about it."

"Quite sufficient," he rapped. "In your amazing interview with Li King Su I detect our only ray of hope...."

§ 2

An interruption came. Dimly—for sounds were muffled in this room—I heard the ringing of a bell. I saw Nayland Smith start. We both listened. We had not long to wait for the next development.

Into the room the huge Nubian came running—followed by the man whom I knew now to be a Dyak. They swept down upon Nayland Smith!

I became tongue-tied. Horror had robbed me of speech.

The man with the mark of Kâli on his brow bent swiftly. I tugged at my bonds. Nayland Smith caught my glance.

Don't worry, Greville," he said. "A hasty removal of prisoners is evidently—"

The Nubian clapped a huge black hand over the speaker's mouth!

I saw Nayland Smith, released from the chair, but rebound by the Dyak expert, lifted in the grasp of the giant Negro. He carried Sir Denis as he might have carried a toy dog under one arm—but he kept his free hand pressed to the captive's mouth.

There came a breathless interval. That dim ringing was renewed. The devotee of Kâli considered me, his eyes lascivious with murder. Then, as the ringing persisted, he grasped my bound ankles, jerked me to the carpet, and dragged me out of the room!

Where, formerly, I had been carried up, now I was hauled down and down, until I knew I was in the cellars of the house.

That I arrived there without sprained wrists or a cracked skull was something of a miracle. Arms fastened behind me, I had nevertheless done all I could to protect my head as I was dragged down many steps to the basement.

Into some dark, paved place, I was finally bundled. I divined, rather than knew, that Nayland Smith lay beside me.

"Sir Denis," I gasped.

Wiry fingers gripped my throat, squeezing me to silence; but: "Here!" Smith replied.

The word was cut off shortly—significantly.

There came a stirring up above—a sound of voices—of movement ... shuffling.

My brain began to work rapidly, despite all the maltreatment my skull had received. This was an unexpected visit of some kind! The house was being cleared of its noxious elements, of its prisoners; made presentable for inspection!

Possibly—the thought set my heart hammering—

Weymouth, after all, had secured some clue which had led him here.

I listened intently.

Short, regular breathing almost in my ear warned me that the slightest sound on my part would result in that strangle grip being renewed.

Yes! It was the police!

There were heavy footsteps in the lobby above—deep voices.

Those sounds died away.

I told myself that the search party had gone up to explore the higher floors—and I wondered who was posing as owner of the house—and what had been done with the body of Li King Su.

The cellar in which I lay possessed drum-like properties. I distinctly heard heavy footsteps on the stairs—descending.

Perhaps the searchers had been unsatisfied! Perhaps they were about to go!

Then I heard, and recognised, a deep voice——

Weymouth!

At that, I determined to risk all.

A significant choking sound which came from the darkness behind might have warned me—for, even as I opened my mouth, a lean, oily smelling hand covered it—a steely grip was on my throat! . . .

"I trust you are satisfied, Inspector?" I heard, in a quavering female voice. "If there is anything else——"

"Nothing further, madam, thank you!" . . . Weymouth! . . . "Evidently she didn't come here. I can only apologise for troubling you."

Receding footsteps . . . murmurs of conversation.

The bang of a street door!

My head dropped back limply as the deathly grip was removed; a whisper came out of the darkness:

"A divine accident—wasted!"

Nayland Smith was the speaker . . . and I knew that that indomitable spirit was very near to despair.

What possibly could have led Weymouth here? Clearly he had no information to justify a detailed search; no warrant. "Evidently she didn't come here. . . ." In those words the clue lay. And who was the old woman of the quavering voice?

Rapidly, these reflections flashed through my mind—but uppermost was a sense of such bitter, hopeless disappointment as I had never known before.

Truly, it was Fate.

Perhaps, as Fah Lo Suee believed, as Li King Su had believed, the day of the West was ended; perhaps we were obstacles in the way of some cataclysmic change, ordained, inevitable—and so must be brushed aside.

When presently we found ourselves back in that room where the figure of Kâli sat, immutable, on a lacquer dias, I told myself that nothing which could happen now could stir me from this dreadful apathy into which I was fallen. And, as had been the case so often in my dealings with this fiendish group, I was wrong.

From my place on the divan I stared across at Nayland Smith where he sat limply in the armchair. Then I looked quickly around.

Some time before I had suspected the tall lacquer cabinet—because of its resemblance to one I remembered at Abbots Hold—of being a concealed door. I had imagined that the figure of Kâli which surmounted it was moving. I had been right.

The masked door opened and Fah Lo Suee came in.

She wore black gloves, carried a white silk shawl, a lace cap, and a pair of spectacles! . . . Her smile was mocking.

I might have known—from her uncanny power of mastering languages and dialects—who the "old woman" had been!

"A difficult moment, Shan," she said composedly. "Something I had not foreseen or provided for. A keener brain—such as yours, Sir Denis—might have challenged the gloves, even in the case of a very eccentric old lady!"

She began to pull them off, revealing those beautiful, long, feline hands.

"But my hands are rather memorable," she added without hint of vanity and simply as a statement of fact. "A late but expected guest was traced here. Fortunately, the taxi-driver upon whose evidence the visit was made was uncertain of the number. But it was very clever of the superintendent—following a telephone call from the lady's last address—to find the man who had driven her from the station."

She turned her long, arrow eyes in Nayland Smith's direction . . . and I saw his jaw harden as he clenched his teeth. I know, now, that already he understood.

"I respect you so much, Sir Denis," she went on, "that I know your removal is vital to my council. But I promise you it shall be swift."

Nayland Smith remained silent.

"A traitor has already paid the price which we demanded. When Li King Su and yourself are found together—the inference will be obvious. And I have arranged for you to be found at the Limehouse end of the Canal."

"Congratulations," he said. "You wear the cloak of your lamented father gracefully."

Perhaps some shade of emotion passed swiftly across the impassive face of Fah Lo Suee; perhaps I only imagined it. But she continued without pause:

"For you, Shan, I have pleasant duties in China—where I must return immediately, my work here undone." Again she stared at Nayland Smith. "But I am not greedy, Shan, and you shall not be lonely."

She clapped her hands.

The door from the lobby opened. . . .

And Rima was pushed into the room by the Nubian!

§ 3

Over those first few moments that followed, I must leave a veil. Exactly what took place I shall never know. The shock of it stupefied me.

". . . They said you were ill, Shan. . . . I came right away without waiting to speak to a soul. . . ."

Those words reached me through a sort of drumming in my head. Now I saw Rima's grave eyes turn to Fah Lo Suee in such a look of loathing horror as I had never seen in them before.

But Fah Lo Suee met that glance without animosity. In her own strange eyes of jade green there was no glint of feminine triumph, no mockery. Only a calm consideration. She had mocked Nayland Smith, she had mocked me: we were her active potent enemies, and she had outwitted us. Rima she regarded with something strangely like a cold compassion.

That God had ever given life to a woman so far above the weaknesses of her sex as Fah Lo Suee was something I could never have believed without convincing evidence. Even her curious infatuation for myself was a mere feline fancy, ordered and contained. She would have sacrificed nothing to it; nor would it long outlast its realisation.

"Shan!" Rima's voice suddenly rose to a high emotional note; she moved forward. "Tell me——"

"Be silent, child," said Fah Lo Suee. "Sit there,"

She indicated an arm-chair. Rima's despairing glance met mine; then she obeyed that quiet, imperious command. Fah Lo Suee signalled to the Nubian to go. He withdrew, not wholly closing the door.

"Shan attracts me," Fah Lo Suee went on. "Apart from which he has qualities which will prove useful when we move in Egypt. But I don't want to steal him from you"—she glanced at Rima—"and he would be unhappy without you."

We were all watching her. There was absolute silence in the room when she ceased speaking. Of the many violent scenes I had known from that dark hour when Sir Lionel's voice—or so I had supposed at the time—called out to me in the wâdi where we were camped, this quiet, deadly interlude before the amazement to come recurs most frequently in my memory.

"It is very simple, Shan"—she turned to me. "Sir Denis has checked me—would always check me. He knows too much of our plans. So do you. The others can wait. If Superintendent Weymouth had come here alone—he would have remained. . . . After you have gone . . . he will become dangerous. But he must wait.

"His arrival here to-night was an unfortunate accident— due to my consideration of your happiness."

I met the steady gaze of those enthralling eyes. . . . "Your happiness. . . ." As though, unwittingly, she had communicated her secret thoughts to me, I grasped the truth; I saw the part that Rima was to play. I, alone, might prove difficult. Rima, helpless in the power of Fah Lo Suee, would make me a pliant slave! Suddenly:

"More and more," said Nayland Smith, "I regret the

absence of Dr. Fu Manchu. I would rather deal with him than with his daughter!"

Fah Lo Suee turned, suddenly.

"Why do you assume my father to be dead?" she asked.

Nayland Smith exchanged a rapid glance with me; then:

"I don't assume anything of the kind," he rapped, with all his old vigour. "I know he's alive!"

"How do you know?"

"That is my business. Kindly confine yourself to a statement of your own."

There were some moments of silence; then:

"Dr. Fu Manchu," said Fah Lo Suee, "is alive—yes. You were always a clever man, Sir Denis. But his age prohibits travel."

I dared not trust myself to look at Nayland Smith. It was incredible.

She didn't know that Fu Manchu was in England!

Smith made no reply.

"The work that he laid down," Fah Lo Suee went on, "I have taken up. The *Si Fan*, Sir Denis, is a power again. But time is precious. The unforeseen visit of Superintendent Weymouth delayed me. There are only two members in England now. They are in this house. They will leave with me. . . . Shan, do you choose that yourself and Rima shall travel as baggage, or will you bow to the inevitable?"

"Agree!" rapped Nayland Smith. "A hundred chances of helping the world present themselves to live man—but not to a synthetic corpse."

"Shan!"

Rima wild-eyed, was staring at me. She sprung up from her chair.

"What?" I asked dully.

"I don't know the meaning of it all—I can only guess; but you wouldn't bargain, Shan?"

Nayland Smith caught my wandering glance, and:

"He would, Rima," he answered. "So would I—if I had the chance! Don't be foolish, little lady. This isn't a game of tennis. It's a game of which you don't know the rules. There's only one thing to play for . . . life. Because, while one of us lives, there's always a chance that that one may win!—Agree,

Greville! It's nine thousand miles to China—and with two active brains alert, anything may happen."

I closed my eyes. This was agony. An age seemed to pass. Had Nayland Smith some scheme behind his words? And where did my duty lie? . . . My duty to Rima; my duty to the world. . . .

"I will agree," I said at last—and my voice was one I could never have recognised, "on the distinct understanding that Rima is not to be harmed or molested in any way—and that Sir Denis is released to-night."

Opening my eyes, I glanced quickly at Fah Lo Suee. Her expression was inscrutable. I looked at Rima. She was staring at me—an uncomprehending stare. . . . Lastly I looked at Nayland Smith.

His steely eyes regarded me wistfully. He twisted his lips in a wry grimace and shook his head, as:

"Your second condition is impossible," Fah Lo Suee replied.

And as she spoke the miracle happened; the thing of which to this very hour I sometimes doubt the reality, seeming, as it does now, rather part of a fevered dream than an actual occurrence.

I don't know what prompted me, as that bell-like voice ceased, to look again at Rima. But I did so.

She was staring past me—at the lacquer cabinet where Kâli sat—the hidden doorway Fah Lo Suee had closed again. I twisted around.

Very slowly—inch by inch—inch by inch—the door was opening! Then, suddenly, it was opened wide. Out of the darkness beyond two figures came; first, the Dyak, who, instant on entering the room, turned again to the lacquered door and dropped on his knees; second the Nubian—who also prostrated himself!

Thirdly, and last, came a figure whose image must remain imprinted on my mind for ever. . . .

It was that of a very tall old man; emaciated to a degree which I had hitherto associated only with mummies. His great height was not appreciable at first glance, by reason of the fact that he stooped very much, resting his weight on a stout stick. He wore a plain black garment, resembling a cassock, and a little black cap was set on his head. . . .

His skull—his fleshless yellow skull—was enormous. I thought that such a brain must be that either of a madman or a genius. And his face, a map of wrinkles, resembled nothing so much as the shrivelled majesty of the Pharaoh Seti I who lies in the Cairo Museum!

Deeply sunken eyes emitted a dull green spark.

But this frail old man radiated such *power* that I was chilled—it seemed to be physical; I could not have experienced a more dreadful sense of impotent horror if the long-dead Pharoah himself had appeared before me. . . .

Those sunken, commanding eyes ignored my existence. Their filmy but potent regard passed the grovelling men, passed me, and was set upon Fah Lo Suee. Then came a sibilant command, utterly beyond my powers to describe:

"Kneel, little thief! *I* am standing. . . ."

I twisted around.

Fah Lo Suee, a chalky quality tingeing the peach bloom of her skin, had lowered that insolent head! As I turned, staring, she dropped to her knees!

And now I saw that Nayland Smith, bound as he was, arms and ankles, had got to his feet. Through the tropical yellow of his complexion, through the artificial stain which still lingered, he had paled.

The hissing voice spoke again.

"Greeting, Sir Denis. Be seated."

Smith's teeth were clenched so hard that his jaw muscles stood out lumpishly. But, relaxing and speaking in a low, even tone:

"Greetings," he replied, "Dr. Fu Manchu."

§ 4

Three times, heavily, Dr. Fu Manchu beat his stick upon the floor.

Two Burmans came in and saluted him.

I knew them. They were the dacoits who had been present at the Council of Seven in el-Khârga.

Dr. Fu Manchu advanced into the room. Extending a bony, clawlike hand, he indicated the kneeling Fah Lo Suee.

And, without a word or glance, eyes lowered, Fah Lo Suee went out with her dreadful escort! It was in my heart to pity her, so utterly was she fallen, so slavishly did that proud woman bow her head to this terrible, imperious old man.

As he passed the prostrate figures of the Nubian and the Dyak, walking heavily and slowly, he touched them each with his stick. He spoke in a low voice, gutturally. They sprang up and approached Rima!

Throughout this extraordinary scene, which had passed much more quickly than its telling conveys, Rima had remained seated—stupefied. Now, realising the meaning of Fu Manchu's last order, she stood up—horror in her eyes.

"Shan! Shan!" she cried. "What is he going to do to me?"

Dr. Fu Manchu beat upon the floor again and spoke one harsh word. The Nubian and the Dyak stood still. No sergeant of the Guards ever had more complete control of men.

"Miss Barton," he said, his voice altering uncannily between the sibilant and the guttural and seeming to be produced with difficulty, "your safety is assured. I wish to be alone with Sir Denis and Mr. Greville. For your greater ease, Sir Denis will tell you that my word is my bond."

He turned those sunken filmed eyes in the direction of the big arm-chair and:

"You needn't worry, Rima," said Nayland Smith. "Dr. Fu Manchu guarantees your safety."

I was amazed beyond reason. Even so fortified, Rima's eyes were dark with terror. A swift flow of words brought the Dyak sharply about to take his instructions. Then he and the Nubian escorted Rima from the room.

I tugged, groaning, at the cords which held me. I stared at Nayland Smith. Was he holding a candle to the devil? How could a sane man accept the assurances of such a proven criminal?

But, as though my ideas had been spoken aloud:

"Do not misjudge Sir Denis," came the harsh voice. "He knows that in warfare I am remorseless. But he knows also that no mandarin of my order has ever willingly broken his promise."

The Nubian had closed the door leading to the lobby. Dr. Fu Manchu had closed that of the false cabinet as he came into the room. No sound entered the arena where this menace to white supremacy and the man whose defences had defied him confronted one another.

§ 5

"It is a strange fact." said Dr. Fu Manchu, "that only the circumstance of your being a prisoner allows of our present conversation."

He paused, watching, watching Nayland Smith with those physically weak but spiritually powerful eyes. The Chinaman's force was incredible. It was as though a great lamp burned in that frail, angular body.

"Yet, now, by a paradox, we stand together."

Resting on his ebony stick, he drew himself up so that his thin frame assumed something of its former height.

"My methods are not your methods. Perhaps I have laughed at your British scruples. Perhaps a day may come, Sir Denis, when you will join in my laughter. But, as much as I have hated you, I have always admired your clarity of mind and your tenacity. You were instrumental in defeating me, when I had planned to readjust the centre of world power. No doubt you thought me mad—a megalomaniac. You were wrong."

He spoke the last three words in a low voice—almost a whisper.

"I worked for my country. I saw China misruled, falling into decay; with all her vast resources, becoming prey for carrion. I hoped to give China that place in the world to which her intellect, her industry, and her ideals entitle her. I hoped to awaken China. My methods, Sir Denis, were bad. My motive was good."

His voice rose. He raised one gaunt hand in a gesture of defiance. Nayland Smith spoke no word. And I watched this wraith of terror as one watches a creature uncreated, who figures hideously in some disordered dream. His sincerity was unmistakable; his power of intellect enormous. When I realised what he defended, what he stood for—and that I, Shan Greville, was listening to him in a house somewhere in London, I felt like laughing hysterically.

"Your long reign, Sir Denis, is ending. A blacker tragedy than any I had dreamt of will end your Empire. It is Fate that both of us must now look on. I thank my gods that the consummation will not be seen by me.

"The woman you know as Fah Lo Suee—it was her pet name in nursery days—is my child by a Russian mother. In her, Sir Denis, I share the sorrow of Shakespeare's King Lear. ... She has reawakened a power which I had buried. I cannot condemn her. She is my flesh. But in China we expect, and exact, obedience. The *Si Fan* is a society older than Buddhism and more flexible. Its ruler wields a sword none can withstand. For many years *Si Fan* has slumbered. Fah Lo Suee has dared to awaken it!"

He turned his dreadful eyes on me for the first time since he had begun to speak.

"Mr. Greville, you cannot know what control of that organisation means! Misdirected, at such a crisis of history as this, it could only mean another world war! I dragged myself from retirement"—he looked again at Nayland Smith—"to check the madness of Fah Lo Suee. Some harm she has done. But I have succeeded. To-night, again, I am lord of the *Si Fan!*"

Quivering, he rested on his stick.

"I had never dreamt," said Nayland Smith, "that I should live to applaud your success."

Dr. Fu Manchu turned and walked to the lacquer door. Reaching it:

"If you were free," he replied, "it would be your duty to detain me. My plans are made. Fah Lo Suee will trouble you no more. Overtake me if you wish—and if you can. I am indifferent to the issue, sir Denis, but I leave England to-night. *Si Fan* will sleep again. The balance of world power will be readjusted—but not as she had planned.

"In half an hour I will cause Superintendent Weymouth—whom I esteem—to be informed that you are here. Miss Barton, during that period, must remain locked in a room above. Greeting and goodbye, Sir Denis. Greeting and goodbye, Mr. Greville."

He went out and closed the door. ...

§ 6

Nearly a year has passed since that night when for the first, and I pray for the last, time I found myself face to face with Dr. Fu Manchu—the world's greatest criminal, perhaps the world's supreme genius—and a man of his word.

Unable to credit the facts, a few minutes after his disappearance, I shouted Rima's name.

She replied—her voice reaching me dimly from some higher room. She was safe, but locked in. . . .

And an hour later, Weymouth arrived—to find Nayland Smith at last disentangled from the cunning knots of the Sea-Dyak!

"It was possible, after all, Greville! But a damned long business!"

I write these concluding notes before my tent in Sir Lionel Barton's camp on the site of ancient Nineveh. Sunset draws near, and I can see Rima, a camera slung over her shoulder, coming down the slope.

We are to be married on our return to London.

Of Dr. Fu Manchu, Fah Lo Suee, and their terrible escort, no trace was ever discovered!

Even the body of Ki King Su was spirited away. Six months of intense and world-wide activity, directed by Nayland Smith, resulted in . . . nothing! "My plans are made," that great and evil man had said.

Sometimes I doubt if it ever happened. Sometimes I wonder if it is really finished. Before me, on the box which is my extemporised writing-desk, lies a big emerald set in an antique silver ring. It reached me only a month ago in a package posted from Hong Kong. There was no note inside. . . .

THE END

THE MASK OF
FU MANCHU

There, enshrined in the darkness, I saw El Mokanna!

CONTENTS

CHAPTER
1. ONE NIGHT IN ISPAHAN
2. WAILING IN THE AIR
3. THE GREEN BOX
4. THE VEILED PROPHET
5. NAYLAND SMITH TAKES CHARGE
6. PERFUME OF MIMOSA
7. RIMA AND I
8. "EL MOKANNA!"
9. THE FLYING DEATH
10. I SEE THE SLAYER
11. THE MAN ON THE MINARET
12. IN THE GHOST MOSQUE
13. THE BLACK SHADOW
14. ROAD TO CAIRO
15. ROAD TO CAIRO (*continued*)
16. A MASKED WOMAN
17. THE MOSQUE OF MUAYYAD
18. DR. FU MANCHU
19. FORMULA ELIXIR VITAE
20. THE MASTER MIND
21. "HE WILL BE CROWNED IN DAMASCUS"
22. THE HAND OF FU MANCHU
23. AMNESIA
24. THE MESSENGER
25. MR. ADEN'S PROPOSAL

CHAPTER

26	A STRANGE RENDEZVOUS
27	THE GREAT PYRAMID
28	INSIDE THE GREAT PYRAMID
29	WE ENTER THE KING'S CHAMBER
30	Dr. FU MANCHU KEEPS HIS WORD
31	THE TRAP IS LAID
32	I SEE EL MOKANNA
33	FACTS AND RUMOURS
34	RIMA'S STORY
35	ORDERED HOME
36	NAYLAND SMITH COMES ABOARD
37	THE RELICS OF THE PROPHET
38	"THE SWORD OF GOD"
39	FLIGHT FROM EGYPT
40	THE SEAPLANE
41	A RUBBER BALL
42	THE PURSER'S SAFE
43	THE VOICE IN BRUTON STREET
44	"THIS WAS THE ONLY WAY——"
45	MEMORY RETURNS
46	FAH LO SUEE
47	IVORY HANDS
48	I REALLY AWAKEN
49	A COMMITTEE OF EXPERTS
50	Dr. FU MANCHU TRIUMPHS
51	WEDDING MORNING
52	Dr. FU MANCHU BOWS

Chapter First

ONE NIGHT IN ISPAHAN

"Shan! Shan!"

Someone calling my name persistently. The voice was faint. I had been asleep, but dreaming hard, an evil from which ordinarily I don't suffer. The voice fitted into my dream uncannily. . . .

I had dreamed I was asleep in my tent in that desolate spot on the Khorassan border, not a hundred yards from the valley called the Place of the Great Magician. No expedition of Sir Lionel's in which I had been employed had so completely got on my nerves as this one.

Persia was new territory for me. And the chief's sense of the dramatic, his innate showmanship (a trait which had done him endless damage in the eyes of the learned societies) had resulted in my being more or less in the dark as to the real object of our journey.

Perhaps, when names now famous are forgotten, that of Sir Lionel Barton will be remembered; he will be measured at his true stature—as the greatest Orientalist of his century. But, big, lovable, generous, I must nevertheless state quite definitely that he was next to impossible to work with.

When he made that historic discovery, when I realised what we had come for and what we had found, I experienced an attack of cold feet from which up to the moment of this queer awakening I had never wholly recovered.

It's a poor joke to dig up a Moslem saint, even if he happens to have been really a heretic. I never remembered to have welcomed anything more than Sir Lionel's decision to trek swiftly south-west to Ispahan. . . .

"*Shan! Shan!*"

That voice again—and yet I could not escape from my dream. I thought that only two stretches of canvas separated me from the long green box, the iron casket containing those strange fruits of our discovery.

Sir Lionel's party was not a large one, but I felt that the

Moslems were not to be relied upon. It is one thing to excavate the tombs of the Pharoahs; it is a totally different thing in the eyes of an Arab to desecrate the resting place of a true believer, or even of a near-true believer.

To Ali Mahmoud, the headman, I would have trusted my life in Mecca; but the six Egyptians, who, together with Rima, Dr. Van Berg, Sir Lionel, and myself made up the party, although staunch enough ordinarily, had occasioned me grave doubts almost from the moment we had entered Persian territory.

As for the Afghan, Amir Khan....

"Shan!"

I threw off the coil of dreams. I opened my eyes to utter darkness. My right hand automatically reached out for the torch—and in the physical movement came recognition of my true surroundings.

Khorassan? I was not in Khorassan. Nor was I under canvas—had not been under canvas for more than a week. I was in a house in Ispahan, and someone was calling me!

I grasped the torch, pressed the button, and looked about.

A scantily furnished room, I saw, its door of unpainted teak, as were the beams supporting its ceiling. I saw a rug of very good quality upon an otherwise uncarpeted floor, a large table littered with papers, photographs, books, and other odds and ends, and, from where I lay in bed, very little else.

My dream slipped into the background. The doubtful loyalty of our Moslem Egyptian workers counted for nothing, since by now they were probably back in Egypt, having been paid off a week before.

But—the green box! the green box was in Van Berg's room, on the floor above . . . and the door directly facing my bed was opening!

I reached down with my left hand. A Colt repeater hung from a nail there. Sir Lionel had taught me this trick. To place a pistol openly beside one's bed is to arm the enemy; to put it under the pillow is simply stupid. In doubtful environment, the chief invariably used a nail or hook, whichever was practicable, between his bed and the wall.

Directing the ray of my torch upon the moving doors, I waited.

As I did so, the door was flung open fully. Light shone upon tousled mahogany-coloured curls and wide-open, startled gray eyes; upon a slim, silk-clad figure!

"Turn the light out, Shan—quick!"

It was Rima who stood in the open doorway.

I switched off the light; but in the instant of pressing the switch I glanced at my watch. The hour was 2 a.m.

Chapter Second

WAILING IN THE AIR

It was one of those situations to which at times I thought the dear old chief took a delight in exposing me. His humour inclined to the sardonic, and in electing, when we left Nineveh, to start off without a break or any leave east into Persia and right up to the Afghan border, he had seriously upset my plans.

Rima, his niece, and I were to have been married on our return to England after the Syrian job. Sir Lionel's change of plan had scotched that scheme. There was laughter in his twinkling eyes when he had notified me of the fact that information just received demanded our immediate presence in Khorassan.

"But what about the wedding, Chief?" I remember saying.

"Well, what about it, Greville?"

"There are plenty of padres in these parts, and the engagement has been overlong. Besides, after all, Rima and I are wandering about in camp together, from spot to spot . . ."

"Greville," he interrupted me, "when you marry Rima, you're going to be married from my town house. The ceremony will take place at St. Margaret's, and I shall give the bride away. I don't care a hoot about the proprieties, Greville. You ought to know that by now. We're setting out for Khorassan to-morrow morning. Rima is a brilliant photographer, and I want her to come with us. But if she prefers to go back to England—she can go."

This was the situation in which my brilliant but erratic chief had involved me. And now, at 2 a.m., Rima, with whom I was hungrily in love, had burst into my room in that queer house in Ispahan, and already in the darkness was beside me.

I wonder, indeed I have often wondered, if my make-up is different from that of other men: definitely I am no squire of dames. But, further, I have sometimes thought that although ardour has by no means been left out of me, I have inherited from somewhere an overweight of the practical; so that at any time, and however deeply my affections might be engaged, the job would come before the woman.

So it was now; for, my arm about Rima's slim, silky waist, her first whispered words in the darkness made me forget how desirable she was and how I longed for the end of this strange interlude, for the breaking down of that barrier unnaturally raised by my erratic chief.

"Shan!" She bent close to my ear. "There was a most awful cry from Dr. Van Berg's room a few minutes ago!"

I jumped up, still holding her. She was trembling slightly.

"I opened my window and listened. His room is almost right over mine, and I felt certain that was where the cry had come from. But I couldn't hear anything."

"Was the voice Van Berg's?"

"I couldn't tell, dear. It was a kind of—scream. Then, as I hurried along to wake you, I heard something else——"

She clung to me tightly.

"What darling?"

"I don't know!" She shuddered violently. "A sort of dreadful *wailing*. . . . Shan! I believe it came from the mosque!"

"Then you called out?"

"I didn't call out till I got right to your door and had it open."

I understood then that I had confused dreaming with reality. The distant voice, as it had seemed to me, had been that of Rima urgently calling at the opened door.

"It's the green box!" she whispered, in an even lower tone. "Shan, I'm terrified! You know what happened on Thursday night! It must have been the same sound. . . ."

That thought was on my own mind. Van Berg had been disturbed on Thursday night by an inexplicable happening, an outstanding feature of which had been a strange moaning sound. The chief had declined to take it seriously; but I knew our American colleague for a man of sound common sense not addicted to nervous imaginings.

And the green box was in his room. . . .

Barefooted, I stepped towards the door, releasing Rima, whom I had been holding tightly.

"Stay here, darling," I said; "unless I call you."

I crept out into the corridor. It was dimly lighted a few

paces along by a high, barred window. Almost opposite in the narrow street stood a deserted mosque, its minaret, from the balcony of which no mueddin had called for many years, overlooking the roof of our temporary residence. Moonlight, reflected from the dingy yellow wall of this mosque, vaguely illuminated the passage ahead of me.

The once holy building had a horrible history and I knew that Rima associated the sound she had heard with the legend of the mosque.

Stock still I stood for a moment, listening.

The house was silent as a vault. It possessed three floors. The rooms beneath on the ground floor contained the stored furniture—or part of it—of the owner from whom Sir Lionel had leased the place. The ground-floor windows were heavily barred, and Ali Mahmoud slept in the lobby; so that none could enter without arousing him.

There were four rooms above, two of them unoccupied. Locked in one were a pair of Caspian kittens, beautiful little creatures with fur like finest silk, destined for the chief's private menagerie, practical zoology being one of his hobbies. In the end, or southeast, room, Dr. Van Berg was quartered. Our records, the bulk of our photographs, and other valuables were in his charge as well as the green box.

No sound disturbed the silence.

I advanced cautiously in the direction of the staircase. The widely open door of Rima's room was on my left. Moonlight poured in upon the polished uncarpeted floor. Her shutters were open.

Pausing for a moment, puzzled, I suddenly remembered that she had opened them when that cry in the night had disturbed her.

Personally, I kept mine religiously closed against the incursions of nocturnal insects, since we were near the bank of the river and no great distance from a fruit market. I had switched off my torch, the reflected light through the high window being sufficient for my purpose. I passed Rima's door—then pulled up short, my nerves jangling.

From somewhere, outside the house, and high up, came a singular sound.

It was a sort of whistle in a minor key, resembling nothing

so much as a human imitation of a police whistle. It changed, passing from a moan to an indescribable wail . . . and dying away.

"Shan, did you hear it? That's the *sound!*"

Rima's voice reached me in a quavering whisper, and:

"I heard it," I answered in a low voice. "For God's sake, stay where you are."

The chief's door was ahead of me, in comparative shadow there at the end of the passage. I could see that it was closed: a teak door, ornamented with iron scrollwork. Sir Lionel was a heavy sleeper. A narrow stair opened on the right and led down to the lobby. No sound reached me from beneath. Evidently Ali Mahmoud had not been aroused.

On my left was a stair to the floor above. I crept up.

My nerves were badly jangled, and creaking of the ancient woodwork sounded in my ears like pistol shots. I gained the top corridor. Two windows faced west, commanding a view of low, flat roofs stretching away to a distant prospect of the river. The moonlight was dazzling. In contrast to the passage below it was like stepping from midnight into high noon.

I paused again for a moment, listening intently.

A sound of scurrying movement reached my ears from beyond Van Berg's closed door. I took a step forward and paused again. Then, my hand on the clumsy native latch:

"Van Berg!" I said softly.

The only reply was a queer soft, plaintive howl.

Let me confess that this nearly unnerved me. A vague but unmistakable menace had been overhanging us from the hour of our momentous discovery in Khorassan. Now, awakened as I had been, my memory repeating over and over again that weird, wailing sound, I recognised that I was by no means at my best.

Clenching my teeth, I raised the latch. . . .

I peered along the narrow room. It extended from the corridor to the opposite side of the house. I saw that the shutters were open in the deep, recessed window. Moonlight reflected from the wall of the mosque afforded scanty illumination.

A sickly sweet perfume hung in the air, strongly resembling that of mimosa, but having a pungency which gripped me by the throat. I pressed the button of my torch.

Some vague thing, indeterminate, streaky, leapt towards me. I shrank back, pistol levelled.... And for the second time I heard *the sound*.

Perhaps I have never been nearer to true panic in my life. That moaning wail seemed to come from outside the house—and from high above. It seemed to vibrate throughout my entire nervous system. It was the most utterly damnable sound to which I had ever listened.

Only my sudden recognition of one of the facts saved me. The Caspian kittens were in the room! I remembered, and gasped in my relief, that the doctor was extremely fond of them. The little creatures, who were very tame, crouched at my feel, looking up at me with their big eyes, appealingly, as it seemed.

A vague stirring came from the depths of the house. The smell of mimosa was overpowering.... Probably Rima had run down and aroused Ali Mahmoud.

These ideas, chaotically, with others too numerous to record, flashed through my mind at the same moment that, stricken motionless with horror, I stood staring down upon Dr. Van Berg, where he lay under the light of my torch.

His heavy body was huddled in so strange a position that, what with anger, regret, fear and other unnameable emotions, I could not at first realise what had happened. He was clothed in silk pajamas of an extravagant pattern which he affected, and his fair hair, which he wore long, hung down over his forehead so that it touched the floor.

He was lying across the green box.

He lay in such a way that his big body almost obscured the box from my view. But now I saw that his powerful arms were outstretched, and that his fingers were locked in a death grip upon the handles at either end.

That long moment of horrified inertia passed.

I sprang forward and dropped upon one knee. I tried to speak, but only a husky murmur came. There was blood on the lid of the box, and a pool was gathering upon the floor beside it. I put my hand under Van Berg's chin and lifted his face. Then I stood upright, feeling very ill.

What I had seen had wiped the slate of consciousness clear

of all but one thing. My fingers quivered on the Colt repeater. I wanted the life of the cowardly assassin who had done Van Berg to death—big, gentle, fearless Van Berg. For here was murder—cold-blooded murder!

A sort of buzzing in my ears died away and left me perfectly cool, with just that one desire for retribution burning in my brain. I heard footsteps—muffled voices. I didn't heed them.

I was staring about the room. Staring at the open window trying to recall details of Van Berg's story of what had happened on the Thursday night. In the room there was no hiding place, and the window was thirty feet above street level. The mystery of the thing was taking hold of me.

"Greville Effendim," I heard.

I glanced back over by shoulder. Ali Mahmoud stood in the open doorway—and I saw Rima's pale face behind him.

"Don't come in, Rima!" I said hastily. "For God's sake, don't come in. Go down and wake the chief."

CHAPTER THIRD

THE GREEN BOX

UPON the horror of that murder in the night, I prefer not to dwell. The mystery of Van Berg's death defied solution. As I recall the tragic event, I can recapture a sharp picture of Sir Lionel Barton arrayed in neutral-coloured pyjamas and an old dressing gown, his mane of grey hair disordered, his deep-set eyes two danger signals, standing massive, stricken, over the dead man.

The bed had been slept in—so much was evident; and about it the strange odour of mimosa clung more persistently than elsewhere.

There was no stranger on the premises. Of this we had assured ourselves. And for a thirty-foot ladder to have been reared against the window of the room and removed without our knowledge, was a sheer impossibility.

Yet Van Berg had been stabbed to the heart from behind—palpably in an attempt to defend the green box: an attempt which had been successful. But, except that his shutters were open, there was no clue to the identity of his assassin, nor to the means of the latter's entrance and exit.

"I didn't hear a sound!" I remember the chief murmuring, looking at me haggard eyed. "I didn't hear that damnable wailing—it might have told me something. Anyhow, Greville, he died doing his job, and so he's gone wherever good men go. His death is on my conscience."

"Why, Chief?"

But he had turned away....

We conformed to the requirements of the fussy local authorities, but got no help from them; and shortly after noon, Mr. Stratton Jean, of the American Legation at Teheran, arrived by air, accompanied by Captain Woodville, a British intelligence officer.

I reflected, when they came in from alighting ground just outside the ancient city, that the caravan route is nearly two hundred and forty miles long, and that in former days a week was allowed for the journey.

It was a strange interview, being in part an inquest upon the dead man. It took place in poor Van Berg's room, which had always served as a sort of office during the time that we had occupied this house in Ispahan.

There was a big table in the corner near the window laden with indescribable fragments, ranging from Davidian armour to portfolios of photographs and fossilised skulls. There was a rather fine scent bottle, too, of blue glass dating from the reign of Haroun-er-Raschid, and a number of good glazed tiles. A fine illuminated manuscript, very early, of part of the Diwan of Hafiz, one of Sir Lionel's more recently acquired treasures, lay still open upon the table, for Van Berg had been busy making notes upon the text up to within a few hours of his death.

The doctor's kit, his riding boots, and other intimate reminders of his genial presence lay littered about the floor; for, apart from the removal of the body, nothing had been disturbed.

That fatal green box, upon which the blood-stains had dried, stood upon the spot where I had found it. The floor was still stained. . . .

Mr. Stratton Jean was a lean Bostonian, gray haired, sallow complexioned, and as expressionless as a Sioux Indian. Captain Woodville was a pretty typical British army officer of thirty-five or so, except for a disconcerting side-glance which I detected once or twice, and which alone revealed—to me, at least, for he had the traditional bored manner—that he was a man of very keen mind.

Mr. Stratton Jean quite definitely adopted the attitude of a coroner, and under his treatment the chief grew notably restive, striding up and down the long, narrow room in a manner reminiscent of a caged polar bear.

Rima, who sat beside me, squeezed my hand nervously, glancing alternately at the two Persian officials who were present, and at her famous uncle. She knew that a storm was brewing, and so did Captain Woodville, for twice I detected him hiding a smile. At last, in reply to some question:

"One moment, Mr. Jean," said Sir Lionel, turning and facing his interrogator. "If Van Berg was a fellow citizen of yours, he was a friend and colleague of mine. You are doing your duty, and I honour you for it. But I don't like the way you do it."

"I just want the facts," said Stratton Jean, dryly.

I saw the colour welling up into Sir Lionel's face and feared an outburst. It was avoided by the intervention of Captain Woodville.

"Thing is, Jean," he drawled lazily, "Sir Lionel isn't used to being court-martialed. He's rather outside your province. But apart from a distinguished military career, he happens to be the greatest Orientalist in Europe."

I waited with some anxiety for the American official's reaction to this rebuke, for it was nothing less than a rebuke. It took the form of a smile, but a very sad smile, breaking through the mask-like immobility of those sallow features.

"You mean, Woodville," he said, "I'm being too darned official for words?"

"Perhaps a trifle stiff, Jean, for a man of Sir Lionel's temperament."

Mr. Stratton Jean nodded, and I saw a new expression in his eyes, yellowed from long residence in the East. He looked at the chief.

"If I've ruffled you, Sir Lionel," he said, "please excuse me. This inquiry is one of the hardest things I've ever had to undertake. You see, Van Berg and I were at Harvard together. It's been a bad shock."

That was straight talking, and in two seconds the chief had Jean's hand in his bear-like grip and had hauled him out of the chair.

"Why in hell didn't you tell me?" he demanded. "We worked together for only two months, but I'd sell my last chance of salvation to get the swine who murdered him."

The air was cleared, and Rima's nervous grip upon my hand relaxed. And that which had begun so formally, was now carried on in a spirit of friendship. But when every possible witness had been called and examined, we remained at a deadlock.

It was Captain Woodville who broached the subject which I knew, sooner or later, must be brought up.

"It is quite clear, Sir Lionel," he said in his drawling way, "that your friend died in endeavouring to protect this iron box.

He pointed to the long green chest upon which the white initials L.B. were painted. Sir Lionel ground his teeth audibly together and began to pace up and down the room.

"I know," he said. "That's why I told you, Greville"—turning to me—"that I was responsible for his death."

"I can't agree with you," Stratton Jean interrupted. "So far as my information goes (Captain Woodville, I believe, is better informed), you were engaged with the late Dr. Van Berg in an attempt to discover the burial place of El Mokanna, sometimes called the Veiled Prophet of Khorassan."

"Veiled Prophet," Woodville interjected, "is rather a misnomer. Actually, Mokanna wore a mask. Isn't that so, Sir Lionel?"

The chief turned and stared at the last speaker.

"That is so," he agreed. They exchanged a glance of understanding. "You know all the facts. Don't deny it!"

Captain Woodville smiled slightly, glancing aside at Stratton Jean; then:

"I know most of them," he admitted, "but the details can only be known to you. As a matter of fact, I'm here to-day because some tragedy of this kind had been rather foreseen. Quite frankly, although I don't suppose I'm telling you anything that you don't know already, you have stirred up a lot of trouble."

Rima squeezed my hand furtively. It was nothing new for her distinguished uncle to stir up trouble. His singular investigations had more than once imperiled international amity.

Chapter Fourth

THE VEILED PROPHET

"You have said, Mr. Jean," said Sir Lionel, "that my particular studies are outside your province, but my interests were shared by Dr. Van Berg. Already he occupied a chair of Oriental literature, but, if he had lived, his name would have ranked high as any. Very well."

He paced up and down in silence for a while, hands locked behind him. The two Persian officials had gone. Those queer discords characteristic of an Eastern city rose to us through the open window: cries of street hawkers, of carriage drivers; even the jangle of camel bells. And there were flies, myriads of flies. . . .

"It was Van Berg who got the clue which set us off upon this expedition—the expedition which was to be his last. Down on the borders of Arabia he picked up a man, an Afghan, as a matter of fact, named Amir Khan. This man told him the story of the spot known locally as the Place of the Great Magician. It's in the No Man's Land between Khorassan and Afghanistan.

"Van Berg, with whom I had been in correspondence for some years, although we had never met, learned that I was in Irak. He was a Persian scholar, and he knew parts of the country well. But of Khorassan and Afghanistan he knew nothing. He got into communication with me. He asked me to share the enterprise. I accepted—as you know, Greville—" he darted one of his quick glances in my direction—"and we moved down and joined Van Berg, who was waiting for us on the Persian border.

"I interviewed the man Amir Khan. I could talk his lingo and so get nearer to the truth than Van Berg had succeeded in doing—"

"I never trusted Amir Khan!" I broke in. "His story was true, and he did his job, but——"

"Amir Khan was a *thug*," the chief continued quietly; "I always knew it. But servants of Kali have no respect for

Mohammed; therefore I was prepared to trust him with regard to the matter in hand. He advanced arguments strong enough to induce me, in conjunction with Van Berg, to proceed with a party, who had been in my employ for more than a year, northeast of Persia. In brief, gentlemen, we went to look for the burial place of El Mokanna, the Hidden One, sometimes called the Veiled Prophet, but, as Captain Woodville has pointed out, more properly the Masked Prophet. . . ."

This was "shop" and overfamiliar. I turned my head and stared from the open window towards a corresponding, ruinous, window of the mosque opposite. The deserted building certainly had a sinister reputation, being known locally as the Ghost Mosque. If this circumstance, together with that eerie sound which had heralded poor Van Berg's death, were responsible, I cannot say. But I became the victim of a queer delusion. . . .

"Mokanna, Mr. Jean," the chief was saying, "about 770 A.D., set himself up as an incarnation of God, and drew to his new sect many thousands of followers. He revised the Koran. His power became so great that the Caliph Al Mahdi was forced to move against him with a considerable army. Mokanna was a hideous creature. His features were so mutilated as to be horrible to see. . . ."

Brilliant green eyes were fixed upon me from the shadow of the ruined window! . . .

"But he was a man. He and the whole of his staff poisoned themselves in the hour of defeat. From that day to this, no one has known where he was buried. His sword, which he wore on ceremonial occasions, and which he called the Sword of God, forged to conquer the world, his New Creed graved upon golden plates, and the mask of gold with which he concealed his mutilated features, disappeared at the time of his death and were supposed to be lost."

I shifted uneasily in my chair. The startling apparition had vanished as suddenly as it had come. Above all things I wanted to avoid alarming Rima. Already I suspected sleepless nights; I realised that she could know no peace in the shadow of the Ghost Mosque with its unholy reputation.

The apparition did not reappear, however; and I turned,

looking swiftly at Rima.

She was watching the chief. Clearly, she had seen nothing.

Walking up and down while speaking, in that manner of a caged bear, Sir Lionel had paused now and was staring at the ominous green box.

"Amir Khan did not lie," he went on. "The tomb-masque that contained the ashes of the prophet is a mere mound of dust to-day; what it concealed was never more than a legend. Its site, though, is strictly avoided—supposed to be haunted by *djinns* and known as the Place of the Great Magician. We camped there, and our excavations were carried out secretly. Few pass that desolate place on the edge of the desert. We found—what we had come to find."

"Is that a fact?" said Stratton Jean in an odd voice.

Sir Lionel nodded, smiling grimly.

"The prophet was dust," he added; "but we found his gold mask, his New Creed engraved upon plates of gold, and his sword, a magnificent blade with a jewelled hilt. There were other fragments—but these were the most important."

He paused and pointed to the green box.

"Those two Persian birds were mighty keen to know what was in this box. I told them it contained priceless records. They pretended to be satisfied, But they weren't. It's a heavy thing to travel—but strong as a safe."

He began to pace up and down again.

"I left the Place of the Great Magician, taking the relics of El Mokanna away in that box! Van Berg and I had a conference before we left; Greville, here, was present. In spite of our precautions, there were rumours flying about, and it was becoming fairly clear that some sort of small but fanatical sect still existed who held the name of El Mokanna in reverence. The desertion of our Afghan guide, Amir Khan, was very significant—wasn't it Greville?"

"It was," I agreed.

At the chief's words I lived again in memory, instantaneously, through those days and nights in that lonely camp, with Rima's presence to add to my anxieties. I knew that we were hundreds of miles from any useful help, and I knew that in some mysterious way the influence of the Veiled Prophet lived, was active, although the Hidden One himself was dead;

that if the truth should leak out, if it should become known that the sacred relics were in our possession, our lives would not be worth a grain of sand!

Almost, in those anxious days and nights, I had come to hate Van Berg, who was the instigator of the expedition, and to distrust Sir Lionel, whose zeal for knowledge had induced him to lead Rima into such peril. His scientific ardour brooked no obstacle. She was a brilliantly clever photographer, and there was a portfolio, now, on poor Van Berg's table, which in the absence of the actual relics constituted a perfect record of our discoveries.

"I improvised a bomb," Sir Lionel went on, "to which I attached a time fuse. We were headed south for Ispahan when all that remained of the tomb-mosque of El Mokanna went up in a cloud of dust."

That wild light, which was more than half mischief, leapt into his eyes as he spoke.

"Although I had covered my tracks, there were consequences which I hadn't counted on. Most of the work had been done at night, but it appears that travellers from a distance had seen our lights. The legendary site of the place was more widely known than we had realised. And when, some time after our departure, which took place after dusk, there was a great explosion and a bright glare in the sky, the result was something totally unforeseen. . . ."

"If I may interrupt you, Sir Lionel," said Captain Woodville quietly, "from this point I can carry on the story. An outcry—'Mokanna has arisen'—swept through Afghanistan. That was the spot at which *I* came into the matter. You had been even more successful than you seem to appreciate. None of the tribesmen who, as you suspect, and rightly, still hold the Mokanna tradition had any idea that you or any human influence had been concerned with the eruption which reduced a lonely ruined shrine to a dusty hollow. A certain fanatical imam took upon himself the duties of a sort of Eastern Peter the Hermit."

The speaker paused, taking a cigarette from his case and tapping it thoughtfully upon his thumb nail. I glanced swiftly over my shoulder. But the cavernous window of the mosque showed as an unbroken patch of shadow. . . .

"He declared that the Masked Prophet had been reborn and that with the Sword of God he would carry the New Creed throughout the East, sweeping the Infidel before him. That movement is gathering strength, Sir Lionel, and I need not tell you what such a movement means to the Indian government, and what it may come to mean for Arabia, Palestine, and possibly Egypt, unless it can be checked."

There came a moment of silence, broken only by the striking of a match and the heavy footsteps of the chief as he restlessly paced up and down—up and down. At last:

"Such a movement would call for a strong leader," said Rima.

Captain Woodville extinguished the match and turned to her gravely.

"We have reason to fear, Miss Barton," he replied, "that such a leader has been found. I suspect also, Sir Lionel—" glancing at the chief—"that he wants what you have found and will stick at nothing to get it. . . ."

Chapter Fifth

NAYLAND SMITH TAKES CHARGE.

"Someone to see you, Greville Effendim."

I raised my eyes from the notes which I had been studying but did not look around. Through the open window in front of the table at which I had been working I could see on the opposite side of the narrow street the sun-bathed wall of that deserted mosque of unpleasant history.

A window almost on a level with that through which I was looking was heavily outlined on one side and at the top by dense shadows. Only that morning I had explored the mosque—penetrating to the gallery behind that window. What I had hoped to find I really don't know. Actually, I had found nothing.

"Show him in, Ali Mahmoud."

I pushed the notes aside and turned, as footsteps on the landing outside told me that my visitor had arrived.

Then I sprang swiftly to my feet. . . .

Something I had vaguely prayed for, something I had not dared to expect, had actually happened! A tall, lean man, with clean-shaven face so sunbaked as to resemble that of an Arab, stood in the doorway.

"Sir Denis! Sir Denis!" I cried. "This is almost *too* wonderful!"

It was Sir Denis Nayland Smith, Assistant Commissioner of Scotland Yard, one of my chief's oldest friends, and the one man in the world whom I would have chosen to be with us now. But the mystery of his appearance had knocked me sideways; and, as he grasped my hand, that lean, tired face relaxed in the boyish smile that I knew and loved; and:

"A surprise?" he snapped in his queer, staccato fashion. "It was a surprise to me too, Greville. If anybody had offered me a hundred to one, three days ago, that I should be in Ispahan now, I should have taken him."

"But . . ." I looked him up and down.

He wore a leather overcoat over a very dilapidated flannel

suit, and, since he was hatless, I saw that his crisp, wavy hair, more heavily silvered in the interval since our last meeting, was disordered.

"But where does Scotland Yard come in?"

"It doesn't come in at all," he returned. "I resigned from Scotland Yard six months ago, Greville. I have been on a sort of secret mission to southern India. I came back via Basra intending to return overland and by air. There is no time to waste, you understand. But at Basra I had news."

"News of what?" I asked, my brain in somewhat of a whirl.

"News that changed my plans," he returned gravely, and his piercing glance fixed me for a moment. "Excuse me if I seem eccentric, but would you mind stepping around the table, Greville, and looking out of the window. I should be glad to know if there is anyone in the street."

Too surprised to reply, I did as he asked. The narrow street was empty as far as I could see it to the left. To the right, where it lay in deep shadow and climbed upward under the lee of the deserted mosque, I could not be so sure that someone, or something, a vague figure, was not lurking. However, after watching for some moments, I determined that the figure existed only in my imagination.

"Nobody," I reported.

"Ah! I hope you're right—but I doubt it."

Nayland Smith had shed his leather coat and was engaged in loading one of those large, cracked briars that I had known so well, with the peculiar cross-cut mixture which he favoured, and which he kept in a pouch at least as dilapidated as his pipe.

The room, which we used as an office, was in better order than during poor Van Berg's time. The bed in which our late colleague had slept had been removed, and I had reduced the place to something like order.

I went to a side table, pouring out a drink. Nayland Smith's eyes were more than normally bright, and his features, I thought, looked almost haggard. He had dropped into an armchair. He took the glass which I handed to him, but set it down in the arm rest, its contents untasted; and:

"Greville," he said, "the hand of destiny may clearly be seen in all this. Where is Barton?"

"I expected him back by now," I replied. "Rima is with him. Do you know what's happened, Sir Denis? Is that why you're here?"

"I know that Dr. Van Berg has been murdered," he returned grimly. "But that isn't why I'm here."

He lighted his pipe absent-mindedly, three matches being used before he was satisfied; then:

"I am here," he went on, "because there is a dangerous movement on the Afghan border and creeping south day by day. Definite orders reached me at Basra. That's why I'm here, Greville. Heaven knows we had enough trouble before, but now that the tribes are rising in response to a mad rumour that El Mokanna, the Masked Prophet, has come out of his tomb to lead them, I don't know where my duty lies."

He had picked up his glass, but he set it down again and fixed me with a steady glance of his steel-gray eyes.

"I suspect that it lies *here!*" he snapped. "Some madness of Barton's is at the bottom of this superstitious rumour, which by now has swept all over the East—Near and Far."

I sustained that stare with great difficulty, and presently:

"You are right, Sir Denis," I admitted. "The truth of the matter I don't know, and I don't think the chief knows it—but I have every reason to believe that poor Van Berg met his death at the hands of some fanatic inspired by this rumour. He died in this room. And the manner of his death remains a mystery to this present hour."

"Barton is mad," said Nayland Smith definitely. "His investigations have caused nearly as much trouble as the zeal of the most earnest missionaries."

He stood up and began to pace the long, narrow room in his restless fashion. In this trick, which betrayed the intense pent-up vitality of the man, he reminded me of the chief. Together, the pair of them emitted almost visible sparks of force.

"Be as brief as you can," he directed. "The clue to the trouble lies here—obscured by now, probably. I have Captain Woodville's report—but it omits almost every essential point. Give me your own story of the death of Van Berg." He stared at me intently. "The peace of the world, Greville, may rest upon your accuracy."

Chapter Sixth

PERFUME OF MIMOSA

"Poor Van Berg," I explained, "slept in this room, which throughout the time that we have been in Ispahan we have used as an office. All the records are kept here, and up to the time of the tragedy the most valuable record of all: a strong iron box, which the chief almost invariably carried with him, and in which it was his custom to deposit valuable finds."

"At the time of Van Berg's death," Nayland Smith said sharply, "what did this box contain?"

"It contained," I replied, "to the best of my knowledge, fifteen plates of thin gold, upon which were engraved the articles of the New Creed; the 'Sword of God,' a very beautiful piece; and a grotesque golden mask—all that remained of El Mokanna, the prophet of Khorassan."

Nayland Smith nodded.

"Van Berg was definitely uneasy from the time that we entered into occupancy of this house. It belongs to a Persian friend of Sir Lionel's—for the chief has friends everywhere; and he arranged in some way that it should be our headquarters in Ispahan. In certain respects it suited us well enough. But, as you can see, it's in a queer district and it lies actually in the shadow of the so-called Ghost Mosque."

"Ghost Mosque!" Nayland Smith echoed. "I don't want to interrupt—but explain more fully what you mean."

"I will do my best. It appears that years ago—I am rather shaky as to dates—an imam of the mosque opposite, who happened to be related to the Grand Sherif of Ispahan, conceived a passion for the favourite wife of the then heir apparent, who formerly had a house near by. They were detected together—so the story goes—inside the gallery of the minaret. The exact details of their fate at the hands of the eunuchs are more lurid than pleasant. But the guilty pair were finally thrown from the gallery to the street below. The mosque has never been used since that day; and the death cries of the victims are supposed to be heard from time to time...."

Nayland Smith tugged at the lobe of his ear irritably, but made no comment; and:

"This circumstance, no doubt," I added, "accounts for the ease with which Sir Lionel obtained possession of so large a house at such short notice. It was shut up on our arrival, and musty from long disuse. I give these details, Sir Denis, first, because you asked for them, and, second, because they have a curious bearing on the death of Van Berg."

"I quite understand."

"The chief related this story with tremendous gusto when we took up our residence here. You know his bloodthirsty sense of humour? But the effect on Rima was dreadful. She's as fit as any man to cope with actual danger and hardship, but the bogey business got completely on her nerves. Personally, I treated it as what it really is—a piece of native superstition. I was altogether more worried about the real purpose of our long delay in Ispahan. I don't know to this present hour, why Sir Lionel hung on here. But my scepticism about the Ghost Mosque got rather a jar."

"In what way?"

"Last Thursday night—that is, two nights before his death—Van Berg aroused me. He said that he had been awakened by a sound which resembled that of a huge bird alighting upon the balcony outside his window."

"This window?" Nayland Smith interrupted, and pointed.

"This window. The shutters were closed, but not latched, and this sound, so he told me, aroused him. He sprang out of bed, switched on the electric torch which lay beside him, and ran across to the shutters. As he did so, he heard a low moaning sound which rose to a wail and then died away. When he threw the shutters open and looked out into the street, there was nobody there."

"Did he examine the woodwork?"

"He didn't say so."

Nayland Smith snapped his fingers and nodded to me to go on.

"Imagine my feelings, Sir Denis, when Rima awakened me on Saturday night saying that she had heard a cry from Van Berg's room, almost immediately above her own (that is, the room, in which we are now), followed, as she crept out of her door to awaken me, by a moaning sound outside the house, and high up in the air!"

"Where is your room?"

"At the farther end of the same corridor below."

"I must inspect this corridor. Go on."

"Rima woke me up—I had been fast asleep. I won't disguise, Sir Denis, the fact that our possession of these relics had become somewhat of a nightmare. When I learned of the disturbance in Van Berg's room above, followed by that strange cry, which I could only suppose to be the same that he himself had heard, I feared the worst... and I was right."

"Did Rima more particularly describe this cry?" Nayland Smith asked impatiently.

"No. But I can do so."

"What?"

"I heard it later myself as I went along the corridor past her room."

"Was the moon up?"

"Yes."

"Was her door open?"

"Wide open."

"Was there any light in her room?"

"Yes—she had opened her shutters and was listening, so I understand, for further sounds from Van Berg's room above."

"Was that when she heard the sound?"

"No. She heard it as she opened her door and came along to me."

"Is there a window facing the door of her room?"

"Yes, almost immediately opposite; in fact, just below where I am standing."

"Good!" rapped Nayland Smith. "Go on."

I stared at him for a moment. I detected something like a glint of satisfaction in the steely gray eyes and began to wonder if he had already seen light where all around was darkness to the rest of us.

"I had just reached Rima's door," I went on, "when I myself heard the extraordinary sound for the first time."

"It was not the cry of a dacoit?"

"It was not."

"Give me some idea of it. Can you imitate it?"

"I fear that's impossible."

"Was it a sound made by a human being? By an animal—by some kind of musical instrument?"

"Frankly, I dare not venture to say. It began with a sort of whistling note, which rose to a shriek and died away in a kind of wail."

Nayland Smith, who had been pacing up and down throughout the whole time that I had been speaking, accelerated his step and began tugging at the lobe of his left ear, in a state of furious irritation or deep reflection—I could not determine which. Until, since I had paused:

"Go on!" he snapped.

"Quite frankly, I was scared out of my life. I called very softly to Rima to go down to the lobby and wake Ali Mahmoud, and I went on upstairs to the corridor outside this door."

"Did you hear anything?"

"Yes; a vague, scuffling sound. I stepped forward to the door and called Van Berg. The scuffling continued, but there was no reply. I opened the door."

"It was not locked, then?"

"No. Van Berg had no occasion to lock his door, since his room, so far as we knew, was inaccessible except by means of the street entrance—and Ali Mahmoud slept in the lobby. I saw that the shutters—those before you—were half open. Two Caspian kittens, pets of the chief, which are now locked in an adjoining room, were in here. Van Berg was very fond of animals, and I imagine that they had been sleeping at the foot of his bed at the time he was aroused."

"You need not tell me where he lay," said Nayland Smith grimly; "the stain is still on the floor. Where was the iron box?"

"He lay across it," I said, and my voice was rather shaky, "clutching the two handles. He had been stabbed from behind with a long, narrow blade, which had pierced right through to his heart. But there was not a soul in the room, and the street below was deserted. Apart from which this window is thirty feet above the ground."

"Did you examine the ledge and the shutters?"

"No."

"Has *anyone* examined them?"

"Not to my knowledge."

Sir Denis stood with his back to me for several moments; then, turning:

"Go on!" he cried. "You must have derived some other impressions. Had the bed definitely been slept in, for instance?"

"Yes, undoubtedly."

"Was Van Berg armed?"

"No. His revolver—a heavy service type—was on a table beside his bed. His flash lamp was still under his pillow."

"Was he a heavy drinker?"

I stared uncomprehendingly.

"On the contrary."

Nayland Smith gave me a steely glance.

"H'm!" he snapped—"amazing! A man, already apprehensive of attack, a man of some experience, wakes to the certain knowledge that there's an intruder in his room—and what does he do? He springs out of bed, unarmed, in semi-darkness—although a flash lamp and a revolver lie under his hand—and throws himself across the iron box. Really, Greville! Reconstruct the scene for yourself. Was Van Berg's behaviour, as you indicate it, *normal?*"

"No, sir Denis," I admitted. "Now that you draw my attention to the curious points, it wasn't. But—good heavens!"

I raised my hand to my forehead.

"Ah!" said he— "forgotten something else?"

"Yes—I had. The perfume."

"Perfume?"

"There was a strange perfume in the room. It resembled mimosa. . . ."

"*Mimosa?*"

"Extraordinarily like it."

"Where was this smell most noticeable?"

"About the bed."

He snapped his fingers and began to walk up and down again.

"Naturally," he murmured. "One small point cleared up . . . but—*mimosa* . . ."

I watched him in silence, overcome by unhappy recollections.

"Where is the iron box now?" he suddenly demanded.

"It's in my room!" roared a great voice—"and I'm waiting for the swine who murdered Van Berg to come and fetch it!"

Sir Denis, in his restless promenade, had reached the window—had been staring out of it, as if considering my statement that it was thirty feet above street level. He turned in a flash—so did I. . . .

Sir Lionel Barton stood in the doorway, and Rima was beside him, a neat, delightful figure in her drill riding kit and tan boots.

If Rima was surprised to learn the identity of the tall man in shabby gray flannels who now turned and confronted her, I can only describe the chief's reaction as that of one half stunned. He fell back a pace—his deep-set eyes positively glaring; then:

"Smith!" he said huskily—Nayland Smith! Am I dreaming?"

The grim face of Sir Denis relaxed in that ingenuous smile which stripped him of twenty years.

"By God!" roared the chief, and literally pounced upon him. "If I were anything like a decent Christian I should say that my prayers had been answered!"

CHAPTER SEVENTH

RIMA AND I

DOWN in the little garden of the house I had a few moments alone with Rima. At some time this garden had been a charming, secluded spot. Indeed, except for a latticed window above, it was overlooked from only one point: the gallery of the minaret. But neglect had played havoc with the place.

The orange trees flourished—indeed, were in full blossom—and a perfect cloak of bougainvillea overhung the balcony below the latticed window. But the flower borders were thickets of weeds and a stone cistern in which a little fountain had long ceased to play was coated with slime and no more than a breeding place for mosquitoes.

"I don't know what it is about Sir Denis Nayland Smith," said Rima. "But I have never experienced such a sense of relief in my life as when I came into that room to-day and found him there."

"I know," I replied, squeezing her reassuringly: "it's the sterling quality of the man. All the same, darling, I shan't feel happy until we're clear of Ispahan."

"Nor shall I, Shan. If only uncle weren't so infernally mysterious. What on earth are we staying on here for?"

"I know no more than you do, Rima. What was the object of this afternoon's expedition? I'm quite in the dark about it!"

"I'm nearly as bad," she confessed. "But at least I can tell you where we went. We went to Solomon Ishak. You know—the funny old jeweller?"

"Solomon Ishak is one of the greatest mysteries of Ispahan. But I understand he gets hold of some very rare antique pieces. Probably the chief is negotiating a deal."

"I don't think so. I had to take along the negatives of about forty photographs, and uncle left me wandering about that indescribable, stuffy shop for more than an hour while he remained locked in an inner room with old Solomon."

"And what became of the photographs?"

"He had them with him but brought them out at the end of

the interview. They are back here now."

"That may explain the mystery," I said reflectively. "The photographs were of the relics of the Prophet, I take it?"

Rima nodded.

"The workmanship on the hilt of the sword has defied even the chief's knowledge," I added. "He probably wanted Solomon Ishak's opinion but didn't care to risk taking the sword itself."

Rima slipped a slender bare arm about my neck and snuggled her head down against my shoulder.

"Oh, Shan!" she whispered. "I have never felt so homesick in my life."

I stooped and kissed her curly hair, squeezing her very tightly; then:

"Rima, darling," I whispered, my lips very close to one half-hidden ear, "when we get to some place a little nearer civilisation, will you come and see the consul with me?"

She made no reply but hid her face more closely against me.

"If the chief still insists on a spectacular wedding, that can come later. But . . ."

Rima suddenly raised her face, looking up at me.

"Next time you ask me, I'm going to say, Yes, Shan. But please don't ask me again until we're out of Ispahan."

"Why?" I asked blankly. "Is there any special reason for this?"

"No," she replied, kissed me on the chin, and nestled down against me again. "But I've promised. And if you are good you'll be satisfied."

I stooped and nearly smothered her with kisses. I suppose my early training was to blame, and I didn't know, or even seek to find out, Rima's views upon the subject. As for the chief, I had known for a long time past that he was thoroughly enjoying the situation.

Had Rima and I openly become lovers, I am convinced he wouldn't have turned a hair. He was a wonderful old pagan, and his profound disrespect for ritual in any form had led to some awkward moments—awkward, that is, for me, but apparently enjoyed by Sir Lionel.

And at the moment that these thoughts were crossing my

mind his great voice came from the window above:

"Break away, there!" he roared. "There's more serious work afoot than making love to my staff photographer!"

I jumped up—my blood was tingling—and turned angrily. But in the very act I met Rima's upcast glance. My mood changed. She was convulsed with laughter; and:

"The old ruffian!" she whispered.

"Come hither, my puritan friend," Sir Lionel continued. "Two cavaliers would have speech with thee!"

Chapter Eighth

"EL MOKANNA!"

A CONFERENCE took place in the chief's room at the end of the long corridor on the first floor of that queer old house.

The place was untidy as only Sir Lionel could make it. There were riding boots on the bed, and strewn about on the floor were such diverse objects as a battered sun helmet, a camera case, odd items of underwear, a pair of very ancient red leather slippers, a number of books—many of them valuable; the whole rising in a sort of mound towards an old cabin trunk, from which one would assume as by an eruption they had been cast forth.

There was a long, high window on the right through which I could see sunshine on the yellow wall of the Ghost Mosque. A low, shallow cupboard occupied the space below this window. Set left of this cupboard was a big table on which lay piled an indescribable litter. There were manuscripts, firearms, pipes, a hat box, a pair of shoes, a large case containing flasks of wine of Shiraz, a big scale map, a beautifully embroidered silk robe, and a fossilised skull.

On a low stool at the foot of the bed stood the grim green iron box.

Sir Denis Nayland Smith was standing staring at the box. The chief had thrown himself into an armchair.

"Greville," said Nayland Smith, "have you ever explored the mosque over the way?"

"Yes," I replied, to his evident surprise. "But I didn't find that it possessed any features of interest. Does it, Sir Lionel?"

"According to Smith," was the reply, "it does!"

"Had you any special reason for exploring the place?" Sir Denis asked.

"I had," I admitted. "I made my way in this morning through a window on the north side. You see, I imagined—it was probably no more than imagination—that I saw someone watching us from there on one occasion——"

"What occasion?"

"The inquiry into Van Berg's death—when Mr. Jean and Captain Woodville were here——"

"Never mentioned this to me!" the chief began, when:

"All I wanted to know," said Nayland Smith rapidly. "Be quiet, Barton." And now he turned. His face had grown very stern. "I want to make it perfectly clear to you both, that we three, and Rima, and Ali Mahmoud, stand in greater peril of our lives, at this present moment, than any of us has ever been before."

"That's putting it pretty strongly, Sir Denis," I said, for I recalled other experiences which I had shared with him.

"Not too strongly," he replied. "I rarely say what I don't mean, Greville. But apart from Rima—I sincerely wish she were a thousand miles from Ispahan—there's a further and a graver consideration. Sir Lionel here—inadvertently, I admit—has stirred up a thing which at this particular stage of world politics is calculated to sway the balance in the wrong direction.

"I know all the facts, Greville"—he threw a quick glance in my direction—"and I assure you that what I say is true. The blowing up of the tomb of El Mokanna revived the tradition of that minor prophet and brought into unexpected prominence certain living believers of his doctrine, of which accident they were not slow to take advantage. I have the names of several men in Afghanistan, Khorassan, and Persia whom I know to be associated with this movement, whether as legitimate fanatics or seekers after power remains to be seen. But the spread of the thing is phenomenal."

The chief had begun to walk up and down the room in that caged-bear fashion of his; and since Nayland Smith was also addicted to promenading in moments of intense thought, the latter checked his own restless movements at the first stride and dropped into an armchair which Sir Lionel had vacated, tugging reflectively at the lobe of his left ear.

His words had chilled me. All my fears, which throughout had centred around Rima, came to a head now. I had known for more than a week past that our little party was the focus of malignant forces. Now, chance, or divine Providence, had sent us the man best equipped to deal with such a situation. But his words held no comfort.

"The way in which this cry of 'El Mokanna' has swept through the East," he continued, speaking in his rapid staccato fashion, "points to organisation. Someone has seized this mighty opportunity. Don't glare at me, Barton. You, and you alone, are responsible for the position in which we find ourselves. Captain Woodville has already told you so, I believe."

I don't think the chief would have remained silent under such treatment from any but Sir Denis. He was certainly glaring, and he continued to glare. But the steely gray eyes met his unfalteringly; and Sir Lionel merely grunted and continued his promenade.

"Our chief enemy," Nayland Smith went on, "recognises the importance of possessing the New Creed, the Sword of God, and the gold mask. This was why poor Van Berg died."

I heard Sir Lionel groan. He halted, and stood with his back to us for some moments.

"The first attempt failed," that cool, even voice went on. "It was attended by very peculiar features; they were not insignificant. But—" he paused for a moment, impressively— "the attempt will be repeated. Our enemy knows that the method by which be obtained access to Van Berg's room has so far defied all investigation. He knows that the green box is no longer in that room—but is here."

"How can you be sure of that?"

"Because Barton has advertised the fact," Nayland Smith returned savagely. "Two Persian officials were present at the inquiry, here, in this house. And they know that the box now rests in Sir Lionel's room. Don't answer, Barton—just listen. And you, too, Greville."

It was hard going for Sir Lionel to swallow his words, but he succeeded in doing so. And with the brief clarity which was one of his peculiar gifts Nayland Smith outlined his plan of defence.

That he seemed to take it for granted that there would be an attack positively terrified me, since Rima was in the house. But what I did not understand at the time was an underlying anger which appeared to be directed against the chief. . . .

"I hope that my presence may be unknown to the enemy," he concluded. "But, frankly, in spite of all the precautions I have taken, I doubt this. I am almost certain that I was covered. The man Amir Khan, originally your guide, has deserted to the other side. This, to me, is particularly, in fact dreadfully, significant. My object, Greville—" evidently he detected bewilderment in my expression—"is this: I mean to bring things to a head."

"What d'you mean?" Sir Lionel demanded, with a sudden angry outburst—"Bring things to a head! Haven't they come to a head already?"

"Listen, Barton," Nayland Smith spoke unusually slowly. "You have taken some risks in your time. But this time you have stirred up something too big for you. Forget that I'm here, but go to work without delay and instruct Ali Mahmoud accordingly, to prepare for departure in the morning. Do everything that occurs to you to make it known that to-night is the last night you will spend under this roof. Upon your success, Barton—I include you, Greville—my plan for discovering the murderer of poor Van Berg will depend. . . ."

Chapter Ninth

THE FLYING DEATH

The extraordinary events of that night brought me nearer to a belief in supernatural agencies than I could have believed myself capable of approaching.

Nayland Smith's programme was perfectly definite. Clearly enough he had formed a theory covering the singular facts of the death of Dr. Van Berg. This theory he bluntly declined to reveal to the chief.

"I'm going to handle this thing, Barton, in my own way," he said firmly. "For once in your life you'll take orders, or stand aside, whichever you please."

In consequence we were disposed in what seemed to me a very strange manner. My own post was in the chief's room, in which our long conference had taken place. I was seated upon a pile of pillows and other odds and ends, screened from the observation of anyone in the room by a large upstanding trunk, the property of Rima.

Through an opening between the wall and the side of this trunk I could see practically the whole of the room, which, as I have already said, was a large one. The shutters of the window above and to my right were closed; only a glimmer of moonlight showed through the slats. In consequence, the place was in semi-darkness, to which, however, after a time, my eyes grew accustomed.

I could see all the objects there very clearly. The window at the further end, that overlooking the street and the side of the mosque, had the shutters closed but not latched. Through the slit between them I could see reflected light on the ancient wall beyond.

The bed, which jutted out along to my left, showed the outline of a heavy body under its sheet. A gray army blanket was rolled across the foot in accordance with Sir Lionel's custom—a provision against the chill of early morning; and the sheet was pulled up right over the pillow so as entirely to conceal the head of the sleeper—another characteristic trick of the chief's in insect-infested countries.

That mound of odds and ends still remained upon the big table, and garments were littered about the floor. On a low stool at the foot of the bed, an object now associated in my mind with murder, stood the long green box. A pistol lay beside me, and I had an electric torch in my pocket.

I anticipated a dreary vigil, nor was I by any means satisfied that the enemy would fall into the trap laid for him by Nayland Smith. Our preparations for departure in the early morning had been almost too ostentatious, in my opinion.

The room was silent as a tomb.

Ali Mahmoud, in the lobby below, would be watching the street intently through the iron-barred grill of the house door. Rima was in one of the rooms above, from which she also commanded a view of the street. Of Sir Denis's position I remained in ignorance, except that definitely he was not in the house....

Time wore on. I grew very restless and cramped. Smoking was prohibited, as well as the making of the slightest sound.

I watched the shutters of the window above the cupboard so long and so intently that my sight became blurred. This, I felt assured, would be the point of attack. I formed dreadful mental pictures of the creature heard many nights ago by poor Van Berg—the thing which had alighted with a sound resembling that caused by the alighting of a heavy bird—in his own words.

What could it be—this flying thing? I conceived horrors transcending the imagination of the most morbid story-tellers.

For the keen weapon which had pierced through Van Berg's back and reached his heart, I substituted a dreadful kind of beak—the beak of a thing not of this world; a flying horror, such as the Arab romancers have conjured up—a ghoulish creature haunting the ancient cemetery just beyond the city walls....

It was the cry of this creature, I told myself, that moaning, wailing cry, which had given rise to the legend of the Ghost Mosque, which had led to this little street becoming deserted, and had made the house in which we lived uninhabitable for so many years.

At which point in my grisly reflections a sound caused me to draw a sharp breath. I crouched, listening intently.

Footsteps!

Someone was walking along the street below. The regular, measured steps paused at a point which I estimated to be somewhere just in front of the door of the house. I anticipated a challenge from Ali Mahmoud, but recalled that Sir Denis's instructions on this point had been implicit.

There was no challenge. The footsteps sounded again, echoing hollowly now, so that I knew the walker to be passing that outjutting wall of the mosque and approaching the dark, tunnel-like archway and the three steps leading to the narrow lane which skirted the base of the minaret.

I heard him mount the three steps; then again he paused....

What would I not have given for a glimpse of him! A passer-by was a phenomenon in that street at night. I dared not move, however. The footsteps continued—and presently died away altogether.

Silence descended again upon this uncanny quarter.

How long elapsed I had no means of judging; probably only a few minutes. But I had begun to induce a sort of hypnosis by my concentrated staring at the slit between the shutters, when—from high up and a long way off, I heard *the sound*....

It brought my mind back in a flash to those horrible imaginings which had absorbed me at the moment that footsteps had broken the stillness. It was coming! ... The flying death!

A sort of horrible expectancy claimed me, as, pistol in hand, I watched the opening between the shutters.

Silence fell again. I could detect no sound either within the house or outside.

Whereupon it happened—the thing I had been waiting for; a thing seemingly beyond human explanation.

There came a faint pattering sound on the narrow ledge outside and below the shutters. A dull impact and a faint creaking of woodwork told of a weight imposed upon the projecting window. Something began to move upward—a dim shadow behind the slats—upward and inward—towards the opening....

The tension of watching and waiting grew almost too keen to tolerate. But my orders were definite, and wait I must.

Beyond that faint straining of woodwork, no sound whatever was occasioned by the intruder. No sign came from below to indicate that Ali Mahmoud had seen anything of this apparition, which indeed, since it had apparently flown through the air, was not remarkable.

Then—the shutters began very silently to open....

Chapter Tenth

I SEE THE SLAYER

The shutter opened so silently and so slowly that only by the closest watching could I detect the movement. There was absolutely no creaking.

A window of the Ghost Mosque on the opposite side of the street, looking like a black smudge on a dirty yellow canvas, came just in line with the edge of the left-hand shutter. And only by the ever increasing gap of yellow between the woodwork and the smudge of shadow, could I tell what was happening.

The effect was slowly to add to the light in the room. So accustomed had I become to the dimness that I felt myself shrinking back farther into my hiding place; although in actual fact the access of light was less, I suppose, than would have been gained by the introduction of a solitary candle.

My ghoulish imaginings came to a head.

Some vampire creature from the ancient cemetery was about to spring in. More than once since the relics of El Mokanna had come into our possession I had laughed at Rima's superstitious terrors, but at this moment I admit frankly that I shared them.

Ispahan lay around me, silent as a city of the past. I might have been alone in Persia. And always the fear was with me that Nayland Smith, for all his peculiar genius, had misjudged the circumstances which had led to the death of Van Berg; that I was about to be subjected to a test greater perhaps than my spiritual strength could cope with.

What I should have done at this moment had I been a free agent, I cannot even guess. But I doubt it I could have remained there silent and watching.

Fortunately, I was under orders. I meant to carry those orders out to the letter. But in honesty I must record that during the interminable moments which elapsed from the time that some incredible creature had alighted outside the window, to the moment that the shutters became fully opened. I doubted the wisdom of Nayland Smith. . . :

A vague mass rose inch by inch over the window ledge; grew higher—denser, as it seemed to me; and, with a wriggling movement indescribably horrible, reached the top of that low cupboard which extended below the window—and crouched or lay there.

I had formed absolutely no conception of outline. The entrance of the nocturnal creature had been effected in such a manner that definition was impossible. This was the point, I think, at which my courage almost touched vanishing point.

What was the thing on top of the cupboard? Something which could fly—something which had no determinate shape. . . .

I knew that the visitor was inspecting the room keenly. To me, as I have said, it seemed to have become brightly illuminated. Colt in hand, I shrank farther and farther away from the narrow opening through which I was peering, until my back was flat against the wall.

That vague outline which disturbed the square of the open window disappeared. A very soft thud which must have been inaudible to ears less keenly attuned than mine told me that the visitant, almost certainly the slayer of Van Berg, had dropped onto the floor and was now in the room with me!

I peered into the darkness left of the big, littered table. Something was approaching the bed . . . going, I thought, *on all fours*.

Definitely, the approaching was oblique—that is, not in my direction. I was conscious of a shock of relief. I had not been seen.

Something glittered dully in the reflected light, and I heard a faint swishing sound, almost the first, expecting the thud, which had betrayed the presence of this nocturnal assassin.

At first it puzzled me, and then, suddenly, to my mind an explanation sprang.

The creature was spraying the bed. . . .

Ideas quickly associated themselves; for at this same moment there was swept to my nostrils an almost overpowering perfume of mimosa—the same that had haunted poor Van Berg's room.

It was some unfamiliar but tremendously potent anaesthetic.

In the instant that realisation came to me, I knew also that the horrible visitor was not a supernatural creature but human. True, his agility was far above the ordinary, and his powers of silent movement were uncanny.

He was evidently armed with some kind of spray; and during the time that its curiously soothing sound continued, I found, so oddly does the mind react to indefinable fear, that my thoughts had wandered. I was thinking about an account I had once read of a mysterious creature known as Springheeled Jack, who terrorised outlying parts of London many years ago.

For the fact remained that this man, now endeavouring to reduce the occupant of the bed to unconsciousness, could apparently spring to high windows, quite beyond the reach of any human jumper, and indeed, beyond the reach of any member of the animal kingdom!

The swishing sound ceased. Absolute silence followed. . . .

Peer intensely as I would, I could detect no trace of another presence in the room. But I knew exactly what was happening. The unimaginable man who had come through the window was crouching somewhere and listening. Probably he was counting, silently, knowing how many seconds must elapse before the unknown drug which smelled like mimosa could reduce the sleeper to unconsciousness—or, perhaps, bring about death. . . .

Distant though I was from the bed, that sickly sweet odour was making me dizzy.

Fully a minute elapsed. No sound could I hear; nor could I detect a movement. But during that age-long minute I observed a vague white patch in the darkness, and presently I identified it. It was made by the initials painted on the green iron box.

And as I watched, this white patch became obscured.

A sound disturbed that all-but-insufferable silence—a sound of heavy breathing. Then, silhouetted against the window . . . I saw the intruder.

I saw a small, lithe body, muscular arms uplifted, the green box born upon the right shoulder.

My hand trembled upon the trigger, but Nayland Smith's instructions had been definite. The man bore the box to the end of the room. Here, shadow from the cupboard swallowed him up. Preceded by very little noise the square outline of the box now appeared upon the top of the cupboard.

He had raised it above his head and placed it there, by which circumstances, since he appeared to be a small man, I was able to judge of his extraordinary strength.

My heart was beating very fast and I realised that I was holding my breath. I inhaled deeply, watching, now, the square of the opened window. A silhouetted arm appeared above the box, then a shoulder, and finally the whole of a lean body.

The midnight visitor was a Negro, or a member of some very dark race, wearing only a black loincloth: his features I could not see.

His movements interested me intensely. Stooping, he bent over the box. Certain metallic sounds told me that the iron handles at either end were being moved.

Then, as I watched . . . the box disappeared!

The black man alone, a crouching silhouette, remained outlined in the open window. The box had gone; incredible fact—but the box had gone! Silently, save for a distant thud that heavy iron chest had been "vanished" from the room as a conjurer vanishes a coin!

An interval followed, my reactions during which I cannot hope to describe, until presently I saw that the crouching figure was performing a sort of hauling movement. This movement ceased.

He stood suddenly upright . . . and disappeared.

CHAPTER ELEVENTH

THE MAN ON THE MINARET

THAT vague supernatural dread which latterly I had shaken off swept back again like a cloud, touching me coldly. The window space was perfectly blank, now. The iron box had gone; the black man had gone. This miracle had been achieved with scarcely any sound!

The legend of Spring-heeled Jack crossed my mind again. Then I was up. My period of enforced inactivity was ended.

I pressed the button of my torch and, springing out from behind the big trunk, directed a ray along the narrow room. The air was still heavy with a vague sickly perfume of mimosa; but I gave no glance at the pillow which had been sprayed with this strange anaesthetic. The bed had been carefully prepared by Nayland Smith to produce the appearance of a sleeper.

"An old dodge of mine, Greville," he had said, "which will certainly fail if the enemy suspects that I am here."

Either the enemy did not suspect, or, like the ancient confidence trick, it was a device which age did not wither nor custom stale. . . .

As though it had been a prearranged cue, that flash of light in the empty room heralded a sound—THE sound . . . an indescribable humming which rose and rose, developed into a sort of wail, then died away like muted roaring. . . .

I must explain at this point that from the moment of the figure's disappearance from the window to that when, switching on the light, I ran forward, only a very few seconds had elapsed.

Leaping upon the low cupboard, and staring down into the street, I witnessed a singular spectacle.

That extraordinary sound, the origin of which had defied all speculation, was still audible, and since it seemed to come from somewhere high above my head, my first instinct was to look up.

I did not do so, however.

At the moment that I sprang into the open window, my glance was instantly drawn *downward*. I saw a figure—that of the black creature who had just quitted the room—apparently suspended in space, midway across the street!

His arms raised above his head, he was *soaring* upward towards a window of the Ghost Mosque!

"Good God!" I said aloud—"it isn't human...."

There came a wild scream. The flying figure faltered—the upraised arms dropped—and he was dashed with a dull thud against the wall of the mosque, some eight feet below the window. From there he fell sheerly to the street below. A second, sickening, thud reached my ears ...

The crack of a pistol, a sharp spurt of flame from the gallery of the minaret far above my head, drew my glance upward now. I saw a black-robed black-faced figure there, bathed in brilliant moonlight, bending over the rail and firing down upon the roof of the mosque below!

Once he fired, and moved further around the gallery. A second time. And then, as he disappeared from view, I heard the sound of a third shot....

Pandemonium awakened in the house about me.

Ali Mahmoud was unfastening the heavy bolt which closed the front door. Rima's voice came from the landing above.

"Shan! Shan! Are you all right?"

"All right, dear!" I shouted.

Turning, I ran along the room and out into the corridor. I heard Barton's great voice growling impatiently in the lobby below. But before I could reach him he had raced out into the street. Ali, rifle in hand, followed him, and I brought up the rear.

Far above, Rima leaned from an open window, and:

"For God's sake, be careful!" she cried. "I can see something moving along the roof of the mosque!"

"Don't worry!" I called reassuringly. "We're all armed."

I was bending over a figure lying in the dust, a figure at which Sir Lionel was already staring down with an indescribable expression. It was that, as I saw now quite clearly, of a small but powerfully built Negro.

He presented an unpleasant spectacle by reason of the fact that he had evidently dashed his skull against the wall of the mosque at the end of that incredible flight from side to side of the street. He wore, as I had thought, nothing but a dark loincloth.

Thrust into this, where it was visible as he lay huddled up and half upon his face, was a dull metal object which gleamed in the light of our torches. For, although moonlight illuminated the minaret and upper part of the mosque, the street itself was a black gully. Stooping, I examined this object more closely.

It was a metal spray, such as dentists use. Its purpose I had already seen demonstrated; then:

"Look at his hands!" the chief said huskily. "What is he holding?"

At first I found it difficult to reply; then I realised that the Negro was clutching two large iron hooks to which had been attached a seemingly endless thread of what looked like catgut, no thicker than the D string of a violin. The truth was still far from my mind; when:

"A West African," Sir Lionel continued—"probably from the Slave Coast. What in hell's name brought such a bird to Persia?"

"Perhaps," I suggested, "he was sold. Slavery is still practised in these parts."

Further speculation on the point was ended by a sudden loud cry from the minaret.

"Stand by, there!"

Sir Lionel, Ali Mahmoud, and I raised our heads. A tall figure draped in a black native robe stood on the gallery. Upright, now, moonlight silvering his hair, I knew him. It was Nayland Smith!

"Ali Mahmoud!" he shouted, "round to the side door of the mosque and shoot anything you see moving. Barton! Stand by the main door, where you can cover three windows. Let nothing come out. Quick, Greville! You know the way into the minaret. Up to me!"

CHAPTER TWELFTH

IN THE GHOST MOSQUE

AN OPEN stone stairway built around the interior wall, afforded a means of reaching the platform of the minaret from that point of entrance to which Nayland Smith had directed me. There was an inner gallery high above my head, to which formerly the mueddin had gained access from a chamber of the mosque.

My footsteps as I clambered upward, breathing hard, echoed around the shell of that ancient tower in a weird, uncanny tattoo. It may seem to have been a bad time for thought, but my brain was racing faster than my feet could carry me.

Some dawning perception of the means by which poor Van Berg had been assassinated was creeping into my mind. In some way the acrobatic murderer had *swung* into the room, probably from one of the windows of the mosque. The hooks which he still clasped in his hands had afforded him a grip, no doubt, and earlier had been hitched to the handles of the iron box which had been swung to its destination in the same way.

But remembering the slender line—resembling a violin string—which we had found attached to those hooks, I met with doubt again. The thing was plainly impossible.

I reached the opening into the gallery and paused for awhile. This gallery extended, right, into darkness which the ray of my torch failed to penetrate. Before me was a low, narrow door, giving access to a winding wooden stair which would lead me to the platform above.

The idea of that passage penetrating into the darkness of the haunted mosque was definitely unpleasant. And casting one final glance along it, I resumed my journey. I stumbled several times on those stairs, which were narrow and dilapidated, but presently found the disk of the moon blazing in my face and knew that I had reached the platform.

"Greville!" came in Nayland Smith's inimitable snappy voice.

"Yes, Sir Denis."

I came out and stood beside him. It was a dizzying prospect as one emerged from darkness. The narrow street upon which our house faced looked like a bottomless ravine. I could see right across the roof of the mosque on one hand, to where Ispahan, looking like a city of mushrooms from which tulip-like minarets shot up, slumbered under a velvet sky, and, left, to the silver river. Then, my attention was diverted.

A dark shape lay almost at my feet, half hidden in shadow. I drew back sharply, looking down; and:

"Damned unfortunate, Greville," said Nayland Smith rapidly.

He was standing near the door out of which I had come, a tall, angular figure, flooded by moonlight on the right, but a mere silhouette on the left. He wore a loose black *gibbeh* which I thought I recognised as the property of Ali Mahmoud. The angularity of his features was accentuated, and the one eye which was visible shone like polished steel. He glanced down.

"I used an extemporised sandbag from behind," he explained, "and I'm afraid I hit too hard. I'm not masquerading, Greville—" indicating his black robe. "I borrowed this to help me to hide in the shadows. Is the other Negro dead?"

"Yes, he dashed his brains out against the wall of the mosque."

"Damnably unfortunate!" Nayland Smith jerked. "I have no personal regrets, but either would have been an invaluable witness. There was a third on the roof of the mosque. His job was to keep a lookout. I missed him twice, but hit him the third time. He managed to get away, nevertheless. But I'm hoping he can't escape from the building."

Dimly, from far below, rose a murmuring of approaching steps and voices. Nayland Smith's shots had awakened the neighbourhood.

"Damn it!" he rapped. "If a crowd gathers, it may ruin everything."

He stooped and removed a loop of that strange tenuous line from a projection of the ornamental stonework decorating the railing of the balcony.

"Look!" he said, and held it up in the moonlight. "It doesn't seem strong enough to support a kitten. Yet the black murderer and the iron box were swung from window to window upon a carefully judged length of it." He thrust the line into his pocket. "I came prepared for wire," he added grimly, and exhibited an implement which I recognised as part of Sir Lionel's kit: a steel wire cutter.

"For heaven's sake, what is it?" I asked.

Even now, I found difficulty in believing that a line no stouter than sewing thread could carry a man's weight.

"I haven't the slightest idea, Greville. But it's tremendously tough. It took a mighty grip to cut through it. Suspended from this balcony, you see, its length carefully estimated, it enabled one of these acrobatic devils to swing from a window of the mosque right onto a corresponding window of the house opposite. It also enabled him to swing the iron box across. But there's work for us!"

He pushed me before him in his impetuous fashion; and:

"There was a *fourth* in the game, Greville," he added . . . "perhaps a fifth. He, or they, were stationed behind the window of the mosque. The controlling influence—the man we're looking for—was there!"

I started down at the wooden stair, Nayland Smith following hard behind me; until:

"One moment!" he called.

I paused and turned, directing the ray of my torch upward. He was fumbling in a sort of little cupboard at the head of the steps, and from it he presently extracted his shoes, and proceeded to put them on, talking rapidly the while.

"It was touch and go when that black devil came up, Greville. I also was black from head to feet; black robe, black socks, and a black head cover, made roughly from a piece of this old *gibbeh*, with holes cut for eyes and mouth! He didn't see me, and he couldn't hear me. I dodged him all round the gallery like a boy dodging around the trunk of a tree! When he made fast the line, on the end of which I could see two large iron hooks, and lowered it, I recognised the method."

He had both his shoes on now and was busily engaged in lacing them.

"It confirmed my worst suspicions—but this can be discussed later. Having lowered it to its approved length, he swung it like a pendulum; and presently it was caught and held by someone hidden behind a window of the mosque. You will find, I think, that there is a still lighter line attached to the hooks. This enabled the Negro, having swung across from the mosque to the house, to haul the pendulum back until the box was safely disposed of. It was as he swung across in turn, that I got busy with the wire cutter."

He came clattering down, and:

"Left!" he said urgently—"into the mosque."

I found myself proceeding along that narrow, mysterious passage.

"Light out!"

As I switched the torch off, he opened a door. I was looking along a flat roof, silvered by moonlight—the roof of the mosque.

"I hit him just before he reached this door. There's a bare chance he may have left a clue."

"A clue to what?"

A considerable group of people had collected in the street, far below, including, I thought, Armenians from across the river, as many excited voices told me. But I was intent upon the strange business in hand; and:

"The sound!" said Nayland Smith; "that damnable, howling sound which was their signal."

No torch was necessary now. The roof was whitely illuminated by the moon. And, stooping swiftly:

"My one bit of luck to-night," he exclaimed. "Look!"

Triumphantly, for I could see his eyes gleaming, he held up an object which at first I was unable to identify, I suppose because it was something utterly unexpected. But presently recognition came. It was a bone . . . a human frontal bone!

"I'm afraid," I said stupidly, "that I don't understand."

"A *bull-roarer!*" cried Nayland Smith. "Barton can probably throw light upon its particular history."

He laughed. A length of stout twine was attached to the bone, and twisting this about his fingers he swung the thing rapidly round and round at ever increasing speed.

The result was uncanny.

I heard again that awesome whining which had heralded the death of Van Berg, which I had thought to be the note of some supernatural nocturnal creature. It rose to a wail— to a sort of muted roar—and died away as the swing diminished. . . .

"One of the most ancient signaling devices in the world, Greville—probably prehistoric in origin. Listen!"

I heard running footsteps, many running footsteps, in the street below—all receding into the distance. . . .

Sir Denis laughed again, shortly.

"Our bull-roarer has successfully dispersed the curious natives!" he said.

Chapter Thirteenth

THE BLACK SHADOW

DAWN was very near when that odd party assembled in the room which we used as an office, the room in which Van Berg had died. Nayland Smith presided, looking haggardly tired after his exertions of the night. He paced up and down continuously. The chief stood near the door, shifting from foot to foot in his equally restless fashion. Rima sat in the one comfortable chair and I upon the arm of it.

A Persian police officer who spoke perfect English completed the party.

"Dr. Van Berg, as you know," said Sir Denis, "died in this room. I have tried to explain how the murderer gained access. The room being higher than Sir Lionel's, the line used was shorter, but the method was the same. I found fingerprints and footmarks on the roof of the mosque and also on the ledge below these shutters. A man stabbed as Van Berg was stabbed bleeds from the mouth; therefore I found no bloodstains. The Negro was swung across, not from the window, but from the *roof* of the mosque. He employed the same device, having quietly entered, of spraying the head of the sleeper with some drug which so far we haven't been able to identify. It smells like mimosa. Fortunately, a portion remains in the spray upon the dead African, and analysis may enlighten us."

"But Dr. Van Berg was stabbed, as I remember?" said the Persian official.

"Certainly!" Nayland Smith snapped. "He had a pair of Caspian kittens sleeping at the foot of his bed. The bed used to stand there, just where you are sitting. They awakened immediately and in turn awakened him. He must have realised what was afoot, and he sprang straight for the box. It was his first and only thought—for already he was under the influence of the drug. The Negro knifed him from behind."

He pointed to a narrow-bladed knife which lay upon a small table.

"He came provided for a similar emergency to-night. . . .

That unhappy mystery, I think, is solved."

"I cannot doubt it," the Persian admitted. "But the strength of this material," touching a piece of the slender yellow-gray line, "is amazing. What is it?"

"It's silkworm gut," Sir Lionel shouted. "I recognised it at once. It's the strongest animal substance known. It's strong enough to land a shark, if he's played properly."

"I don't agree with you, Barton," Nayland Smith said quietly. "It certainly *resembles* silkworm gut, but it is infinitely stronger."

Before the chief could reply:

"A very singular business, Sir Lionel," the suave official murmured. "But I am happy to learn that no Persian subject is concerned in this murderous affair."

There was a pause, and then:

"A fourth man was concerned," said Nayland Smith, speaking unusually slowly. "He, as well as the Negro whom I wounded, has managed to get away. Probably there are exits from the mosque with which I am unacquainted?"

"You suggest that the fourth man concerned was one of our subjects?"

"I suggest nothing. I merely state that there was a fourth man. He was concealed in a window of the mosque."

"Probably another of these Negroes—who are of a type quite unfamiliar to me. . . ."

"They are Ogboni!" shouted the chief. "They come from a district of the Slave Coast I know well! They're members of a secret Voodoo society. You should read my book *The Sorcerers of Dahomey*. I spent a year in their territory. When I saw that bull roarer there—" he pointed to the frontal bone with the twine attached, which also lay upon the small table—"it gave me the clue. I knew that these West African negroes were Ogboni. They're active as cats and every bit as murderous. But I agree with Smith, that they were working under somebody else's direction."

The Persian official, a dignified and handsome man of forty-odd, wearing well tailored European clothes, raised his heavy brows and smiled slightly.

"Are you suggesting, Sir Lionel," he asked, "that the religious trouble, which I fear *you* have brought about, is at the bottom of this?"

"I am," the chief replied, glaring at him truculently.

"It's beyond doubt," said Nayland Smith. "The aim of the whole conspiracy was to gain possession of the green box."

The Persian continued to smile.

"And in this aim it would seem that the conspirators have been successful."

"They certainly managed to smuggle the box out of the mosque," Nayland Smith admitted grimly, "although one of the pair was wounded, as I know for a fact."

Our visitor stood up.

"Some sort of rough justice has been done," he said. "The actual assassin of your poor friend Dr. Van Berg has met his deserts, as has his most active accomplice. The green box, I believe, contained valuable records of your recent inquiries in Khorassan. . . ."

His very intonation told me unmistakably that he believed nothing of the kind. . . .

"I feel, Sir Lionel, that this may represent a serious loss to Oriental students—nor can I imagine of what use these—records can be to those who have resorted to such dreadful measures to secure them."

The chief clapped his hands, and Ali Mahmoud came in. The Persian official stooped and kissed Rima's fingers, shook hands with the rest of us, and went out. There was silence for a few moments, and then:

"You know, Barton," said Nayland Smith, pacing up and down rapidly, "Ispahan, though quite civilised, is rather off the map; and frankly—local feeling is against you. I mean this Mokanna movement is going to play hell in Persia if it goes on. As you started it—you're not popular."

"Never have been," growled the chief; "never expect to be."

"Not the point," rapped Smith. "There's going to be worse to come—when they know."

A silence followed which I can remember more vividly than many conversations. Rima squeezed my arm and looked up at me in a troubled way. Sir Denis was not a man to panic. But he had made it perfectly clear that he took a grave view of the situation.

Sir Lionel had fenced with the local authorities throughout, knowing that they could have no official information regarding the relics—since, outside our own party (and now Captain Woodville and Stratton Jean), nobody but Amir Khan knew we had found them.

At the cost of one life in our camp and two in their own the enemy had secured the green box . . . but the green box was empty! I knew now why the chief had been so conscience-stricken by the death of Van Berg; I knew that the relics had never been where we all supposed them to be from the time that we came to Ispahan.

Van Berg had died defending an empty box. . . .

Sir Lionel began to laugh in his boisterous fashion.

"We've scored over them, Smith!" he shouted, and shook his clenched fist. "They had Van Berg—but we got a pair of the swine to-night! Topping it all—they've drawn a blank!"

His laughter ceased, and that wonderful, lined old face settled down again into the truculent mask which was the front Sir Lionel Barton showed to the world.

"It's a poor triumph," he added, "to pay for the loss of Van Berg."

Nayland Smith ceased his promenade at the window and stood with his back to all of us, staring out.

"I don't know where you've hidden the relics, Barton," he said slowly, "but I may have to ask you to tell me. One thing I do know. This part of the East is no longer healthy for any of us. The second attempt has failed—but the third . . ."

"What are you suggesting?" Sir Lionel growled; "that I give 'em up? Suppose it came to that. Who am I dealing with?"

Nayland Smith did not turn. But:

"I believe I can tell you," he answered quietly.

"Then tell me! Don't throw out hints. Speak up, man!"

At that, Nayland Smith turned and stared at the speaker, remaining silent for some moments. At last:

"I flew here in a two-seater from Basra," he replied. "There was no other aircraft available in the neighbourhood. I have already made arrangements, however. Imperial Airways have lent us a taxi. You must realise, Barton, the position is serious."

Something in his manner temporarily silenced the chief; until:

"I do realise it," he admitted grudgingly. "Some organiser has got hold of this wave of fanaticism which my blowing up of El Mokanna's tomb started, and he realises—I suppose that's what you're driving at?—that production of the actual relics would clinch the matter. Am I right?"

"You are!" said Nayland Smith. "And I must ask you to consider one or two facts. The drug which was used in the case of Van Berg, and again last night, is, I admit unfamiliar. But the method of employment is not. You see what I mean?"

Rima's grip on my arm tightened; and:

"Shan," she said, looking up at me, "it was what happened two years ago in England!"

The chief's face was a study. Under tufted eyebrows he was positively glaring at Nayland Smith. The latter continued:

"Rima begins to realise what I mean. The device for passing from house to house without employing the usual method of descending to the street is also familiar to me. It was *experience*, and nothing else, that enabled me to deal with the affair of last night."

He paused, and I found my mind working feverishly. Then, bringing that odd conversation to a dramatic head, came a husky query from Sir Lionel.

"Good God! Smith!" he said. "*He* can't be behind this?"

The emphasis on "he" resolved my final doubt.

"You're not suggesting, Sir Denis," I asked, "that we are up against *Dr. Fu Manchu?*"

Rima clutched me now convulsively. Once only had she met the stupendous genius, Dr. Fu Manchu, but the memory of that one interview would remain with her to the end of her days, as it would remain with me.

"If I had had any doubts, Barton," said Nayland Smith, "your identification of the murderer and his accomplice would have settled them. They belong, you tell me, to a secret society on the Slave Coast."

He paused, staring hard at Sir Lionel.

"I believe that there is no secret society of this character, however small or remote, which is not affiliated to the organisation known as the Si-Fan. That natives of the Pacific Islands are indirectly controlled by this group, I know for a fact; why not Negroes of West Africa? Consider the matter from another angle. What are natives of the Slave Coast doing in Persia? Who has brought them here?

"They are instruments, Barton, in the hands of a master

schemer. For what object they were originally imported, we shall probably never know, but their usefulness in the present case has been proved. There can be no association between this West African society and the survivors of the followers of El Mokanna. These Negroes are in the train of some directing personality."

It was morning, and the East is early afoot. From a neighbouring market street came sounds of movement and discords human and animal. Suddenly Sir Denis spoke again.

"If any doubt had remained in my mind, Barton, it would have been removed last night. You may recall that just before the first signal came, someone passed slowly along the street below?"

"Yes! I heard him—but I couldn't see him."

"I heard him, too!" I cried. . . .

"I both heard him and *saw* him," Nayland Smith continued—"from my post on the minaret. Action was impossible—unfortunately—in the circumstances. But the man who walked along the street last night just before the second attempt on the green box . . . was Dr. Fu Manchu!"

Chapter Fourteenth

ROAD TO CAIRO

WEARY though I was of all the East, nevertheless, Cairo represented civilisation. I think I have never felt a greater wave of satisfaction than at the moment when, completing the third and longest stage of our flight from Ispahan, we climbed down upon the sands of Egypt.

Dr. Petrie was there to meet us; and the greeting between himself and Sir Denis, while it had all the restraint which characterises our peculiar race, was nevertheless so intimate and affectionate that I turned away and helped Rima down the ladder.

When the chief, last to alight, joined his old friend, I felt that Rima and I had no further part in the affair.

It should have been a happy reunion, but a cloud lay over it—a cloud which I, personally, was helpless to dispel.

Dr. Petrie, no whit changed since last I had seen him, broke away from Sir Denis and the chief and hugged Rima and myself in both arms. The best of men are not wholly unselfish; and part of Petrie's present happiness was explainable by something which I had overheard as he had grasped Nayland Smith's hand:

"Thank God, old man! Kara is home in England...."

Mrs. Petrie, the most beautiful woman I have ever met (Rima is not jealous of my opinion), was staying with Petrie's people in Surrey, where the doctor shortly anticipated joining her.

I was sincerely glad. For the gaunt shadow of Fu Manchu again had crept over us, and the lovely wife whom Petrie had snatched from that evil genius was in safe keeping beyond the reach of the menace which stretched over us even here.

Nevertheless, this was a momentary hiatus, if no more than momentary. Rima extended her arms, raised her adorable little head, and breathed in the desert air as one inhaling a heavenly perfume.

"Shan," she said, "I don't feel a bit safe, yet. But at least we are in Egypt, *our* Egypt!"

Those words "our Egypt" quickened my pulse. It was in Egypt that I had met her, and in Egypt that I had learned to love her. But above and beyond even this they held a deeper significance. There is something about Egypt which seems to enter the blood of some of us, and to make that old, secret land a sort of super-motherland. I lack the power properly to express what I mean, but over and over again I have found this odd sort of cycle operating—suggesting some mystic affinity with the "gift of the Nile," which, once recognised, can never be shaken off.

"Our Egypt!" Yes, I appreciated what she meant. . . .

Dr. Petrie had his car waiting, and presently we set out for Cairo. Our pilot, Humphreys, had official routine duties to perform, but arrangements were made for his joining us later.

The chief, with Nayland Smith and Rima, packed themselves in behind, and I sat beside Dr. Petrie in front. Having cleared the outskirts of Heliopolis and got out onto the road to Cairo:

"This last job of yours, Greville," said Petrie, "in Khorassan, has had its echoes even here."

"Good heavens! You don't tell me!"

"I assure you it is so. I hadn't the faintest idea, until Smith's first message reached me, that this extraordinary outburst of fanaticism which is stirring up the Moslem population (and has its particular centre at El Azhar) had anything to do with old Barton. Now I know."

He paused, steering a careful course through those immemorable thoroughfares where East and West mingle. Our pilot had just tricked sunset, and we drove on amid the swift, violet, ever changing dusk; dodging familiar native groups; a donkey-rider now and then—with villas shrinking right and left into the shadows, and dusty palms beginning to assume an appearance of silhouettes against the sky which is the roof of Egypt.

"It may have reached me earlier than it reached the authorities," Dr. Petrie went on; "I have many native patients. But that the Veiled Prophet is re-born is common news throughout the native quarter!"

"This is damned serious!" said I.

Petrie swept left to avoid a party of three aged Egyptians

trudging along the road to Cairo as though automobiles had not been invented.

"When I realised what lay behind it," Petrie added, "I could only find one redeeming feature—that my wife, thank God! was in England. The centre of the trouble is farther east, but there's a big reaction here."

"The centre of the trouble," rapped Nayland Smith, evidently having overheard some part of our conversation, "is here, in your car, Petrie!"

"What!"

The doctor's sudden grip on the wheel jerked us from the right to the centre of the road, until he steadied himself; then:

"I don't know what you mean, Smith," he added.

"He means the big suitcase which I have with me!" the chief shouted. "It's under my feet now!"

We were traversing a dark patch at the moment with a crossways ahead of us and a native café on the left. Petrie, a careful driver, had been trying for some time to pass a cart laden with fodder which jogged along obstinately in the middle of the road. Suddenly it was pulled in, and the doctor shot past.

Even as Sir Lionel spoke, and before Petrie could hope to avert the catastrophe, out from the nearer side of this café, supported by two companions, a man (apparently drunk or full of hashish) came lurching. I had a hazy impression that the two supporters had sprung back; then, although Petrie swerved violently and applied brakes, a sickening thud told me that the bumpers had struck him. . . .

A crowd twenty or thirty strong gathered in a twinkling. They were, I noted, exclusively native. Petrie was out first—I behind him—Nayland Smith came next, and then Rima.

Voices were raised in high excitement. Men were gesticulating and shaking clenched fists at us.

"Carry him in," said Petrie quietly. "I want to look at him. But I think this man is dead. . . ."

On a wooden seat in the café we laid the victim, an elderly Egyptian, very raggedly dressed, who might have been a mendicant. A shouting mob blocked the doorway and swarmed about us. Their attitude was unpleasant.

Nayland Smith grabbed my arm.

"Give 'em hell in their own language!" he directed. "You're a past master of the lingo."

I turned, hands upraised, and practically exhausted my knowledge of Arab invective. I was so far successful as to produce a lull of stupefaction during which the doctor made a brief examination.

Rima throughout had kept close beside me; Nayland Smith stood near the feet of the victim—his face an unreadable mask, but his piercing gray eyes questioning Petrie. And at last:

"Where's Barton?" said Petrie astonishingly, standing upright and looking about him—from Rima to myself and from me to Nayland Smith.

"Never mind Barton," said the latter. "Is the man dead?"

"Dead?" Petrie echoed. "He's been dead for at least three hours! He's rigid . . . Where's Barton?"

Chapter Fifteenth

ROAD TO CAIRO (continued)

Sir Denis forming the head of the wedge, the four of us fought our way out of the café to the street, Petrie and I acting as Rima's bodyguard.

The hostility of the crowd was now becoming nasty. The mystery of the thing had literally turned me cold. Then, to crown it all, as we gained the open, I was just in time to see the chief, standing beside Petrie's car, deliver a formidable drive to the jaw of a big Nubian and to see the Negro sprawl upon his back.

"A *frame-up*, Smith!" came his great voice, as he sighted us. "To me, Cavaliers! We're in the hands of the Roundheads!"

So strange a plot I could never have imagined, but its significance was all to obvious. The chief's cry was characteristic of the man's entire outlook on life. He was a throwback to days when personal combat was a gentleman's recreation. His book *History and Art of the Rapier* might have been written by a musketeer, so wholly was the spirit of the author steeped in his bloodthirsty subject. This boyish diablerie it was which made him lovable, but perhaps as dangerous a companion as any man ever had.

One thing, however, I could not find it in my heart to forgive him: that he should expose Rima to peril consequent upon his crazy enthusiasms. I had come to want her near me in every waking moment. Yet now, with that threatening crowd about us and with every evidence that a secret enemy had engineered this hold-up, I found myself wishing that she, as well as Mrs. Petrie, had been safe in England.

How we should have fared, and how that singular episode would have ended, I cannot say. It was solved by the appearance of a member of one of the most efficient organisations in the world: a British-Egyptian policeman, his tarbush worn at a jaunty angle, his blue tunic uncreased as though it had left the tailor's only that morning. His khaki breeches were first class, and his very boots apparently unsoiled by the dust. He elbowed his way into the crowd—aloof, alone, self-contained, all powerful.

I had seen the same calm official intrusion on the part of a New York policeman, and I had witnessed it with admiration in London. But never before had I welcomed it so as at the appearance of this semi-military figure that night on the outskirts of Cairo.

Gesticulating Egyptians sought to enlist his sympathy and hearing. He was deaf. It dawned upon me that the casual onlookers had been deceived as completely as ourselves. We were regarded as the slayers of the poor old mendicant. But the appearance of that stocky figure changed everything.

As we reached Barton:

"Is the case safe?" snapped Nayland Smith, glancing down at the Negro, now rapidly getting to his feet.

"It is," the chief replied grimly. "That's what they were after."

Sir Denis nodded shortly and turned to the police officer.

"*Your* car, sir?" asked the latter. "What's the trouble?"

"Remains to be investigated! You turned up at the right moment. My name is Nayland Smith. Have you been advised?"

The man started—stared hard, and then:

"Yes, sir." He saluted. "Two days ago. Carry on, sir. I'll deal with all this."

"Good. You're a smart officer. What's your name?"

"John Banks, sir, on special duty here to-night."

"I'll mention you at headquarters. . . ."

CHAPTER SIXTEENTH

A MASKED WOMAN

"I AM not prepared to believe," said Sir Lionel, walking up and down the big room reserved for him at Shepheard's "that even Dr. Fu Manchu could have had a stock of dead men waiting on the road from Heliopolis."

"Neither am I," said Nayland Smith. "We may have avoided earlier traps. Those three old fellows, Petrie—" turning to the Doctor—"who seemed so reluctant to get out of your way, you remember, and the cart laden with fodder. I don't suggest for a moment, Barton, that that poor old beggar was killed to serve the purpose; but Petrie here is of opinion that he died either from enteritis or poisoning, and the employment of a body in that way was probably a local inspiration on the part of the agents planted at that particular stage of our journey. He was pushed out, to the best of my recollection, from a shadowy patch of waste ground close beside the café. Where he actually died, I don't suppose we shall ever know, but—" tugging at the lobe of his left ear—"it's the most extraordinary trick I have ever met with, even in my dealings with. . ."

He paused, and Rima finished the sentence:

"Dr. Fu Manchu."

There came an interval. The shutters of the window which overlooked the garden were closed. Muted voices, laughter, and a sound of many footsteps upon sanded paths rose to us dimly. But that group in the room was silent, until:

"Only *he* could devise such a thing," said the chief slowly," and only you and I, Smith, could go one better."

He pointed to a battered leather suitcase lying on a chair and began to laugh in his own boisterous fashion.

"I travel light, Smith!" he cried, "but my baggage is valuable!"

None of us responded to his mood, and Sir Denis stared at him very coldly.

"When is Ali Mahmoud due in Cairo?" he asked.

That queer question was so unexpected that I turned and stared at the speaker. The chief appeared to be quite taken aback; and:

"He'll do well if he's here with the heavy kit in four days," he replied. "But why do you ask, Smith?"

Nayland Smith snapped his fingers irritably and began to walk up and down again.

"I should have thought, Barton," he snapped, "that we knew one another well enough to have shared confidences."

"What do you mean?"

"Simply what I say. If it conveys nothing—forget it!"

"I shan't forget it," said the chief loweringly, his tufted brows drawn together. "But I shall continue to conduct my own affairs in my own way."

"Good enough. I'm not going to quarrel with you. But I should like to make a perfectly amiable suggestion."

"One moment," Petrie interrupted. "We're all old friends here. We've gone through queer times together, and after all—there's a common enemy. It's useless to pretend we don't know who that common enemy is. You agree with me, Smith? For God's sake, let's stand four square. I don't know all the facts. But I strongly suspect—" turning to Sir Denis—"that *you* do. You're the stumbling block, Barton. You're keeping something up your sleeve. Lay all the cards on the table."

The chief gnawed his moustache, locked his hands behind him, and stood very upright, looking from face to face. He was in his most truculent mood. But at last, glancing aside from Petrie:

"I await your amiable suggestion, Smith," he growled.

"I'll put it forward," said the latter. "It is this: A Bibby liner is leaving Port Said for Southampton tomorrow. I suggest that Rima secures a berth."

Rima jumped up at his words, but I saw Petrie grasp her hand as if to emphasise his agreement with them.

"Why should I be sent home, Sir Denis?" she demanded. "What have I done? If you're thinking of my safety, I've been living for months in remote camps in Khorassan and Persia, and you see—" she laughed and glanced aside at me—"I'm still alive."

"You have done nothing, my dear," Sir Denis returned, and smiled in that delightful way which, for all his seniority, sometimes made me wonder why any woman could spare me a thought while he was present. "Nor," he added, "do I doubt your courage. But while your uncle maintains his present attitude, I don't merely fear—I know—that all of us, yourself included, stand in peril of our lives."

There was an unpleasant sense of tension in the atmosphere. The chief was in one of his most awkward moods—which I knew well. He had some dramatic trick up his sleeve. Of this I was fully aware. And he was afraid that Sir Denis was going to spoil his big effect.

Sir Lionel, for all his genius, and despite his really profound learning, at times was actuated by the motives which prompt a mischievous school-boy to release a mouse at a girl's party.

Incongruously, at this moment, at least from our point of view, a military band struck up somewhere beneath; for this was a special occasion of some kind, and the famous garden was en fête. None of us, however, were in gala humour; but:

"Let's go down and see what's going on, Shan," said Rima. She glanced at Sir Lionel. "Can you spare him?"

"Glad to get rid of him," growled the chief. "He's hand and hoof with Smith, here, and one of 'em's enough. . ."

And so presently Rima and I found ourselves crossing the lobby below and watching a throng entering the ballroom from which strains of a dance band came floating out.

"What a swindle, Shan!" she said, pouting in a childish fashion I loved. "I'm simply dying for a dance. And I haven't even the ghost of a frock with me."

We were indeed out of place in that well dressed gathering, in our tired-looking travelling kit. For practically the whole of our worldly possessions had been left behind with the heavy gear in charge of Ali Mahmoud.

After several months more or less in the wilderness, all these excited voices and the throb and drone of jazz music provided an overdose of modern civilisation.

"I feel like Robinson Crusoe," Rima declared, "on his first day home. Do you feel like Man Friday?"

"Not a bit!"

"I'm glad, because you look more like a Red Indian."

Exposure to sun and wind, as a matter of fact, had beyond doubt reduced my complexion to the tinge of a very new brick, and I was wearing an old tweed suit which for shabbiness could only be compared with that of gray flannel worn by Sir Denis.

Nevertheless, I thought, as I looked at Rima, from her trim glossy head to the tips of her small gray shoes, that she was the daintiest figure I had seen that night.

"As we're totally unfit for the ballroom," I said, "do you think we might venture in the garden?"

We walked through the lounge with its little Oriental alcoves and out into the garden. It was a perfect night, but unusually hot for the season. Humphreys, our pilot, joined us there, and:

"You know, Greville," he said grinning, "I don't know what you've been up to in Khorassan, or wherever it is. But somebody in those parts is kicking up no end of a shindy."

He glanced at me shrewdly. Of the real facts he could know nothing—unless the chief had been characteristically indiscreet. But I realised that he must suspect our flight from Persia to have had some relation to the disturbances in that country.

"I should say you bolted just in time," he went on. "They claim a sort of new Mahdi up there. When I got to Cairo this evening I found the news everywhere. Honestly, it's all over the town, particularly the native town. There's a most curious feeling abroad, and in some way they have got the story of this Veiled bloke mixed up with the peculiar weather. I mean, it's turned phenomenally hot. There's evidently a storm brewing."

"Which they put down to the influence of El Mokanna?"

"Oh, what nonsense!" Rima laughed.

But Humphreys nodded grimly, and:

"Exactly," he returned. "I'm told that a religious revival is overdue among the Moslems, and this business may fill the bill. You ought to know as well as I do, Greville, that superstition is never very far below the surface in even the most cultured Oriental. And these waves of fanaticism are really incalculable. It's a kind of mass hypnotism, and we know the creative power of thought."

I stared at the speaker with a new curiosity. He was revealing a side of his nature which I had not supposed to exist. Rima, too, had grown thoughtful.

"Someone would have to lead this movement," she suggested. "How could there be followers of a Veiled Prophet if there were no Veiled Prophet?"

"I'm told that up at El Azhar," Humphreys replied seriously, "they are proclaiming that there is a Veiled Prophet—or, rather, a Masked Prophet. He's supposed to be moving down through Persia."

"But it's simply preposterous!" Rima declared.

"It's likely to be infernally dangerous," he returned dryly. "However," brightening up, "I notice you're devoid of evening kit, Miss Barton, same as Greville. But as I'm attired with proper respectability, I know of no reason why we shouldn't dance out here. The band's just starting again."

Rima consented with a complete return of gaiety. And as her petite figure moved off beside that of the burly airman, I lighted a cigarette and looked around me. I was glad she had found a partner to distract her thoughts from the depression which lay upon all of us. And, anyway, I'm not much of a dancing man myself at the best of times.

Up under the leaves of the tall palms little coloured electric lamps were set, resembling fiery fruit. Japanese lanterns formed lighted festoons from trunk to trunk. In the moonlight, the water of the central fountain looked like an endless cascade of diamonds. The sky above was blue-black, and the stars larger and brighter than I remembered ever to have seen them.

Crunching of numberless feet I heard on the sanded paths; a constant murmur of voices; peals of laughter rising sometimes above it all—and now the music of a military band.

There were few fancy costumes, and those chiefly of the stock order. But there was a profusion of confetti—which seems to be regarded as indispensable on such occasions, but which I personally look upon as a definite irritant. To shed little disks of coloured paper from one's clothing, cigarette case, and tobacco pouch wherever one goes for a week after visiting a fête of this kind is a test of good-humour which the Southern races possibly survive better than I do.

I strolled round towards the left of the garden—that part farthest from the band and the dancers—intending to slip into the hotel for a drink before rejoining Rima and Humphreys.

Two or three confetti fiends had pot shots at me, but I did not find their attentions stimulating. In fact, I may as well confess that this more or less artificial gaiety, far from assisting me to banish those evil thoughts which claimed my mind, seemed to focus them more sharply.

Sir Denis and the chief, when I had left them, were still pacing up and down in the latter's room, arguing hotly; and poor Dr. Petrie was trying to keep the peace. That Sir Lionel had smuggled the Mokanna relics out of Persian territory he did not deny, nor was this by any means the first time he had indulged in similar acts of piracy. Nayland Smith was for lodging them in the vault of the Museum: Sir Lionel declined to allow them out of his possession.

He had a queer look in his deep-set eyes which I knew betokened mischief. Sir Denis knew too, and the knowledge taxed him almost to the limit of endurance, that the chief was keeping something back.

A sudden barrage of confetti made me change my mind about going in. Try how I would, I could not force myself into gala humour, and I walked all around the border of the garden, along a path which seemed to be deserted and only imperfectly lighted.

Practically everybody was on the other side, where the band was playing—either dancing or watching the dancing. The greater number of the guests were in the ballroom, however, preferring jazz and a polished floor to military brass and al fresco discomfort. I had lost my last cigarette under the confetti bombardment, and now, taking out my pipe, I stood still and began to fill it.

Dr. Fu Manchu!

Nayland Smith believed that agents of Dr. Fu Manchu had been responsible for the death of Van Berg and for the theft of the green box. This, I reflected, could mean only one thing.

Dr. Fu Manchu was responsible for the wave of fanaticism sweeping throughout the East, for that singular rumour that a prophet was reborn, which, if Humphreys and Petrie were to be believed, El Azhar already proclaimed.

My pipe filled, I put my hand in my pocket in search of matches, when—a tall, slender figure crossed the path a few yards ahead of me.

My hand came out of my pocket, I took the unlighted pipe from between my teeth, and stared . . . stared!

The woman, who wore a green, sheath-like dress and gold shoes, had a delicate indolence of carriage, wholly Oriental. About one bare ivory arm, extending from just below the elbow to the wrist, she wore a massive jade bangle in six or seven loops. A golden girdle not unlike a sword belt was about her waist, and a tight green turban on her head.

Her appearance, then, was sufficiently remarkable. But that which crowned the queerness of this slender, graceful figure, was the fact that she wore a small half-mask; and this half-mask was apparently of gold!

That the costume was designed to represent El Mokanna there could be no doubt. This in itself was extraordinary, but might have been explained by that queer wave of native opinion which was being talked about everywhere. It was such an illconsidered jest as would commend itself to a crazy member of the younger set.

But there was something else. . . .

Either I had become the victim of an optical delusion, traceable to events of the past few days, or the woman in the gold mask was Fu Manchu's daughter!

Chapter Seventeenth

THE MOSQUE OF MUAYYAD

Normally the air would have been growing chilly by now, but on the contrary a sort of oppressive heat seemed to be increasing. As the alluring figure crossed diagonally and disappeared into a side path, I glanced upward.

The change was startling.

Whereas but a few minutes before the stars had been notably bright, now not a star was visible. A dense black cloud hung overhead, and, as the band stopped, I noted a quality of stillness in the atmosphere such as often precedes a storm.

These things, however, I observed almost subconsciously. I was determined to overtake the wearer of the gold mask; I was determined to establish her identity. All those doubts and fears which I had with difficulty kept at bay seemed to swoop down upon me as if from the brooding sky.

An imperfect glimpse only I had had of long, tapering ivory fingers. But I believed there was only one woman in the world who possessed such hands—the woman known as Fah Lo Suee, the fascinating but witch-like daughter of the Chinese doctor.

Slipping my pipe back into my pocket, I stepped forward quickly, turning right, into a narrow path. Owing, I suppose, to the threatening skies, a general exodus from the garden had commenced, and since I was walking away from the hotel and not towards it, I met with no other guests.

I had hesitated only a few seconds before starting in pursuit. Nevertheless, there was no sign of my quarry. I pulled up, peering ahead. A sudden doubt crossed my mind.

Had Fah Lo Suee seen me? And did she hope to slip away unmasked? If so, she had made a false move.

For a glance had shown that, now, she could not possibly avoid me. She had turned left, from the narrow path, and was approaching the railings of the garden at a point where there was a gate.

I chanced to know that this gate was invariably locked . . . She had nearly reached it when I began to walk forward again, slowly and confidently. Her movements convinced me even in the semi-darkness that my conjecture had been correct. This was Fu Manchu's daughter, beyond any shadow of doubt.

I was not twelve paces behind her when she came to the gate. She stooped, and, although I heard no sound—the gate swung open! I saw her for a moment, a tall, slim silhouette against lights from the other side of the street; then the gate clanged to behind her.

Without even glancing over her shoulder, although I knew she must have heard my approach, she turned left in the direction of Sharia Kamel, still at that leisurely, languid pace.

I ran to the gate—it was locked!

This discovery astounded me.

By what means obtained, I could not even guess, but clearly this strange woman possessed a key of the disused entrance. I contemplated scaling the railings, but realised the difficulty of the operation. There was only one thing for it.

I turned and ran back to the hotel, hoping I might meet no one to whom I should feel called upon to give an explanation of my eccentric conduct.

There came an ominous rumbling, and I saw with annoyance that crowds were pouring in at the entrance. However, I made a rush for it; earned some stinging comments on the part of guests into whom I bumped—dashed across the lobby and out onto the terrace.

A line of cars and taxicabs was drawn up outside. This I had time to note as I went flying down the steps. I turned sharply right.

I was only just in time. A wonderfully slender ankle, an arched instep, and a high-heeled golden shoe provided the only clue.

The woman had just entered a car stationed, not outside the terrace of the hotel, but over by the arcade opposite. At the very moment that I heard the clang of its closing door, the car moved off, going in the direction of Esbekiyeh Gardens.

I ran to the end of the rank of waiting cabs and cars, and, grabbing an Egyptian driver who brought up the tail of the procession:

"Look!" I said rapidly in Arabic, and pulled him about,

"where I am pointing!"

The hour being no later than ten o'clock, there was still a fair amount of traffic about. But I could see the car, a long, low two-seater, proceeding at no great speed, in the direction of the Continental.

"You see that yellow car? The one that has just reached the corner!"

The man stared as I pointed; and then:

"Yes, I see it."

"Then follow it! Double fare if you keep it in sight!"

That settled the matter. He sprang to the wheel in a flash. And whilst I half knelt on the seat, looking back, he turned his cab with reckless disregard of oncoming traffic and started off at racing speed. . . .

Other cars were in the way, now, but I could still discern that in which the woman had driven off. I saw it turn left. I bent forward, shouting to the driver.

"They have turned left—did you see?"

"Yes."

An English policeman shouted angrily as my driver swerved to avoid a pedestrian and drove madly on. But the magic of a double fare infected him like a virus. He took the corner by the Gardens, when we reached it, at breakneck speed, and foreseeing disaster if this continued:

"Take it easy!" I shouted, leaning forward. "I can see them ahead. I don't want to catch them—only to keep them in sight."

The man nodded, and our progress became less furious. The atmosphere remained oppressive, but a few stars began to creep out overhead, and I saw ragged borders of the black cloud moving away over the Mokattam Hills. Rumbling of thunder grew more distant.

I could see the car ahead very clearly, now, for indeed we were quite near to it. And I found time to wonder where it could possibly be going.

We were leaving the European city behind and heading for the Oriental. In fact, it began to dawn upon me that Fah Lo Suee was making for the Muski—that artery of the bazaar streets, hives of industry during the day, but desolate as a city of the dead at night.

I was right.

The last trace of native night life left behind us, I saw the yellow car, proceeding in leisurely fashion, head straight into that deserted thoroughfare. My driver followed. We passed a crossways but still carried on, presently to turn right. I saw a mosque ahead, but my brain was so excited that at the moment I failed to identify it. My knowledge of native Cairo is not extensive at the best.

We left the mosque behind, the narrow street being far from straight and I in a constant fever lest we should lose sight of the yellow car. Then, I saw it—just passing another, larger mosque.

"Where are we?" I asked.

"Sukkariya," he replied, slowing down still more and negotiating a right-angle turn.

Empty shops and unlighted houses were all about us. For some time now we had met not a single pedestrian. It was utterly mystifying. Where could the woman possibly be heading for?

"Where does this lead to?"

"Mosque of Muayyad-Bab ez Zuwela. . . ."

Fah Lo Suee, of course, must have known now that she was pursued, but this I considered to be unavoidable, since in that maze of narrow streets that only a native driver could have negotiated, to lose sight of her for a moment would have meant failure.

Right again went the long, low French car.

"Don't know the name," my driver announced nonchalantly.

We turned into the narrowest street we had yet endeavoured to negotiate.

"Pull up!" I ordered sharply.

The place was laden with those indescribable smells which belong to the markets of the East, but nowhere could I see a light, or any evidence of human occupation. Narrow alleys intersected the street—mere black caverns.

Ahead, I saw the yellow car moving away again. But, for the second time that night, I had a glimpse of an arched instep, of a golden shoe.

Fah Lo Suee had alighted from the car, which evidently someone else was driving, and had walked into a narrow alley not twenty yards along.

I jumped out.

"Stay here," I ordered. "Don't move, whatever happens, until I come back."

I set out at the double, pulling up when I gained the entrance to the alley, and peering into its utter blackness. I heard the distant rumbling of thunder. It died away into oppressive silence.

No sound of footsteps reached me, and there was no glimmer of light ahead.

CHAPTER EIGHTEENTH

Dr. FU MANCHU

I BEGAN to grope my way along a dark, unevenly paved passage, but I had taken no more than two steps forward when the folly of my behaviour crashed upon me like a revelation. If the woman who had disappeared somewhere ahead were indeed she whom we had known as Madame Ingomar, what a fool I was to thrust myself into this rat trap!

For a man to experience such terrors in regard to a woman may seem feeble; but from bitter experience I knew something of the weapons at command of Fah Lo Suee. That I might be mistaken about the identity of the gold mask was remotely possible, but no more than remotely so.

In a few fleeting seconds I reviewed the queer episode from the moment when I had seen that green-robed figure in Shepheard's garden—and I realised with bleak certainty that her behaviour had been directly to one end and to one end only. A trap had been baited . . . and I had fallen into it like the veriest fool.

I pulled up sharply, stretching out my hands to learn if any obstruction lay ahead. In the heat of the chase I had thrown precaution aside. I realised now, too late, that I was unarmed, alone; no one but the driver of the taxicab had the slightest idea where I had gone.

This same counsel came in the same moment that panic threatened. What else I could have done if the woman were not to escape unmasked was not clear. But to have sent a message to Smith, to Petrie, to the chief, before setting out, seemed, now, a more reasonable course.

And as the things which I had not done presented themselves starkly before me, a wave of that abominable perfume of mimosa which to the end of my days I must associate with the death of poor Van Berg was swept into my face. . . .

It stifled me, engulfed me, struck me dumb. I remember that I tried to cry out, recognising in this awful moment that my only chance was to attract the attention of the Egyptian driver.

But never a sound came, only an increase of darkness, a deadly sickness, and a maddening knowledge that among fools in the land of Egypt I might claim high rank. . . .

My next impression was of acute pain in the left ankle. My head was swimming as though I had recently indulged in a wild debauch, and my eyelids were so heavy that I seemed to experience physical difficulty in raising them.

I did raise them, however, and (a curious circumstance, later to be explained) my brain immediately began to function from the very moment that I had smelled that ghastly perfume.

My first thought, now, overlapped my last before unconsciousness had claimed me. I thought that I lay in that nameless alley somewhere behind the Mosque of Muayyad and that in falling I had twisted my ankle. I expected darkness, but I saw light.

Raising my hands, I rubbed my aching eyes, staring about me dazedly. I was furiously thirsty, but in absolute possession of my senses. I looked down at my ankle, which pained me intensely, and made a discovery so remarkable that it engaged my attention even in the surroundings amid which I found myself.

I was lying on a divan; and about each of my ankles was fastened a single loop of dull, gray-yellow line resembling catgut and no thicker than a violin string. Amazing to relate—there were apparently *no knots!*

One of these loops was drawn so tightly as to be painful, and a single strand, some twelve inches long, connected the left ankle with the right. I struggled to my feet—and was surprised, since I knew I had been drugged, to find that my muscular reactions were perfectly normal.

Evidently my common sense was subnormal (or I am slow to profit by experience); for, resting one foot firmly on the floor, I kicked forward with the other, fully anticipating that this fragile link would snap.

The result must have been comic; but I had no audience. I kicked myself backward with astonishing velocity, falling among the cushions of the divan, from which I had not moved away!

Fortunately, the tendon escaped serious injury; but this

first experiment was also the last. I had, tardily, recognised my bonds to be of that mysterious substance which had figured in our Ispahan adventure. I should not have been more helpless, save that I could shuffle about the room, if iron fetters had confined me.

I lay where I had fallen, gazing about. And I knew, as I had known in the very moment of opening my heavy-lidded eyes, that this was an amazing room in which I found myself.

It was a long, low salon, obviously that of an old Egyptian house, as the woodwork, a large *mushrabiyeh* window, and the tiling upon part of the wall clearly indicated. There were a few good rugs upon the floor, and light was furnished by several lamps, shaded incongruously in unmistakable Chinese fashion, which swung from the wooden ceiling.

The furniture was scanty, some of it Arab in character but some of it of Chinese lacquer. Right and left of the recessed window (which, wrongly, as after events showed, I assumed to overlook a street adjoining that alleyway behind the mosque) were deep bookcases laden with volumes. These, to judge from their unfamiliar binding, might have been rare works.

There were a number of glass cases in the room, containing most singular objects. In one was what looked like a living human head, that of a woman. But, as I focused my horrified gaze upon it, I saw that it was an unusually perfect mummy head. In another, which was obviously heated, I saw growing foliage and, watching it more closely, realised that a number of small, vividly green snakes moved among the leaves. A human skeleton, perfect, I thought, even to the small bones, stood in a rack in a gap between the bookcases. The window recess was glazed to form a sort of small conservatory, and through the glass, dimly, I could see that bloated flesh-coloured orchids were growing.

I stood up again, testing my injured ankle. It pained intensely, but the tendon had survived the jerk. I began to shuffle forward in the direction of a large, plain wooden table, resembling a monkish refectory table, before which was set one of those polished, inlaid chairs which are produced in the bazaars of Damascus.

There were some of those strange-looking volumes upon this table, as well as a number of scientific instruments, test tubes, and chemical paraphernalia. As I stood up, I saw that the table was covered with a sheet of glass.

Changing my position, other glass cases came into view; they contained rows of chemical bottles and apparatus. The place was more than half a laboratory. And I noticed, looking behind me, that there was a working bench in one corner fitted with electrical devices, although of a character quite unfamiliar.

The truth came subconsciously ahead of its positive confirmation. There were three doors to the salon, perfectly plain white teak doors. And in the very moment that I recognised a peculiar fact—viz: that they possessed neither bolts, handles, nor keyholes—one of these doors opened and slid noiselessly to the left.

I found myself alone with Dr. Fu Manchu.

Chapter Nineteenth

FORMULA ELIXIR VITAE

HE WORE a green robe upon which was embroidered a white peacock, and on the dome of his wonderful skull a little cap was perched—a black cap surmounted by a coral ball. The door slid silently to behind him, and he stood watching me.

Once and once only, hitherto, had I seen the mandarin Fu Manchu. He had impressed me, then, as one of the most gigantic forces ever embodied in a human form: but amazing—and amazingly horrible—he seemed, now, as he stood looking at me, to have shaken off part of the burden of years under which he had stooped on that unforgettable night in London.

He carried no stick; his long, bony hands were folded upon his breast. He was drawn up to his full, gaunt height, which I judged to be over six feet. His eyes, which were green as the eyes of a leopard, fixed me with a glance so piercing that it extended my powers to the full to sustain it.

There are few really first-class brains in the world to-day, but no man with any experience of humanity, looking into those long brilliant eyes could have doubted that he stood in the presence of a super-mind.

I cannot better describe my feelings than by saying I felt myself to be absorbed; mentally and spiritually sucked empty by that awful gaze.

Even as this ghastly sensation, which I find myself unable properly to convey in words, overwhelmed me, a queer sort of film obscured the emerald eyes of Dr. Fu Manchu, and I experienced immediate relief.

I remembered in that fleeting moment a discussion between Nayland Smith and Dr. Petrie touching this phenomenal quality of Fu Manchu's eyes, which the doctor frankly admitted he had never met with before, and for which he could not account.

Walking slowly, but with a cat-like dignity, Fu Manchu crossed to the long table, seating himself in the chair. His slippered feet made no sound. The room was silent as a tomb.

The scene had that quality which belongs to dreams. No plan presented itself, and I found myself tongue-tied.

Fu Manchu pressed the button of a shaded lamp upon a silver pedestal, and raising a small, pear-shaped vessel from a rack, examined its contents against the light. It contained some colourless fluid.

His hands were singular: long, bony, flexible fingers, in which, caricatured, as it were, I saw the unforgettable ivory fingers of Fah Lo Suee.

He replaced the vessel in the rack and turned to a page of one of those large volumes which lay open beside him. Seemingly considering it, he began to speak absent-mindedly.

His voice was as I remembered it, except that I thought it had acquired greater power: guttural but perfectly clear. He gave to every syllable its true value. Indeed, he spoke the purest English of any man I have ever heard.

"Mr Greville," he said, "I trust that any slight headache which you may have experienced on awakening has now disappeared."

I stood watching him where he sat, but attempted no reply.

"Formerly," he continued, "I employed sometimes a preparation of Indian hemp and at other times various derivatives of opium with greater or less success. An anaesthetic prepared from the common puffball for many years engaged my attention also; but I have now improved upon these."

He extended one long, green-draped arm, picking up and dropping with a faint rattling sound a number of brownish objects which looked like dried peas and which lay in a little tray upon the table.

"Seeds of a species of *Mimosa pudica*, found in Brazil and in parts of Asia," he continued, never once glancing in my direction. "I should like you to inform our mutual friend Dr. Petrie, whom I esteem, that Western science is on the wrong track, and that the perfect anaesthetic is found in *Mimosa pudica*. You succumbed to it to-night, Mr. Greville, and you have been unconscious for nearly half an hour. But if you were a medical man you would admit that the effects are negligible. The mental hiatus, also, is bridged immediately. Your first conscious thought was liked with your last. Am I right?"

"You are right," I replied, looking down at my feet and wondering if a sudden spring would enable me to get my hands around that lean throat.

"Your reflexes are normal," the slow, guttural voice continued. "The visceral muscles are unimpaired; there is no cardiac reaction. You are even now contemplating an assault upon me." He turned to another page of the large volume. "But consider the facts, Mr. Greville. You are still young enough to be impetuous: permit me to warn you. That slender thread which confines your ankles, and which I understand Sir Lionel Barton mistook for silkworm gut, is actually prepared from the flocculent secretion of *Theridion*—a well known but interesting spider. . . .

"You seem to be surprised. The secret of that preparation would make the fortune of any man of commerce into whose hands it might fall. I may add that it will *not* fall into the hands of any man of commerce. But I am wasting time."

He stood up.

"I have studied you closely, Mr. Greville, in an endeavour to discern those qualities which have attracted my daughter."

I started violently and clenched my fists.

"I find them to be typically British," the calm voice continued, "and rather passive than active. You will never be a Nayland Smith, and you lack that odd detachment which might have made our mutual friend, Dr. Petrie, the most prominent physician of the Western world had he not preferred domesticity with an ex-servant of mine."

Inch by inch I was edging nearer to him as he spoke.

"You cannot have failed to note an improvement in my physical condition since last we met, Mr. Greville. This is due to the success of an inquiry which has engaged me for no less a period than twenty-five years."

He moved slowly in the direction of the *mushrabiyeh* window, and, frustrated, I pulled up.

"These orchids," he continued, extending one bony hand to the glass case which occupied the recess, "I discovered nearly thirty years ago in certain forests of Burma. They occur at extremely rare intervals—traditionally only once in a century, but actually with rather greater frequency. From these orchids I have at last obtained, after twenty-five years of study, an essential oil which completes a particular formula—"

he suddenly turned and faced me—"the formula *elixir vitae* for which the old philosophers sought in vain."

Transfixed by the glare of those green eyes, I seemed to become rigid: their power was awful. I judged Fu Manchu to be little short of seventy, but as he stood before me now I appreciated in the light of his explanation, more vividly than I had understood at the moment of his entrance, how strangely he had cheated time.

I was fascinated but appalled—fascinated by the genius of the Chinese doctor; appalled by the fact that he employed that genius, not for good, but for evil.

"You are a very small cog, Mr. Greville," he continued, "in that wheel which is turning against me. If I could use you, I would do so. But you have nothing to offer me. I bear you no ill-will, however, and I have given my word to my daughter—whom you know, I believe, as Fah Lo Suee—that no harm shall come to you at my hands. She is a woman of light loves, but you have pleased her—and I have given my word."

He spoke the last sentence as one who says, "I have set my royal seal to this." And indeed he spoke so with justice. For even Sir Denis, his most implacable enemy, had admitted that the word of Dr. Fu Manchu was inviolable. Volition left me. Facing this superhuman enemy of all that my traditions stood for, I found my mental attitude to be that of a pupil at the feet of a master!

"My daughter's aid was purchased to-night at the price of this promise," Dr. Fu Manchu added, his voice displaying no emotion whatever. "I had thought that I could use you to achieve a certain end. But consideration of the character of Sir Lionel Barton has persuaded me that I cannot."

"What do you mean?" I asked, my voice sounding unfamiliar.

"I mean, Mr. Greville, that you love him. But you love a shell, an accomplishment, a genius if you like; but a phantom, a hollow thing, having no real existence. Sir Lionel Barton would sacrifice you tomorrow—to-night—to his own ambitions. Do you doubt this?"

It was a wicked thought, and I clenched my teeth. But God knows I recognised its truth! I knew well enough, and Rima knew too, that the chief would have sacrificed nearly everything and almost everybody to that mania for research, for achievements greater than his contemporaries' which were his gods. That we loved him in spite of this was, perhaps, evidence of our folly or of something fine in Sir Lionel's character, something which outweighed the juggernaut of his egoism.

"For this reason"—Dr. Fu Manchu's voice rose to a soft, sibilant note—"I have been compelled slightly to modify my original plans."

Returning to his chair, he seated himself. I was very near to him now, but:

"Sit down!" he said.

And I sat down, on an Arab stool which stood at one end of the table and which he indicated with a bony extended forefinger.

Since that all but incredible interview I have tried to analyse my behaviour; I have tried to blame myself, arguing that there must have been some course other than the passive one which I adopted. Many have thought the same, but to them all I have replied: "You have never met Dr. Fu Manchu."

He rested his long hands before him upon the glass covering of the table. And, no longer looking in my direction:

"Sir Lionel Barton has served me for the first time in his life," he said, his voice still touching that high, sibilant note. "By discovering and then destroying the tomb of El Mokanna he awakened a fanaticism long dormant which, properly guided, should sweep farther than that once controlled by the Mahdi. And the Mahdi, Mr. Greville, came nearer to achieving his ends than British historians care to admit. Your Lord Kitchener—whom I knew and esteemed—had no easy task."

He suddenly turned to me, and I lost personality again, swamped in the lake of two green eyes.

"The Mokanna may be greater than the Mahdi," he added. "But his pretensions must survive severe tests. He must satisfy the learned Moslems of the Great Mosque at Damascus, and later pass the ordeal of Mecca. This he can do who possesses the authentic relics. . . ."

Vaguely, I groped for the purpose behind all this. . . .

"I would not trust Sir Lionel Barton to respond even to that demand about to be made upon him, if Dr. Petrie and Sir Denis Nayland Smith were not there. Since they are—I am satisfied."

He struck a little gong suspended on a frame beside his chair. One of the three doors—that almost immediately behind him, opened; and two of those dwarfish and muscular Negroes entered, instantly carrying my mind back to the horrors of Ispahan.

They wore native Egyptian costume, but that they were West Africans was a fact quite unmistakable.

"New allies of mine, Mr. Greville," said the awful Chinaman, "although old in sympathy. They have useful qualities which attract me."

He made a slight signal with his left hand, and in an instant I found myself pinioned. He spoke gutturally in an unfamiliar tongue—no doubt that of the Negroes. And I was led forward until I stood almost at his elbow.

"This document is precious," he explained, "and I feared that you might attempt some violent action. Can you read from where you stand?"

Yes, I could read—and reading, I was astounded. . . .

I saw a note in my own handwriting, addressed to Rima; phrased as I would have phrased it, and directing her to slip away and to join me in a car which would be waiting outside Shepheard's! Particularly, the note impressed upon her that she must not confide in anyone, but must come *alone*. . . .

I swallowed audibly; and then:

"It's a marvellous forgery," I said.

"Forgery!" Dr. Fu Manchu echoed the word. "My dear Mr. Greville, you wrote it with your own hand during that period of thirty minutes' oblivion to which I have drawn your attention. My new anaesthetic"—he drooped some of the dried seeds through his long fingers—"has properties approaching perfection."

My arms held in a muscular grip:

"She will never be fool enough to come," I exclaimed.

"Not to join *you?*"

"She will run back when she finds I am not there."

"But you will be there."

"What?"

"When one small obstacle has been removed—that which the obstinacy of Sir Lionel Barton has set before me—your behaviour, Mr. Greville, will excite Dr. Petrie's professional interest. I wish it were in my power to give him some small demonstration of the potentialities, which I have not yet fully explored, of another excellent formula."

A sudden dread clutched me, and I found cold perspiration breaking out all over my body.

"What are you going to do with me?" I asked—"and what are you going to do with Rima?"

"For yourself, you have my word . . ." the green eyes which had been averted turned to me again; "and I have never warred with women. I am going to recover the relics of the Masked Prophet and return them to those to whom they properly belong. You are going to assist me."

I clenched my teeth very tightly.

Dr. Fu Manchu stood up and moved with his lithe, dignified gait, to one of the glass cases. He opened it. Speaking over his shoulder:

"If you care to swallow a cachet," he said, "this would suffice. The liquid preparation"—he held up a small flask containing a colourless fluid—"is not so rapid. Failing your compliance, however, an injection is indicated."

He stood with his back to me. The grip of the two dwarfish Negroes held me as in iron bands. And I found myself studying the design of the white peacock which was carried from the breast of the doctor's robe, over the shoulders and round to the back. I watched his lean yellow neck, and the scanty, neutral-coloured hair beneath his skullcap; the square, angular shoulders, the gaunt, cat-like poise of the tall figure. He seemed to be awaiting a reply.

"I have no choice," I said in a dry voice.

Dr. Fu Manchu replaced the flask which he held in one bony hand and selected a small wooden box. He turned, moving back towards the table.

"The subcutaneous is best," he murmured, "being most rapid in its effect. But the average patient prefers the tablets. . . ."

He opened a leather case which lay upon the table and extracted a hypodermic syringe. Unemotionally he dipped the point into a small vessel and wiped it with a piece of lint. Then, charging it from a tiny tube which he took from the box, he stepped towards me.

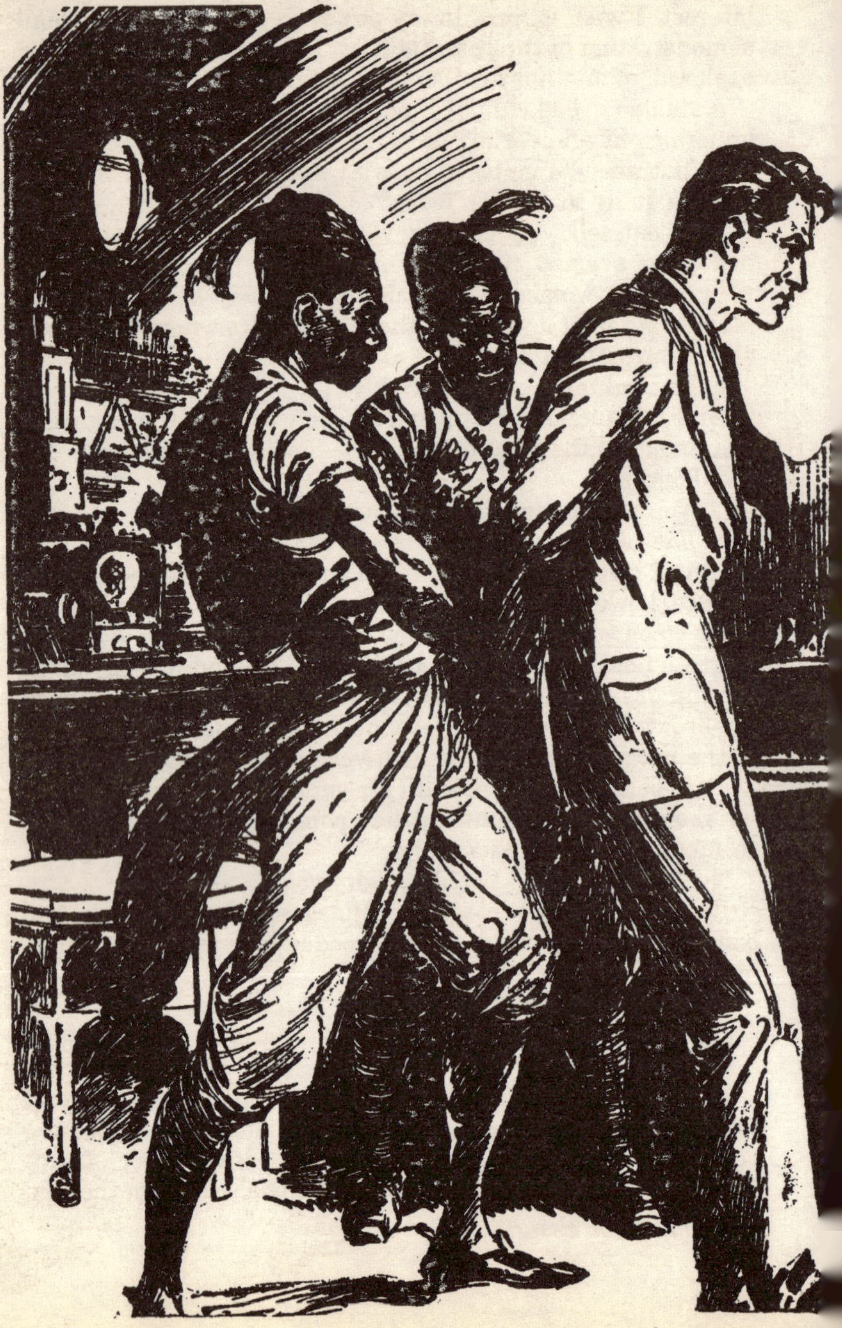

In an instant I found myself pinioned. . . . "This document is precious," he explained. "Can you read from where you stand?"

Chapter Twentieth

THE MASTER MIND

I REMEMBER saying, as that master physician and devil incarnate thrust back the sleeve of my tweed jacket and unfastened my cuff link:

"Since I have your word, Dr. Fu Manchu, you are loosing a dangerous witness on the world!"

The needle point pierced my flesh.

"On the contrary," the guttural voice replied without emotion, "one of your own English travellers, Dr. McGovern, has testified to the fact that words and actions under the influence of this drug—which he mentions in its primitive form as *kaapi*—leave no memory behind. I have gone further than the natives who originally discovered it. I can so prescribe as to induce fourteen variations of amnesia, graded from apparently full consciousness to complete anaesthesia. The patient remains under my control in all these phases. Anamnesis, or recovery of the forgotten acts, may be brought about by means of a simple antidote. . . . ."

He extracted the needle point.

"This preparation"—he laid the syringe on the glass-topped table and indicated the working bench—"might interest Sir Denis."

I experienced a sudden unfamiliar glow throughout my entire body. A burning thirst was miraculously assuaged. Whereas, a moment before, my skin had been damp with perspiration, now it seemed to be supernormally dry. I was exhilarated. I saw everything with an added clarity of vision. . . .

Some black, indefinable doubt which had been astride me like an Old Man of the Sea dropped away. I wondered what I had been worrying about. I could perceive nothing wrong with the world nor with my own condition and place in it.

Dr. Fu Manchu took up a dull white flask, removed the stopper, and dipped a slender rod into the contents.

"This, Mr. Greville"—holding up a bar of metal—"is Sheffield steel."

He dropped upon the bar some of the liquid adhering to the rod.

"Now—observe..."

In obedience to a slight signal, the Negroes released my arms; one with surgical scissors, cut the fastenings from my ankles....

But I was conscious of no desire to attack the speaker. On the contrary, I recognised with a sudden overwhelming conviction the fact that my own happiness and the happiness of everyone I knew rested in his hands! He was all-powerful, beneficent, a superman to be respected and obeyed.

I watched him, entranced. Holding the steel bar in his bony fingers, he snapped it as though it had been a stick of chocolate!

"Had I been a burglar, Mr. Greville, this small invention would have been of value to me. You see, even *I* have my toys..."

He turned and walked slowly from the room with that dignified, yet cat-like gait which I knew. As lightning flickers in a summer sky, the idea crossed my mind that once I had feared, had loathed this Chinese physician. It disappeared, leaving me in a state of mental rapture such as I had never known.

I rejoiced that I was to serve Fu Manchu. Of the details of my mission I knew nothing, but that it aimed at the ultimate good of us all, I did not doubt. We were in charge of an omnipotent being; it was not for us to question his wisdom.

Led by one of the Slave Coast Negroes whose broad shoulders and slightly bandy legs lent him a distinct resemblance to an ape dressed in human clothing, I found myself passing rapidly along a dimly lighted passage. I was delighted at my discovery that these active little men resembled apes. It seemed to me, in that strange mood, one worthy of reporting to the chief—an addition to scientific knowledge which should not be lost.

I understood, and it was a deep-seated faith, why Dr. Fu Manchu had willing servants all over the world. Hitherto I had merely existed: this was *life*. I laughed aloud, and snapped my fingers in time to my swift footsteps.

Down a flight of stairs I was led. A silk-shaded lamp on the landing afforded the only light, but I was aware of a surety of foot which would have enabled me to negotiate the most perilous mountain path with all the certainty of a wild goat. An iron-barred and studded door was opened, and I looked out into a square courtyard.

No cloud obscured the sky, now, which seemed to be filled with a million diamonds.

A landaulet stood before the steps. Respecting its driver, I could be sure only of one thing in that semi-darkness: he wore a *tarbush* and was therefore presumably an Egyptian.

The Negro opened the door for me, and I stepped in. One of the headlights was switched on momentarily, and I saw a heavy gate being opened. Then, the driver had swung out into a narrow street. It was not that behind the Mosque of Muayyad....

Through a number of such narrow streets, with never a light anywhere, we went at fair speed. I found myself constantly chuckling at the surprise which I had in store for Rima and the chief. Its exact character was not apparent to me, but I was perfectly satisfied that when the time came all would be well.

A shock of doubt, which passed quickly, came, when leaving the last of these streets we bumped up an ill-made road, turned sharply, and at greatly accelerated speed set off along a straight tree-bordered avenue. Beyond question this was the road from Gizeh to Cairo!

Mental confusion resembling physical pain claimed me in that moment. My drugged brain, of course, was trying to force realities upon me. The spasm passed. There was some good reason for this circuitous route....

And now we were nearing Cairo. The moment of the great revelation was fast approaching.

I took very little heed of passing automobiles or pedestrians, nor did I note by what route the driver made his way through to the Sharia Kamel. But almost exactly at the spot where Fah Lo Suee had entered the yellow car, that is, nearly opposite Shepheard's, we pulled up.

"Stand here, please, in the light," said the driver, springing out and opening the door for me, "where she can see you when I find her."

"I know," I replied eagerly; "I understand perfectly."

The man nodded and ran across to the terrace steps. The number of waiting cars was not so great as at the time of my departure, but it was obvious that revelry still proceeded.

So unusually warm was the night that fully half a dozen tables on the terrace were occupied by dancers who had evidently come there to seek comparative quiet. Dimly I could hear strains of music. One thing I knew urgently I must avoid above all others—I must not be seen by anyone who knew me.

It was vitally important that Rima alone should know what was afoot.

I saw the driver go up the steps. He looked about him swiftly and then went into the hotel. He was carrying my letter. I became the victim of a devouring impatience.

Rima was not well known at Shepheard's and perhaps it might prove difficult to find her, unless she chanced to be in her room. All would be lost if Sir Lionel got to know, or even if Sir Denis or Dr. Petrie should suspect what was afoot.

My impatience grew by leaps and bounds.

A group of four people came out onto the terrace, walking down the strip of carpet towards the steps. I shrank back apprehensively. One was a big, heavily built man, and for a moment I mistook him for the chief, until I saw that he wore evening kit. A car drew up, and the party drove away.

Suspense became all but intolerable. Evidently some difficulty was being experienced in finding Rima, and the moments were precious—each one adding to the chances of detection. I found myself regarding failure of the plot with absolute horror!

Such was the genius of Dr. Fu Manchu. . . .

The doors revolved again. The Egyptian driver came out, walked to the head of the steps, and signaled to me.

I stepped forward into the roadway where I must be clearly visible from the terrace. Rima came out, dressed as I had seen her last, hatless and flushed with excitement. She held an open letter in her hand—mine. And she was staring eagerly across the street in quest of me.

None of the people seated on the terrace took any notice of these manoeuvres; indeed, as I realised joyfully, there was nothing extraordinary in a man calling to pick up a girl from a dance.

Rima saw me, raced down the steps, and ran across.

I noticed, with a quick pang of sorrow—which, however, instantly gave place to that thrilling exaltation which was the keynote of my mood—that she was, or recently had been, very frightened. She threw her arms around me with a little gasping cry and looked into my eyes.

"Shan, Shan darling! You have terrified us all! Wherever have you been? Whose car is this?"

"It is *his* car, dearest," I replied. "Quick! get in. It's important that nobody should see us."

"*His* car?"

As I half lifted her in onto the cushions she grasped my arm and looked up with startled eyes at me. The chauffeur already was back at the wheel.

"Shan dear, whatever do you mean? Sir Denis got in touch with police headquarters half an hour ago. And Uncle is simply raving. Dr. Petrie has asked everybody he knows in the hotel if you were seen to leave."

I held her close as the car moved off, but she began to tremble violently.

"Shan!—my dear, my dear!" she cried, and pulled my head down, trying to search my eyes in that semidarkness. "For God's sake, where are we going?"

"We are going to *him*," I replied.

"My God! He's mad!"

The words were barely audible—a mere whisper. Thrusting both hands against my breast, Rima tried to push me away—to free herself. Already we had passed the Continental.

"You don't understand, darling. . . ."

"God help me, Shan, I *do!* Make him stop! Make him stop, I tell you!"

An English policeman was on duty at the corner, and as we raced past him, I saw him raise his arm. Rima, wrenching free, leaned from the window, and:

"Help!" she screamed.

But I drew her forcibly back, putting my hand over her mouth before she could utter another word.

"My darling!" I said, holding her very close. "You will spoil everything! You will spoil everything!"

She relaxed and lay very still in my arms. . . .

The way was practically deserted, now, and we passed few lighted patches, but I could see her big, upcast eyes fixed upon me with an intensity of expression which puzzled me. I could see, too, that she had grown very pale. She did not speak again, but continued to watch me in that strange manner.

She seemed to be communicating some silent message and to be changing my mood, cooling that feverish exaltation.

What had she asked? Where we were going? Yes, that was it. . . . And where *were* we going? Mental turmoil like a physical pain claimed me again as I tried to grapple with that question. . . .

CHAPTER TWENTY-FIRST

"HE WILL BE CROWNED IN DAMASCUS"

I HAVE related what really happened on that night in Cairo in the proper order of those events—but in their order as I knew it later. As a matter of fact, quite a long interval elapsed, as will presently appear, before I was able to recall anything whatever from the time when I set out in pursuit of Madame Ingomar to that when I acted as a decoy in the abduction of Rima.

A master player had used me as a pawn. The very seat of reason had been shaken by a drug not to be discovered in any pharmacopœia. These events and those which immediately followed I was to recover later. I must return now to the conclusion of a phase in my life which I still consider the most remarkable any man has known. . . .

★   ★   ★

"Shan dear, I know you are very sleepy, but it's getting cold, and very late. . . ."

I stirred dreamily, opening my eyes. I was pillowed on a warm ivory shoulder, a bare arm encircled my neck, and the silvery voice which had awakened me was tenderly caressing. I hugged my fragrant pillow and felt no desire to move.

A long jade earring touched me coldly. Soothing fingers stroked my hair, and the silvery voice whispered:

"Truly, Shan, you must wake up! I'm sorry, dear, but you must."

Reluctantly I raised my head, looking into brilliant green eyes regarding me under half lowered lashes. Their glance was a caress as soothing as that of the slender fingers.

Fah Lo Suee, I mused languidly, conscious of nothing but a dreamy contentment, and thinking what perfect lips she had, when, smiling, she bent and whispered in my ear:

"Love dreams are so bitter-sweet because we know we are dreaming."

But yet I was reluctant to move. I could see a long reach of the Nile, touched to magic by the moon. *Dahabeahs* were moored against the left bank, their slender, graceful masts forming harmonious lines against a background of grouped palms and straggling white buildings. Of course! I was in Fah Lo Suee's car; her arms were about me. I turned my head, looking over a silken shoulder to where a bridge spanned the Nile. It must be very late, I mused, later than I had supposed; the Kasr el-Nil bridge was deserted.

Memory began to return—or what I thought then to be memory—from the moment when I determined to follow Fah Lo Suee from the garden of Shepheard's. . . . I had been uncertain of her identity until she had removed the gold mask. . . .

"I think someone has been watching, Shan, and I am positively shivering. I am going to drive you back now."

I sat bolt upright, one hand raised to my head, as Fah Lo Suee bent slightly and started the car. With never another glance aside, she drove on, presently to turn, right, into the maze of Cairo's empty streets.

Furtively I watched the clear profile of the driver. It was beautiful, and strangely like that of the mystery queen, Nefertiti, whose cold loveliness has caused so much controversy. The small chin was delicately but firmly modelled, the straight nose from a strictly classical standpoint was perhaps too large, but very characteristic. I exulted in the knowledge that this brilliant and alluring woman had selected me— Shan Greville—from the rest of mankind.

Cairo's streets were depopulated as the streets of sleeping Thebes; and at the corner of Sharia el-Maghriabi, which I recognised with a start of awakening, Fah Lo Suee pulled up.

I did not know then, but I knew later, the real character of a kind of wave of remorse which swept over me. It was, of course, my true self fighting against this strange abandonment, partly drug-induced and partly hypnotic, which held me voluptuously. . . .

Rima! How could I ever face Rima? What explanation could I offer which she would accept? And Sir Denis! Oddly enough, it was his grim brown face which appeared most vividly before me in that odd moment of clarity: the chief and Dr. Petrie were mere shadows in a mist background. . . .

I had held a link of a deathly conspiracy in my hand. I could have snapped it; my duty was plain. Instead, I had passed the hours in dalliance with Fah Lo Suee! I clutched my head, trying to recall where we had gone. I could not believe that I had spent the night like some callow undergraduate on a petting party; but:

"You must walk from here, Shan," said Fah Lo Suee. "I dare not drive you any farther."

She linked her arms about me and crushed her lips against mine, her long, narrow eyes closed. And in the complete surrender of that parting embrace I experienced a mad triumph which no other conquest could have given me. Rima, Nayland Smith, the chief—all were forgotten!

"Good-night, dear! And remember me until we meet again. . . ."

I stood on the pavement struggling with the most conflicting emotions, as the car swept around in the empty Sharia el-Maghrabi and disappeared in the direction of Ismailia. The perfume of that parting kiss still lingered on my lips. As a man marooned, condemned, forgotten, I stood there—I cannot say for how long. But at last I turned and stared about me.

Cairo was asleep. What did it matter? I laughed aloud— and began to walk back to Shepheard's.

I met never a soul in the Sharia Kamel, until just before reaching the terrace. At this point, where there are a number of shops lying back from the street, a hideous object, a belated beggar man, suddenly emerged from the shadows.

Ragged, bearded, indescribably filthy, he hobbled upon a crude crutch. As he ranged up beside me, muttering unintelligibly, I thrust my hand into my trouser pocket, found some small coins, and dropped them in his extended palm.

"He will be crowned in Damascus," said the mendicant, and hobbled away. . . .

I despair of making my meaning clear; but those words formed the termination of what I can only term the *second phase* of my dream-like experience. Oddly enough, they remained with me: I mean, when all else was forgotten, I remembered the words, "He will be crowned in Damascus."

For, as they were spoken, and as I listened to the *tap-tap-*

tap of the mendicant's crutch receding in the distance, a complete mental black-out came for a third time in that one night!

All that I have related of my experience with Fah Lo Suee, as well as that which went before, I was to recall later, as I shall presently explain; but, so far as I knew at the time, in effect what occurred was this:

I found myself standing, swaying rather dizzily, and with a splitting headache, looking towards the steps of Shepheard's with the words buzzing in my ears: "He will be crowned in Damascus."

The sound of the crutch had died away, and I had no idea who had spoken those words! I know now, of course, that they formed part of an amazing sequence of hypnotic suggestions; that they were my cue for *final forgetfulness*. At the time, I merely knew that, wondering when and where I had heard that sentence spoken, I staggered forward, trying to remember why I was there—and what business had brought me to Cairo.

Then came *true* memory—I mean memory without interference.

I had reached the foot of the steps when the facts returned to me.... That narrow alley behind the Mosque of Muayyad! From the moment I had entered it until the present, I was conscious of nothing but darkness!

How had I reached the Sharia Kamel? I asked myself. Could I have walked? And where had I heard those words: "He will be crowned in Damascus"?

Shepheard's was in darkness, and it suddenly occurred to me to look at my wrist watch.

Three a.m.

Heavy-footed, I mounted the steps. The door was barred, but I pressed the bell. In the interval of waiting for the night porter to open, I cudgeled my brains for an explanation of what had happened.

I had followed Fu Manchu's daughter (of her identity I was all but certain) in a taxicab. I should remember the man. Leaving him at a corner near the Bab ez-Zuwela, I had unwisely run on into a narrow alleyway; and then?

Then.... I had found myself a few steps away from the point at which I now stood at three in the morning!

The night porter unbarred the door.

At this point a belated beggar suddenly emerged

from the shadows, muttering unintelligibly

Chapter Twenty-second

THE HAND OF FU MANCHU

The night porter, who knew me well, stared like a man who sees a ghost.

"Good heavens, Mr. Greville!"

I saw that the lobby was in the hands of an army of cleaners, removing traces of the night's festivities. A man standing over by the hall porter's desk turned and then came forward quickly.

"Where is Sir Lionel Barton?" I had begun when:

"Are you Mr. Shan Greville?" the stranger asked.

He was an alert-looking man wearing dinner kit and carrying a soft felt hat. There was something about him which was vaguely familiar.

"I am," I replied.

The hall porter had stepped back as the newcomer arrived upon the scene, but he continued to stare at me, in a half-frightened way.

"My name is Hewlett. I'm in charge of police headquarters in the absence of Superintendent Weymouth. I was never more pleased to see a man in my life than I am to see you, Mr. Greville."

I shook his hand mechanically, noting that he was looking at me in a a queer fashion; and then:

"Where is Sir Denis?" I asked rapidly, "and Miss Barton?"

Hewlett continued to look at me, and I have since learned that I presented a wild-eyed and strange appearance.

"All your friends, Mr. Greville," he replied, "are out with the search party, operating from Bab el-Khalk. I came back here ten minutes ago for news. I'm glad I did."

"Where are they searching?" I asked dazedly.

"All around the neighbourhood of the Bab ez-Zuwela—acting on information supplied by the taxi-man who drove you there."

"Of course," I muttered; "he returned here and reported my absence, I suppose?"

Hewlett nodded. His expression had changed somewhat, had become very grave.

"You look completely whacked," he said. "But, nevertheless, I'm afraid I must ask you to come along and join Sir Denis. My car is just round the corner."

My confusion of mind was such that I thought the search (which presumably had been for me) would now be continued in the hope of discovering the hiding place of Fah Lo Suee.

"Very well," I replied wearily. "I should like a long drink before we start, and then I shall be entirely at your service."

"Very well, Mr. Greville."

I gave the necessary orders to the night porter, whose manner still remained strange, and dropped upon a lounge. Hewlett sat down beside me.

"In order that we don't waste one precious moment," he went on, "suppose you tell me exactly what happened to-night?"

"I'll do my best," I said, "but I fear it's not going to help very much."

"What? How can that be?"

"Because the most important period is a complete blank."

Whereupon I related my movements in the garden that night: how I had seen a woman, whom I was convinced was none other than the daughter of Fu Manchu, going out by that gate of the garden which I had supposed always to be locked. How I had run through to the front of the hotel just in time to see her entering a car which waited upon the other side of the street.

"Describe this car," said Hewlett eagerly.

I did so to the best of my ability, stressing its conspicuous yellow colour.

"I have no doubt that my driver's account is more accurate than mine," I continued. "He knew the names of all the streets into which we turned, with the exception of the last."

"He led us there," said Hewlett with a certain impatience, "but we drew a complete blank. What I want you to tell me, Mr. Greville, is into which house you went in that street."

I smiled wryly, as the night porter appeared, bearing refreshments on a tray.

"I warned you that my evidence would be a disappointment," I reminded him. "From that point up to the moment when I found myself standing outside Shepheard's, here, my memory is a complete blank."

Hewlett's expression became almost incredulous.

"But what happened?" he demanded. "The man tells us that he saw you run into a narrow turning on the left, as the yellow car—your description of which tallies with his—was driven off. He followed you a moment later and found no trace whatever. For heaven's sake, tell me, Mr. Greville, what happened?"

"I had fallen into a trap," I replied wearily. "I was drenched with some kind of anaesthetic. I don't know how it was applied. Perhaps a cloth saturated in it was thrown over my head. Unconsciousness was almost instantaneous. Beyond telling you that this drug, which was used in the murder of Dr. Van Berg in Persia, has a smell resembling that of mimosa, I can tell you nothing more—absolutely nothing!"

"Good heavens!" groaned Hewlett, "this is awful. Our last hope's gone!"

My brain seemed to be spinning. I was conscious of most conflicting ideas; and suddenly:

"Wait a moment!" I cried. "There *is* one other thing. At some time—I haven't the faintest idea when, but at some time during the night I heard the words, 'He will be crowned in Damascus'!"

"By whom were they spoken?"

I shook my head impatiently.

"I have no recollection that they were spoken by anybody. I merely remembered them, just before I came up the steps a little while ago. When and where I heard them I haven't the slightest idea. But I'm ready, Mr Hewlett. I'm afraid I can't be of the least assistance, but all the same I'm at your service."

He stood up, and I detected again that queer expression upon his face.

"I suppose," I added, "Miss Barton is in her room?"

Hewlett bit his lip and glanced swiftly aside. He was a man suddenly and deeply embarrassed. In a grave voice which he tried to make sympathetic:

"It's hard to have to tell you, Mr. Greville," he replied, "but it's for Miss Barton we are searching."

"*What!*"

I had turned, already heading for the door, when those words fell upon my ears. I grasped the speaker by both shoulders and, staring into his eyes like a madman, I suppose:

"Miss Barton! What do you mean? What do you mean?" I demanded.

"Go steady, Mr. Greville," said Hewlett, and gripped my forearms tightly, reassuringly. "Above all things, keep your nerve."

"But—" my voice shook almost hysterically—"she was with Reggie Humphreys, the Airways pilot . . . I left her dancing with him!"

"That was a long time ago, Mr. Greville," was the reply, spoken gently. "Half an hour after the time you mention, there was a perfect hue and cry because *you* had disappeared. The hotel was searched, and finally Sir Denis got through to my office. Then the cabman turned up reporting your disappearance and where it had taken place. He reported to the central police station, first, and then came on here."

"But," I began, "but when——"

"I know what you're going to ask, but I can't answer you, because nobody seems to know. There's only one scrap of evidence. An Egyptian chauffeur brought a note to one of the servants here and requested him to give it to Miss Barton. He telephoned to her room, found her there, and she immediately came down. From that moment the man (I have examined him closely) lost sight of her. But his impression, unconfirmed, is that she ran out onto the terrace. From which moment, Mr. Greville, I regret to say, nothing has been seen or heard of her."

Chapter Twenty-third

AMNESIA

My frame of mind when the new day broke, is better left to the imagination. I was convinced that my brain could not long sustain such stress. Maltreated already by an administration of some damnable drug, this further imposition was too great. I sat in the chief's room in the light of early morning. Birds were flying from tree to tree outside in the garden; and I could hear the sound of a broom as a man below swept the sanded path.

Sir Lionel had gone to his room to rest, and Dr. Petrie had been recalled to his house by professional duties. Nayland Smith walked up and down in front of the open window. He looked haggard—a sick man; and his eyes were burning feverishly. Suddenly he stopped, turned, and stared at me very hard.

"Look at me, Greville," he said, "and listen closely."

His words were spoken with such a note of authority that I was startled out of my misery. I met that steady glance, as:

"He will be crowned in Damascus," said Nayland Smith distinctly.

I felt my eyes opening more widely as if under the influence of that compelling stare. Even as I realised that this was a shot at random, and grasped the purpose of the experiment, it succeeded—in a measure.

For one incalculable instant I saw with my mind's eye an incredibly dirty old beggarman, hobbling along on a crutch. My expression must have given the clue, for:

"Quick!" rapped Nayland Smith; "what are you thinking about?"

"I am thinking," I replied in a flat, toneless voice, which during these last agonising hours I had come to recognise as my own, "that those words were spoken by a very old man, having one leg and carrying a crutch."

"Keep your mind on that figure, Greville," Nayland Smith ordered; "don't lose it, but don't get excited. You are sure it was a crutch—not a stick?"

I shook my head sadly. I thought I knew what he was driving at. Dr. Fu Manchu, on the one occasion (so far as I remembered) that I had ever set eyes on him, had supported his weight upon a heavy stick.

"It was a crutch," I replied. "I can hear the tap of it, now."

"Did it *crunch*? Was the man walking on gravel—or sand?"

"No, a clear tap. It must have been on stone."

"Did he speak in English?"

"Yes. I am almost sure the words were spoken in English."

"Did he say 'Damas' or 'Damascus'?"

"Damascus."

"Anything else?"

"No—it's all gone again."

I dropped my head into my hands as Nayland Smith began to walk up and down before the window.

"Do you know, Greville," he said, speaking slowly and deliberately, "that your memory of those words—for I am perfectly convinced that you really heard them—relieves my mind of a certain anxiety in regard to Rima."

I looked up.

"What ever do you mean?"

"It confirms my first opinion that her disappearance was arranged, and arranged with fiendish ingenuity, by the Fu Manchu group. This can only mean one thing, Greville. She has been abducted for a definite purpose. Had it been otherwise, in these rather disturbed times, I should have feared that her abduction had been undertaken for personal reasons. You understand what I mean?"

I nodded miserably.

Nayland Smith stepped across and laid his hand upon my shoulder.

"Buck up, old chap. I think I know how you feel. But there's nothing to despair about. Take my word for it: we shall have news of her before noon."

Hoping, doubting, I looked up at the speaker.

"You don't say that just to try to ease my mind?"

"To do so would be false kindness. I say it because I believe it."

"You mean . . .?"

"I mean that Rima is to be used as an instrument to bring Sir Lionel to reason."

"By heavens!" I sprang up, hope reborn in my heart. "Of course! Of course! It will be a case of ransom!"

"Rima's life against the relics of the Prophet," Nayland Smith returned dryly. He begun to walk up and down again. "And this time, Greville, the enemy will score. Not even Barton could hesitate."

"Hesitate!" I cried. "Why, if he has to be forced to give them up at the point of a gun—give them up he shall!"

"I don't think such persuasion will be necessary, Greville. Barton is a monument of selfishness where his professional enthusiasms are concerned, but he has a heart, and a big one at that."

I dropped back into my seat again. A flood of relief had swept over me, for I believed Nayland Smith's solution of the mystery to be the correct one. Truth to tell, I was physically tired to the point of exhaustion; yet sleep, I knew, was utterly impossible. And I sat there, watching that apparently tireless man; haggard, but alert, bright-eyed, pacing up and down—up and down—his brain as clear and his nerves as cool as if he were fresh from his morning bath. Even the chief, who had the constitution of a healthy ox, had collapsed some time before and was now sleeping like a log.

I was conscious of an acute pain in the tendon behind my left ankle, and stooping, I began to rub it. As I did so:

"What's the matter?" Nayland Smith asked sharply.

"I don't know," I replied, and lifting my foot I rolled my sock down and examined the painful spot.

"By Jove! something has cut in there. And my other ankle is painful, too, but in front."

"Let me see," he said rapidly. "Rest both feet on this chair here."

Whereupon he stooped and examined my ankles with the utmost care, and finally:

"You have been tied," he said, "and from the appearance of your ankles, brutally tied, with some very thin but presumably very strong material." He glanced up, smiling sourly. "I think, Greville, I have a length of that same mysterious material carefully preserved among my belongings!"

He watched me steadily, and I knew what he hoped for.

"No!" I shook my head sadly. "I have undoubtedly been tied, as you surmise, but I have no recollection whatever of the matter."

"Damn!" he rapped, and stood upright. "I can't help you in this case. There's no cue word, you see, to arouse that drugged memory. By heaven, Greville—" he suddenly shook his clenched fist in the air—"if I and those behind me can defeat the genius of this one old man, we shall have accomplished a feat which Homer might have sung. He is stupendous!"

He ceased suddenly and began to stare at me again.

"H'm!" he added. "I am forgetting how to keep my head in difficult moments. I have allowed elementary routine to go to the winds. Have you by any chance examined the contents of your pockets since you returned?"

"No!" I replied in surprise; "it never occurred to me."

"Be good enough to turn out all your pockets and place their contents upon this table."

Mechanically I obeyed. A wallet, a pipe, a pouch, a cigarette case, I extracted from various pockets and laid down upon the table. A box of matches, a pocketknife, a bunch of keys, some loose money, a handkerchief, a trouser button, two toothpicks, and an automatic lighter which never functioned but which I carried as a habit.

"That's the lot," I announced dully.

"Anything missing?"

"Not that I can remember."

Nayland Smith took up my cigarette case, opened it, and glanced inside.

"How many cigarettes were in your case when you left?"

I paused for a moment, and then:

"None," I replied confidently. "I remember dropping my last in the garden, here, just before I sighted Fah Lo Suee."

He took up my pipe: it was filled but had not been lighted.

"Odd! Isn't it?" he asked. "Remember anything about this!"

I dropped my weary head into my hands again, thinking hard, and at last:

"Yes," I replied. "I remember that I never lighted it."

Nayland Smith sniffed at the tobacco, opened my pouch and sniffed at the contents, also; then:

"Is your small change all right?"

"To the best of my recollection."

"Examine the wallet. You probably know exactly what you had there."

I obeyed; and at the first glance, I made a singular discovery.

A small envelope of thick gray paper containing a bulky

enclosure protruded from one of the pockets of the wallet!

"Sir Denis!" I said excitedly, "this wasn't here. This doesn't belong to me!"

"It does now," he replied grimly, and, stooping, he pulled out the envelope from the wallet which I held in my hand.

"'Shan Greville, Private,'" he read aloud. "Do you know the writing?"

I stared at the envelope which he had placed on the table before me. Yes, that handwriting was familiar—hauntingly familiar, but difficult to place. Where had I seen it before?

"Well?"

It was queer, square writing, the horizontal strokes written very thickly, and the ink used was of a peculiar shade of green. I looked up.

"Yes, I have seen it—somewhere."

"Good. As it is addressed to you and marked 'private,' perhaps you had better open it."

I tore open the small square envelope. It contained a single sheet of the same thick, gray paper folded in which was a little piece of muslin, a tiny extemporised bag, tied with green silk. It contained some small, hard object, and I placed it on the table glancing at Nayland Smith, and then began to read the note written in green ink upon the gray paper. This is what I read:

> I do not want you to suffer because of what I have been compelled to do. You love Rima. If she does not come back—trust me. I am not jealous. I send you a tablet which must be dissolved in a half litre of matured white wine, and which you must drink as quickly as possible. I trust you also—*to burn this letter*. To help you I say: He will be crowned in Damascus.

This I read aloud, then dropped the letter on the table and glanced at Nayland Smith. He was watching me fixedly.

"'He will be crowned in Damascus,'" he echoed. "Quick! Do those words, now, take you back any further?"

I shook my head.

"Do you know the writing? Think."

"I am thinking. Yes, I have it! I have only seen it once before in my life."

"Well?"

"It's the writing of Fu Manchu's daughter—Fah Lo Suee!"

Sir Denis snapped his fingers and began to walk up and down again.

"I knew it!" he snapped. "Greville! Greville! It's the old days over again! But this time we're dealing with a she-devil. And dare we trust her? Dare we trust her?"

I was untying the little packet, and from it I dropped an ordinary-looking tablet, small, round, and white, which might have been aspirin, upon the table.

"Personally," I said, with a ghastly attempt at a smile, "I would as soon think of following the instructions in her letter as of jumping out of that window."

Nayland Smith continued to walk up and down.

"For the moment I express no opinion," he replied. "I may have a better knowledge of the mentality of Eastern women than you have, Greville. And I may have paid a high price for my knowledge. But don't misunderstand me."

I picked up the tablet and was in the act of throwing it out into the garden, when:

"Don't do that!" He sprang forward and grasped my wrist. "You leap to conclusions too hastily. Think! Thought is man's prerogative. You definitely recognise this as the writing of Fu Manchu's daughter? Granting it even to be a forgery—what then?" He stared at me coldly. "Can you conceive of any object which would be served by bringing your death about in so complicated a manner?"

It was a new point of view—but a startling one.

"Frankly, no." I admitted. "But we have had experience in the past, Sir Denis, of remarkable behaviour on the part of persons subjected to the poisons of Dr. Fu Manchu."

"You are thinking of an attempt once made unconsciously by Rima to murder *me*?" he suggested. I had thought of this. Don't imagine I haven't taken it into account. But no agent of Dr. Fu Manchu, with such an object in mind, could be so clumsy as this."

He pointed to the tablet upon the table.

"I suppose you're right," I said dully. "But all the same, you are not suggesting that I should follow out these instructions?"

Nayland Smith shook his head.

"I am merely suggesting," he answered, "that you should keep this remarkable clue. It may have its uses later."

Already he was sniffing at the paper and envelope, scrutinising the writing—holding the sheet up to the light—examining its texture.

"Very remarkable," he murmured, and, tuning, stared at me fixedly.

Personally, I was on the verge of collapse and knew it. My brain was a veritable circus; my body was deadly weary. Desperately though anxiety rode me, I would have given all I had for one hour of sleep, of forgetfulness, of relief from this fever which was burning me up. Nayland Smith came forward and, seating himself beside me, put his arm around my shoulders.

"Listen, Greville," he said. "Petrie is due back in a few minutes, now. He won't have long to spare. But I'm going to make him put you to sleep. You understand?"

I had never in my life stood so near to the borders of hysteria.

"Thanks," I replied; "of course I do. And I'll submit to it; but there's a proviso . . ."

"What is it?"

"Not for more than an hour. I can't bear the thought of lying like a log while I might be of use to her."

He gripped my tightly for a moment, and then stood up.

"You are off duty," he snapped dryly. "I'm in charge, and you'll take my orders. When Petrie comes, you'll do exactly as Petrie directs. In the meantime, have I your permission to examine and photograph this letter? You will then, quite properly, wish to destroy it, as your correspondent directs."

I agreed. At which very moment the door was thrown open and Petrie came in. One glance he cast at Sir Denis, and then directed that searching professional gaze upon me; the analytical look of a diagnostician. I saw that he was not favourably impressed.

"Smith," he said, with another glance at Sir Denis, "our friend here must sleep."

Nayland Smith nodded.

"It's not going to be easy," Petrie continued; "you're most terribly overwrought, Greville. But if you share my opinion that sleep is necessary, I think I can manage you."

"I do," I replied.

"In that event, the matter is simple enough. We will go up to your room, now."

CHAPTER TWENTY-FOURTH

THE MESSENGER

"WAKE-UP, old chap, there's good news!"

I opened my eyes to find myself staring up into the face of Nayland Smith. My brain was confused; I could not coordinate circumstances, and:

"What is it?" I asked drowsily; "what's the time?"

"Never mind the time, Greville. Wake up! There's work for you."

Then full consciousness came. But before I had time to clear the borderland:

"He will be crowned in Damascus," said Nayland Smith staring intently into my eyes.

His gaze held me; but in the moment that he spoke I had seen that Dr. Petrie stood behind him, that I was lying in my room. Even as I realised what he was endeavouring to do, I realised also that he had partially succeeded.

For my memory was thrown back as he willed it to be, to the pavement of the Sharia Kamel. Dawn, as I recalled the scene, was not far off. And I was walking in the direction of Shepheard's. Out of the shadows of the recess where the shops lie back, a ragged figure approached me, whining for *bakshish*. I saw him clearly; every line and lineament of his dirty face, his straggly gray beard, his ragged garments, his crutch. I could hear it tapping on the pavement....

I saw myself give him alms and turn away; I heard his words: "He will be crowned in Damascus." I knew again the mystification which had descended upon me in that moment; and felt the depth of wonder about where I had been and of how I came to find myself in that place, at that time.

Starting up in bed:

"It was an old *beggarman*," I cried hoarsely, "in the Sharia Kamel, who spoke those words!"

And while Nayland Smith and Petrie listened eagerly I told them all that I had remembered. And, concluding:

"What's the news?" I demanded, now fully awake, and

conscious that my hours of sleep had given me new life.

"It's as I predicted, Greville," Nayland Smith replied. "She is being held to ransom."

I sprang out onto the floor. Queerly enough, that news came like balm to my troubled mind. Rima was in the hands of Dr. Fu Manchu! A dreadful thought, one would suppose—but better, far, far better than doubt. One thing at least I knew definitely: that if terms had been demanded by the Chinaman, it remained only strictly to carry them out.

The most evil man I had ever known, he was also, according to his own peculiar code, the most honourable. I met Nayland Smith's glance and knew that he understood me.

"I have burned your letter, Greville," he said quietly.

"Thank you," I replied. "And now, tell me: Who brought the news?"

"The messenger is in Barton's room," Dr. Petrie answered, watching me with keen professional interest. "How do you feel? Fairly fit?"

"Thanks to you, I feel a new man."

Nayland Smith smiled and glanced aside at Petrie.

"You may recall," he said, "that no less an authority than Dr. Fu Manchu always regarded your great talents as wasted, Petrie!"

CHAPTER TWENTY-FIFTH

MR ADEN'S PROPOSAL

"LEAVE this to me, Barton," Nayland Smith said sharply. "If you interfere in any way I won't be answerable for the consequences."

Sir Lionel clenched his fists and glared at our visitor; then, crossing, he stood with his back to us, looking out of the window. He was dishevelled, unshaven, wrapped in his dilapidated old dressing gown, and in a mood as dangerous as any I had ever known.

Professional duties had compelled Dr. Petrie to leave, and so there were four of us in the long pleasant room, with its two windows overlooking the garden. I was little better groomed than the chief, for I had been fast asleep five minutes before, thanks to Petrie's ministrations. But Sir Denis, although his grey suit had seen much wear, looked normally spruce.

I stared with murderous disfavour at a man seated in an armchair over by the writing table.

Heavily built, he wore the ordinary morning dress of a business man, and indeed was of a type which one may meet with in any of the capitals of the world. His face, inclined to be fat, was of a dead white colour. Thick iron-gray hair was cut close to his skull, and he had a jet-black moustache. I hated his dark, restless eyes.

"This is Mr.—er—Aden," Nayland Smith continued; "and as the business upon which he has come interests you personally, Greville, I thought you should be present."

Mr. Aden bowed and smiled. My detestation grew by leaps and bounds.

"Mr. Aden is a solicitor practising in Cairo. By the way—" suddenly turning to our visitor—"I believe I met your brother some years ago."

"That is not possible," said the Greek; and his oily voice did nothing to redeem his character in my eyes.

"No?" Sir Denis queried rapidly. "Not a Mr. Samarkan, onetime manager of the New Louvre Hotel in London? But surely?"

Mr. Aden visibly started, but endeavoured to conceal the fact with an artificial cough and a swiftly upraised hand.

"You are mistaken, Sir Denis," he declared suavely, "not possibly in the resemblance, but certainly in the relationship. I never *heard* of Mr. Samarkan."

"Indeed!" snapped Nayland Smith, and turned aside. "Let it pass, then. Briefly, Greville the position is this: Mr.—er—Aden, here in the ordinary way of his professional duties—"

"Damned nonsense!" shouted the chief, stamping one slippered foot upon the floor, but not turning around. "He's one of the gang and an impudent liar!"

"Barton!" Nayland Smith interrupted angrily, "I have requested you to leave this matter to me. If you insist upon interrupting, I shall order you to do so."

"Order be damned!"

"I have the necessary authority."

Some few moments of ominous silence followed, during which Nayland Smith stood staring at the broad back of Sir Lionel. The latter remained silent, and:

"Very well," Sir Denis went on. "As I was explaining, Greville, Mr.—er—the name persistently escapes me . . ."

"Adrian Aden," our visitor prompted smoothly.

"Yes. Mr. Aden has been instructed by one of his clients to approach Barton professionally."

"The situation is difficult," Mr. Aden explained, extending a fat white hand. "But what could I do? I act for the great interests in Egypt. I cannot afford to offend."

"Ah!" shouted the chief, "truth at last! I admit you're not the man to offend Dr. Fu Manchu."

"Dr. Fu Manchu?" Mr. Aden murmured. "That name also is unfamiliar to me."

Nayland Smith glanced in Barton's direction, snapped his fingers irritably, and:

"The name of your client it is unnecessary to discuss at the moment," he said. "But I gather your instructions to be these: A body of religious fanatics has abducted Miss Rima Barton. Your client has learned that she will be returned unharmed if the demands of these religious fanatics are complied with?"

"Ah!" beamed Mr. Aden, "but this is common sense, Sir Denis. How perfectly you understand my position."

"If *you* understood it," growled the chief, "you would know that you might be kicked through the window at any moment."

"This is the lowest and foulest kind of blackmail," I broke in savagely. "If you are what you claim to be, a solicitor, you deserve to be struck off the rolls."

"Really, Greville," said Nayland Smith, "you are unduly hard upon Mr. Aden. I have no doubt that he has undertaken infinitely more delicate cases."

Mr. Aden shot a quick glance at the speaker, but either missed the point or professed to do so.

"You speak hastily, Mr. Greville," he replied. "I act for those who would help you."

"His clients, you see, Greville," Nayland Smith continued dryly, "seem to know all that goes on in the Near East. They deeply deplore the outrage which has been committed—I understood you to say so, Mr. Aden."

"Oh, but completely!"

"And they suggest a means by which Miss Barton's release may be secured. In fact, the exact terms are mentioned, I believe?"

"But certainly!" but certainly!" the Greek assured him. "They claim, these religious people, that Sir Lionel Barton has stolen property which belongs to them."

To my intense surprise the chief did not speak, did not move.

"They say also, my clients inform me, that, if this property is returned, the missing lady will also be returned."

"Quite reasonable," Sir Denis murmured. "Have you details of the property which they claim has been stolen?"

"I have it here."

Mr. Aden opened a portfolio lying beside him on the floor and extracted a sheet of paper.

"A sword or scimitar of Damascus steel inlaid with gold, having a curved, double-edged blade and the hilt encrusted with emeralds, rubies, and pearls . . . ."

He slipped on a pair of horn-rimmed spectacles, the better to read, and continued:

"A mask of thin gold finely engraved; and fifteen thin gold plates sixteen inches long by twelve inches wide, bearing the text of the New Koran of El Mokanna."

He ceased speaking, took off his spectacles, and looked up.

As he did so, Sir Lionel turned. And before Nayland Smith could check him:

"Suppose I admitted that I had these things in my possession," he said, glaring down upon the white-faced Greek, "what would you do?"

"I should believe you."

"Thanks. But how much better off would Rima be?"

"Barton," said Nayland Smith, "absolutely for the last time—will you either shut up or get out!"

The chief plunged his hands into the pockets of his dressing gown, glared down at the Greek again, and glared at Sir Denis. Then, walking across to a settee, he threw himself upon it, stamping his feet on the floor.

"We will assume," Nayland Smith continued, "that the objects you enumerate are actually in Sir Lionel's possession. What next?"

"I understand that those who have her in charge will give up Miss Barton in exchange for these relics."

"Under what conditions?"

I was positively boiling over, and hot words leapt to my tongue; but Sir Denis stared me down.

"You will bring those things which I have specified to an appointed place," Mr. Aden replied, "and there you will meet Miss Rima Barton."

"Sounds like an ambush," Nayland Smith snapped.

The Greek shrugged his fat shoulders.

"I should be glad to communicate any other suggestion you might care to make. But first—my instructions on this point are explicit—" he turned with unconcealed nervousness to Sir Lionel: "I must see these items, please," he held up the sheet of paper, "and notify my clients that all is correct."

"Don't speak, Barton," said Nayland Smith. "The suitcase is under the settee, just by your feet. Haul it out, unstrap it, unlock it, and comply with Mr. Aden's request."

The chief's face grew positively purple as he angrily sustained the fixed stare of Sir Denis.

"Neither Greville nor I can understand your hesitation," the latter added. "Nothing else counts while Rima is in the hands of—Mr. Aden's client."

At those words Sir Lionel's furious glare was transferred to

Mr. Aden, upon whose white forehead I could see beads of perspiration. Then he stooped, hauled forth the heavy suitcase, and unfastened it.

Out from the interior he lifted and laid upon a small table those priceless relics of the Masked Prophet, the possession of which had brought about such disaster and in its consequences driven me to the verge of madness.

Chapter Twenty-sixth

A STRANGE RENDEZVOUS

We sat on the terrace in a corner near the entrance to the American Bar. It was getting on towards lunch time, and this was a fairly busy season in Cairo. I had seen several people I knew but had deliberately avoided them. Now I faced Sir Lionel across the cane-topped table, and:

"There's one thing I can't stand, Greville," he said, "and that's being ordered about! Latterly, I've had too much of it—altogether too much of it." He brought his fist down on the table with a bang. "But we shall see who scores in the end. As for that slimy swine Aden, he's no more a solicitor than I'm a barber."

"Wrong again, Barton," came quietly, and glancing up I saw that Nayland Smith had just come through the doors behind us.

"I'm apparently always wrong," growled the chief.

"Not always," said Sir Denis, drawing up a chair. "But it happens that the Mr. Samarkan whom I mentioned an hour ago—you remember him, of course?"

"My memory isn't failing me, Smith! He died in England, in those damned caves—near my own place. Of course I remember him! Thanks to you, the sticky business was hushed up!"

"Ah!" murmured Nayland Smith, and his stern face suddenly broke into a smile.

That smile rather cleared the air.

"You know, Barton," he went on, "although you're the last man to admit it, you've been behaving like a sick cow ever since Rima disappeared. I understand your feelings, but I don't understand why you should vent them on your friends. However (it was Petrie who gave me the clue), the record of M. Samarkan—one-time manager of a hotel no great distance from this, and, later, of the New Louvre in London—is filed at Scotland Yard. Therefore I happen to know that he had a brother. I know also that his brother changed his name by deed poll and took out naturalisation papers."

He paused, staring hard at Sir Lionel.

"I saw the resemblance, of course," the chief admitted, "but . . ."

"So did I," Nayland Smith went on. "But it was Petrie who placed him. I have just been checking up on the gentleman. He has a legal practice in Cairo, as he stated. But it's of a very shady character."

"So I imagine," I interjected.

"In short, there's no doubt whatever that his main source of revenue is the affairs of the Si-Fan. He's one of their spies, and an agent of Dr. Fu Manchu, as his brother was before him."

Simply eaten up with impatience and anxiety, I could scarcely contain myself during this conversation. And, as Sir Denis paused again:

"This doesn't help me in the least to understand," I said, "why you let the brute slip!"

"Same here," growled the chief. "Personally, I should have thrown him out of the window."

Sir Denis lay back in his chair, giving an order to a waiter who had just come up; and, as the man went away:

"Your primitive tactics, Barton," he remarked coldly, "would probably result in the total disappearance of Rima. If that's what you are after—take charge."

"But——" the chief began.

"There's no 'but'!" snapped Nayland Smith impatiently. "We have absolutely no clue to Rima's whereabouts. Greville, here, has been doped—his brain on that point is useless. The man you wanted to throw out of the window probably knows no more than we know. But he's a link—a link which *you* would have snapped!"

He paused so suddenly, staring obliquely across the street at a high window, that automatically I turned and looked in the same direction. And as I looked, I saw what he had seen.

From the window of a native house—for Shepheard's borders closely upon the Oriental city—a woman was leaning out, apparently watching us where we sat on the stoep. She withdrew from the window immediately, but as she did so I turned and met a piercing glance from Sir Denis.

"Was I right, Greville?"

I nodded.

"I *think* so."

Even without his confirmation I should have been certain that Fah Lo Suee had been watching us from across the street!

I jumped up.

"Let's search the house!" I cried. "I know you have powers, Sir Denis!"

My excitement had attracted attention, and I suddenly realised with embarrassment that a number of people were looking at me.

"Sit down, Greville," was the quiet reply. "Your tactics are as bad as Barton's."

I dropped back in my chair and met his steady gaze—not, I believe, with too great an amiability.

"What the devil's all this about?" growled the chief. "I can't see anything."

"Outside your particular province," Nayland Smith returned, "you rarely *do* see anything. Petrie, with his stolid mentality, is worth both of you put together when it comes to grasping facts. If I hadn't been here last night, Barton, all Cairo would know now that Rima was missing."

"Why shouldn't all Cairo know?"

"Because it would result in her being smuggled away. If you can't see that, you can see nothing."

Nevertheless, I could not refrain from glancing up at that high window at which, I was assured, Fu Manchu's daughter had been stationed—watching us. And Nayland Smith suddenly detected this.

"For heaven's sake!" he snapped irritably, "pretend you didn't see her." He pulled out pouch and pipe and threw them down on the table. "I must smoke!"

As he began to load the cracked old briar:

"What I want to know——" Sir Lionel began.

"What you want to know," Sir Denis took him up, "is why I selected so strange a meeting place. If you'll be good enough not to interrupt me, I'll explain. Ah! here's Petrie."

I saw the doctor, who had just come up the steps, looking about in search of us, and standing up I waved my hand. He nodded, and threading his way among the tables, joined us.

"Sit down, Petrie," said Nayland Smith; "here's a chair. You will notice that, anticipating your arrival, I thoughtfully ordered a drink for you."

"Tell me, Smith," Petrie began eagerly, "have you come to terms? For God's sake, say that you have."

"I have, old man," Nayland Smith replied, laying his hand upon the speaker's arm, and squeezing it reassuringly. "But neither Barton nor Greville seems to appreciate my purpose."

"Fah Lo Suee——" I began, glancing towards that window across the street.

"Greville!" snapped Sir Denis, "there will be plenty of time later; at the moment I wish to explain the position to Petrie."

His manner was overbearing to the point of rudeness. I felt like a recruit in the hands of a company sergeant major. But I suffered it and took out my cigarette case.

"I have arranged," he continued, "with Mr. Aden—who is, as you suspected, Petrie, a brother of the lamented Samarkan——"

"I knew it!" Petrie cried.

"You were right," Nayland Smith admitted, "and I am indebted to you for the clue. But, as I was saying, I have arranged that the relics of the Masked Prophet—which God knows have caused sufficient misery already—shall be handed over to those who demanded them, and Rima returned to us to-night at twelve o'clock in the King's Chamber of the Great Pyramid."

Probably no more perfect registration of astonishment could have been achieved by any Hollywood star than that now displayed by Dr. Petrie. He stared from face to face in positive bewilderment, and:

"You think what I think, Petrie," the chief shouted; "that it's stark raving lunacy!"

"Frankly, I don't know what to think," Petrie confessed. "It sounds fantastic to a degree. Really, Smith, in the circumstances . . ."

Sir Denis, having failed to light up with the first match, turned irritably to the speaker.

"Have you ever had occasion to observe, Petrie," he inquired acidly, "that my average behaviour tends to the absurd?"

"Not at all."

"Very well." He struck a second match. "I will quote, from

memory, the terms of the agreement to which Barton and I have set our hands, witnessed by Greville, here."

The second match failed also. Laying his pipe upon the table:

"The phrasing doesn't matter," he went on, "but the hub of the thing is this:

"Dr. Fu Manchu's agent was authorised to propose that at a meeting place to be mutually agreed on, but one not less than half a mile from any inhabited dwelling, no more than two persons should present themselves with the relics of the Prophet. Of the other part it was agreed that no more than two persons should be with Rima. Rima having been accepted on our side, and the relics on the other, all should be permitted to depart unmolested."

"Well?" said the chief, leaning across the table; "it was playing into our hands!"

"Listen," Nayland Smith's even voice continued: "Knowing with whom I was dealing, I made a further condition. It was this: that after the interchange of valuables (pardon me, Greville, but I don't quite know how otherwise to express myself) there should be a ten minutes' truce. Note the time—*ten minutes.*"

"I still remain in the dark," I confessed.

"So do I," said Petrie.

"Wait!" the chief growled, watching Nayland Smith intently. "I begin to see—I think I begin to see."

"Good for you, Barton," was the reply. "I naturally anticipated an ambush. If Fu Manchu can secure what he wants and at the same time dispose of two people in the world who know much of himself and his methods, this would be a master stroke. I looked for loopholes in the agreement. While the doctor would not hesitate to murder any of us, he is incapable of dishonouring his bond. I played for safety."

"Hopeless!" I exclaimed. "It appears to me that to-night we are walking with our eyes open right into a trap."

"Wait!" With a third match the speaker got his pipe going. "By the courtesy of Mr. Aden it was left to me to suggest this meeting place. And I selected the King's Chamber of the Great Pyramid. It was a momentary inspiration, and I may have been wrong. But consider its advantages."

He paused, and now we were all watching him intently.

"Apart from the condition that we shall be represented by no more than two persons at the meeting place, there is no clause in the agreement prohibiting our being *covered* by as many persons as we care to assemble!

"Police headquarters are advised. To-night at twelve o'clock Gizeh will be deserted; there's no moon. A cordon will be drawn around the Pyramid. Nothing in my agreement with Mr. Aden prohibits this. When Rima is brought there from whatever place they have her in hiding, the fact will be reported to me."

"By heaven!" cried the chief, and banged the table so violently that Petrie's glass was upset; but, as if not noticing the fact. "By heaven! This is sheer genius, Smith. Your pickets will get her on the way?"

"It's possible."

Sir Lionel laughed boisterously and clapped his hands for a waiter.

"They won't even get——" he began—and then paused.

I saw Sir Denis watching him, and I realised that he, as well as I, had noticed that schoolboy furtiveness creeping over Sir Lionel's face. The arrival of the waiter interrupted us temporarily, but then:

"You see, Greville," said Sir Denis, turning to me eagerly, "even if they slip past the pickets, and we have to enter the Pyramid, those inside will be at our mercy. Because the police will close around the entrance behind us, and——"

"And there's only *one* entrance!" I concluded. "I see it all! We can't fail to regain the relics?"

"This would be playing into our hands," cried the chief, "if Fu Manchu agreed to it. We began cheering too soon! I admit the brilliancy of the scheme, Smith; I can see your point, now. But when a meeting place half a mile from any inhabited dwelling was suggested, Fu Manchu hadn't thought about the Great Pyramid! He's a devil incarnate and could probably work conjuring tricks almost anywhere else within the terms of the agreement. But the Pyramid! He'll veto the whole thing when the slimy Aden reports."

"I had fully anticipated it," Nayland Smith admitted, "but only ten minutes ago, just before I joined you, the arrangement was confirmed on the telephone."

"By whom!" I asked.

"By the only voice of its kind in the world—by the voice of Dr. Fu Manchu."

"Good God!" I exclaimed—"then he's *here*, in Cairo!"

Chapter Twenty-seventh

THE GREAT PYRAMID

WE SET out at eleven-thirty in Petrie's car.

I suppose, of all the dark hours I have known, this was as black as any. I rested upon Sir Denis Nayland Smith as upon a rock.... If he should fail me—all was lost.

That his singular plan was a good one I had accepted as a fact; failing this acceptance, I should have been in despair. Perhaps it was the aftermath of drugs to the influence of which I had been subjected; but I was in an oddly *muted* frame of mind. Frenzy had given place to a sort of Moslem-like resignation; a fatalistic, deadening recognition of the fact that if Rima, who was really all that mattered to me in the world, should have come to harm, life was ended.

At the village, where few lights were burning when we passed, a British policeman was on duty. Nayland Smith checked Petrie, and leaning out of the car:

"Anything passed?" he asked rapidly.

"Nothing much, sir. Two or three hotel parties. I've noticed a lot of funny-looking Bedouins about here to-night, but I suppose that's nothing to do with the matter."

"Making for Gizeh?"

"No, sir. They all went that way—into the village."

"Go ahead, Petrie."

As we swung around onto that long, straight tree-lined avenue which leads to the Plateau of Gizeh, I counted three cars which passed us, bound towards Cairo. There was nothing ahead, and nobody seemed to be following. As the hotel came into view:

"We have time in hand," said Petrie, "shall I drive right ahead?"

"Pull up," Nayland Smith directed sharply.

An Egyptian, who might have been a dragoman, had sprung from the shadow of the wall bordering the gardens of Mena House, where during the day a line of cars and camels may be seen. Nayland Smith craned out.

313

"Who is it?" he asked impatiently.

"Enderby, Sir Denis. You met me at headquarters to-day."

"Right! What have you to report?"

"Not a thing! I have four smart gyppies watching with me, and we have checked everybody. There's absolutely nothing to report."

"Leave the car here, Petrie," said Nayland Smith, "we have time to walk. It may be better."

Petrie backed the car in against the wall, and we all got out. The "Arab" whose name was Enderby, and whom I took to be a secret service agent, conversed aside with Sir Denis for some time. Then, saluting in the native manner, he withdrew and disappeared into the shadows again.

"Queer business," said Nayland Smith, pulling the lobe of his ear. "A gathering of the heads of the many orders of dervishes is taking place in the Village to-night. As a rule they don't mix . . . And why at Gizeh?"

"Don't like the sound of it myself," the chief growled; but:

"D'you mind grabbing the case, Greville?" said Nayland Smith tersely.

With ill-concealed reluctance, Sir Lionel passed his leather suitcase into my possession; and we started up the sandy slope.

I had abandoned speculation—almost abandoned hope; having, in fact, achieved acceptance of the worst. Diamond stars gleamed in an ebony sky. The Great Pyramid, most wonderful, perhaps, of the structures of man, blotted out a triangle of the heavens. Our feet crunched on the sandy way. We were sombrely silent.

At one point, as we turned the bend at the top of the road, I remember that I wondered, momentarily, what the others were thinking about; and particularly if Sir Denis's confidence remained unimpaired. My own, alas, had long since deserted me. . . .

And dervishes were assembling at Gizeh. That certainly was odd. Why, as Nayland Smith had asked, at Gizeh?

Just as we were topping the slope a man appeared, apparently from nowhere, and so suddenly that I was startled out of my confused reverie. Petrie, who was beside me, grabbed my arm; and then:

"You're early, Sir Denis," said a voice.

I knew it at once: it was that of Hewlett, Acting Superintendent of Police.

"Not so loud," snapped Nayland Smith. "What's the news?"

"None, I regret to say, sir."

"You mean no one has entered The Pyramid?"

"Not a soul—if I can rely on my men!"

My heart sank—went down to zero. The scheme, the fantastic scheme, had failed. He was dealing with a super-mind, and Fu Manchu was laughing at him. It was unthinkable that the Chinese doctor should have exposed any of his agents to a danger so obvious.

"How many men have you here?"

"Sixty. The place is entirely surrounded."

"What does this mean, Smith?" Petrie asked urgently. He turned to Hewlett, whom he evidently knew well, and: "How long have you been covering the Pyramid?" he added.

"Since the guides knocked off," was the reply. "If anybody's smuggled through in the interval, he must have been invisible."

"It's a booby trap," said the chief shortly. "You've ruled me out, Smith, and perhaps it doesn't matter. But, by heaven——"

"Disappear, Hewlett," Nayland Smith directed tersely; and as Hewlett obediently merged into the shadows: "I don't know what this means, Petrie," he went on, "any more than you do. From the evidence, and I count it pretty sound, nobody has gone into the place to-night since sunset. But three of us have signed an agreement with an enemy I would strangle with my own hands if I had the opportunity, but with an enemy who has one redeeming virtue: he always keeps his word. We must keep ours."

"He's spotted the cordon," Sir Lionel growled, "and he's called his men off."

"We have stuck strictly to the terms of the understanding. He must have anticipated that we should do our utmost to arrest his agents immediately the ten-minute truce ended."

"Then he finds he can't cope with the situation. He's backed out—"

"My God!" I groaned, "where's Rima? She can't possibly be here!"

"Wait and see!" snapped Nayland Smith.

His words were spoken so savagely that I recognised the tension under which he was labouring and regretted my emotional outburst.

"I'm sorry, Sir Denis," I said. "It's vital to me, and——"

"It's equally vital to *me!* I'm not risking Rima's life for any pet theory, Greville. I'm doing my damnest to make sure she's returned safely."

His words made me rather ashamed of myself.

"I know," I replied. "I'm terribly worked up."

"Barton," came a tense order, "get in touch with Hewlett, and stand by, here. You too, Petrie."

"I hate you for this," said the chief violently.

"Hate on! You are too damned impetuous for the job before us. . . ."

Together, he and I set out.

I glanced back once, and Sir Lionel and Dr. Petrie presented a spectacle which might have been funny had my sense of humour been properly alert. Dimly visible, for the night was velvety dark, they stood looking after us like schoolboys left outside a circus. . . .

And presently I found myself alone with Nayland Smith at the foot of that vast, mysterious building which has defied the researches of Egyptologists and exercised the imaginations of millions who have never seen it. Personally, I had lived down that sense of mystery which claims any man of average intelligence when first he confronts this architectural miracle.

Sir Lionel had carried out an inquiry here in 1930, just prior to our excavations on the site of Nineveh. I knew the Great Pyramid inside out, remembering the job more vividly because Rima had been absent in England during the time, the chief having given her leave of absence which he refused to grant to me.

We had reached the steps which led to the opening; and:

"You're in charge now," said Nayland Smith. "Lead, and I'll follow. Give me the case."

CHAPTER TWENTY-EIGHTH

INSIDE THE GREAT PYRAMID

IN THAT little bay in the masonry which communicates with the entrance we stood and, turning, looked back.

Sixty men surrounded us; but not one of them was in sight. At some point there in the darkness, Sir Lionel and Dr. Petrie were probably watching. But in the absence of moonlight we must have been very shadowy figures, if visible at all. I looked down upon the mounds and hollows of the desert, and I could discern away to the left those streets of tombs whose excavation had added so little to our knowledge. There were two or three lighted windows in Mena House. . . .

"Go ahead, Greville," said Nayland Smith. "From this point onward I am absolutely in your hands."

I turned, switching on the flash lamp which I carried, and began to walk down that narrow passage, blocked at its lower end, which leads to the only known entrance to the interior chambers. Familiar enough it was, because of the weeks I had spent there taking complicated measurements under Sir Lionel's direction—measurements which had led to no definite results.

We came to the end where the old and new passages meet. Our footsteps in the silence of that densely enclosed place aroused most eerie echoes; and in the flattened V where the ascent begins:

"Stand still, Greville," Sir Denis directed.

I obeyed. My light already was shining up the slope ahead. In silence we stood, for fully half a minute.

"What," I asked, are you listening for?"

"For anything," he replied in a low voice. "If I had not spoken to Dr. Fu Manchu in person on the telephone to-day, Greville, I should be prepared to swear that you and I were alone in this place to-night."

"I have no reason to suppose otherwise," I replied. "The pickets have seen no one enter. What have we to hope for?"

"Nothing is impossible—particularly to Dr. Fu Manchu. He

accepted my terms and the meeting place. In short he declared himself. And, though contrary to normal evidence, I shall be greatly surprised if when we reach the King's Chamber, we do not find his representatives there with Rima."

I could not trust myself to reply, but led on, up the long, sloping, narrow way which communicates with the Great Hall, that inexplicable, mighty corridor leading to the cramped portals of the so-called King's Chamber. At the mouth of that opening beyond which the Queen's Chamber lies, Nayland Smith, following, grasped my arm and brought me to a halt.

"Wait," he said; "listen again."

I stood still. Some bats, disturbed by our lights, circled above us. My impatience was indescribable. I imagined Rima, a captive, being dragged along these gloomy corridors. I could not conceive it; I did not believe she was in the place.

But until I had reached that dead end which is the King's Chamber, my doubts could not be resolved; and this delay imposed by Nayland Smith was all but intolerable, the more so since I could not fathom its purpose.

I have never known a silence so complete as that which reigns inside the Great Pyramid. No cavern of nature has ever known it, for subterraneously there is always the trickle of water, some evidence of nature at work. Here, in this vast monument, no such sounds intrude.

And so, as we stood there listening, save for the whirl of bat wings, we stood in a silence so complete that I could hear myself breathing. When Nayland Smith spoke, although he spoke in a whisper, his voice broke that utter stillness like the blow of a hammer.

"Listen! Listen, Greville! Do you hear it?"

Chapter Twenty-ninth

WE ENTER THE KING'S CHAMBER

VERY dimly it came to my ears. From whence it proceeded I could not even imagine. . . . In those surroundings, at that hour, it possessed a quality of weirdness which was chilling:

The dim note of a gong!

Its effect was indescribably uncanny; its purpose incomprehensible. In the harsh light of the flash lamps I saw Nayland Smith's features set grimly.

"For heaven's sake, what's that?" I whispered.

"A signal," he replied in a low voice, "to advise *someone* we are here. God knows how any of them got in, but you see, Greville, I was right. We are not alone!"

"There's something horrible about it," I said uneasily.

I glanced upward into the darkness we must explore.

"There is," Nayland Smith agreed quietly. "But it has a good as well as a bad aspect. The good that it seems to imply ignorance of our cordon; the bad, that it proves certain persons to have entered the Pyramid to-night unseen by the pickets."

Silence, that dead silence which is characteristic of the place, had fallen about us again like a cloak. Honestly, I believe it was only the thought of Rima which sustained me. It was at this moment that the foolhardiness of our project presented itself starkly to my mind.

"Aren't you walking into a trap, Sir Denis?" I said. "*I* don't count from the point of view of Dr. Fu Manchu, but——"

"But," he took me up, "as an expert, can you tell me how Dr. Fu Manchu's agents, having disposed of me here—which admittedly might be convenient—could hope to profit? At the moment, six men are watching the entrance. A further sixty are available if anything in the nature of an Arab raid should be attempted."

"I agree. But the *gong*. If they got in unseen, surely they can get out?"

He stared at me; his eyes were steely in that cold light.

"I had hoped you might have overlooked this fact," he said,

"because it reduces us to our only real safeguard: the word of Fu Manchu! In all the years that I have fought for his destruction, Greville, I have never known him to break it. We shall go unmolested for ten minutes after Rima is restored to us! Then—unleash the dogs of war! Carry on."

"Ten minutes after Rima is returned to us!" . . . Did the light of his faith in the word of Fu Manchu truly burn so bright?

I led on and upward—and presently we found ourselves in that awe-inspiring black corridor which communicates with the short passage leading to the room called the King's Chamber, but which (as Sir Lionel has always maintained) in its very form destroys at a blow the accepted theory, buttressed by famous names, that this majestic pile was raised as the tomb of Khufu.

Automatically, I directed the light of my lamp farther upward. The vast, mysterious causeway was empty, as far as the feeble rays could penetrate.

We mounted to the ramp on the left side and climbed onward. Ages of silence mantled us, and, strangely, I felt no desire to give voice to the many queries which danced in my brain. An image led me on; I seemed to hear my voice speaking a name:

Rima!

I climbed more swiftly.

This might be a trap; but according to available evidence, no one had entered the Pyramid that night; but plainly I had heard the gong . . . and dervishes were gathering at Gizeh. . . .

We reached the horizontal passage to the King's Chamber; and instinctively both of us paused. I stared back down the slope as far as the light of my lamp would reach. Nothing moved.

"Will you be good enough to take over the duties of pack mule, Greville," said Nayland Smith crisply.

He handed me the case. The entrance to the place yawned in front of us. Sir Denis took a repeater from his pocket, examined it briefly, and slipped it back. Then, shining a light into the low opening:

"Follow closely," he directed.

For one instant he hesitated—any man living would have hesitated—then, ducking his head and throwing the light forward along the stone passage, he started forward. I followed; my disengaged hand gripped an automatic.

I saw the end of the passage as Nayland Smith reached it; I had a glimpse of the floor of that strange apartment which many thousands have visited but no man has ever properly comprehended; and then, following him in, I stood upright in turn.

As I did so, I drew a sharp breath—indeed, only just succeeded in stifling a cry. . . .

A bright light suddenly sprang up! So lighted, the place presented an unfamiliar aspect. No bats were visible. The chamber looked more lofty, but for that very reason more mysterious. The lamp which shed this brilliant illumination—a queer, globular lamp—was so powerful that I could not imagine from what source its energy was derived.

It stood upon a small table, set close beside the famous coffer; and behind it, so that the light of this lamp shone down fully upon him, a man—apparently the sole occupant of the King's Chamber—was seated in a rush chair of a type common in Egypt. He wore a little black cap surmounted with a coral ball, and a plain yellow robe. His eyes were fixed steadily upon Sir Denis.

It was Dr. Fu Manchu!

CHAPTER THIRTIETH

DR. FU MANCHU KEEPS HIS WORD

Nayland Smith stood quite still, the ray of his torch shining down on the floor at his feet. Those incredible green eyes beyond the globular lamp watched him unblinkingly.

As I supposed at the time—although, of course, I was wrong—I had seen Dr. Fu Manchu once only in my life. And as I saw him now, an astounding change presented itself. That wonderful face, on which there rested an immutable dignity, seemed to be the face of a younger man. And the power which radiated from the person or this formidable being was of a character which I could never hope to portray. He seemed to exude force. The nervous energy of Sir Denis was of a kind which could almost literally be felt, but that which emanated from Dr. Fu Manchu vibrated with an intensity which was uncanny.

How long a time elapsed in the utter silence of that strange meeting place before a word was spoken, I cannot say, but the dragging seconds seemed interminable.

The atmosphere was hot—stiflingly hot. My head seemed to be swimming. I glanced swiftly at Nayland Smith. His teeth were clenched tightly, and I knew that his right hand, which he held in his pocket, rested upon a Colt repeater. I could not guess what or whom he had expected to meet, but every lineament of his stern face told me that he had never anticipated meeting the Chinese doctor.

It was the latter who broke that unendurable silence.

"We meet again, Sir Denis—a meeting which I observe you had not anticipated. Yet you might have done so."

Fu Manchu spoke coldly, unemotionally, and except for certain gutturals and at other times an odd sibilant, his English was perfect, deliberate to the point of the pedantic, but carrying no trace of accent. I remembered that, according to Petrie, the Chinese doctor spoke with facility in any of the civilised languages, as well as many savage tongues and dialects.

I had eagerly read all that my friend had written about him, during the years that he and Sir Denis had warred almost constantly with their great adversary, my reading embracing hundreds of Petrie's notes which had never been published. Memories returned to me now, as I found myself face to face with this great but evil man. I wish I possessed the doctor's facility of style. His pen, I think, could have done greater justice to a scene in attempting which I find my own more than halting.

"You saw me in Ispahan," the calm voice continued. Its effect in that enclosed chamber was indescribable. "Prior to which, you had recognised my methods. You had tricked those acting for me, and I arrived too late to rectify their errors of judgment, for which, however, two paid with their lives."

Nayland Smith continued to watch the speaker, but uttered never a word.

"Perhaps my personal appearance in that street on the night of my second attempt to secure the relics was an indiscretion. But I had lost faith in my agents. You foiled me, Sir Denis. You saw me; I did not see you. You seem to have overlooked the fact that I walked without the aid of a stick."

Nayland Smith visibly stared—but did not speak.

"Sir Lionel Barton's box-trick," Fu Manchu went on—his peculiar utterance of the chief's name producing a horrifying effect upon my mind—"necessitated this hasty journey to Egypt, at great personal inconvenience. I arrived an hour after you. Therefore, Sir Denis, since you know with whom you are dealing, and since with my present inadequate resources I have none about me upon whose service I can rely, is there anything singular in my meeting you personally?"

"No." Sir Denis spoke at last, never taking his gaze from that lined, yellow face. "It is characteristic of your gigantic impudence."

No expression of any kind could be read upon Dr. Fu Manchu's face, except that his eyes, long, narrow, and of a brilliant green colour which I can only term unnatural, seemed momentarily to become slightly filmed.

"You have played the only card which we couldn't defeat," Sir Denis went on; "and here—" he pointed to the case which I had set upon the floor—"is your price. But, before we proceed further . . ."

I knew what he was about to say, and I said it for him,

shouted it, angrily:

"Where is Rima?"

For one instant the long green eyes flickered in my direction. I felt the force of that enormous intellect, and:

"She is here," said Dr. Fu Manchu softly. "I said she would be here."

The last words were spoken as if nothing could be more conclusive. I was on the point of challenging them, but, somehow, there was that in their utterance which seemed unchallengeable. The crowning mystery of the thing presented itself nakedly before me.

How had Fu Manchu gained access to this place, the entrance to which had been watched from sunset? How had Rima been smuggled in?

"Your motives," said Nayland Smith, speaking in the manner of one who holds himself tightly on the curb, "are not clear to me. This movement among certain Moslem sects—which, I take it, you hope to direct—must break down when the facts are published."

"To which facts do you more particularly refer?" the Chinese doctor inquired sibilantly.

"The fact that an extemporised bomb was exploded in the tomb of El Mokanna by Sir Lionel Barton, and that the light seen in the sky on that occasion was caused in this manner; the fact that the relics were brought by him to Egypt and returned to the conspirators under coercion. What becomes of the myth of a prophet reborn when this plain statement is made public?"

"It will not affect the situation in any way; it will be looked upon as ingenious propaganda of a kind often employed in the past. And since neither Sir Lionel Barton nor anyone else will be in a position to *prove* that the relics were ever in his possession, it will not be accepted."

"And your own association with the movement?"

"Is welcome, since the ideals of the Si-Fan are in harmony with the aims of those Moslem sects you have mentioned, Sir Denis. Subterfuge between us is useless. This time I fight in the open. One thing, and one thing only, can defeat the New Mokanna . . . his failure to produce those evidences of his mission which, I presume, you bring to me to-night. . . ."

His strength and the cool vigour of his utterance had now,

as I could see, arrested Sir Denis's attention as they had arrested mine; and:

"I congratulate you," he said dryly. "Your constitution would seem to be unimpaired by your great responsibilities."

Dr. Fu Manchu slightly inclined his head.

"I am, I thank you, restored again to normal health. And I note with satisfaction that you, also, are your old vigorous self. You have drawn a cordon of Egyptian police around me—as you are entitled to do under the terms of our covenant. You hope to trap me, and have acted as I, in your place, should have acted. But I know that for ten minutes after our interview is concluded I am safe from molestation. I am not blind to the conditions. My safety lies in my knowledge that you will strictly adhere to them."

He clapped his hands sharply.

What I expected to happen, I don't know. But Nayland Smith and I both glanced instinctively back to the low opening. What actually happened transcended anything I could have imagined.

A low shuddering cry brought me swiftly about again.

"Shan!"

Rima, deathly pale in the strange light of that globular lamp, was standing upright behind the granite coffer!

My heart leapt, and then seemed to stop, as she fixed her wide-open eyes upon me appealingly. And Sir Denis, that man of steel nerve, exhibited such amazement as I had never known him to show in all the years of our friendship.

"Rima!" he cried. "Good God! Have you been lying there, hiding?"

"Yes!" she turned to him. I saw that her hands were clenched. "I promised." She glanced down at the motionless, high-shouldered figure seated before her. "It was *my* part of the bargain."

Describing a wide circle around the sinister Chinaman, she ran to me, and I had her in my arms. I could feel her heart beating wildly. I held her close, stroking her hair: she was overwrought, on the verge of collapse. She was whispering rapidly—incoherently—of her fears for my safety, of her happiness to be with me again, when those low even tones came:

"I have performed what I promised, Sir Denis. It is now your turn. . . ."

Chapter Thirty-first

THE TRAP IS LAID

My last recollection as I stopped and went out must always remain vivid in my mind.

Those golden records of the Masked Prophet, one of the unique finds in the history of archaeology, lay glittering upon the narrow table under the light of that strange globular lamp. Dr. Fu Manchu, his long pointed chin resting upon his crossed hands, his elbows upon the table, watched us unfalteringly.

One grave anxiety was set at rest. In reply to a pointed question of Nayland Smith's, he had assured us that Rima had not been subjected to "damnable drugs or Lama tricks" (Sir Denis's own words). And, fearing and loathing Dr. Fu Manchu as I did, yet, incredible though it may seem, I never thought of doubting his word. A hundred and one questions I was dying to ask Rima, but first and foremost I wanted to find the sky above by head again.

The Great Corridor was empty from end to end. And, I leading and Nayland Smith bringing up the rear, we stumbled down to the point where it communicates with the narrower passage. Here I turned, and looked back as far as the light of my lamp could reach.

Nothing was visible. I could only think that Dr. Fu Manchu remained alone in the King's Chamber. . . .

I glanced at Rima. She was clenching her teeth bravely, and even summoned up a pallid smile. But I could see that she was close to the edge of her resources.

"Hurry!" snapped Nayland Smith. "Remember—ten minutes!"

But even when, passing the lowest point, we began to mount towards open air, somehow, I could not credit the idea that Dr. Fu Manchu had carried out this business unaided. I paused again.

"It was here that we heard," I began——

As though my words had been a cue, from somewhere utterly impossible in those circumstances to define, came the dim note of a gong!

Rima clutched me convulsively. In that age-old corridor, in the heart of the strangest building erected by the hands of man, it was as uncanny a sound as imagination could have conjured up.

"Don't be afraid, Rima," came Nayland Smith's voice. "It's only a signal that we are on the way up!"

"Oh!" she gasped, "but I can't bear much more. Please get me out, Shan!—get me out. . ."

I led on as swiftly as possible. Had Rima collapsed, it would have been no easy task to carry her along that cramped passage. But the purpose of those signals, apart from the mystery of the hiding place of whoever gave them, was a problem we were destined never satisfactorily to solve.

As we had arranged, five men with Dr. Petrie were immediately outside the entrance.

"Thank God, Petrie," said Nayland Smith hoarsely. "We've got her! Here she is! Take care of her, old man."

Whereupon, at sight of the Doctor, Rima's wonderful fortitude deserted her. She threw herself into his arms with a muffled scream and began to sob hysterically.

"Rima, dear," I exclaimed, "Rima!"

Petrie, supporting her with one arm, waved to me to go on, at the same time nodding reassuringly.

"Come on, Greville," said Nayland Smith. "She's in safe hands, and better without you at the moment."

We had arranged—I confess I had never dared to hope that our arrangements would be carried out—to take her to Mena House. Down on the sands at the foot of the slope Sir Lionel and Hewlett were stationed. And, as I jumped from the last step:

"Have you got her, Greville? Is she safe?" the chief asked hoarsely.

"Yes, she's with Petrie. She's broken down, poor little lady—and I don't wonder," Nayland Smith replied. "But she's come to no harm, Barton. Keep out of the way—leave her to Petrie."

"Where has she been? How did it happen?"

"It's impossible to ask until the nerve storm has worn itself out. Anything to report, Hewlett?"

"I'm staggered, Sir Denis! But thank God you have Miss Barton! There's only one thing. A few minutes after you went in, as we were closing up on the Pyramid, we heard a most awful wailing sound. . . ."

"A *bull-roarer*, Smith!" the chief shouted. "But God knows where the nigger was hidden: we never had a glimpse of him."

Nayland Smith glanced aside at me.

"Possibly the opposite number of the *gong* signal," he whispered. "But what came first?—and how did one signaler hear the other?"

I saw Hewlett glancing at the dial of an illuminated wrist watch.

"Three minutes to go, Sir Denis," he announced. "How many are inside?"

"One only," Nayland Smith replied, in a curiously dull voice.

"Only one!" the chief cried incredulously.

"One, but the biggest *one* of all."

"What! You don't mean . . ."

"Exactly what I do mean, Barton. We left Dr. Fu Manchu alone in the King's Chamber."

"Good God! Then for all his cunning—"

"He's trapped!" Hewlett concluded. "How he got in, and how he got Miss Barton in, is entirely beyond me. But that he can never get out, is certain."

He spoke truly; for other than the Grand Hall or Great Corridor along which we had recently come, there is no entrance to the King's Chamber—and the two exits from the Pyramid were guarded.

CHAPTER THIRTY-SECOND

I SEE EL MOKANNA

Dr. Petrie gave Rima a sleeping draught and saw her off to bed in the big hotel on the edge of the desert. In spite of all our precautions, news had leaked out that something was afoot.

Whereas, at the time of our arrival, the place had been quiet, with few lights showing, now an air of excitement prevailed. People who seemed to have hastily dressed were standing about in groups. We had smuggled Rima in by a side entrance. But in the lobby and on the terrace outside I met many curious glances.

And there was another, altogether more disturbing circumstance. In the roadway, and by the gate usually haunted by dragomans during the day, a group of some forty natives had assembled, of a type not usually met with there. They were men from the desert villages for the most part, and although all were oddly silent, I overheard several furtive asides which I construed as definitely hostile.

I recognised the black turbans of the *Rifaiyeh* and the red of the *Ahmadiyeh*. *Senussi* I saw among them too—and the white headdresses of many *Kadiriyeh*. . . .

These were the dervishes who had gathered at Gizeh Village!

Wildly impatient as I was to join the party at the Pyramid, it was impossible for me to leave for some time. Petrie was with Rima, whom he had placed under the care of a resident nurse. She kept waking up and calling piteously for me. Twice I had been brought to her room to pacify her. Her frame of mind was most mysterious. She seemed to be obsessed with the idea that some harm had befallen me.

The second time, after she had gone to sleep contentedly, clasping my hand, I had managed to slip away without awakening her. And now, as I roamed restlessly about the lobby, Dr. Petrie suddenly appeared.

"She's right enough now, Greville," he reported, "and Mrs. Adams is with her. A most reliable woman."

"Dare we start?" I asked.

"Certainly! my car's outside. But we shall be too late for——"

I knew what he would have said; equally, I knew why he hesitated. The physical facts of the situation were beyond dispute; but the more I had considered the matter, the more clearly I had appreciated the fact that a man of Dr. Fu Manchu's intellect would never voluntarily have walked into such a mouse trap.

No one knew how he had entered the Pyramid nor how Rima had been taken there. Furthermore, he had introduced that singular lamp into the place, the table and the Arab chair. Now, in addition, he had the relics of the Prophet.

As we walked down the sanded drive to the road, observed with great curiosity by several residents who obviously suspected that our business was a strange one, we came face to face with that ominous gathering of Arabs near the gate. I saw at a glance that reinforcements had joined them. The black turbans of the *Rifaiyeh* predominated now. "This looks unwholesome, Greville," said Petrie in an undertone. "What are all these fellows doing here at this time of night?"

"They are the dervishes! Evidently they assembled at Gizeh Village and then marched here. I have been prowling about for some time, waiting for reports about Rima, and I watched them gathering."

We were among them now. Although they made way for us, I liked their attitude less and less.

"Tribesmen of some sort," said Petrie close to my ear. "Except in ones and twos, these birds are rarely seen."

As we reached his car, which stood a little to the left of the entrance, I looked back uneasily. The dervishes seemed to be watching us.

"What the devil's afoot?" Petrie asked, grasping the wheel. "I should think they meant mischief, if they were armed."

He started slowly up the slope; and as we passed that silent company I looked into many flashing eyes close beside the window. But no one attempted to obstruct us.

"A very queer business," Petrie muttered. "Smith should

know at once. It can hardly be a coincidence."

We met several stragglers of the same type on that short winding road which leads up to the plateau, presumably going to join those already assembled outside Mena House. But the doctor's mind, as well as my own, now focused upon the major problem; and as we turned the final bend and the great black mass of the Pyramid loomed above us:

"You know, Greville," said Petrie, "a load has been lifted from my mind. Honestly, I don't think the possession of the relics of Mokanna will do much to help the movement. Rima's safety would be cheap at the price of every relic in the Cairo Museum."

"I feel much the same about it," I admitted. "Although, of course, those things are unique."

"Unique be damned!" said Petrie. "Hello! who's this?"

It was a police officer standing with upraised arm.

"You can't pass this way, sir," he shouted, and came forward as Petrie pulled up.

We both got out, but the night, as I have said, was very dark. And as we did so, the policeman directed the ray of the lamp upon us.

"Oh!" he added. "It's Dr. Greville and Mr. Petrie, isn't it?"

Petrie laughed.

"The other way about, officer," he replied.

"You'll have to walk from here. Those are my orders, sir."

"It makes no difference. We couldn't have driven much further, anyway. Is there any news?"

"Not that I've heard, sir. I understand that they're still searching inside——"

"What!" I exclaimed. "There's nothing to search—only two rooms. That is, unless they're searching Davidson's shaft."

"Come on, Greville," said Petrie curtly. "Let's go and see for ourselves. You may be of use here. You ought to know every nook and cranny of the place."

"I do, but so does the chief—and he's on the spot."

We were challenged again as we reached the foot of the Pyramid, by a sergeant whom I took to be in charge of the cordon.

"O.K., sir," he said when he saw me.

"What's happened? Who's inside?"

"The acting superintendent, sir, Sir Denis Nayland Smith, and Sir Lionel Barton. Three men with them."

"And no one has come out?"

"Not a soul, sir."

Petrie turned to me in the darkness.

"Shall we go up?" he said.

We found four men on duty when we had climbed up to the entrance. They passed us immediately, and I was about to lead the way in when a muffled voice reached me from the interior.

"I tell you it's a trick, Smith! He's slipped out in some way. . . ."

The chief.

I stepped back again and felt, for I could not see their faces, an atmosphere of tension among the four police officers on duty.

"There's treachery. Somebody's been bought over."

That loud, irascible voice was drawing nearer; and:

"It's all but incredible, Greville," said Petrie, in a low voice; "but evidently Fu Manchu has managed to get out as mysteriously as he got in!"

"I hope there's no question about *us*, sir," came sharply; and one of the four men, whom on close inspection I recognised for a sergeant, stepped forward. "I'm responsible to the acting superintendent, so I don't care what the other gentleman says. But you can take my word for it that nobody has come out of this place to-night, since you came out with the lady and Sir Denis."

"We don't doubt it, Sergeant," Petrie replied. "Sir Denis won't doubt it, either. You mustn't pay too much attention to Sir Lionel Barton. He's naturally very disturbed."

"That may be, sir—" the man began; when:

"Who's on duty, here?" bellowed the chief, suddenly appearing out of the opening.

"One moment, Sir Lionel," a quiet voice interrupted; and I saw Hewlett grasp his arm. "*I* am responsible for the men on duty. Sergeant!"

"Sir?"

"Have you anything to report?"

"Nothing, sir."

"It's some damned trick!" growled the chief.

Nayland Smith came out last, saw me in the darkness, and:

"Is everything all right, Greville?" he asked eagerly.

"We managed to get her to sleep," Petrie replied. "Everything is all right. But this business passes my comprehension, Smith."

"It does!" the latter rapped. "But, needless to say, I anticipated it."

"It's a trick!" the chief shouted. "The man's a conjurer: always was. How did he get Rima in? Damn it! Can't we ask her?"

"You'll ask her nothing to-night, Barton," Petrie returned quietly. "And you'll ask her nothing in the morning until you have my permission."

"Thanks!" was the reply. "I'll remember you in my will." He was, in short, in a towering rage, and: "Where's Greville?" he finished up.

"Here I am."

"D'you think it feasible that Fu Manchu could have slipped up into one of the construction chambers?"

"No, I don't."

"Neither do I. Even if he did, he's got to come down sometime."

"What are these construction chambers, Greville?" Nayland Smith asked in a low voice.

"Five low spaces above the King's Chamber," I replied, "terminating in a pointed roof, generally supposed to have been intended to relieve the stress on the room below."

"Any way into them?"

"Yes—by means of a long ladder."

"Is there anything in what Barton says?"

"Hardly. In any event, there is only one way out!" I turned to Sir Lionel. "Have you searched the shaft, Chief?"

"No!" he growled—"I haven't. And what's more I'm not going to. Have the damn place closed and watched; that's all that's necessary."

Nayland Smith turned to Hewlett.

"You must arrange for the Pyramid to be closed to visitors for the remainder of the week. And have men on duty at the entrance day and night."

"Very good," said Hewlett; "I'll see to it."

We had climbed down again to the base, and my feet were on the sand, when an idea occurred to me.

"By heavens! Sir Denis," I cried. "It isn't safe to leave just four men there to-night."

"Why?" he snapped.

"You remember the meeting of dervishes reported by Enderby? Well—they are here—fifty or sixty strong!"

"Where?"

"Just this side of Mena House."

"A rescue!" said the chief hoarsely. "They mean to rush the entrance! Fu Manchu is hiding inside!"

I could see Nayland Smith pulling at the lobe of his ear.

"They began to gather about midnight," said Hewlett. "It's been reported."

"Who are they?"

"Mostly men from outlying villages, and as Mr Greville says, members of various dervish orders."

"I don't like this," rapped Nayland Smith. The Mahdi organised the dervishes, you know. What's your opinion, Hewlett?"

"I haven't one. I can't make it out—unless, as Sir Lionel suggests, they are going to attempt to rush us ... But, by jove! here they come!"

We had set out down the slope and nearly reached that point where Petrie and I had left the car. Now, we pulled up like one man.

Dimly visible in the darkness of the night, their marching feet crunching upon the sand, we saw a considerable company of Arabs approaching from the opposite direction.

"It might be dangerous," Nayland Smith muttered, "if it weren't for the fact that sixty armed men are still on duty."

And as he spoke, that onward march ceased as if in response to some unspoken order. Vaguely, although at no great distance from where we stood, we could see that strangely silent company. The policeman who had stopped Petrie's car suddenly appeared.

"What do I do about his, sir?" he asked, addressing Hewlett. "They look nasty to me."

"Do nothing," was the reply. "We have the situation well in hand."

"Very good, sir."

We were near enough now to the crowd on the edge of the plateau to be able to distinguish the colours of robes and turbans—white, black, green and red; a confused blurred mass, but divisible into units. And as I looked doubtingly in their direction, suddenly I saw a hundred arms upraised, and in a muted roar their many voices reached me:

"*Mokanna!*"

Whereupon, unanimous as worshippers in a cathedral, they dropped to their knees and bowed their heads in the sand!

"Good God! What's this?"

Nayland Smith was the speaker.

We all turned together, looking back to the northern face of the Great Pyramid. And as we did so, I witnessed a spectacle as vivid in my mind to-night as it was on the occasion of its happening.

Perhaps two thirds of the way up the slope of the great building, but at a point which I knew to be inaccessible to any climber, a figure appeared. . . . Even from where I stood, it was visible in great detail—for the reason that this figure was brilliantly lighted!

Many explanations occurred to us later of how this illumination might have been produced. We recalled the globular lamp in the King's Chamber; several such lamps, masked from the viewpoint of the onlookers and placed one step below the figure, backed by reflectors, would, I think, have accounted for the phenomenon. But at the time, no solution offered.

Personally, I was conscious of nothing but stark amazement, For there, enshrined in the darkness, *I saw El Mokanna!*

I saw a tall, majestic figure, wearing either a white or a very light green robe. The face was concealed by a golden mask and surmounted by a tall turban. Upraised in the right hand glittered a sword with a curved blade . . .

A weird chanting arose from the dervishes. I didn't even glance back. I was staring—staring at that apparition on the Pyramid. Distant shouting reached me—orders, as I realised. But I knew, had known it all along, that no climber could reach that point.

Then, as suddenly as it had appeared, the apparition vanished.

The lights had been extinguished or covered: such was the conclusion to which we came later. But at the time the effect was most uncanny. And as the figure vanished, again, from the dervishes, came a loud and now triumphant shout:

"*Mokanna!*"

In the dead silence which followed:

"Fu Manchu has set us a problem," said Nayland Smith. "Either he or some selected disciple has been posing as the reborn prophet, from Afghanistan right down to the border of Arabia. You understand the dervish gathering, now, Hewlett?"

A murmuring of excited conversation reached us. The assembly of Arabs, palpably come there as to a tryst, was dispersing and already returning down the slope.

"It was urgent," Sir Denis went on; "hence the abduction of Rima. This was an *appointment* with the leaders of the *Senussi* and other fanatical orders. He had tricked them hitherto, but if the real relics had once been placed beyond his reach detection sooner or later was inevitable. This spark, Greville—" he turned to me in the darkness—"is going to light a bonfire. The Mokanna promises to be a greater problem that the Mahdi."

Whereupon the chief began to laugh!

That laughter was so unexpected, and indeed so eerie in the circumstances, that I found in it some quality of horror.

"He's tricked us, Smith!" he shouted. "He's tricked us! But, by God, I've tricked *him!*"

Chapter Thirty-third

FACTS AND RUMOURS

The story of the second Masked Prophet, although extreme precautions were taken by the British secret service and by Sir Denis Nayland Smith, nevertheless leaked out and into the newspapers of Europe and America. It is well known to-day to everybody, so far as externals go.

Journalistic espionage triumphed even before the prophet appeared in Egypt. That ominous disturbance moving from Afghanistan down through Persia was paragraphed in the London *Daily Telegraph*, in the *Times* of New York and in *Le Temps* of Paris. The Indian papers had fairly long accounts.

When that strange rumour, hitherto unsupported by tangible evidence, reached Egypt, a special correspondent of the *Daily Mail* interviewed prominent Moslems. With one exception these denied all knowledge of the matter. The one—a learned imam whose name I have forgotten, but which may be found in the files of the newspaper in question—admitted that news of this movement had come to him. But, he informed his interviewer, it was confined to members of certain unorthodox sects; therefore he was not in a position to express any opinion regarding it.

This interview must have taken place, I suppose, at about the time that we reached Cairo. It was not prominently featured; but later came a column account by the same correspondent, of a second gathering of Wise Men, numbering not three, but according to his estimate, seventy; and a story of the apparition on the Great Pyramid which closely corresponded to the truth.

Since no other newspaper carried this story, I can only suppose that the correspondent of the *Daily Mail* was staying at Mena House.

Throughout these exacting days I lived in a state of unrelieved suspense. The watch on the Pyramid had had no results; the place was opened again to the public. Rima, who narrowly escaped a serious breakdown, was not fit to be moved for some time. Indeed, during the first forty-eight hours, Dr. Petrie was unable to conceal his anxiety.

The chief remained at Shepheard's awaiting the return of Ali Mahmoud with the heavy baggage; but I had moved to the hotel by the Pyramids in order to be near Rima. She suffered from a strange delusion that I was dead, and my presence was frequently required to reassure her. Later, I learned the origin of this obsession, which at the time puzzled me, as it puzzled Petrie.

Acting partly, I think, upon that one memory which remained to me of the hiatus preceding Rima's abduction, Sir Denis had proceeded in a Royal Air Force plane to Damascus.

The chief during this period was wrapped in one of his most impossible moods. A score of times I tried to discuss the mystery of Fu Manchu's disappearance; and:

"Your measurements were wrong, Greville," was his invariable conclusion.

Characteristically, he did not question his own!

He referred, of course, to the investigation which we had carried out there, based upon his conviction that there were other chambers in the Great Pyramid. Sceptical as I had been at the time, I was disposed now to believe that Sir Lionel's extraordinary imagination had not misguided him.

Failing the existence of other chambers, and, more astounding still, of another exit, the escape of Dr. Fu Manchu was susceptible of no material explanation. The later apparition of the Masked Prophet at an inaccessible point on the northern slope, might have been accounted for by daring trickery.

But these were trying days indeed. Knowing, as everyone knows who has spent much time among Orientals, that news travels among them faster than radio can carry it, I killed many idle hours in the native quarter, listening to the talk of shop-keepers, peddlers and mendicants.

In this way, thanks to my knowledge of vernacular Arabic, I kept abreast of the Mokanna movement. Probably I knew, before Nayland Smith and the British intelligence service knew, that the threat of that uprising grew less day by day. It had proved abortive; something had gone wrong. I used to report to the chief such scraps of rumour as reached me. They seemed to afford him matter for amusement.

"We'll sail in the next P. & O., Greville," he said one night. "Rima should be fit enough by then. It's high time we were out of Egypt. I'm only waiting for Ali Mahmoud. . . ."

Chapter Thirty-fourth

RIMA'S STORY

AND then at last came a day when Petrie announced to me privately that Rima was ready, was anxious, to be questioned; to tell her own story.

"Only you and I, Greville," he stipulated. "It remains dangerous ground, and Barton is liable to prove an irritant...."

We had tea with her, Petrie and I, on the balcony of her room overlooking the Pyramids. It was Sunday. The tourist season now was in nearly full flower. Camels with grotesquely poor riders paced up the slope to that little plateau which contains two of the wonders of the world: the Great Pyramid and the Sphinx. There were many cars. In the garden, smart Egyptians and their women occupied the best tables, regarding English, French, and American tourists with thinly veiled amusement.

Rima looked almost ethereal after her strange nervous illness, but so utterly desirable that I felt a savage urge to take her in my arms and stifle her with kisses. But, now that the fear phase had passed, I saw that she regarded me with a queer aloofness.

When her story was told, I understood....

"Of course, Shan, Dr. Petrie has made it all clear to me. You should be grateful to him, dear. I think he has saved me from...

"It was that night when you called for me at Shepheard's—but of course, I'm forgetting; you know nothing about it! You see, Shan, after your disappearance on the evening of our arrival, I was simply in a frenzy. They kept it from me for a long time—Uncle and Sir Denis and the doctor. But at last they had to tell me, of course.

"I didn't know what to do with myself. I began to think that my crazy behaviour was attracting attention—and I rushed up to my room. I hadn't been there more than five minutes when one of the servants bought me a note—from *you!*"

"It was a forgery!" I cried. "It must have been!"

"Don't interrupt, Greville," said Petrie quietly. "These are the *facts*. Remember that they relate to a period during which your own evidence is not available."

Good heavens! it was true. A great part of that night was a blank to me. . . .

"It was from *you*," Rima went on. "You asked me to tell no one, but to come out at once and join you. . . . I couldn't wait for the lift: I simply raced downstairs and out onto the terrace. An Egyptian chauffeur in a blue uniform met me and showed me where you were waiting——"

"*I* was waiting! Where?"

"Just opposite the hotel, beside a French landaulet. Of course, I ran across to you. Shan! you simply *hauled* me in! You were grim to the nth degree! But I was so utterly happy that at first I thought of nothing except that I had found you again.

"Then, Shan—oh, heavens . . . Shan!"

"Don't let the memory upset you, Rima," said Petrie. "It's all passed and done with. You know, my dear, he's the *third* victim, as I have told you. All three of us, Greville, at various times, have had similar experiences at the hands of our Chinese friend."

"I understand," I replied, watching Rima; "I begin to understand. Go on, darling."

"It came to me, my dear, that you were *mad!* I saw, in a flash, what had happened—because something like it had once happened to *me*. I fought with you—oh, my God, how I fought; it was terrible! Then, when I realised it was useless, I tried to *will* you to know what you were doing.

"We passed through Gizeh Village and were out on the causeway to here when the driver pulled up suddenly. A tall man dressed in black was standing in the roadway. He came forward to the right of the car—and I recognised him——

"It was Dr. Fu Manchu!"

"Rima!"

"I began to collapse. I couldn't stand much more. He spoke to you. I didn't hear the words; but—Shan . . . you fell back on the seat as though you were—*dead*. . . .

"It was the last straw. I believe I made a fool of myself—or they may have drugged me; but I passed away.

"When I opened my eyes again, after a thousand years of nightmare, I found myself in a strange but delightful room. I was lying on a couch wrapped in a silk dressing gown; and an old negress sat sewing near me. . . .

"It turned out to be part of a suite in a house which must have been right outside Cairo; because all I could see from the little windows in the *mushrabiyeh* screens was miles and miles of desert. I suppose the negress was a servant of Dr. Fu Manchu, but she was certainly a sweet old thing.

"My first waking thought, Shan, was about you! But the old woman could tell me nothing. She merely said over and over again, 'Don't fret, honey child; it will sure be all right.'

"I spent a whole day in those three small rooms. It was quite impossible to get out, and the old negress never left me. No one else came near us. She did all she could to make me comfortable, but I refused to touch food. I have never passed through such a day in my life. I felt myself to be slowly going mad with suspense. Once, a long way over the desert, I saw some camels; that was towards evening. Otherwise, I saw nothing. . . .

"At sunset the negress lighted the lamps; and she had only just done so when I heard the sound of a gong somewhere in the house below.

"By this time I was in a state of suppressed frenzy, and when I heard that sound I wanted to shriek. The old woman gave me a warning glance, whispered, 'Don't fret, honey child; it will sure be all right,' and went and stood by the door.

"I heard footsteps outside; the door was unlocked—and Dr. Fu Manchu came in!

"He was dressed as I remembered him in London—but the horrible thing was that he seemed to be much *younger!* I must have been nearer to crashing than I knew at the time; for I can't recall one word that he said to me, except that he made me understand, Shan, that your life depended upon *me*.

"Evidently he saw that I was likely to collapse at any moment. He spoke to the old negress in some language I had never heard—and then forced me to drink a glass of some rather sweet white wine.

"After that I remember him watching me very intently and speaking again. His voice seemed to fade away, and his awful eyes to grow larger and larger——"

"Like a green lake!" I burst in, "which swallowed you up! I know. I know!"

"*How* do you know?" Petrie asked sharply. "When did you derive that curious impression?"

He was studying me keenly: and at once I grasped the significance of my words. They echoed some submerged memory of the hiatus! But, in the moment of uttering them, that memory slipped back again into the limbo of the subconscious.

"No good, Doctor," I said, shaking my head. "You were right—but it's gone! Go on, Rima."

Rima, who seemed intuitively to have seized upon the purpose underlying Petrie's question, looked at me pathetically, and then:

"I *know* you know, Shan dear," she went on. "But you can't remember—nor can I. Because I woke in a gloomy stone chamber, lighted by a round green lamp——"

"The King's Chamber, Greville," Petrie interpolated. "Rima had never seen it before, it seems."

"Dr. Fu Manchu was sitting by a small table, and there was a big stone sarcophagus just behind him. I was standing in front of him. There was no one else there; and the *silence* was dreadful.

"'Behind this coffer,' he said, and pointed with an incredibly long finger, 'you will find a mattress and cushions. Lie there, whatever happens, and make no sign—until I clap my hands. Then stand up. Shan Greville's life depends upon you. This is *your* part of the bargain.'

"I heard a gong—somewhere a long way off.

"'To your place,' said Dr. Fu Manchu in that voice which seems to make every word sound like a command, 'and remember, when I clap my hands. . . .'

"What happened after that, Shan, you know."

CHAPTER THIRTY-FIFTH

ORDERED HOME

ON THE following night Rima returned to Cairo. I remember, as Sir Lionel and I sat in the lounge waiting for her to join us for dinner, that my mind was more nearly at ease than it had been for many days. When presently Rima appeared, although she looked perhaps rather more than normally pale, she had nevertheless contrived to efface any signs of her recent ordeal.

"In the absence of Dr. Petrie," I said, "I prescribe a champagne cocktail."

The patient approved of the prescription.

"What about you, Chief?"

"Whisky and soda," Sir Lionel growled, staring towards the entrance door. "Where the devil's Petrie?"

"A busy medical man," I replied, summoning a waiter, "is always excused social appointments. Isn't he, Chief?"

"Has to be, I suppose."

As I gave the order I found myself thinking about the doctor's earlier days, when, a struggling suburban practitioner in London, he had first found himself involved in the web of Dr. Fu Manchu. His published journals of those singular experiences which he had shared with Sir Denis, had created such world-wide interest that to-day, as I knew, he was independent of the proceeds of his profession. But he was, as someone had said of him, a born healer; and he had the most extensive practice of any English physician in Cairo. Evidently my thoughts were reflected upon my face; for

"What are you grinning about?" the chief demanded.

"I was wondering," I replied, "if Sir Denis will allow me to publish an account of the story of the Masked Prophet."

"You published an account, as you term it," Rima interrupted, "of what happened in the Tomb of the Black Ape and afterwards. I didn't think it was too flattering to me, but I know you made a lot of money out of it. I don't really think, Uncle—" turning and snuggling up against Sir Lionel—"that it's quite fair, do you? Shouldn't *we* have a share?"

"Yes." The chief stared at me with smothered ferocity. "You've written me up in a painfully frank way, Greville, now I come to think about it . . . Ah! Here's Petrie!"

As he spoke, I saw the doctor come in from the terrace at a brisk pace. There was urgency in his manner, and when, sighting us, he hurried forward I realised that he was ill at ease.

His first thought, however, was for his patient; and dropping into a chair beside Rima, he looked at her in that encompassing manner which comes to a man who for many years has practised as a physician.

"Quite restored, I see," he said, and glanced critically at the cocktail. "Only one, Rima. Excitants are not desirable . . . yet!"

Seeing me about to call a waiter:

"As I'm rather late, Greville," he went on, "let's go in to dinner; if possible, find a quiet table, as there's something I have to tell you."

"Knew it!" said the chief loudly, watching the speaker. "Got something on your mind, Petrie. What is it?"

"You're right," Petrie admitted, smiling slightly. "I don't quite know what to make of it."

"Nor do I," Sir Lionel replied, "unless you tell me what it is."

"A long message from Smith in Damascus. It was relayed over the telephone. That's what detained me. But don't let us talk about it now."

We stood up and walked along the corridor, which is a miniature jewel bazaar, to the dining room. I had arranged for a quiet table at the farther end, and presently, when we were all seated and the chief, who was host, had given his orders:

"This message is disturbing, in a way," said Petrie. "There's a Dutch steamer of the Rotterdam Lloyd Line, the *Indramatra*, leaving Port Said tomorrow night for Southampton; and Smith insists that, baggage or no baggage, you must all leave in her!"

"What!" Sir Lionel cried so loudly that many heads were turned in our direction. "He must be mad. I won't budge an inch—not one inch—until Ali Mahmoud arrives with the gear."

Dr. Petrie looked grave.

"I have the message here," he continued; "and when I have read it to you, possibly you may change your mind.... Dr. Fu Manchu has been in Damascus. He has disappeared. Smith has every reason to believe that he is on his way here—to Cairo. His mission, Barton is to see *you!*"

Chapter Thirty-sixth

NAYLAND SMITH COMES ABOARD

THE *Indramatra* lay off the pontoon, opposite the Custom House at Port Said; and it was a night sailing. Ali Mahmoud had arrived in the nick of time; I could see him now from where I stood, supervising the shipment of the heavy baggage.

That curious sustained murmur, a minor chord made up of human voices, audible whenever cargo is being worked in this odd portal of the East, came to my ears, as I craned out watching the pontoon. I had left Rima, a stewardess, and two coolies busily unpacking trunks; for Rima had something of her uncle's gift for making people work enthusiastically in her interests. Part of her personal baggage had been deposited in her cabin, and, having explored the first of her trunks:

"There isn't a thing that's fit to wear!" she had declared. . . .

I had considered it prudent to join the chief.

That experienced old traveller had secured a suite with bath, at the Cairo office. Admittedly, the ship was not full, but, nevertheless, someone else had been pencilled in for this accommodation ahead of him. The someone else (a Member of Parliament, he turned out to be) was reduced to an ordinary double cabin, and the purser was having a bad quarter of an hour.

Sir Lionel, armed with a whisky and soda, was sprawling on the little sofa in his sitting room, his feet resting upon a stout wooden chest. He reminded me of an old buccaneer, gloating over ill-gotten treasure; and:

"Has Smith arrived?" he demanded.

"No. I'm just going up to make inquiries, chief . . ."

And so, now, I found myself craning out and watching the pontoon. It would be nearly an hour before the *Indramatra* sailed, but I could not imagine, since Sir Denis had missed us in Cairo, how he hoped to reach Port Said before we left. Nevertheless, he had advised us to expect him.

I glanced down at Ali Mahmoud, patiently checking the items of our baggage destined for the hold, and experienced a pang of regret in parting from him. Then again I stared towards the shore. I saw the headlights of a car which was being driven rapidly along the waterfront. I saw it pull up just short of the Custom House.

No other steamer was leaving that night, and although, admittedly, this might have been a belated passenger, something told me that it was Nayland Smith.

I was right.

Above the clatter of machinery and minor drone of human voices, with the complementary note of water lapping at the ship's side, a clamour reached me from the shore. There was urgency in the sound. And as I watched, I saw a police launch which had been lying just off the pontoon, run in, in response to a signal. A few moments later, and the little red craft was describing a flattened arc as she headed out rapidly for the *Indramatra*.

One glimpse I had in a momentary glare of the searchlight, of a man seated in the stern, and then I was hurrying down to the lower deck. I had no more than reached the head of the ladder when Nayland Smith came bounding up. As I greeted him:

"Quick!" he snapped and grasped my arm. "The purser's office—where is it? I don't know this ship."

"This way, Sir Denis."

Pushing past groups of passengers, mostly planters and officials from the Dutch East Indies, we went racing across to the purser's office. As I had expected, a number of people were waiting to interview that harassed official, but the curtain was drawn over his door, and I could hear an excited voice within. Sir Denis never hesitated for a moment. He rapped loudly, jerked the curtain aside, and:

"Mr. Purser!" he said, "I regret that I don't know your name—my apologies. But it is vitally urgent that I should see you for a few moments."

The purser, a Sumatra-born Dutchman, stout and normally good-humoured, I judged, at the moment was not in an amiable mood. Mr. John Kennington, M.P., a fussy little man resembling Tweedledee in spectacles, was literally dancing about in his room.

"I say it's an outrage, sir," he was exclaiming, "an outrage. This fellow, Sir Lionel Barton, this travelling mountebank, has almost literally thrown me out of a cabin which I reserved in

Cairo. As a British Member of Parliament, I wish to state——"

"I don't know your name, sir," said the purser, looking up wearily at Sir Denis—he spoke excellent English, for the Dutch are first-class linguists; "mine is Voorden: but you can see that I am very much engaged."

"Such a state of affairs," Mr. Kennington continued, extending his rotund person in the manner of a frog about to burst, "such a state of affairs would not be tolerated for a moment in the P. & O."

That, of course, was a slip, and put the purser on our side at once. His growing distaste for the angry passenger was reflected upon normally placid features.

"The P. & O., sir," said Nayland Smith, "is an admirable line, to which I can give you a personal introduction ensuring excellent accommodation."

Mr. Kennington paused, turned, and looked up at the grim face of the speaker; then:

"Possibly, sir, you may know that Members of Parliament, travelling officially, are afforded certain facilities——"

"I do know it, and I feel sure that your complaint is a just one. But since you are a Member of Parliament, you will naturally do everything in your power to assist me. A matter of national urgency demands that I should have two minutes' private conversation with Mr. Voorden."

Mr. Kennington blew himself up again.

"My dear sir," he replied, "I must take this opportunity of pointing out to you that I have certain rights here."

Sir Denis's temper, never of the best, was growing dangerously frayed.

"Mr. Voorden," he said quietly, "I don't know this gentleman's name, but have I your permission to place him in the alleyway until our very urgent business is concluded?"

The purser's broad face broke into a smile. It was a suggestion after his own heart; and:

"May I ask you, Mr Kennington," he said, addressing the outraged M.P., whose features were now assuming a hectic florid hue, "to allow me two minutes with this gentleman? His business, I think, is important."

"Important!" the other exploded. "Important! By heavens, sir, Rotterdam shall hear of you—Rotterdam shall hear of you!"

He expelled himself from the cabin.

"Here is my card, Mr. Voorden," said Sir Denis, laying a card upon the purser's table: "but in order to save your time and my own, I called upon the Dutch consul on my way to the docks. He was unable to accompany me, but he sends this note."

He laid upon the table a sheet of paper bearing the letterhead of the Dutch consulate in Port Said. The purser put on a pair of horn-rimmed glasses and read the note. Mr Kennington, not far away, might be heard demanding an interview with the captain.

"Sir Denis Nayland Smith," the purser, sanding up, "I am at your service. What can I do for you?"

"Thank you," said Sir Denis, and shook his hand. "Your passenger list, if you please. I want the name of everyone joining the ship at this port."

"Certainly! that is very simple. You will also wish to know, of course, what accommodation they have reserved?"

"Exactly."

A moment later Nayland Smith was bending over a plan of the ship, in close consultation with the purser. I moved to the curtain, drew it aside, and stepped into the alleyway. Mr. Kennington had discovered the second steward and was insisting that that official should conduct him to the captain. I had it in mind to endeavour to pacify the infuriated little man, when the matter was taken out of my hands.

"Sir Lionel Barton is the person's name," shouted Mr. Kennnigton—"who the devil may I ask is Sir Lionel Barton?"

Unfortunately for Mr. Kennington, at that moment Sir Lionel appeared on the scene.

"Does anybody want me?" he inquired in his deep gruff voice.

Mr. Kennington turned and looked up into that sun-baked, truculent mask. He tried bravely to sustain the glare of deepset eyes beneath tufted brows. But when he spoke, it was with a notable lack of confidence.

"Are you Sir Lionel Barton?"

"I am. Did you want me?"

The second steward escaped, leaving Mr. Kennington to fight his battle alone.

"There seems to be some misunderstanding about our cabins," he said in a tone of gentle melancholy. . . .

CHAPTER THIRTY-SEVENTH

THE RELICS OF THE PROPHET

THERE was some pretty straight talking in the chief's room five minutes later. Rima was not present.

"I have the outline of the thing complete, Barton," said Nayland Smith, puffing furiously at his pipe. "For God's sake, don't interrupt. Just listen. My time is brief. The man Amir Khan blundered onto the location of Mokanna's tomb in some way and up to the time of his disappearance, was undoubtedly acting on his own. I take it you paid him well for his information."

"I did."

Sir Denis nodded.

"He did not belong to that obscure sect, an offshoot of true Mohammedanism, which still holds the tradition of the New Koran. But he knew more than they do, because he knew where the prophet was buried. He was a *thug*; you always knew this. And he deserted because he was recalled by his immediate chief. The laws of *thuggee* (which I don't profess to understand) are very binding upon devotees. His chief learned what had happened; and his chief—"

"Was one of the Fu Manchu group!" Sir Lionel interrupted. "And so. . . ."

"And so the news reached the doctor. Where he was at the time, we shall probably never know—but he acted swiftly. The possibilities were tremendous. Islam is at least as divided as Christianity. A religious revival is long overdue. The man and the occasion, only, were wanted. Here was the occasion. Dr. Fu Manchu found the man."

"Whom did he find?"

"I don't know. Listen, and I will tell you all I know. In every religion there are secret sects. I have maintained for many years, in the face of much opposition from learned sources— and from you—that the organisation known as the Si-Fan embodies the greater part of these dissentients——"

"Rot!"

"Such a movement, reinforced by the backing of the Si-Fan,

would almost certainly have tipped the scale. This was what Dr. Fu Manchu saw. The arising of the prophet was staged for him when you blew up that lonely tomb in Khorassan. This he acted upon with the results which we know. Interested parties in the Moslem world were only too ready to receive the new prophet. His material qualities they were prepared to overlook. But it happens—and a memory of Greville's gave me the clue to the truth—that a certain fanatical sect, having representatives at Damascus and also at Mecca, possess or claim to possess copies of the New Koran."

"That's true," said the chief, shifting his feet uneasily, for he was sprawling upon the settee. "I've seen 'em. I knew what I was up against, Smith."

Nayland Smith looked at Sir Lionel with a sort of reluctant admiration.

"You're a remarkable man, Barton," he admitted. "If a modicum of discretion had been added to your outfit, much of this trouble might have been avoided."

"What trouble?" the chief shouted. He kicked at the wooden chest. "Where's the trouble? I've tricked every damned fool among them. And, by heaven! I've tricked Dr. Fu Manchu himself. You all wondered why I hung on so long in Ispahan——"

He began to laugh loudly; but:

"I know *now*," said Nayland Smith.

And he spoke the words so coldly that the chief's laughter was checked.

"I thought," he went on, "that you were bluffing in Cairo. I know your schoolboy sense of humour. It was a dramatic surprise to me, although I may not have shown it, when your old suitcase was opened before Mr. Aden and I saw the sword, the mask, and the gold plates."

He jumped out of his chair and began to move from foot to foot, since there was no room for him to promenade.

"I carried out my contract with Dr. Fu Manchu—Rima's life being the price at stake—in what I believed to be all honesty. Don't speak, Barton—let me finish. Dr. Fu Manchu is the most ghastly menace to our present civilisation which has appeared since Attila the Hun. He is an old man, but, by some miracle which I can only ascribe to his gigantic power, he is as forceful to-day as he was in the first hour that I ever set eyes on him in a forest of Burma. That's agreed. He has one virtue. According to his admittedly peculiar code—he is a man of honour."

"Stop!"

Sir Lionel was up, now, his strong hands clenched, his eyes glaring upon the speaker.

"Stop, Smith! I won't take it from you or from any man. I may have broken every other commandment, but I have never lied."

"Have I accused you of lying?" Sir Denis's voice was very cool.

"Practically, yes."

"You remained in Ispahan until Solomon Ishak, perhaps the finest craftsman in the East, had duplicated the relics of the prophet. Oh, it was clever work, Barton. But . . ."

"Well," growled the chief, still glaring at him. "But, what . . . ? Didn't the man Aden or Samarkan or whatever his name is—pass the stuff that we showed him in Shepheard's? Did I or did you undertake to deliver up anything else? We had Rima back, and we handed over the duplicates." Furiously he kicked the box. "Ali Mahmoud had the relics. He brought them from old Soloman Ishak back to Cairo, and from Cairo on board here. And there they are!"

He dropped back onto the settee, his mouth working evilly, for he was in murderous humour. But Nayland Smith continued to watch him calmly.

"It would be reviving an ancient libel to say that you argue like a Jesuit, Barton," he remarked coldly.

"Thanks!" snapped the chief. "You have probably said enough."

I think I have never felt more unhappy in my life. The facts now revealed to me were astounding; the ethics of the thing beyond me. But it was ghastly that these two old friends—men of first-rate genius in their separate spheres—should thus be almost at one another's throats.

Loyalty to the chief forbade my siding with Sir Denis, yet in my heart I knew that the latter was right. The price had been Rima's life; and Sir Lionel had played a faked card.

It didn't surprise me; and since he had succeeded, I had it in my heart to forgive him, but:

"You know chief," I said, "I can see what Sir Denis means.

So don't boil over. We were in the wrong."

I hadn't meant it; I am not clever enough to have thought of it; but that use of "we" rather did the trick. Sir Lionel relaxed and looked at me in an almost kindly way.

"You think so, Greville?" he growled.

"Well, it was the devil of a risk, and Dr. Fu Manchu," Nayland Smith snapped, "discovered the substitution in Damascus, on the very day, I believe, that I arrived there. By means of what secret knowledge held by certain imams of the Great Mosque he anticipated that the forgery would be detected, I don't know."

He paused—his pipe had gone out, and he struck a match; then:

"*Someone* spoke from the pulpit that evening. The huge mosque was packed to the doors. I have never seen such mass fanaticism in my life."

"Were you there?" asked the chief with sudden boyish enthusiasm.

"I was."

"Good old Smith!"

And in those words I recognised the fact that the storm had blown over.

"The speaker wore a green turban, a green robe, and a thick gold mask."

"It was Fu Manchu!"

"I am still inclined to doubt it. I don't think I could mistake him. If it were he, then he has thrown off the burden of thirty years. He held his audience in the palm of his hand, as I know Fu Manchu can do. But the virility of his voice . . ."

And as he spoke, a sort of half-memory stirred in my brain. It passed—leaving a blank.

"There were doubters there. And that very night, as I believe, the substitution was discovered. The new Mahdi opened brilliantly, Barton, but he met with a definite check in Damascus. What actually happened I naturally don't profess to know. But—" he pointed to the wooden chest on the floor of the cabin—"are they in there?"

"They are!" said the chief triumphantly.

"The rumour is already spreading—you know how news travels in these parts—that Mokanna is an impostor. I need

"Someone *spoke from the pulpit that evening*

I have never seen such a mass fanaticism in my life"

not add that our Intelligence Department is zealously fostering this. Only one thing could save the situation." He pointed again to the chest. "I don't know where Dr. Fu Manchu is, but from my knowledge of his methods I should predict that he is not far from Port Said at the present moment."

Those words sent a cold shudder down my spine.

"He's too late," growled Sir Lionel; "we sail in fifteen minutes."

"I know," Nayland Smith returned. "But while I'm aware that I am wasting words, if I were in your shoes, Barton, I should be disposed to send Ali Mahmoud ashore with that crate and sail in comfort."

"You'd do nothing of the sort!" shouted the chief, jumping up again. "You know it as well as I do."

"Very good. I've a few suggestions to make before I go ashore. I can't possibly leave Egypt for at least another week, when I hope that Petrie will be ready to join me."

Chapter Thirty-Eighth

"THE SWORD OF GOD"

"BOLT the door, Greville," said Sir Lionel.

I did as he directed. His stateroom presented an appearance of untidiness which, even for the chief, touched the phenomenal. He had unpacked the wooden crate, and the floor was littered with straw and paper.

It proved to contain three packages tied up in canvas; one, long and narrow, which enwrapped the sword of the prophet; another, the heaviest, rectangular and perhaps eight inches thick; and a smaller one, which was obviously some kind of box.

"Get busy with the big package," he directed energetically. "Untie the string, but don't cut it. We shall want to use it again."

"Very good," I said resignedly, and set to work.

The *Indramatra* had just pulled out from her berth, Nayland Smith and the Company's agent being the last two visitors to go down the ladder. Rima was in her cabin busily unfolding frocks which had been folded for weeks and about the condition of which she was in complete despair.

What Sir Lionel's object could be in unpacking these treasures, now that at last we had escaped with them, was a problem which defeated me. But mad though he was, there was generally some method in his madness.

"Gad! what a beauty!" he cried.

He had unwrapped the scimitar and was gazing upon it with the eyes of a lover. Indeed I knew, had known for many years, that the chief's heart was wholly in the past. He worshipped these relics of strange men and wild times, although his collections, of which he had one in each of his several houses, must have broken the heart of any museum curator. Priceless pieces were as likely to be found upon the floor, or on the seat of a chair where a careless visitor might sit upon them, as anywhere else. But the fact remained that his enthusiasm was genuine.

"You're a hell of a long time with the plates," he growled.

"These knots want a bit of coping with."

"Give it to me and unpack the mask."

I complied only too willingly.

"Can you see anything lying about, Greville, remotely resembling the Sword of God?—any fitting we could tear down?"

I began to laugh. The purpose of the chief's toil had become evident. He was at his favourite trick again.

"Really," I said, looking up from the floor where I was kneeling untying the box containing the mask, "I don't know what you have in mind, but short of seizing the ship, I can't see how anybody is going to gain access to the purser's safe."

"Can't you?" he growled. "Did you see how anybody was going to gain access to that room in Isphahan? I know more about the methods employed by Dr. Fu Manchu than you do, Greville. And as I told Smith just now, I think nothing of safes at any time. We shouldn't have the stuff now if I thought as you do."

"True enough," I admitted, and took out a delicate and exquisite mask from the box which held it.

"Gad!" exclaimed Sir Lionel in a low voice—"What a beauty! Unique, Greville, absolutely unique! This one item would make the reputation of any collector."

He paused in his task, stood up, and stared about him. Then from a battered leather hat box he took an old sun helmet, emptied a cigar box onto the bed (it contained quite a dozen cigars) and put the gold mask in their place. Tying the box with a piece of string, he dropped it into the helmet, returning the latter to its leather case. He threw the case on the settee.

"A very clever American," he remarked—"one Edgar Allan Poe—laid it down that the best place to hide a thing was where everyone could see it. Ha! here's what you want, Greville."

An umbrella belonging to Rima had somehow strayed into his cabin, left there in error by a steward, no doubt when the baggage had come aboard. She had bought it in Cairo. It was short, with a fancifully carved handle of glass, representing the Sphinx.

"Wrap it up," he said; "that's splendid."

He laughed, in his loud, boisterous fashion. And something of his crazy humour began to infect me also. His treatment of a menace which had overhung us darkly for so long, which already had cost several lives and had stirred up the beginnings of a promising Arab rising, was stimulating, to say the least.

I wrapped up the umbrella in the canvas packing, tying it with care; and Sir Lionel, having unfastened the gold plates, examined them lingeringly. I knew he would have liked to devote hours to that examination, but the time was not now.

"Where's the Burberry?" he asked.

I pointed to an open door communicating with his bedroom; my old Burberry hung upon a hook there.

He nodded, wrapped the sheets of thin gold in pieces of newspaper, and slipped them into the big pocket of the coat, which contained them quite easily.

"Let me see!" he cried.

I exhibited the parcel I had just completed.

"Not bad," he commented; "I think it will pass. Now, to seal it."

Crossing to a little writing table, and kicking all sorts of litter out of his way as he went, he opened a box containing odds and ends of stationery, and presently found a piece of sealing wax. Lighting many matches and dropping a quantity of wax upon the carpet, he sealed several of the knots, pressing his signet ring upon each of them. Then, holding up the finished product, he laughed like a schoolboy.

"Number one ready!" he cried. "Ah! you have done another. What did you put in the box?"

"Nothing," I replied; "the weight of the mask is negligible."

"Hand me that thin atlas over there," he directed.

From a pile of books thrown carelessly on the floor, I collected the volume to which he referred. It was roughly of about the same size and shape as the fifteen gold plates laid together. It was also very heavy.

"Good enough!" he said, weighing it in his hand. "Hello! Who's this? Don't open, Greville."

Someone was rapping on the cabin door.

"Who's there?" roared Sir Lionel.

"Steward, sir. Miss Barton has asked me to inquire if an umbrella which is missing has been brought in here."

"No," roared the chief, "it hasn't Never seen it."

"Do you mind if I take a look round, sir?"

"I mind very much. I'm busy. Go away!"

He stood upon the settee, drew the curtain aside, and peered through a porthole.

"We're clear of shore, Greville," he reported. "By heaven! I've tricked him this time!"

A few minutes later we completed the third parcel to his satisfaction, and:

"Cut along to your cabin," he directed; "you haven't far to go. Carry your Burberry over your arm;, you can hold the sword underneath it."

"Very good. Where shall I put them?"

"Put the sword under your bed for the time being, and hang the Burberry in the bathroom, or anywhere. I'll come along presently and decide definitely. But first we must see the purser."

Unbolting the door, we sallied forth. I went along to my cabin and then rejoined Sir Lionel. Stewards were still coming and going, carrying stray items of baggage, the ship being in that state of unrest which prevails on leaving port.

"I don't trust these Javanese," the chief whispered. "Every one of them might belong to Dr. Fu Manchu."

I felt rather disposed to agree with him. But Nayland Smith had been insistent upon our leaving by the first available ship, and failing the *Indramatra*, we should have had to wait for three days.

Passengers were standing about at the foot of the stairs in the neighbourhood of the purser's room, examining notices and making aimless inquiries of almost every European member of the crew who passed. Carrying our strange burdens, we came to the purser's door.

"I simply refuse to occupy a cabin," an excited voice was shouting within, "in which the running water resembles beer. It's scandalous, sir, scandalous!"

"Our friend Kennington," said the chief, unceremoniously jerking the curtain aside and walking in. "Good-evening, purser. Sorry to trouble you, but I have some valuables which I wish to leave in your care."

"Very good, Sir Lionel," said the harassed officer, turning in his chair and looking up at us.

"One of them looks a bit bulky for the safe. Perhaps we can manage."

Mr. Kennington, blown up to his full dimensions, was standing at the farther end of the room, glaring. On further examination he was a singular-looking object. His rotundity seemed positively artificial, so suddenly did it develop, and his dark eyes, behind horn-rimmed spectacles, did not seem to belong to his red and choleric face. He had carroty hair, close-cut and an absurd little moustache.

"I will not be side-tracked in this manner, sir," he cried, as the purser, standing up, turned and unlocked the big safe. "I have already been given accommodation other than that which I reserved, and now..."

"And now," said the chief, looking him up and down in his most truculent and intolerant manner, "you have been given tap water which resembles beer."

"I have, sir. And I will not tolerate it for one moment—not for one moment!"

"Neither should I," said the chief, "if I were a teetotaller. Are you a teetotaller?"

"I am, sir."

"And a member of the Labour party, I take it?"

"Certainly."

"Funny thing, Greville," said Sir Lionel, looking at me, "how these enemies of capital always insist upon the best accommodation. But——"

"By a little readjustment," said the purser, "I can manage your three sealed packages, Sir Lionel."

He reclosed and locked the massive safe.

"And now you will want a receipt for them."

He sat down at his table again.

"I have registered my protests, sir," said Mr. Kennington sternly; "my second protest since I came on board this ship. Since you don't seem to propose to attach any importance to it, I shall make a point of placing the matter before the captain."

He bowed with absurd dignity and went out.

"You know, gentlemen," said Voorden, taking a printed form

from a case on his table, "one passenger like that puts years on a ship's purser. According to his passport, Mr. Kennington does not travel much, which perhaps accounts for it. Ah, well!" he sighed wearily, filling in the form, "I suppose it's the sort of thing that the company pays me for. There you are, sir."

Sir Lionel thanked him, folded up the receipt, and placed it in his pocket case. As we went out and were crossing towards the stairs, I heard Mr. Kennington talking to the chief steward.

"I insist upon a table to myself, steward."

"I will do my best, sir."

"It would be pleasant for everybody concerned," said the chief in a loud voice, "if some travellers would insist upon a *ship* to themselves, and stay on board for the rest of their lives."

Whereupon he began to laugh thunderously.

Chapter Thirty-ninth

FLIGHT FROM EGYPT

I STOOD at the after end of the promenade deck, my arm very tightly about Rima. Together, we watched the lights of Egypt fading in the distance. It was good to be together after that brief but dreadful hiatus in Cairo, but yet, although neither of us spoke, I knew we shared a common regret. It was true we had known sorrow in Egypt, but we had known great happiness there, and the happiness outweighed the sorrow.

It was growing late, and we had the starboard side of the deck to ourselves; a few passengers lingered in the smoke-room, but nearly everybody was in bed. It would have been good to have Nayland Smith with us, but he and Dr. Petrie hoped to be in London in time for the spectacular wedding which Sir Lionel had planned for us.

Personally, I looked forward to that function with the utmost horror. But I was not at all sure that Rima didn't secretly enjoy the prospect. Rima had been a very popular débutante two years before; and I knew the chief would enjoy himself to the top of his bent in circulating paragraphs among gossip writers, and in employing his genius for showmanship to make our wedding a successful public entertainment.

In fact, having few friends of my own in London, and knowing that Rima had many, I felt that those days in the Mediterranean which lay ahead would be the last for a long time during which I should have her to myself.

No words were necessary between us. I just held her very closely, and she nestled against me in perfect contentment, while together we watched the lights of Port Said growing more and more dim upon the horizon.

Only nine passengers had joined the *Indramatra* there, including our own party of thee. They had been checked up by Nayland Smith, and not one of them came within the shadow of suspicion. Other than these six first-class passengers and ourselves, no one had come aboard in Egypt, nor had the crew been reinforced. I remembered Sir Denis's parting words:

"Unless, which isn't impossible, since we're dealing with Dr. Fu Manchu, an agent of his has been smuggled aboard disguised as cargo, it would appear, Greville, that, for once in his life, the doctor has missed fire."

It was cold comfort, since I had reason to know that the doctor rarely missed fire. And I hugged Rima so closely that she demanded a kiss and received many. . . .

When at last, and very reluctantly, I turned in that night, common sense told me that Sir Lionel had pulled off his daring trick and risked Rima's life in the process. But, once in Europe, I believed that we had little to fear on this score, since the religious-political unity of the relics by then would have become nil. Only by their immediate recovery could Dr. Fu Manchu hope to re-establish the claims of the new prophet, already challenged by reason of their absence. A week would make all the difference.

But, in destroying this daring scheme of the greatest, and most evil man I had ever known, what had we done?

His mentality was incalculable. I believed him too great to waste an hour of his time in so futile a purpose as vengeance. But in this I knew that I might be mistaken. He was a Chinaman, and I knew little of Chinese mentality. He was unscrupulous, valuing human life no more highly than the blades of grass one treads upon. But in this he conformed to his own peculiar code.

No desire for personal aggrandisement inspired him, Nayland Smith had assured me. He aimed to lift China from the mire into which China had fallen. He was, according to his peculiar lights, a great patriot. And, this I knew, according to those same peculiar lights, he was scrupulously honourable.

True, the terms he had extorted upon the strength of the abduction of Rima had been blackmail at its vilest, but blackmail of a kind acceptable to his own code. We had agreed to his terms and had set our names to that agreement. Such implicit trust had he placed in our English honour that he had met us alone—the gesture of a great man if a great villain.

And in all good faith on the part of Nayland Smith and myself we had tricked him! Would he have tricked us in that way? Was it what his inscrutable Chinese conscience would regard as fair warfare, or was it not?

I doubted, and, to be perfectly honest, I feared. I had warned Rima to bolt her door before I said good-night to her, and now, entering my own cabin, I did the same. I made sure that the sword of God was in my golf bag concealed among the clubs, and the gold plates in the pocket of my Burberry before I began to undress. The wooden chest, nailed up again, stood at the end of a blind alleyway leading to the chief's suite.

The Mediterranean was calm as a great lake, and there was little motion perceptible from stem to stern of the *Indramatra*, My cabin was forward on the port side and only two removed from that occupied by Sir Lionel. These cabins opened on a narrow gallery overlooking the dining saloon, and Rima's was nearly opposite my own.

I had experienced a pang of uneasiness on realising that the stewards were almost exclusively Javanese, some of them of a very Mongolian type: silent, furtive, immobile, squatting like images at the corner of nearly every alleyway—their slippers beside them, their faces expressionless.

To-night, however, they had all disappeared. The ship was silent, the saloon a dark well. Only faint vibrations from the screw propellers and that creaking of woodwork inseparable from a ship at sea, disturbed the stillness.

I had only partially unpacked, and feeling very wide awake, I began to grope among my baggage for a tin of tobacco which I had bought just before leaving Cairo. I had determined to smoke a final pipe before turning in. A final drink would have been welcome, but I doubted if I could obtain one.

Following some searching, I discovered the tobacco, and I had just raised the lid and begun to fill my pipe when there came a soft rapping upon the door of the cabin. . . .

CHAPTER FORTIETH

THE SEAPLANE

I CONFESS that I was reluctant to open my door. It was perhaps not surprising after the strain which had been imposed upon me during those past few weeks; but I was conscious of a definite decline of morale. I had many unhappy memories and some dreadful ones: not the least of these that strange lacuna in Cairo, throughout which I had obviously been a passive instrument of the Chinese doctor's will

The rapping was repeated, rather more insistently, but yet not loudly.

I laid my pipe down on the bed and moved towards the cabin door. Save for that slight creaking of woodwork as the ship rode a barely perceptible swell, there was no sound.

"Who's there?" I said sharply, but without shooting the bolt back.

"Urgent radio message for Mr. Greville."

I heaved a sigh of relief which must have been audible beyond the door, shot the bolt back, and there stood a Marconi operator.

"I shouldn't have disturbed you in the ordinary way," he explained, "but the message was marked 'Immediate delivery.'"

"Thanks," I said; "I hadn't turned in."

I took the flimsy envelope.

"Good-night," I added.

"Good-night, sir."

I returned and bolted the door. Then, tearing open the message, I read eagerly.

SOMETHING WILL BE ATTEMPTED TO-NIGHT STOP
STAY AWAKE AND KEEP A SHARP LOOK-OUT
                              NAYLAND SMITH

I dropped the message on the bedcover. From what possible source was such an attempt to be looked for? And what should I do?

Lighting my pipe, I stared at the golf bag propped in a corner of the cabin, a strange repository for a relic which already had such a bloody history; but in Sir Lionel's opinion a better one than the purser's safe.

Cudgel my brains as I would—and I was very wide awake now—I could conceive of no plan—even assuming the real whereabouts of the damnable relics to be known to our enemies—whereby they could obtain possession of them, otherwise than by an open raid on my cabin and that of the chief.

It was preposterous! Even if it were admissible that Fu Manchu had servants among the native members of the crew—what could they do?

Yet, here was the message. What in Heaven's name did it mean?

One thing I determined upon: to obey Nayland Smith's instructions. I would mount guard until daylight, when the normal life of the ship would be resumed. Then, if nothing had occurred, I might safely assume the danger past.

With this laudable object in view, I removed my coat and threw myself on the bed, taking up a booklet issued by the shipping company and illustrated with charts showing the mileage between ports of call.

I read on industriously. Once I thought I detected a faint sound out in the alleyway, but, putting the pamphlet down and listening intently it presently resolved itself into a variation of that endless creaking. I realised that the gentle, soothing motion had become more marked; the swell was slightly increasing.

How long I pursued my reading, I cannot say, for, as often occurs at such times, although I imagined myself to be wide awake, I was actually tired out, and probably no more than a few minutes later I was fast asleep.

I suppose I slept lightly, for there could be little doubt about what awakened me. I know that I sat up with a start, and at first was utterly confused by my surroundings. Ash was on the counterpane where I had dropped my pipe; fortunately, it had not set fire to it. I sat listening.

Above the noise of creaking woodwork and the dim vibration of the shaft, a new sound was perceptible. I glanced at my watch. I had slept for two hours.

Stepping to my cabin door, I shot the bolt, opened, and looked out into the alleyway. Darkness and silence. Nothing moved. I returned and even more plainly, now, could hear this new disturbance.

I had carefully closed the porthole, having painful memories of the acrobatic methods employed by agents of Dr. Fu Manchu. I unscrewed the bolts and opened it. The sound became much louder; and curiosity grew overpowering. I was as widely awake as ever now, and I determined to go up on deck for a moment.

I had discovered that my cabin door possessed a key—which is unusual in English ships. I locked it, went quietly along the alleyway, and mounted the stairs. Not a soul was about. Both entrances were closed, but the sound had seemed to come from the port side, and therefore I opened the port door and stepped out on deck.

It was a clear, starry night. And as I looked upward and aft my theory was confirmed.

Some kind of heavy aircraft, to judge from the deep drone of her propellers, was flying on a parallel course and rapidly overtaking the *Indramatra*. I went up the ladder to the boat deck, thinking I could obtain a better view. In this I was right.

She was, I thought, a seaplane, but by reason of her position in relation to the ship, and the darkness of the night, I could not be sure of this. I glanced forward to the bridge.

The officer of the watch was out on the port wing, his glasses directed upwards; and I had time to wonder if the rigid discipline of the Dutch Mercantile Marine necessitated his logging the occurrence.

I turned and went back to my cabin. The seaplane, for such I now clearly saw it to be, had passed the ship, and was some little distance ahead of us.

About to pass the alleyway communicating with the chief's suite, I pulled up in doubt. The light was bad, but I could not see the wooden crate which formerly had contained the relics of the prophet.

I tiptoed along, to make sure. Undoubtedly, the crate was gone!

This, of course, might have been accounted for in several ways; yet I was practically certain that the crate had been there when I turned in. I entered my own cabin, and automatically plunged my hand in the golf-bag. The Sword of God was safe. I felt the pendulous pocket of my Burberry in the wardrobe—and the New Creed remained in its hiding place.

I had just slipped into my pyjamas when again came a knocking on the cabin door.

From the jump which I gave, I knew how badly my nerves had suffered.

"Who is it?" I cried.

"Very sorry, Mr. Greville! Marconi again."

I opened the door.

"It's all right," I said, smiling without effort, for frankly I was relieved. "What is it this time?"

"It's another urgent message. It looks as though we had a crook aboard!"

"What!"

I took the radiogram and read:

NO M P NAME OF KENNINGTON IN PRESENT COMMONS STOP ADVISE PURSER AT ONCE AND INTERROGATE PASSENGER

        NAYLAND SMITH

Looking up, I met the glance of the operator.

"It's queer, isn't it?" he commented. "But I don't see much point in waking the purser at this time of night. Are you by any chance connected with the English police, sir?"

"No. My correspondent is."

"Oh, I see. Well if you want to wake the purser, I can show you his room."

"I'll think it over," I replied. "I know where to find you if I decide to see him."

"Right aft on the boat deck," he said, and turned.

"Good-night!"

"Good-night."

I had just reclosed the door, and sitting down was considering Nayland Smith's second message when there came a sudden lull; a queer stillness. At first, I could not account for it. Then, I knew what had happened.

The engines had been rung off.

Chapter Forty-first

A RUBBER BALL

In much the same way, I suppose, as the stopping of a clock will awake a sleeper, the stoppage of the propellers awakened many passengers in the *Indramatra*. As I pulled on a dressing gown and hurried out into the alleyway, voices and movements were audible all about me.

Then, staring across the yawning black gap of the dining saloon, I saw Rima, dishevelled, but adorably dishevelled, endeavouring to adjust a hastily grasped bathrobe. Her glance met mine from the opposite gallery.

"Oh, Shan!" she cried. "What's happened? I didn't get to sleep until about half an hour ago; I thought I heard knockings and voices. . ."

"I don't know, darling. I'm going to find out."

No sound came from the chief's cabin: doubtless he was fast asleep. Rima and I apparently were the only two passengers sufficiently curious about the stoppage of the engines to have left our rooms. As I joined her at the foot of the staircase the *Indramatra* got under way again but was putting about, as I could plainly detect.

"We're turning back!" exclaimed Rima. "Let's go up and see what's happening."

We went up, and having fought with the fastenings of the starboard door, finally got out on deck. The night was clear enough, and I could see no sign of any craft ahead.

We mounted the ladder to the boat deck. I saw the commander, a seaman of the old school, who, with his fine face and pointed grey beard, might have posed for Vandyck, going forward to the bridge, muffled in a top coat.

Holding Rima tightly as we craned over between two boats, I saw what had happened.

The seaplane floated on an oily swell about three lengths away from us. Assuming her to be in difficulties, the officer of the watch had put the ship about. And now, the *Indramatra's* searchlight cast a sudden dazzling glare upon the sea; and I saw something else:

An object which looked like a big football was moving in the direction of the seaplane in the wake of a swimmer wearing a life jacket, who, striking out lustily, was apparently towing the ball behind him!

"What ever's that?" Rima whispered.

From the bridge of the *Indramatra* came a roar through a megaphone; the commander doubtless: but since he spoke in Dutch, I could not follow his words. The engines were rung off again. We lay-to very near the sea-and-air craft; but no reply came from her crew.

The swimmer, towing his singular burden, grasped one of the floats. I saw that a ladder had been thrown down to assist him, and as I watched, he began to clamber up. At which moment:

"Greville!" came a hoarse voice. "What the hell's happening?"

I turned, still holding Rima tightly—and there was the chief, wrapped in his untidy dressing gown.

"I don't know," I replied. "But I'm glad you're here. I have news for you——"

Another challenge came from the bridge—and brought forth no response. The swimmer climbed on board the seaplane. All that I could make out of him was that he wore bathing kit and had a cap upon his head. The light touched him momentarily.

That object which resembled a football was hauled up; and, as we watched, I saw the propellers started. There was some commotion before they cleared away. Men were climbing aboard, clearly visible in the glare of the searchlight. Then the seaplane was off, skimming over the surface of the Mediterranean like a seagull; presently to take to the air, rise, bank sharply and sweep back for the coast of Egypt.

I heard, dimly, a bell, and the engines came to life again. The *Indramatra* was being put back on her course.

Chapter Forty-second

THE PURSER'S SAFE

As we regained the main deck, it became evident that something extraordinary was afoot. The purser, in uniform, but wearing a white muffler in lieu of a collar, was standing by the door of his room with the second engineer and another officer. He looked very pale, I thought, and as Sir Lionel came in Voorden fixed a rather wild gaze upon him.

Before he had time to speak, the captain also hastily dressed, appeared from an alleyway and joined the group.

"Something's wrong!" Rima whispered.

A sort of embarrassed hush descended when we came down; then:

"Sir Lionel Barton, I believe?" said the captain, stepping forward. "Your name is well known in my country. But I have not before had the pleasure of meeting you. My name is Vanderhaye."

"How d'you do, Captain," growled the chief, and shook hands. "What's the trouble?"

The captain glanced at the purser and shrugged helplessly.

"I'm afraid, sir," said the latter, addressing Sir Lionel, "that you have suffered a heavy loss."

"What!"

"It is," explained Captain Vanderhaye, his steady blue eyes fixed upon the chief, "a case of minor piracy. Nothing of the kind has ever occurred to me in the forty years I have been at sea. I regret your loss, Sir Lionel, more deeply because it has happened in my ship. But here are the facts: you may judge if I or my officers are to blame."

He stepped to the door of the purser's room, which, as I saw now, was open, and indicated the keyhole with an outstretched finger. The chief, Rima and I, grouped around him, and as I bent forward I saw a really amazing thing.

Where the keyhole had been, as the fitting belonging to a brass flap clearly indicated, was a jagged hole, perhaps an inch and a half in diameter, going clean through the door!

It was sufficiently obvious that such a tunnel must have destroyed the lock, leaving the door at the mercy of any intruder.

"This," said the captain, "is strange enough. How such a thing could be done silently I cannot explain. But be good enough to step inside."

He entered the office. The chief's face was very grim, but, knowing him, I could see that he was stifling a smile. Rima stayed very close to me.

"Look!"

Captain Vanderhaye was pointing to the big safe. The pale-faced purser stood beside him, watching us almost pathetically. And, as I looked, I wondered; looking longer—my wonder grew.

In one hand the commander held a lock, with the other he pointed to a gap, roughly square and some six or seven inches across, in the steel door of the safe.

"This steel," he said, and tapped the lock, "has been cut through like a piece of cheese. No blow lamp could have been used—it would have taken too long and would have aroused some of the people in neighbouring cabins. But see——"

He ran his forefinger along the edge of the cut-out lock. The frayed steel crumbled away like biscuit!

Placing the lock on the purser's table, he shrugged his broad shoulders.

"It is magic!" he declared. "A safebreaker armed with some new thing of science. What can I say? He sprang overboard with his booty and was picked up by that strange seaplane." He swung the door widely open. "Look for yourselves. Nothing has been disturbed, except. . . ."

"Your three sealed parcels, Sir Lionel," said the purser huskily, "which were here, in the bottom of the safe. They are gone!"

Chapter Forty-third

THE VOICE IN BRUTON STREET

IN THE absence of Rima and the chief, the big gloomy house in Bruton Street overpowered me. But with characteristic disregard of my personal wishes Sir Lionel that morning had carried Rima off to Norfolk—true, for two days only. But London, much as I had longed to see it again, can be a lonely spot for a man with few friends.

By common consent, that most singular episode on the high seas had been hushed up as far as possible. It took its place, of course, in the ship's log.

Examination of the cabin occupied by the pseudo Member of Parliament revealed the fact that two of his three trunks were empty, and that the third contained discarded clothing—and a pneumatic pump. A life jacket was missing from its place; and the crate which had once held the relics (broken open) was discovered in his bathroom. He had taken the precaution of examining this first, thereby exhibiting a knowledge of Sir Lionel's methods!

That the floating ball had contained the sealed packages stolen from the purser's safe was beyond dispute. He had brought this remarkable piece of equipment for that purpose. It was, I suppose, a large rubber bag in two sections which could be hermetically screwed together and then inflated by means of a pump, when, assuming its contents to be not too heavy, it would float.

The method employed in opening the safe, as the captain had said, was a new development in burglary. Later, looking back upon my profound mystification, the genius of Dr. Fu Manchu has positively awed me; for I know now, although I did not know then, that he himself, with that sardonic humour peculiarly his own, had demonstrated this very process in that untraceable house outside Cairo!

Who was the man posing as "Mr. Kennington"?

Obviously his appearance was due to a cunning disguise. My impression of the swimmer who had climbed into the seaplane was that of a slender, athletic figure. He had been a wonderful actor, too, admirably chosen for his rôle, since by drawing attention to himself at the outset he had completely lulled everyone's suspicion—even deceiving Nayland Smith. . . .

These queer memories often claimed my mind at the most unlikely moments. We had been absent from England more than a year and had brought back a stack of stuff to be disposed of and catalogued. This tedious business, the chief invariably left to me.

I was three deep in appointments with British Museum authorities, the Royal Society, and others too numerous to mention.

The bloodstained relics of Mokanna occupied a case to themselves in the famous Museum Room at Bruton Street. Sir Lionel had several properties in England, one of which, however, he had recently sold. His collection was distributed among the others, but the gems were in London.

Already, as I had anticipated, he had opened his campaign of publicity for the wedding. With characteristic disregard for the conventions, he had insisted that I must put up at his house. And during the past few days, almost every time I had gone out with Rima I had found our path beset by Press photographers. On more than one occasion I had bolted—to save myself from committing an assault.

Rima and the chief left by an eleven o'clock train for Norfolk, and, a busy day's work now concluded, I looked forward to a dull evening. However, by chance I picked up an old acquaintance at the club; we did a show together and then went on to supper, killing time quite agreeably. For a few hours, at any rate, I forgot my more or less constant longing for Rima.

She was already swamped in appointments with costumiers, hat makers, and others, and had gone to Norfolk to rest, specifying that she would be absent for only two days. She would have refused to go at all, I am sure, under ordinary circumstances; but Mrs. Petrie was meeting her there. Petrie and Sir Denis were already homeward bound, and the chief had planned the return to Norfolk to synchronise with their arrival in London.

If Sir Lionel ever enters paradise, it is beyond doubt that he will reorganise the angels. . . .

I parted from my friend at the top of the Haymarket in the neighbourhood of one o'clock and decided to walk back to Bruton Street. As I set out, going along deserted Piccadilly, a panorama of the recent years unrolled itself before my mind. The giant shadow of Fu Manchu lay over all my memories.

There had been a time, and this not so distant, when I should have hesitated to walk alone along Piccadilly at one o'clock in the morning; but in some queer fashion my feelings in regard to Dr. Fu Manchu had undergone a change.

Since that unforgettable interview in the Great Pyramid, I had formed an impression of his greatness which, oddly enough, gave me a sense of security. This may be difficult to understand, but what I mean is that I believed him too big to glance aside at one so insignificant as myself. If ever I stood in his way, he would crush me without hesitation; at the moment he had nothing to gain by intruding upon my humble existence.

So I mused, staring about me as I walked. His resources, I realised, were enormous, apparently inexhaustible, as the daring robbery from the *Indramatra* on the high seas had shown; but the motive which had actuated this could inspire Dr. Fu Manchu no longer.

There had been a short paragraph in *The Times* that morning (confirming the latest news from Sir Denis) which indicated that the Mokanna rising, or threat of a rising, sometimes referred to as the "Coming of the New Mahdi," had subsided almost as suddenly as it had arisen. The explanation of the *Times* correspondent was that the leader of the movement, whose identity remained unknown, had proved to be an impostor.

There was a fair amount of traffic in Piccadilly, but there were few pedestrians. I lighted my pipe. Crossing to the corner of Bond Street I saw a constable patiently testing the fastenings of shop doors. My thoughts flashed back to the many market streets of the East I had known. . . .

I began to feel pleasantly sleepy. Another busy day was before me; the chief was preparing a paper dealing with Mokanna relics which he would read before the Royal Society. Embodying, as it did, the truth about the abortive rising of the Masked Prophet, it was calculated to create a tremendous sensation, doubtless involving Notes between the Persian Legation and the Foreign Office. This, of course, which any normal man must have wished to avoid, was frankincense and myrrh in the nostrils of Sir Lionel.

At eleven o'clock four famous experts had been invited to examine the relics: Hall-Ramsden of the British Museum; Dr. Brieux of Paris; Professor Max Eisner—Germany's greatest Orientalist; and Sir Wallace Syms of the Royal Society.

I think the chief's hasty departure had something to do with this engagement. He avoided his distinguished contemporaries as one avoids a pestilence. I had rarely known such a meeting which had not developed into a fight.

"Better wait for the Royal Society night, Greville," he had said. "Then I can go for the lot of 'em together!"

Turning into Bruton Street, I saw it deserted as far as Berkeley Square. Sir Lionel's house was one of the few not converted to commercial use; for this once favoured residential district is being rapidly absorbed into the shopping zone. He had had tempting offers for the property; but the mere fact that others were so anxious to buy was sufficient to ensure his refusal to sell. The gloomy old mansion, which he rarely occupied, but where a staff of servants was maintained, cost him somewhere in the neighbourhood of two thousand a year to keep empty.

I was in sight of the entrance, guarded by two miniature obelisks, and was already fumbling for my key when an odd thing occurred.

The adjoining house had been up for sale ever since I could remember. It was unoccupied and plastered all over with auctioneers' boards—a pathetically frequent sight in Mayfair. And as I passed the iron railing guarding the area of the basement—indeed, had my foot on Sir Lionel's steps—a voice called me by name.

"Shan!"

The voice came from the basement of the empty house!

It was a woman's voice; not loud, but appealing. My heart leapt wildly. In tone it was not unlike the voice of Rima!

I turned back, staring down into the darkness below. An illusion, I thought. Yet I could have sworn it was a human voice. And as I stood there looking down:

"Shan!" it came again, more faintly.

It chilled me! it was uncanny—but investigate I must. I looked up and down the street; not a soul was in sight. Then, pushing open the iron gate, I descended the steps to the little sunken forecourt.

There was no repetition of the sound, and it was very dark down there in the area. But I could see that a window of the empty house had been taken out, and it occurred to me that the call had come from someone inside. Standing by the frameless window:

"Who's there?" I cried.

There was no reply.

Yet I knew that a second time I could not have been mistaken. Someone had called my name. I must learn the truth. My pipe gripped firmly between my teeth, and, ignoring accumulated dust on the ledge, I climbed over a low sill and dropped into the gloom of the deserted house. I put my hand into my topcoat pocket in search of matches. . . .

Chapter Forty-fourth

"THIS WAS THE ONLY WAY..."

A PARALYSING grip seized my ankles; my arms were pinioned behind me, and an impalpable something was pressed over my mouth! I experienced a sudden sharp pain in my arm, as though something had seared the flesh. Then . . . I realised that, struggle as I might, I was helpless—helpless as a child!

That I had walked into a trap laid by common footpads was the thought that flashed across my mind. But the presence of a woman, of a woman who knew my name, promptly banished it. I had walked into a trap—yes! But the identity of the one who had baited that trap suddenly forced itself upon my brain with all the reality of a vision: long, narrow, brilliantly green eyes seemed to be looking into mine out of the darkness. . . .

I was spurred to a great effort for safety. I exerted every nerve and sinew in a violent bid for liberty.

Good heavens! *what* was it that had me at its mercy! Surely no human hands gripped my ankles; no arms of flesh and blood could hold a struggling, muscular man, immovable!

Yet, so I was held—immovable! My strivings were utterly futile: no sound of quickened breathing, nothing to show that my struggles inconvenienced these unseen captors. No flinching; no perceptible tremor of the hands—if hands they were—that had locked themselves about me.

I swore in an agony of furious impotence. But only a groan escaped from the pad held over my mouth. Then, I stood still—tensed nervously. . . . The crowning strangeness of the thing had suddenly been borne home to me.

Held captive though I was, no attempt had been made on my personal possessions, no word had been spoken! Nothing had moved—nothing breathed. Indeed, although I stood but a few yards from a Mayfair street, there was something awful in the stillness—something uncanny in the silent strength which held me.

Doubts were dispelled; the cold water of nervous fear trickled down my spine. For what is more fearful than utter helplessness in the face of an enemy? I was afraid—grimly, dreadfully afraid.

I felt chilled, too, as though by the near presence of ice. The pad was not pressed so tightly over my mouth as to be stifling, but nevertheless I held my breath, listening. Save for the thumping of my heart, not a sound could I hear.

Then, from afar off, as though from a remote room of the empty house, came a voice—a wonderful and a strange voice, penetrating, sweet, and low; the voice of a woman. Although the speaker seemed to be far away—very far away—the impression was not as that of a loud voice heard in the distance; it was that of a soft, caressing voice which carried clearly every word to my ear, from some other place; almost from some other world.

"You have nothing to fear, Shan," it said. "No harm shall come to you. This was the only way."

The voice ceased . . . and then, I was free!

For several seconds, an unfamiliar numbness, the spell of the hidden speaker, lay upon me. I stood stock still, questioning my sanity. Then natural instincts reasserted themselves. I lashed out right and left, with hand and foot, might and main!

A gashed knuckle was my only reward—caused by a window casement. With fingers far from steady, at last I found the matches, struck one and looked quickly about me.

I was alone!

The unsatisfactory light showed a large kitchen, practically stripped; a big, dirty cooking range at one end, torn wall paper, and general odds and ends upon the floor; an old whitewash pail in a corner—my pipe lying at my feet. Absolutely nothing else. I ran to the only door which I could see.

It was locked.

The cupboards! . . . both were empty!

My fourth match smouldered down to my fingers, and, as a man in a dream, I climbed out again into the well of the area, looking up at dirty vacant windows, plastered over with house agents' bills.

"What the devil!" I said aloud.

A voice answered from immediately above me.

"Hello, there!"

I turned with a start. It was a policeman—a real substantial constable; the same, I thought, whom I had seen examining shop doors in Bond Street.

"What's your game, eh?"

He was standing by the iron gate, looking down at me. My first impulse was to tell him the truth. I was conscious of a crying necessity for someone to confide in. Then, the thought of the question which had already flashed through my own mind restrained me: such a tale would be discredited by any, and by every policeman in the force.

"It's all right, constable," I said, going up the steps. "I thought I heard a row in this house, so I went in to investigate. But there seems to be no one there."

The man's attitude of suspicion relaxed when he had had a good look at me.

"I live next door," I went on, "and was just about to go in when I heard it."

"What sort of a row, sir?"

"Don't know exactly," I replied—"scuffling sounds."

The officer looked surprised.

"Can't be rats, can it?" he mused. "Been inside?"

"I looked in through that broken kitchen window."

"Nobody there?"

"No, nobody."

"Think I'll take a look round."

He went down the steps, shot a light into the broken window, and finally climbed over, as I had done. He examined the kitchen, trying the door which I knew to be locked; then:

"Must have been mistaken, sir," he said; "the place has been empty for years. But I believe it's been sold recently and is going to be converted into flats."

He walked up the steps and approached the front entrance, directing his light through the glass panels into an empty hallway, at the same time ringing the bell, though with what idea I was unable to conjecture.

"Nobody here," he concluded. "Nothing to make it worth anybody's while, is there?"

"I shouldn't think so," I agreed; and, entirely contrary to regulations, slipped a ten-shilling note into his hand. "Sorry I have been unable to find you a case, though."

"Right-ho!" the constable grinned; "better luck next time. Good-night, sir."

"Good-night," I said, taking out my key and opening Sir Lionel's door.

As I hung up my hat and coat I stood in the lobby trying to get my ideas into some kind of order. What, exactly, had happened?

Had I fallen victim to a delusion?—was my brain slightly out of gear? And if so, where had delusion ceased and actuality commenced? I had spoken to the constable; this was beyond dispute. But had I ever heard that strange voice? Had I ever been gripped as in a vice and listened to those words? And if I had, what did it all mean? Who could profit by it?

If, as I suspected—and the suspicion was abominable—we had blown the trumpet of triumph too soon, why should Fu Manchu, or anyone associated with him, stoop to a meaningless practical joke?

I stared about the lobby with its curious decorations, and up the fine old staircase to where a row of Saracen armour stood on guard. The servants had long since retired, and there was not a sound to be heard in the house. Pushing open the dining-room door, I turned up one of the lights.

There was cold supper on the buffet, which Betts invariably placed there. I helped myself to a stiff whisky and soda, extinguished the light, and went upstairs.

Needless to say that I was badly shaken, mystified, utterly astounded. Aimlessly I opened the door of the Museum Room, turning up all the lamps.

Walking in, I dropped into one of the big settees, took a cigarette from a box which lay there, lighting it and staring about me. I was surrounded by the finest private collection of its kind in Great Britain. Sir Lionel's many donations to public institutions contained treasures enough, but here was the cream of a lifetime of research.

Directly facing me where I sat, in a small case which had been stripped for the purpose, were the fifteen gold plates of the New Koran mounted on little wooden easels; the mask above them, and the magnificent Sword of God suspended below. A table with paper, writing material, lenses, and other conveniences, was set not far away, in preparation for the visit of the experts in the morning.

And I sat, dully gazing at all this for fully five minutes—or so I estimated at the time.

As a matter of fact, I may have remained there longer; I have no recollection of going upstairs, but it is certain that I did not fall asleep in the Museum Room. I remember that a welcome drowsiness claimed me as I sat there, and I remember extinguishing my cigarette in an ash tray.

Of my movements from that point onward I retain no memory whatever!

CHAPTER FORTY-FIFTH

MEMORY RETURNS

MY NEXT impression was of acute pain in both ankles. My head was swimming as after a wild night, and my eyelids seemed to be weighted with lead. I raised them, however, by what I felt to be a definite muscular effort. And, curious circumstances—very curious indeed, as I came to realise later—my brain immediately began to function from the last waking moment I have recorded; namely, from the moment when, seated in the Museum Room, I began to feel very drowsy.

My first thought now was that I had fallen asleep on the settee in some unnatural position, which might account for the pain in my ankles. I looked about me. . . .

I was certainly lying on a divan, as I had supposed; but my ankles were fastened together by a single strand of that dull, yellowish-gray material resembling catgut, and no thicker than a violin string, which had played a part in the death of poor Dr. Van Berg in Ispahan!

My fragile bonds were fastened so tightly as to be painful, and I struggled to my feet. Wedging one foot firmly against the floor, I kicked forward with the other, supposing that the slender link would snap.

The result was that I kicked myself backwards!

I fell among the cushions of the divan, aware that I had badly strained a tendon. Helpless, bewildered, struggling with some memory ever growing, I lay where I had fallen, looking about me. And this was what I saw:

A long, low salon—that, I thought, of an old Egyptian house; parts of the walls were tiled, and a large *mushrabiyeh* window formed a recess at one end. there were some rugs upon the floor, and the room was lighted by a number of lamps having shades of a Chinese pattern which swung from the wooden ceiling. The furniture, scanty, was of mixed Arab and Chinese character. There were deep bookcases laden with volumes in most unfamiliar bindings as well as a number of glass cabinets containing most singular objects.

In one was something which at first I took to be a human head, that of a woman. But, focusing my gaze upon it, I realised that it was an unusually perfect mummy head. In another were some small green snakes, alive. I saw a human skeleton; and in a kind of miniature conservatory which occupied the recess formed by the *mushrabiyeh* window, queer-looking orchids, livid and ugly, were growing.

A definite conviction claimed my mind that I had been in this room before. But—perhaps the most remarkable feature of the experience—it reached my brain in just the same way that such impressions reach us in everyday life. I thought, "This has all happened before." The only difference was that my prophetic anticipations lasted much longer than is normally the case.

Upon a long, wooden table, resembling a monkish refectory table, lay a number of open volumes among test tubes and other scientific paraphernalia. Standing up, I saw that the table was covered with glass.

Then, turning around, I realised that in many other cabinets hitherto invisible were rows of chemical bottles and apparatus. I was, then, in a room which was at least partly a laboratory; for in one corner I saw a working bench with electrical fittings. There were three doors to the room, of old, bleached teak. They possessed some peculiarity which puzzled me, until I recognised wherein it lay:

These doors had neither latches, handles, nor keyholes. And as I grasped this curious fact, one of them slipped noiselessly open.

And Dr. Fu Manchu came in . . .

All who have followed my attempts to record the strange and tragic events which followed upon Sir Lionel Barton's discovery of the tomb of El Mokanna, will recognise at this point something which I was totally unable to recognise at the time:

I was living again through that hiatus in Cairo; bridging the gap which led to the loss of Rima! That everything in the room, every word spoken by the Chinese doctor, seemed familiar, was natural enough; since I had seen those things and heard those words before.

Again that compelling glance absorbed me. The green,

globular lamp upon a silver pedestal was lighted on the long table. And I watched the Chinaman, with long, flexible, bony fingers, examining the progress of some chemical experiment in which he had evidently been engaged at the time of quitting the room.

He spoke to me of this experiment and of others; of the new anaesthetic prepared from mimosa; of the fabrication of spider web—a substance stronger than any known to commerce. He discussed his daughter, Nayland Smith, and Dr. Petrie; and he spoke of the essential oil of a rare orchid found in Burma, which for twenty-five years he had studied in quest of what the old philosophers called the elixir of life.

And I knew, watching him, that he had thrown off the burden of many years, had cheated man's chiefest enemy—Time.

He went on to criticise the chief, stripping him bare of all his glamour, placing his good qualities in the scale against the colossal egoism of the man. "You love a shell," he said, "an accomplishment, a genius, if you like, but a phantom, a hollow thing, having no real existence."

So it went on to the point where I was forced to submit to an injection of that strange new drug in which the Chinese doctor evidently took such pride.

I experienced a sudden and unfamiliar glow throughout my entire body. I became exhilarated; some added clarity of vision came to me. And presently I took my orders from Dr. Fu Manchu as a keen subaltern takes orders from his colonel.

Exulting in the knowledge that by reason of my association with the great Chinese physician, I was above the trivialities of common humanity, god-like, superior, all-embracing, I set out for Shepheard's—intent only upon bringing Rima within the fold of this all-powerful genius.

When we pulled up opposite the hotel, and the driver had run across with my note, I knew a fever of impatience—I could scarcely contain myself. But at last I saw her come out, my letter in her hand, saw her run down the steps.

Then, we were together, and my heart was singing with gladness. . . . I was taking her to Dr. Fu Manchu!

She could not understand; I knew that she could never understand until she had stood face to face with that great and wonderful man, as I had done.

And at first I tried to pacify her, holding her very close. She fought with me, and even endeavoured to attract the attention of a British policeman. But at last she lay passive in my arms, watching me. And I grew very uneasy.

I was assailed by odd doubts. We were far out on the road to Gizeh when suddenly the car pulled up. I saw Dr. Fu Manchu standing beside me.

"You have done well," he said; "you may rest now. . . ."

CHAPTER FORTY-SIXTH

FAH LO SUEE

"SHAN, dear, I know you are very sleepy, but it's getting cold and late too."

I stirred lazily, opening my eyes. I was pillowed on a warm shoulder, a bare arm encircling my neck. That silvery voice had awakened me. A long jade earring touched my cheek coldly, and caressing fingers stroked my hair.

Yes! I was with Fah Lo Suee, somewhere on the banks of the Nile. And I was content—utterly, rapturously content.

"Love dreams are bitter-sweet, Shan, because we know we are dreaming. . . ."

I could see a long reach of the river, silver under the moon, *dahabeahs* moored against the left bank, where groups of palms formed a background for their slender, graceful masts.

"I think someone has been watching, Shan; I am going to drive you back to Shepheard's now."

And as she drove, I watched the delicate profile of the driver. She was very beautiful, I thought. How wonderful to have won the love of such a woman. She linked her arms about me and crushed her lips against mine, her long, narrow eyes closed.

In the complete surrender of that embrace I experienced a mad triumph, in which Rima, Nayland Smith, the chief, all, were forgotten.

CHAPTER FORTY-SEVENTH

IVORY HANDS

I CLOSED my eyes again, pressing my face against that satin pillow. I felt I could have stayed there forever.

"You know, Shan," Fah Lo Suee's voice went on—that silvery voice in which I seemed to hear the note of a bell—"you have often hated me and you will hate me again."

"I could never hate you," I said drowsily.

"I have tricked you many times; for, although I love you, Shan, you are really not very clever."

"Cleverer men than I would give all for your kisses," I whispered.

"That is true," she replied, without vanity; for with much of his powerful brain she had also inherited from the Chinese doctor a philosophy by virtue of which she judged herself equally with others. "But I find hatred hard to accept."

I kept my eyes obstinately closed. Some vague idea was stirring in my brain that when I opened them that act would herald the end of this delicious interlude.

She was so slender—so exquisite—her personality enveloped me like a perfume.

"I have given you back the memory of forgotten hours, Shan. There is no disloyalty in what I have done. Your memories can only tell you again what you know already: that my father is the greatest genius the world has ever known. The old house at Gizeh is deserted again, even if you could find it. Your other memories are of me."

I clutched her tightly.

"Why should you leave me?"

She clung to me for a moment, and I could hear her heart beating; then:

"Because the false is valueless to me, and the true I can never have."

The words were so strangely spoken, in so strange a voice, that at last I opened my eyes again . . . and, astounded, broke free from Fah Lo Suee's clinging arms and stared about me.

I was in the Museum Room in Bruton Street!

A silk dressing gown I had over my pyjamas; a pair of Arab slippers were on my feet. Fah Lo Suee, in a pale green frock which did full justice to her perfect back and shoulders, was lying among the cushions beside me, her fur coat on the floor near by.

She was watching me under half-lowered lashes—doubting me, it would seem. There was more of appeal than command in those emerald green, long, wonderful eyes. Staring about the room, I saw everything was as I had left it; and:

"Well?" Fah Lo Suee murmured, continuing to watch me.

I turned and looked down at her where she lay.

And, as her glance met mine, I was claimed, submerged, swept away by such a wave of desire for this woman as I had never known for anyone in the whole of my life. I dropped to the floor, clasping her knees.

"You cannot—you must not—you dare not go!"

Her lips rippled in a smile—those perfect lips which I realised I adored; and then very wistfully:

"If only that were true!" she murmured.

"But it is!" I knelt upon the settee, grasping her fiercely, and looking into those eyes which beckoned to me—beckoned to me.... "Why do you say that? How can you doubt it?"

But she continued to smile.

And then, as I stooped to kiss her, she thrust her hands, slender, exquisite ivory hands against me, and pushed me back. I would have resisted—

"*Shan!*" she said.

And although the word was spoken as an appeal, yet it was a command; and a command which I obeyed. Yes, she was right. There was some reason—some reason, which escaped me—why we must part. I clutched my head feverishly, thinking—thinking. What could that reason by?

"I am going, dear. You mustn't come down to the door—I know my way."

But I sprang up. She had stooped and was taking up her cloak. Mechanically, I slipped it about her shoulders. She leaned back as I did so and submitted to my frenzied kisses. At last, releasing herself, and pulling the cloak about her slim body:

"Good-bye, Shan dear," she said, brokenly, but with a determination which I knew I had no power to weaken. "Please go back to bed—and go to sleep."

Hot tears burned behind my eyes. I felt that life had nothing left for me. But—I obeyed.

Passing out onto the landing where suits of Saracen armour stood on guard, I watched Fah Lo Suee descend the broad staircase. A light burned in the lobby, as was customary, and, reaching the foot of the stairs, she turned.

With one slender, unforgettable, indolent hand, she beckoned to me imperiously.

I obeyed her order—I moved towards the staircase leading to the floor above. I had begun to go up when I heard the street door close. . . .

CHAPTER FORTY-EIGHTH

I REALLY AWAKEN

"Nine o'clock, sir. Are you ready for your tea?"

I opened my eyes and stared into the face of Betts. Upon a salver he carried the morning papers and a pile of correspondence. Placing them upon the table, he crossed and drew back the curtains before the windows.

"A beautiful morning again, sir," he went on; I hope this will continue until the happy day."

I sat up.

"Shall I bring your tea, sir?"

"Yes, please do."

As that venerable old scoundrel, whose job was one of those which every butler is looking for, went out of the room, I stared about me in search of my dressing gown.

There it was, thrown over the back of an armchair—upon which also I saw my dress clothes. I jumped out of bed, put on the old Arab slippers, and then the dressing gown.

Never in my life had I been visited by so singular, so vivid a dream . . . a dream? Where had dreaming left off? I must make notes while the facts were clear in my memory.

I went out and down to the library; grabbed a writing pad and a pencil. I was on the point of returning upstairs when that query, "Where had dreaming left off?" presented itself in a new aspect.

Dropping pad and pencil, I hurried along the gallery and into the Museum Room. . . .

I could not forget that Petrie, that man of scientific mind, had once endeavoured to shoot his oldest friend, Sir Denis, under some damnable influence controlled by Dr. Fu Manchu. And had I not myself seen Rima, actuated by the same unholy power, obeying the deathly orders of Fah Lo Suee?

The Museum Room looked exactly as I had left it—except that Betts, or one of the maids, had cleaned the ash tray in which I remembered having placed the stub of a cigarette. The table prepared for my eleven o'clock appointment was in order. Everything was in order.

And—that which above all engaged my particular attention—the small case containing the relics of Mokanna showed no signs of disturbance. There were the mask, the plates, and the sword.

I returned to the library for pencil and writing pad. If I had dreamed, it had been a clairvoyant dream, vivid as an actual experience. It had given me certain knowledge which might prove invaluable to Nayland Smith.

Perhaps analysis of that piece of slender twine which I knew was in Sir Denis's possession would show it to be indeed composed of spider web. I wondered if the mystery of the forcing of the safe on the *Indramatra* had been solved for me. And I wondered if the liquid smelling strongly of mimosa which still remained in that spray found upon the dead Negro in Ispahan would respond to any test known to science?

Strangest fact of all, I loathed the memory of Fah Lo Suee!

I was ashamed, humiliated, utterly overcome by those dream recollections. I had desired her, adored her, covered her with kisses. While now—my true, waking self—I knew that there was only one woman in all the world for me . . . and that woman was Rima!

CHAPTER FORTY-NINTH

A COMMITTEE OF EXPERTS

PROFESSOR EISNER was the first of the experts to arrive. I knew his name, of course, but he himself proved something of a surprise. He had iron-grey hair cut close to a very fine skull, and wore a small monocle. He was otherwise clean-shaven, presenting in his walk, his build, his manner, an Englishman's conception of the typical Prussian cavalry officer.

He was shown into the big Syrian room on the ground floor, where suitable refreshments had been prepared by Betts, and proved on acquaintance to be a charming as well as a clever man.

Then came the Frenchman, Dr. Brieux, a very different type. He wore a caped overcoat and a large black soft hat. I saw him approaching from the window, as a matter of fact, and predicted to myself that he would stop at the door and ring the bell. I was right. Here was the traditional scholar—stooping, with high, bald brow, scanty white hair and beard, and large, horn-rimmed glasses.

He greeted Professor Eisner very coldly. I didn't know it at the time, but they held directly opposite views regarding the date when the Khuld Palace in Old Baghdad was deserted in favour of the Palace of the Golden Gate. A heated controversy had raged in the learned journals between these two distinguished Orientalists. I fear I had overlooked this.

I know and love the Near East and its peoples; their arts and crafts, and the details of their domestic life. But this hairsplitting on a matter of dates is something quite outside my province.

The learned Englishmen were late: they arrived together; and I was glad of their arrival. Professor Eisner was sipping a glass of the chief's magnificent old sherry and nibbling some sort of savoury provided by Betts; Dr. Brieux, hands behind him, was staring out of the window, his back ostentatiously turned to his German confrère.

When Mr. Hall-Ramsden of the British Museum and Sir

Wallace Syms of the Royal Society had chatted for a time with the distinguished visitors, I led the way upstairs to the Museum Room.

As I have mentioned I had prepared everything early the night before. My notes, a map of our route, a diary covering the period we had spent in the Place of the Great Magician, and one or two minor objects discovered in the tomb of the prophet, were ready upon the table.

At all costs (such were the chief's instructions) I had to avoid giving away any of the dramatic points—he had made a list of them—which he proposed to spring upon the Royal Society.

This was not in the remotest degree my kind of job. I hated it from the word Go! The dream or vision which had disturbed my sleep during the night continued to haunt me. I was uncertain of myself—uncertain that the whole episode was not some damnable aftermath to that drug which had taken toll of several hours of my life in Cairo.

At the best of times I should have been ill at ease, but on this occasion I was doubly so. However, I attacked the business. Removing the mask, the plates, and the sword from the cabinet in which they rested, I placed them upon the big table.

Professor Eisner claimed the gold plates with a motion resembling that of a hawk swooping upon its prey. Dr. Brieux took up the mask between delicate, nervous fingers, and peered at it closely through the powerful lenses of his spectacles. Hall-Ramsden and Sir Wallace Syms bent over the Sword of God.

I glanced at my notes, and, realising that nobody was listening to me, intoned the situation, condition, external appearance, and so forth, of the half-buried ruin which had been the tomb of the Mokanna. Finally:

"Here are the photographs to which I have referred, gentlemen," I said, opening a portfolio containing more than three hundred photographs taken by Rima. "If any questions occur to you, I shall be glad in Sir Lionel's absence to answer them to the best of my ability."

I had gone through this painful duty quite automatically. Now, I had time to observe the four specialists. And looking at them where they sat around the big table, I sensed at once a queer atmosphere.

Mr. Hall-Ramsden glanced at me furtively, but catching my eye resumed a muttered colloquy with Sir Wallace Syms. Professor Eisner and Dr. Brieux seemed to have discovered common ground. The doctor, holding up the mask, was talking with tremendous rapidity, and the professor, alternately tapping the plates and pointing to the sword seemed to be agreeing, judging from his short ejaculations of *"Ja, ja!"*

"Can I assist you in any way, gentlemen?" I asked somewhat irritably.

As the chief officer of the expedition which had discovered the relics, I felt that I was receiving scant courtesy. But, as I spoke, four pairs of eyes were turned upon me.

There came a moment of silence, as I looked from face to face; and then it was the German professor who spoke:

"Mr. Greville," he said, "I understand that you were present when Sir Lionel Barton opened the tomb of El Mokanna?"

"Certainly I was present, Professor."

"This was what I understood." He nodded slowly. "Were you actually present at the time that these relics were unearthed?"

His inquiry was made in a way kindly enough, but it jagged me horribly. I looked from face to face, meeting with nothing but unfathomable glances.

"Your question is a strange one," I replied slowly. "Ali Mahmoud, the headman in charge of our party, was actually first among us to see anything of the relics: he saw a corner of one of those gold plates. I was the first to see an entire plate (I think it was ninth in the series, as a matter of fact). Sir Lionel, and Rima, his niece, as well as the late Dr. Van Berg, were present when the treasure was brought to light."

Professor Eisner had a habit of closing his left eye; betokening concentration, no doubt; and, now, his right eye—a cold blue eye—focused upon me through the little monocle, registered something between incredulity, amusement and pity.

Sir Wallace I knew for an avowed enemy of the chief. Regarding Hall-Ramsden's attitude, I knew nothing. Of Professor Eisner Sir Lionel had always spoken favourably, but I was aware that he regarded Dr. Brieux as a mere impostor.

But now, under the gaze of that magnified blue eye, I realised that the authenticity of these treasures, which had nearly led to a Holy War in the East, was being questioned by the four men seated about the table!

Instantly I pictured the scene if Sir Lionel had been present! Hall-Ramsden might have put up a show, and the German looked like a man of his hands: but as for the other two, I was confident that they would have been thrown bodily downstairs. . . .

"Gentlemen," I said, "you seem to share some common opinion about the relics of El Mokanna. I should be glad to know your views."

A further exchange of glances followed. I realised that in some way my words had created embarrassment. Finally, having cleared his throat, it was Hall-Ramsden who answered me.

"Mr. Greville," he said, "I have heard you well spoken of, and, personally, I should not think of doubting your integrity. Sir Lionel Barton—" he cleared his throat again—"as an Orientalist of international reputation, is naturally above suspicion."

Dr. Brieux blew his nose.

"Since it has been arranged for Sir Lionel to address the Royal Society next Thursday on the subject"—he extended his hand towards the objects on the table—"of these relics, I recognise, of course—we all recognise—that there must be some strange mistake, or else . . ."

He hesitated, glancing about as if to seek help from one of his confrères.

"That Barton," Sir Wallace Syms continued—"whose sense of humour sometimes betrays him—has seen fit to play a joke upon us!"

By this time I was thoroughly angry.

"What the devil do you mean, Sir Wallace?" I asked.

My anger had one immediate effect. Professor Eisner stood up and approached me, putting his arm about my shoulders.

"My young friend," he explained, "something has gone wrong. It will all be explained, no doubt. But be calm."

His manner quietened me. I recognised its sincerity. And, giving me a kind of final reassuring hug:

"I shall not be surprised to hear," he went on, "that you have not examined these relics recently. Eh?"

"Not," I admitted, "since they were put in the case."

"Since you placed them in the case, eh? Now, you have already a considerable reputation, Mr. Greville. I have talked with you, and you know your subject. Before we say any more, please to look at this sword."

He stepped to the table, took up the Sword of God, returned, and handed it to me. My anger was still simmering as I took the thing up and glanced at it. Having done so:

"Well," I replied, "I have looked. What do you expect me to say?"

"To say nothing—yet." Again that reassuring arm was around my shoulders. "But to look, examine carefully—"

"It's simply absurd!" came the voice of Dr. Brieux.

"If you please!" snapped the Professor sharply—"if you please! What you have to say, Doctor can wait for a moment."

Amid a silence which vibrated with hostility, I examined the blade in my hand. And I suppose, as I did so, my expression changed.

"Ah! you see, eh?" said the German.

And while I stared with horrified eyes at the blade, the inlay, the hilt, he had darted to the table, almost immediately to return with one of the gold plates. Relieving me of the sword. he placed the inscribed tablet in my hands.

"It is beautifully done!" He almost whispered the words, very close to my ear; "and rubbed down very fine. But look . . ."

He held a glass before my eye—one of those which I had provided for this very purpose.

I looked—and I knew!

Tossing the plate down, I faced the three men around the table. Professor Eisner remained beside me.

"Gentlemen," I said—"my apologies. I can only ask you to remain silent until this mystery has been cleared up. I will try, to the best of my ability, to explain."

The sword, the plates, and the mask, which I had exhibited to these four experts, were, beyond any shadow of doubt, *the duplicates made by Solomon Ishak.* . . .

Chapter Fiftieth

DR. FU MANCHU TRIUMPHS

Thanks to Rima's photographs, I proved my case. The blade of the sword, as I realised, had been provided by Soloman Ishak. It closely resembled the sword of the prophet, but differed in several essential particulars.

The stones in the hilt (the hilt had been reproduced exactly) were genuine and must have cost the chief some hundreds of pounds; but they were much smaller than those shown in the photograph; and some of them badly flawed.

Under a powerful lens the plates shrieked forgery aloud. I learned later that they had been photographed from Rima's negatives onto the gold and then engraved by Solomon's workmen. Closely examined, the newly cut gold betrayed the secret.

The mask was the most perfect duplicate I have ever handled; but the two large jewels were reconstructed; and the delicate engravery, magnified, betrayed itself in the same way as that upon the plates.

However, a friendly atmosphere was re-established before the party broke up. I had admitted—could see no alternative—that Sir Lionel had a duplicate set made in Persia. And it was obvious that this was the set which now lay upon the table.

When and where the substitution had taken place, I left to the imagination of my visitors. They were sympathetic in a way, but the Englishmen were laughing at me; and the Frenchman, who had come from Paris especially to view the relics, was very plainly annoyed.

Professor Eisner alone seemed to understand and to sympathise. He was the last to leave, and:

"Mr. Greville," he said in parting, "Sir Lionel Barton has touched deep, secret influences in this matter. He has been clever—very clever; but they have been more clever still. Eh? You will find out one day when this trick was done."

But as from the window I watched him swinging down Bruton Street with the walk of a dragoon, I knew that I had nothing to find out. I already knew where dreaming had ended and reality had begun. And I knew why Fah Lo Suee had whispered: "You will live to hate me...."

I was still trying to get a call through to the chief, whose Norfolk number was a private extension, when Betts came in and announced:

"Sir Denis Nayland Smith and Dr. Petrie, sir."

I hung up the receiver and positively sprang to meet them. They were waiting for me in the room on the left of the lobby, the room in which I had received my learned visitors that morning. I suppose my expression must have betrayed me, for I saw, as I ran in, that both had sensed the fact that there was something wrong.

"What is it, Greville?" snapped Nayland Smith—"Barton? Rima?"

"Both safe," I replied. "This is a delightful surprise! You are a whole day ahead of your schedule!"

"Flew from Marseilles," said Sir Denis.

"But something is wrong with you," Dr. Petrie declared, holding onto my hand and looking at me searchingly.

I nodded, smiling, although I was far from mirthful.

"Suppose you prescribe a drink, Doctor!" I suggested; "I feel badly shot away. Then I will try to explain the position."

It occupied me longer than I could have supposed; involving as it did an account of what had happened since I had parted from my friend on the previous night, right up to my recent interview with the four experts.

Long before I had reached the end of it, Nayland Smith was pacing up and down the room in his restless fashion, having relighted his pipe three or four times. But at last, when that strange story was ended:

"Amazing," he snapped, "but ghastly." He turned to Petrie. "I told you that Fu Manchu would be in England ahead of us."

"You did," the doctor agreed.

"He is here?" I exclaimed.

"Undoubtedly, Greville. He keeps a close watch upon his beautiful daughter! Your dream, as it seemed to you, was of course no dream at all. You were subjected last night, in the basement of the adjoining house, to the treatment referred to by Dr. Fu Manchu; an injection in your arm. Petrie can probably discover the mark. Eh, Petrie?"

"Possibly," the doctor replied guardedly. "But I can make an examination later, Smith. Please carry on."

"Very well. Later, you were given that 'simple antidote' which he mentioned. You remember now those lost hours in Cairo. And some of your memories, Greville, are most illuminating. I can see Hewlett and myself searching the Sukkariya quarter, when actually the house for which we were looking was somewhere out at Gizeh!

"The drug used by Fu Manchu (obviously that mentioned by McGovern) renders the subject peculiarly susceptible to suggestion. I suppose you appreciate that you had your instructions from Fah Lo Suee, who was awaiting your return in the adjoining empty house, to open the door for her at a specified time?"

"I *must* have opened it," I returned blankly; " for, otherwise, how did she get in?"

"You certainly *did* open it; just as certainly as you once aided in the abduction of Rima from Shepheard's in Cairo!

"She substituted the duplicates, which of course she had brought with her, for the real relics, and presumably handed the latter to an accomplice in waiting. The phase which followed, Greville—" he smiled that inimitable smile—"is one which I prefer to forget."

"Let's all agree to forget it," said Petrie.

"Dr. Fu Manchu is the greatest master of drugs this old world of ours has ever known. His daughter is an apt pupil. I believe she has a sincere affection for you, Greville—God knows why! But, since you did not dream, we have the word of Fu Manchu that no harm will come to you. Frankly, I think Barton has got off lightly—"

"So do I!" Petrie interrupted again.

"After all, even in this stage of laxity, there are things which are not done. The word of a prison governor to a convict is as sacred as any man's word to any other man; and according to my view, which may be peculiar, Barton doubled on Dr. Fu Manchu. I believe that super-devil to be too great a character to waste a moment upon revenge. But in the circumstances, Greville, if you don't mind, I should like to get through to Sir Lionel—and there's someone there whom Petrie is dying to speak to. . . ."

Chapter Fifty-first

WEDDING MORNING

Upon the events of the next few days I prefer not to dwell. At my first interview with Sir Lionel following the loss of the relics of the Masked Prophet, I believed for one hectic moment that he would attempt to strangle me with his own hands.

Perhaps it was the presence of Nayland Smith, alone, which prevented him from making an assault. I can see him now, pacing up and down the Museum Room, clenching and relaxing his big fists, and looking murder from underneath tufted eyebrows.

"No possible blame attaches to Greville," said Sir Denis.

The chief growled inarticulately.

"And I would remind you that in somewhat similar circumstances, and not long ago, you personally assisted the same lady to open the Tomb of the Black Ape, in the Valley of the Kings, and to walk away with its contents. Rather a good parallel, I think?"

Sir Lionel stood still, staring hard at the speaker, then:

"Damn it!" he admitted—"you're right!"

He transferred his stare to Petrie, and finally to me.

"Forget my somewhat harsh criticisms, Greville," he said. "Unlike Smith, I often say more than I mean. But this cancellation of my address to the Royal Society is going to set poisoned tongues wagging."

This was true enough. Not only had he been deprived of that hour of triumph in anticipation of which he had lived for many months past, but unpleasant whispers were going around the more scholarly clubs. Scotland Yard, working secretly, had put its vast machinery in motion in an endeavour to trace Fah Lo Suee.

They failed, as indeed we all knew they must fail. Servants of Dr. Fu Manchu perused secret avenues of travel upon which the Customs and the police apparently had no check. There was a theory held at Scotland Yard, and shared, I believe, by our old friend Weymouth, that the Chinese doctor worked in concert with what is known as the "underworld".

This theory Nayland Smith declined to entertain.

"His organisation is infinitely superior to anything established among the criminal classes," he declared. "He would not stoop to use such instruments."

However, the chief's resiliency of character was not the least amazing of his attributes; and within forty-eight hours he was deep in a book dealing with the Masked Prophet, of which he designed to publish a limited edition, illustrated by selected photographs of Rima's.

"I don't know why I allow you to issue your rotten accounts of my expeditions, Greville!" he shouted one day, when I entered the library and found him at word.

He was surrounded by masses of records and untidy heaps of manuscript notes, portfolios, and what-not. Two shorthand typists were in attendance.

"Their scientific value is nil, and they depict me personally as a cross between a large ape and a human half-wit. . . ."

In the meantime he had relaxed no jot of his publicity campaign upon my wedding, to which an added piquancy was given by what happened at the Athenæum Club.

Following a heated argument there with Sir Wallace Syms, the chief challenged him to a duel within hearing of fully twelve members!

This resulted in a crop of spicy paragraphs, practically all of which included a reference to the forthcoming ceremony at St. Margaret's. My horror of this ceremony grew with almost every passing hour.

I had been pestered by interviewers and gossip writers for particulars of my family history, my interests in sport, and other purely personal matters, until I was reduced to a state of nerves as bad as anything I had known in the most evil times of the past.

A popular débutante two years before, Rima had spent one hectic season in London under the wing of Lady Ettrington, Sir Lionel's younger sister and a chip of the old block whom I wholeheartedly detested.

Rima's decision to abandon society and to join her eccentric uncle in the capacity of photographer had bought down upon her head the wrath of Lady Ettrington. Her later decision to marry me, instead of some society idler, had resulted in my name being written in large letters in her ladyship's Black Book.

The apartment once known as the breakfast room at Bruton Street, but which the chief had had converted into a sort of overflow library, was rapidly filling up with wedding presents. Rima's waking hours were distributed between hat shops, hairdressing establishments, and modistes.

Sometimes she would meet me for lunch, at other times she was too busy. Women, however, never seem to tire under this particular kind of stress. One such day would have exhausted me. Of presents to the bridegroom there were notably few. Such friends as I had were distributed all over the world.

Among all this fuss and bother and the twittering of Rima's bridesmaids (only two of whom I had ever met before), I felt a good deal of an outsider. To me the whole thing was unspeakably idiotic—a waste of time and as utterly undignified an exhibition as only a spectacular wedding can offer.

The chief, however, was enjoying himself to the top of his bent, sparing no expense to make the entertainment a popular one. The number of people who had accepted invitations appalled me.

I knew many of them by name, but few of them personally; and in cold print it appeared that the bridegroom would be the least distinguished person present at the church.

In many respects those days were the worst I have ever lived through. . . .

But I moved under a cloud. Since the loss of the relics I had felt in some indefinable way that of actual danger from Dr. Fu Manchu there was none. His last project had failed; but I was convinced that failure and success alike left him unmoved. Over and over again I discussed the matter with Nayland Smith and Petrie, and with Superintendent Weymouth, who had been staying somewhere in the Midlands but who was now back in London prior to returning to Cairo.

"In the old days," he said on one occasion, "Fu Manchu was operating under cover, and he stuck at nothing to get rid of those who picked up any clue to his plans. From what you tell me now it appears that in this last job he had nothing to hide."

This, then, was not the shadow which haunted me: it was the memory of Fah Lo Suee. . . .

To what extent aided by those strange drugs of which her father alone possessed the secret I was unable to decide, but definitely she had power to throw some sort of spell upon me, under which I became her helpless slave. Rima knew something, but not all, of the truth.

She knew that I had followed Fah Lo Suee from Shepheard's that night in Cairo, but of what had happened later she knew nothing; nor of what had happened in Bruton Street.

But something there was which she knew and had known from the first: that Fah Lo Suee possessed a snake-like fascination to which I, perhaps any man, was liable to succumb. And she knew that this incalculable woman experienced a kind of feline passion for me.

Often, when we had been separated, I surprised a question in her eyes. Perhaps she knew that I dreaded meeting Fu Manchu's daughter as greatly as she dreaded it herself.

And all the time, while I looked on, feeling like a complete stranger, arrangements for the wedding proceeded. Sir Lionel dictated chapter after chapter of his book, and at the same time several papers to scientific publications which he occasionally favoured with contributions; interviewed representatives of the Press, quarrelled with the caterers responsible for the reception; wrote insulting letters to *The Times*; in short, thoroughly enjoyed himself.

I pointed out to him, one day, that since Rima and I would have to live upon my comparatively slender income, our married life would be something of an anti-climax to our wedding.

"You've got a good job!" he shouted. "Damn it! I pay you a thousand a year!—and you must make something out of your ridiculous books!"

The discussion was not carried any further. I realised that it was one I should never have begun.

I had his sister Lady Ettrington to cope with, also. She issued an ultimatum to the effect that she would not be present in the church unless it was arranged that I took up my residence elsewhere than under the same roof as her niece Rima. This led to a tremendous row between brother and sister. It took place in the room where the presents were assembled: a draw, in which both parties exhibited the celebrated Barton temperament in its most lurid form.

"You can go to the devil!" was Sir Lionel's final politeness. "As to being in the church, personally I don't remember having invited you. . . ."

It had all blown over, however, which was the way with storms in this peculiar family; and being awakened by Betts one morning, that privileged old idiot opened the curtains and announced:

"The happy day has arrived, sir. . . ."

CHAPTER FIFTY-SECOND

DR. FU MANCHU BOWS

NOT being a society reporter, the wedding at St. Margaret's must be taken for granted in this account. Suffice to say that it duly took place.

My best man was first rate, and Rima looked so lovely that I was almost reconciled to this dreadful occasion. The crowd inside the church was small in comparison with the crowd outside. Sir Lionel's gift of showmanship would have put C.B. Cochran out of business, had the chief decided to plunge into the theatrical sphere.

He sailed into the church through a solid avenue of humanity with that dainty bride on his arm, smiling cheerfully, right and left, as who should say, "What did I tell you? Isn't she a beauty?"

My own entrance took place in a sort of merciful haze, out of which, dimly, I heard reassuring words from my best man. The ceremony itself stunned me.

I am no believer in the marriage service, and neither is Sir Lionel. He would not for the price of a kingdom have taken those awful vows demanded by the priest, but he thoroughly enjoyed hearing me commit myself to that which he would never have undertaken.

When we came out again into the sunshine (as the sentimental Betts had prayed this was a glorious day) a battery of cameras awaited us.

We escaped finally in a Rolls two-seater—one of Sir Lionel's presents to the bride—in which he had insisted we must drive away, although frankly I was in no fit condition for the job.

However, I managed it without mishap—to find a second camera battery awaiting us in Bruton Street....

Inside the house I found myself lost in a maze of unfamiliar faces. It was like a first night at a London theatre. Even the servants were strangers, many of them, although Sir Lionel had reinforcements there from other of his establishments.

One fleeting glimpse I had of Petrie's beautiful wife. She

waved to me from a distant corner and then disappeared before I could reach her. A queer situation: *I* was the cause, the centre, of this gathering—and I didn't seem to know a soul!

The room containing the wedding presents looked promising. I saw Betts there presiding over a sort of extemporised snack-bar. I also saw a detective whom I had chanced to meet in London two years before. He winked at me solemnly—the first man I had recognised at my own wedding reception.

It was one of the queerest experiences of my life. And, owing to my association with Sir Lionel, my days had been far from humdrum.

Exactly what occurred in the interval preceding that strange intrusion which must form the end of this chronicle I cannot definitely state. At one moment I was with Rima; in the next I had lost her. . . . I exchanged greetings with Nayland Smith—and then found myself talking to a perfect stranger. . . . Petrie expressed a wish to drink my health . . . and we were separated on our way to the buffet. . . .

Over the heads of a group of perfect strangers I presently caught the eye of Betts. He signaled to me.

I extricated myself from the crowd and joined him.

"A somewhat belated visitor, sir, wishes to add his congratulations on this happy day."

"Who is he, Betts?"

Betts extended a salver, with a perfect gesture. Jostled on all sides, I took up a card, and read:

Dr. Fu Manchu

There was no address; just those three words.

I became suddenly unaware of everything, and of everybody about me, except Betts and the card of Dr. Fu Manchu. I spoke—and my voice seemed to come from far away.

"Did you—*see* the visitor?"

"I showed him up to the Museum Room, sir, which, having been locked, is the only suitable room in the house to-day. He expressed a wish to see you *alone*, sir."

"Is *he* alone?"

"Yes, sir. . . ."

A band had started playing somewhere.

People spoke to me on my way: I don't know who they were.

One idea, one idea only was burning in my brain: this was a trap, a trap into which the doctor expected that all his enemies assembled in that house would fall!

A final question I threw at Betts:

"He's a tall man?"

"Very tall, sir, and distinguished; Chinese, I believe. . . ."

I battled my way to the staircase. Couples were seated upon it fully halfway up. I heard the chief's loud laugh and had a hazy impression that Nayland Smith formed one of the group in the lobby.

They were the two for whom this trap had been laid!

While disavowing any claims to heroism, I must state here that I mounted those stairs to the Museum Room fully expecting to meet destruction. I was determined to meet it alone. The plan should fail. With moderate luck, I might escape; but, even if I crashed, the Chinese doctor would have been foiled.

Sounds of voices, laughter, music, followed me as I threw open the door guarded left and right by phantoms clothed in Saracen armour.

The museum room was empty!

For a moment I doubted the evidence of my senses. After all, was it credible that Fu Manchu should have presented himself at Sir Lionel's house? Was it possible that he could have crossed the lobby without being recognised by one of the many present who knew him?

I was aware, of course, that the room had three doors; but, even so, escape to the street without detection was next to impossible.

But definitely there was no one there!

Then, on the table, that memorable table which I had prepared for the private view of the relics, I saw that a small parcel lay.

A dimmed clamour of voices and music reached me, with which mingled the traffic hum of Bruton Street.

Neatly wrapped and sealed it lay before me; that package which I believed to contain—death.

The motives which actuated me I realise now, looking back, were obscure; but I opened the parcel and found it to consist of a small casket apparently of crystal, carved (as I supposed at the time) in a pattern of regular prisms which glittered brightly in the sunlight.

An ebony box was inside the casket. A sheet of thick, yellow notepaper, folded, lay on the lid of the box. I opened the box.

It was lined with velvet; and, resting upon the velvet, I saw a string of pink pearls coiled around a scarab ring.

My brain performed a somersault. Someone was calling my name, but I didn't heed the interruption. I was unfolding the sheet of thick, yellow notepaper. It was neither headed nor dated. In jet-black, cramped writing it contained these words:

To Mr. Shan Greville.
Greeting.

You have suffered at my hands, because unwittingly you have sometimes obstructed me. I bear you no ill will. Indeed, I respect you—for you are an honourable man; and I wish you every happiness.

The pearls are for your bride. They are the only perfectly matched set of a hundred pink pearls in the world. The casket is also for her. She is beautiful, brave, and virtuous, a combination of qualities so rare that the woman possessing them is a jewel above price. It is set with eighty flawless diamonds and was made to the order of Catherine of Russia—who was brave, but neither beautiful nor virtuous.

The ebony box is for you. It will interest Sir Lionel Barton. It bears engraved upon it the seal of King Solomon and came from his temple. The ring, also, I request you to accept. It is the signet ring of Khufu—supposed builder of the Great Pyramid.

Commend me to Sir Denis Nayland Smith, to Dr. Petrie, and to Kâramenèh, his wife, and convey my good wishes to Superintendent Weymouth.

I desire you every good fortune.
Greeting and Farewell.

            FU MANCHU.

THE END

FU MANCHU'S BRIDE

CONTENTS

CHAPTER

1. FLEURETTE
2. A PURPLE CLOUD
3. THE BLOODSTAINED LEAVES
4. SQUINTING EYES
5. THE BLACK STIGMATA
6. "654"
7. IVORY FINGERS
8. "BEWARE . . ."
9. FAH LO SUEE
10. GREEN EYES
11. AT THE VILLA JASMIN
12. MIMOSA
13. THE FORMULA
14. IN MONTE CARLO
15. FAIRY TRUMPET
16. THE DACOIT
17. THE ROOM OF GLASS
18. DR. FU MANCHU
19. THE SECRET JUNGLE
20. DREAM CREATURES
21. THE HAIRLESS MAN
22. HALF-WORLD
23. THE JADE PIPE
24. COMPANION YAMAMATA
25. THE LIFE PRINCIPLE

CHAPTER

26 THE ORCHID
27 IN THE GALLERIES
28 EVIL INCARNATE
29 PURSUIT
30 NAYLAND SMITH
31 FU MANCHU'S ARMY
32 RECALL
33 I OBEY
34 DERCETO
35 THE SECTION DOORS
36 THE UNSULLIED MIRROR
37 THE GLASS MASK
38 THE GLASS MASK (Concluded)
39 SEARCH IN STE CLAIRE
40 THE SECRET DOCK
41 "I SAW THE SUN"
42 THE RAID
43 KÂRAMENÈH'S DAUGHTER
44 OFFICER OF THE PRÉFET
45 ON THE DESTROYER
46 WE BOARD THE *LOLA*
47 DR. PETRIE
48 "IT MEANS EXTRADITION"
49 MAÎTRE FOLI
50 "THE WORK GOES ON"

CHAPTER FIRST

FLEURETTE

ALL the way around the rugged headland, and beyond, as I sat at the wheel of the easy-running craft, I found myself worrying about Petrie. He was supposed to be looking after *me*. I thought that somebody should be looking after him. He took his responsibilities with a deadly seriousness; and this strange epidemic which had led the French authorities to call upon his expert knowledge was taxing him to the limit. At luncheon I thought he had looked positively ill; but he had insisted upon returning to his laboratory.

He seemed to imagine that the reputation of the Royal Society was in his keeping. . . .

I had hoped that the rockbound cove which I had noted would afford harbourage for the motorboat. Nevertheless, I was pleasantly surprised when I found that it did.

The little craft made safe, I waded in and began to swim through nearly still water around that smaller promontory beyond which lay the bay and beach of Ste Claire de la Roche. Probably a desire to test my fitness underlay the job; if I could not explore Ste Claire from the land side, I was determined to invade it, nevertheless.

The water was quite warm, and it had that queer odour of stagnation peculiar to this all but tideless sea. I swam around the point, and twenty yards out from the beach my feet touched bottom.

At the same moment I saw her. . . .

She was seated on the smooth sand, her back towards me, and she was combing her hair. As I stumbled, groped, and began to make my way inland, I told myself that this sole inhabitant of Ste Claire was probably one of those fabulous creatures, a mermaid—or, should I say, a siren.

I halted, wading ashore, and watched her.

Her arms, her shoulders, and her back were beautiful. Riviera salt and sun had tanned her to a most delectable shade of brown. Her wavy hair was of a rich red mahogany colour. This was all I could see of the mermaid from my position in the sea.

I made the shore without disturbing her.

It became apparent, then, that she was not a mermaid; a pair of straight, strong, and very shapely brown legs discredited the mermaid theory. She was a human girl with a perfect figure and glorious hair, wearing one of those bathing suits fashionable in Cannes. . . .

What it was, at this moment, which swamped admiration and brought *fear*—which urged me to go back—to go back—I could not imagine. I fought against this singular revulsion, reminding myself that I was newly convalescent from a dangerous illness. This alone, I argued, accounted for the sudden weird chill which had touched me.

Why, otherwise, should I be afraid of a pretty girl?

I moved forward.

And as I began to walk up the gently sloping beach she heard me and turned.

I found myself staring, almost in a frightened way, at the most perfect face I thought I had ever seen. Those arms and shoulders were so daintily modelled that I had been prepared for disillusionment: instead, I found glamour.

She was bronzed by the sun, and, at the moment, innocent of make-up. She had most exquisitely chiselled features. Her lips were slightly parted showing the whitest little teeth. Big, darkly fringed eyes—and they were blue as the Mediterranean—were opened widely, as if my sudden appearance had alarmed her.

I may have dreamed, as some men do, of flawless beauty, but I had never expected to meet it; when:

"How did *you* get here?" the vision asked and rolled over onto one elbow, looking up at me.

Her voice had a melodious resonance which suggested training, and her cool acceptance of my appearance helped to put me more at ease.

"I just swam ashore," I replied. "I hope I didn't frighten you?"

"Nothing frightens me," she answered in that cool, low tone, her unflinching eyes—the eyes of a child, but of a very clever and very inquisitive child—fixed upon me. "I was certainly surprised."

"I'm sorry. I suppose I should have warned you."

Her steady regard never wavered; it was becoming disconcerting. She was quite young, as the undisguised contours of her body revealed, but about her very beauty there hovered some aura of mysteriousness which her typically nonchalant manner could not dispel. Then, suddenly, I saw, and it greatly relieved me to see, a tiny dimple appear in her firm round chin. She smiled—and her smile made me her slave.

"Please explain," she said; "this isn't an accident is it?"

"No," I confessed; "it's a plot."

She shifted to a more easy position, resting both elbows on the sand and cupping her chin in two hands.

"What do you mean 'a plot'?" she asked, suddenly serious again.

I sat down, peculiarly conscious of my angular ugliness.

"I wanted to have a look at Ste Claire," I replied. "It used to be open to inspection and it's a spot of some historical interest. I found the road barred. And I was told that a certain Mahdi Bey had bought the place and had seen fit to close it to the public. I heard that the enclosed property ran down to the sea, so I explored and saw this little bay."

"And what were you going to do?" she asked, looking me over in a manner which struck me as almost supercilious.

"Well..." I hesitated, hoping for another smile. "I had planned to climb up to Ste Claire, and if I should be discovered, explain that I had been carried away by the current which works around the headland and been compelled to swim ashore."

I watched eagerly for the dimple. But no dimple came. Instead, I saw a strange, far-away expression creep over the girl's face. In some odd manner it transformed her; spiritually, she seemed to have withdrawn—to a great distance, to another land; almost, I thought, to another world. Her youth, her remarkable beauty, were transfigured as though by the occult brush of a dead master. Momentarily, I experienced again that insane desire to run away.

Then she spoke. Her phrases were commonplace enough, but her voice too was far away; her eyes seemed to be looking right through me, to be fixed upon some very distant object.

"You sound enterprising," she said. "What is your name?"

"Alan Sterling," I answered, with a start.

I had an uncanny feeling that the question had not come

from the girl herself, although her lips framed the words.

"I suppose you live somewhere near here?"

"Yes, I do."

"Alan Sterling," she repeated; "isn't that Scotch?"

"Yes, my father was a Scotsman—Dr. Andrew Sterling—but he settled in the Middle West of America, where I was born."

The mahogany curls were shaken violently. It was, I thought, an act of rebellion against that fey mood which had claimed her. She rose to her knees, confronting me; her fingers played with the sand. The rebellion had succeeded. She seemed to have drawn near again, to have become human and adorable. Her next words confirmed my uncanny impression that in mind and spirit she had really been far away,

"Did you say you were American?" she asked.

Rather uncomfortably I answered:

"I was born in America. But I took my degree in Edinburgh, so that really I don't quite know what I am."

"Don't you?"

She sank down upon the sand, looking like a lovely idol.

"And now please tell me *your* name," I said; "I have told you mine."

"Fleurette."

"But Fleurette what?"

"Fleurette nothing. Just Fleurette."

"But, Mahdi Bey——"

I suppose my thoughts were conveyed without further words, for:

"Mahdi Bey," Fleurette replied, "is——"

And then she ceased abruptly. Her glance strayed away somewhere over my shoulder. I had a distinct impression that she was listening—listening intently for some distant sound.

"Mahdi Bey," I prompted.

Fleurette glanced at me swiftly.

"Really, Mr. Sterling," she said, "I must run. I mustn't be caught talking to you."

"Why?" I exclaimed. "I was hoping you would show me over Ste Claire."

She shook her head almost angrily.

"As you came out of the sea, please go back again. You can't come with me."

"I don't understand why——"

"Because it would be dangerous."

Composedly she tucked a comb back into a bag which lay upon the sand beside her, picked up a bathing cap, and stood up.

"You don't seem to bother about the possibility of my being drowned!"

"You have a motorboat just around the headland," she replied, glancing at me over one golden shoulder. "I heard your engine."

This was a revelation.

"No wonder you weren't frightened when I came ashore."

"I am never frightened. In fact, I am rather inhuman, in all sorts of ways. Did you ever hear of Derceto?"

Her abrupt changes of topics, as of moods, were bewildering, but:

"Vaguely," I answered. "Wasn't she a sort of fish goddess?"

"Yes. Think of me, not as Fleurette, but as Derceto. Then you may understand."

The words conveyed nothing at the time, although I was destined often to think about them, later. And what I should have said next I don't know. But the whole of my thoughts, which were chaotic, became suddenly focused . . . upon a sound.

To this day I find myself unable to describe it, although, as will presently appear, before a very long time had elapsed I was called upon to do so. It more closely resembled the note of a bell than anything else—yet it was not the note of a bell. It was incredibly high. It seemed at once to come from everywhere and from nowhere. A tiny sound it was, but of almost unendurable sweetness: it might be likened to a fairy trumpet blown close beside one's ear.

I started violently, looking all around me. And as I did so, Fleurette, giving me no parting word, no glance, darted away!

Amazed beyond words, I watched her slim brown figure bounding up a rocky path, until, at a bend high above, Fleurette became invisible. She never once looked back.

And then—the desire to get away, and as soon as possible, from the beach of Ste Claire de la Roche claimed me again, urgently. . . .

Chapter Second

A PURPLE CLOUD

When presently I climbed on board the motorboat and pushed off, I found myself to be in a state of nervous excitement. But as I headed back for the landing place below Petrie's tiny villa, I grew more and more irritated by my memories.

Fleurette was not only the most delightful but also the most mysterious creature who had ever crossed my path; and the more I thought about her, reviewing that odd conversation, the nearer I drew to what seemed to be an unavoidable conclusion. Of course, she had been lying to me—acting the whole time. A beautiful girl in the household of a wealthy Egyptian—in what capacity was she there?

Common sense supplied the answer. It was one I hated to accept—but I could see no alternative. The queer sound which had terminated that stolen interview, I preferred not to think about. It didn't seem to fit in. . . .

As I secured the boat to the ring and started a long, hot climb up to the Villa Jasmin, I found myself wondering if I should ever see Fleurette again, and, more particularly, if she wanted to see *me*.

I supposed Mme Dubonnet had gone into the village to do her midday shopping, which included an *apéritif* with one of her cronies outside a certain little café. Petrie I knew would be hard at work in the laboratory at the bottom of the garden.

Mixing myself a cool drink, I sat down on the flower-draped verandah and allowed my glance to stray over the well stocked little kitchen garden. Beyond and below were more flower-covered walls and red roofs breaking through the green of palm and vine, and still beyond was a distant prospect of the jewel-like Mediterranean.

I reflected that this was a very pleasant spot in which to recuperate. And then I began to think about Fleurette. . . .

No doubt my swim had overtired me, but stretched out there in a deck-chair, the hot sun making my skin tingle agreeably, I presently fell asleep. And almost immediately, as

I suppose, I began to dream.

I dreamed that I lay in just such a deck chair, under an equally hot sun, on a balcony or platform of an incredibly high building. I have since decided that it was the Empire State Building in New York. I was endowed with telescopic vision. Other great buildings there were, with mile after mile of straight avenues stretching away to the distant sea.

The sky was sapphire blue, and a heat haze danced over the great city which lay at my feet.

Then there came a curious, high sound. It reminded me of something I had heard before—but of something which in my dream I could not place. A cloud appeared, no larger than my hand, on the horizon, miles and miles away—over that blue ocean. It was a purple cloud; and it spread out, fan-wise, and the sections of the fan grew ever larger. So that presently half of the sky was shadowed.

And then a tiny glittering point, corresponding, I thought, to the spot where the hinge of this purple shadow-fan should have been, I saw a strange jewel. The fan continued to open, to obscure more and more the sky.

It was advancing towards me, this shadowy thing; and now the jewel took shape.

I saw that it was a dragon, or sea serpent, moving at incredible speed towards me. Upon its awful crested head a man rode. He wore a yellow robe which, in the light focused upon him, for the sun was away to my left as I dreamed, became a golden robe.

His yellow face glittered also, like gold, and he wore a cap surmounted by some kind of gleaming bead. He was, I saw a Chinaman.

And I thought that his face had the majesty of Satan—that this was the Emperor of the Underworld come to claim a doomed city.

So much I saw, and then I realized that the dragon carried a second rider: a woman, robed in queenly white and wearing a jewelled diadem. Her beauty dazzled me, seeming more than human. But I knew her. . . .

It was Fleurette.

The purple shadow-fan obscured all the sky, and complete darkness came. The darkness reached me, and where there had been sunshine was shadow. I shuddered and opened my eyes, staring up, rather wildly, I suppose.

Dr. Petrie had just stepped onto the verandah. His shadow touched me where I lay.

"Hullo, Sterling," he said briskly. "What's wrong? been overdoing it again?"

I struggled upright. Then, in a moment, I became fully awake. And as I looked up at Petrie, seated on the low wall beside a big wine jar which had been converted into a flower pot, I realized that this was a very sick man.

He wore no hat, and his dark hair, liberally streaked with grey, was untidy—which I knew to be unusual. He was smoking a cigarette and staring at me in that penetrating way which medical men cultivate. But his eyes were unnaturally bright, although deep shadows lay beneath them.

"Been for a swim," I replied; fell asleep and dreamed horribly."

Dr. Petrie shook his head and knocked ash from his cigarette into the soil in the wine jar.

"Blackwater fever plays hell even with a constitution like yours," he replied gravely. "Really, Sterling, you mustn't take liberties for a while."

In pursuit of my profession, that of an orchid hunter, I had been knocked out by a severe attack of blackwater on the Upper Amazon. My native boys left me where I lay, and I owed my life to a German prospector who, guided by kindly Providence, found me and brought me down to Manaos.

"Liberties be damned, doctor," I growled, standing up to mix him a drink. "If ever a man took liberties with his health, that man is yourself! You're worked to death!"

"Listen," he said, checking me. "Forget me and my health. I'm getting seriously worried."

"Not another case?"

He nodded.

"Admitted early this morning."

"Who is it this time?"

"Another open-air worker, Sterling, a jobbing gardener. He was working in a villa, leased by some Americans, as a matter of fact, on the slope just this side of Ste Claire de la Roche——"

"Ste Claire de la Roche?" I echoed.

"Yes—the place you are so keen to explore."

"D'you think you can save him?"

He frowned doubtfully.

"Cartier and the other French doctors are getting in a perfect panic," he replied. "If the truth leaks out, the Riviera will be deserted. And they know it! I'm rather pessimistic myself. I lost another patient to-day."

"What!"

Petrie ran his fingers through his hair.

"You see," he went on, "diagnosis is so tremendously difficult. I found *trypanasomes* in the blood of the first patient I examined here; and although I never saw a tsetse fly in France, I was forced to diagnose sleeping sickness. I risked Bayer's 205—" he smiled modestly—"with one or two modifications of my own; and by some miracle the patient pulled through."

"Why a miracle? It's the accepted treatment, isn't it?"

He stared at me, and I thought how haggard he looked.

"It's one of 'em," he replied—"for sleeping sickness. But this was *not* sleeping sickness!"

"What!

"Hence the miracle. You see, I made cultures; and under the microscope they gave me a shock. I discovered that these parasites didn't really conform to any species so far classified. They were members of the sleeping sickness family, but *new* members. Then—just before the death of another patient at the hospital—I made a great discovery, on which I have been working ever since—"

"*Over*working!"

"Forget it." He was carried away by his subject. "D'you know what I found, Sterling? I found *bacillus pestis* adhering to one of the parasites!"

"*Bacillus pestis?*"

"Plague!"

"Good God!"

"But—here's the big point: the *trypanasomes* (the parasites which cause sleeping sickness) were a new variety, as I have mentioned. *So was the plague bacillus*. It presented obviously new features! Crowning wonder—although you may not appreciate it—parasite and bacillus affiliated and working in perfect harmony!"

"You've swamped me, doctor," I confessed. "But I have a hazy idea that there's something tremendous behind this."

"Tremendous? There's something *awful*. Nature is upsetting her own laws—as we know them."

This, from Dr. Petrie, gave me something to think about.

My father had been invited to lecture at Edinburgh—his old university—during Petrie's first year, and a close friendship had sprung up between the keen student and the visiting lecturer. They had corresponded ever since.

During my own Edinburgh days the doctor was established in practice in Cairo; but I spent part of one vacation as his guest in London. And another fast friendship resulted. He had returned from Egypt on that occasion to receive the medal of the Royal Society for his researches in tropical medicine. I remember how disappointed I had been to learn that his wife, of whose charm I had heard many rumours, was not accompanying him on this flying journey.

His present visit—also intended to be a brief one—had been prolonged at the urgent request of the French authorities. Petrie's reputation had grown greater with the passage of years, and learning that he was in London, they had begged him to look into this strange epidemic which threatened southern France, placing the Villa Jasmin at his disposal. . . .

Three weeks later I was invalided home from Brazil. Petrie, who had had the news from my father, met the ship at Lisbon and carried me off to the Villa Jasmin to recuperate under his own watchful eye.

I fear I had proved to be a refractory patient.

"You didn't see the other case, did you?" Petrie asked suddenly.

"No."

"Well." He set down his glass. "I wish you would come along to the hospital with me. You must have met with some queer diseases on the Amazon, and you know the Uganda sleeping sickness. There's this awful grin—proof of some sort of final paroxysm—and particularly what Cartier calls the 'black stigmata.' Your bulb hunting has taken you into a few unwholesome places; have you ever come across anything like it?"

I began to fill by pipe.
"Never, doctor," I replied.
The sound of a distant gun boomed through the hot silence.
A French battleship was entering Villefranche Harbour. . . .

CHAPTER THIRD

THE BLOODSTAINED LEAVES

"GOOD GOD! it's ghastly! Cover him up again, doctor. I shall dream of that face."

I found myself wondering why Providence, though apparently beneficent, should permit such horrors to visit poor humanity. The man in the little mortuary—he had been engaged in a local vineyard—had not yet reached middle age when this new and dreadful pestilence had cut him off.

"This," said Petrie, "is the really singular feature."

He touched the dead man's forehead. It was of a dark purple colour from the scalp to the brows. The sun-browned face was set in a grin of dreadful malignancy and the eyes were rolled upward so that only their whites showed.

"What I have come to recognize as the characteristic sign," Petrie added. "Subcutaneous haemorrhage but strangely localised. It's like a purple shadow, isn't it? And when it reaches the eyes—finish."

"What a ghastly face! I have seen nothing like it anywhere!"

We came out.

"Nor have I!" Petrie confessed. "The earlier symptoms are closely allied with those of sleeping sickness but extraordinarily rapid in their stages. Glandular swellings always in the armpit. This final stage—the black stigmata, the purple shadow, which I have managed to avert in some of the other cases, is quite beyond my experience. That's where plague comes in.

"But now for the most mysterious thing of all—in which I am hoping you can really help me. . . ."

If anyone had invited me to name Dr. Petrie's outstanding characteristic, I should have said "modesty."

Having run the car into its garage, Petrie led the way down the steep rocky path to a shed a hundred yards from the villa, which he had fitted up as a laboratory.

We entered. The laboratory was really an enlarged gardener's hut which the absent owner of Villa Jasmin had converted into a small studio. It had a glass window running along the whole of one side. A white-topped table now occupied a great part of the space before it, and there was a working bench in a corner opposite the door. In racks were rows of test tubes, each bearing a neatly written label, and there were files of specimen slides near the big microscope.

I noted the new pane of glass in a section of window which had been cut out one night less than a month ago when some strange burglar had broken in and explored the place. Since that time Petrie had had steel shop-blinds fitted to the interior of the windows, which could be closed and locked at night.

He had never secured any clue to the identity of the intruder or formed any reasonable theory as to what his object could have been.

At the moment, several of the windows were open, and sunlight streamed into the place. There was a constant humming of bees in the garden outside. Petrie took up a little sealed tube, removed the stopper, and shook out the contents of the tube into a glass tray. He turned to me, a strange expression upon his haggard brown face.

"Can you identify this, Sterling?" he asked. "It's more in your line than in mine."

I found it to consist of several bruised leaves, originally reddish purple in colour, attached to long stalks. I took up a lens and examined them carefully, the doctor watching me in silence. I saw, now, that there were pollen-like fragments adhering to a sticky substance exuded by the leaves.

There were some curious brown blotches, too, which at first I took to be part of the colouring, but which closer examination showed to be due to a stain.

"It's *drosophyllum*," I murmured—"one of the fly catching varieties, but a tropical species I have not come across before."

Petrie did not interrupt me, and:

"There are stains of what looks like dark brown mud," I went on, "and minute shiny fragments of what might be pollen—"

"It isn't pollen," Petrie broke in. "It's bits of the wing and body of some very hairy insect. But what I'm anxious to know, Sterling, is this—"

I put down the lens and turned to the speaker curiously. His expression was grimly serious.

"Should you expect to find that plant in Europe?"

"No, it isn't a European variety. It could not possibly grow even as far South as this."

"Good. That point is settled."

"How do you account for the stains?"

"I don't know how to account for them," Petrie replied slowly, "but I have found out what they are."

"What are they?"

"Blood!—and what's more, human blood."

"Human blood!"

I stopped, at a loss for words.

"I can see I am puzzling you, Sterling. Let me try to explain."

Petrie replaced the fragments in the tube and sealed it down tightly.

"It occurred to me this morning," he went on, "after you had gone, to investigate the spot where our latest patient had been at work. I thought there might be some peculiar local condition there which would give me a new clue. When I arrived, I found it was a piece of steeply terraced kitchen garden—not unlike our own, here. It ended in a low wall beyond which was a clear drop into the gorge which connects Ste Claire with the sea.

"He had been at work up to sunset last evening about halfway down, near a water tank. He was taken ill during the night, and this morning developed characteristic symptoms....

"I stood there—it was perfectly still; the people to whom the villa is leased are staying in Monte Carlo at present—and I listened for insects. I had gone prepared to capture any that appeared."

He pointed to an equipment which lay upon a small table.

"I got several healthy mosquitoes, and other odds and ends. (Later examination showed no trace of parasite in any of them.) I was just coming away when, lying in a little trench where the man had apparently been at work up to the time that he knocked off—I happened to notice *that*...."

He pointed to the tube containing the purple leaves.

"It was bruised and crushed partly into the soil."

He paused, then:

"Except for the fragments I have pointed out," he added, "there was nothing on the leaves. Possibly a passing lizard had licked them... I spent the following hour searching the neighbourhood for the plant on which they grew. I drew blank."

We were silent for some time.

"Do you think there is some connection," I asked slowly, "between this plant and the epidemic?"

Petrie nodded.

"Of course," I admitted, "it's certainly strange. If I could credit the idea—which I can't —that such a species could grow wild in Europe, I should be the first to agree with you. Your theory is that the thing possesses the properties of a carrier, or host, of these strange germs; so that anyone plucking a piece and smelling it, for instance, immediately becomes infected?"

"That was not my theory," Petrie replied, thoughtfully. "It isn't a bad one, nevertheless. But it doesn't explain the blood-stains."

He hesitated.

"I had a very queer letter from Nayland Smith to-day," he added. "I have been thinking about it ever since."

Sir Denis Nayland Smith, ex-Assistant Commissioner of Metropolitan Police, was one of Petrie's oldest friends, I knew, but:

"This is rather outside his province, isn't it?" I suggested.

"You haven't met him," Petrie replied, labouring his words as it seemed. "But I think you will. Nayland Smith has one of the few first-class brains in Europe, and *nothing* is outside his——"

He ceased speaking, staggered and clutched at the table edge. I saw him shudder violently.

"Look here, doctor," I cried, grasping his shoulders, "you are sickening for 'flu or something. You're overdoing it. Give the thing a rest, and——"

He shook me off. His manner was wild. He groped his way to a cupboard, prepared a draught with unsteady hands, and drank it. Then from a drawer he took out a tube containing a small quantity of white powder.

"I have called it 654," he said, his eyes feverishly bright. "I haven't the pluck to try it on a human patient. But even if Mother Nature has turned topsy-turvy, I believe this may puzzle her!"

Watching him anxiously:

"Strictly speaking, you ought to be in bed," I said. "Your life is valuable."

"Get out," he replied, summoning up the ghost of a smile. "Get out, Sterling. My life's my own, and while it lasts I have work to do. . . ."

Chapter Fourth

SQUINTING EYES

I SPENT the latter part of the afternoon delving in works of reference which I had not consulted for many months, in an endeavour to identify more exactly the leaves so mysteriously found by Petrie.

To an accompaniment of clattering pans, old Mme Dubonnet was preparing our evening meal in the kitchen and humming some melancholy tune very cheerily.

Petrie was a source of great anxiety. I had considered 'phoning for Dr. Cartier, but finally had dismissed the idea. That my friend was ill he had been unable to disguise; but he was a Doctor of Medicine, and I was not. Furthermore, he was my host.

That he was worried about his wife in Cairo, I knew. Only the day before he had said, "I hope she doesn't take it into her head to come over—much as I should like to see her." Now, I shared that hope. His present appearance would shock the woman who loved him.

Fleurette—Fleurette of the dimpled chin—more than once intruded her image between me and the printed page. I tried to push these memories aside.

Fleurette was the mistress of a wealthy Egyptian. Despite her name, she was not French. She was, perhaps, an actress. Why had I not thought of that before? Her beautifully modulated voice—her composure. "Think of me as Derceto. . . ."

"In *Byblis gigantea*, according to Zopf, insect-catching is merely incipient," I read. . . .

She could be no older than eighteen—indeed, she might be younger than that. . . .

And so the afternoon wore on.

Faint buzzing of the Kohler engine, and a sudden shaft of light across the slopes below, first drew my attention to approaching dusk. Petrie had turned up the laboratory lamps.

I was deep in a German work which promised information, and now, mechanically, I switched on the table lamp. Hundreds of grasshoppers were chirping in the garden; I could hear the purr of a speedboat. Mme Dubonnet continued to sing. It was a typical Riviera evening.

The shadow of that great crag which almost overhung the Villa Jasmin lay across part of the kitchen garden visible from my window, and soon would claim all our tiny domain. I continued my studies, jumping from reference to reference and constantly consulting the index. I believed I was at last on the right track.

How long a time elapsed between the moment when I saw light turned up in the laboratory and the interruption, I found great difficulty in determining afterwards. But the interruption was uncanny.

Mme Dubonnet, working in the kitchen, French fashion, with windows hermetically sealed, noticed nothing.

Already, on this momentous day, I had heard a sound baffling description; and it was written—for the day was one never to be forgotten—that I should hear another.

As I paused to light a fresh cigarette, from somewhere outside—I thought from the Corniche road above—came a cry, very low, but penetrating. . . .

It possessed a quality of fear which chilled me like a sudden menace. It was a sort of mournful wail on three minor notes. But a shot at close quarters could not have been more electrical in its effect.

I dropped my cigarette and jumped up.

What was it?

It was unlike anything I had ever heard. But there was danger in it, creeping peril. I leaned upon the table, staring from the window upward, in the direction from which the cry seemed to have come.

And as I did so, I saw something.

I have explained that a beam of light from the laboratory window cut across the shadow below. On the edge of this light something moved for a moment—for no more than a moment—but instantly drew my glance downward.

I looked. . . .

A pair of sunken, squinting eyes, set in a yellow face so evilly hideous that I was tempted then, and for sometime later, to doubt the evidence of my senses, watched me!

Of the body belonging to this head I could see nothing; it

was enveloped in shadow. I saw just that evil mask watching me; then—it was gone!

As I stood staring from the window, stupid with a kind of horrified amazement, I heard footsteps racing down the path from the road which led to the door of Villa Jasmin.

Turning, I ran out onto the verandah.

I reached it at the same moment as the new arrival—a tall, lean man with iron-grey, crisply virile hair, and keen, eager eyes. He had the sort of skin which tells of years spent in the tropics. He wore no hat, but a heavy topcoat was thrown across his shoulders, clockwise. Above all, he radiated a kind of vital energy which was intensely stimulating.

"Quick," he said—his mode of address reminded me of a machine gun—"where is Dr. Petrie? My name is Nayland Smith."

"I'm glad you have come, Sir Denis," I replied; and indeed I spoke sincerely. "The doctor referred to you only to-day. My name is Alan Sterling."

"I know it is," he said, and shook hands briskly; then:

"Where is Petrie?" he repeated. "Is he with you?"

"He is in the laboratory, Sir Denis. I'll show you the way."

Sir Denis nodded, and we stepped off the verandah.

"Did you hear that awful cry?" I added.

He stopped. We had just begun to descend the slope.

"*You* heard it?" he rapped in his staccato fashion.

"I did. I have never heard anything like it in my life!"

"*I* have! Let's hurry."

There was something very strange in his manner, something which I ascribed to that wailing sound which had electrified me. Definitely, Sir Denis Nayland Smith was not a man susceptible to panic, but some fearful urgency drove him to-night.

I was about to speak of that malignant yellow face when, as we came in sight of the lighted windows of the laboratory:

"How long has Petrie been in there?" Nayland Smith asked.

"All the afternoon. He's up to his eyes in work on these mysterious cases—about which, perhaps, you know?"

"I do," he replied. "Wait a moment. . . ."

He grasped my arm and pulled me up just at the edge of the patch of shadow. He stood still, and I could tell that he was listening intently.

"Where's the door?" he asked suddenly.

"At the farther end."

"Right."

He set off at a run, and I followed past the lighted window. Petrie was not at the table nor at the bench. I was puzzled to account for this, and already vaguely fearful. A premonition gripped me, a premonition of something horrible. Then, I had my hand on the door and had thrown it open. I entered, Sir Denis close behind me.

"Good God! Petrie! . . . Petrie, old man . . ."

Nayland Smith had sprung in and was already on his knees beside the doctor.

Petrie lay in the shadow of his working bench, in fact, half under it, one outstretched hand still convulsively gripping its edge!

I saw that the apparently rigid fingers grasped a hypodermic syringe. Near to his upraised hand was a vessel containing a small quantity of some milky fluid; and the tube of white powder which he had shown to me lay splintered, broken by his fall, on the floor a foot away.

In those few fleeting seconds I saw Sir Denis Nayland Smith, for the first and last time in my knowledge of him, fighting to subdue his emotions. His head dropped into his upraised hands, his fingers clutched his hair.

Then he had conquered. He stood up.

"Lift him!" he said hoarsely—"out here, into the light."

I was half stunned. Horror and sorrow had me by the throat. But I helped to move Petrie farther into the middle of the floor, where a central light shone down upon him. One glance told me the truth—if I had ever doubted it.

A sort of cloud was creeping from his disordered hair, down over his brow.

"Heaven help him!" I whispered. "Look—look! . . . the purple shadow!"

Chapter Fifth

THE BLACK STIGMATA

The laboratory was very silent. Through the windows, which still remained open, I could hear the hum of the Kohler engine in its little shed at the bottom of the garden—the chirping of crickets, the clucking of hens.

There was a couch littered with books and chemical paraphernalia. Sir Denis and I cleared it and laid Petrie there.

I had telephoned Dr. Cartier from the villa.

That ghastly purple shadow was creeping farther down my poor friend's brow.

"Shut the door, Sterling," said Nayland Smith sharply.

I did so.

"Stand by," he went on, and pointed.

Petrie, who wore a woollen pullover with long sleeves when he was working late, had evidently made an attempt to peel it off just before coma had claimed him.

"You see what he meant to do," Nayland Smith went on. "God knows what the consequences will be, but it's his only chance. He must have been fighting it off all day. The swelling in his armpit warned him that the crisis had come."

He examined the milky liquid in a small glass measure.

"Have you any idea what this *is*?"

I indicated the broken tube and scattered white powder on the floor.

"A preparation of his own—to which I have heard him refer as '654.' He believed it was a remedy, but he was afraid to risk it on a patient."

"I wonder?" Sir Denis murmured. "I wonder——"

Stooping, I picked up a fragment of glass to which one of Petrie's neatly written labels still adhered.

"Look here, Sir Denis!"

He read aloud:

"'654.' 1 grm. in 10 c.c. distilled water: intravenous."

He stared at me hard, then:

"It's kill or cure," he rapped. "We have no choice...."

"Shouldn't we wait for Dr. Cartier?"

"Wait!" His angry glare startled me. "With luck, he'll be here in three quarters of an hour. And life or death in this thing is a matter of *minutes*! No! Petrie must have his chance. I'm not an expert—but I can do my best. . . ."

I experienced some difficulty in assisting at what followed; but Nayland Smith, his course set, made the injection as coolly as though he had been used to such work for half a lifetime. When it was done:

"If Petrie survives," he said quietly, "his own skill will have saved him—not ours. Lay that rug over him. It strikes one as chilly in here."

The man's self-mastery was almost superhuman.

He crossed to close the windows—to hide his face from me. Even that iron control had its breaking point. And suddenly the dead silence which fell with the shutting of the windows was broken by the buzzing of an insect.

I couldn't see the thing, which evidently Sir Denis had disturbed, but it was flying about the place with feverish activity. Something else seemed to have arrested Sir Denis's attention: he was staring down at the table.

"H'm!" he muttered. "Very queer!"

Then the noise of the busy insect evidently reached his ears. He turned in a flash and his expression was remarkable.

"What's that, Sterling?" he snapped. "Do you hear it?"

"Clearly. There's a gadfly buzzing about."

"Gadfly—nothing! I have recently spent many hours in the laboratory of the School of Tropical Medicine. That's why I'm here! Listen. Did you ever hear a gadfly that made that noise?"

His manner was so strange that it chilled me. I stood still, listening. And presently, in the sound made by that invisible, restless insect, I detected a difference. It emitted a queer *sawing* note. I stared across at Nayland Smith.

"You've been to Uganda," he said. "Did you never hear it?"

At which moment, and before I had time to reply, I caught a glimpse of the fly which caused this peculiar sound. It was smaller than I had supposed. Narrowly missing the speaker's head, it swooped down onto the table behind him, and settled upon something which lay there—something which had already attracted Sir Denis's attention.

"Don't move," I whispered. "It's just behind you."

"Get it," he replied, in an equally low voice; "a book, a roll of paper—anything; but for God's sake don't miss it. . . ."

I took up a copy of the *Gazette de Monte Carlo*. One of poor Petrie's hobbies was a roulette system which he had never succeeded in perfecting. I rolled it and stepped quietly forward.

Nayland Smith stood quite still. Beside him, my improvised swatter raised, I saw the insect distinctly. It had long, narrow, brownish wings and a curiously hairy head. In the very moment that I dashed the roll of paper down, I recognized the object upon which it had settled.

It was a spray of that purple-leaved *drosophyllum*, identical except that it was freshly cut, with a fragment which I knew to be sealed in a tube somewhere in Petrie's collection!

"Make sure," said Sir Denis, turning.

I repeated the blow. Behind us, on the couch Petrie lay motionless. Sir Denis bent over the dead insect.

"Don't you know what this is, Sterling?" he demanded.

"No. Flies are a bit outside my province. But I can tell you something about the purple leaves. . . ."

Taking the roll of paper from me, he moved the dead fly further forward upon the polished table-top where direct light fall upon it; then:

"Hullo!" he exclaimed.

He snatched up a lens which lay near by and bent over the insect, peering down absorbedly.

I turned and looked towards the couch were Petrie lay, and I studied his haggard features. I could detect no evidence of life. The purple shadow showed like a bruise on his forehead; but I thought that it had not increased.

Yet I believed he was doomed, already dying, and my thoughts jumped feverishly to that strange plant upon the table—and from the plant to the yellow face which so recently had leered at me out of the darkness.

Was it conceivable—could it be—that some *human agency* directed this pestilence?

I turned, looking beyond the bent, motionless figure of Nayland Smith, out into the dusk—and a desire to close the steel shutters suddenly possessed me.

This operation I completed without drawing a single comment from Sir Denis. But, as that menacing dusk was shut out, he stood upright and confronted me.

"Sterling," he said, and there was something in his steady gaze which definitely startled me—"have you, as a botanist, ever come across a true *genus-hybrid?*"

"You mean a thing between a lily and a rose—or an oak growing apples?"

"Exactly."

"In the natural state, never—although some curious hybrids have been reported from time to time. But many freaks of this kind can be *cultivated*, of course. The Japanese are experts."

"Cultivated? I agree. But nature, in my experience, sticks to the common law. Now here, Sterling—" he indicated the table—"lies an insect which, from the sound it made when flying, I took to be a tsetse fly——"

"A tsetse! Good heavens! *Here?*"

He smiled grimly.

"Well outside its supposed area," he admitted, "and above its usual elevation. I thought you might have recognized its note, as you have travelled in the flybelt. However, I was right—up to a point. It definitely possesses certain characteristics of *glossina*, the tsetse fly; notably the wings, which are typical. You see, I have been taking an intensive course on this subject! But can you imagine, Sterling, that it has the legs and head of an incredibly large *sand-fly?* The thing is a nightmare, an anachronism; it's a sort of giant *flying flea!*"

His words awakened a memory. What had Petrie said to me, earlier in the evening? . . . that "even if Nature is turning topsy-turvy, I think I can puzzle her! . . ."

"Sir Denis," I broke in, "I think you should know that Petrie found, in the blood of a patient, some similar freak—a sort of hybrid germ, which I lack the knowledge to describe to you. He found sleeping sickness and plague combined——"

"Good God!"

I thought that the lean, sun-baked face momentarily grew yet more angular.

"You know," he interrupted, "that tsetse carries sleeping

sickness? Sand-fly is suspect in several directions. But the rat-flea (and this is more like a flea than a sand-fly) is the proved cause of plague infection.... Am I going mad?"

He suddenly crossed and bent over Petrie. He examined him carefully and in detail. The fact dawned upon me that Sir Denis Nayland Smith had more than a smattering of the medical art. I watched in silence while finally he took the temperature of the unconscious man.

"There's no change," he reported. "'654' seems already to have checked its progress. But this coma.... Dare we hope?"

"I don't know what to hope, or what to believe, Sir Denis!"

He nodded.

"Nor do I. The nature of my job has forced me to pick up some elements of medicine; but this is a specialist's case.... However, tell me about these leaves—the leaves which seemed to attract the fly...."

I told him briefly all that I knew of the insect-catching plant.

"The specimen which Petrie has preserved," I concluded, "bears traces of human blood."

Sir Denis suddenly grabbed the lens again and bent over the purple leaves on the table-top. A moment he looked, then turned.

"So does this!" he declared. "Fresh blood."

I was dumb for a matter of seconds; then:

"The insect which I partly crushed?" I suggested.

He shook his head irritably.

"Quantity too great. These leaves have been *sprayed* with blood!"

"How, in heaven's name, did they get here? And how did that damnable fly get here?"

He suddenly clapped his hands upon my shoulders and stared at me fixedly.

"You're a man of strong nerve, Sterling," he said, "and so I can tell you. They were *brought* here. And—" he pointed to the still body on the couch—"for *that* purpose."

"But——"

"There are no 'buts.' I left the car in which I had been driven over from Cannes some distance back on the road tonight, and walked ahead to look for this villa, the exact location of which my driver didn't know. I had nearly reached the way in when I heard a sound."

"I heard it too."

"I know you did. But to you it meant nothing—except that it was horrible; to me, it meant a lot. You see, I had heard it before."

"What was it? I shall never forget it!"

"It was the signal used by certain Burmans, loosely known as dacoits, to give warning to one another. If poor old Petrie had come across this new species of tsetse fly—he would have begun to think. If he had heard that cry . . . he would have *known!*"

"He would have known what?" I asked, aware of a growing excitement communicated to me by the speaker.

"He would have known what he was up against." He raised his fists in a gesture almost of despair. "We are children!" he said vehemently, momentarily taken out of himself. "What do you know of botany, and what does Petrie know of medicine beside Dr. Fu Manchu?"

"Dr. Fu Manchu?" I echoed.

"A synonym for Satan—evil immutable; apparently eternal."

"Sir Denis——" I began.

But he turned aside abruptly, bending again over the motionless body of his old friend.

"Poor Kâramanèh!" he murmured.

He was silent a while, then, without looking around:

"Do you know his wife, Sterling?" he asked.

"No, Sir Denis; we have never met."

"She is still young, as we count tears to-day. She was a child when Petrie married her—and she is the most beautiful woman I have ever known. . . ."

As he spoke I seemed to hear a soft voice saying, "Think of me as Derceto" . . . Fleurette! Fleurette was the most beautiful woman I had ever *seen*. . . .

"She was chosen by a master—who rarely makes mistakes."

His manner and his words were so strange that I may be forgiven for misunderstanding.

"A master? Do you mean a painter?"

At that, he turned and smiled. His smile was the most

440

boyish and disarming I had ever met with in a grown man.

"Yes, Sterling, a painter! His canvas, the world; his colours, the human races. . . ."

This was mystery capping mystery, and certainly I should never have left the matter there; but at this moment we were interrupted by a series of short staccato shrieks.

I ran to the door. I had recognized the voice.

"Who is it?" Sir Denis snapped.

"Mme Dubonnet."

"Housekeeper?"

"Yes."

"Keep her out."

I threw the door open—and the terrified woman tottered into my arms.

"M. Sterling," she panted, hysterically—"something terrible has happened! I know—I know—something terrible has happened!"

"Don't worry, Mme Dubonnet," I said, and endeavoured to lead her away. "Dr. Petrie——"

"But I must tell the doctor—it concerns him. As I look up from my casserole dish I see at the window just above me—a face—a dreadful yellow face with cross eyes. . . ."

"Rather a quandary, Sterling," Sir Denis cut in, standing squarely between the excited woman and the insensible man on the couch. "One of those murderous devils is hanging about the place. . . ."

Dimly I heard the sound of an insistent motor horn on the Corniche road above, nearing the head of that narrow byway which debouched from the Corniche and led down to the Villa Jasmin.

"The ambulance from the hospital!" Sir Denis exclaimed in relief.

Chapter Sixth

"654"

Mme Dubonnet, still shaking nervously, was escorted back to her quarters. Petrie, we told her, was down with a severe attack of influenza and must be moved immediately. The appearance of the yellow face at the window, mendacity had failed to explain; and the old lady announced that she should lock herself into the kitchen until such time as someone could take her home.

She was left lamenting, "Oh, the poor, dear kind doctor! . . ."

Cartier had come in person, with two orderlies and a driver. The bearded, round-faced little man exhibited such perfect consternation on beholding Dr. Petrie that it must have been funny had it not been tragic. He dropped to his knees, bending over the insensible man.

"The black stigmata!" he muttered, touching the purple-shadowed brow. "I am too late! The coma. Soon—in an hour, or less, the final convulsions . . . the end! God! it is terrible. He is a dead man!"

"I'm not so sure," Sir Denis interrupted. "Forgive me, doctor; my name is Nayland Smith. I have ventured to give an injection——"

Dr. Cartier stood up excitedly.

"What injection?" he demanded.

"I don't know," Sir Denis replied calmly.

"What is this?"

"I don't know. I used a preparation of Petrie's which he called '654.'"

"654!"

Dr. Carter dropped upon his knees again beside the insensible man.

"How long," he demanded, "since the shadow appeared?"

"Difficult to say, doctor," I replied. "He was alone here. But it hasn't increased."

"How long since the injection?"

Nayland Smith shot out a lean brown wrist and glanced at

a gun-metal watch in a leather strap.

"Forty-three minutes," he reported.

Cartier sprang to his feet again.

"Dr. Smith!" he cried excitedly—and I saw Sir Denis suppress a smile—"this is triumph! From the time that the *ecchymosis* appears, it never ceases to creep down and down to the eyes! It has remained static for forty-three minutes, you tell me? This is triumph!"

"Let us dare to hope so," said Sir Denis gravely.

When all arrangements had been completed and the good Dr. Cartier had grasped the astounding fact that Nayland Smith was not a confrère but a super-policeman:

"It's very important," Sir Denis whispered to me, "that this place should be watched to-night. We have to take into consideration—" he gripped my arm—"the possibility that they fail to save Petrie. The formula for '654' *must* be somewhere here!"

But we had searched for it in vain; nor was it on his person.

The driver of the car in which Sir Denis had come, agreed, on terms, to mount guard over the laboratory. He remained in ignorance of the nature of Petrie's illness; but Dr. Cartier assured us there was no danger of direct infection at this stage.

And so, poor Petrie having been rushed to the isolation ward, Nayland Smith going with the ambulance, I drove Mme Dubonnet home, leaving the chauffeur from Cannes on guard. Returning, I gave the man freedom of the dinner which Fate had decreed that Petrie and I were not to eat, lent him a repeater, and set out in turn for the hospital.

This secret war against the strange plague which threatened to strip the Blue Coast of visitors and prosperity had aroused the enthusiasm of the whole of that small hospital staff.

Petrie, with other sufferers from the new pestilence, was lodged in an outbuilding separated from the hospital proper by a stretch of waste land. A porter, after some delay, led me through this miniature wilderness to the door of the isolation ward. The low building was dominated by a clump of pines.

A nursing sister admitted me, conducting me in silence along a narrow passage to Petrie's room.

As I entered, and the sister withdrew, I saw at a glance the cause of a suppressed feverish excitement which I had detected even in the bearing of the lodge porter.

Dr. Cartier was in tears. He was taking the pulse of the unconscious man. Nayland Smith, standing beside him, nodded to me reassuringly as I came in.

The purple shadow on Petrie's brow had encroached no further—indeed, as I thought, was already dispersing!

Dr. Cartier replaced his watch and raised clasped hands.

"He is doing well," said Sir Denis. "'654' is the remedy . . . but what, exactly is '654'?"

"We must know!" cried Dr. Cartier emotionally. "Thanks to the good God, he will revive from the coma and tell us. We must know! There is no more that I or any man can do now. But Sister Thérèse is a treasure among nurses, and if there should be a development, she will call me immediately. I shall be here in three minutes. But tomorrow? What can we do? We must know!"

"I agree," said Sir Denis quietly. "Don't worry any more about it. I think you are about to win a great victory. I hope, as I have told you, to recover a copy of the formula for '654'—and as Dr. Petrie's safety is of such vital importance, you have no objections to offer to my plan?"

"But none!" Cartier replied. "Except that this seems unnecessary."

"I never take needless risks," said Sir Denis drily.

But when Cartier was gone:

"I am going into Nice," Sir Denis said, "now, to put a phone call through to London."

"What!"

"There's a definite connection, Sterling, between the appearance in Petrie's laboratory of a new species of tropical fly at the same time as an unfamiliar tropical plant—the latter bloodstained!"

"So much is obvious."

"The connecting link is the Burmese dacoit whom I heard and you and Mme Dubonnet saw. He was the servant of a dreadful master."

A question burned on my tongue, but:

"Sister Thérèse is all that Carter claims for her—I have

interviewed the sister. She will attend to the patient from time to time. But I'm going to ask you to do something, Sterling, for me and for Petrie."

"Anything you like. Just say the word."

"You see, Sterling, since Petrie left London and came here, he had kept in close touch with Sir Manston Rorke, of the School of Tropical Medicine—one of the three big names, although I doubt if he knows more than Petrie. Some days ago, Sir Manston called me up. He had formed a remarkable opinion."

"What about?"

"About the French epidemic. Two cases, showing identical symptoms, occurred in the London dock area, and he had had news of several in New York and of one in Sydney, Australia. Having personally examined the London cases (both of which terminated fatally) he had come to the conclusion that this disease was not an ordinary plague. Briefly, he believed that it was being induced artificially!"

"Good heavens, Sir Denis! I begin to believe he was right."

Nayland Smith nodded.

"I invited him to suggest a motive, and he wavered between a mad scientist and a Red plot to decimate unfriendly nations! In my opinion, he wasn't far short of the truth; but here's the big point: I have reason to believe that Petrie submitted to Sir Manston the formula for '654'—and I'm going to Nice to call him up."

"God grant he has it," I said, glancing at the bed where the sick man lay.

"Amen to that. But in the meantime, Sterling—I may be away two hours or more—it's vitally important that Petrie should not be alone for one moment."

"I quite follow."

"So I want you to stand by here until I get back. What I mean is this—I want you to sit tight beside his bed."

"I understand. You may count on me."

He stared at me fixedly. There was something almost hypnotic in that penetrating look.

"Sterling," he said, "you are dealing with an enemy more cunning and more brilliant than any man you have ever met East or West. Until I return you are not to allow a soul to *touch* Petrie—except Sister Thérèse or Cartier."

I was startled by his vehemence.

"It may be difficult," I suggested.

"I agree that it may be difficult; but it has to be done. Can I rely upon you?"

"Absolutely."

"I'm going to dash away now, to put a call through to Manston Rorke. I only pray that he is in London and that I can locate him."

He raised his hand in a sort of salute to the insensible man, turned, and went out.

CHAPTER SEVENTH

IVORY FINGERS

I THOUGHT of many things during the long vigil that followed. The isolation ward harboured six patients, but Petrie had been given accommodation in a tiny private room at one end. The corresponding room at the other end was the sanctum of Sister Thérèse.

It was a lonely spot, and very silent. I heard the sister moving about in the adjoining ward, and presently she entered quietly, a fragile little woman, her pale face looking childishly small framed in the stiff white headdress of her order. Deftly and all but noiselessly she went about her duties; and, watching her, I wondered, as I had often wondered before, from whence came the unquestioning faith which upheld such as Sister Thérèse and in which they found adequate reward for a life of service.

"You are not afraid of infection, M. Sterling?" she asked, her voice very low and gentle.

"Not at all, Sister. In *my* job I have to risk it."

"What do you do?"

"Hunt for new species of plants for the Botanical Society—and orchids for the market."

"But how fascinating! As a matter of fact, there is no danger of infection at this stage."

"So I am told by Dr. Cartier."

"It is new to us, this disease. But it is tragic that Dr. Petrie should fall a victim. However, as you see——"

She pointed.

"The stigmata?"

Sister Thérèse shuddered.

"It is so irreligious! But Dr. Cartier, I know, calls this mark the black stigmata. Yes—it does not increase. Dr. Petrie may conquer. He is a wonderful man. You will moisten his poor lips from time to time? I am praying that he may be spared to us. Good-night, M. Sterling. Ring for me if he moves."

She withdrew in her gentle, silent way, leaving me to my

thoughts. And by some queer mental alchemy these became transmuted into thoughts of Fleurette. I found myself contemplating in a sort of cold horror the idea of Fleurette infected with this foul plague—her delicate beauty marred, her strong young body contorted by the work of some loathsome, unclassified bacillus.

And then I fell to thinking about those who had contracted this thing, and to considering what Nayland Smith had told me. What association was there to explain a common enmity between London dock labourers and Dr. Petrie?

I stared at him as the thought crossed my mind. One of the strangest symptoms of this horror which threatened France was the period of complete coma preceding the end. Petrie looked like a dead man.

A searching wind, coming down from the Alps, had begun to blow at sunset. The pines, some of which almost overhung the lonely building, hushed and whispered insidiously. I construed their whispering into a repetition of the words "Fleurette—Derceto. . . ."

If dear old Petrie survived the crisis, I told myself, tomorrow should find me once more on the beach of Ste Claire de la Roche. I might have misjudged Fleurette. But even if she were the mistress of Mahdi Bey, she was very young and so not past praying for.

I had just formed this resolution when a new sound intruded upon the silence of the sickroom.

There was only one window—high in the wall which marked the end of the place. As I sat near the foot of Petrie's bed, this window was above on my left.

And the sound, a faint scraping, seemed to come from there.

I listened to the hushing of the pines, thinking that the wind had grown higher and that some outstretched branch must be touching the wall. But the wind seemed to have decreased, and the whisper, "Fleurette—Derceto," had become a scarcely audible sigh.

Raising my head, I looked up. . . .

A yellow hand, the fingers crooked in a clutching movement—a threat it seemed—showed for a moment, then disappeared, outside the window!

Springing to my feet, I stared wildly. How long had I been sitting there, dreaming, since Sister Thérèse had gone? I had no idea. My imagination pictured such an evil, mask-like face as I had seen at the Villa Jasmin—peering in at that high window.

One of the dacoits (the name was vaguely familiar, although I had never been in Burma) referred to by Nayland Smith must be watching the place!

Was this what he had feared? Was this why I had been left on guard?

What did it mean?

I could not believe that Dr. Petrie had ever wronged any man. Who, then, was hounding him to death, and what was his motive?

Literally holding my breath, I listened. But there was no repetition of the scraping sound. The climber—the window was twelve feet above ground level—had dropped silently at the moment that I sprang from my chair.

To rush out and search was obviously not in orders. My job was to sit tight. I was pledged to it.

But the incident had painted a new complexion on my duties.

I watched that high window keenly and for a long time. Then, as I was on the point of sitting down, a slight sound brought me upright at a bound. I realised that my nerves were badly overtuned.

The door opened, and Sister Thérèse came in, in her unobtrusive, almost apologetic way.

"A lady has called to see Dr. Petrie," she said. "To see Dr. Petrie!"

"How could I refuse her, M. Sterling?" Sister Thérèse asked gently. "She is his wife!" The little sister glanced wistfully at the unconscious man. "And she is such a beautiful woman."

"Great heavens!" I groaned—"this is going to be almost unendurable. Is she very—disturbed, Sister?"

Sister Thérèse shook her head, smiling sadly.

"Not at all. She has great courage."

Just as poor Petrie had feared—his wife had come from Cairo—to find him . . . a doomed man.

"I suppose she must come in. But his appearance will be a

frightful shock to her. . . ."

Anticipating a tragic interview, I presently turned to meet Mrs. Petrie, as Sister Thérèse showed her into the room. She was, I saw, tall and slender, having an indolent grace of bearing totally different from affectation. She was draped in a long wrap of some dark fur beneath which showed the edge of a green dress. Bare, ivory ankles peeped below its fringe and she wore high-heeled green sandals with gold straps.

She had features of almost classic chiselling and perfectly moulded lips. But her eyes were truly remarkable. They were incredibly long, of the true almond shape, and brilliant as jewels. By reason of the fact that Mrs. Petrie wore a little green beret-like hat set on one side of her glossy head, from which depended a figured gold veil, I could not determine the exact colour of those strange eyes: the veil just covered them.

Her complete self-possession reassured me. She glanced at Petrie, and then, as Sister Thérèse silently retired:

"It is very good of you, Mr. Sterling," she said—and her voice had an indolent, soothing quality in keeping with her personality—"to allow me to make this visit."

She seated herself in a chair which I placed for her beside Petrie's bed.

So this was "Kâramanèh"? I had not forgotten that strange name murmured by Nayland Smith as he had bent over Petrie. "The most beautiful woman I have ever known. . . ."

And that Mrs. Petrie was beautiful none could deny; yet for some reason her appearance surprised me. I had not been prepared for a woman of this type. Truth to tell, although I didn't recognize the fact then, I had subconsciously given Mrs. Petrie the attributes of Fleurette—a flower-like tender loveliness wholly removed from the patrician yet exotic elegance of this woman who sat looking at the unconscious man.

Having heard of her passionate love for the doctor, I was surprised, too, by her studied self-possession. It was admirable, but, in a devoted wife, almost uncanny . . .

"I could do no less, Mrs. Petrie," I replied. "It is very brave of you to come."

She was bending forward, watching the sick man.

"Is there—any hope?" she asked.

"There is every hope, Mrs Petrie. In other cases which the

doctors have met with, the appearance of the purple shadow has meant the end."

"But in this case?"

She looked at me, her wonderful eyes so bright that I thought she was suppressing tears.

"In Petrie's case, the progress of the disease has been checked—temporarily, at any rate."

"How wonderful," she whispered—"and how strange."

She bent over him again. Her movements were feline in their indolent grace. One slender ivory hand held the cloak in place; the long nails were varnished to a jewel-like brightness. I wondered how these two had met, and how such markedly different types had ever become lovers.

Mrs. Petrie raised her eyes to me again.

"Is Dr. Cartier following some different treatment in—my husband's case?"

The nearly imperceptible pause had not escaped me. I supposed that a wave of emotion had threatened to overcome her when she found that name upon her lips and realised that the man himself tottered on the brink of the Valley.

"Yes, Mrs Petrie; a treatment of your husband's known as '654.'"

"Prepared, I suppose, by Dr. Cartier?"

"No—prepared by Petrie himself just before he was seized with illness."

"But Dr. Cartier, of course, knows the formula?"

That caressing voice possessed some odd quality of finality; it was like listening to Fate speaking. Not to reply to any question so put to one would have been a task akin to closing one's ears to the song of the Sirens. And the darkly fringed eyes, which, now, owing to some accident of reflected light, I thought were golden, emphasized the soft command.

Indeed, I was on the point of answering truthfully that no one but Petrie knew the formula when an instinct of compassion gave me strength to defy that powerful urge. Why should I admit so cruel a truth?

"I cannot say," I replied, and knew that I spoke the words unnaturally.

"But of course it will be somewhere in my husband's possession? No doubt in his laboratory?"

Her anxiety—although there was no trace of tremor in her velvety tones—was nevertheless unmistakable.

"No doubt, Mrs Petrie," I said reassuringly—and spoke now with greater conviction, since I really believed that the formula must be somewhere among Petrie's papers.

She murmured something in a low voice—and, standing up, moved to the head of the bed.

Whereupon, my difficulties began. For, as Mrs. Petrie bent over the pillow, I remembered the charge which had been put upon me, remembered Nayland Smith's words: "You are not to allow a soul to *touch* him——"

I got up swiftly, stepped around the foot of the bed, and joined Mrs. Petrie where she stood.

"Whatever you do," I said, "don't touch him!"

Slowly she stood upright; infinitely slowly and gracefully. She turned and looked into my eyes.

"Why?" she asked.

"Because—" I hesitated: what could I say?—"because of the possibility of infection."

"Please don't worry about that, Mr. Sterling. There is no possibility of infection at this stage, Sister Thérèse told me so."

"But she may be wrong," I urged. "Really, I can't allow you to take the risk."

Perhaps my principles ride me to death; I have been told that they do. But I had pledged my word that no one should touch Petrie, and I meant to stick to it. Logically, I could think of no reason why this woman who loved him should not stroke his hair, as I thought she had been about to do. It was almost inhuman to forbid it. Yet, by virtue of Sir Denis's trust in me, forbid it I must.

"It may be difficult," I remembered saying to him. *How* difficult it was to be, I had not foreseen!

"Surely," she said, and her soft voice held no note of anger, "the risk is mine?"

Mrs. Petrie bent again over the pillow. She was on the point of resting those slender, indolent hands on Petrie's shoulders.

She intended, I surmised, to kiss his parched lips. . . .

Chapter Eighth

"BEWARE..."

As those languorous ivory hands almost rested on Petrie's shoulders, and the full red lips were but inches removed from the parched blue lips of the unconscious man, I threw my arms around Mrs. Petrie and dragged her away!

She was light and resilient as a professional dancer. I had been forced to exert considerable strength because of her nearness to the doctor. She was swept back, lying against my left arm and looking up at me in a startled yet imperious way, which prepared me to expect an uncomfortable sequel.

During one long moment she remained motionless, our glances meeting. Her cloak had slipped, exposing a bare arm and shoulder. I was partly supporting her and trying frenziedly to find words to excuse my apparent violence, when, still looking up at me, she turned slightly.

"Why did you do that?" she asked. "Was it . . . to save me from contagion?"

The cue was a welcome one; I seized it gladly.

"Of course!" I replied, but knew that my assurance rang false. "I warned you that I should not allow you to touch him."

She continued to watch me, resting in the crook of my arm; and I had never experienced such vile impulses as those which goaded me during those few seconds. The most singular promptings were dancing in my brain. I thought she was offering me her lips, or, rather, challenging me to reject the offer. With a movement so slight that it might have been accidental, she seemed to invite me to caress her.

Yes, most utterly damnable thing, I, in whose blood there runs a marked streak of Puritanism, I, with poor Petrie lying there in the grip of a dread disease, suddenly wanted to crush this woman—his wife—in my arms!

It was only a matter of hours since I had met Fleurette on the beach of Ste Claire de la Roche and had become so infatuated with her beauty and charm that I had been thinking about her almost continuously ever since. Yet here I stood fighting against a sudden lawless desire for the wife of my best friend—a desire so wild that it threatened to swamp everything—friendship, tradition, honour!

Perhaps I might have conquered—unaided. I am not prepared to say. But aid came to me, and came in the form of what I thought at the time to be a miracle. As I looked down into those enigmatical, mocking eyes, in a silence broken only by the hushing of the pines outside the window—a voice—a groaning, hollow voice, a voice that might have issued from a tomb—spoke.

"Beware . . . *of her*," it said.

Mrs. Petrie sprang back. A fleeting glimpse I had of stark horror in the long, narrow eyes. My heart, which had been beating madly, seemed to stop for a moment.

I twisted my head aside, staring down at Petrie.

Was it imagination—or did I detect a faint quivering of those swollen eyelids? Could it be *he* who had spoken? That slight movement, if it had ever been, had ceased. He lay still as the dead.

"Who was it?" Mrs Petrie whispered, her patrician calm ruffled at last. "Whose voice was that?"

I stared at her. The spell was broken. The glamour of those bewitched moments had faded—dismissed by that sepulchral voice. Mrs. Petrie's eyelashes now almost veiled her long, brilliant eyes. One hand was clenched, the other hidden beneath her cloak. My ideas performed a complete about-turn. Some sudden, inexplicable madness had possessed me, from the consequences of which I had been saved by an act of God!

"I don't know," I said hoarsely. "I don't know . . ."

Chapter Ninth

FAH LO SUEE

The end of that interview is hazy in my memory. Concerning one detail, however, I have no doubt: Mrs. Petrie did not again approach the sick man's bed. Despite her wonderful self-discipline, she could not entirely hide her apprehension. I detected her casting swift glances at Petrie and—once—upwards towards the solitary window.

That awful warning, so mysteriously spoken— could have related only to *her*. . . .

I rang for Sister Thérèse and arranged that the night concierge should conduct the visitor to her car. I suspected that the neighbourhood was none too safe.

Mrs. Petrie gave me the address of a hotel in Cannes, asking that she be kept in touch. She would return, she said, unless summoned earlier, at eight in the morning. She had fully regained her graceful composure by this time, and I found myself wondering what her true nationality could be. Her languid calm was hard to reconcile with wifely devotion: indeed, I had expected her to insist upon remaining.

And when, with a final glance at Petrie and an enigmatical smile to me, she went out with Sister Thérèse, I turned and stared at the doctor. I could detect no change whatever, except that it seemed to me that the purple shadow on his brow was not so dark.

Could it be he who had spoken?

His face was dreadfully haggard, looking almost emaciated, and his lips dry and cracked, were slightly parted so as to expose his teeth. In that unnatural smile I thought I saw the beginning of the death grin which characterized this ghastly pestilence.

He did not move, nor could I detect him breathing. I glanced at the window, high above my head, where not so long before I had seen those crooked yellow fingers. But it showed as a black patch in the dull white mass of the wall.

The pines began whispering softly again: "Fleurette—

Derceto...."

If Petrie had not spoken—and I found it hard to believe that he had—whose was the voice which had uttered the words, "Beware... of her?"

I had ample time to consider the problem and many others as well which had arisen in the course of that eventful day. Dr. Cartier looked in about eleven o'clock, and Sister Thérèse made regular visits.

There was no change to be noted in Petrie's condition.

It was a dreary vigil; in fact, an eerie one. For company I had an apparently dead man, and some of the most horrible memories which one could very well conjure up as a background for that whispering silence.

At some time shortly after midnight I hard swift footsteps coming along the passage which led to Petrie's room. The door opened, and Nayland Smith walked in.

One glance warned me that something was amiss.

He crossed and stared down at Petrie in silence, then turning to Sister Thérèse, who had entered behind him:

"I wonder, Sister," he said rapidly, "if I might ask you to remain here until Dr. Cartier arrives, and allow Mr. Sterling and myself the use of your room?"

"But of course, with the greatest pleasure," she replied, and smiled in her sweet, patient way.

Together we went along the narrow corridor and presently came to that little room used by the nurse on duty. It was very simple and very characteristic.

There was a glass-fronted cabinet containing medicines, dressings, and surgical appliances. Beside a little white table was placed a very hard white enamelled chair. An open book lay on the table; and the only decoration was a crucifix on the distempered wall.

Sir Denis did not speak for a moment, but paced restlessly to and fro in that confined space twitching at the lobe of his ear—a habit which I later came to recognize as indicative of deep thought.

Suddenly he turned and faced me.

"Sir Manston Rorke died early yesterday morning," he said, "from an overdose of heroin or something of that kind!"

"What!"

I had been seated on the edge of the little table, but at that I sprang up. Sir Denis nodded grimly.

"But was he—addicted to drugs?"

"Apparently. He was a widower who lived alone in a flat in Curzon Street. There was only one resident servant—a man who had been with him for many years."

"It's Fate," I groaned. "What a ghastly coincidence!"

"Coincidence!" Sir Denis snapped. "There's no coincidence! Sir Manston's consulting rooms in Wimpole Street, where he kept all his records and pursued his studies, were burgled during the night. I assume that they found what they had come for. A large volume containing prescriptions is missing."

"But, if they found what they came for——"

"That was good enough," he interrupted. "Hence my assumption that they did. Sir Manston had a remarkable memory. Having destroyed the prescription book, the next thing was to destroy . . . that inconvenient memory!"

"You mean—he was *murdered?*"

"I have little doubt on that point," Sir Denis replied harshly. "The butler has been detained—but there's small hope of learning anything from him, even if he knows. But I gather, Sterling—" he fixed a penetrating stare upon me—"that a similar attempt was made here to-night."

"*Here?* Whatever do you mean, Sir Denis?"

But even as I spoke the words I thought I knew, and:

"Why, of course!" I cried—"the dacoit!"

"Dacoit," he rapped. "What dacoit?"

"You don't know? But, on second thoughts, how could you know! It was shortly after you left. Someone looked in at the window of Petrie's room——"

"Looked in?" He glanced up at the corresponding window of Sister Thérèse's room. "It's twelve feet above ground level."

"I know. Nevertheless, someone looked in. I heard a faint scuffling—and I was just in time to catch a glimpse of a yellow hand as the man dropped back."

"Yellow hand?" Sir Denis laughed shortly. "Our cross-eyed friend from the Villa Jasmin, Sterling! He was spying out the land. Shortly after this, I suggest, the *lady* arrived?"

I stared at him in surprise.

"You are quite right. I suppose Sister Thérèse told you?

Mrs. Petrie came a few minutes afterwards."

"Describe her," he directed tersely.

Startled by his manner, I did my best to comply, when:

"She has green eyes," he broke in.

"I couldn't swear to it. Her veil obscured her eyes."

"They are green," he affirmed confidently. "Her skin is the colour of ivory, and she has slender, indolent hands. She is as graceful as a leopardess, of the purring which treacherous creature her voice surely reminded you?"

Sir Denis's sardonic humour completed my bewilderment. Recalling the almost tender way in which he had spoken the words, "Poor Kâramanèh," I found it impossible to reconcile those tones with the savagery of his present manner.

"I'm afraid you puzzle me," I confessed. "I quite understood that you held Mrs. Petrie in the highest esteem."

"So I do," he snapped. "But we are not talking about Mrs. Petrie!"

"Not talking about Mrs. Petrie! But——"

"The lady who favoured you with a visit to-night, Sterling, is known as Fah Lo Suee (I don't know why). She is the daughter of the most dangerous man living to-day, East or West—Dr. Fu Manchu!"

"But, Sir Denis!"

He suddenly grasped my shoulders, staring into my eyes.

"No one can blame you if you have been duped, Sterling. You thought you were dealing with Petrie's wife: it was a stroke of daring genius on the part of the enemy——"

He paused; but his look asked the question.

"I refused to permit her to touch him, nevertheless," I said.

Sir Denis's expression changed. His brown eager face lighted up.

"Good man!" he said in a low voice, and squeezed my shoulders, then dropped his hands. "Good man."

It was mild enough, as appreciation goes, yet somehow I valued those words more highly than a decoration.

"Did she mention my name?"

"No."

"Did you?"

I thought a while, and then:

"No," I replied. "I am positive on the point."

"Good!" he muttered, and began to pace up and down again. "There's just a chance—just a chance *he* has overlooked me. Tell me, omitting no detail that you recall, exactly what took place."

To the best of my ability, I did as he directed.

He interrupted me once only: when I spoke of that sepulchral warning—

"Where was the woman when you heard it?" he rapped.

"Practically in my arms. I had just dragged her back."

"The voice was impossible to identify?"

"Quite."

"And you could not swear to the fact that Petrie's lips moved?"

"No. It was a fleeting impression, no more."

"It was after this episode that she subjected you to her hypnotic tricks?"

"Hypnotic tricks!"

"Yes—you have narrowly escaped, Sterling."

"You refer," I said with some embarrassment for I had been perfectly frank—"to my strange impulses?"

He nodded.

"No. It was the voice which broke the spell."

He twitched his ear for some moments, then:

"Go on!" he rapped.

And when I had come to the end:

"You got off lightly," he said. "She is as dangerous as a poised cobra! And now, I have another job for you."

"I'm ready."

"Hurry back to Villa Jasmin—and call me up here if all's well there. Have you a gun?"

"No. I lent mine to the chauffeur."

"Take this." He drew an automatic from his topcoat pocket. "Drive like hell and shoot if necessary. You are a marked man. . . ."

As I hurried out, Dr. Carter hurried in.

"Ah!" Nayland Smith exclaimed. "I regret troubling you, doctor; but I want you to examine Petrie very carefully."

"What! there is some change?"

"I don't know. That's what I want you to find out."

Chapter Tenth

GREEN EYES

The two-seater which had been placed at Petrie's disposal was no beauty, but the engine was fairly reliable, and I set out along the Corniche about as fast as it is safe to travel upon such a tortuous road.

I suppose it had taken me a ridiculously long time to grasp the crowning horror which lay behind this black business. As I swung around the dangerous curves of that route, the parapet broken in many places and the mirror of the Mediterranean lying far below on the right, my brain grew very active.

The discovery of a fly-catching plane near the place where a man had been seized by this frightful infection, coupled with our finding later a similar specimen in Petrie's laboratory, had suggested pretty pointedly that human agency was at work. Yet, somehow, in spite of the apparition of that grinning yellow face in the kitchen garden of the villa, I had not been able to realize, or not been able to believe, that human agency was actually *directing* the pestilence.

Sir Denis Nayland Smith had adjusted my perspective. Someone, apparently a shadowy being known as Fu Manchu, was responsible for these outbreaks!

And the woman who had posed as Petrie's wife, the woman who had tried, and all but succeeded in her attempt to bewitch me, was of the flesh and blood of this fiend. She was Chinese; and her mission had been—what?

To poison Petrie—as Sir Manston Rorke had been poisoned?

As I swung into the lighted tunnel cut through the rock, I laughed aloud when that seeming absurdity presented itself to my mind.

A new disease had appeared in the world. Yes; of this, I had had painful evidence. It was possibly due, according to Sir Denis, to the presence in France of an unfamiliar fly—what he had called a genus-hybrid.

So much I was prepared to admit.

But how could any man be responsible for the appearance of such an insect, anywhere and at any time; much less in such widely separated places as those which had been visited by the epidemic?

The Purple Shadow...

I had nearly reached the end of the rock cutting. There was a dangerous corner just ahead; and I had allowed my thoughts to wander rather wide of the job in hand. A big car, a Rolls-Royce, appeared suddenly. The driver—some kind of African, as I saw—was taking so much of the road on the bend that no room was left for me.

Jamming on the brakes, I pulled close in against the wall of the tunnel... and I acted only just in time.

The driver of the Rolls checked slightly and swept right—missing me by six inches or less!

I had a clear, momentary view of the occupants of the car which had so nearly terminated my immediate interest in affairs....

How long I stayed there after the beautiful black-and-silver thing had purred away into the darkness, I don't know. But I remember turning round and staring over the folded, dusty hood in a vain attempt to read the number.

The car had two occupants.

In regard to one of those occupants I wondered if the wild driving of the Negro chauffeur and my preoccupation with the other had led me to form a false impression. Because, when the Rolls had swept on its lordly way, I realised that my memory retained an image of something not entirely human.

A yellow face buried in the wings of an upturned fur collar I had certainly seen: a keen wind from the Alps made the night bitingly cold. The man wore a fur cap pulled down nearly to his brows, creating a curious mediaeval effect. But this face had a placid, almost godlike immobility, gaunt, dreadful, yet sealed with power like the features of a dead Pharoah.

Some chance trick of the lighting might have produced the illusion (its reality I could not admit); but about the second traveller I had no doubts whatever.

Her charming head framed—as that other skull-like head was framed—in the upturned collar of a fur coat... I saw Fleurette!

And I thought of a moss-rose. . . .
I turned to the wheel again.
Fleurette!

She had not seen me, had not suspected that I was there. Probably, I reflected, it would not have interested her to know.

But her companion? I tested the starter, wondering if it would function after the shock. I was relieved to find that it did. The Rolls was miles away, now, unless the furious driving of the African chauffeur had led to disaster. . . . That yellow face and those glittering green eyes—I asked myself the question: Could this be Mahdi Bey?

Somehow I could not believe the man with Fleurette to be an Egyptian. Yet, I reflected, driving on, there had been that about him which had conjured an image to my mind . . . the image of Seti the First—that King of Egypt whose majesty had survived three thousand years. . . .

CHAPTER ELEVENTH

AT THE VILLA JASMIN

The car in which Nayland Smith had come from Cannes was standing just where the steep descent to the little garage made a hairpin bend. I supposed that the man had decided to park there for the night. But I was compelled to pull in behind, as it was impossible to pass.

I walked on beyond the bend to the back of the bungalow. A path to the left led around the building to the little verandah; one to the right fell away in stepped terraces, skirting the garden and terminating at the laboratory.

My mind, from the time of that near crash with the Rolls up to this present moment, had been preoccupied. The mystery of Fleurette had usurped my thoughts. Fleurette—her charming little bronzed face enveloped in fur; a wave of her hair gleaming like polished mahogany. Now, as I started down the slope, a warning instinct spoke to me. I found myself snatched back to dangerous reality.

I pulled up, listening; but I could not detect the Kohler engine.

Some nocturnal flying thing hovered near me; I could hear the humming of its wings. Vividly, horribly, I visualised that hairy insect with its glossy back, and almost involuntarily, victim of a swift, overmastering and sickly terror, I began striking out right and left in the darkness. . . .

Self-contempt came to my aid. I stood still again.

The insect, probably some sort of small beetle, was no longer audible. I thought of the fly-haunted swamps I had known, and grew hot with embarrassment. The Purple Shadow was a ghastly death; but Petrie had faced it unflinchingly. . . .

Natural courage returned. A too vivid imagination had betrayed me.

I reached the laboratory and found it dark and silent. This was not unexpected. I supposed that the man had turned in on the couch. He was a tough type who had served in the

French mercantile marine; I doubted if he were ever troubled by imagination. He had been given to understand, since this was the story we had told to Mme Dubonnet, that Petrie was suffering from influenza. He had accepted without demur Dr. Cartier's assurance that there was no danger of infection.

Walking around to the door I rapped sharply.

There was no reply.

Far below I could see red roofs peeping out of purplish shadow, and, beyond, the sea gleaming under the moon; but by reason of its position the laboratory lay in darkness.

Having rapped several times without result, I began to wish that I had brought a torch, for I thought that then I could have looked in at the window. But even as the idea crossed my mind I remembered that the iron shutters were drawn.

Thus far, stupidly, I had taken it for granted that the door was locked. But failing to get a response from the man inside, I now tried the handle and found, to my great surprise, that the door was unlocked.

I opened it. The laboratory was pitch black and reeked of the smell of mimosa.

"Hullo, there!" I cried. "Are you asleep?"

There was no reply, but I detected a sound of heavy breathing as I groped for the switch. When I found it, the lamps came up very brightly, dipped, and then settled down.

"My God!" I groaned. The man from Cannes lay face downward on the couch!

I ran across, and tried to move him. He was a big, heavy fellow, and one limply down-stretched arm, the fingers touching the floor, told me that this was no natural repose. Indeed, the state of the place had prepared me for this.

It was not merely in disorder—it had been stripped. Petrie's specimen slides and all the documents which were kept in the laboratory had been removed!

The smell of mimosa was everywhere; it was getting me by the throat.

I rolled the man over on his back. My first impression, that he had been drinking heavily, was immediately dispelled. He was insensible but breathing stertorously. I shouted and shook him, but without avail. My Colt automatic, which I had lent him, lay upon the floor some distance away.

"Good heavens!" I whispered, and stood there, listening.

Except for the hum of the engine in its shed near by, and the thick breathing of the man on the couch, I could hear nothing. I stared at the chauffeur's flushed features.

Was it . . . the Purple Shadow?

My medical knowledge was not great enough to tell me. The man might have been stunned by a blow or be suffering from the effects of an anaesthetic. Certainly, I could find no evidence of injury.

It was only reasonable to suppose that whatever the marauders had come to look for, they had found. I decided to raise the metal shutters and open a window. That stifling perfume, for which I was wholly at a loss to account, threatened to overpower me. I wondered if the searchers had upset a jar of some queer preparation of Petrie's.

How little I appreciated at that moment the monumental horror which lay behind these opening episodes in a drama destined to divert the whole course of my life!

I came out of the laboratory. Some kind of human contact—sympathy—assistance was what I most desired. Leaving the lights on and the door and window open, I began to make my way up the steep path bordering the kitchen garden, towards the villa. I had slipped my own automatic into my pocket and so was now doubly armed.

In my own defence I think I may say that blackwater fever leaves one very low, and, as Petrie had warned me, I had been rather overdoing it for a convalescent. This is my apologia for the fact that as I climbed up that narrow path to the Villa Jasmin I was conscious of the darkest apprehension. I became convinced, suddenly but quite definitely, that I was being watched.

I had just stepped onto the verandah and was fumbling with the door key when I heard a sound which confirmed my intuition. . . .

From somewhere behind me, near the laboratory which I had just left, came the call, soft but unmistakable, on three minor notes, of a dacoit!

I flung the door open and turned up the light in the small, square lobby. Then I reclosed the door. What to do was the problem. I thought of the man lying down there helpless—at the mercy of unguessed dangers. But he was too heavy to carry, and at all costs I must get to the phone—which was here in the villa.

I threw open the sitting-room door and entered the room in which, that evening, I had quested through the works in several languages for a clue to the strange plant discovered by Petrie. I switched on the lamps.

What I saw brought me up sharply with a muttered exclamation.

The room had been turned upside down!

Two cabinets and the drawers of a writing table had been emptied of their contents. The floor was littered with papers. Even the bookshelves had not escaped scrutiny. A glance showed me that every book had been taken from its place. They were not in their right order.

Something, I assumed, had disturbed the searchers....

What?

Upon this point there was very little room for doubt. That cry in the garden had given warning of my approach. To whom?

To someone who must actually be in the villa now!

My hand on the butt of an automatic, I stood still, listening. I was unlikely ever to forget the face I had glimpsed at the end of the kitchen garden. It was possible that such a horror was stealthily creeping upon me at the present moment. But I could hear no sound.

I thought of Petrie—and the thought made me icily and murderously cool. Petrie—struck down by the dread disease he had risked his life to conquer; a victim, not of Fate, but of a man—

A man? A fiend! a devil incarnate he must be who had conceived a thing so loathsome.

Dr. Fu Manchu!

Who was this Dr. Fu Manchu of whom even Nayland Smith seemed to stand in awe? A demon—or a myth? Indeed, at the opening stage of my encounter with the most evil and the most wonderful man who, I firmly believe, has ever been incarnated, I sometimes toyed with the idea that the Chinese doctor had no existence outside the imagination of Sir Denis.

All these reflections, more or less as I have recorded them, flashed through my mind as I stood there listening for evidence of another presence in the villa.

And although I heard not the faintest sound, I *knew*, now, that someone was there—someone who was searching for the formula of "654," and, therefore, not a Burmese bodyguard or other underling, but one cultured enough to recognize the formula if it should be found!

Possibly . . . Dr. Fu Manchu!

I stepped up to the writing desk, upon which the telephone stood—and in doing so noticed that the shutters outside the window had been closed. First and foremost, I must establish contact with Sir Denis. I thought I should by justified in reporting that the enemy had not yet found the formula.

The automatic in my right hand, I took up the receiver in the left. Because of the position of the instrument, I was compelled to turn half away from the open door.

I could get no reply. I depressed the lever; there was no answering ring. . . .

A light sound, and a change in the illumination of the room, brought me about in a flash.

The door was closed.

And the telephone line was dead—cut. . . .

I leapt to the door, grasped the handle, and turned it fiercely. I remained perfectly cool—which is my way of seeing red. The door was locked.

At which moment the lights went out.

Chapter Twelfth

MIMOSA

I LISTENED intently, not knowing what to expect. That this was a prelude to an attack on my life, I did not doubt.

The room was now in complete darkness, for, as I had already noted, the outside shutters had been closed. There were two points from which this attack was to be apprehended: the door or the window. There was no chimney, heat being provided by a stove the pipe of which was carried out through an aperture in the wall high up near the ceiling.

At first I could not hear a sound.

Very cautiously I bent and pressed my ear to the thin panelling of the door. Now, I detected movement—and, furthermore, sibilant whispering. I could hear my own heart beating, too.

After a lapse of fully a minute, I became certain that *someone else* was standing on the other side of the door, listening, as I was listening.

A murderous rage possessed me.

It was unnecessary to recall Sir Denis's instructions: "Don't hesitate to shoot." I did not intend to hesitate . . . I was anxious for an opportunity. Petrie's haggard face was always before my mind's eye. And if Nayland Smith were correct, Sir Manston Rorke also had been foully done to death by this callous, foul group surrounding the creature called Fu Manchu.

A very slight movement upon the woodwork now enabled me to locate the exact position of the one who listened.

I hesitated no longer.

Standing upright, I clapped the nose of my automatic against the panel at a point about waist high and fired through the door. . . .

The report in that tiny enclosed space was deafening, but the accuracy of my judgment was immediately confirmed. A smothered, choking cry and a groan followed by the sound of a heavy fall immediately outside told me that my shot had not gone astray.

Braced tensely, I stood awaiting what would follow. I anticipated an attempt to rush the room, and I meant to give an account of myself.

What actually happened was utterly unexpected.

Someone was opening the outer door of the villa; then I heard a low voice—and it was a woman's voice!

I had stepped aside, anticipating that my own method might be imitated, but now headless of risk, I bent and listened again. A faint smell of burning was perceptible where I had fired through the woodwork.

That low, musical voice was speaking rapidly—but not in English, nor in any language with which I was familiar. It was some tongue containing strange gutturals. But even these could not disguise the haunting music of the speaker's tone.

The woman called Fah Lo Suee was outside in the lobby. . . .

Then I heard a man's voice, a snarling, hideous voice, replying to her; and, I thought, a second. But of this I could not be sure. . . .

They were dragging a heavy body out onto the verandah. There came a choking cough. Such was my mood that I could have cheered aloud. One of the skulking rats had had his medicine!

As those movements proceeded in accordance with rapidly spoken orders in that unforgettable voice, I turned to considerations of my own safety. Tiptoeing across the room and endeavouring to avoid those obstacles the position of which I could remember, I mounted on to the writing table.

Slipping the automatic into my pocket I felt for the catch of the window, found it, and threw the window open: the shutters, I knew, I could burst with a blow, for they were old, and the fastener was insecure.

I moved farther forward, resting upon one knee, and raised my hands.

As I did so, a ghastly thing happened—a thing unforeseen. I was faced by a weapon against which I had no defence.

Pouring down through the slats of the shutters came a cloud of vapour. I was drenched, saturated, blinded by *mimosa!* A faint hissing sound accompanied the discharge; and as I threw one arm across my face in a vain attempt to shield myself from the deadly vapour, this hissing sound was repeated.

I fell onto both knees, rolled sideways, and tried to throw myself back.

But the impalpable abomination seemed to follow me. I was enveloped in a cloud of it. I tried to cry out—I couldn't breathe—I was choking.

A third time I heard the hissing sound, and then I think I must have rolled from the table onto the floor. My impression at the time was of falling—falling into dense yellow banks of cloud, reeking of mimosa. . . .

Chapter Thirteenth

THE FORMULA

"Sterling, Sterling! wake up, man! You're all right now."

I opened my eyes as directed, and apart from a feeling of pressure on the temples, I experienced no discomfort.

I was in my own bed at the Villa Jasmin!

Nayland Smith was standing beside me, and a bespectacled, bearded young man whom I recognized as one of Dr. Cartier's juniors was bending down and watching me anxiously.

Without any of that mental chaos which usually follows unconsciousness, I remembered instantly all that had happened, up to the moment that I had rolled from the table.

"They drugged me, Sir Denis," I said, "but I can tell you all that happened."

"The details, Sterling. I have already reconstructed the outline." He turned to the doctor. "You see, this drug apparently has no after effects."

The medical man felt my pulse, then turned in amazement to Sir Denis.

"It is truly astounding," he admitted. "I know of no property in any species of mimosa which could explain this."

"Nevertheless," rapped Sir Denis, "the smell of mimosa is still perceptible in the sitting room."

The French doctor nodded in grave agreement. Then as I sat up—for I felt as well as I had ever felt in my life——

"No, please," he insisted, and laid his hand upon my shoulder: "I should prefer that you lie quiet for the present."

"Yes, take it easy, Sterling," said Nayland Smith. "There was another victim here last night."

"The man in the laboratory?"

"Yes; but he's none the worse for it. He dozed off on the couch, he tells me, and they operated in his case, I have discovered, by inserting a tube through the ventilator in the wall above. He sprang up at the first whiff, but never succeeded in getting to his feet."

"Please tell me," I interrupted excitedly, "is there any blood in the lobby?"

Sir Denis shook his head grimly.

"I take it that *you* are responsible for the shot-hole through the door?"

"Yes, and I scored a bull!"

"The lobby is tiled. They probably took the trouble to remove any stains. Apart from several objects and documents which they have taken away, they have left everything in perfect order. And now, Sterling—the details."

Sir Denis looked very tired; his manner was unusually grave; and:

"Before I begin," he said rapidly—"Petrie? Is there any change?"

The Frenchman shook his head.

"I am very sorry to have to tell you, Mr. Sterling," he replied, "that Dr. Petrie is sinking rapidly."

"No? Good God! Don't say so!"

"It's true!" snapped Nayland Smith. "But tell me what I want to know—I haven't a minute to waste."

Filled with a helpless anger, and with such a venomous hatred growing in my heart for the cruel, cunning devil directing these horrors, I outlined very rapidly the events of the night.

"Even now," said Nayland Smith savagely, "we don't know if they have it."

"The formula for '654'?"

He nodded.

"It may have been in Rorke's study in Wimpole Street, or it may not; and it may have been here. In the meantime, Petrie's case is getting desperate, and no one knows what treatment to pursue. Fah Lo Suee's kindness towards yourself, following a murderous assault upon one of her servants, suggests success. But it's merely a surmise. I must be off!"

"But where are you going, Sir Denis?" I asked, for he had already started towards the door. "What are *my* orders?"

He turned.

"Your orders," he replied, "are to stay in bed until Dr. Brisson gives you permission to get up. I am going to Berlin."

"To Berlin?"

He nodded impatiently.

"I spent some time with the late Sir Manston Rorke," he went on rapidly, "at the School of Tropical Medicine, as I have already told you. And I formed the impression that Rorke's big reputation was largely based upon his friendship with Professor Emil Krus, of Berlin, the greatest living authority upon Tropical Medicine.

"I suspected that Rorke almost invariably submitted proposed treatments to the celebrated German, and I hope—I *only* hope—that Petrie's formula '654' may have been sent on to the Professor for his comments. I have already been in touch by telephone with Berlin, but Dr. Emil Krus proved to be inaccessible.

"The French authorities have placed a fast plane and an experienced pilot at my service, and I leave in twenty minutes for the Templehof aerodrome."

I was astounded—I could think of no words; but:

"It is Dr. Petrie's only chance," the Frenchman interrupted. "His condition is growing hourly worse, and we have no idea what to do. It is possible that the great Krus"—there was professional as well as national jealousy in his pronunciation of the name—"may be able to help us. Otherwise——"

He shrugged his shoulders.

"You see, Sterling?" said Nayland Smith. "Take care of yourself."

He ran out.

I looked up helplessly into the bespectacled face of Dr. Brisson. Dawn was breaking, and I realized that I must have been insensible for many hours.

"Such friendship is a wonderful thing, doctor," I said.

"Yes. Sir Denis Nayland Smith is a staunch friend." Brisson replied; "but in this—there is more than friendship. The south of France, the whole of France, Europe, perhaps the world, is threatened by a plague for which we know of no remedy. The English doctor Petrie has found means to check it. If we knew what treatment should follow the injection of his preparation '654' we could save his life yet."

"Is it, then, desperate?"

"It is desperate. But as surely you can appreciate, we could also save other lives. If a widespread epidemic should threaten to develop, we could inoculate. I do not understand, but it seems that there is *someone* who opposes science and favours the plague. This is beyond my comprehension, but one thing is clear to me: only Dr. Petrie, who is dying, and Professor Krus—perhaps—know how to fight this thing. You see? It may be that the fate of the world is at stake."

Indeed I saw, and all too plainly.

"Have the police been informed of the outrages here last night?" I asked.

The Frenchman shrugged his shoulders, and his bearded face registered despair.

"In this matter I am distracted," he declared, "and I have ceased even to think about it. Sir Denis Nayland Smith, it seems, has powers from Paris which override the authorities of Nice. The Department is in his hands."

"You mean that no inquiry will be made?"

"Nothing—as I understand. But as I confessed to you, I do not understand—at all."

I sprang up in bed—my brain was superactive.

"This is awful!" I exclaimed—"I must do something—I must *do* something!"

Dr. Brisson rested his hands upon my shoulders.

"Mr Sterling," he said, and his eyes, magnified by the powerful lenses of his spectacles, were kindly yet compelling, "what you should do—if you care to take my advice, is this: you should rest."

"How can I rest?"

I sank back on the pillows, while he continued to watch me.

"It is difficult, I know," he went on. "But what I tell you, Dr. Cartier would tell you, and your friend Dr. Petrie, also. You are a very strong man, full of vigour, but you have recently recovered from some severe illness. This I can see. The Germans are very clever—but we in France are not without knowledge. For at least four hours, you should sleep."

"How can I sleep?"

"There is nothing you can do to help your friend. All that experience has taught us, we are doing. I offer you my advice. An orderly from the hospital is in the lobby and will remain there until he is relieved. Your housekeeper, Mme Dubonnet, will be here at eight o'clock. Please take a small cachet which I have in my bag, and resign yourself to sleep."

I don't know to what extent the doctor's kindly and deliberate purpose influenced me, but as he spoke I recognized how weary I was.

The hiatus induced by that damnable mimosa drug had rested me not at all: my brain was active as from the moment that I had succumbed to it. My body was equally weary.

"I agree with you, doctor," I said, and grasped his hand. "I don't think I need your cachet. I am dead tired. I can sleep without any assistance."

He nodded, and smiled.

"Better still," he declared. "Nature is always right. I shall close the shutters and leave you. Ring for your coffee when you awake. By then, if Sir Denis's instructions have been carried out, the telephone will have been repaired, and you can learn the latest news about Dr. Petrie."

I remember seeing him close the shutters and walk quietly out of the room. I must have been very tired . . . for I remember no more.

Chapter Fourteenth

IN MONTE CARLO

I WOKE late in the afternoon.

Body, brain, and nerves had been thoroughly exhausted; but now I realized that my long sleep had restored me.

Mme Dubonnet was in the kitchen, looking very unhappy. The telephone had been repaired that morning, she told me, but it was all so mysterious. The house had been disturbed, and there were many things missing. And the poor dear doctor! They had told her, only two hours before, that there was no change in his condition.

I turned on the bath taps and then went to the telephone.

Dr. Brisson was at the hospital. In answer to my anxious inquiry, he said in a strained, tired voice that there was nothing to report. He could not conceal his anxiety, however.

Something told me that dear old Petrie's hours were numbered. Sir Denis Nayland Smith had not been in touch.

"I trust that he arrived safely," he concluded, "and succeeded in finding Dr. Emil Krus."

"I shall be along in about an hour."

"Nothing of the kind, my dear Mr. Sterling, I beg of you. It would only add to our embarrassment. You can do nothing. If you would consent to take my advice again, it would be this: drive out somewhere to dinner. Try to forget this shadow, which unfortunately you can do nothing to dispel. Tell the housekeeper where you intend to go, so that we can trace you, should there be news—good or bad."

"It's impossible," I replied; "I feel I must stand by."

But the tired, soothing voice at the other end of the line persisted. A man would relieve Mme Dubonnet at the villa just before dusk; "And," Brisson concluded, "it is far better that you should seek a change of scene, if only for a few hours. Dr. Petrie would wish it. In a sense, you know, you are his patient."

In my bath, I considered his words. Yes, I suppose he was right. Petrie had been insistent that I should not overdo things—mentally or physically. I would dine in Monte Carlo, amid the stimulating gaiety of the strangest capital in the world.

I wanted to be at my best in this battle with an invisible army. I owed it to Petrie—and I owed it to Nayland Smith.

In spite of my determination, it was late before I started out. The orderly from the hospital had arrived. He had nothing to report. Sir Denis was of opinion, I learned, that there was just a possibility of a further raid upon the Villa Jasmin being attempted, and the man showed me that he was armed.

He seemed to welcome this strange break in his normal duties. I told him that I proposed to dine at Quinto's Restaurant. I was known there, and he could get in touch, or leave a message, at any time.

Then, heavy-hearted, but glad in a way to escape, if only for a few hours, from the spot where Petrie had been stricken down by his remorseless, hidden enemy, I set out for Monaco.

Some new and strange elements had crashed into my life. It was good to get away to a place dissociated from these things and endeavour to see them in their true perspective.

The route was pathetically familiar.

It had been Petrie's custom on two or three evenings in the week to drive into Monte Carlo, dine and spend an hour or so in the Casino. He was no gambler—nor am I—but he was a very keen mathematician, and he got quite a kick out of pitting his wits against the invulnerable bank.

I could never follow the principle of his system. But while, admittedly, we had never lost anything, on the other hand, we had not gained.

My somewhat morbid reflections seemed to curtail the journey. I observed little of the route, until I found myself on the long curve above Monte Carlo. Dusk had fallen, and that theatrical illumination which is a feature of the place had sprung into life.

I pulled up for a moment, looking down at the unique spectacle—wonderful, for all its theatricality. The blazing colour of the flower beds, floodlighted from palm tops; the emerald green of terraced lawns, falling away to that ornate frontage of the great Casino.

It is Monte Carlo's one and only "view", but in its garish way it is unforgettable.

I pushed on down the sharp descent to the town, presently halting before the little terrace of an unpretentious restaurant. Tables were laid under the awning, and already there were many diners.

This was Quinto's, where, without running up a ruinous bill, one may enjoy a perfect dinner and the really choice wines of France.

The genial maître d'hôtel met me at the top of the steps, extending that cosmopolitan welcome which lends a good meal an additional savour. Your true restaurateur is not only an epicure; he is also a polished man of the world.

Yes, there was a small table in the corner. But I was alone to-night! Was Dr. Petrie busy?

I shook my head.

"I am afraid he is very ill," I replied cautiously.

Hitherto the authorities had succeeded in suppressing the truth of this ghastly outbreak so near to two great pleasure resorts. I had to guard my tongue, for an indiscreet word might undo all their plans of secrecy.

"Something serious?" he asked, with what I thought was real concern: everybody loved Petrie.

"A serious chill. The doctors are afraid of pneumonia."

Quinto raised his hands in an eloquent Southern gesture.

"Oh, these chilly nights!" he exclaimed. "They will ruin us! So many people forget to wrap themselves up warmly in the Riviera evenings. And then—" he shrugged—"they say it is a treacherous climate!"

He conducted me to a table in an angle of the wall, and pointed out, as was his custom, notabilities present that evening.

These included an ex-Crown Prince, Fritz Kreisler, and an internationally popular English novelist residing on the Côte d'Azur.

The question of what I should eat and what I should drink was discussed as between artists; for the hallmark of a great maître d'hôtel is the insidious compliment which he conveys to his patron in conceding the latter's opinions to be worthy of the master's consideration.

When the matter was arranged and the wine-waiter had

brought me a cocktail, I settled down to survey my fellow guests.

My survey stopped short at a table in the opposite corner.

A man who evidently distrusted the chill of the Southern evenings sat there, his back towards me. He wore a heavy coat, having an astrakhan collar; and, what was more peculiar at dinner, he wore an astrakhan cap. From my present point of view he resembled pictures I had seen of Russian nobleman of the old régime.

Facing him across the small square table was *Fleurette!*

Over one astrakhan-covered shoulder of her companion our glances met. Dim light may have created the illusion, but I thought that that flower-like face turned pale, that the blue eyes opened very wide for a moment.

I was about to stand up, when a slight, almost imperceptible movement of Fleurette's head warned me unmistakably not to claim the acquaintance.

Chapter Fifteenth

FAIRY TRUMPET

I asked myself the question: had the gesture been real, or had I merely imagined it?

Fleurette wore a light wrap over a vary plain black evening frock. Her hair smouldered under the shaded lights so that it seemed to contain sparks of fire. She had instantly glanced aside. I could not be wrong.

At first I had experienced intense humiliation, but now my courage returned. True, she had not conveyed the message: "Don't speak to me." But it had been in the nature of a warning, an admission of a mutual secret understanding, and in no sense a snub.

She was not, than, inaccessible. She was hedged around, guarded, by the jealous suspicions of her Oriental master.

I could doubt no longer.

The man seated with his back to me was the same I had seen in the car driven by the Negro chauffeur. Despite his nonconformity to type, this was Mahdi Bey. And Fleurette, for all her glorious, virgin-like beauty, must be his mistress.

She deliberately avoided looking in my direction again.

Her companion never moved: his immobility was extraordinary. And presently, through the leaves of the shrubs growing in wooden boxes, I saw the black-and-silver Rolls, almost directly opposite the restaurant.

My glance moved upward to the parapet guarding a higher road which here dips down and forms a hairpin bend.

A man stood there watching.

Difficult though it was from where I sat to form a clear impression of his appearance, I became convinced, nevertheless, that he was one of the tribe of the dacoits . . . either the same, or an opposite number, of the yellow-faced horror I had seen in the garden of the Villa Jasmin!

And at that moment, as my waiter approached, changing the plates in readiness for the first course, I found myself swept back mentally into the ghastly business I had come there to forget. I experienced a sudden chill of foreboding.

If, as I strongly suspected, one of the murderous Burmans were watching the restaurant—did this mean that I had been followed there? If so, with what purpose? I no longer stood between Petrie's enemies and their objective . . . but:

I had wounded, probably killed, one of their number. I had heard much of the implacable blood feuds of the Indian thugs; it was no more than reasonable to suppose that something of the same might prevail among the dacoits of Burma.

I glanced furtively upward again. And there was the motionless figure leaning against the parapet.

In dress there was nothing to distinguish the man from an ordinary Monaco workman, but my present survey confirmed my first impression.

This was one of the yellow men attached to the service of Dr. Fu Manchu.

I cast my memory back over the route I had so recently traversed. Had any car followed me? I could not recollect that it was so. But, on the other hand, I had been much abstracted, driving mechanically. . . . Dusk had fallen before I had reached Monaco. If an attempt were contemplated, why had it not taken place upon the road?

The problem was beyond me. . . . But there stood the watcher, motionless, by the parapet.

And at this very moment, and just as the wine-waiter placed a decanter of my favourite Pommard before me, I had a remarkable experience—an experience so disturbing that I sat quite still for several seconds, my outstretched hand poised in the act of taking up the decanter.

Close beside my ear—as it seemed, out of space, out of nowhere—that same high, indescribable note became audible; that sound which I believe I have already attempted to describe as the call of a fairy trumpet. . . .

Once before, and once only, I had heard it—on the beach of Ste Claire de la Roche.

Some eerie quality in the sound affected me now, as it had affected me then. It was profoundly mysterious; but one thing was certain. Unless the sound were purely a product of my own imagination, or the result of some trouble of the inner ear—possibly an aftermath of illness—it could not be coincidence that on the two occasions that I had heard it Fleurette had been present.

My hand dropped down to the *couvert*—and I looked across at her.

Her eyes were fixed on the face of her companion, who sat with his back to me, in that dreamy, far-away regard which I remembered.

Then her delicate lips moved, and I thought, although I could not hear her words, that she was replying to some question which he had addressed to her.

And, as I looked and realised that she was speaking, that strange sound ceased as abruptly as it had commenced.

I saw Fleurette glance aside; her expression changed swiftly. But her eyes never once turned in my direction. I stared beyond her, up through the leaves of the shrubs and towards the parapet on the other side of the street.

The Burman had disappeared. . . .

CHAPTER SIXTEENTH

THE DACOIT

"You are wanted on the telephone, Mr. Sterling."

I started as wildly as a man suddenly aroused from sleep. A dreadful premonition gripped me icily. I stood up.

"Do you know who it is?"

"I believe the name was Dr. Cartier, sir."

In that moment Fleurette and her mysterious companion were forgotten; the lurking yellow man faded from my mind as completely as he had faded from my view. This was news of Petrie; and something told me it could only be bad news.

I hurried through the restaurant to the telephone booth, and snatched up the receiver.

"Hullo, hullo!" I called. "Alan Sterling here. Is that Dr. Cartier?"

Brisson's voice answered me: his tone prepared me for what was to come.

"I mentioned Dr. Cartier's name in case you should not be familiar with my own, Mr. Sterling. I would not have disturbed you—for you can scarcely have begun your dinner yet—had I not promised to report any news at once."

"What is it?" I asked eagerly.

"Prepare yourself to know that it is bad."

"Not . . . ?"

"Alas—yes!"

"My God!"

"There was no final convulsion—no change. '654' might have saved him—if we had known what treatment to pursue after the first injection. But the coma passed slowly into . . . death."

As I listened to those words, a change came over my entire outlook on the future. A cold rage, and what I knew to be an abiding rage, took possession of me. The merciless fiends, for no reason that I could possibly hope to imagine, had ended an honourable and supremely useful life; that kindly personality which had lived only to serve had been snatched away, remorselessly.

Very well. . . . It was murder, calculated, callous murder. This was a game that two could play. What I had done once, I could do again, and again—and every time that I got within reach of any of the foul gang!

Dr. Fu Manchu!

If such a person existed, I asked only to be set face to face with him. That moment, I vowed, should be his last—little knowing the stupendous task to which I vowed myself.

Fah Lo Suee—a woman; but one of them. The French had not hesitated to shoot female spies during the World War. Nor should I, now.

I had reached the head of the steps when Victor Quinton touched my shoulder. Details were indefinite, but my immediate objective was plain. One of the Burmans was covering my movements. I planned to find that Burman; and—taking every possible precaution to insure my own getaway—I planned to kill him. . . .

"You have had bad news, M. Sterling?"

"Dr. Petrie is dead," I said, and ran down the steps.

I suppose many curious glances followed; perhaps Fleurette had seen me. I didn't care. I crossed the street and walked up the opposite slope. A man was lounging there, smoking a cigarette—a typical working-class Frenchman; and I remembered that he had stood there for part of the time during which the dacoit had watched the restaurant.

"Excuse me." I said.

The man started and turned.

"Did you chance to see an Oriental who stood near you here a few minutes ago?"

"But yes, m'sieur. Someone I suppose off one of those foreign yachts in the harbour? He had gone only this last two minutes."

"Which way?"

He pointed downward.

"Toward the Jardin des Suicides," he replied smiling.

"Suitable spot, if I catch him there," I muttered; then, aloud: "Drink my health," I said, thrusting a note into his hand. "I shall need your kind wishes."

"Thank you, m'sieur—and good night. . . ."

I remember starting the car and driving slowly down the

slope to the corner by the Café de Paris. I had no glimpse of the Burman. Here, viewing the activity which surges around the Casino, seeing familiar figures at the more sheltered café tables, noticing a gendarme in an Offenbach uniform, a hotel bus—I pulled up.

My determination remained adamant as ever; but I suddenly recognized the hopelessness of this present quest. I must cast my hook wisely; useless to pursue one furtive shark. My place was beside Cartier, beside dear old Petrie—in the centre of the murderous school. . . .

I set out. I had not dined; nor had I tasted my wine. But I was animated by a vigorous purpose more stimulating than meat and drink.

That purpose, as I view it now, was vengeance. Some part of me, the Highland, had seen the Fiery Cross. I was out for blood. I had consecrated myself to a holy cause: the utter destruction of Dr. Fu Manchu and of all he stood for.

Petrie dead!

It was all but impossible to accept the fact—yet. I dreaded my next meeting with Sir Denis: his hurt would be deeper even than my own. And throughout the time that these bitter reflections occupied my mind, I was driving on, headlong, my steering controlled by a guiding Providence.

Without having noted one landmark on the way, I found myself high up on the Corniche road. Beyond a piece of broken parapet outlining a sharp bend I could see twinkling lights far ahead, and below were, I thought, the lights of Ste Claire de la Roche. I slowed up to light my pipe.

The night was very still. No sound of traffic reached my ears.

I remembered having stuck a spare box of matches in a fold of the canvas hood. I turned to get it . . .

A malignant yellow race, the eyes close-set and slightly oblique, stared into mine!

The dacoit was perched on the baggage rack!

What that hideous expression meant—in what degree it was compounded of animosity and of fear caused by sudden discovery—I didn't pause to consider. But that my own cold purpose was to be read in my face the Burman's next move clearly indicated.

Springing to the ground, he began to run....

He ran *back:* I had no chance to turn the car. But I was out and after him in less time than it takes me to record the fact. This was a murder game: no quarter given or expected!

The man ran like Mercury. He was already twenty yards away. I put up a tremendous sprint and slightly decreased his lead. He glanced back. I saw the moonlight on his snarling teeth.

Pulling up, I took careful aim with the automatic—and fired. He ran on. I fired again.

Still he ran. I set out in pursuit; but the dacoit had thirty yards' start. If he had ever doubted, he knew, now, that he ran for his life.

In a hundred yards I had gained nothing. My wind was not good for more than another hundred yards at that speed. Then—and if I had had enough breath I should have cheered—he stumbled, tottered, and fell forward onto hands and knees!

I bore down upon him with grim determination. I was not ten feet off when he turned, swung his arm, and something went humming past my bent head!

A knife!

I checked and fired again at close range.

The Burman threw his hands up, and fell prone in the road. . . .

"Another one for Petrie!" I said breathlessly.

Stooping, I was about to turn him over, when an amazing thing happened.

The man whipped around with a movement which reminded me horribly of a snake. He threw his legs around my thighs and buried fingers like steel hooks in my throat!

Dragging me down—down—remorselessly down—he grinned like a savage animal cornered but unconquerable......
The world began to swim about me; there was a murmur in my ears like that of the sea.

I thought a car approached in the distance.... I saw bloody foam dripping from the dacoit's clenched teeth....

CHAPTER SEVENTEENTH

THE ROOM OF GLASS

WHEN I opened my eyes my first impression was that the dacoit had killed me—that I was dead—and that the Beyond was even more strange and inconsequential than the wildest flight of Spiritualism had depicted.

I lay on a couch, my head on a pillow. The cushions of the couch were of a sort of neutral grey colour; so was the pillow. They were composed, I saw, of some kind of soft rubber and were inflated. I experienced considerable difficulty in swallowing, and raising a hand to my throat found it to be swollen and painful.

Perhaps, after all, I was not dead; but if alive, where in the known world could I be?

The couch upon which I lay—and I noted now that I was dressed in white overalls and wore rubber-soled shoes!—was at one end of an enormously large room. The entire floor, or that part of it which I could see, was covered with this same neutral grey substance which may have been rubber. The ceiling looked like opaque glass, and so did the walls.

Quite near to me was a complicated piece of apparatus, not unlike, I thought, a large cinematograph camera, and mounted on a movable platform. It displayed a number of huge lenses, and there were tiny lamps here and there in the amazing mechanism, some of them lighted.

A most intricate switchboard was not the least curious feature of this baffling machine. Farther beyond, suspended from the glass ceiling, hung what I took to be the largest arc lamp I had ever seen in my life. But although it was alight, it suffused only a dim purple glow, contributing little to the general illumination.

Half hidden from my point of view stood a long glass table (or a table composed of the same material as the ceiling and the walls) upon which was grouped the most singular collection of instruments and appliances I had ever seen, or even imagined.

Huge glass vessels containing fluids of diverse colours, masses of twisted tubing, little points of fire, and a thing like an Egyptian harp, the strings of which seemed to be composed of streaks of light which wavered and constantly changed colour, emitting a ceaseless crackling sound. . . .

I closed my eyes for a moment. My head was aching furiously, and my mouth so parched that it caused me constantly to cough, every cough producing excruciating pain.

Then I opened my eyes again. But the insane apartment remained. I sat up and swung my feet to the floor.

The covering had the feeling of rubber, as its appearance indicated. My new viewpoint brought other objects within focus. In a white metal rack was ranged a series of vessels resembling test tubes. The smallest was perhaps a foot high, and from this the others graduated like the pipes of an organ, creating an impression in my mind of something seen through a powerful lens.

Each tube was about half filled with some sort of thick fluid, and this, from vessel to vessel, passed through shades from deepest ruby to delicate rose pink.

I stood up.

And now I could see the whole of that fabulous room. I perceived that it was a kind of laboratory—containing not one instrument nor one system of lighting with which I was acquainted!

Other items of its equipment now became visible, and I realised that a continuous throbbing characterised the whole place. Some powerful plant was at work. This throbbing, which was more felt than heard, and the crackling of those changing rays, alone disturbed the silence.

Still doubting if I really lived, if I had been rescued from the *thug*, I asked myself—assuming it to be so—who was my rescuer, and to what strange sanctuary had he brought me?

No human figure was visible.

And now I observed a minor but a curious point: the rubber couch upon which I had been lying was placed in a corner. And upon the floor-covering were two black lines forming a right angle. Its ends, touching the walls, made a perfect square—in which I stood.

I looked about that cavernous place, pervaded by a sort of

violent light, and I realized that certain pieces of apparatus, and certain tables, were surrounded by similar black marks upon the floor.

Apparently there was no door, nor could I find anything resembling a bell. If this were not mirage—or death—what was this place in which I found myself; and why was I there alone?

I set out to explore.

One step forward I made, and had essayed a second, when I recall uttering a loud cry.

As my foot crossed the black mark on the floor, a shock ran through my body which numbed my muscles! I dropped to my knees, looking about me—perhaps, had there been any to see, as caged animals glare from their cages. . . .

What did it mean? That some impassable barrier hedged me in!

The shock had served a double purpose: it had frightened me intensely—this I confess without hesitation; but as I got to my feet again I knew that also it had revived that cold, murderous rage which had governed my mind up to the moment that the dacoit had buried his fingers in my throat.

"Where the devil am I?" I said aloud; "and what am I doing here?"

I sprang forward . . . and fell back as though a cunning opponent had struck me a straight blow over the heart!

Collapsed on the rubber-covered floor I lay quivering—temporarily stunned. I experienced, now, not so much fear as awe: I was a prisoner of the invisible.

But, looking about at the nameless things which surrounded me, I knew that the invisible must be controlled by an intelligence. If this were not death—I had fallen into a trap.

I rose up again, shaken, but master of myself. Then I sat down on the couch. I felt in the pocket of my overalls—and found my cigarette case! A box of Monaco matches (which rarely light) was there also. I lighted a cigarette. My hands were fairly steady.

Some ghostly image of the truth—a mocking reply to those doubts which I had held hitherto—jazzed spectrally before me. I stared around, looking up at the dull, glassy roof, and at unimaginable instruments and paraphernalia which lent this place the appearance of a Martian factory, devoted to experiments of another age—another planet.

Then I sprang up.

A panel in one of the glass walls slid open. A man came in. The panel closed behind him. He stood, looking in my direction.

CHAPTER EIGHTEENTH

DR. FU MANCHU

HE WORE a plain yellow robe and walked in silent, thick-soled slippers. Upon his head was set a little black cap surmounted by a coral bead. His hands concealed in the loose sleeves of his robe, he stood there, watching me.

And I knew that this man had the most wonderful face that I had ever looked upon.

It was aged, yet ageless. I thought that if Benvenuto Cellini had conceived the idea of executing a death-mask of Satan in gold, it must have resembled very closely this living-dead face upon which my gaze was riveted.

He was fully six feet in height and appeared even taller by reason of the thickly padded slippers which he wore. For the little cap (which I recognized from descriptions I had read to be that of a mandarin of high rank) I substituted mentally the astrakhan cap of the traveller glimpsed in the big car on the Corniche road; for the yellow robe, the fur-collared coat.

I knew at the instant that he entered that I had seen him twice before; the second time, at Quinto's.

One memory provoked another.

Although in the restaurant he had sat with his back towards me, I remembered now, and must have noted it subconsciously at the time, that tortoiseshell loops had surrounded his yellow pointed ears. He had been wearing spectacles.

Then, as he moved slowly and noiselessly in my direction, I captured the most elusive memory of all——

I had seen this man in a dream—riding a purple cloud which swept down upon a doomed city!

The veil was torn—no possibility of misunderstanding remained. Those brilliant green eyes, fixed upon me in an unflinching regard, conveyed as though upon astral rays a sense of force unlike anything I had known. . . .

This was Dr. Fu Manchu!

My Gothic surroundings, the man's awesome personality, my attempt to cross the black line surrounding an invisible prison, these things had temporarily put me out of action. But now, as this definite conviction seized upon my mind, my hand plunged to my pocket.

Flesh and blood might fail to pass that mysterious zone; perhaps a bullet would succeed.

The man in the yellow robe now stood no more than ten feet away from me. And as I jerked my hand down, a sort of film passed instantaneously over those green eyes, conveying a momentary—but no more than momentary—impression of blindness. This phenomenon disappeared in the very instant that I came to my senses—in the very instant that I remembered I was wearing strange garments. . . .

How mad of me to look for a charged automatic in the pocket of these white overalls!

I set my foot upon the smouldering cigarette which I had dropped, and with clenched fists faced my jailer; for I could no longer blink the facts of the situation.

"Ah! Mr. Sterling." he said, and approached me so closely that he stood but a pace beyond the black line. "Your attempt to explore the radio research room caused a signal to appear in my study, and I knew that you had revived."

His voice had a guttural quality, the sibilants being very stressed. He spoke deliberately, giving every syllable its full value. I suppose, in a way, he spoke perfect English, yet many words so treated sounded wholly unfamiliar so that I knew I had never heard them pronounced in that manner before.

I could think of nothing to say. I was helpless, and this man had come to mock me.

"You seem to have a disregard for the sanctity of human life," he continued, "unusual in Englishmen. You killed one of my servants at the Villa Jasmin—a small matter. But your zeal for murder did not end there. Fortunately, I was less than half a mile behind at the time, and I had you carried to a place of safety before some passing motorist should be attracted by the spectacle of two bodies in the Corniche road. You mortally wounded Gana Ghat, head of my Burmese bodyguard."

"I am glad to hear it," I replied.

Those green eyes watched me immutably.

"Rejoice not unduly," he said softly. "I wished you no harm, but you have thrust yourself upon me. As a result, you find yourself in China—"

"In *China!*"

I heard the note of horror in my own voice. My glance strayed swiftly around that incredible room, and returned again to the tall, impassive, yellow-robed figure.

Good heavens! it was a shattering idea—yet not wholly impossible. I had no means of knowing how long I had been unconscious. The dreadful theory flashed through my mind that this brilliant madman—for I could not account him sane—had, by means of drugs, kept me in a comatose condition, and had had me transported in some private vessel from France to China.

I tried to challenge those glittering green eyes—but the task was one beyond my powers.

"You left me no choice," Dr. Fu Manchu went on. "I can permit no stranger to intrude upon my experiments. It was a matter of deciding between your death—which would not have profited me—and your services, which may do so."

He turned slowly and walked in the direction of the hidden glass door. He glanced at me over his shoulder.

"Follow," he directed.

Since at the moment I could see no alternative to obedience, I stepped cautiously forward.

There was no shock when I passed the black line, but I continued to move warily across that silent floor, in the direction of the opening in which the Chinaman stood, glancing back at me.

The idea of springing upon him the moment I found myself within reach crossed my mind. But —*China!* If I should actually be in China, what fate awaited me in the event of my attack being successful?

I knew something of the Chinese, having met and employed many of them. I had found them industrious, kindly, and simple. My knowledge of the punishments inflicted by autocratic officials in the interior was confined entirely to hearsay. Certain stories came back to me, now, counselling prudence. If Nayland Smith were correct, it would be a good deed to rid the world of this Chinese physician—even at the price of a horrible martyrdom.

But I might fail . . . and pay the price nevertheless.

These were my thoughts as I drew nearer and nearer to the glass door. I had almost reached it when Fu Manchu spoke again.

"Dismiss any idea of personal attack," he said in a soft voice, the sibilants more than usually pronounced. "Accept my assurance that it could not possibly succeed. Follow!"

He moved on, and I crossed the threshold into a small room furnished as a library. Many of the volumes burdening the shelves were in strange bindings, and their lettering in characters even less familiar. There was a commodious table upon which a number of books lay open. Also, there was a smell in the room which I thought I identified as that of burning opium; and a little jade pipe lying in a bronze tray served to confirm my suspicion.

The library was lighted by one silk-shaded lantern suspended from the ceiling, and by a queer globular lamp set in an ebony pedestal on a corner of the table.

So much I observed as I crossed this queer apartment, richly carpeted, and came by means of a second doorway into the largest glasshouse I had seen outside Kew Gardens. Its floor was covered with that same rubber-like material used in the "radio research room."

The roof was impressively lofty, and the vast conservatory softly lighted by means of some system of hidden lamps. Tropical heat prevailed, and a damp, miasmatic smell. There were palms there, and flowering creepers, rare shrubs in perfect condition, and banks of strange orchids embedded amid steaming moss.

Chapter Nineteenth

THE SECRET JUNGLE

The place was a bulb-hunter's paradise, a dream jungle, in parts almost impenetrable by reason of the fact that luxurious growths had overrun the sometimes narrow paths.

I discovered as we proceeded that it was divided into sections, and that the temperature, in what was really a series of isolated forcing houses, varied from tropical to subtropical. The doors were very ingenious. There was a space between them large enough to accommodate several persons, and a gauge set beside a thermometer which could be adjusted as one door was closed before the next was opened.

Let me confess that I myself had ceased to exist. I was submerged in the flowers, in the jungle, in the vital, intense personality of my guide. This was phantasy—yet it was not phantasy. It was a mad reality: the dream of a super-scientist, a genius whose brilliance transcended anything normally recognised, expressed in rare foliage, in unique blooms.

Dr. Fu Manchu consented to enlighten me from point to point.

At an early stage he drew my attention to species which I had sought in vain in the forests of Brazil; to orchids which Borneo, during one long expedition, had failed to reveal to me: Indian varieties and specimens from the Burmese swamps. . . .

"This is mango-apple, a fruit which first appeared here two months ago. . . . Notice near its roots the beautiful flowers which occasion the heavy perfume—*Cypripedium-Cycaste;* a hybrid cultivated in these houses successfully for the first time . . . the very large blooms are rose-peonies—scentless, of course, but interesting. . . ."

At one point in a very narrow path, overhung by a most peculiar type of hibiscus in full bloom, he paused and pointed.

I saw pitcher plants of many species, and not far away *drosophyllum*—of that kind of which I had already met with two specimens.

"These insectivorous varieties," said Dr. Fu Manchu, "have proved useful in certain experiments. I have outlined several inquiries, upon which I shall request you to commence work shortly, relating to this interesting subject. We come now to the botanical research room..."

He opened a door, and with one long-nailed yellow hand beckoned me imperiously to follow.

I obeyed.

He closed the door and adjusted the gauge, continuing to speak as he did so.

"You will work under the direction of Companion Herman Trenck——"

"What!" His words aroused me from a sort of stupor. "Dr. Trenck? Trenck died five years ago in Sumatra!"

Dr. Fu Manchu opened the second door, and I saw a beautifully equipped laboratory, but much smaller than that in which I had first found myself.

A Chinaman wearing white overalls resembling my own bowed to my guide and stood aside as we entered.

Bending over a microscope was a grey-haired, bearded man. I had met him once; twice heard him lecture. He stood upright and confronted us.

No possibility of doubt remained. It was Herman Trenck... who had been dead for five years!

Dr. Fu Manchu glanced aside at me.

"It will be your privilege, Mr. Sterling," he said, "to meet under my roof many distinguished dead men."

He turned to the famous Dutch botanist.

"Companion Trenck," he continued, "allow me to introduce to you your new assistant, Companion Alan Sterling, of whose work I know you have heard."

"Indeed, yes," said the Dutchman cordially, and advanced with outstretched hand. "It is a great pleasure to meet you, Mr. Sterling, and a great privilege to enjoy such assistance. Your recent work in Brazil for the Botanical Society is well known to me."

I shook hands. I was a man in a dream. This was a dream meeting.

Of the bona fides of Dr. Trenck in life there could never have been any question. His was one of the great names in botany. But now, I thought, I had entered a spirit world, under the guidance of a master magician.

"If you will pardon me," said Trenck, "there is something here to which I must draw the doctor's attention."

I made no reply. I stood stricken silent, now most horribly convinced that my first impression had been the true one—that definitely I was dead. And I watched, as that tall, gaunt figure in the yellow robe bent over the microscope. Herman Trenck studied his every movement with intense anxiety; and presently:

"Not yet," said the Chinaman, standing upright. "But you are very near."

"I agree," said the Dutch botanist earnestly.

"That I am still wrong?"

"It is more probable, doctor, that *I* am wrong...."

And it was at this moment, while I firmly believed that I had stepped into the other world, that a phrase flashed through my mind, spoken in a low, musical voice: "Think of me as Derceto...."

Fleurette!

This thought was powerful enough to drag me away from that phantasmal laboratory—powerful enough to make me forget, for a moment, Dr. Fu Manchu, and the dead Dutch botanist who talked with him so earnestly.

Was Fleurette also a phantom?

Did Fleurette belong to the life of which until recently I had believed myself to form a unit, or was she one of the living-dead? In either case, she belonged to Dr. Fu Manchu; and every idea which I had formed respecting her was scrapped, swept away by this inexorable tidal wave which had carried me into a ghost world....

A new thought: Perhaps this was insanity!

In the course of my struggle with the dacoit I might have received a blow upon the skull, and all this be but a dream within a dream: delirium, feverish fancy...

Through all these chaotic speculations a guttural voice issued a command:

"Follow."

And dumbly, blindly I followed.

CHAPTER TWENTIETH

DREAM CREATURES

I FOUND myself in a long, gloomily lighted corridor.

My frame of mind by this time was one which I cannot hope to convey in words. In a setting fantastic, chimerical, I had found myself face to face with that eerie monster whose existence I had seriously doubted—Dr. Fu Manchu. I had been made helpless by means of some electrical device outside my experience. I had seen botanical monstrosities which challenged sanity . . . and I had shaken the hand of a dead man!

Now, as I followed my tall, yellow-clad guide:

"The radio research room," he said, "in which you recently found yourself, is in charge of Companion Henrik Ericksen."

This was too much; it broke through the cloud of apathy which had been descending upon me.

"Ericksen!" I exclaimed—"inventor of the Ericksen Ray? He died during the World War—or soon after!"

"The most brilliant European brain in the sphere of what is loosely termed radio. Van Rembold, the mining engineer, also is with us. He 'died,' as you term it, a few months before Ericksen. His work in the radium mines of Ho Nan has proved to be valuable."

Yet another door was opened, and I entered into half light to find myself surrounded by glass cases, their windows set flush with the walls and illuminated from within.

"My mosquitoes and other winged insects," said Dr Fu Manchu. "I am the first student to have succeeded in producing true hybrids. The subject is one which possibly does not interest you, Mr. Sterling, but one or two of my specimens possess characteristics which must appeal even to the lay mind."

Yes; this was delirium. I recognized now that connecting link, which, if sought for, can usually be found between the most fantastic dream and some fact previously observed, seemingly forgotten, but stored in that queer cupboard which we call the subconscious.

The ghastly fly which had invaded Petrie's laboratory—this

was the link!

I proceeded, now, as a man in a dream, convinced that ere long I should wake up.

"My principal collection," the guttural voice went on, "is elsewhere. But here, for instance, are some specimens which have spectacular interest."

He halted before the window of a small case and, resting one long, yellow hand upon the glass, tapped with talon-like nails.

Two gigantic wasps, their wasted bodies fully three inches long, their wingspan extraordinary, buzzed angrily against the glass pane. I saw that there was a big nest of some clay-like material built in one corner of the case.

"An interesting hybrid," said my guide, "possessing saw-fly characteristics, as an expert would observe, but with the pugnacity of the wasp unimpaired, and its stinging qualities greatly increased. Merely an ornamental experiment and comparatively useless."

He moved on. I thought that such visions as these must mean that I was in high fever, for I ceased to believe in their reality.

"I have greatly improved the sand-fly," Dr. Fu Manchu continued; "a certain Sudanese variety had proved to be most amenable to treatment."

He paused before another case, the floor thickly sanded, and I saw flea-like, winged creatures nearly a large as common houseflies. . . .

"The spiders may interest you. . . ."

He had moved on a few steps. I closed my eyes, overcome by sudden nausea.

The dream, as is the way with such dreams, was becoming horrible, appalling. A black spider, having a body a large as a big grapefruit, and spiny legs which must have had a span of twenty-four inches, sat amidst a putrid-looking litter in which I observed several small bones, watching us with eyes which gleamed in the subdued light like diamonds.

It moved slightly forward as we approached. Unmistakably, it was watching us; it had intelligence!

No horror I had ever imagined could have approximated to this frightful, gorged insect, this travesty of natural laws.

"The creature," said Dr. Fu Manchu, "has a definitely

developed brain. It is capable of elementary reasoning. In regard to this I am at present engaged upon a number of experiments. I find that certain types of ant respond also to suitable suggestion. But the subject is in its infancy, and I fear I bore you. We will just glance at the bacteria, and you might care to meet Companion Frank Narcomb, who is in charge of that department."

I made no comment—I was not even shocked.

Sir Frank Narcomb—for some time physician to the English royal family, and one of the greatest bacteriologists in Europe, had been a friend of my father's!

I had been at Edinburgh at the time of his death, and had actually attended his funeral in London!

A door set between two cases slid open as my guide approached it. In one of these cases I saw an ant-hill inhabited by glittering black ants, and in the other, a number of red centipedes moving over the leaves of a species of cactus, which evidently grew in the case. . . .

In a small but perfectly equipped laboratory a man wearing a long white coat was holding up a test tube to a lamp and inspecting its contents critically. He was quite bald, and his skull had a curious, shrivelled appearance.

But when, hearing us enter, he replaced the tube in a rack and turned, I recognized that this was indeed my father's old friend, aged incredibly and with lines of suffering upon his gaunt face, but beyond any question Sir Frank Narcomb himself!

"Ah, doctor!" he exclaimed.

I saw an expression of something very like veneration spring into the tired eyes of this man who, in life, had acknowledged none his master in that sphere which he had made his own.

"The explanation eludes me," he said. "Russia persistently remains immune!"

"Russia!"

I had never heard the word spoken as Dr. Fu Manchu spoke it. Those hissing sibilants were venomous.

"Russia! It is preposterous that those half-staved slaves of Stalin's should survive when stronger men succumb. *Russia!*"

With the third repetition of the name a sort of momentary frenzy possessed the speaker. During one fleeting instant I looked upon this companion of my dream as a stark maniac. The madman discarded the gown of the scientist and revealed himself in his dreadful, naked reality.

Then, swiftly as it had come, the mood passed. He laid a long yellow hand upon the shoulder of Sir Frank Narcomb.

"Yours is the most difficult task of all, companion," he said. "This I appreciate, and I am arranging that you shall have more suitable assistance." He glanced in my direction, and I saw that queer film flicker across his brilliant eyes. "This is Mr. Alan Sterling, with whom, I am informed, you are already acquainted."

Sir Frank stared hard. As I remembered him he had been endowed with a mass of bushy white hair; now he was a much changed man, but the shrewd, wrinkled face remained the same. Came a light of recognition.

"Alan!" he said, and stretched out his hand. "It's good to meet you here. How is Andrew Sterling?"

Mechanically I shook the extended hand.

"My father was quite well, Sir Frank," I replied in a toneless voice, "when I last heard from him."

"Excellent! I wish he could join us."

In the circumstances, I could think of nothing further to say, but:

"Follow!" came the guttural order.

And once more I followed.

CHAPTER TWENTY-FIRST

THE HAIRLESS MAN

Our route led up a flight of stairs, rubber-covered like every other place I had visited, with the exception of that strange study pervaded with opium fumes.

"The physiological research room," Dr. Fu Manchu said, "would not interest you. It is very small in this establishment, although Companion Yamamata, who is at present in charge, is engaged upon a highly important experiment in synthetic genesis."

We entered a long, well lighted corridor, with neat white doors right and left, each bearing a number like those in a hotel. These doors were perfectly plain and possessed neither handles nor keyholes.

"Some of the staff reside here," my guide explained.

He pressed a button in the wall beside a door numbered eleven, and the door slid noiselessly open. I saw a very neat sitting room, with other rooms opening out of it.

"Temporarily . . ." the guttural voice continued.

There was a strange interruption.

A sort of quivering note sounded, a gong-like note, more a vibration of the atmosphere than an actual sound. But Dr. Fu Manchu stood rigidly upright, and his extraordinary eyes glanced swiftly left along the corridor.

"Quick!" he said harshly, "inside! And close the door—there is a corresponding button in the wall. One pressure closes the door; two open it. Remain there until you are called, if you value your life. . . ."

His harsh imperious manner had its effect. Some of the secret of this strange man's power lay in the fact that he never questioned his own authority, or the obedience of those upon whom he laid his orders.

The force behind those orders was uncanny.

With no other glance in my direction he set off along the corridor, moving swiftly, yet with a sort of cat-like dignity.

With his withdrawal, some part of my real self began to

clamour for recognition. I hesitated on the threshold of the little room, watching him as he went. And when the tall figure, with never a backward glance, disappeared where the corridor branched right, something like a cold wave of sanity came flooding back to my brain.

This was neither delirium nor death! It was mirage. This place was real enough—the long corridor and the white doors—but the rest was hypnotism; a trick played for what purpose I could not imagine, by a master of that dangerous art!

That the woman called Fah Lo Suee was an adept, Sir Denis had admitted. This was her father, and her master.

Those living-dead men were phantoms, conjured up by his brain and displayed before me as an illusionist displays the seemingly impossible. Those vast forcing houses, the big laboratory, the horrible insects in their glass cases! It was perhaps his method of achieving conquest of my personality, submerging me and then using me.

Very well! I was not conquered yet. I could still fight!

That curious throbbing, as of a muted gong, continued incessantly.

What did it mean? What was the explanation of Dr. Fu Manchu's sudden change of manner and his hurried departure?

"Close the door . . . and remain there until you are called, if you value your life!"

These had been his words. He had spoken with apparent sincerity.

And now, as I watched, I saw a strange thing. At the foot of the stairs which we had ascended, I saw a door dropping slowly from the roof. I could feel the slight vibration of the mechanism controlling it.

I glanced swiftly left, along the corridor.

A similar door was descending just where the passage branched off!

They were stone doors, or something very like them, such as are used in seagoing ships. Was this the meaning of that constant vibrating note which now was beginning to tell upon my nerves?

What had happened? Had fire broken out? If so, I might

well be trapped between the two doors, for I knew of no other exit. Further reflection assured me that these devices could not be intended for use in such an emergency as fire. What then was their purpose, and what was it that Dr. Fu Manchu had feared?

The answer came, even as the question flashed into my mind.

Heralded by a hoarse, roaring sound, a *Thing*, neither animal nor human, a huge, naked, misshapen creature resembling an animated statue by Epstein, burst into view at the end of the corridor!

It had a huge head set upon huge shoulders. The head was hairless, and the entire face, trunk, and limbs glistened moistly like the skin of an earthworm. The arms were equally massive; but I saw that the hands were misformed, the fingers webbed, and the thumbs scarcely present.

The legs were out of all proportion to that mighty trunk, being stumpy, dwarfed, and terminating in feet of a loathsome pink colour—feet much smaller than the great hands, but also webbed.

From the appalling glistening, naked face, two tiny eyes set close together beside a flattened nose with distended nostrils, glared redly, murderously in my direction.

Uttering a sound which might have proceeded from a wounded buffalo, the creature hurled itself towards me. . . .

Chapter Twenty-second

HALF-WORLD

I SPRANG back, looking wildly right and left for the button which controlled the door.

The worm-man was almost upon me, and transcending all fear of a violent death was the horror of contact with those moistly glistening limbs. The control button proved to be on the right. I pressed it.

And the door began to close rapidly and smoothly.

In the very instant of its closing, a loathsome moist mass appeared at the narrowing opening.

My heart leapt and then seemed to stop. I thought that one of those great pink arms was about to be thrust through. Judging the door to be a frail one, I looked in those few instances upon a fate more horrible than any which had befallen man since prehistoric times.

The door closed.

And now came a hollow booming, and a perceptible vibration of the floor upon which I stood.

That unnameable thing was endeavouring to batter a way in! I inhaled deeply, and knew such a sense of relief as I could not have believed possible under the roof of Dr. Fu Manchu.

The door was of metal. Not even the unnatural strength of the monster could prevail against it.

All sounds were curiously muted here; but one harsh bellow of what I took to be frustrated rage reached me very dimly. Then silence fell.

I pressed my ear against the enamelled metal but could hear nothing save a vague murmuring, with which was mingled the rumble of those descending doors.

Thereupon I stood upright; and as I did no, a stifled exclamation brought me sharply about.

Fleurette was in the room just behind me!

She wore a blue-and-white pyjama suit and blue sandals. Her beautiful eyes registered the nearest approach to fear which I had seen in them. She had told me, I remembered, that nothing frightened her, but to-day—or to-night, for I had lost all count of time—something had definitely succeeded in doing so. Her face, which was so like a delicate flower, was pale.

"You!" she whispered, "what are *you* doing here?"

I swallowed, not without difficulty. I suffered from an intense thirst, and my throat remained very sore by reason of its maltreatment at the hands of the dacoit.

My heart began jumping in quite a ridiculous way.

Yet I suppose the phenomenon was not so ridiculous, for Fleurette was more lovely than I had ever believed a woman could be. Oddly enough, her beauty swamped the last straw of reality upon which I had clutched in the corridor with its rows of white doors and which had remained with me up to the moment that the worm-man had appeared. I sank back again into a sea of doubt, from which, agonisingly, I had been fighting to escape.

Fleurette was dead! *I* was dead! This was a grim, a ghastly half-world, horribly reminiscent of that state which Spiritualists present to us as the afterlife.

"I have joined you," I replied.

My words carried no conviction even to myself.

"What?"

Her expression changed; she watched me with a new, keen interest.

"I have joined you."

Fleurette moved towards me and laid one hand almost timidly upon my shoulder.

"Is that true?" she asked, in a low voice.

I had thought that her eyes were blue, but now I saw that they were violet. The life beyond, then was a parody of that which we had lived on earth. I had seen travesties of my own studies in those monstrous houses; I had met with the fabulous Dr. Fu Manchu; I had watched men still pursuing the secrets they had sought in life—amid surroundings which were a caricature of those they had known during their earthly incarnation.

Horror there was, in this strange borderland, but, as I looked into those violet eyes, I told myself that death had its recompenses.

"I am glad you are here," said Fleurette.

"So am I."

She glanced aside and went on rapidly:

"You see, I have been trained not to feel fear, but whenever I hear the alarm signal and know that the section doors are being closed—I feel something very like it! I don't suppose you know about all this yet?" she added.

Already normal colour was returning to those rose-petal cheeks, and she dropped into a little armchair, forcing a smile.

"No," I replied, watching her; "it's unpleasantly strange."

"It must be!" She nodded. "I have lived among this sort of thing on and off as long as I can remember.

"Do you mean *here?*"

"No; I have never been here before. But at the old place in Ho Nan the same system is in use, and I have been there many times."

"You must travel a lot," I said, studying her fascinatedly, and thinking that she had the most musical voice in the world.

"Yes, I do."

"With Mahdi Bey?"

"He nearly always comes with me: he is my guardian, you see."

"Your guardian?"

"Yes." She looked up, a puzzled frown appearing upon her smooth forehead. "Mahdi Bey is an old Arab doctor, you know, who adopted me when I was quite tiny—long before I can remember. He is very, very clever; and no one in the world has ever been so kind to me."

"But, my dear Fleurette, how did you come to be adopted by an Arab doctor?"

She laughed: she had exquisite little teeth.

"Because," she said, and at last that for which I had been waiting, the adorable dimple, appeared in her chin, "because I am half an Arab myself."

"What!"

"Don't I look like one? I am sunburned now, I know; but my skin is naturally not so many shades lighter."

"But an Arab, with violet eyes and hair like . . . like an Egyptian sunset."

"Egyptian, yes!" She laughed again. "Evidently you detect

the East even in my hair!"

"But," I said in amazement, "You have no trace of accent."

"Why should I have?" She looked at me mockingly. "I am a most perfect little prig. I speak French also without any foreign accent; Italian, Spanish, German, Arabic, and Chinese."

"You are pulling my leg."

That maddening dimple reappeared, and she shook her head so that glittering curls danced and seemed to throw out sparks of light.

"I know such accomplishments are simply horrible for a girl—but I can't help it. This learning has been thrust upon me. You see, I have been trained for a purpose."

And as she spoke the words, dancing, vital youth dropped from her like a cloak. Those long-lashed eyes, which I had an insane desire to kiss, ceased to laugh. Again that rapt, mystical expression claimed her face. She was looking through me at some very distant object. I had ceased to exist.

"But, Fleurette," I said desperately, "*what* purpose? There can be only one end to it. Sooner or later you will fall in love with—somebody or another. You will forget your accomplishments and everything. I mean—it's a sort of law. What other purpose is there in life for a woman?"

In a faraway voice:

"There is no such thing as love," Fleurette murmured. "A woman can only *serve*."

"Whatever do you mean?"

"You are new to it all. You will know tomorrow or perhaps even to-night."

I had taken a step in her direction when something arrested me—drew me up sharply.

Like a fairy trumpet it sounded, again, that unaccountable call which I had heard twice before—coming from nowhere; from everywhere; from inside my brain!

Fleurette stood up, giving me never another glance, and moved to that end of the room opposite to the door by which I had entered. She touched some control hidden in the wall. A section slid open. As she crossed the threshold, she turned: I could see a lighted corridor beyond.

"The danger is over now," she said. "Goodbye."

I stood staring stupidly at the blank expanse of wall where

only a moment before Fleurette had been, when I heard a sound behind me. I turned sharply.

The white door was open! The woman whom Nayland Smith had called Fah Lo Suee stood there, looking at me.

With the opening of the door a faint vibration reached my ears. The "section doors" (so Fleurette had described them) were being raised. Fah Lo Suee wore what I took to be a Chinese dress, by virtue of its style, only; for it was of a patternless, shimmering gold material. Her unveiled eyes were green as emeralds; their resemblance to those of the terrible doctor was unmistakable.

"Please come," she said; "my father is waiting for you."

Chapter Twenty-third

THE JADE PIPE

As I followed that slim, languorous figure, mentally I put myself in the witness box. And this was the question to which I demanded an answer:

Am I alive or dead?

On the whole, I was disposed now to believe that I was alive. Therefore, I put this second question:

Am I sane?

To which query I could find no answer.

If the occurrences of the last few hours were real, then I had stepped into a world presumably under the aegis of Dr. Fu Manchu, and presumably in China, where natural laws were flouted; their place taken by laws created by the Chinese physician.

At the foot of the stairs, Fah Lo Suee turned sharply left and opened one of the sliding doors which seemed to be common in the establishment. She beckoned me to follow, and I found myself in a carpeted, warmly lighted corridor. She bent across me to reclose the door.

"You must forget all that is past and all that is puzzling you," she whispered urgently, speaking close to my ear. "My father knows that you and the little Rose-petal are acquainted. Don't speak—listen. He will question you, and you will have to answer. When you go to Yamamata's room, do not fear the injection. But all that you are told will happen when you have received the Blessing of the Celestial Vision, *see that you carry out.* . . . Pretend—it is your only chance. Pretend! I will see you again as soon as possible. Now follow me."

These strange words she had spoken with extraordinary rapidity, as she had bent over me, apparently fumbling with the button which controlled the door.

And now, with that slow, lithe, cat-like walk in which again I recognized her father, she moved ahead, leading me. My brain was working with feverish rapidity.

The little Rose-petal!

This must be the Chinese name of Fleurette. Our association, I gathered, did not meet with the approval of Dr. Fu Manchu. And what was the Blessing of the Celestial Vision? This I had yet to learn.

At the end of the corridor I saw a small green lamp burning before an arched opening. Here Fah Lo Suee paused, signalling me to be silent.

"Remember," she whispered.

The green light in the little lamp flickered, and a heavy door of panelled mahogany slid aside noiselessly.

"Go in," said Fah Lo Suee.

I obeyed. The door closed behind me, and a whiff of air laden with fumes of opium told me that I was in that queer study which, presumably, was the sanctum of Dr. Fu Manchu.

One glance was enough. He was seated at the big table, his awful but majestic face resting upon one upraised palm. The long nails of his fingers touched his lips. His brilliant eyes fixed me so that I experienced almost a physical shock as I met their gaze.

"Sit down," he directed.

I discovered that a Chinese stool was set close beside me. I sat down.

Dr. Fu Manchu continued to watch me. I tried to turn my eyes aside, but failed. The steel-grey eyes of Sir Denis Nayland Smith were hard to evade, but I had never experienced such a thralldom as that cast upon me by the long, narrow, green eyes of Dr. Fu Manchu.

All my life I had doubted the reality of hypnotism. Sir Denis's assurance that Fah Lo Suee had nearly succeeded in hypnotising me at the hospital had not fully registered; I had questioned it. But now, in that small, opiated room, the reality of the art was thrust upon me.

This man's eyes held a power potent as any drug. When he spoke, his voice reached me through a sort of mist, against which something deep within—my spirit, I suppose—was fighting madly.

"I have learned that you are acquainted with the little flower whose destiny is set upon the peak of a high mountain. Of this, I shall ask you more later. She is nature's rarest jewel: a perfect woman.... You have, unwittingly as I believe, thrust yourself into the cogs of the most delicate machine ever set in motion."

I closed my eyes. It was a definite physical effort, but I achieved it.

"Now, when you are about to devote your services to the triumph of the Si-Fan, consider the state of the world. The imprint of my hand is upon the nations. Mussolini so far has eluded me; but President Hoover, who stood in my path, makes way for Franklin Roosevelt. Mustapha Pasha is a regrettable nuisance, but my organization in Anatolia neutralises his influence. Von Hindenburg! the old marshal is a granite monument buried in weeds . . . !"

Persistently I kept my eyes closed. This dangerous madman was thinking aloud, communicating his insane ideas to a member of the outer world, and at the same time pronouncing my doom—as I realized: for the silence of the father confessor is taken for granted. . . .

"Rumania, the oboe of the Balkan orchestra . . . I have tried to forget King Carol—but negligible quantities can upset the nicest equation by refusing to disappear. A man ruled by women is always dangerous—unless his women are under my orders. . . . Women are the lever for which Archimedes was searching, but they are a lever which a word can bend. You may have heard, Alan Sterling, that I have failed in my projects. But consider my partial successes. I have disturbed the currencies of the world. . . ."

That strange, guttural voice died away, and I ventured to open my eyes and to look at Dr. Fu Manchu.

He had lighted a little spirit lamp which formed one of the items upon the littered table, and above the flame, on the end of a needle, he was twirling a bead of opium. He glanced up at me through half-closed eyes.

"Something upon which Science has not improved," he said softly. "Yes, I could hasten the crisis which I have brought about, if I wished to do so."

He dropped the bead into the jade bowl of a pipe which lay in a tray beside him.

"Here is a small brochure," he went on, and took a book from a table rack, thrusting it in my direction. "*Apologia Alchymiae*—a restatement of alchemy. It is the work of a

London physician—Mr. Watson Councell, whose recent death I regret, since otherwise I should have solicited his services. There are five hundred copies of this small handbook in circulation. Singular to reflect, Alan Sterling, that no one has attempted the primitive method of manufacturing synthetic gold, as practised by the alchemists and clearly indicated in these few pages. For fable is at least as true as fact. Gold...."

He placed the stem of the pipe between his yellow teeth... "I could drown the human race in gold!"

"But Russia is starving, and the United States undernourished. The world is a cheese, consuming itself.... Even China—my China..."

He fell silent—and I watched him until he replaced the little pipe in its tray and struck a gong which stood near to his left hand.

A pair of Chinamen, identical in appearance, and wearing identical white robes, entered behind me—I suddenly found one at either elbow. Their faces resembled masks carved in old ivory and mellowed by the smoke of incense.

Dr. Fu Manchu spoke a few rapid words in Chinese—then:

"Companion Yamamata will see you," he said, his voice now very drowsy, and that queer film creeping over his brilliant eyes; "he will admit you to the Blessing of the Celestial Vision, by which time I shall be ready to discuss with you certain points in regard to the future and to instruct you in your immediate duties."

One of the Chinese servants touched me upon the shoulder and pointed to the open doorway. I turned and walked out.

Chapter Twenty-fourth

COMPANION YAMAMATA

I PRESENTLY found myself in a typical reception room of a consulting surgeon. I was placed in a chair around which were grouped powerful lights for examination purposes. Companion Yamamata, who was scrutinizing some notes, immediately stood up and introduced himself, peremptorily dismissing the Chinamen.

He was young and good-looking in the intellectual Japanese manner; wore a long white coat having the sleeves rolled up; and as he rose from the table where he had been reading the notes, he laid down a pair of tortoiseshell-rimmed glasses and looked at me with humorous, penetrating eyes. He spoke perfect English.

"I am glad that you are becoming a Companion, Mr. Sterling," he said. "Your province of science is not mine, but I am given to understand by Trenck that you are a botanist of distinction. Your medical history—" he tapped the pages before him—"is good, except for malarial trouble."

I stared at him perhaps somewhat stupidly. His manner was utterly disarming.

"How do you know that I have had malaria?" I asked. "I don't think I display any symptoms at the moment."

"No, no, not at all," he assured me. "But, you see, I have your history before me. And this malaria has to be taken into account, especially since it culminated in blackwater fever so recently as three months ago. Blackwater, you know, is the devil!"

"I do know," said I grimly.

"However," he displayed gleaming teeth in a really charming smile, "I am accustomed to these small complications, and I have prepared the dose accordingly. Will you please strip down to the waist. I always prefer to make the injection in the shoulder."

He stepped to a side table and took up a hypodermic syringe, glancing back at me as he did so.

"Suppose I object?" I suggested.

"Object?" He wrinkled his brow comically. "Object to enthusiasm?—object to be admitted to knowledge conserved for hundreds of centuries?—to salvation physical as well as intellectual? Ha, ha! that is funny."

He went on with his preparations.

I reviewed the words of the woman Fah Lo Suee.

To what extent could I rely upon them? Did they mean that for some reason of her own she was daring to cross the formidable mandarin, her father? If so, what was her reason? And supposing that she had lied or had failed, what was this Blessing of the Celestial Vision to which I should be admitted?

I suspected that it was the administration of some drug which would reduce me to a condition of abject mental slavery.

That there was vast knowledge conserved in this place, that experiments ages ahead of any being carried out in the great cultural centres of the world were progressing here, I could not doubt; I had had the evidence of my own eyes. But to what end were these experiments directed?

Something of my thoughts must have been reflected upon my face, for:

"My dear Mr. Sterling," said the Japanese doctor, "it is so useless to challenge the why and demand the wherefore. And you are about to be admitted to the Company of the Si-Fan. A new world which trembles in the throes of birth will be your orange, of which you shall have your share."

I made to stand up—to confront him. I could not move! And Dr. Yamamata laughed in the most good-humoured manner.

"Many jib at the last fence," he assured me, "but what is to be, will be, you know. Allow me to assist you, Mr. Sterling."

He stepped behind me, and with the adroit movement of a master of jiu-jitsu, peeled my overalls down over my shoulders, pinioning my arms. He unbuttoned my shirt collar.

"Injections are always beastly," he admitted. "For myself, they induce a feeling of nausea; but sometimes they are necessary."

I experienced a sharp stab in the shoulder and knew that the needle point of the syringe had been thrust into my flesh. I clenched my teeth; but I was helpless. . . .

He was cleaning the syringe at a wash-basin on the other

side of the room. His manner was that of a dental surgeon who has deftly made a difficult extraction.

"A pleasant glow pervades your body, no doubt?" he suggested. "You see, I am accustomed to these small operations. It will be succeeded, I assure you, by a consciousness of new power. No task which may be set—and the tasks set by the doctor are not simple ones—will prove too difficult."

He replaced the parts of the syringe upon a glass rack and began to wash his hands.

"When you are rested I shall prescribe a whisky-and-soda, which I know is your national beverage, and then you will be ready for your second interview with the doctor."

He glanced back at me smilingly.

"Is my diagnosis correct?"

"Perfectly." I replied, conscious of the fact that no change whatever had taken place in my condition, and mindful of the words of that strange, evil woman.

I had a part to play. Not only my own life, but other lives—thousands, perhaps millions—depended upon my playing it successfully!

"Ah!" he beamed delightedly, and began to dry his hands. "Sometimes novitiates shout with joy—but blackwater has somewhat lowered your normal vitality."

"Nevertheless," I replied, grinning artificially, "I feel that I want to shout."

"Then, shout!" he cried, revealing those gleaming teeth in a happy smile. "Shout! the chair is disconnected. Jump about! Let yourself go! Life is just beginning!"

I moved. It was true . . . I could stand up.

"Ah!" I cried, and stretched my hands above my head.

It was a cry and a gesture of relief. Fah Lo Suee had tricked the Japanese doctor! And I was free—free in mind and body . . . but in China, and under the roof of Dr. Fu Manchu!

"Splendid!" Yamamata exclaimed, his small, bright eyes registering pure happiness. "My congratulations, Companion Sterling. We will drink to the Master who perfected this super-drug—which makes men giants with the hearts of lions."

He took up a decanter and poured out two liberal pegs of whisky.

"There was a slight *faux-pas* earlier this evening," he went on. "A nearly perfected *homonculus*—not in your province, Companion, but I am an enthusiast in my own—escaped from the incubator. The formula is, of course, the doctor's. I had contributed some small items to its perfection, and the specimen who disturbed the household had points of great interest."

He added soda to the whisky and handed a glass to me. I resigned myself to this gruesome conversation and merely nodded. Yamamata raised his glass.

"Comrade Alan Sterling—we drink to the Mandarin Fu Manchu, master of the world!"

It was a badly needed drink, and I did not challenge his toast; then:

"The specimen had enormous physical strength," he went on, "and that blind elemental fury which characterises these products—a fact recognised even by Paracelsus. The section doors had to be closed. And I felt dreadfully guilty."

I drank down half the contents of my tumbler; and:

"What became of . . . the thing?" I asked.

"Most regretfully," Yamamata replied, shaking his head, "the vital spark expired. You see, the temperature of the corridors was unsuitable."

"I see——"

I stopped short.

That clear, indefinable sound or vibration which I had first heard upon the beach of Ste Claire de la Roche came to me again. I saw Yamamata raise one hand and press it against his ear. The sound ceased.

"Dr. Fu Manchu is waiting for you," he said.

He extended both hands cordially, and I grasped them.

For a moment I had all but forgotten my part; in the horror of the story of that *life* which was not human, which had been bred, I gathered, in an incubator. . . .

But now, in time—I remembered.

"I am going to kneel at his feet," I said, endeavouring to impart a quality of exaltation into my voice.

And as I spoke, the smile vanished from the face of Dr. Yamamata as writing sponged from a slate.

"We *all* kneel at his feet," he said solemnly.

Chapter Twenty-fifth

THE LIFE PRINCIPLE

Drenched in the opium fumes of that stygian room, I stood again before Dr. Fu Manchu. His eyes were brilliant as emeralds, the pupils mere pin-points, and he lay back in a padded chair, watching me. I had thought out the words which I would speak, and I spoke them now.

"I salute the Master of the World," I said, and bowed deeply before him.

That the Blessing of the Celestial Vision produced some kind of mental exaltation was clear to me. This I must enact; but it was a mighty task which rested upon my shoulders. That cold hatred which had possessed me at the moment that the news of Petrie's death had come, now again held absolute sway. I knew that Sir Denis Nayland Smith had not romanced when he had said that this man was Satan's own—apparently eternal.

At whatever cost—my life was nothing in such a contest!—I would help to throw him down. *I* would be the feeble instrument which should prove that the was *not* eternal.

He was monstrous—titanic—dreadful—hell's chosen emissary. But if I could live, if I could hope to trick this gigantic evil brain, I would find means to crush him; to stamp him out; to eradicate this super-enemy of all that was clean and wholesome.

I could not forget the dead men in his workshops. This monster clearly possessed knowledge transcending natural laws. He laughed at God. No matter! he was still human—or so I must continue to believe.

The price of doubt was insanity. . . .

He watched me a while in silence and then:

"In two hours, Companion Sterling," he said, "you will be called for duty. This is your private telephone."

He handed to me what looked like a signet ring, made of some dull white metal. I had to clench my teeth at the moment of contact with those long, talon-like nails; but I took the ring and stared at it curiously.

"It is adjustable," Dr. Fu Manchu continued. "Place it upon that finger which you consider most suitable. It is an adaptation—much simplified by Ericksen—of the portable radio now in use among the French police. It does not convey the spoken word. Morse code is used. You know it?"

"I regret to say that I do not."

"It is simple. You will find a copy of the code in your room. The call note used by Ericksen is highly individual, but inaudible a short distance away from the *receiver*. Companion Trenck will call you to-night for duty and give you further particulars."

As he spoke, I started—suppressing an exclamation.

A queer whistling note had sounded, almost in my ear, and some vague grey shape streaked past me, alighted upon the big table with its litter of strange books and implements, and with a final spring settled upon the yellow-robed shoulder of Dr. Fu Manchu!

Out from a ball of grey fur, a tiny, wizened face peered at me. One of those taloned hands reached upward and caressed the little creature.

"Probably the oldest marmoset in the world." said the guttural voice. "You would not believe me if I told you Peko's age."

And as the Chinaman spoke, the wizened little creature perched upon his shoulder looked down into that majestic, evil face, made a mocking, whistling sound, and clutched with tiny fingers at the little skullcap which Dr. Fu Manchu wore.

"I shall not detain you now. Urgent matters call me. You may possibly have noticed that Professor Ascheim and Dr. Hohlwag of Berlin have found *hormone*—the life principle—in coal deposits. It will prove to be *female*. The *male* I had already found. It is expressed in a rare orchid which possesses the property of extracting this essence of life from certain Burmese swamps which have absorbed it during untold centuries. . . .

"It flowers at regrettably long intervals. Companion Trenck is endeavouring to force some specimens forward under special conditions."

He struck the little gong beside him upon the table.

Almost instantaneously, as though he had arisen from the floor like an Arab genie, one of the white-clad Chinese servants appeared, in the doorway to the right of, and behind, Dr. Fu Manchu's chair.

A guttural order was spoken; the servant bowed to me and stood aside.

I bowed deeply to that strange figure in the padded chair, the tiny, wrinkled-face monkey crouched upon his shoulder—and went out.

I was conducted back to the long corridor with its rows of white-painted doors. That numbered eleven was opened by the Chinese servant, and I found myself in the small, comfortably appointed sitting room. My silent guide indicated an adjoining bedroom with a bathroom opening out of it; whereupon I dismissed him.

As the sliding door closed and I found myself alone, I examined more particularly these apartments which had been allotted to me. They were beautifully appointed. Silk pyjamas lay upon the temptingly turned-down bed; and though I had never felt in greater danger in the whole of my life, the lure was one I could not resist.

I recognised a weariness of brain and body which demanded sleep. I made a brief survey of the three rooms before turning in, but although I failed to find any means of entrance or exit other than that opening upon the corridor, that such another exit existed, I knew.

Nevertheless, nature triumphed. . . .

I cannot remember undressing, but I vaguely recall tucking my head into the cool pillow. I was asleep instantly.

The sleep that came to me was not dreamless.

I stood again, a spectator unseen, in the opium-laden atmosphere of Dr. Fu Manchu's study. Fleurette sat in a high-backed chair, her eyes staring straight before her. The long yellow hand of Fu Manchu was extended in her direction, and a large disc, which appeared to be composed of some kind of black meteoric stone, was suspended from the ceiling of the room and was slowly revolving.

As I watched, its movements became more and more rapid, until presently it resembled a globe throwing out ever changing sparks of light.

The room, Fleurette, the Chinese doctor disappeared. I found myself fascinatedly watching those sparks, their ever changing colour.

As I watched, a picture formed, mistily, and then very

clearly, so that presently it resembled a miniature and very sharp cinematograph projection.

I saw the Templehof aerodrome at Berlin. I had been there several times and knew it well. I saw Nayland Smith descend from a plane and hurry across the ground to where a long, low, powerful police car awaited him.

The car drove off. And as in a moving picture, I followed it.

It skirted Berlin and then headed out into a suburb with which I was not acquainted. Before a large house set back beyond a thick shrubbery the car pulled up, and Sir Denis, springing out, opened the gate and ran up a path overarched by trees.

A crown of people was assembled before the house. I saw fire engines and men uncoiling a hose. Through all these, angrily checking their protests, Nayland Smith forced his way, and began to run towards the house ...

Something touched me coldly.

In an instant I was awake—in utter darkness—my heart thumping.

Where was I?

In the house of Dr. Fu Manchu! . . . and someone, or something, was close beside me.

Chapter Twenty-sixth

THE ORCHID

"Do not speak—nor turn on the light!"

Fah Lo Suee! Fah Lo Suee was somewhere in the room beside me. . . .

"Listen—for there are some things you must know to-night. First, look upon yourself as in China. For although this is France——"

"France! I am still in France?"

"You are in Ste Claire de la Roche. . . . It makes no difference; you are in China. No one can leave here day or night without my father's consent—or mine. Very soon now he opens his war upon the world. He will almost certainly succeed; he has with him some of the finest brains in science, military strategy, and politics which Europe, Asia, and America have ever produced. . . ."

I resigned myself to the magic of her voice.

But if I was indeed in Ste Claire, it remained to be seen if no one could leave. . . .

This house, she told me, was a mere outpost, used chiefly as a base for certain experiments. Elsewhere she had allies of her own, but in Ste Claire, none. . . .

"For you see I do not agree with all that my father plans—especially his plans concerning Fleurette."

"Fleurette! What are these plans?"

"Ssh!" Cool fingers were laid upon my arm. "Not so loudly. It is about her I came to tell you. She was chosen—before her birth—for this purpose. She had Eastern and Western blood; her pedigree on both sides is of the kind my father seeks. I am his only child. It will be Fleurette's duty to give him a son."

"What! Good God! You mean he *loves* her?"

Fah Lo Suee laughed softly.

"How little you know him! She is part of our experiment—the success of which is of political importance. But listen," she lowered her voice. "*I* do not wish this experiment to take place. . . . Soon, very soon, we shall be leaving France.

Fleurette—I think—has found *love*. She is of a race, on her mother's side, to whom love comes swiftly..."

"Do you mean..."

"I mean that if you want Fleurette I will help you. Is that direct enough? It was for this reason I emptied the syringe and recharged it with a harmless fluid. I had seen... once, in the bay; again, in this room...."

She had seen me on the beach! Hoping—doubting—trying to think, to plan, I listened....

Fah Lo Suee had gone.

That voice which seemed to caress the spirit, in which there was a fluttering quality like the touch of butterfly wings, and sometimes a hard, inexorable purpose which made me think of the glittering beauty of a serpent, had ceased. The presence of the sorceress was withdrawn.

The room remained in utter darkness; yet I seemed to see her gliding towards the door, and I envisioned her as a slender ivory statue created by some long-dead Greek, and endowed with life, synthetic but potent, by a black magician whose power knew no bounds.

I waited, as I had promised to wait until I thought that fully a minute had elapsed; then I groped for the switch, found it, and flooded the room with light.

The door, visible from where I lay, I saw to be closed, nor had I heard it open. The location of the other door I did not know.

But I was the sole occupant of the place.

I had still half an hour before I should be summoned to the strange duties which awaited me—half an hour in which to think, to try to plan.

Going into the bathroom, I turned on the taps. Shaving materials and every other toilet necessity were provided in lavish form. I remembered that I had to memorize the Morse code, and leaving the taps running I returned to the little sitting room and took up a chart of Morse which lay there on the table.

A brief inspection satisfied me that I could learn it in a few hours. I have that kind of brain which can assimilate exact information very rapidly.

I returned to the bathroom and mechanically proceeded....

To what extent could I rely upon the dreams, or what had seemed to be a dream, which had preceded the visit of Fah Lo Suee? There was no evidence, so far as I could see, to indicate that one episode, was more real than the other.

Perhaps the woman's visit had been part of the same dream—or perhaps I had dreamed neither! That almost miraculous experiments in radio and television were being carried out in these secret laboratories, I could not doubt. It might be that that queer scene, resembling one in the cave of some mediaeval astrologer, had actually taken place; that for some reason, accidentally or purposefully, I had become a witness of it.

"There is as much truth in fable as in fact," Dr. Fu Manchu had said, when he had drawn my attention to the handbook of the modern alchemist.

Perhaps the lost Sybilline books upon which much of the policy of ancient Rome was based were not mere guesses but scientific prophecy. Perhaps Fu Manchu had discovered Fleurette to possess the fabulous powers once attributed to the Cumæn oracle. . . .

I considered the strange things which Fah Lo Suee had told me, but greater significance lay, I thought, in the facts which she had withheld. Nevertheless, some glimmering of an enormity about to be loosed upon the world was penetrating even to my dull mind.

For good or evil, I must work in concert with this treacherous woman. Her purpose was revealed, and it was one which I understood. In her alone lay safety, not only for myself, but for Western civilisation.

I had just completed dressing when that tiny penetrating sound seemed to vibrate throughout my frame. It sustained one long note and then ceased; no attempt was made to send me a message other than the signal which told me that my six hours' watch had commenced.

The door slid open, and one of the white-robed Chinamen appeared in the opening, inclining his head slightly and indicating that I should follow him. I slipped the code book into a pocket of my overall. . . .

Exit without leave (which only Fu Manchu has power to give) was out of the question, Fah Lo Suee had assured me. Failing outside assistance, there was no means of leaving save by the main gate.

This was the problem exercising my mind as I followed my silent guide downstairs and along to the botanical research room.

I found the famous Dutch botanist in a state of great scientific excitement. Already I was partly reconciled to the indisputable fact that he had died some years earlier in Sumatra. He led me to a small house where artificial sunlight prevailed.

About the mummy-like roots of some kind of dwarf mangrove which grew there, a bank of muddy soil steamed malariously. The place stank like an Amazon forest in the rainy season.

"Look!" said Trenck, with emotion.

He pointed; and, creeping up from the steaming mud, I saw tender flesh-coloured tendrils clasping the swampy roots.

"The orchid of life!" Trenck cried. "The doctor so terms. But imagine! Watch this thermometer—watch it as though your life depended, Mr Sterling! Here is a culture of *fourteen days!* In its natural state in Burma, flowering occurs at intervals of rarely less than eighty years! Do you realise what this means?"

I shook my head rather blankly.

"Come, Companion! It means that if we can produce flowers, and I expect these buds to break within the next few hours, no one of us, no member of the Si-Fan, shall ever die except by violence!"

Probably my expression had grown even more blank, for:

"The doctor has not told you?" he went on excitedly. "Very well! The knowledge which we accumulate is common to us all, and it is my privilege to explain to you that from this orchid the doctor has obtained a certain oil. It is the missing ingredient for which the old alchemists sought. It is the Oil of Life!"

As he spoke, mentally I conjured up the face of Dr. Fu Manchu, recalling the image which had occurred to me—that of Seti the First, the Egyptian Pharaoh. Could it be possible that this Chinese wizard had solved a problem which had taunted the ages?

"He spoke of it," I said, "but gave me no details. How old

then is Dr. Fu Manchu?"

Trenck burst out laughing.

"Do you think," he cried, his voice rising to a note almost hysterical, "that a man could know what *he* knows in one short span of life? How can I tell you? It is only necessary to prevent the veins from clogging as in vegetable life. The formula which first came into his possession demanded an ingredient no longer obtainable. For this, after nearly thirty years' inquiry, he found a substitute in the oil expressed from this Burmese orchid. Ah! I must go. It is tantalizing to leave at such a moment, but regulations must be obeyed. But I forget; you are a novice. I will show you how to call be if a bud breaks."

He hurried back to the laboratory and pointed to a dial set upon the wall. He illustrated its simple mechanism, and it was not unlike that of a dial telephone.

"You see," he said, "my number is ninety-five."

He twisted the mechanism until the number ninety-five appeared in a small, illuminated oval.

At which moment I heard again that strange vibrating note which had so intrigued me on the beach at Ste Claire.

Trenck pressed a button, and the number ninety-five disappeared from the illuminated space, and that incredibly high sound which was almost like the note of a bat ceased.

"At the moment that a bud begins to break," he said, "you will call me? It would be tragic for a new world to open before us in all its perfection and Father Time to cut us off before we could enjoy it. Eh? I envy you your hours of duty; they may bring the honour of being the first man to witness a thing which shall revolutionise human life!"

Chapter Twenty-Seven

IN THE GALLERIES

MY COURSE was already set.

That there would be some kind of night patrol—probably one of those immobile Chinamen—I could not doubt. But since I had no orders to the contrary, I was presumably entitled to proceed wherever I pleased, definitely within the botanical department, and by presumption elsewhere, always supposing that the communicating doors were not locked.

Complete silence descended upon the laboratory, which was not more than twenty feet square. I found it necessary to keep reminding myself of the fact that in the eyes of those surrounding me, including the formidable Dr. Fu Manchu himself, I had become a Companion of the Si-Fan, a devotee of the cause, a blind slave of the Chinese doctor.

The more I considered the situation, the more obvious it became that I had only one person to fear—Fah Lo Suee! Fah Lo Suee alone knew that I was still the captain of my soul.

She counted on my interest in Fleurette to ensure my complicity. She thought—and she was right—that I would hesitate at nothing to save the lovely Rose-petal from that unimaginable fate mapped out for her by the insane master of so many destinies.

And as I paced up and down that silent room I tried to work out where my duty lay.

Fah Lo Suee clearly took it for granted that I could not escape from the place: this remained to be seen! But assuming that I did escape, and my absence be noted, this would precipitate some catastrophe, at the nature of which I could little more than guess.

Fleurette would be lost to me forever! Sir Frank Narcomb and the rest—what would be their fate?

Moreover, recognising the imminence of his danger, Fu Manchu might open his war on the world!

Yet, now that I knew myself to be not in China, but in Ste Claire de la Roche, my determination to endeavour to get in touch with Nayland Smith was firmly established: the route alone remained doubtful.

And upon this point I formed a sudden resolution.

I had noted that in one of the houses—the first which I had entered with Dr. Fu Manchu, and the loftiest; that in which many fantastic species of palms grew—there was a spiral staircase leading to a series of gangways. By means of these presumably the upper foliage of the trees could be inspected.

From up there, I thought, I might obtain a view of whatsoever lay outside, and thus get my bearings. Otherwise, I was just as likely to penetrate farther and farther into this maze of laboratories and workshops, as to find a way out of it.

I had one chance, and I didn't know what it was worth. But given anything like decent luck, I proposed to risk it.

For a minute or more I looked in through the observation window to the small house flooded with synthetic sunshine, where those queer, flesh-like orchids were clambering up from steaming mud around the contorted mango roots. They seemed to be moving slightly, as is the way with such plants, in a manner suggesting the breathing of a sleeping animal.

I moved on to the door which communicated with the first of the range of forcing houses, or the last in the order in which I had inspected them. It was the one containing the pitcher plants and other fly-catching varieties.

It was dimly lighted within, and the door slid open as I pressed the control button. I closed it, adjusted the gauge, then opened the inner door and went in.

The steamy heat of the place attacked me at once. It was like stepping out of a temperate clime into the heart of a jungle. The air was laden with perfumes—pleasant and otherwise; the predominant smell being that of an ineffable rottenness which characterises swampy vegetation.

I threaded my way along a narrow path. So far, I had met with success—probably all the doors were unfastened.

It proved to be so, nor did I meet a soul on the way.

And when at last I stood in the most imposing house of all, palms towering high above my head, I became conscious of an apprehension against which I must fight . . . that the note of recall would suddenly sound in my brain.

Yet to discard the metal ring would have been folly.

There was an odd whispering among the dim palm-tops, for the place was but half lighted. It felt and smelled like a tropical forest. Much of the glass comprising the walls was semi-opaque. What lay beyond, I had no means of finding out.

I moved cautiously along until I came to that spiral staircase I had noted. It was situated at no great distance from the doorway through which I had originally entered.

Cautiously I began to ascend, my rubber-soled shoes creating a vague thrumming sound upon the metal steps. I reached the top of the first staircase and saw before me a narrow gangway with a single handrail—not unlike those found in engine rooms.

Palm boles towered about me, and fronds of lower foliage extended across the platform. I advanced, sometimes ducking under them, to where vaguely I had seen a second stair leading higher. I mounted this until I found myself among the tops of wildly unfamiliar trees; narrow galleries branched off in several directions. I selected one which seemed to lead to the glass wall. I saw queer fruit glowing in the crowns of trees unknown. Normally I could not have resisted inspecting it more closely; but to-night my professional enthusiasms must be subdued: a task of intense urgency claimed me.

Then, I had almost come to where one gangway joined another running flat against the glass wall, up very near to the arching roof, when I pulled up, inhaled deeply, and clutched at the hand rail....

Uttering a shrill whistling sound, *something* swung from a golden crest on my right, perched for a moment on the rail, not a yard from where I stood, chattering up at me and sprang into bright green foliage of an overhanging palm!

My heart was beating rapidly—but I tried to laugh at myself.

It was Fu Manchu's marmoset!

I had begun to move on again when once more I pulled up.

Surely it was not the doctor's custom to allow his pet to roam at large in these houses? It had presumably escaped from its usual quarters, and sooner or later the doctor, or someone else, would see it.

I stood still, listening. I could hear nothing save the faint whispering of the leaves.

Moving on to the side gallery, I saw ahead of me through

glass windows a rugged slope topped by a ruined wall, and beyond the wall an ancient building. Stepping slightly to the right, I could see more of the place—a narrow street descending in cobbled steps, and another more modern building, from the arched entrance of which light shone out upon the cobbles. Looking higher, I saw a cloudless sky gemmed with stars.

This, beyond doubt was the back of Ste Claire, and these huge forcing houses were built against the slope which ran down from it to the sea.

In other words, as I stood, the sea was behind me. I must seek an exit in that direction. I walked back along the gangways to the head of the spiral staircase, seeing nothing of Peko, the marmoset, on my way.

I descended; proceeded along the second gallery to the lower stair, and so reached the rubber covered floor again.

Instantly, I noticed something which pulled me up dead in my tracks . . . an unmistakable smell of *opium!*

I turned slowly, fists clenched, looking towards those doors which I knew to communicate with the study of Dr. Fu Manchu.

Good heavens! what did this mean?

Both doors, the inner and the outer, were open!

From where I stood I could see the farther wall of the room—I could see a silk lantern suspended from the ceiling; some of the books in their barbaric bindings; the thick carpet; and even that Chinese stool upon which I had sat.

Not a sound reached me.

Something, perhaps a natural cowardice, was urging me to go back—to go back, but I conquered it, and went forward— very cautiously.

I believe I had rarely done anything so truly praiseworthy as when I crossed the space between those two doors, and, craning forward inch by inch, peeped into the study.

Chapter Twenty-eighth

EVIL INCARNATE

I WITHDREW my head with hare-like rapidity and clenched my teeth so sharply, stifling an exclamation, that I heard the click as they came together.

Dr. Fu Manchu was seated in the big throne-like chair behind the writing table.

One glimpse only I had of him in profile, but it had wrecked my optimism—reduced me to a state of helpless despair.

I stood now on the threshold, not daring to move, scarce daring to breathe. He was seated, I had seen in that lightning glimpse, his head resting against the back of the padded chair, bolt upright, his yellow taloned hands clutching the arms. It was like a vision of a Pharoah dead upon his throne.

The open doors were explained: he had heard me approaching. He was waiting for me! . . . What explanation could I offer?

So much more than my own life was at stake, that I stood there, aware that a cold perspiration had broken out upon my skin, fighting for composure, demanding of my dull brain some answer to the inquisition to which at any moment I expected to be submitted.

Silence!

Not a sound came from that study out of which opium fumes floated to my nostrils.

It was possible, it was just possible, that he had not heard my approach. This being so, it was also possible that he did not know the identity of the intruder whom, presumably, he had heard mounting or dismounting the iron staircase. . . .

I might creep back, and if questioned later, brazen the thing out. One objective I must keep in mind—my freedom!

Silence!

The sickly smell of opium mingling with a damp miasma from the palm house. So still it was that I could hear my heart beating, and hear—or thought I could hear—that faint rustling in the tree-tops, that curious communion among tropical leaves which never ceases, day or night.

I began to recover courage.

After all, my duties were of a character which rendered wakefulness difficult. What more natural as a botanist than that I should keep my mind alert by inspecting the unique products of those wonderful houses? Finding these doors open, what more natural than that I should investigate?

Very cautiously, very quietly, I bent forward again, and this time ventured to look long and steadily.

Like Seti the First, Dr. Fu Manchu sat in his throne chair. I knew that I had never seen so majestic an outline, nor so wonderful a brow, such tremendous power in any human lineaments. He was motionless, his hands resting upon the dragon chair-arms; he might have been carved from old ivory.

My rubber-soled shoes making no sound, I stepped into the room and stood watching him closely. His eyes were closed. He was asleep, or—

I glanced at the jade-bowled pipe which lay upon the table before him. I sniffed the fumes with which the room was laden.

Drugged!

Here was the explanation which I had been slow to grasp.

Dr. Fu Manchu was in an opium trance . . . possibly the only sleep which that restless, super-normal brain ever knew!

I glanced rapidly about the room, wondering if any other man, not enthralled by the Blessing of the Celestial Vision, had ever viewed its strange treasures and lived to tell the world of them.

And now, as I stood there in the presence of that insensible enemy of Western civilisation, I asked myself a question: What should I do?

If I could find a way out of this maze I believed I had a fighting chance to escape from Ste Claire. I was in China only in the sense that this place was under the domination of the Chinese doctor. Actually, I was in France; my friends were within easy reach if I could get in touch with them.

Why should I not kill him?

He had killed Petrie—dear old Petrie, one of the best friends I had ever had in life: he had killed, for no conceivable reason, those other poor workers in vineyards and gardens.

And, according to Sir Denis, this was but the beginning of the sum of his assassinations!

I stood quite close to him; only the big table divided us. And I studied the majestic, evil mask which was the face of Dr. Fu Manchu.

He was helpless, and I was a young, vigorous man. Would it be a worthy or an unworthy deed? It is an ethical point which to this day I have never settled satisfactorily.

All I can say in defence of my inaction is that, confronting Dr. Fu Manchu, helpless and insensible, I knew, although my reason and my Celtic blood rose in revolt against me, that something deep down in my consciousness bade me not to touch him!

Supreme Evil sat enthroned before me, at my mercy—perhaps the nearest approach to Satan incarnate which this troubled world has ever known. . . . And perhaps, for that strange reason, inviolable.

I dared not lay a finger upon him—and I knew it!

No! I must pursue my original plan—gain my freedom.

The mahogany-arched recess communicated, I knew, with a corridor at the end of which was a stair leading to the rooms with white doors. The door which faced the table opened into the big laboratory called the radio research room.

Which of these should I attempt?

I had decided upon that leading to the laboratory when something occurred to me which produced a chill at my heart.

The opened doors into the palm house!

Who had opened them, since, obviously, Dr. Fu Manchu had not done so?

I stood quite still for a moment; then turned slowly and looked out into that misty jungle beyond.

Someone had come out of this room during the time that I had been creeping about upon those gangways in the palm-tops. A patrol? A patrol who, having heard me, would now be waiting for me. . . .

I listened; but no sound came from that tropical jungle. And now dawned a second thought. One acquainted with the iron routine of that place would never have left both doors open!

What did it mean?

An urge to escape from this drug-laden room, from the awful still figure in the carven chair, seized me.

I stepped softly towards the archway—only to realise that the control was hidden. I could see no trace of one of those familiar glass buttons, resembling bell pushes, which took the place of door-knobs in this singular household. Perforce, then, I must try my luck in the radio research room.

Beside the door facing Dr. Fu Manchu I could see the control button which opened it. I turned, pressed that button . . . and the door slid silently open.

I stepped out into the violet-lighted laboratory.

Looking swiftly right and left I could see no one. The place was empty, as when I had first discovered myself in its vastness. Almost directly at my feet a black line was marked upon the rubber floor.

I inhaled deeply. Could I cross it?

Clenching my teeth, I stepped forward. Nothing happened. I was free of the radio research room!

But now my case was growing desperate. I could not believe myself to be the only person awake in that human ant-hill. Sooner or later I must be detected and challenged. My only chance was to find another way out of the radio research room. And now it occurred to me that there might be none!

Avoiding those black marks upon the dull grey floor which outlined the settings of certain pieces of mechanism and of tables laden with indefinable instruments, I walked in the direction of the further end of the dimly lighted place, until I came to the glass wall.

A great part of it was occupied by shelves containing stores of all kinds. I knew that the door—if a door existed—must be somewhere in the opening between the shelves.

Desperately I began to search for it.

Chapter Twenty-ninth

PURSUIT

I COULD see no indication of a control in the first recess which I explored. But the wall was divided into panels or sections, framed in narrow strips of some dull white metal, and experience had taught me that any one of these might be a hidden door.

I groped hopelessly, as I had groped along the wall of the apartment which had been allotted to me, seeking for the hidden exit by which Fleurette and, later, Fah Lo Suee, had gone out.

A slight sound in that vast, silent room brought me twisting about.

As I turned, my down-stretched hands pressed against the glass panel behind me. I could see nothing to account for the sound which I had heard, or imagined I had heard . . . but I felt the glossy surface upon which my hand rested sliding away to the right!

I turned again—and looked up an uncarpeted staircase to where, far above, a silk-shaded lantern hung upon a landing.

Doubting, hesitating, I looked alternately at the stairway and back along the laboratory. This way led upward, and my route was downward to the sea. But, what was more important—I must learn the secret of these doors! There might be others yet to be negotiated. I determined to experiment.

The door had slid open to the right. I remembered that my hand had rested at a point about three feet from the floor. I pressed now right of the door, but there was no response. I pressed to the left. The door remained open. Baffled, I stepped back—and the door closed, swiftly and silently!

The principle was obscure, but the method I had solved.

I opened it again and stepped in to the foot of the stairs.

How did I close it now?

The solution of this problem evaded me. I began to mount the stairs—and as my foot touched the first step, the door closed behind me!

I mounted, silent in my rubber-soled shoes, reached the landing and looked about me, wondering what I should do next.

A short, dark passage opened to the right, and another, longer one, to the left. At the end of the latter I saw a green light burning. I could hear no sound. I determined to explore the shorter passage first. I began to tiptoe along it; then I paused and stood stock still.

The door at the foot of the stairs had opened, and someone had come through . . .

I was being followed!

A momentary panic touched me. Had the opium sleep of Dr. Fu Manchu been an elaborate pretence? Could it be that he, after all, had been watching me throughout?—that it was this dreadful being himself who was upon my track?

I hurried to the end of that narrow passage; but there were doors neither right nor left, nor at its terminus.

It was wood-panelled, and I looked about desperately for one of the control buttons. Suddenly I saw one, pressed it, and the door slid open.

I filled my lungs with sharp night air, and I looked upon the stars. I stood on a paved terrace bordered by a low parapet. Below me lay a rocky gorge cloaked in vegetation. Beyond was the sea, and instinct told me, the beach of Ste Claire.

Steps descended on the left. I made no attempt to close the door, but began hurrying down.

Rock plants, ferns, cacti, grew upon the wall. Moonlight painted a sharp angle of shadow upon the steps. I came to a bend and turned. The steps below were completely in shadow. I began to grope my way down.

And at the third step I pulled up sharply and listened.

Someone had come out onto the terrace above: he was following me!

I had yet to find my way to the sea; but having won freedom from the house of Dr. Fu Manchu and gained the clean free air, it would be a dead man that this tracker carried back again. And unless he shot me down before coming to close quarters, there would be a classic struggle at some point between this and the beach. . . .

The insidious atmosphere of that secret place, as I realised now, had taken its toll of my spirit. But under the stars—free—free from that ghastly thralldom, my cold hatred of the Chinese doctor and of all his works and his creatures surged back upon me chokingly.

Fleurette!

The dark schemes of Fah Lo Suee could never save her. One hope only I had, and I included Fleurette in it optimistically, for no word of love had ever passed between us.

I must find Nayland Smith—surround this scorpion's nest—and put an end to the menace which threatened the peace of the world.

Courage came to me: I felt capable of facing even Dr. Fu Manchu himself.

And throughout this time I had been groping my way down dark steps; and now I came to yet another bend. Thus far I had made no sound. I stood still, listening: and clearly I heard it . . . footsteps following me.

It was eerie—uncanny.

Whomever it might be, the Chinese doctor or one of his creatures, why had he not challenged me—why this silent pursuit? I could only suppose that a trap awaited me.]

Someone was on guard at the foot of the stairs, and the one who followed was content to make sure that I did not double back.

Some impassable obstacle lay between me and the beach. It might be—and the thought turned my heart cold—such an obstacle as I had once met with in the radio research room!

In that event, I should be trapped.

I pulled up, groping upon the wall beside the steps. Some kind of creeping plant grew there in profusion, indeterminable in the darkness. I pulled it aside and craned over, looking down.

Below, as I dimly saw, was a sheer descent of a hundred feet or more. These steps were built around the face of the gorge. Lacking ropes, there was no other means of reaching the beach.

This discovery determined my course.

Unknown dangers were ahead, but a definite enemy was on my trail. Even now, as I stood there listening, I could hear him cautiously descending, step by step.

He exercised great precaution, but in the silence of the night, nevertheless, I could detect his movements. I must deal with him first. Moreover, as I recognised, I must deal with him speedily. This stealthy pursuit was taking toll of my nerves.

I pictured to myself Dr. Fu Manchu, some strange death in his hand, stalking me—the man who had presumed to trick him—cat-like, cruel, and awaiting his own moment to spring.

I looked about me: my eyes were becoming used to semi-darkness. I taxed my brain for some scheme of dealing with the tracker.

And as I began again to grope my way down the steps and came to another bend, a possible plan presented itself. The next flight, branching away at a sharp angle, was palely lighted by the moon. A sharp shadow-belt cut anglewise across the first three steps.

Making as little noise as possible, I hauled myself up on the parapet; not without injury, for a spiny kind of cactus grew there. But I finally reached the desired position, squatting in dense shadow.

With the advantage which this take-off gave me, I aimed to wait until my follower reached the bend, and then to spring upon his back and hurl him down the steps, trusting to break his neck and to save my own. . . .

I had no more than poised myself for the spring when I heard him on the last step of the shadowy stairs.

He paused for a long time—I could hear him breathing. I clenched my fists and prepared to spring. . . . He took a pace forward.

For one instant I saw his silhouette against the light.

"My God!" I cried. *"You!"*

It was *Nayland Smith!*

CHAPTER THIRTIETH

NAYLAND SMITH

"THANK God I found you, Sterling," said Nayland Smith when the first shock of that meeting was over. "It's a break-neck job in the dark, but I think we should be wise to put a greater distance between ourselves and the house. Do you know the way?"

"No."

"I do, from here. I discovered it to-night. There are five more flights of stone steps and then a narrow path—a mere goat track on the edge of a precipice. It ultimately leads one down to the beach. There may be another way, but I don't know it."

"But," said I, as we began to grope our way downward, "when we get to the beach?"

"I have a boat lying off, waiting for me. We have a lot to tell each other, but let's make some headway before we talk."

And so in silence we pursued our way, presently coming to the track of which Nayland Smith had spoken, truly perilous navigation in the darkness; a false step would have precipitated one into an apparently bottomless gorge.

Willy-nilly, I began listening again for that eerie recall note which I was always expecting to hear, wondering what would happen if it came and I did not obey—and what steps would be taken in the awful house of Dr. Fu Manchu.

Some parts of the path were touched my moonlight, and here we proceeded with greater confidence. But when it lay, as it often did, in impenetrable shadow overhung by great outjutting masses of rock, it was necessary to test every foot of the way before trusting one's weight to it.

At a very easy gradient the path sloped downward until, at the end of twenty minutes' stumbling and scrambling, it ended in a narrow cutting between two huge boulders. Far ahead, framed in their giant blackness, I saw the moon glittering on the sea, and white-fringed waves gently lapping the shore.

Clear of the cutting—which Nayland Smith appeared to distrust—he dropped down upon a pebbly slope.

"Phew!" he exclaimed. "One of the strangest experiences of a not uneventful life!"

I dropped down beside him; nervous excitement and physical exertion had temporarily exhausted me.

"There's definitely no time to waste," he went on, speaking very rapidly. "It might be wiser to return to the boat. But a few minutes' rest is acceptable, and I doubt if they could overtake us now. Bring me up to date, Sterling, from the time you left Quinto's restaurant. I have interviewed the people there, and your movements as reported, prior to the moment when you drove away in Petrie's car, struck me as curious. You crossed and spoke to a man who was standing on the opposite side of the street. Why?"

"I had seen one of the dacoits watching me, and I wanted to find out which way he had gone."

"Ah! and did you find out?"

"Yes."

"Good. Go ahead, Sterling, and be as concise as you can."

Whereupon I told him, endeavouring to omit nothing, all that had taken place. Frankly, I did not expect to be believed, but Nayland Smith, who in the darkness was busily loading his pipe, never once interrupted me until I came to the incident where, escaping from the worm-man, I had turned to find Fleurette in the room.

"Who is this girl?" he rapped; "and were did you meet her?"

"Perhaps I should have mentioned the incident before, Sir Denis," I replied, "but naturally I did not believe it to have any connection with this ghastly business. I met her on the beach, out there."

And I told him as shortly as possible of my first meeting with Fleurette.

"Describe her very carefully," he directed tersely.

I did so in loving detail.

"You say she had violet eyes?"

"They appear sometimes very dark violet; sometimes I have thought they were blue."

"Good. Go on with the story."

I went on; telling him of Fah Lo Suee's intervention and of how she had tricked the Japanese surgeon; of my second interview with Dr. Fu Manchu, and even of the dream which

I had had. Then, of Fah Lo Suee's midnight visit, outlining what she had told me. Finally, I described my escape, and the opium sleep of Dr. Fu Manchu. Sir Denis had lighted his pipe and now was smoking furiously.

"Amazing, Sterling," he commented. "You seem actually to have seen what took place in Berlin. You have correctly described my movements up to the time that I reached the house of Professor Krus. This can have been no ordinary dream. It is possible that his girl possesses a gift of clairvoyance which Dr. Fu Manchu uses. And it rather appears that, given suitable circumstances, her visions, or whatever we should term them, are communicated to your own brain. Have you ever dreamed of her before?"

"Yes," I replied, my heart giving a sudden leap. "I fell asleep at the villa Jasmin shortly after our first meeting, and dreamed that I saw her and Dr. Fu Manchu—whom I had never met at the time—riding in a purple cloud which was swooping down upon a city . . . I thought, New York."

"Ah!" rapped Nayland Smith. "My theory was right. There was once another woman, Sterling, who, under hypnotic direction from Dr. Fu Manchu, possessed somewhat similar gifts. The doctor is probably the most accomplished hypnotist in the world. Many of his discoveries are undoubtedly due to his employment of these powers. And it would seen that there is some mental affinity between this girl's brain and your own."

My heart beat faster as he spoke the words.

"But as to what happened in Berlin: I arrived to find the Professor's laboratory in flames!"

"What!"

"The origin of the fire could not be traced. Incendiarism was suspected by the police. Briefly, the place was burned to a shell, in spite of the efforts of the fire brigade. . . . It is feared that the Professor was trapped in the flames."

"Dead?"

"At the time of my hurried departure, the heat remained too great for any examination of the ruins. But from the moment that Dr. Krus was seen to enter his laboratory, no one attached to his household ever saw him again."

"Good heavens!"

I groaned, "the very gods seem to have been fighting against poor Petrie."

"The gods?" Nayland Smith echoed grimly.

"The gods of China—Fu Manchu's China. . . ."

"Whatever do you mean, Sir Denis?"

"The burglary at Sir Manston Rorke's," he rapped, "Sir Manston's sudden death—the fire at Professor Krus's laboratory, and his disappearance: these things are no more coincidences than Fah Lo Suee's visit to the hospital where Petrie lay. Then—something else, which I am going to tell you."

He rested his hand upon my knee and went on rapidly:

"I dashed back to the aerodrome: there was nothing more I could do in Berlin. There came a series of unaccountable delays—none of which I could trace to its source. But they were deliberate, Sterling, they were deliberate. Someone was interested in hindering my return. However, ultimately I got away. It was late in the afternoon before I reached the hospital. I had had the news—about Petrie—when I landed, of course.

He stopped for a moment, and I could tell he was clenching his pipe very tightly between his teeth; then:

"As is the custom," he went on, "in cases of pestilence in a hot climate, they had. . . buried him."

I reached out and squeezed his shoulder.

"It hit *me* very hard, too," I said.

"I know it did. There is a long bill against Dr. Fu Manchu, but you don't know all yet. You see, the history of this brilliant Chinese horror is known to me in considerable detail. Although I didn't doubt your word when you assured me that Fah Lo Suee had not touched Petrie in the hospital, you may recall that I questioned you very closely as to where she was sitting during the greater part of her visit?"

"I do."

"Well!" He paused, taking his pipe from between his teeth and staring at me in the darkness. "She had brought something—probably hidden in a pocket inside her cloak—"

"You mean—"

"I mean that she *succeeded* in the purpose of her visit. Yes, Sterling! Oh, no blame attaches to you. That hell-cat is nearly as brilliant an illusionist as her illustrious father. Briefly, when Cartier and Brisson gave me a detailed account of the symptoms which had preceded the end—I was not satisfied,"

"Not satisfied of what?"

"You shall hear."

He paused for a moment and grasped my arm.

"Listen!"

We sat there, both listening intently.

"What did you think you heard?" I whispered.

"I am not certain that I heard anything; but it may have been a vague movement on the path. Are you armed?"

"No."

"I am. If I give the word—run for it. I'll bring up the rear. The boat is hidden just under the headland. They will pull in, and we can wade out to them."

CHAPTER THIRTY-FIRST

FU MANCHU'S ARMY

"Your disappearance on the road from Monte Carlo," Nayland Smith went on, "puzzled me extraordinarily. The guiding hand behind this business had ceased to be a matter of speculation: I knew that we were dealing with Dr. Fu Manchu. But where you belonged in the scheme was not clear to me. I had urgent personal work to do, necessitating the bringing of pressure to bear on the French authorities. Therefore, I delegated to a local chief of police the task of tracing your movements step by step, on the night of your disappearance.

"This was undertaken with that admirable thoroughness which characterises police work here, and involves a house-to-house inquiry along many miles of the Corniche road. In the meantime, working unremittingly, I had secured the powers which I sought. . . . Petrie's grave—a very hurried one—was reopened. . . ."

"What!"

"Yes; it was a pretty ghastly task. In order to perform it in secrecy we had to close the place and post police upon the roads approaching it. However, it was accomplished at last, and the common coffin in which the interment had taken place was hauled up and laid upon the earth."

"My God!" I groaned.

"I have undertaken some unpleasant duties, Sterling, but the sound of the screws being extracted and the thought that presently——"

He broke off and sat silent for a while.

"It was done at last," he went on, "and I think I came nearer to fainting than I have ever been in my life. Not from horror, not from sorrow; but because my theory—my eleventh-hour hope—had proven to have a substratum of fact."

"What do you mean, Sir Denis?"

"I mean that Petrie was not in the coffin!"

"Not in the coffin! . . . It was empty?"

"Not at all." He laughed grimly. "It contained a body right

enough. The body of a Burman. The mark of Kali was on his brow—and he had died from a shot wound in the stomach."

"Good heavens! The dacoit who——"

"Exactly, Sterling! Your late friend of the Villa Jasmin, beyond doubt. You will observe that Dr. Fu Manchu finds uses for his servants—dead, as well as living!"

"But this is astounding! What does it mean?"

Quite a long time elapsed before Sir Denis replied:

"I don't dare to hope that it means what I wish it to mean," he said; "but—Petrie was not buried."

I was literally breathless with astonishment, but at last:

"Whenever can so amazing a substitution have taken place?" I asked.

"The very question to which I next applied myself," Nayland Smith replied. "Half an hour's inquiry established the facts. The little mortuary, which, I believe, you have visited, is not guarded. And his body, hastily encased, as I have indicated, lay there throughout the night. The mortuary is a lonely building, as you may remember. For Dr. Fu Manchu's agents such a substitution was a simple matter."

"What do you think?" I broke in.

"I don't dare tell you what I think—or hope. But Dr. Fu Manchu is the greatest physician the world has ever known. Come on! Let's establish contact with the police boat."

He stood up and began to walk rapidly down to the beach. We had about reached the spot where first I had set eyes upon Fleurette, when a boat with two rowers and two men in the stern shot out from shadow into moonlight and was pulled in towards us.

Sir Denis suddenly raised his arm, signalling that they should go about.

I watched the boat swing round and saw it melt again into the shadows from which it had come. I met the glance of eyes steely in the moonlight.

"An idea has occurred to me," said Sir Denis.

I thought that he watched me strangely.

"If it concerns myself," I replied, "count on me for anything."

"Good man!"

He clapped his hand on my shoulder.

"Before I mention it, I must bring you up to date. Move

back into the shadow."

We walked up the beach, and then:

"I checked up on the police reports," he went on. "That dealing with Ste Claire was the only one which I regarded as unsatisfactory. Ste Claire, as you probably know, was formerly an extensive monastery; in fact, many of the vineyards in this neighbourhood formerly yielded their produce to the Father Abbot. When the community dispersed, it came into the possession of some noble family whose name I have forgotten. The point of interest and the point which attracted me was this:

"The place is built on a steep hillside, opening into a deep cleft which we have just negotiated, rather less than a mile in length. The chief building, now known as a villa, but reconstruction of the former monastery, is surrounded by one or two other buildings—and there is a little straggling street. It has been the property for the last fifteen years of a certain wealthy Argentine gentleman, regarding whose history I have set inquiries on foot.

"More recently, the lease was taken over by one Mahdi Bey, of whom I have been able to learn very little—except that he practised as a physician in Alexandria at one time, and is evidently a man of great wealth. He it was who closed Ste Claire to the public. However, the police in the course of their inquiries paid a domiciliary visit some time during yesterday afternoon. They were received by a majordomo who apologised for the absence of his master, who is apparently in Paris.

"They were shown over the villa and the adjoining houses, occupied now, I gather, by dependents of the Bey. No information was obtained upon the subject of your disappearance.

"But, in glancing through the police report, bearing in mind that I was definitely looking for a place occupied by Dr. Fu Manchu, a process of elimination showed me that of all the establishments visited, Ste Claire alone remained suspect.

"The Argentine owner had built a number of remarkable forcing houses. The police, under my directions and unaware of the reasons for them, were ostensibly searching for an escaped criminal, which enabled them tactfully to explore the various villas en route. I noted in their report that they had merely glanced into these houses, nor did I come upon any account of the enormous wine cellars, enlargements of natural caves, which, I was informed, lay below the former monastery.

"The character and extent of Dr. Fu Manchu's new campaign dawned upon me suddenly, Sterling. I wonder if it has dawned upon you?"

"I'm afraid it hasn't," I confessed. "I have alternated between the belief that I was dead and the belief that I was delirious almost throughout the time that I have been in that house. But knowing now that what I saw was not phantasy, I am still in doubt, I must confess, as to the nature of this 'war' which threatens."

"It's nature is painfully clear," Nayland Smith rapped. "Somewhere in this place there are thousands—perhaps millions—of those damnable flies! The deaths of which we know were merely experimental. The cases were watched secretly, with great interest, by Dr. Fu Manchu or his immediate agents. It was the duty of one of his servants—probably a Burman—to release one of these flies in the neighbourhood of the selected victim. I have learned that they seek shadow during the daytime, and operate at dusk and in artificial light. Directly there was presumptive evidence that the fly had bitten the selected subject, it was the duty of Fu Manchu's servant to place a spray of this fly-catching plant—the name of which I don't know—where it would attract the fly.

"To make assurance doubly sure, the seductive leaves were sprayed with human blood! Vegetable fly-papers, Sterling—nothing less!"

"My God! It's plain enough to me now."

"Such experiments have apparently been carried out all over the world.

"That Dr. Fu Manchu—or the si-Fan, which is the same thing—has international agents, I know for a fact. This means that collections of these flies, which have been specially bred to carry the new plague and to spread it, exist at unknown centres in various parts of Europe, Asia, Africa and Australia—also, doubtless, in the Continent of America.

"Of all those seeking it, Petrie alone discovered a treatment which promised to be successful! Dr. Fu Manchu's allies would of course be inoculated against the plague. But do you see, Sterling, do you see what Petrie did, and why he stood in the Chinaman's way?"

I hesitated. I was beginning to grasp the truth, but before I could reply:

"The formula for '654' would have been broadcast to the medical authorities of the world, in the event of a general outbreak. This would have shattered Fu Manchu's army."

"Fu Manchu's army?"

"An army, Sterling, bred and trained to depopulate the white world! An army of *flies*—carrying the germ of a new plague; a plague for which medical science knows no remedy!"

I was awed, silenced.

"Police manned a boat in the neighbouring bay," Nayland Smith went on; "I distrusted the sound of a motor. They told me that there was a little beach attached to Ste Claire. And in this again I recognised such a spot as Fu Manchu would have chosen.

"At dusk, I waded ashore, ordering the boat to lie off in the shadow of the cliff. I was acting unofficially; I was outside the law if I should be wrong; but I had left a sealed envelope with the Chief of Police, telling him upon what evidence I had acted—if I should not return.

"I walked up the strip of sand, reached the pebbles, and had just come to the big boulders, when I saw a speedboat heading in! I took cover behind one of the boulders and waited.

"It came right in. The police had orders not to show themselves unless they received a prearranged signal. A man waded ashore through the shallow water, and the boat immediately set out again, and soon had disappeared around the headland.

"I watched him come through the gap between the boulders. He was wearing gum boots and went very silently. But I was rubber-shod, and could go silently too. I followed him. It was a difficult business, because of the fact that part of the path, more then than now, wad bathed in moonlight. But it evidently never occurred to the man to look back.

"In this way, unconsciously he led me to the foot of the steps, and I followed him, flight by flight, to the top. I was craning over the parapet when he opened he door; but, nevertheless, it took me nearly ten minutes to find how it worked."

"Do you mean to say that you broke into that house alone?"

"Yes. It was a one-man job: two would have bungled it."

I could find no words with which to reply. It was a privilege merely to listen to a man at once so clear-headed and so fearless.

"I was first attracted," he went on, "by the long corridor at the end of which a green light burned. There was not a sound in the place, and so I explored this corridor first. I discovered a sliding door operated by one of the button controls, and I opened it."

He paused—laughing shortly.

"I asked you to describe Fleurette particularly," he went on, "because my first investigation led me to Fleurette's bedroom!

"Yes, Sterling, the palace of the Sleeping Beauty. I could see her in the reflected moonlight, one arm thrown over her head, and her face turned towards the window. Your description was that of an artist. I agree with you; she is beautiful. Yet it wasn't her beauty which pulled me up, nor even the knowledge that I had made a mistake: it was something else."

"What?" I asked eagerly.

"I knew her, Sterling! Yes! I know who she is, this mystery girl who has taken such a hold upon you."

"But, Sir Denis, do you mean . . ."

"I understand your eagerness, and you shall hear everything later. I was anxious to learn the colour of her eyes. You see, they were closed; she was asleep. I retired without disturbing her. I next descended the stairs . . ."

"Good God! I wish I had your nerve!"

"Really, I had very little to fear."

"You may think so—but please go on, Sir Denis."

"My guide, of course, had disappeared, but I found a square space with corridors opening right and left. The trail of wet rubber boots gave me the clue. The imprint of fingers on a panel three feet from the floor enabled me to open the door. I found myself in that insane laboratory—"

"Insane is the word," I murmured.

"It was empty. It was permeated by a dim violet light. And as I entered—the door closed! I was particularly intrigued by a piece of mechanism resembling an ancient Egyptian harp."

"I noticed it, also."

"I determined to investigate more closely, but there was a black mark on the floor surrounding the table on which this piece of mechanism stood..."

"Say no more, Sir Denis! I have had the same experience."

"Oh! Is that so? This rather checked me. I observed that such a mark ran entirely around the laboratory close to the wall: you may have failed to notice this? And I can only suppose that this system of checking intruders has been disconnected in relation to the doors because the unknown man who had unwittingly acted as my guide was expected.

"As the idea flashed across my mind, I had no more than time to duck when the man in question came out!

"A panel slid open on the left-hand wall, and a Chinaman, still wearing wet gum boots, closed the door behind him, crossed the laboratory, opened another door on the farther side, and disappeared.

"I waited for a while, listening to a sort of throbbing which alone disturbed the silence, and then I too ventured to open that door. Do you know what I found?"

"I can guess."

"I found myself face to face with Dr. Fu Manchu...."

Chapter Thiry-second

RECALL

"For the last twenty years, Sterling, I have prayed for an opportunity to rid the world of this monster. My automatic was raised; I could have shot him where he sat. He hadn't a chance in a million. You know the room? I saw you come out of it.

"He was seated in that throne-like chair behind the big table, and his marmoset, that wizened little creature which I haven't seen for fifteen years, was asleep on his shoulder. The reek told me the story—Dr. Fu Manchu has always been addicted to opium. He was asleep."

"I know!" I groaned.

"You evidently conquered the same temptation. But I am still wondering if we are right. When I decided that I couldn't shoot him as he slept, I cursed my own ridiculous prejudices. A hundred, perhaps a thousand deaths lay at this man's door—yet, it was impossible.

"I looked at him, seated there, and his crimes made a sort of bloody mountain behind him. I have never known so keen a temptation in my life, and I have never felt so deeply a self-contempt in resisting one.

"Suddenly I observed a door on the right of his chair, and I knew that Dr. Fu Manchu as an adversary might be disregarded for the moment. There was a button beside this door. I opened it and saw a second, a pace beyond. I opened this also.

"And I found myself looking into a tropical jungle! At which moment the marmoset awakened, uttered its shrill, whistling cry, and whirled past me, disappearing among the trees in that misty place. . . .

"I turned, my automatic raised, watching Fu Manchu. He didn't move. I ventured to take a step into that huge glass-house. I looked all about me, at the banks of flowers, and up into the palm-tops. Further exploration would be madness, I thought. I had achieved my purpose.

"My next step was to get out, undetected, as I had got in. I had just turned, intent upon the idea of creeping back into the room of Fu Manchu, when I heard a sound of soft footsteps up among the palm-tops.

"This hastened my action. Without attempting to close the communicating doors, I crept back across the carpet of the study and out into the big laboratory. I hesitated there for a moment; but finally I closed the door. I stood still, listening.

"But apart from the throbbing, which apparently never ceased, there was no movement to be perceived.

"Avoiding the black marks, I set out, moving rapidly to the right. As I neared the wall at the end of that huge place, which, as you have probably realised, is built entirely underground, an unpleasant fact dawned upon me.

"I could not remember at which point I had entered! And the blank spaces on the wall offered no clue.

"I was making tentative experiments when I heard someone come out from Dr. Fu Manchu's study. . . . I dived to cover.

"The black marks upon the floor I knew I must avoid, and I had just found a hiding place when someone began to walk along the laboratory towards me! Beyond the fact that he wore white overalls I had no means, from the position which I occupied, of identifying him.

"I saw this figure go up to a recess between two tall cases. The walls being divided into panels by a sort of metal beading, I was determined to make no mistake, and I crept forward in order to watch more closely.

"In my eagerness, I allowed one foot to intrude upon a black mark surrounding an instrument resembling a searchlight. The shock which ran up my leg brought me flatly to the floor. I cursed under my breath and lay there prone.

"When I ventured to look up, the man in the white overalls had disappeared.

"The wall displayed its former even surface. But I knew where the door was, and I knew that I could open it by pressing hard three feet from the floor.

"Evidently, I had not been detected. I allowed fifty of sixty seconds to elapse, and then, in turn, I opened the door. I saw a flight of stairs ahead of me, and recognised them for those which I had descended. As I crept cautiously onto the first step, the door closed behind me.

"I waited, listening.

"Very faintly, for these mechanisms are beautifully adjusted, I heard a door above being opened. I remembered it: it was the door by which I had come in.

"The rest, Sterling, you know. An unknown man, for I had never had a glimpse of your face, and your attire was unfamiliar, was moving somewhere between me and the shore which I desired to reach."

He stopped, and:

"What's that?" he whispered.

An elfin note, audible above the faint sound of the sea, had reached my ears, as it had reached his.

"Someone is calling me," I said, "my absence has been noted."

Chapter Thirty-third

I OBEY

I OFTEN remember the silence which fell between us at that moment. I thought I knew what Nayland Smith was thinking—perhaps because I was thinking the same myself.

"It's asking a lot, Sterling," he said at last. "I have a good old-fashioned police whistle in my pocket, and there's a police boat standing by. But I told you a while ago that an idea had occurred to me."

Remembering what Sir Denis had done that night, how, alone, he had penetrated to this secret stronghold of Dr. Fu Manchu, I set my course, and when next he spoke, I was glad I had done so. His idea was mine!

"What's the mechanism?" he asked sharply. "You said, I think, it was a ring?"

I slipped the ring from my finger and handed it to him. Already I saw his plan, and my part in it. But I was full out for the rôle he had allotted to me, although I doubted seriously if I should live to see it through.

He stood up, and silhouetted against the skyline I saw him tugging at the lobe of his ear; then:

"I have no right to ask what I am going to ask, Sterling," he began.

"I had thought of it already," I interrupted. "I am game. This is a fight to a finish, and you are in charge, Sir Denis. Just give me my orders."

He reached out and grasped my shoulder.

"Unless my calculations are wildly at fault, Sterling, Petrie is up there, in that house—dead or alive—I don't know which. But I *want* to know, before I make my next move."

Dimly I saw him slip the adjustable ring upon his finger, and then:

"I will come back to the door," he said. "The whistle will be audible from that point to the men in the boat. Make straight for the dial—the one Herman Trenck explained to you. The curse is, you don't know Morse."

"I have the code in my pocket."

"It isn't easy to work from printed instructions," he rapped back. "What I have in mind is this: If you are not suspected, just call your number. What is it?"

"103," I replied. "It's on the ring."

"Good enough. Failing such a message within a period of ten minutes, I shall raid the house at once: I have it covered."

"That's quite clear, Sir Denis."

"In the event of your giving me the O.K., I shall wait for the Morse message—but I shall wait only half an hour. The plain call again will tell me. Try to find out if Petrie is there—and if he is alive or dead. One sustained note to mean that he is there, but dead: two short ones, that he is there, but alive."

And as he spoke he was urging me forward, up the path, grasping my arm and firing me with that vital enthusiasm of which he had such an abundant store.

"There may be difficulties about the missing ring," I suggested.

"A point I had been considering," he returned. "Have you any suggestions? You know the place better than I do. Where might you have lost it?—where would it be difficult to find?"

"Among the aquatic plants," I replied; "some of them grow in deep water."

"Good!" he snapped. "Let it be the aquatic plants. Do your damnedest in the next half hour to find old Petrie; then run for it. I shall be waiting for you. . . ."

We proceeded now in silence, groping our way along that perilous path. Once again I found myself listening for that high, strange call note; but it never came.

We mounted the many stone steps and reached the terrace. I saw a dim light shining out upon the pavement. The door was open.

"I left it open," said Nayland Smith, in a low voice. "I'll stay here. Send me the signal as soon as you are assured of your own safety." He grasped my hand hard. "Good luck! In half an hour . . ."

As I reached the open door and realised that I was about to enter again the house of Dr. Fu Manchu, a qualm touched me, for which I hope I may be forgiven.

It passed as swiftly as it came. It was succeeded by a feeling of shame, by a memory of what Sir Denis had done that night.

I stepped inside, looking swiftly right and left. The green lamp still burned at the end of the long corridor. And remembering who was sleeping there, I watched it lingeringly. Then I looked down the stairs, and I stood still, listening.

No one was in sight, and there was not a sound audible. I pressed my finger upon the control button twice; the door closed. Then I began to descend the stairs.

Reaching the foot, I groped with my hand upon the panel which I knew concealed the door. Presently it responded, and bathed in that dim violet light I saw the great laboratory ahead of me.

It was empty.

I stepped forward—and the door closed behind me. I began to cross the rubber-covered floor, heading for Dr. Fu Manchu's study.

This was the supreme moment.

I was disposed to think that it was he, awakening, who had summoned me. I lost count of time as I stood before that blank wall, charging myself with cowardice, flogging my failing courage.

At last I took the plunge . . . and the door opened.

He sat there like the mummy of Seti the First, upright on his throne. Opium still held him in its grasp. A jungle smell was mingling now with the poppy fumes, for the doors leading into the great palm house remained open. The marmoset was crouching on that yellow shoulder, not did he stir as I went tiptoe across the carpet.

So far, I was safe.

I closed the first door, hurried to the second, and closed that also. I hadn't the courage to pause to adjust the gauge. I ran through the place, ducking to avoid overhanging branches, many of them flower-laden. And coming to the next door I pulled up and listened.

There was no pursuit.

From thence onward, I adjusted all the gauges, until, opening the final door, I stepped into the botanical research room, from which I had set out upon that memorable pilgrimage. . . .

Stock still I pulled up on the threshold.

Fleurette stood there watching me!

Chapter Thirty-fourth

DERCETO

"Fleurette!" I exclaimed.

She wore a silk wrap over night attire; sandals on her slim brown feet. She watched me gravely.

"Fleurette! Who called me?"

"*I* called you."

"But"—I was astounded—"how did you know—?"

"I know most of the things that go on here," she returned calmly.

I moved nearer to her and looked at the dial close to which she was standing. My number—103—was registered upon it; and:

"How often did you call me?" I asked.

"Twice."

Her unmoving regard, in which there was an unpleasant question, began to disturb me.

My conception of her as a victim of the powerful and evil man who sought to destroy white civilisation was entirely self-created. I remembered that she had been reared in this atmosphere from birth; and conscious of an unpleasant chill I realised that she, whom I had regarded as a partner in misfortune, an ally, might prove to be the means of my unmasking. I decided to be diplomatic.

"Yes—of course you called me twice," I replied.

The second call would have been taken by Nayland Smith! How would he have read it?

"Why didn't you come?" she asked. "Where were you?"

Her beautiful eyes were fixed upon me with a regard which I found almost terrifying. An hour before, an instant before, I would have met her gaze gladly, happily; but now—I wondered.

After all, the romance between this girl and myself existed only in my own imagination. It was built upon nothing but a stairs of sand—her remarkable beauty. She was, as Dr. Fu Manchu had said, that most rare jewel—a perfect woman.

But I—I was far removed from a perfect man. Vanity had

blinded me. She belonged body and soul to the group surrounding the Chinese doctor. And perhaps it was no more than poetic justice that she and none of the others should expose me.

"I was in the palm house. I had never seen such trees. And, as you know, I am a botanist."

"But you were a long time coming" she insisted. "You are sure you were alone?"

As if a black cloud had lifted, I saw—or dared to hope that I saw—the truth in the regard of those sunset violet eyes. Or was it vanity, self-delusion, again? But, moving nearer to her:

"Alone!" I echoed. "Who could be with me at this hour of the night?"

And now at last, unfalteringly, I looked into her eyes.

"The Princess is very beautiful," she said, in a low voice.

"The Princess?"

I had no idea at the moment to whom she referred; but chaotically, delightfully, it was as I had dared to hope!

My sudden wild passion for this exquisite, unattainable girl had not failed utterly of its objective. She was sufficiently interested to be jealous! And now, watching her, it dawned upon me to whom she referred.

"Do you mean Fah Lo Suee?"

She made a little grimace and turned aside.

"I wondered why you had joined us," she murmured. "If she is Fah Lo Suee to you—I know. I was merely curious. Goodnight."

"Fleurette!" I cried. "Fleurette!"

She turned and walked away.

She did not look back.

I sprang forward, threw my arms around her and held her. Even so, she did not look back; she merely stood still. But my doubts, my diffidence, were gone: my heart was singing....

She had given me that age-old sign which is woman's prerogative. The next move was mine. Revelation was so sudden, so wholly unexpected, that it swept me out of myself. To my shame I confess that, although vast issues hung in the balance, establishment of an understanding with Fleurette was the only thing in life at which at that moment I aimed.

I had fallen irrevocably in love with her at first sight.

Recognition of the fact that she was interested produced a state of mind little short of delirium.

"Fleurette!" I said, holding her tightly and bending close to her averted head, "that woman you call the Princess I call Fah Lo Suee because I was told that that was her name: I know her by no other. She means nothing more to me than I thought I meant to you. I had seen her once only in my life before I came here...."

I checked my words: I had been on the point of saying too much. Fah Lo Suee had told me, "She has Eastern blood in her, and to Eastern women love comes suddenly." Of all that Fu Manchu's daughter had revealed, this alone I was disposed to believe.

Fleurette turned quickly and looked up at me.

Nothing, I think, short of sudden death could have checked me then.

Raising my left hand to her shoulder, I twisted her about, so that I had her clasped in my arms. And stooping to those delicious, tremulous lips, I kissed her until we both were breathless.

One instantaneous moment there was of rebellion, and then such exquisite surrender that when presently she buried her lovely little head in my shoulder, so that I could feel her heart beating, I think there was in the whole world no happier man than I.

There was an old tradition in my family of which my mother had told me—that we were slow to hate but quick to love. Fleurette and I were well met. I doubted if mutual love had ever been unmasked under circumstances more peculiar....

What she told me did not fully register at the time, nor, perhaps, were my questions those which Nayland Smith would have selected. Nevertheless, I learned much respecting this queer household of Dr. Fu Manchu.

I began to realise the greatness of the menace which he represented; because, through Fleurette, the knowledge came to me that many who served him loved him.

Perhaps, among the lower orders of his strange entourage, fear was his sceptre. But, as I gathered—and I dared not speak a word to shatter that ideal—Fleurette's sentiments were those of profound respect.

Mahdi Bey, her guardian, had taught her to look upon the

Chinese doctor as upon a man supreme among men. It was an honourable fate to be chosen by the Prince who one day would rule the world—be its Emperor. . . .

Fleurette had received a remarkable education, embracing the icy peaks of sexless philosophy to which she had been taught to look up in a Buddhist monastery in the north of China to the material feminism of a famous English school. Yet she remained completely human; for she lay in my arms whispering those replies to my eager questions!

She had not been denied the companionship of men, but always, in whichever part of the world she had chanced to find herself, had been constantly accompanied and never left alone in the society of others for more than those few minutes which Western social custom demands. There were girls of good family and of her own age in some of the larger establishments. But as to how they came to be there I was unable to form any idea: apparently they had been selected purely as companions for Fleurette. . . .

Fah Lo Suee, to whom she referred as "the Princess," she distrusted, but evidently feared. Fah Lo Suee, it seemed, had partisans of her own among the many leaders of this mysterious movement which Fleurette called the Si-Fan. Regarding the political side of the organisation, she clearly knew next to nothing. That a great war was pending in which Dr. Fu Manchu expected to overthrow all opposition, she was aware: the character of this war she did not seem even to suspect.

Without recourse to the Ericksen telephone, Dr. Fu Manchu was able to call her, she told me—and she was compelled to go to him.

He sometimes made her look into a disk in which strange images appeared. . . .

There were times—of which to-night was an instance—when his influence dropped from her—unaccountably; when she questioned the meaning of her life—and followed her own impulses. Those times, beyond doubt, although I did not tell her so, corresponded to the doctor's bouts of opium-smoking.

"Why did you tell me to think of you as Derceto?"

Fleurette laughed, but not happily.

"Because you found me on the shore—and to love me meant destruction. . . ."

During the greater part of the telling of her strange story, she had lain in my arms—and there had been silent intervals. But at last I seemed to hear the crisp voice of Sir Denis demanding that I should put duty first. . . .

CHAPTER THIRTY-FIFTH

THE SECTION DOORS

"He is here," said Fleurette. "Leave the door open, I will call if anyone comes."

At that moment, as I crossed the threshold into a small white bedroom, even Fleurette was forgotten. Petrie, pale as I had never seen him, his hair blanched as by the brushes of ten years, lay there, watching me!

There was a dull flush on his forehead where the Purple Shadow had been.

"Petrie, old man!" I whispered—"Petrie! . . . Thank God!"

Had I not met other dead men in the house of Dr. Fu Manchu, this must have been a moment of stupefaction. . . .

He nodded weakly and smiled—the same patient smile which I knew, even extending his hand, which I grasped between both my own.

"This," I said, "is a miracle."

"I agree." His voice was very low. "I must have the constitution of a rattlesnake, Sterling. For I have not only survived the new plague—but an injection of the preparation known as 'Fu Manchu *katalepsis*' or briefly—'*F. katalepsis.*'"

"You *know* all this?"

"Yes; I even knew that you were here. But this is no time—"

He stopped, breathlessly, and I realised how weak he was.

"Don't tire yourself," I urged, grasping his shoulder. "Sir Denis is waiting for the news."

"Nayland Smith!" His eyes lighted up. "*He* is here?"

"Yes—standing by, outside."

Petrie clenched his teeth; closed his eyes. I recognised all this news had meant to him; then:

"There is only one thing you must wait for," he said. "Give me that scribbling block from the table, Sterling, and a pencil."

I did as he directed—I could see that it would be useless to object.

"Lift me up," he went on. "It's going to be a struggle to write, but it has to be done—in case—of—accidents"

"What Petrie? Why is all this necessary?"

He shook his head and began very slowly to write. Bending over him, I saw that he was writing a prescription.

The truth dawned upon me!

"'654'?"

He nodded, and went on writing. For a moment he paused, and:

"This must be circulated throughout the world," he whispered weakly—"without delay."

He glanced over what he had written, and nodded his wish to be laid back upon the pillows. This accomplished, I tore the sheet off the block, folded it, and slipped it into a pocket of my overall.

"Now, bolt!" he whispered. "Bolt for your life while there's a chance. Everything depends upon your success."

I had turned to go—when, unaided, he sat upright in bed, his eyes fixed upon the open door.

"Alan!" I heard softly.

I turned in time to see Fleurette's head hurriedly withdrawn. Someone was coming!

"Sterling! Sterling!" Petrie clutched my shoulder: his eyes were suddenly wild. "*Who* was that at the door?"

"A friend . . . you need not be afraid . . . Fleurette."

"Fleurette? My God! Am I growing delirious?"

I assisted him back onto his pillows. His manner was alarmingly strange.

"Who is she?"

"She is a victim of Dr. Fu Manchu—but we are going to get her away."

"Great heaven!" He closed his eyes. "Can it be true? Is it possible? . . . Don't wait, Sterling—go . . . go!"

Indeed I knew that I had no alternative; and squeezing his hand hard I ran out of the room.

Fleurette was standing just beyond the door, which she closed instantly upon my appearance.

"Someone is coming!" she said, in a low voice. "I think it is Companion Yamamata. Quick!—this way!"

She led me along a short passage to the head of a descending stair.

"Don't make a noise," she warned.

We crept to the bottom, my arm about her waist.

"Who is Dr. Petrie?" she whispered. "He stared at me as though he knew me; yet I have never seen him in my life before."

"He is one of my oldest friends," I replied, "and unfortunately I hadn't time to ask him. But I saw how he looked at you. Yes! he thinks he knows you."

And now I wondered what knowledge was common to Dr. Petrie and Sir Denis but not shared by me. . . .

Both had recognised Fleurette!

We turned a corner, and I saw that we stood directly under a little green lamp.

"There is your way," said Fleurette—"straight ahead. It is the only door onto the terrace."

At which moment I realised that we were standing directly outside her room!

"Darling, at last!" I exclaimed, and felt my heart leap. "Come on! Hurry! There isn't a moment to waste!"

She slipped by me and opened the door of her room. I stared at her in blank amazement—and her expression baffled me. She took my hand, pulled me gently forward . . . and then closed the door.

"Someone might see or hear us in the corridor," she said. "We are safe here. Please say good-bye to me."

"What!"

She watched me, and in the dim light of that room which Nayland Smith had described as the Palace of the Sleeping Beauty her eyes looked like violets wet with dew.

"What did you think I meant to do?" she asked softly. "I have never cared for anyone before. I suppose I am to blame because I cared for you? But although you have not told me— I know what you think of Dr. Fu Manchu . . . of all of us. You belong to the poor ignorant world. You are not really one of us. You are a spy."

I tried to take her in my arms, but she eluded me.

"Fleurette! This is madness!"

"The world is mad—Alan." That moment of hesitation before my name was a rainbow. "But you belong to it, and you must go back. I should hate to believe that you could think me capable of deserting those who have never denied me anything as long as I can remember. No, dear, I sink or swim with my friends! I am betraying them, now, by letting you go. But the moment you have reached safety—I shall warn them."

"Fleurette!"

"If I could love you without wronging them, I would—but I can't." She rested her hands on my shoulders. "Please say good-bye to me. You must hurry—you must hurry!"

Then she was in my arms, and as her lips met mine I knew that the greatest decision of my life was being asked of me.

The philosophy of a young girl, crazy though it may be, is intensely difficult to upset—and beyond doubt there was fatalism in Fleurette's blood. Yet—how could I let her go?

My heart seemed to be beating like a steam hammer. I wanted to pick her up, to carry her from that accursed house. She began to plead.

"If you force me to go," I said, "I shall get you back—follow you if necessary all around the world."

"It would be useless. I can never belong to you—I belong to *him*."

I wanted to curse the name of Fu Manchu and to curse all his works. Knowing, as I knew, that he was a devil incarnate, a monster, an evil superhuman, the monument which he stood for in the mind of this beautiful child—for she was little more—was a shrine I yearned to shatter.

Yet, for all the frenzy of passion which burned me up, enough of common sense remained to warn me that this was not the time; that such an attempt must be worse than futile.

I held her tightly, cruelly, kissing her eyes, her hair, her neck, her shoulders. I found myself on the verge of something resembling hysteria.

"I can't leave you here!" I said hoarsely; "I won't—I daren't. . . ."

A dim throbbing sound had become perceptible. This at first I had believed to be a product of excitement. But now Fleurette seemed to grow suddenly rigid in my arms. . . .

"Oh, God!" she whispered. "Quick! *quick!* Someone has found out! Listen!"

A cold chill succeeded fever.

"They are closing the section doors! Quick, for your life . . . and for *my* sake!"

It was inevitable. For *her* sake?—yes! If I should be found there...

She sprang to the control button.

The door remained closed.

She twisted about, her back pressed against the door, her arms outstretched—such terror in her eyes as I had hoped never to see there.

"All the doors have been locked as well," she whispered. "It is impossible to get out!"

"But, Fleurette!" I began.

"It's useless! It's hopeless!"

"But if I am found here?"

"It's unavoidable now."

"I could hide."

"No one can hide from him. He could force me to tell him."

Her lips began to tremble, and I groaned impotently, knowing well that I could do nothing to comfort her—that I, and I alone, was the cause of this disaster about to fall.

And through those dreadful moments, the vibration of the descending doors might faintly be detected, together with that muted gong note which I had learned to dread.

"There must be something we can do!"

"There is nothing."

Silence.

The section doors were closed.

And in that stillness I seemed to live again through years of life. I had in my pocket the means of saving the world. Useless, now! Within call, perhaps within sight from the terrace, eagerly awaiting me, were Sir Denis—freedom—sanity!

And here was I, helpless as a mouse in a trap, awaiting... what?

My heart, which had been beating so rapidly, seemed to check, to grow cold; my brain jibbed at the task.

What would be Fleurette's fate if I were discovered there, in her room, by Dr Fu Manchu?

Chapter Thirty-sixth

THE UNSULLIED MIRROR

Many minutes elapsed, every one laden with menace. Then—came that eerie note which I knew.

Fleurette stood quite still. Used now to its significance and purpose, I could detect the dots and dashes of the Morse alphabet, given at a speed which only an adept could have followed.

The sound ceased.

Fleurette dropped into an armchair, looking up at me, hopelessly.

"They are searching for you," she said, in a dull tone. "*He* doesn't know yet."

I stood there dumb of tongue and numb of brain for long moments; then ideas began to come. Someone had called me—possibly Trenck—and I had not replied. Nayland Smith had received those messages.

What had they been, and how had he construed them?

This uncertainty only added to the madness of the situation. I had an idea born of experience.

"Fleurette," I said, dropping upon my knees beside her, "why could I not have come in here as you came into my room when the alarm sounded?"

She looked at me; her face was like a beautiful mask: immutable, expressionless.

"It would be useless," she replied. "No one can lie to Dr. Fu Manchu."

And I accepted the finality of those words, for I believed it. I sprang upright. I had become aware of a faint distant vibration.

"Can the doors be raised separately?"

"Yes; any one of them can be raised alone."

I stepped across the room and pressed the control button. There was no response. I bent close to the metal, listening intently. I formed the impression, and it was a definitely horrible impression, that the control doors were being raised, one by one . . . that someone was approaching this room in which

I was trapped with Fleurette.

Beyond doubt, that ominous sound was growing nearer—growing in volume. And finally the vibration grew so great that I could feel it upon the metal against which my head rested.

I stepped back—my fists automatically clenched.

The door slid open—and Dr. Fu Manchu stood there watching me!

His majestic calm was terrible. Those long, brilliant eyes glanced aside, and I knew that he was studying Fleurette.

"Woman—the lever which a word can bend," he said softly.

He made a signal with his long-nailed hand, and two of his Chinese servants sprang in.

I stepped back debating my course.

"Heroics are uncalled for," he added, "and could profit no one."

For an instant I glanced aside at Fleurette.

Her beautiful eyes were raised to Dr. Fu Manchu, and her expression was that of a saint who sees the Holy Vision!

He spoke rapidly in Chinese and entered the room, giving me not another glance. My arms were grasped and I found myself propelled forcibly out into the corridor. The strength of these little immobile men was amazing.

The section door at the corner where those stairs terminated which led down to the radio research room was not yet fully raised: two feet or more still protruded from the slot in the ceiling which accommodated it.

Our human brains possess very definite limitations: mine had reached the edge of endurance. . . .

My memory registers a blank from the moment that I left Fleurette's room to that when I found myself seated in a hard, high-backed chair in the memorable study of Dr. Fu Manchu. Beside me, Yamamata was seated, and at the moment at which I suppose my brain began to function again—suddenly that door which I knew led into the palm house opened—and Fah Lo Suee came in.

She wore a bright green pyjama suit and was smoking a cigarette in a jade holder. One glance I received from her unfathomable eyes—but if it conveyed a message, the message failed to reach me.

She closed the door by which she had entered and dropped onto a little settee close beside it.

I glanced at Yamamata. His yellow skin was clammy with perspiration. In doing so, I noticed that the door in the archway was open—and now through the opening came Dr. Fu Manchu; silent—with cat-like dignity.

The door closed behind him.

Yamamata stood up, and so did Fah Lo Suee. It was farcically like a court of law. I wrenched my head aside, clenching my teeth. My passion for Fleurette had thrown true perspective out of focus.

This man who assumed the airs of an emperor was, in fact, a common criminal: the hangman awaited him. And then I heard his guttural voice:

"Stand up!"

All that was *me*, all that I had proudly been wont to regard as my personality, fought against this command—for a command it was. Yet—the plain fact must be recorded: I stood up. . . .

He took his seat in the dragon-carved chair behind the big table. I had kept my eyes deliberately averted, but now, in the silence which followed, I stole a glance at him. He was staring intently at Fah Lo Suee.

Suddenly he spoke:

"Companion Yamamata," he said softly, "you may go."

Yamamata sprang up; I saw his lips move, but no sound issued from them. He bowed, and opening the door which led into the big laboratory, went out, closing it behind him.

Dr. Fu Manchu began to speak rapidly in Chinese, and at the end of the first sentence Fah Lo Suee, dropping her jade cigarette holder into a bronze tray upon the floor, came down to her knees on the carpet and buried that evilly beautiful face in upraised hands—delicate ivory hands—patrician hands—shadows, etherialised, of those of her formidable father.

He continued to speak, and she shrank lower and lower, but spoke no word—uttered no sound. Then:

"Alan Sterling," he said, suddenly expressing himself in English; "the ill-directed cunning of one woman and the frailty of another have taken your fate out of my control. There are men to whom women are dangerous—you, unhappily, would seem to be one of them."

And as he spoke, the remarkable fact disclosed itself to me that, although Fah Lo Suee had spoken no word, already he *knew* her part in the conspiracy!

Good heavens! A suspicion sprang to my mind: Had Fah Lo Suee been watching? Was it *she* who had trapped me with Fleurette? Was this the end to which she had preserved my life: Fleurette's swift ruin, my own speedy death?

In its classic simplicity the scheme was Chinese, I thought.

I looked at her where she crouched, abject.

The voice—the strange, haunting voice—spoke on:

"Millions of useless lives cumber the world to-day. Among them I must now include your own. The ideal state of the Greek philosopher took no count of these. There can be no human progress without selection; and already I have chosen the nucleus of my new state. The East has grown in spirit, while the West has been building machinery. . . .

"My new state will embody the soul of the East.

"I am not ready yet for my warfare against the numerous but helpless army of the rejected. The Plagues of Egypt I hold in my hands, but I cannot control the course of the sun. . . .

"It may be that you, a gnat on the flywheel, have checked the machinery of the gods. Alone, you could never have cast a shadow upon my path: one of my own blood is the culprit."

He stuck a little gong which hung close to his hand upon the table, and the door facing me as I sat opened instantaneously and silently. One of those white-robed, image-like Chinamen entered, to whom Fu Manchu spoke briefly, rapidly.

The men bowed and went out. Fah Lo Suee's slender body seemed to diminish. She sank down until her head touched the carpet.

Dr. Fu Manchu tapped with a long nail upon the table, glancing aside at her where she crouched.

"Your Western progress, Alan Sterling," he said, "has resulted in the folly of women finding a place in the councils of state. That myth you call 'chivalry' has tied your hands and stricken you mute. In the China to which I belong—a China which is not dead but only sleeping—we use older simpler, methods. . . . We have *whips*. . . ."

The door suddenly opened again, and two powerfully built negresses entered. Their attire consisted of red-and-white striped skirts fastened by girdles about their waists.

Dr. Fu Manchu addressed them rapidly, but now, I knew, he was not speaking Chinese.

He ceased, and pointed.

One of the negresses stooped; but even as she did so, Fah Lo Suee sprang to her feet with an elastic movement, turned flaming eyes upon that dreadful figure in the high-backed chair, and then, a negress at either elbow, walked out into the palm house beyond.

I glanced at Dr. Fu Manchu, and he caught and held that glance. I realised that I was incapable of turning my eyes away.

"Alan Sterling," he said, "it is my purpose to save the world from itself. And to this end there must be a great purging. Today or tomorrow, my dream will be fulfilled. One of those bunglers acting for what is sometimes termed Western civilisation may bring about my death by violence. There is none to succeed me.... My daughter—trained for a great purpose, as few women have been trained and endowed with that physical perfections of a carefully selected mother, inherits the taint of some traitor ancestor....

"I desire that a son shall succeed to what I shall build. The mother of that son I have chosen. Sex determination is a problem which at last I have conquered. Neither love nor passion will enter into the union. But if you, Alan Sterling, have cast a shadow of either upon the unsullied mirror which I had patiently burnished to reflect my will . . . then the work of eighteen years is undone."

His guttural voice sank lower and lower, and the last few words sounded like a sibilant whisper....

He struck the gong twice....

I found myself seized by my arms and lifted off the chair in which I had been seated! Two of his Chinamen—unheard, unsuspected—had entered behind me.

Brief guttural words, and I was swung around, as Dr. Fu Manchu stood up, tall, gaunt, satanic, and from a hook upon the wall took down a whip resembling a Russian knout.

As I was swept about to face the door which communicated with the radio research room, one horrifying glimpse I had in the palm house, dimly lighted, of an ivory body hanging by the wrists....

CHAPTER THIRTY-SEVEN

THE GLASS MASK

In a frame of mind which I must leave to the imagination, I paced up and down the little sitting room of the apartment numbered eleven.

I was alone, and the door was unopenable; some ten minutes before, I had heard the section doors being closed, also. Whichever way my thoughts led me, I found stark madness lurking there.

Fleurette! What would be the fate of Fleurette? For Dr. Fu Manchu was not human in the accepted sense of the word. He was a remorseless intelligence. Where he could not use, he destroyed. Perhaps he would spare Fleurette because of her remarkable beauty. But spare her—for what?

Petrie! He was helpless indeed, desperately ill. And as for myself, I suffered those hundred deaths which the coward is said to die, during the unaccountable period that I paced up and down that small room.

My mad passion for Fleurette had brought this down upon all of us! In those feverish moments while I had been pleading with her, I should have been clear of this ghastly house. My freedom meant the safety of the world. I had sacrificed this to my own selfish desires. Only by wrecking the elaborate organisation of the Si-Fan—the scope of which hitherto I had never suspected—could I hope to win Fleurette.

Fool—mad fool!—to have supposed that a newly awakened passion could upset traditions so carefully emplanted and nurtured.

What was happening?

I tried to work out what Nayland Smith would be likely to do—to estimate the chances of a raid taking place before it was too late. I could not forget the imperturbable figure in the yellow robe.

That Dr. Fu Manchu was prepared for such an emergency as this it was impossible to doubt. His manner had not been that of a criminal trapped.

I pressed my ear against the door and listened. . . .
But I could detect no sound.

I crossed to the further wall, in which I knew there was another door, but one I had never been able to open. I listened there also, for I remembered that there was a corridor beyond.

Silence. I was shut into a narrow section of the house between barriers of steel.

I estimated that fully an hour elapsed. I knew from experience that these apartments were practically soundproof. My brain was a phantom circus, and I was rapidly approaching a state of nervous exhaustion.. My frame of mind had been all but unendurable when I had thought that I was dead, when I had thought that I was in a state of delirium. But now, knowing that the horrors accumulated about me, the monstrosities, parodies of nature, the living dead men, the incalculable machines were real and not figments of fevered imagination—now, when I should have been most sane, I was more likely to lose my mental poise than at any time during the past.

A dream which I had scarcely dared to entertain had come true—only to be shattered in the very hour of its realisation. That I should ever leave this place alive, I did not believe for a moment. But surely no man had ever held so much in his hands, ever needed life as I needed it at this moment, when I knew I faced death.

I dropped down into a little armchair—one in which I remembered miserably Fleurette had sat—and buried my face in my hands.

If only I could conjure up one spark of hope—find something to think about which did not lead to insanity!

Then I sprang to my feet. It had reached me unmistakably . . . that dim vibration which told of the section doors being raised!

What did it mean?

That my fate had been decided upon and that they were coming for me? I crossed and pressed the control button. There was no response.

Again, as in Fleurette's room earlier that night, I felt like a mouse in a trap. It could profit no one, myself least of all, but a determination came to me at this moment which did much to steady me.

I would die fighting.

I tested the weight of the little armchair in which I had been seated. It was about heavy enough for my purpose. I would hurl it at whoever entered.

I pulled open the drawers of a large cabinet which occupied a great portion of one wall. It contained laboratory appliances, presumably belonging to a former occupant, and including a glass mask and rubber gloves. But I found no weapon there.

A pedestal lamp stood upon the table. I wrenched the flex from it, removed the lamp and the shade, and realised that it made a very good club. Armed with this I would rush out and see what account I could give of myself in the corridors.

This useless plan made, I stood there waiting. At least, there would be action to come.

The muted rumbling of the doors continued. Once again, setting the lamp stand upon the carpet beside me, I tested the control—but without result.

That rumbling and the queer throbbing gong note which accompanied it could be heard distinctly when I pressed my head against the framework. But now, abruptly, it ceased.

The section doors were raised. . . .

Yet again I tried the control, but uselessly. I stood there waiting, dividing my attention between the wall with its hidden entrance and the door which I knew.

But silence prevailed; nothing happened.

For fully five minutes I waited, not knowing what to expect, but full of my plan for a fighting finish. At last I determined that I could bear this waiting no longer. Again I tested the control. . . .

The door slid noiselessly open!

What I could see of the corridor outside seemed to be more dimly lighted than usual. There was another white door nearly opposite. A faint, putrid smell reached my nostrils.

Cautiously I crept forward, and peeped out, looking along the passage.

A strange humming sound seemed to be drawing nearer to the light shining out from the room behind me. And then . . .

I sprang back, stifling a scream that was truly hysterical. The passage was held by an army of flies, of ants, of other nameless things which flew and crawled and scurried. . . . And, not three feet away, watching me with its hideously intelligent eyes, crouched that monstrous black spider I had seen in the glass case. . . .

CHAPTER THIRTY-EIGHTH

THE GLASS MASK (Concluded)

FRENZIEDLY I closed the door, shutting out those flying and crawling horrors.

Then I began a grim fight—a fight to conquer shaken nerves. That long period of waiting had taken its toll; but the terrors of the corridor, crowned by the apparition of that giant spider "capable of primitive reasoning," had taxed me beyond the limit.

What had happened?

Was this a plan, premeditated?—or had some action on the part of Nayland Smith resulted in a disturbance of this ghastly household?

I dismissed the idea that Dr. Fu Manchu had released this phantom army merely to compass my own death. I had intruded—unwittingly, as he had admitted—upon the delicate machinery of his purpose. But brief though my acquaintance had been with the Chinese doctor, I was not prepared to believe him capable of stooping from that purpose, even momentarily, in response to the promptings of jealousy or of any lower human impulse.

Therefore, if what I had seen conformed to some plan, this plan was not directed against myself, although I might be included in it. If it were the result of accident, of panic on the part of a household disturbed by unexpected events, it could only mean that the doctor had departed—fled before the menace of Nayland Smith!

And by virtue of the fact that I was exercising my brain in hard reasoning, I regained control of that courage which, frankly, had been slipping. And a memory came....

In my frantic search for some weapon with which to put up a fight for life, I had hauled out the drawers of a big cabinet which occupied nearly the whole of one wall of the sitting room in which I now stood.

Among the objects, useless at the time, which I had discovered had been a glass mask of the kind chemists wear.

I formed a desperate resolution. I ran to the drawer in which the mask lay, and slipped it over my head. I saw now that my white overalls, which were made of some unfamiliar material, were adapted to the wearing of this mask: the collar could be turned up and buttoned to the equipment. I fixed it in place, bending before the mirror in the bathroom and contemplating my hideous image.

The rubber gloves!

These, also, I discovered could be attached to my sleeves in a certain manner so that nothing could penetrate between glove and sleeve. My final discovery, that the trousers of the white overalls might be tucked inside the tops of the shoes which a strap was attached for the purpose, convinced me.

Courage returned. I was equipped to face the terrors of the corridor.

I would have given much for a gun, or even a handy club, but in the end I was reduced again to the lamp standard.

Clutching this in my hand, I reopened the door. There was some system of ventilation in the curious mask which I wore—but nevertheless breathing was difficult.

I stood looking along the passage.

The black horror, the giant spider—which, for some reason, although it may have been comparatively harmless, I feared more than anything else—had disappeared. The air was thick with flies; I could hear them vaguely. Some had settled upon the walls. I saw that they were of various kinds.

One of the huge wasps flew straight against my glass mask. I ducked wildly, striking at it—not confident yet in my immunity.

The thing flew by—I heard the fading buzz of its passing....

I came to the end of the corridor and looked down the stairs. My wits were far from clear. At all costs I must remember the route. I found as I stood there that I could remember only that by which Dr. Fu Manchu had first conducted me.

Another way there was, and I had gone by it. The route I remembered would lead me through the bacteriological research room. From thence onward I knew my course.

All the doors were open.

At the entrance to the room where I had seen Sir Frank Narcomb, I pulled up. My knowledge of bacteria was limited;

but if the insects were free—so presumably were the germs. . . .

I glanced down at my feet. Large ants, having glittering bodies, were swarming up over the lashings of my overalls!

Stamping madly, I stooped, brushing the things off with my rubber gloves. I saw a centipede wriggling away from my stamping feet. Panic touched me. I ran through the room and out into a short passage beyond.

In that dimly lighted place, surrounded by windows behind which the insects lived, I saw that the doors of the cases were open. Some of the things still hovered about their nests, but many of the cases were empty.

There was no one in the passage beyond—which was even more dimly lighted; but I stepped upon some wriggling thing and heard the crunch of its body beneath my rubber-shod foot.

The sound sickened me.

I pressed on to the botanical research room. A glance showed that it had been partly stripped. I stared through the observation window into that small house where the strange orchids had been under cultivation. They had disappeared.

Looking about at the shelves, I realised that much of the apparatus had been taken away. The doors leading into the first of the big forcing houses were open.

I passed through, and immediately grasped the explanation of something which had been puzzling me: namely, that the escaped insects were scarcely represented here, whereas the corridors beyond were thick with them, flying and crawling.

A sharp change in the atmosphere offered an explanation.

Windows, as well as doors, were open here, admitting a keen night air borne by a wind from the Alps.

Those things were seeking warmth in the interior of the place. And already, so delicate are such plants, I saw that many of the tropical flowers about me were drooping—would soon be dead.

What did this mean?

It was probably part of a plan to destroy such results of those unique experiments as could not be removed.

With every step I advanced the air grew colder and colder—and destruction among the unique products through which I passed was such that I could find time for a moment of regret in the midst of my own engrossing troubles. The palm house, in common with every other place I had visited, was deserted. The doors leading into Dr. Fu Manchu's study were open . . . I could see light shining out.

Here was the crux of the situation. Here if anywhere I should meet with a check.

Despite the keenness of the air, I was bathed in perspiration, buckled up in my nearly airtight outfit.

I advance slowly, step by step, until I could look into the study. Then I stood still, staring through the glass mask—which had grown very misty—at a room stripped of its exotic trappings!

The furniture alone remained. This destruction, then, which I had witnessed, was the handiwork of Dr. Fu Manchu himself—or so I must suppose. For here was clear evidence that he had fled, taking his choicest possessions with him.

I paused there for only a few moments; then I ran out into the great radio research room.

Of the masses of unimaginable mechanisms which had cumbered the room, only the heaviest remained. The instruments had gone from the tables. Many shelves were bare. Three intricate pieces of machinery, including that which I had thought resembled a moving-picture camera, were there, but wretched—shattered—mere mounds of metallic fragments upon a grey floor!

There were no insects visible in the big room, which was as cold as a cavern, Indeed, as Nayland Smith had pointed out, a cavern, practically, it was. Doors I had not known to exist were open in the glass walls, but I ran the length of the place and sprang up the stairs beyond.

The door did not close behind me. The whole of that intricate mechanism had been locked in some way.

Gaining the top corridor I glanced swiftly to the right.

A cold grey light—the light of dawn—was touching the terrace.

Chapter Thirty-ninth

SEARCH IN STE CLAIRE

I RAN forward.

"Hands up!" came swiftly.

And even as I obeyed that order, I groaned, filled with such bitterness of spirit as I had rarely known.

On the very threshold—freedom in sight—I was trapped again!

A group of semi-human figures surrounded me in the half light: creatures goggle-eyed, with shapeless heads, to which were attached trunk-like appendages! I raised my hands, staring helplessly about that ghoulish party closing in upon me.

"Search him!" came the same voice, staccato, but curiously muffled.

But now, hearing it, I grasped the truth!

The hideous headdresses of the men surrounding me were gas masks!

"*Sir Denis!*" I cried, and knew that my own voice was at least as muffled as his.

The leader of the party was Nayland Smith!

Something very like unconsciousness threatened me. I had not fully appreciated how wrought up I was until this moment. Sights and sounds merged into an indistinguishable blur. But presently, out of this haze, I began to apprehend that Nayland Smith was talking to me, his arm about my shoulders.

"Not a soul has left Ste Claire, Sterling; it's covered from the land and from the sea. When your first message reached me——"

"I sent no message! But what was it?"

"You sent no message?"

"Not a thing! Nevertheless, I think I know who did. What did you take it to mean?"

"According to the system we had arranged, it meant that Petrie was there—but dead. There was a second, much later, which quite defeated me."

"I don't know who sent the second. But it's true Petrie is there—and when I saw him last, *alive*."

"Sterling, Sterling! you are sure?"

"I spoke to him. And—by heavens! I had almost forgotten——"

I plunged a rubber-clad hand into the pocket of my overall, and pulled out the creased and folded sheet of paper.

"The formula for '654.'"

"Thank God! Good old Petrie! Quick! give it to me."

Nayland Smith had discarded his helmet temporarily, and I my glass mask. He dashed away down the steps, leaving me standing there, looking about me.

Six or eight men were by the open door, their heads hidden in gas equipment, and I realised now that they must be French police. I felt very much below par, but the keen night air was restoring me, and after an absence of no more than two or three minutes Sir Denis came running back.

"I don't think, Sterling," he said in his rapid way, "that the doctor's campaign was ripe to open. It depended, I believe, upon climatic conditions. But in any event '654' will be in possession of the medical authorities of the world to-night.

"Petrie's wish is carried out!"

"I should have raided an hour ago, Sterling, if I had had the foresight to equip the party suitably. We were here before I realised the nature of the death trap into which I might be leading them. I once saw a party of detectives in a Limehouse cellar belonging to Dr. Fu Manchu die the most dreadful deaths. . . .

"The Chief of Police was at the main gate, and I consulted with him. He quite naturally wanted to waive my objections; but I persisted. The delay was caused by the quest for gas masks, of which there is not a large supply in the neighbourhood. When they were obtained, the men on duty here reported that the door had been opened from inside but that none had come out. I had rejoined them only a few minutes when you appeared."

"Yet the place is deserted!"

"What?"

"Part of it is infested with plague flies and other horrors, but there is no trace of a human being anywhere."

"Come on!" he snapped, and readjusting his helmet. "Are you fit, Sterling?"

"Yes."

I buttoned myself up in my grim equipment. Followed by the police party, I found myself again in the house of Dr. Fu Manchu.

Unhesitatingly I began to run towards the green lamp at the end of the corridor which marked the position of Fleurette's room—when all the lights went out!

"What's this?" came a muffled exclamation.

The ray of a torch cut the darkness; then many others. Every member of the party was seemingly provided. Someone thrust a light into my hand and I went racing along to the door of Fleurette's room.

One glance showed me that it was empty....

"I forgive you, Sterling," came hoarsely, "but you are wasting time."

The party tore down the stairs, Nayland Smith and I leading.

"Petrie's room!" came huskily, "that first...."

We dashed across the dismantled radio research laboratory, eerie in torchlight, through the empty study where Dr. Fu Manchu, wrapped in a strange opium dream, had sat in his throne chair, and on through those great forcing houses where trees, shrubs, and plants to which Dame Nature had never given her benediction wilted in the keen air sweeping through open doors.

Hoarse exclamations told of the astonishment experienced by the police party following us as we dashed through those exotic mysteries. Then, mounting the stair and coming to the corridor with its white, numbered doors, I became aware of a crunching sound beneath my feet.

I paused, and shone the light downward.

The floor was littered with dead and comatose insects, swift victims of this change of temperature! The giant spider had succumbed somewhere, I did not doubt; yet even now I dreaded the horror, dreaded those reasoning eyes.

"We turn right here!" I shouted, my voice muffled by the mask.

I ran along the passage and in at the open door of that room in which I had seen Petrie.

The room was empty!

"They have taken him!" groaned Nayland Smith. "We're too late. What's that?"

A sound of excited voices reached me dimly. Then came a cry from the rear. The men under the local Chief of Police had joined us; they had come in by the main entrance.

Yet neither group had discovered a soul on the premises!

"Spread out!" cried Nayland Smith—"parties of two! There's some Chinese rathole. A big household doesn't disappear into thin air. Come on, Sterling! our route is downward, not up."

We pressed our way through the throng of men behind us, Nayland Smith and the Chief of Police repeating the orders.

Sir Denis beside me, I raced back along the way we had come; and although every door appeared to be open, there was seemingly none in that range of rooms other then those I knew. We searched the big forcing houses, meeting only other muffled figures engaged upon a similar task.

But apparently the doors leading into Dr. Fu Manchu's study and those which communicated with the botanical research room were the only means of entrance or exit!

Out into the big dismantled laboratory we ran. There were two open doors in the wall opposite our point of entrance.

"This one first!" came in a muffled voice.

Sir Denis and I ran across to an opening in the glass wall.

"The Chinaman who arrived in the speedboat went this way," he shouted.

Shining our torches ahead, we entered—and found a descending stair. Our light failed to penetrate to the bottom of it.

"Stop, Sir Denis!" I cried.

Wrenching off the suffocating glass mask, I dropped it on the floor, for I saw that in the darkness he had already discarded his gas helmet.

"We must assemble a party—we may be walking into a trap."

He pulled up and stared at me; his face was haggard.

"You are right," he rapped. "Get three or four men, and notify Furneaux—he's in charge of the police—which way we have gone."

I ran back across the great empty hall from which that curious violet light had gone, and shouted loudly. I soon assembled a party, one of whom I despatched in search of the Chief of Police, and, accompanied by the others, I rejoined Nayland Smith.

We left one man on duty at the door.

Nayland Smith leading, and I close behind him, we began to descend the stairs into the subterranean mystery of Ste Claire.

Chapter Fortieth

THE SECRET DOCK

"This is where the Chinaman went," he said. "It speaks loudly for the iron rule of the doctor, Sterling, that although this man had presumably brought important news, not only did he avoid awakening Fu Manchu, but he even left the doors of the palm house open. However, where did he go? That's what we have to find out."

A long flight of rubber-covered stairs descended ahead of us. The walls and ceiling were covered with that same glassy material which prevailed in the radio research room. I counted sixty steps and then we came to a landing.

"Look out for traps," rapped Nayland Smith, "and distrust every foot of the way."

We tested for doors on the landing, but could find none. A further steep flight of steps branched away down to the right.

"Come on!"

The lower flight possessed the same characteristics as the higher, and terminated on another square landing. A long corridor showed beyond—so long that the light of our torches was lost in it.

"One man to stand by here," came the crisp order—"and keep in contact with the man at the top."

We pressed on. We were now reduced to a party of four. There were several bends in the passage, but its general direction, according to my calculations, was southerly.

"This is amazing," muttered Nayland Smith. "If it goes on much farther, I shall being to suspect that it is a private entrance to the Casino at Monte Carlo!"

Even as he spoke, another bend unmasked the end of this remarkable passage. Branching sharply down to the right, I saw a further flight of steps—rough wooden steps; and the naked rock was all about us.

"What's this?"

"We must be down to sea level."

"Fully, I should think."

Sir Denis turned; and:

"Fall out another man," he directed; "patrol between here and the end of the passage. Keep in contact with your opposite number, a shot to be the signal of any danger. Come on!"

A party of three, we pressed on down the wooden steps. There was a greater chilliness in the air, and a stale smell as of ancient rottenness. Another landing was reached, wooden planked: roughly hewn rock all about us. More wooden stairs, inclining left again.

These terminated in an arched, crudely octagonal place which bore every indication of being a natural cave. It was floored with planks, and a rugged passage, similarly timbered, led yet farther south—or so I estimated.

"Stay here," Nayland Smith directed tersely. "Keep in touch with the man at the top."

And the last of the police party was left behind.

Sir Denis and I hurried on. Fully a hundred yards we went—and came to a yawning gap, which our lights could not penetrate. Moving slowly now, we reached the end of the passage.

"Careful!" warned Sir Denis. "By heavens! what's this?"

We stood on a narrow wharf!

Tackle lay about; crates, packing cases, coils of rope. And the sea—for I recognised that characteristic smell of the Mediterranean—lapped its edge!

But not a speck of light was visible anywhere. The water was uncannily still. One would not have suspected it to be there.

"Lights out!" snapped Sir Denis.

We extinguished our lamps. Utter darkness blanketed us: we might have stood in a mine gallery.

"Don't light up!" came his voice. "I should have foreseen this. But even so, I don't see how I could have provided against it. . . . My God! what's that?"

A dull sustained note, resembling that of a muted gong, vibrated eerily through the stillness. . . In fact, now that he had drawn my attention to it, I believed that it had been perceptible for some time, although hitherto partly drowned by the clatter of our rubber soles upon wooden steps.

For one moment I listened—and knew . . .

"You were right, Sir Denis," I said; "this place isn't deserted. Someone is closing *the section doors!*"

"Quick! for your life! Back to the stairs! . . ."

We turned and ran into the wooden-floored tunnel; our feet made a drumming sound upon the planks. The man left on duty at the foot of the stairs was missing. Up we went helter-skelter, neither of us doubting the urgency. We met with no obstruction and, breathing hard, began to race up the higher flight.

Neither patrol was to be seen. I suspected that they had gone back along the corridor to establish contact with the man at the farther end.

In confirmation of my theory came the sound of a shot, curiously muffled and staccato, from some point far ahead.

We pulled up, panting and—staring. . . .

A section door was descending, cutting us off from the corridor! It was no more than three feet from the ground, and falling—falling—inch by inch. . . .

"We daren't risk it!" groaned Nayland Smith. "If we did, and weren't crushed, we should be shut in between this and the next."

I heard shouting in the corridor beyond; a sound of racing feet. But even as I listened and watched, the dull grey metal door was but fifteen inches above floor level, and:

"We must try back again," I said hoarsely.

"There must be some way out of that place, even if we have to swim for it."

"There's no way out," Sir Denis rapped irritably. "The entrance is below sea level."

"What!"

"You saw the patches of oil on the wharf?"

"I did. But—"

"Nevertheless, we'll go back. There may be some gallery communicating with another exit."

We began to descend again.

I was trying to think, trying to see into the future. An appalling possibility presented itself to my mind: that this might be the end of everything! So tenacious is the will to live in all healthy animals that predominant above every other consideration at the moment towered that of how to escape from this ghastly cavern.

Nayland Smith's torch—he was leading by a pace—shone upon the oil-stained planking of the wharf.

"Lights out!"

In complete darkness we stood there. That warning note which indicated the closing of the section doors had ceased.

They were closed.

Failing our discovery of another way out, rescue depended upon the forcing of many such obstacles!

Considering what I knew of the equipment of Ste Claire, I realised that the whole of the party within its walls must be cut off one from another in the innumerable sections. Lacking intelligent work on the part of someone outside—and I believed the Chief of Police to be inside—it was a hopeless task to attempt to calculate how long we might have to wait for that rescue.

And now a voice—a voice once heard never to be forgotten—broke the silence: it echoed eerily from wall to wall of the cavern.

"Sir Denis Nayland Smith . . ."

It was Dr. Fu Manchu speaking!

My heart throbbed painfully, and I choked down an exclamation:

"You are not called upon to answer if it please you to remain silent, but I know that you are there. I may add that you will remain there for a considerable time. Apart from certain personal inconvenience, Sir Denis, do not congratulate yourself upon having altered my plans. Dr. Petrie's experiments were a menace more serious than any intrusion of yours. The impossibility of adapting my flying army to certain Russian conditions was an obstacle which in any event I had not succeeded in surmounting. However, Dr. Petrie is with me now, and his proven genius in my own special province should be of some service in the future."

I could hear Nayland Smith breathing hard close beside me, but he spoke no word.

"Mr. Alan Sterling," the guttural, mocking voice continued, "I have reconstructed your brief romance with Fleurette. It is regrettable. I remain uncertain if I can efface your handiwork. . . ."

I doubted if any man had ever participated in so fantastic a scene; and now, as if to crown its phantasy, Sir Denis spoke out of the darkness beside me.

"Who built your submarine?" he asked in an ordinary conversational tone.

And with that courtesy proper between lifelong enemies Dr. Fu Manchu replied:

"My submersible yacht was designed by Ernst von Ebber, whose 'death' some ten years ago you may recall. But it incorporates many new features of Ericksen. It was built at my yard on the Irrawaddy, in your beloved Burma.

"I must leave you. If I do so with a certain reluctance, this is due to the fact that I always pay my gambling debts. My life was at your mercy, Sir Denis—and you held your hand...."

Chapter Forty-first

"I SAW THE SUN"

Silence.

That guttural, imperious voice had ceased.

"No lights—yet!" came harshly from Nayland Smith. "He has paid the debt. He won't pay twice!"

And in that clammy darkness I stood waiting—and listening.

Sir Denis began speaking again, close to my ear, in a low voice.

"Where did you place him?"

"Almost directly opposite to where we stand—"

"But higher up?"

"Yes."

"I agree. There's some gallery there. We must move warily. I gather that you are a powerful swimmer?"

My heart sank. Keyed up though I was to the supreme object—escape, contemplation of plunging into that still, cavernous water appalled me.

"Fairly good—but I'm rather below par at the moment!"

"That is understood, Sterling. Only vital issues at stake could demand such an effort. As a matter of fact, I believe this pool to be no more than fifty or sixty yards from side to side. My own powers as a swimmer being limited, I trust I am right. I might manage once across!"

"What's your plan, Sir Denis?"

"This: If we show ourselves again we may be shot down; but this we can test: I suggest that we place a light on the edge of the wharf, as a beacon, and that you slip quietly into the water. There's a ladder near to where we stand. Getting your direction from the light, swim across."

"I'm game. What next?"

"Find out if there is any way of climbing up."

"In this utter darkness?"

"Palpably impossible! But you have probably swum across a river before now, carrying your valuables under your hat?"

"I have seen it done."

"My rubber tobacco pouch, which is unusually large, will comfortably accommodate the automatic which I am now slipping into it, and also one of the flash lamps. . . . Pass yours to me."

Silently, I groped in the blackness, found Sir Denis's outstretched hand, and transferred my lamp to him.

"I am tying up the pouch in a silk handkerchief," he murmured. . . . "here we are—come nearer. . . ."

As I moved cautiously forward, I felt his grasp on my shoulder; some of the man's amazing vitality was imparted to me: I warmed to the ordeal.

"Tie the loose ends under your chin," he directed.

And as I endeavoured to the best of my ability to carry out his directions, he went on, speaking in a low voice but urgently:

"If you can get ashore, use the light to find a way up. Keep the gun in your other hand. If you can make no landing, swim back. Is it clear—and can you do it?"

"It's clear, Sir Denis; and failing interference I think I can do it."

"Good man! Now, grab my arm, and when I move back move with me!"

I felt him stoop . . . then suddenly a light sprang up at my feet!

"Back," he muttered.

He drew me back three paces, and, watching, I saw the light move—it moved slowly towards us . . . became stationary . . . moved again!

"I tied a piece of string to it," he murmured in my ear.

The silence, save for those low-spoken words, remained unbroken, until:

"No snipers!" rapped Sir Denis. "Dr. Fu Manchu retains his one noble heritage. His word is his bond. Get busy, now Sterling! I'll place the light. . . ."

Of that swim across the cavern I prefer not to think; therefore I shall not attempt to describe it. The temperature of the water was much lower than in the open sea.

At a point which I estimated to be not more than fifty yards from the wharf, I touched a rock bottom. I experimented, cautiously; found a foothold; and began to grope forward.

Shelves of rock met my questing fingers. I managed to scramble out of the water. Then, half sitting on a ledge, I unfastened my curious headdress and, gripping the tobacco pouch between my teeth, extracted the lamp. I continued to hold it so, the automatic still inside, while I directed a ray of light upward.

It was no easy climb, but I saw that there was a shelf of rock ten or twelve feet up. It sloped at an easy gradient to what looked like a small cave in the wall of the cavern.

I turned, looking back.

The faint beam of light from the lamp, gleaming on that still pool, pointed almost directly towards me.

I began to climb.

There were fewer difficulties than I had looked for. Without very great exertion, I gained the shelf and started for the gap in the rock. When I reached it, I hesitated for a moment. It was much higher and wider than I had thought it to be from below.

Taking the tobacco pouch from between my teeth, I grasped Nayland Smith's automatic—and went forward.

I found myself in a rock passage not unlike that which we had negotiated on the other side of the pool, except that it was not boarded and that it sloped steeply downward.

Shining my light ahead, I followed this passage.

Its temperature was bitingly low for a naked man: but a tang of the sea came to my nostrils which drew me on.

The passage wound and twisted intricately, growing ever lower and narrower. I pushed on.

There was nothing to show that it was used: it looked like untouched handiwork of Nature; untravelled, undiscovered. The gradient grew so steep as to resemble a crude stair. I stumbled to the foot of it....

And I saw the sun rising over the Mediterranean!

I shouted, exultantly! I was a sun worshipper!

I stood in a tiny pebbled bay, locked in by huge cliffs. The sea lay before me, but neither to right nor to left could I obtain a glimpse of any coastline.

There was some hint of a path leading steeply upward on one side. I examined it closely. Yes! at *some* time it had been traversed!

Five paces up, I found a burned match!

I turned back, running in my eagerness. And, in a fraction of the time taken by my outward journey, I found myself at the mouth of the passage, staring across the pool to where that feeble beacon beckoned.

"Sir Denis!" I cried, and waved my flashlight—"swim across! *We're out!*"

CHAPTER FORTY-SECOND

THE RAID

I LOOKED out across the sea, shimmering under a cloudless morning sky, then turned and stared at my companion. He was hatless, but his crisp grey hair in which were silver streaks was of that kind which defies rough usage and persistently remains well groomed.

His tanned skin, upon which in that keen light many little lines showed, and the fact that he was unshaven added to the gauntness of his features. He wore a grey flannel suit and rubber-soled shoes. The suit was terribly wrinkled, and his tie, which I had watched him knotting, was not strictly in place; but nevertheless I felt that Sir Denis Nayland Smith presented a better front to the world than I did at that moment.

In that keen profile I read something of the force which lies behind a successful career; and looking down at the dirty white overalls in which I was arrayed, a wave of admiration swept over me—admiration for the alert intelligence of my companion in this strange adventure. Who but Sir Denis would have thought of bundling our scanty possessions into a small packing case, and towing it behind him on that same piece of string which had served in his test to unmask a possible sniper?

He was examining the match upon the rock path which alone had given me a clue to the fact that escape from this secret spot was possible. Then I spoke:

"Sir Denis," I said, it's a great privilege to have helped you in any way. You are a very remarkable man."

He turned and smiled; his smile was thirty years his junior.

"I suppose you must be right, Sterling," he replied, "otherwise, I shouldn't have survived. But——"

He stopped.

And blotting out the triumph of our escape from the cavern which Dr. Fu Manchu had thought to be a Bastille came reality—memories—sorrow.

Petrie had gone to join the ranks of those living dead men. . . .

Fleurette!

Fleurette was lost to me forever! No doubt my change of mood was reflected on my face; for:

"I know what you're thinking, Sterling," Sir Denis added, "but don't despair—yet, There's still hope."

"What!"

"That this path leads somewhere and does not just lose itself among the rocks, I have little doubt. My own impression is that it leads to the beach of Ste Claire. But this is not the chief point of interest."

"To me, it seems to be."

"What do you regard as the most curious features of our recent experience?"

I considered for a moment, then:

"The mystery of Dr. Fu Manchu's motive in remaining behind," I replied, "and the greater mystery of how and when he joined his submersible yacht—whatever a submersible yacht may be."

Nayland Smith nodded rapidly.

"You are getting near to it," he rapped. "I am satisfied that the opening above the water cave at the top of the rocks was the place from which he spoke to us. And I think we are unanimous on the point that there is no other means of exit but his. Therefore, I have been asking myself for the last ten minutes: why did he come by this roundabout route when he could have boarded his craft at the wharf, as no doubt the other members of his household did. It's rather a hazardous guess, but one I like to make."

"What is it, Sir Denis?"

"I don't think he joined the submarine at all."

"What!"

"Whatever the construction of that craft may be, it would offer serious obstacles to the transporting of a sick man."

"Good heavens! You think——"

"It is just possible that Petrie has been taken another way, under the personal care of the doctor."

"But," I protested, "that climb up the rocks?"

"Could easily be performed by native bearers carrying a

stretcher or litter, and descent to this point is easy."

"But—" I pointed along the faintly pencilled track.

Nayland Smith shook his head.

"Not that way, Sterling," he admitted. "A motorboat has been lying here. Look—there are still traces of oil at the margin of the water, and the beach slopes away very sharply."

"You think Dr. Fu Manchu has been taken to some landing place farther along the coast, where a car awaited him?"

"That is the point we have to settle. Only one of two roads could serve—the Great Corniche or the Middle. All cars using them are being challenged and searched."

"Then, by heaven! we may have him yet!"

"Knowing him better than you do, I look upon that as almost too much to hope for, Sterling. However, suppose we begin our climb."

We set out.

A wild eleventh-hour hope was mine, that not only Petrie but Fleurette might be with Dr. Fu Manchu, and that this delay might prove to be his undoing. I did not know how far to take his words literally—but I remembered that he had said, "Dr. Petrie is with me." Yes, there was still a ghost of a chance that all was not lost yet.

The path was one of those which would not have appalled a hardened climber, but mountaineering had never been my enthusiasm. One thing was certain: Dr. Fu Manchu and his party had never come this way.

It wound round and round great gnarled crags, creeping higher and ever higher. I was glad to be wearing rubber-soled shoes, although I am aware that experienced mountaineers reject them.

At one point it led us fully a mile inland, climbing very near to the rim of a deep gorge and at an eerie height above the sea. It was a mere tracing, much better suited to a goat than to a human being. Never once did it touch any practicable road, but now led seaward again, until we found ourselves high up on the side of a dizzy precipice, sheer above the blue Mediterranean.

"Heavens!" muttered Nayland Smith, clutching at the rocky wall at his right hand. "This is getting rather too exciting!"

"I agree, Sir Denis."

At a point which was no more than eighteen inches wide, I was tempted to shut my eyes, but knew that I must keep them open and go on.

"Heaven knows who uses such a path as this," he muttered.

We rounded the bluff and saw that our way lay inland again. The slope below was less steep, and there was dense vegetation upon its side. Nayland Smith pulled up, and under one upraised hand, stared hard.

"It is difficult to recognise from this point," he said, "but here is the bay of Ste Claire, as I suspected."

And now that crazy path began to descend, leading us lower and lower.

It was very still there, and the early morning air possessed champagne-like properties. And suddenly Sir Denis turned to me:

"Do you hear it, Sterling?" he snapped.

Distinctly, in the silence, although it seemed to come from a long way off, I had detected the sound to which he referred—a distant shouting, and an almost incessant booming sound.

"It seems incredible," he continued, "but they are evidently still trying to force a way into the house! Come on, let's hurry—there's much to do, and very little time to do it."

We ran down the remaining few yards of the path and found ourselves upon the beach—that beach of which I had dreamed so often—but always with the dainty, sun-browned figure of Fleurette seated upon it.

Sir Denis, whose powers of physical endurance were little short of phenomenal, ran across, making for that corresponding path upon the other side which led to the seven flights of steps communicating with the terrace of the villa. . . .

We mounted at the double.

I saw that the main door had been forced and the shutters torn from an upper window against which a ladder rested.

The booming sound, which had grown louder as we approached, was caused by the efforts of a party of men under a bewildered police officer endeavouring to force the first of the section doors at the top of the steps which led down to the radio research room.

Sir Denis made himself known to the man—who had not been a member of the original party. And we learned the astounding fact that with the exception of four, the whole of that party, including the Chief of Police, remained locked inside the house—nor had any sound or message come from them!!

A man was at work with a blow-lamp, supported by others with crowbars.

Expert reinforcements were expected at any moment; and—a curious feature of the situation—although there was a telephone in the villa, no message had come over it from within, nor had any reply been received when the number was called. . . .

Chapter Forty-third

KÂRAMANÈH'S DAUGHTER

In the course of the next few minutes I had my first sight of Ste Claire de la Roche.

A paved path circled the house. There were ladders against several windows; ways had been forced into the outer rooms, and the villa proper was in possession of the police. But I knew that the real establishment was far below, and that it was much more extensive than that more or less open to inspection.

Crashing and booming echoed hollowly from within.

The front of the villa, by which I mean that part which faced towards the distant road, was squat and unimpressive. An entrance had been forced from this point also, and there were a number of police hurrying about.

A little cobbled street, flanked by a house with an arched entrance, presented itself. Beside the house, in a cavern-like opening, a steep flight of steps disappeared into blackness. The top of a ladder projected above the parapet on my right, and, looking over, I saw that part of the glass roof of one of the forcing houses visible at this point had been smashed and a ladder lowered through the gap.

Dim voices reached me from far below. I wondered if any of the raiding party had been found in that section.

But Nayland Smith was hurrying on down the slope. And now we came to a long, sanded drive. There was a wall on the left, beyond which I thought lay a kitchen garden and a sheer drop on the right.

Sweeping around in a northerly direction, the drive led to gates of ornate iron scrollwork, which were closed, and I saw that two police officers were on duty there.

The gates were opened in response to a brief order, and we hurried out into a narrow, sloping lane. I remembered this lane. It wandered down to the main road; for I had penetrated to it in my earliest attempt to explore Ste Claire de la Roche, and had been confronted with a "No thoroughfare" sign.

"There's a police car at the corner," said Nayland Smith; "we must take that."

No cars had been found in the stone garage attached to the villa, and I wondered what had become of that which had once belonged to Petrie, and which must have been hidden on the night of my encounter with the dacoit on the Corniche road.

A sergeant of police was standing by the car. He reported that a motorcyclist patrol had just passed. All cars using both roads had been challenged and searched throughout the night in accordance with Sir Denis's instructions. But no one had been detained.

Nayland Smith stood there twitching at the lobe of his ear; and my heart sank, for I thought that he was about to admit defeat.

"He may have gone by sea down to Italy," he said; "it is a possibility which must not be overlooked. Or, by heavens!—"

He suddenly dashed his fist into the palm of his left hand.

"What, Sir Denis?"

"He may have had a yacht standing by! He got away from England in that manner on one occasion."

"It is also just possible," I began . . .

"I know," Sir Denis groaned. "My theory lacks solid foundation—he may have joined the submarine?"

"Exactly."

"His delay might be due merely to his sense of the dramatic—which is strong. Get in, Sterling."

He turned to the sergeant in charge of the car.

"Officer of the Préfet," he rapped and jumped in behind me.

To endeavour to reconstruct the ideas which passed through my mind during that early morning drive would be futile, since they consisted of a taunting panorama of living-dead men; the flowerlike face of Fleurette appearing again and again before that ghostly curtain, and set in an expression of adoration which formed my most evil memory. I could not banish the image of Petrie, could not accept the fact that he had joined the phantom army of Dr. Fu Manchu.

Nayland Smith sat grimly silent, until at last:

"Sir Denis," I said, "this is not time to talk of my personal affairs, but—something which happened in Petrie's room has been puzzling me."

"What is that?" he snapped.

"Fleurette kept watch at the door—she had led me there—while I slipped in to see him. Just before I left, he caught a glimpse of her, and——"

"Yes?" said Sir Denis, with a sudden keen interest in his eyes. "What did he do?"

"He sat up in bed as though he had seen an apparition. He asked in a most extraordinary voice who it was that had looked into the room. I had to leave—it was impossible to stay. But there is no doubt whatever that he recognised her!—although, as she told me afterwards, she had never seen Petrie in her life."

I paused, meeting his eager regard; and then:

"You also thought you recognised her, Sir Denis," I went on, "and evidently you were not wrong. I can't believe I shall ever see her again, but, if you know, tell me: Who is she?"

He drew a deep breath.

"You told me, I think that you had never met Kâramanèh—Petrie's wife?"

"Never."

"She was formerly a member of the household of Dr. Fu Manchu."

"It seems impossible!"

"It does, but it's a fact, nevertheless. I seem to remember telling you that she was the most beautiful woman I have ever known."

"You did."

"On one side she's of pure Arab blood, of the other I am uncertain."

"Arab?"

"Surely. She was selected for certain qualities, of which her extraordinary beauty was not the least, by Dr. Fu Manchu. Petrie upset his plans in that direction. Now, it is necessary for you to realise, Sterling, that Petrie, also, is a man of very good family—of sane, clean, balanced stock."

"I am aware of this, Sir Denis; my father knows him well."

Sir Denis nodded and went on:

"Dr. Fu Manchu has always held Petrie in high esteem. Very few people are aware of what I am going to tell you—possibly even your father doesn't know. But a year after Petrie's marriage to Kâramanèh, a child was born."

"I had no idea of this."

"It was so deep a grief to them, Sterling, that they never spoke of it."

"A grief?"

"The child, a girl, was born in Cairo. She died when she was three weeks old."

"Good heavens! Poor old Petrie! I have never heard him even mention it."

"You never would. They agreed never to mention it. It was their way of forgetting. There were curious features about the case to which, in their sorrow they were blind at the time. But when, nearly a year later, the full facts came into my possession, a truly horrible idea presented itself to my mind."

"What do you mean, Sir Denis?"

"Naturally, I whispered no word of it to Petrie. It would have been the most callous cruelty to do so. But privately, I made a number of enquiries; and while I obtained no evidence upon which it was possible to act, nevertheless, what I learned confirmed my suspicion. . . .

"Dr. Fu Manchu is patient, as only a great scientist can be."

He paused, watching me, a question in his eyes. But as I did not speak:

"When I entered that room, which I described to you as the Palace of the Sleeping Beauty, I received one of the great shocks of my life. Do you know what I thought as I looked at Fleurette asleep?"

"I am trying to anticipate what you are going to tell me."

"I thought that it was Kâramanèh—*Petrie's wife!*"

"You mean——"

"I mean that, even with her eyes closed, the likeness was uncanny, utterly beyond the possibility of coincidence. Then, when you described to me their unusual quality—and Kâramanèh's eyes are her crowning beauty—I knew that I could not be mistaken."

Positively I was stricken dumb—I could only sit and stare at the speaker. No words occurred to me.

"Therefore, poor Petrie's recognition does not surprise me. It may seem amazing, Sterling, almost incredible, that a child less than three weeks old could be subjected to that treatment upon which much of Fu Manchu's monumental knowledge rests: the production of artificial catalepsy; but a fact which by now must have dawned upon you. He is not only the greatest physician alive to-day, he is probably the greatest physician who has ever been."

"Sir Denis——"

The car was just pulling up before the police headquarters.

"There's no doubt whatever, Sterling!" He grasped my arm firmly. "Think of what the doctor has told you about her—think of what she has told you about herself—so much as she knows. There isn't a shadow of doubt. Fleurette is Petrie's daughter, and Kâramanèh is her mother! Buck up, old chap, I know how you must feel about it—but we haven't abandoned hope yet."

He sprang out and ran in at the door, brushing past an officer who stood on duty there.

Chapter Forty-fourth

OFFICER OF THE PRÉFET

In the large but frigid office of M. Chamrousse, Préfet of the Department, that sedate, grey-bearded official spoke rapidly on the telephone and made a number of notes upon a writing block, Sir Denis snapping his fingers impatiently and pacing up and down the carpet.

I had no idea of his plan, of what he hoped for. My state of mental chaos was worse than before. Fleurette Petrie's daughter! From tenderest infancy she had lived as those others lived whom he wanted for his several purposes: a dream-life!

And now—Petrie himself . . .

In upon my thoughts broke the magisterial voice of the man at the big table.

"Here is the complete list, Sir Denis Nayland Smith," he said. "You will see that the only private vessel of any tonnage which has cleared a neighbouring port during the last twelve hours is this one."

He rested the point of his pencil on the paper. Nayland Smith, bending eagerly over him, read the note aloud:

"M. Y. *Lola*, of Buenos Aires; four thousand tons; owned by Santos da Cunha."

He suddenly stood upright, staring before him.

"Santos da Cunha?" he repeated. "Where have I heard that name?"

"Curiously enough," said M. Chamrousse, "the villa at Ste Claire was formerly the property of this gentleman, from whom it was purchased by Mahdi Bey."

Sir Denis dashed his fist into the palm of his hand.

"Sterling!" he cried—"there's hope yet! there's hope yet! But I have been blind. This is the Argentine for whose record I am waiting!" He turned to the Préfet. "How long has the *Lola* been lying in Monaco?"

"Nearly a week, I believe."

"And she left?"

"Soon after dawn, Sir Denis—as I read in this report."

"You see, Sterling! you see?" he cried.

He turned again to the Préfet, and:

"The *Lola* must be traced," he said rapidly—"without delay. Please give instructions for messages to be sent to all ships in the neighbourhood, notifying position of this motor yacht when sighted."

"I can do this," said the other gravely, inclining his head.

"Next, is there a French or British warship in port anywhere along the coast?"

M. Chamrousse raised his eyebrows.

"There is a French destroyer in the harbour of Monaco," he replied.

"Please notify her commander to be ready to leave at a moment's notice—in fact, the instant I get on board."

That peremptory manner, contempt for red tape and routine, which characterised Sir Denis in emergencies, had the effect of ruffling the French official.

"This, sir," he replied taking off his spectacles and tapping them on the blotting pad, "I cannot do."

"Cannot?"

The other shrugged.

"I have no such powers," he declared. "It is in the province of the naval authority. I doubt if even the admiral commanding the Mediterranean Fleet could take it upon himself to do what you ask of me."

"Perhaps," rapped Nayland Smith, "in these circumstances, you will be good enough to put a call through to the Ministry of Marine in Paris."

M. Chamrousse shrugged his shoulders and looked mildly surprised.

"Really——" he began.

"My authority from the British Foreign Office," said Sir Denis, with a sort of repressed violence, "is such that any delay you may cause must react to your own discredit. The interests of France as well as those of England are involved in this matter. Damn it, M. Chamrousse! I am *here* in the interests of France! Must I go elsewhere, or will you do as I ask?"

The Préfet resignedly took up the telephone and gave instructions to the outer office that Paris should be called.

Nayland Smith began again to pace up and down the carpet.

"You know, Sir Denis Nayland Smith," M. Chamrousse began in his dry, precise voice, "it is perhaps a little unfair to me that I am so badly informed regarding this matter. All the available police have been rushed to Ste Claire and, according to my latest reports, are locked up there. I am in the dark about this—I am tied hand and foot. Paris instructed me to place myself at your disposal, and I have done so, but the reputation of Mahdi Bey, whom I have met several times socially, is quite frankly above suspicion. To me the whole thing is incomprehensible; and now you demand——"

In this unemotional outburst I saw the reason of the Préfet's coldness towards Sir Denis. He resented the action of Paris. Sir Denis realised this also; for checking his restless promenade he turned to face the little bearded man.

"Such issues are at stake, M. Chamrousse," he said, "and my own blunders have so confounded me, that perhaps I have failed in proper courtesy. If so, forgive me. But try to believe that I have every reason for what I do. It is of vital importance that the yacht *Lola* should be detained."

I accept your assurance upon these matters, Sir Denis," said M. Chamrousse.

But I thought from the tone of his dusty voice that he was somewhat mollified.

Conversation ceased, and unavoidably I dropped back into that valley of sorrowful reflection from which this verbal duel between Sir Denis and the French official had temporarily dragged me.

Fleurette was Petrie's daughter!

This was the amazing fact outstanding above the mist and discord which ruled my brain. It might be that they were together; but, once Petrie should have fully recovered from his dangerous illness, I did not doubt that he would be forced to accept that Blessing of the Celestial Vision from which I had so narrowly escaped; and then . . .

If my influence had "not tarnished the mirror," in Dr. Fu Manchu's words—a ghastly union of unknown age and budding youth would be consummated!

I could not face the idea. I found myself clenching my fists and grinding my teeth.

At which moment, the connection with Paris was made; M. Chamrousse stood up, bowed courteously, and handed the receiver to Sir Denis.

The latter—in voluble but very bad French—proceeded to tread heavily on the toes of the Paris official at the other end of the line. I had learned that he, in moments of stress, was prone to exhibit a truculence, an indifference to the feelings of others which underlay and may have been the driving power behind that brusque but never uncourteous manner which characterised him normally.

He was demanding to speak to the Minister in person and refusing to be put off.

"At home and asleep? Be so good as to put me through to his private number at once!"

M. Chamrousse had taken his stand on the carpet upon which Nayland Smith so recently had paced up and down; listening to the conversation, he merely shrugged, took out a cigarette, and lighted it with meticulous care.

However, it must be recorded to the credit of Sir Denis that his intolerant language—which was sometimes frankly rude—achieved its objective.

He was put through to the sleeping Minister. . . .

No doubt there is much to be said for direct methods in sweeping aside ill-informed opposition. In the Middle West of America, my father's home, I had learned to respect the direct attack as opposed to those circumlocutory manouevres so generally popular in European society.

To the unconcealed surprise of M. Chamrousse, Sir Denis's demands were instantly conceded!

I gathered that authoritative orders would be transmitted immediately to the commander of the destroyer lying in the harbour at Monaco; that every other available unit in the fleet would be despatched in quest of the submarine. In short, it became evident during this brief conversation that Sir Denis wielded an authority greater than even I had suspected.

When presently he replaced the receiver and sprang to his feet, the effect upon M. Chamrousse was notable.

"Sir Denis Nayland Smith," he said, "I congratulate you—but you fully realise that in this matter I was indeed helpless!"

Sir Denis shook his hand.

"Please say no more! Of course I understand. But if you would accept my advice, it would be this: proceed personally to Ste Claire, and when you have realised the difficulties of the situation there, you will be in a position to deal with it."

Some more conversation there was, the gist of which I have forgotten, and then we were out in the car again and speeding along those tortuous roads headed for Monaco.

"Much time has been wasted," rapped Nayland Smith; "only luck can help us now. Failing a message from some ship which has sighted the yacht *Lola*, it's impossible to lay a course. Probably the *Lola* has a turn of speed which will tax the warship in any event. But lacking knowledge of her position, we can't even start.

"I don't doubt she will have been sighted. There's a lot of shipping in those waters."

"Yes, but the bulk of it is small craft, and many of them carry no radio. However, we are doing all that lies in our power to do."

CHAPTER FORTY-FIFTH

ON THE DESTROYER

FROM the bridge of the destroyer I looked over a blue and sailless sea. The speed of the little warship was exhilarating, and I could see from the attitude of her commander beside me that this break in peace-time routine was welcome rather than irksome.

I glanced towards the port wing of the bridge where Nayland Smith was staring ahead through raised glasses.

Somewhere astern of where I stood, somewhere in the slender hull, full out and quivering on this unexpected mission, I knew there were police officers armed with a warrant issued by the Boulevard du Palais for the arrest of Dr. Fu Manchu.

And as the wine of the morning began to stir my blood, hope awakened. The history of Fleurette lay open before me like a book. And all that had seemed incomprehensible in her character and her behaviour, lover-like, now I translated and understood. She had been cultivated as those plants in the forcing houses had been cultivated.

The imprint of Dr. Fu Manchu was upon her.

Yet through it all the real Fleurette had survived, defying the alchemy of the super-scientist: she was still Petrie's daughter, beautiful, lovable, and mine, if I could find her. . . .

I set doubt aside. Definitely, we should overtake the South American yacht. News had come from a cruising liner ten minutes before we had reached Monaco Harbour: the *Lola*, laid on a southerly course, was less than twenty miles ahead.

But, since the *Lola* also must have picked up the message, we realised that the course of the motor yacht would in all probability have been changed. Nevertheless, ultimate escape was next to impossible.

Yet again that damnable thought intruded: the *Lola* might prove to be a will o' the wisp; Fu Manchu, Fleurette, and Petrie not on board!

It appeared to me that the only thing supporting Nayland

Smith's theory and his amazing reaction to it was the fact that the *Lola* had not answered those messages sent out by the French authority.

At which moment Sir Denis dropped the glasses into their case and turned.

"Nothing!" he said grimly.

"It is true," the commander replied; "but they have a good start."

A man ran up to the bridge with a radio message. The commander scanned it.

"They are clever," he reported. "But all the same they have been sighted again! They are still on their original course."

"Who sends the report?" asked Nayland Smith.

"An American freighter."

"The air arm is strangely silent."

"We must be patient. Only two planes have been dispatched; they are looking also for a submarine—and there are many miles of sea to search."

He took up the glasses. Nayland Smith, hands thrust in his pockets, stared straight ahead.

The destroyer leaped and quivered under the lash of her merciless engines, a living, feverish thing. And this reflection crossed my mind: that the Chinese doctor, wherever he might be at that moment, was indeed a superman; for he is no ordinary criminal against whom warships are sent out. . . .

Another message was brought to the bridge; this one from a flying officer. The *Lola* was laid-to, less than five miles off and nearly dead on our course!

"What does this mean?" rapped Nayland Smith. "I don't like it a bit."

I was staring ahead, straining my eyes to pierce the distance. . . . And now, a speck on the skyline, I saw an airplane flying towards me.

"Coming back to pilot us," said the commander; "they know the game is up!"

A further message arrived. The Lola was putting a launch off at the time that the airman had headed back to find us. No submarine had been sighted.

"By heavens!" cried Nayland Smith, "I was right. His under-water craft *is* waiting for him in the event of just such an emergency as this! Instruct the plane to hurry back!"

The order was despatched. . . .

I saw the pilot bank, go about, and set off again on a course slightly westward of our own.

The commander spoke a few more orders rapidly, and we crept into line behind the swiftly disappearing airman. We must have been making thirty-five knots or more, for it was only a matter of minutes before I saw the yacht—dead ahead.

"The launch is putting back!" said Nayland Smith. "Look!"

The little craft was just swinging around the stern of the yacht! And now we were so near that I could see the lines of the *Lola*, a beautiful white-and-silver ship, with a low, graceful hull and one squat yellow funnel with a silver band.

"By heavens!" I shouted, "we're in time!"

The naval air pilot was circling now above the yacht. That submarine was somewhere in the neighbourhood it seemed reasonable to suppose, unless it had been the purpose of the launch's crew to head back for shore: a possibility. But no indication of an under-water craft disturbed the blue mirror of the Mediterranean.

The commander of the destroyer rang off his engines.

Chapter Forty-sixth

WE BOARD THE "LOLA"

WE WATCHED the launch return to the ladder of the yacht and saw her crew mount. The launch was already creeping up to her davits when the boat from the destroyer reached the ladder.

A lieutenant led with an armed party, Nayland Smith followed, then came the French police; and I brought up the rear.

A smart-looking officer—Portuguese, I thought—took the lieutenant's salute as he stepped on deck. Never, I think, in the experiences which had come to me since I had found myself within the zone of the Chinese doctor, had I been conscious of quite that sense of pent-up, overpowering emotion which claimed me at this moment.

Fleurette! Petrie! Were they here?

The sea looked like a vast panel which some Titan craftsman had covered with blue enamel, and the French warship might have been a gaunt grey insect trapped inside the pigment.

"Sir Denis," I said suddenly, in a low voice—"If the submarine is really in our neighbourhood—"

"I had thought of it," he rapped. "It was impossible to identify the man in the stern of the launch. But unless it was Dr. Fu Manchu, in which event he's on board here, our safety is questionable!"

"Take us to the captain," said the lieutenant sharply.

The yacht's officer saluted and led the way.

Armed men were left on duty at the ladder-head and at the foot of the stair leading up to the bridge. The bridge proved to be deserted. Two men were posted there, and we followed on into the chart house.

This was small but perfectly equipped, and it had only one occupant: a tall man wearing an astrakhan cap and a fur-trimmed overcoat. His arms folded, he stood there facing us as we entered . . .

Emotion almost choked me; triumph, with which even yet a dreadful doubt mingled. Nayland Smith's jaw squared as he stood beside me staring across the room.

No greetings were exchanged.

"Who commands this yacht?" the lieutenant demanded.

And in that cold guttural voice, so rarely touched by any trace of human feeling:

"I do," Dr. Fu Manchu replied.

"You failed to answer an official call sent out to all shipping in these waters."

"I did."

"You are accused of harbouring persons wanted by the police, and I have the authority to search this vessel."

Dr. Fu Manchu stood quite still; his immobility was mummy-like.

Nayland Smith stepped aside to make way for the senior police officer from Nice. As the man entered, Sir Denis merely pointed to that tall, dignified figure. The detective stepped forward.

"Is your name Dr. Fu Manchu?"

"It is."

"I hold a warrant for your arrest. You must consider yourself my prisoner."

Chapter Forty-seventh

Dr. PETRIE

"Come in," said a low voice.

Sir Denis stood stock still for one age-long moment, his hand resting on the door knob. Then he pulled open the white cabin door.

In a bed under an open porthole Petrie lay! His eyes, darkly shadowed, were fixed upon us. But his expression as Nayland Smith sprang forward was one I shall never forget.

"Petrie! Petrie, old man! . . . Thank God for this!"

Sir Denis's face I could not see—for he stood with his back to me, grasping Petrie's upstretched hand. But I could see Petrie; and knew that he was so overwhelmed by emotion as to be incapable of words. Sir Denis's silence told the same story.

But when at last that long, silent handgrasp was relaxed:

"Sterling!" said the invalid, smiling—"you have done more than merely to save my life. You have brought back a happiness I thought I had lost forever. Smith, old man—" he looked up at Sir Denis—"get a radio off to Kara in Cairo at the earliest possible moment! But break the news gently. She will be mad with joy!"

He looked at me again.

"I understand, Sterling, that what you have found you want to keep?"

At that Nayland Smith turned.

"I trust your financial resources are adequate to the task, Sterling?" he rapped, but with a smile on his tired face—and it was a smile of happiness.

"Does she know?" I asked, and my voice was far from steady.

Petrie nodded.

"Go and find her," he said. "She will be glad to see you."

I went out, leaving those lifelong friends together. I returned to the deck.

What must there not be that Petrie had to tell Sir Denis

and he to tell Petrie? It was, I suppose, one of the most remarkable reunions in history. For Petrie had died and had been buried, and was restored again to life. And Sir Denis had crowned his remarkable career with the greatest accomplishment in criminal records—the arrest of Dr. Fu Manchu. . . .

The attitude of the members of the crew of the *Lola* strongly suggested that the vessel was used for none but legitimate purposes. One by one they were being submitted to a close interrogation by the French detective and his assistant in a forward cabin.

I had heard the evidence of the chief navigating officer and of the second officer. The vessel belonged to Santos da Cunha, an Argentine millionaire, but he frequently placed it at the disposal of his friends, of whom Dr. Fu Manchu (known to them as the Marquis Chûan) was one. It was the Marquis's custom sometimes to take charge, and he, according to these witnesses was a qualified master mariner and a fine seaman!

His personal servants, of whom there were four, had come on board at Monaco; from this dehumanised quartette I anticipated that little would be learned. The ship's officers and crew denied all knowledge of a submarine. When the engines had been stopped by Dr. Fu Manchu and the launch ordered away, they had obeyed without knowing for what purpose those orders had been given.

Personally, I had no doubt that the under-water craft lay somewhere near, but that the doctor had decided to sacrifice himself alone rather than to order the submarine to surface when the coming of the French airman had warned him that his movements were covered.

Why?

Doubtless because he had recognised his own escape to be impossible. . . .

I reached the cabin in which I knew Fleurette to be, rapped, opened the door, and went in.

She was standing just inside—and I knew that she had been waiting for me. . . .

I forgot what happened immediately afterwards; I lived in another world. . . .

When, at last, and reluctantly, I came to earth again, the first idea which I properly grasped was that of Fleurette's almost insupportable happiness because she had learned that she really possessed a father—and had met him!

Her eagerness to meet her mother resembled a physical hunger.

It was not easy to see these strange events through her eyes. But, listening to her, watching her fascinatedly, tears on her dark lashes as she sometimes clutched me, nervously, excitedly, it dawned upon me that there is probably a great void in the life of one who has never known father or mother.

Her happiness was clouded by the knowledge that she had gained it at the price of the downfall of Dr. Fu Manchu. I tried to divert the tide of her thoughts, but it was useless.

She, and she alone, was responsible. . . .

It was clear to me that Petrie—sensing that exulted estimate which Fleurette had made of the character of the incalculable Chinaman—had done nothing to disturb her ideals.

How long we were there alone I don't know; but at last:

"Really, darling," said Fleurette, "you must go back. I am not going to move. I dare not face——"

I tore myself away; I returned to Petrie's cabin.

Nayland Smith was there. The two were deep in conversation: they ceased speaking as I entered.

"I have solved a mystery for you," Sir Denis began, looking up at me. "You recall, when Petrie lay in the grip of the purple plague and Fah Lo Suee was there, the voice which warned you to beware of her?"

"Yes."

"*I* was the speaker, Sterling!" said Petrie.

Save for the queer blanching of his hair, he seemed to me now to be restored to something almost resembling his former self. Happiness is the medicine of the gods. He had met a beautiful girl, in whom, as in a mirror, he had seen his wife; had known that this was the daughter snatched from them in babyhood. Then, within a few hours, he had been rescued from a living death to find Nayland Smith at his bedside.

"I suspected it; but at the time I found it hard to believe."

"Naturally!" Sir Dennis was the speaker. "But I have just learned a remarkable and at the same time a ghastly thing, Sterling. Victims of the catalepsy induced by Dr. Fu Manchu remain *conscious*."

"What!"

"It is difficult to make you understand," Petrie broke in, "what I passed through. Evidently my preparation '654' is fairly efficacious. If you had known what to do next, I should have survived all right. I was insensible, but the injection of Dr. Fu Manchu's virus to induce catalepsy restored me to consciousness!

"How long after it had been administered, I don't know. Incidentally, that hell-cat made the injection in my thigh, under the sheet, while she sat beside the bed. Oh! you're not to blame, Sterling."

"She inherits her father's genius," Sir Denis murmured.

"As I saw her last," I said savagely, "she was suffering for it."

"What? I don't know about this."

"He flogged her. . . ."

Sir Denis and Petrie exchanged glances.

"Details can wait," rapped the former. "Inhuman though the sentiment may be, I cannot find it in my heart to be sorry."

"Can you imagine, Sterling," Petrie went on, "that from the time I recovered consciousness and found Fah Lo Suee in the room, I was aware of everything that happened?"

"You don't mean——"

Sir Denis nodded shortly.

"Yes . . . even that," Petrie assured me. "Somehow, when I saw that she-cat coiling herself about you, I forced speech—I tried to warn you. It was the last evidence of which I was capable to show you that I still lived!

"I heard myself pronounced dead; I saw Cartier's tears. I was hurried away—a plague case. The undertakers dealt with me, and I was put into a coffin."

"My God!" I groaned, and wondered at the man's fortitude.

"Do you know what I thought, Sterling, as I lay there in the mortuary?—I prayed that nothing would interfere with the plans of Dr. Fu Manchu! For the purpose of it all was clear to me. And I knew—try to picture my frame of mind!—that if my friends should upset his plans, I should be——"

"Buried alive!"

Nayland Smith's voice sounded like a groan.

"Exactly, old man. You have noticed my hair? That was

when it happened. When I heard the screws being removed, and saw two evil-looking Burmans bending over me—or rather, I saw them at rare intervals, for it was impossible to move my eyes—I sent up a prayer of thankfulness!

"They lifted me out—my body, of course, was quite rigid, placed me in a hammock and hurried me out to a car in the lane beyond. Of the substitution of which you have told me, I saw nothing. I was taken by road to Ste Claire, carried to the room in which you found me, Sterling, and placed in the care of a Japanese doctor who informed me that his name was Yamamata.

"He gave me an injection which relaxed the rigidity, and then a draught of that preparation which looks like brandy but tastes like death.

"You and I, Smith—" he glanced aside at Sir Denis—"have met with it before!"

"Is Dr. Yamamata on board?" I asked.

"No. I was carried in a sort of litter down to that water cave which Smith tells me you have visited, across it in a collapsible boat which I assume is part of the equipment of the submarine; and from there up to a rock tunnel and down to the beach. A launch belonging to this yacht was waiting, in which I was brought on board. Dr. Fu Manchu in person superintending. Fleurette was with us. We joined the yacht in sight of Monaco. I resigned myself to becoming a subject of the new Chinese Emperor of the World."

CHAPTER FORTY-EIGHTH

"IT MEANS EXTRADITION"

I HAD rarely, if ever seen a display of Gallic emotion to equal that of Dr. Cartier when he entered Petrie's room in the Hôtel de Paris in Monte Carlo.

He beheld before him a man whom he had certified to be dead; whom he had seen buried. Perhaps his behaviour was excusable. Brisson, who was with him, controlled himself better.

"Because I am the cause of this," said Petrie, "I naturally feel most embarrassed. But you may take it, Cartier, that weakness now is the only trouble. It's a question of getting me on my feet again."

"I will arrange for a nurse."

The door opened, and Fleurette came in.

As her accepted lover, the incense of worship which the Frenchmen silently offered should perhaps have been flattering. Oddly enough, I resented it.

"This is my daughter, gentlemen," said Petrie—with so much pride and such happiness in his voice that all else was forgotten.

She crossed and seated herself at his side, clasping his outstretched hand.

"This, dear, is Dr. Cartier . . . Dr. Brisson, my friends and allies."

Fleurette smiled at the French doctors. That intoxicating dimple appeared for a moment in her chin, and I knew that they were her slaves.

"I shall require no other nurse," Petrie added.

It was hard to go; but a nod from Fleurette gave me my dismissal. With a few words of explanation I left the room.

Sir Denis was waiting for me in the lobby.

"I hate to drag you away, Sterling," he said. "But if any sort of progress has been made at Ste Claire, you can probably help."

We joined a car which was waiting. I could not fail to recall in the early stages of the journey, that night when, learning at Quinto's that Petrie was dead, I had launched what was meant to be a vendetta.

I had set out to seek the life of any servant of Dr. Fu Manchu who might cross my path!

And even now, when the fact had become plain to me that the unscrupulous methods of the great Chinaman, his indifference to human life, were not dictated by any prospect of personal gain but belonged to an ideal utterly beyond my Western comprehension, I did not regret the death of that Burmese strangler with whom I had fought to a finish on the Corniche road.

"The big villa at Ste Claire," said Nayland Smith, "has obviously been a European base of the group for many years past. It's impossible to close one's eyes to the fact, Sterling, that this Si-Fan movement, whatever it may embody, has gained momentum since the days when I first realised the existence of Dr. Fu Manchu. You have told me that he claims to be responsible for that financial chaos which at that moment involves the whole world. That he had defeated age, I know. And I gather that he professes to have solved the mystery of the Philosopher's Stone."

We were clear of Monaco now, and mounting higher and higher.

"In all this, there is one thing which we must bear in mind: it has taken me many years to learn as little as I know of the Mandarin Fu Manchu. But at last I have discovered his term of official office, and with many blanks I have built up something of his pedigree.

"Tell me," I said eagerly.

"He administered the Province of Ho Nan, under the Empress. Judging by the evidence which I have accumulated, he appeared to be of the same age in those days as he appears now!

"What ever age is the man?"

"Heaven only knows, Sterling! This I doubt if we shall ever find out. He is affiliated to those who once ruled China. His place in the scheme of things, I take it, may be compared to that once held by the Pretender, in England. But he has a legitimate claim to the title of Prince."

"Sir Denis, this is amazing!"

"Dr. Fu Manchu is the most amazing figure living in the world to-day. He holds degrees of four universities. He is a Doctor of Philosophy as well as a Doctor of Medicine. I have reason to believe that he speaks every civilised language with facility; and I know that he represents a movement which already had pushed Europe and America very near to the brink—and which, before long, may push both of them right over."

"You have prevented that, Sir Denis. An army is helpless without its leader."

I glanced aside at him as we sped along the Corniche road: he was tugging at the lobe of his ear.

"How do we know that he *is* the leader?" he snapped. "Think of the living-dead whom we chance to have identified. How many more belong to the Si-Fan whose identities we don't even suspect? His 'submersible yacht,' the existence of which, even if I had doubted Dr. Fu Manchu's word (and this I have never doubted), is established by the disappearance of every member of his household! The French authorities have never had so much as a suspicion that such a vessel was on their coasts!

"That pool may have been known to the monks in the old days; but you will search for it in vain in Baedeker. Do you grasp what I mean, Sterling? We in the West follow our well trodden paths; no one of us sees more than the others see. But, under the street along which we are walking, at the back of a house which we have passed a hundred times, lies something else—something unsuspected.

"These are the things that Dr. Fu Manchu has discovered—or rediscovered. This is the secret of his influence. He is behind us, under us, and over us."

"At the moment," I said savagely, "he is in a French prison!"

"Why?" murmured Nayland Smith.

"What do you mean?"

"His submersible yacht, for a sight of which I would give much, is almost certainly armed—probably with torpedoes, improved by Ericksen or some other specialist possessing a first-class brain stolen form the tomb to work for Dr. Fu Manchu. Therefore why did he submit to arrest?"

"I don't follow."

"I agree that the circumstances were peculiar, and possibly I am pessimistic. But I am not satisfied. I have been in touch with the Foreign Office. The Naval resources of Europe already will be combing the Mediterranean for the mysterious submarine. But—" he turned, and I met the glance of the steel-gray eyes—"do you think they will find it?"

"Why not?"

He snapped his teeth together and pulled out from his pocket a very large and dilapidated rubber pouch, and at the same time a big-bowled and much charred briar. I recognised the pouch, remembering when and where I had last seen it.

"I thought I had lost that for you, Sir Denis!" I said.

"So did I," he rapped; "but I found it on my way down. It's an old friend which I should have hated to lose. Hello! here we are."

As he began to charge his pipe, the driver of the car had turned into that steeply sloping lane which led up to the iron gates of the Villa Ste Claire.

"I don't expect to learn anything here, Sterling," said Sir Denis, "which is worth while. But there's no other line of investigation open at the moment. Dr. Fu Manchu's arrest is a very delicate matter. He has already applied to his Consul, and demanded that the Chinese Legation in Paris shall be notified of the state of affairs! To put the thing in a nutshell: unless there is some evidence here—and I don't expect to find it—to connect him with the recent outrages in the neighbourhood or to establish his association with the epidemic, which is frankly hopeless, it means extradition."

"Have you arranged for it?" I asked eagerly.

"Yes. But even if we get him back to England—and I know his dossier at Scotland Yard from A to Z——"

He paused and stuffed the big pouch into his pocket; some coarse-cut mixture which overhung the bowl of his briar lent it the appearance of a miniature rock garden.

"What!"

"The law of England has many loopholes."

CHAPTER FORTY-NINTH

MAÎTRE FOLI

THE absence of reporters from Ste Claire, the gate of which was guarded by police, amazed me.

"There are some things which are too important for publicity," said Sir Denis. "And in France, as well as in England, we have this advantage over America: we can silence the newspapers. The only witnesses of any use in a court of law which we have captured so far are the four Chinese bodyservants of the doctor's who were on board the yacht. Some of these you can identify, I believe?"

"Three of them I have seen before."

Sir Denis opened the door of the car. We had reached the end of that sanded drive which swept around the side of the villa and terminated near the southerly wing of the terrace.

"Have you ever tried to interrogate a Chinaman who didn't want to commit himself?" he asked.

"Yes, I have employed Chinese servants, and I know what they can be like."

Nayland Smith turned to me—he was standing on the drive.

"They are loyal, Sterling," he snapped. "Bind them to a tradition, and no human power can tear them away from it. . . ."

Many of the section doors had been forced, but more than half the party remained imprisoned. Under instructions from Sir Denis, I gathered, a party had been landed in that tiny bay which was the sea-bound terminus of the exit from the water cave. Suitably prepared, they had landed there, and were operating upon the first of the section doors in order to liberate members of the raiding party trapped in that long glass-lined corridor. The local Chief of Police was still among the missing.

"I think," said Sir Denis, "we can afford to overlook infection from the hybrid flies, and even from other insects which you have described to me. Those used experimentally by Dr. Fu Manchu—for instance, the fly in Petrie's laboratory—

seem to have survived the evening chill. But you may have noticed that there has been a drop in the temperature during the last two days. I think it was these eccentricities of climate which baffled the doctor. His flying army couldn't compete with them."

We spent an hour at Ste Claire; but it was an hour wasted.

When, presently, we left for Nice, where Dr. Fu Manchu was temporarily confined, I reflected that if Ste Claire was a minor base of the Si-Fan, as Fleurette had given me to understand, then the organisation must be at least as vast as Sir Denis Nayland Smith believed.

Ste Claire was a scientific fortress; its destruction in one way and another represented a loss to human knowledge which could not be estimated. His section doors had checked pursuit of the doctor so effectively that, failing my adventurous swim across the pool and discovery of that other exit, the fugitive could conveniently have landed from the motor yacht *Lola* at any one of many ports before the radio had got busy with his description.

I wondered if the measures taken to ensure secrecy would prove to be effective.

The very air was charged with rumours; the Nice police had caught the infection. Such suppressed excitement prevailed that the atmosphere vibrated with it.

Dr. Fu Manchu had declined to be transported to Paris until he had had an opportunity of consulting with his legal adviser. In this he was acting within his rights, as he had pointed out; and the departmental authorities, at a loss, welcomed the arrival of Sir Denis.

M. Chamrousse awaited us, his magisterial dignity definitely disturbed. . . .

There was a guard before the doubly locked door, but in due course it was opened. The Préfet conducted Sir Denis and myself into the apartment occupied by Dr. Fu Manchu.

This officially was a cell; actually, a plainly furnished bed-sitting room.

At the moment of my entrance the scene was unreal—wholly chimerical. During my acquaintance with the Chinese doctor I had formed the opinion, reinforced later by what I had heard from Sir Denis of the monstrous tentacles of the organisation called Si-Fan, that ordinary frail human laws did not apply to this man who transcended the normal.

And, as I saw him seated in a meanly furnished room, this feeling of phantasy, of unreality, claimed me.

It was just as fantastic, I thought, as the mango-apple; the tsetse fly crossed with the plague flea; the date palms growing huge figs; the black spider which could reason....

He had discarded his astrakhan cap and fur coat, and I saw that he wore a yellow robe of a kind with which I was familiar. Chinese slippers were upon his feet. Something strikingly unusual in his appearance at first defeated me; then I realised what it was. He did not wear the little cap which hitherto he had worn.

For the first time I appreciated the amazing frontal development of his skull. I had never seen such a head. I had thought of him as resembling Seti the First; but the great king had the skull of a babe in comparison with that of Dr. Fu Manchu.

He sat there watching us as we entered. There was no expression whatever in that wonderful face—a face which might well have looked upon centuries of the ages known to man.

"I shall be glad to see you, Sir Denis," came the guttural, imperturbable voice, "and Mr. Sterling may also remain. Pray be seated."

He fixed a glance of his emerald-green eyes upon the préfet, and I knew and sympathised with the effect which that glance had upon its recipient. The dignified official backed towards the door. Sir Denis saved his dignity.

"It may be better if you leave us for a few moments, M. Chamrousse," he whispered....

When we were alone:

"Alan Sterling," said Dr. Fu Manchu.

And prisoner though he was, he was not so truly a prisoner as I; for he had caught and held my glance as no other man in the world had ever had power to do. I knew that my will was helpless. A dreadful sense of weakness possessed me, which I cannot hope to make clear to anyone lacking experience of that singular regard.

"I speak as one," the guttural voice continued, "who may be at the end of his career. You lack brilliance, but you have qualities which I respect. You may look upon Dr. Petrie's daughter as your woman, since she has chosen you. Take her, and hold her—if you can."

He turned his eyes away. And it was as though a dazzling light had been moved so that I could see the world again in true perspective; then:

"Sir Denis," he continued.

I twisted aside and looked at Nayland Smith. His jaws were clenched. It was plain that every reserve of his enormous vitality, mental energy, his will, was being called upon as he stared into the face of the uncanny being whom he had captured, who was his prisoner.

"In order that we may understand one another more completely," the imperious voice continued, "I desire to make plain to you, Sir Denis Nayland Smith, that the laws of France, the laws of England, the laws of Europe, are cobwebs which I blow aside. It is your wish that I shall be carried to Paris, and thence to London. You believe that your English courts can end my labours. . . .

"I have this to say to you: the work of a world reformer is a work in which there is no sleep—no rest. That which he achieves is always in the past, as he moves forward upon his endless path. Himself, he is alone—always looking into the future. You have fought me; but because you are untiring as myself, you have stimulated. You have checked me. But you cannot hold back the cloudburst nor stifle the volcano. I may fall—thanks to you. But what I have made stands granite fast.

"Ask me no questions: I shall answer none."

I stared again at Sir Denis. His profile was as grimly masklike as that of the Chinaman. He made no reply.

"Maître Foli," Dr. Fu Manchu continued, "my French legal adviser, has been detained unavoidably, but will be here at any moment."

CHAPTER FIFTIETH

"THE WORK GOES ON"

When presently we left the apartment of Dr. Fu Manchu, Nayland Smith's face was very stern.

"He was rather obscure," I said.

"Obscure?"

He turned his piercing grey eyes upon me with a glance almost scornful.

"I thought so."

Whereupon Sir Denis smiled, that rare smile which when it came must have disarmed his bitterest enemy. He grasped my arm.

"Dr. Fu Manchu is never obscure," he said; "he spoke the plain truth, Sterling. And truth is sometimes a bitter pill."

"But—Maître Foli! He is one of the greatest advocates in France!"

"Certainly. What did you expect? Surely you know that Dr. Fu Manchu never looks below excellence—living or dead! I warned you that Fu Manchu arrested and Fu Manchu convicted were totally different matters."

We returned to the office of the préfet, and:

"Hello!" Sir Denis exclaimed—"he's here!"

A stooping but imposing figure was seated in the leathern armchair before the table of the préfet. M. Chamrousse, not yet entirely his own man, following his encounter with the formidable Chinaman, was listening with every mark of deference to his distinguished visitor. The latter ceased speaking, and the préfet stood up as we entered.

"Sir Denis," said Chamrousse, "This is Maître Foli—Dr. Fu Manchu's legal adviser."

Maître Foli stood up and bowed very formally.

I had recognised him immediately from his photographs published during the progress of a Paris *cause célèbre* in which he had secured the vindication of his client—a distinguished officer accused of espionage. I judged his age to be close to seventy; his yellow face was a map of wrinkles rendered more conspicuous by a small, snow-white moustache and a tiny tuft of beard under the lower lip.

He was buttoned up in a black, caped overcoat from the lapels of which bulged a flowing tie; and a wide-brimmed hat lay on the carpet beside a bulky portfolio. A close-fitting silk skullcap lent him a mediæval appearance, which was lost when he adjusted large, slightly tinted spectacles in order more closely to observe us.

It was a memorable situation.

"Your reputation is well known to me, Maître Foli," said Sir Denis.

"Indeed, yes," M. Chamrousse murmured, bowing to the famous lawyer.

"But the identity of your present client surprises me."

"Sir Denis Nayland Smith," Maître Foli replied in a harsh, strident voice, "I have acted for Dr. Fu Manchu over a period of some forty years."

"Is that so?" Sir Denis muttered drily.

"You and I do not see eye to eye in the matters which we know about. You have behaved, and behaved honourably, in accordance with your principles, Sir Denis. Dr. Fu Manchu has followed another star. His codes are those of a civilisation different from ours—and older. A day will come, must come, when you will recognise your outlook—as I have recognised mine—to be limited. His manner of warfare appals you—yet I can only regret, Sir Denis, that a man of your great capacity should have been called upon to oppose the inevitable over a period of so many years."

He stood up.

"Thank you," said Sir Denis.

"Will you be good enough—" Maître Foli bowed to the préfet and to Nayland Smith—"to grant me an interview with my client? I desire that this interview should not be interrupted—a desire which I am entitled to express."

The French official glanced at Sir Denis, who nodded. Maître Foli took up his bulky portfolio and went out, walking very slowly and much stooped. M. Chamrousse followed him.

I stared at Nayland Smith, who had begun to pace up and down the carpet restlessly.

"This man Foli is going to oppose extradition!" he rapped.

"If he succeeds—and he rarely fails—Fu Manchu will slip through our fingers!"

Presently M. Chamrousse returned, shrugging apologetically.

"Such is the law," he said, "and the eminence of Maître Foli offers me no alternative. This Fu Manchu is a political prisoner. ..."

A messenger entered to announce the arrival of the Chinese consul.

"Do you mind, M. Chamrousse," said Sir Denis, "if I see this gentleman privately for a few minutes?"

"But not at all."

Sir Denis nodded to the speaker and walked rapidly out of the room. Five to ten minutes elapsed, during which there was little conversation between M. Chamrousse and myself, and then:

"The appearance of the great Foli in this case gives me a heavy sense of responsibility," M. Chamrousse declared.

"I fully understand."

A further interval of silence; and then, heralded by the sound of a bell and the unlocking of doors, Maître Foli rejoined us, portfolio under his arm.

M. Chamrousse sprang to his feet.

"Gentlemen," said the famous lawyer, groping for that wide-brimmed hat which he had left upon the floor beside his chair, "I am returning at once in order to get in touch with the Chinese Legation in Paris."

"The Chinese consul is here, Maître Foli."

That stooping bur dignified figure turned slowly.

"I thank you, M. Chamrousse; but this affair is outside the sphere of minor officialdom."

M. Chamrousse rang a bell; a clerk appeared, who showed Maître Foli out of the office. At the door he turned.

"Gentlemen," he said, "I know that you look upon me as your enemy; but your enemy is my client. I am merely acting for him."

He bowed and went out. The door closed.

Perhaps half a minute had elapsed when it was flung open again and Nayland Smith hurried in.

"Was that Maître Foli who left a moment ago?" he rapped.

"Yes," M Chamrousse replied. "He is anxious to get into immediate touch with the Chinese Legation in Paris."

Sir Denis stood stock still, then:

"Great heavens!" he said in a low voice—and looked at me almost wildly—"it's not impossible! It's not impossible——"

"What do you mean, Sir Denis?"

"The Blessing of the Celestial Vision!"

His words were a verbal thunderbolt; his meaning was all too clear.

"Sterling! Good God! Follow me."

He rushed from the room, along the passage to the cell occupied by Dr. Fu Manchu. A guard was on duty at the door. He opened it in response to Sir Denis's order. We entered. M. Chamrousse was close behind.

A man was seated where Dr. Fu Manchu had sat; one in figure not unlike whom we had come to seek. But . . .

"Great heavens!" cried Nayland Smith. "He wasn't relying on loopholes of the law! He was relying on his genius as an illusionist!"

The man in the yellow robe bowed.

It was Maître Foli!

"Sir Denis," he said, in his harsh, strident voice, "I have served my purpose for which I have been retained by Dr. Fu Manchu for a period of more than thirty years. I am honoured; I am happy. I crown a successful career with a glorious deed . . ."

The light in his eyes—their wild fanaticism—told me the truth. Maître Foli was a Companion; a victim of those arts which I had so narrowly escaped!

"I shall be committed to a French jail—my sentence may be a long one. I am too old for Devil's Island; but in any event what does it matter? The Prince is free! The work goes on. . . ."

THE END